THE

"Captivating!
A lush and sweeping novel
that sparkles with fascinating characters."
—**Julie Garwood**

He came to her, took her hand and spread the long, slim fingers wide, running his thumb over each in a careful, intent way. He turned the hand over and looked at the palm.

"No scar," he said. "The burn healed a long time ago. Do you remember the night you got it?"

The night San Francisco burned down. The night she and Sophy nearly perished in that inferno of a theater. The night she thought he was dead.

"I remember. I couldn't find you and then I saw you come running. . . ."

"You knew then that I loved you. You know it now."

Strange how the heart could seem to stop and then suddenly start again. She said, "I never . . ."—her voice faltered—"I never thought I'd hear you say that, not ever in my life."

She reached out, needing to touch him, and his arms went around her, banishing fear and loneliness. It was sweet, so sweet to be held by him, safe, supported, loved. Then she whispered, "Why, *why* did you marry her?"

LIGHTS ALONG THE SHORE

"LIGHTS ALONG THE SHORE is a skillfully written saga and wonderfully entertaining. Filled with memorable characters and fascinating period detail, it is an enthralling tale and first-rate. I thoroughly enjoyed it."

—Laurie McBain

"Diane Austell's LIGHTS ALONG THE SHORE is a feast of historical fact and memorable characters, seasoned by the dramatic events of California's early statehood."

—Marianne Willman

LIGHTS ALONG THE SHORE

Diane Austell

BANTAM BOOKS
NEW YORK · TORONTO · LONDON · SYDNEY · AUCKLAND

LIGHTS ALONG THE SHORE

A Bantam Fanfare Book / February 1992

FANFARE *and the portrayal of a boxed "ff" are trademarks of Bantam Books, a division of Bantam Doubleday Dell Publishing Group, Inc.*

ISBN 0-553-29331-1

Published simultaneously in the United States and Canada

Bantam Books are published by Bantam Books, a division of Bantam Doubleday Dell Publishing Group, Inc. Its trademark, consisting of the words "Bantam Books" and the portrayal of a rooster, is Registered in U.S. Patent and Trademark Office and in other countries. Marca Registrada. Bantam Books, 666 Fifth Avenue, New York, New York 10103.

PRINTED IN THE UNITED STATES OF AMERICA

RAD   0 9 8 7 6 5 4 3 2 1

*For my husband, the man who has opened
all the doors for me*

LIGHTS ALONG
THE SHORE

BOOK ONE

Chapter 1

Her baptismal name was Maria Catherine, but everyone called her Marin. The inscription in the family Bible in the parlor was almost forgotten. From the upper hall she could see the table where the big book rested, open at the first chapter of Ecclesiastes, Papa's favorite. He read it so often at Sunday prayers that she could recite it by heart, liking the sound of the poetry without understanding it.

" 'Vanity of vanities, all is vanity,' " she said to herself, moving closer to the stairs, " 'and vexation of spirit.' " She leaned over the banister, listening.

Below, all was quiet, unnaturally so, considering that it was ten o'clock on a busy Monday morning. At least a half dozen servants were always in the house, and the Gentrys' domestics had no notion of unobtrusive service. They chattered, squabbled, or sang as they worked, often accomplishing all three at once, but today no one was singing; no quick cascade of Spanish jokes or insults disturbed the morning hush.

At breakfast the maids had served the food in icy silence, with only one short, sharp exchange when Luz bumped Josefina, causing her to drop the coffeepot and invoke the entire Holy

Family loudly enough for Mama to scold her. Josefina, a sensitive girl, ran weeping to the kitchen while Luz continued to serve breakfast with a satisfied smile.

The moment the meal ended, the other servants found chores outdoors, as far from trouble as possible. Marin hurried upstairs and had been hiding in her bedroom ever since, waiting for the storm that was sure to come. When it did, she would be free to leave the house unseen by her mother or any other authority.

She pulled off her flat-heeled shoes and stuffed them into her canvas carryall, and at that moment there was a burst of spluttering Spanish downstairs, followed by a long, drawn-out shriek that would have been bloodcurdling to anyone who did not know Josefina. Marin smiled. The forces of darkness had invaded the kitchen again, which meant that she could soon leave unobserved.

Light footsteps clicked toward the back of the house. A soft, deceptively calm voice floated above the agonized gush of Spanish Marin heard tumbling through the kitchen door. Poor Mama.

Another shriek, and then *"Madre de Dios, ayúdame!"* echoed through the house. Aunt Delphine raced up the stairs, her skirt hiked above her ankles, her graying blond hair straggling from its net. She passed Marin without a glance and vanished behind her own bedroom door. Marin's lips curled in affectionate contempt. It was Delphine's usual cowardly retreat in the face of difficulty; her door would remain shut for hours.

The howling from below intensified, and experience told her that the moment for escape had come. She slipped the straps of the carryall over her arm and tiptoed to the top of the stairs. The hall below was empty. Mama was trapped in the kitchen with the hysterical maid; Papa had gone to the upper range sometime before dawn; her little sister, Sophy, was swinging in the orchard behind the back garden; and her brother, Ethan, had left on a mission of his own immediately after breakfast. Ethan wouldn't carry tales anyway, for he and Marin had long ago negotiated a contract: Marin shut her eyes to Ethan's activities, and he in turn never interfered with her. On the few occasions one of them had broken the contract, retribution by the injured party had been swift and terrible. As a result, violations were rare.

Assured that the way was clear, Marin ran down the stairs and passed through the silent parlor, cool and dim in morning shadows. Beyond the front door a broad veranda encompassed three sides of the house, shaded by a balcony and an overhanging roof. Mateo, her father's stable-boy, was at the side of the house brushing the chestnut mare until her russet coat shone and whistling through his teeth. Two Mexican babies played on the grass in the front yard, undisturbed by the commotion inside the house, and at the corner of the porch old Chispa sat, wrapped in a dirty blanket, grinding her day's corn in a stone bowl. Mama wouldn't like that, not on the front porch.

Chispa spoke very little English. Marin decided to risk a meeting and sauntered by the old woman, murmuring "*Buenos días.*" Chispa nodded and smiled, revealing her one remaining tooth. Marin hopped off the porch, circled the children, and started down the hill, feeling her mother's eyes on her back, prepared to be caught and ordered back to the house at any moment.

At the bottom of the hill Marin turned onto the road with a little dance step of joy. No lessons, no sewing, no listening to the wails from the kitchen today. A twinge of sympathy for Rose stung her briefly, but after all, it was Mama's job to deal with servants. She sat down on a rock beside the road, dug shoes and stockings out of her pack, and then, properly shod, swung down the narrow road that followed the boundary between James Gentry's Little Mountain Ranch and the great Fontana—Nicolas Cermeno's empire—which embraced thousands of acres of fertile grazing country. A few miles to the south and west, two other ranches touched Fontana and Little Mountain to form what would have appeared on a map as a star-shaped meeting point. One was the second-largest ranch in the district, John Baldwin's La Gracia. The other was Longridge, the Severance family's ranch. Together these four holdings contained much of the land from the Carquinez straits to the southern end of the bay.

There were no fences. The wiry, small, long-horned cattle wandered where they pleased, and no one worried much about whose animals were where. They were branded, they could be separated when separation was necessary, the land was limitless, and there was more than enough food and water for all, was it not so?

In that early May of 1847 the soft California sun gave promise of summer, and the translucent air was sweet with the smell of growing things—wild oats and cultivated barley and the bursting buds on peach, pear, orange, and lemon trees. The wild grass would turn gold when summer came, but now it was still green from winter rains and swept over the gentle hills like a lawn in a gigantic garden. Many of the wildflowers had already blown their brilliant colors on the wind and gone to seed, but blue and pink lupine still grew in patches, and orange-gold poppies ignited in the sun.

Beyond the hills the grass continued in huge tracts of unmarked land, unmarked because every man knew where his property ended and another's began, and there was no need for surveys and legal documents among gentlemen. Then came the great bay, a glittering inland sea held captive by a long peninsula. On the western side of the bay sandy hills curved down to a gap through which water flowed into the Pacific; then the hills rose to curve and enclose again. At one of the coves below those hills a few traders lived in flea-ridden tents and shacks, an encampment they called Yerba Buena. On this morning lead-colored clouds hung above Yerba Buena, clouds that could mean a late spring storm, but Marin dismissed the possibility. There were often storms over on the peninsula that never reached this side of the water.

The bay was fed by many rivers flowing down from the Sierra mountains, and it was to a small branch of one of these rivers that she headed, carrying her lunch, a sketchpad, and the novel her friend, Celia Baldwin, had lent her in secret. Celia's father, John Baldwin, was almost as famous for his library as for his money-making ability, and if he wanted a book forbidden by the home government in Mexico City, he simply had it smuggled in. Often he ordered entertaining novels for Celia and she passed them on to Marin, who hid them from her parents. Rose disapproved of novels as mind-weakening, and James looked askance at books from a Catholic household, but to Marin anything Celia Baldwin had was desirable. She was beautiful, she lived in luxury at La Gracia, and men had fought duels over her. Marin's admiration for Celia was almost as great as her envy.

But today painful emotions such as jealousy and dissatisfaction did not trouble her. Today it was spring, and she felt pretty, and the yellow mustard blooming on both sides of the road was higher than her head. A month from now, when the heat came on, it would shrivel into brown straw, but today it was fresh and young, a golden mass of delicate blossoms blowing and bending on long, thin stalks.

Like sunlight . . . I am walking through clouds of sunlight, she thought, and gave an exuberant leap, an act beneath her dignity if anyone had been watching. She strode on down the dusty road, stretching her legs to see how far apart she could set her footprints, an energetic fifteen-year-old with hair so red, it seemed to catch fire in the sun, and fresh good looks untouched by disappointment, or failure, or heartbreak. Inner character had not yet set its mark on her face, nor had experience withered expectations. A certain wariness in her dark, intelligent eyes revealed doubt that the world was quite the agreeable place it seemed, but most of the time her thoughts centered on immediate troubles or pleasures, and most of the time she was happy.

On this particular sunny day she felt that life had been designed especially for her, and seized by unreasoning happiness, she stopped in the middle of the road and whirled in a circle, watching her blue-flowered skirt stand out. How pretty the dress, how pretty the day! She had stolen her freedom, she was meeting a man secretly beside a secluded riverbank, and Mama would never suspect. There were many things Mama didn't know about, innocent little adventures that harmed no one and were a lot of fun, but that Mama, in her strictness, would disapprove of if she knew. Rose Gentry considered the Morgan family trashy—John Wesley Morgan especially—and would never understand his appeal even if Marin were so unwise as to try to explain it.

The truth was, John Wesley made her feel beautiful and desirable, and that was all she wanted. Wars might come and governments topple, empires might be lost and men like her father build new empires, but only one thing really mattered—to be a great belle like Mama and Aunt Delphine in the old days, or Celia Baldwin right now. She had studied Celia's hairstyles, her bearing, even her tone of voice, and still had not figured out what it was about the girl that captivated so many men.

And there was Sophy, who looked so much like Rose. In two or three years she would be the belle of the Gentry family, and what would Marin do then?

Her father was the most important person in her life—her teacher and her kindest critic. It was he who told her that she had the best brain in the family and tried to teach her to use it. He discussed with her his own political and religious ideas, lent her books with passages marked and comments in the margins, and gave reasoned, thoughtful answers to her questions. Some of what he said was beyond her understanding, but over time she absorbed much of his thinking. She was his favorite, she knew it as surely as if he had said so, and the knowledge warmed her. Once he had cupped her chin in his callused hand and said, "You're out of the common mold, my girl. You'll be a stunner one day, and then the men will jump to your tune." And he had laughed and pinched her cheek. She was not sure what a stunner was, but the part about men jumping to her tune was clear enough and she waited none too patiently for it to happen. Up to now the only man at her beck and call had been John Wesley Morgan.

Three miles ahead, farther than she intended to walk, lay the beginning of Longridge, an ill-fitting name for a California ranch, as stuffy as its owner, Malcolm Severance. The Severances were the Gentrys' only neighbors who were both American and Protestant (except for the Morgans, who did not count), but although there was some visiting back and forth, close friendship had not developed.

Relations between the Severances and the Spanish rancheros were equally reserved. Even the easygoing Californians found it hard to like Malcolm Severance, an austere New Englander with lofty standards and inflexible opinions, and although Elizabeth, his wife, tried to be neighborly, there was a reticence and dignity about her that made genuine intimacy impossible. Their daughter was a different matter. Logan Severance lacked the beauty that might have brought suitors buzzing around, but her intelligence and warm heart attracted many friends. A retiring girl, she seemed out of place in the robust Severance family, rather like a modest flower struggling to bloom in a lustily overgrown garden, but she had strong opinions and, unassuming as she was, stood by them firmly. Marin had once heard her boldly contradict her father and make the flat statement that Elizabeth Cady Stanton and Lucretia Mott were right—women should have the vote. Her mother had looked down at her hands and said nothing, her brothers had grinned, and her frowning father had delivered a ten-minute lecture on the place of Woman as the helpmeet and dependent of Man. Marin loved Logan for that bit of audacity as much as for her kindliness and good humor. And there was one other attraction Logan held, which Marin admitted to no one but herself—her lean-hipped, broad-shouldered, quietly charming brother, Stuart. He was the real reason she had chosen the river as a meeting place with John Wesley; along this road there was always the chance that she might, quite by accident, run into Stuart Severance.

From the woods just ahead came the sound of a horse being ridden at a moderate pace, and she stepped off the road. Papa could have decided to come home for his midday meal, and he might make her go back with him. As she dived behind the mustard hedge, she saw a big, rangy man on a bay stallion riding into the shade of the oak grove. The horse was decked out with a tooled saddle and silver-trimmed bridle, but the man was carelessly dressed in a worn leather jacket and twill pants stuffed into unpolished knee-high boots. He wore a red bandana at the open neck of his shirt, his wide-brimmed hat was set at a jaunty angle, and he was singing in a fine baritone:

> Now you are come all my grief is removed,
> Let me forget that so long you have roved,
> Let me believe that you love as you loved
> Long, long ago, long ago.

He held the last note soulfully and then laughed to himself. Marin sat down in disgust. It was Stuart's older brother, Vail. He was Ethan's friend, not hers, and the few times he had noticed her he'd simply said, "Hello, Red," and then ignored her. It was a rude nickname, and he was a rude man. Her hair was auburn, not red, and he ought to be able to tell the difference.

Vail had a lady-killer's reputation, and because of it there was considerable interest in his activities and countless tidbits of gossip floating around, the most unlikely rumor being that he had studied medicine at Harvard College. She didn't believe it. He did not look or act like a doctor, and he did not practice medicine in a country where real doctors were almost unknown and badly needed. In California men who claimed any medical knowledge at all had long waiting lists of patients and could name their own price.

He was away from home a good part of the time, traveling to Monterey and San Diego and sometimes all the way down to Valparaiso, Chile, as business agent for Longridge ranch. During visits home most of his energy was spent hunting, gambling on cards and cockfights, and, to the displeasure of his father, pursuing every pretty Spanish girl in the area, even married women—a dangerous pastime among a people almost morbidly protective of female virtue. Ethan admired him, and as far as possible imitated his dress, his manners, and his habits of living, which were, Marin gathered, unmentionable in the presence of ladies.

But Stuart—Stuart was so different. Handsomer, kinder, more appealing in every way. Everyone knew about the barely suppressed antagonism between the brothers—they had never been the best of friends, Logan admitted—and it was only because of Stuart's even temper and inherent reasonableness that they did not clash more often. Peeking through the bushes at the man on the horse, Marin thought she could see in his face the intractable qualities that made him so hard to get along with. No wonder Malcolm Severance was said to prefer his younger son.

Across the open field two riders appeared, pounding their

horses' flanks with their hats and hallooing, and she knew by their riding style that it was her brother, Ethan, and his friend Michael Morgan, tearing over the rough ground in a flat-out gallop that risked their animals and their necks. They pulled up on the road in an abrupt maneuver, coming to a dead stop in seconds and causing their horses to rear on powerful legs. Marin, watching Ethan calm his skittish horse, thought with a swell of pride that in this country of superb horsemen, he was the finest rider of them all, and so handsome, too, with his shining blond hair and slim, well-muscled body. He and Michael Morgan were both twenty-one, and both stood an inch above six feet, but Michael seemed shorter, thick-chested and square, without Ethan's grace or his dashing charm.

Ethan trotted toward Vail, who had reined in and waited with a smile in the dappled shade of the oaks.

"We're going to find Pa and talk him into selling Michael that chestnut mare he's been wanting."

Sell, indeed, sniffed Marin behind the hedge. Michael Morgan never had any money. He'd have to work for the mare—*if* Papa would let her go. She was a beauty, and Marin wanted the animal for herself.

Ethan said, "Come with us—you can get supper at our house tonight."

"I'm afraid I can't." The broad *a* of Boston in Vail's voice fell oddly on Marin's ears, accustomed as she was to her own family's soft Southern speech. "I'm on my way to Fontana to sell Nicolas on our bull. My father's trying to convince him he'll make more money if he breeds up his scrawny cows."

Malcolm Severance had imported a magnificent bull and demonstrated what improved bloodlines could do, but so far only James Gentry had been impressed enough to use the bull on his own stock. The Spanish rancheros could not be bothered. The land was vast, the supply of cattle unlimited; tallow and hides shipped out on American, English, and Russian ships brought them all the goods they needed and all the luxuries, too. The quantity of meat remaining after slaughter was an embarrassment, and they left most of it decaying on the hills for the wolves and vultures. Stockbreeding meant work, and time was better spent cockfighting, hunting, riding, and giving parties. Why look for work and give better meals to the wolves?

At the mention of Fontana, Ethan's eyes sparkled. "Give Prudencia my respects."

Vail laughed. It was well known that Prudencia Cermeno's

name did not match her character. Her brother Nicolas was hard pressed to keep her in line.

"I'll do that."

As Vail spurred past them, Michael and Ethan called after him several crude suggestions as to what he could do to Prudencia if he caught her alone. Then they dug the long rowels of their spurs—cruel devices—into their horses and leaped off in a sudden full gallop, disappearing into the grove of oaks before Marin could scramble from her hiding place. She came back onto the road, stepped daintily over the horse droppings, and stopped to brush her skirt free of grass, not noticing the horseman riding down the hill behind her.

From the crest of the hill James Gentry had observed with amusement the three young horsemen talking in the road and his daughter hiding behind the golden mustard hedge. What was she up to? Whatever it was, he would bet a year's production of hides that Rose didn't know about it.

Marin's instinct was correct as to her father's feeling for her—she was his favorite child—but he loved all his children and had watched them grow toward adulthood with a shrewd, dispassionate eye. Sophy was his baby and now going through a bad patch as she entered her teens. But her spirit was sweet, her fundamental nature sunny, and he trusted she would survive the difficult years just ahead and come out well on the other side. Ethan was his only son, the bearer of his name, but he saw that young man's limitations clearly and lived in the hope that increased maturity would fit the boy to take over the great ranch James expected to hand on to him.

Of all his children, his elder daughter interested him most. A pity she was not a boy, for she had a superior mind and the drive to make her intelligence count for something. He knew her faults—obstinacy, bossiness, and, worse, a scorching temper—and blamed the temper on his wife's Italian heritage, not seeing in Marin the exact image of himself. She had one other flaw that worried him more. Unfortunately Marin did not always tell the truth.

Once when he had caught her in an especially outrageous lie, he had taken her on his knee and said, "You must not tell stories, chicken, for people who do become known for it. Then when you are telling the truth and most need to be believed, no one will believe you." Sometimes he thought his words had produced the desired effect, other times . . . But after all, children did lie, mostly to avoid punishment. As a boy he had gone all around the mulberry bush himself to keep his father from discovering minor transgressions, and life had taught him that deceit did not pay in the long run. Marin's childish deviousness was a deficiency that time and experience would correct.

She was also unswervingly loyal and loving, with a generous, optimistic spirit—fine qualities that made any little defects insignificant. All in all, he was most pleased with her and had a sneaking admiration even for some of her flaws, since so many of them were his own.

His small, sturdy mustang slid on the loose rocks and caught itself surefootedly, and stones rattled into the gully. Marin looked up and froze.

He jumped his horse across the ditch, and she smiled as happily as if she were glad to see him. "Oh, Papa, the boys just went off to the upper range looking for you."

He rode up to her. "They'll have a long look. Where are you headed, chicken? Does your mother know you're here?"

"Um, yes. Papa, are you going to sell Michael the chestnut?"

"Is that what he's after? Probably not. I haven't heard yet where you're going."

"Just to the creek for a picnic." She pulled her lunch out of her pack, said winningly, "Enough for both of us," and held her breath.

"Thank you, pet, no. I'll take myself home, as your mother is expecting me." He almost laughed at her relief. "Be home well before dark. We'll have visitors this evening, and Mama needs your help."

Uncle Cole and his sons. Boring, boring. "Yes, Papa, I'll come back right after lunch."

He smiled down at her, a forceful man, deep-chested and black-haired, with the weathered, ruddy skin of one who has lived his life outdoors and the same look of liveliness that was in her face. He was too soft with her, he knew it. Like a restive horse, she needed a stern, steady hand—but she was only a child and so pretty, looking up at him with the innocence of angels in her eyes. There was time enough for discipline. Though he did wonder what in hell she was up to.

He laid his hand on her bright hair, warm and shining in the hot sun, said, "You should have your bonnet," and "Be home early, mind," and trotted off toward home.

She watched until he was out of sight and then walked into the woods.

John Wesley Morgan was on the creek bank skimming stones

across the shimmering, slow-moving water, a tall boy, almost seventeen, and bulky like his brother, Michael, with the same square face, the same light brown hair worn long, and a stubble on his chin where he was trying to raise a beard. His eyes were different though, brown and prominent, and shining with impatience. Michael, in spite of his boyish rowdyism, had a kindliness that Marin vaguely recognized and knew that John Wesley lacked.

He watched as she descended the bank. An astonishing change had come over the skinny little girl he had first met last summer, and he relished the new, enticing softness of her arms and breasts, wondering how her body managed to be so pleasantly round and at the same time so slender. She moved with fluid grace on long, slim legs, like a blossom fluttering on a tall stem. He knew what her legs looked like, although they were now always hidden under skirts that swept the ground, for he'd caught many flashing glimpses of them last year, when she still hiked her short dresses above her knees to go wading or climb on a horse.

But that was a long time back, before she put her skirts down and became a proper young lady. He hadn't paid much attention to her legs then; now he thought about them a good part of the time. One of his favorite diversions was imagining Marin Gentry in various stages of undress, and speculating as to how he could catch her alone with no clothes on at all.

She was smart, too, and he didn't resent it, for many times her clever tongue had gotten them out of scrapes that could have led to punishment. She awed him, this slip of a girl who could talk him into anything and make his heart pound when she smiled; she knew so much he didn't know and had been so many places he would never see, fabled places like New York City and Valparaiso. She always had her nose in a book, reading about the places she hadn't been and planning to go there. The truth was, though he would have endured torture rather than admit it, John Wesley was afraid of her.

"I thought you weren't coming," he said as she sat down and spread out her skirt so that the lace showed to advantage.

She shrugged. "I was lucky to get away. Luz put the evil eye on Josefina again, and I sneaked out while Mama was trying to quiet her down."

She made no further explanation, and John Wesley understood. Josefina and Luz were rivals for the affections of James Gentry's chief vaquero, Gabriel Navarro, a sly, shifty-eyed fellow, excellent with horses and cattle but, in Marin's opinion, hardly the kind of man to inspire violent devotion. The girls were from Yucatan, more Mayan than Spanish, and in her desperation Luz had brushed aside her superficial Catholicism and reached into the weaponry of her ancient Indian forebears, using the evil eye on Josefina, a power they both believed in to the bottom of their superstitious souls. Many times the family had found Josefina on the floor and watched her come out of apparent deep unconsciousness screaming that Luz had set the devil on her. James shocked his wife by stating that he wished Gabriel would set up housekeeping with both girls so he could have peace in his home, except that they would surely kill each other. With a frown Rose had changed the subject, and Marin refrained from saying that Papa's solution made sense.

She laid out the lunch on the grass, and she and John Wesley ate and talked companionably. Only last fall they had hammered together the remnants of a barn door found near the abandoned house at the edge of the woods and launched it into the stream, intending to sail down to the big river, across the bay, and into the ocean to China or the Sandwich Islands. They had climbed aboard, water had bubbled through the cracks, and their craft had sunk under them. It settled into soft mud, leaving them standing in a humiliating two feet of cold water, their feet sinking in muck, slimy green vegetation wrapping around their legs as they struggled to the bank.

Looking back at that fiasco, Marin found it impossible to believe that she had ever been so ridiculously young. Her sixteenth birthday wasn't so very far away, and many of the Spanish girls, daughters of great families, were wives and even mothers at fourteen. The thought of marriage led directly to Stuart Severance, and she pushed away the alluring image of that young man and dug in her bag for her sketchpad. It wasn't smart to dream of one man while you were in the company of another.

She braced the pad against her knees and began to draw the bending willow on the opposite bank, wishing John Wesley would go away so she could get on with the novel hidden in the bottom of her bag. He sprawled beside her, watching her face and thinking that her hair looked like wild honey, red-gold honey with the sun shining through it, making her eyes a delicious shock when she lifted them and looked at him. They were enormous, those eyes—shining black, sending pleasant ripples through him. You didn't expect black eyes with the red hair and white, white skin. It was those Italians, he supposed, back somewhere in her mother's family. Italians were dark, like Spaniards.

But John Wesley was wrong. Rose Gentry's father had been an

Italian from Milan, a northern Italian as blue-eyed and blond as a Swede. Marin's black eyes came from the daughter of a Scots borderer who had married into the English Gentrys; from her, too, had come the red hair, a subtle red that flamed in the light and muted in shadow to the honey gold that bewitched John Wesley.

He thought about putting his hands in that hair and letting the silk fall through his fingers. He thought about tracing her dark, arching brows and then drawing one finger down the slightly tilted tip of her nose and along the line of her cheeks, rosy cheeks curving around high cheekbones like a juicy, ripe peach. If he bit that peach . . . not a good idea. He could wrestle Marin down, but she was strong for a girl, a fighter who would kick, bite, and gouge when really mad.

She raised her hand to smooth her long hair, knowing he was watching her, managing with the motion to show off the lovely line of her breasts. She had no idea that he had finished his inventory of her face and, progressing to better things, was taking off her clothes in his mind.

In disbelief she looked down. His long, knobby hand had traveled up her back and was sneaking around to the inviolable, never-to-be-touched front part of her. She swiped at his hand with her sketchpad and leaped to her feet, swinging both fists and shouting. He held her off with one long arm, trying to explain and apologize. Damn. She'd be mad at him for weeks, and he had been planning to wheedle an invitation to eat at her house tonight. Mrs. Gentry didn't like him much, but she set a good table. Marin aimed a vicious kick, and he danced back out of reach. She swung again with her fist, missed, and in passionate frustration shouted, "I'll kill you! I'll . . ." She searched for the ultimate threat. "I'll tell your sister!"

He dropped his arm and vaulted away. Glenna was a good Christian woman. If she found out, life wouldn't be worth living. From behind a tree he tried reason.

"Listen, Marin, I said I was sorry . . ."

She scrabbled in the grass, found a good-size rock, and hurled it in his direction. It struck the tree near his head, and splinters of bark flew in his face. Without further argument he took off toward home, leaving her in the clearing shouting after him, her face red with outrage.

If at that moment she had been told that there was a connection between his wandering hands and her increasingly expert attempts to dazzle him, she would have denied it with honest indignation, for she was a product of a society that came close to denying the existence of things sexual, where fear and fascination were locked in perpetual struggle and guilt was the constant companion of most people. Marin loved to flirt whenever she could find a male to practice on; a young man's admiration was a marvelous builder of self-esteem and could effectively counter, at least for a little while, the sense of unworthiness that sometimes oppressed her. But though she had grown up on a horse farm and could quote chapter and verse from James's studbook, she had little idea of what went on between married people in their bedrooms or between young men like Ethan and available girls like Fermina Victoria. Like most well-bred young women of her time, she suspected, but she did not know, and so it was easy to force down unclean, depraved ideas and believe she had never thought them. What could it be that drew Ethan to Fermina? Why did men like Vail Severance risk real danger to pursue the charming but well-guarded Spanish ladies? Why did John Wesley try to put his hands on her every time they were alone? It was a mystery that gave her such an odd, uneasy feeling, she decided not to think about it.

With no man present to impress, she pulled Celia Baldwin's novel from her bag and stretched out on the grass. A smile curled the corners of her mouth. She'd scared the daylights out of that wicked boy; he had gone leaping across the meadow like a rabbit with the hounds on his trail. Then, in moments, she forgot him and was lost in a tale of love between a dashing man and a beautiful woman, the kind of grand passion she greatly desired for herself.

The sun climbed the sky and slowly dipped while she read through to the tragic end of the book. Tears rolled down her face. She put out her tongue and licked a tear, liking the salty taste. She looked down at the slow-flowing stream, cool, serene, dark green, carrying on its surface spring blossoms blown down by wind that still bore the last faint sting of winter.

It was a lovely, lonely land, underpopulated and tranquil, and its silence pressed on her with gentle melancholy Her thoughts returned to John Wesley. He loved her and would do anything for her, and it was her beauty and charm that had brought him to such a pass, just as had happened with the heroine in the book. It was wonderfully heady, this sense of mastery over another human being, and though part of her said she was heartless, the rest of her delighted in it and wanted to experience more.

Her wants, in fact, were legion. She wanted a white silk dress, a floating cloud of silk to emphasize the purity of her complexion and the flame of her hair; she wanted men clustering around her, begging for her kind attention; she wanted to live in a house full of elegant possessions, to dance all night and not be tired in the morning, to go away for days and not explain when she got home; she wanted her freckles to disappear from her nose, and her hair to grow to her knees; she wanted . . . oh, most of all she wanted a man to love her, a strong, wise man who didn't mind that she wasn't a good person. Then the hollow places inside her would be filled and the aching loneliness would end.

It was a secret, this inner pain, one she had never told anyone, not even Papa. Especially not Papa, for he would never understand. Wasn't she loved? he would demand with hurt and indignation. Didn't he and Mama love her and do for her constantly? Yes, of course, she would have to reply. She needed their love and would die without it, and yet there was another kind of love that she hungered for as a starving man hungered for food. Not the heroics and high-flown speeches in the books she read; they were thrilling, but innate common sense told her that was not the way life was. It was something else she craved—to be known utterly by one man, every flaw and frailty down to the darkest part of her nature, and loved anyway.

She knew she lied when she should not. Each time it happened she swore she would never do it again, but when the next time came and a bending of the truth seemed necessary—either to get herself out of trouble or to make others behave as they should— she did it.

Not even her father could have told her why. He did not know that his cheerful, effervescent little girl had been born with a gift that was also a curse: acute awareness of the dangers in the world combined with a finely honed survival instinct. He never understood that the protective instinct that kept her off large, temperamental horses until she was sure she could control them also led her into lies—how else to manage people and events, how to keep herself safe?

There was such confusion inside her along with the fear— anger, bewilderment, loneliness, contradictory urges bumping and jostling, dark thoughts, secret longings, devils in her soul that she would never admit to, not if she died for it. The analytic mind that James admired would not let her rest, for she saw in herself qualities she did not like, while all around were the serene, honest faces of family and friends. Why was everyone else so good when she was not? She did not guess that behind social courtesies and religious lip service everyone else hid feelings like hers, indulged in hypocrisies, struggled with ignoble urges and often lost the battle. She did not know that loneliness was at the center of human experience and was never healed, only eased by distractions. And being ignorant of these things, she reached blindly for comfort, thinking that once she was loved by the right man, she would be happy forever. For some months now she had believed that the right man was Stuart Severance.

A drop of water landed on her book. She brushed it away, and another landed on her head. From the west came a muttering rumble. The iron gray clouds, gathered seaward all the day, were moving inland across a sky turned drab and ominous. The cheerful late afternoon sun had vanished.

She grabbed up her possessions and scuttled through the trees to the abandoned house on the meadow's edge where she and John Wesley had played last year when they were children.

As she stepped inside, the downpour began, and she looked back once into the wavering curtain of rain. Then she turned into the main room of the house. It was a small adobe building with walls three feet thick, and the room was empty except for a leather-thonged settee sagging in front of the cold, black fireplace. She shivered and rubbed her bare arms briskly. There were sticks of firewood festooned with cobwebs in the corner. She wished she had some matches.

A cutting wind whipped through the open doorway, and she went back and jerked at the door. One corner was jammed against the dirt floor of the porch, and she could not move it. The wind blew rain against her, and she retreated into the house and climbed the stairs to the second floor. There were three rooms upstairs, and all were empty. Whoever had lived here and left had stripped the house when he went. In a corner of the largest room she found a coarse blanket that smelled faintly of horses. She wrapped it around her and lay down on the floor, and in this position, flat on her stomach, the book under her nose and the blanket keeping away most of the chill, she settled down to wait out the storm.

The light faded until reading became impossible, and she laid the book aside. Several times in the last hour the rain had slackened enough that she considered a dash for home, knowing that her mother would be passing from annoyance to worry. But then a burst of rain would crash against the roof, and she would sink again into a doze under the warm, scratchy blanket.

It was dark when voices and footfalls echoed below. She roused from sleep and sat up. Someone had managed to wrench the stubborn door free, for it shut with a bang. The murmur of voices was louder. There was the sound of wood being dumped and a clatter as something heavy was dragged across the floor. Wrapped in her blanket, she crept to the doorway and peered through the broken balustrade. There were Indians in the hills, wild Indians never tamed by the missions, who did not like whites and sometimes raided lonely ranch houses. But the intruders were not Indians.

The dusty settee had been pushed closer to the fireplace, and Prudencia Cermeno was brushing at it gingerly. She sat down, arranging her silk shawl around her shoulders with plump white hands. Vail Severance knelt before the pile of wood on the grate. He struck a match, and a small gold flame flared and grew, lighting the center of the room and making the shadows in the corner blacker. Marin shivered, wishing she were as close to that lovely, warming fire as Prudencia. Then she forgot the cold and settled down to watch as Prudencia snapped open the fine ivory fan dangling at her wrist and fluttered her stubby black lashes.

"Ah, Señor Severance . . ." Her voice was soft, insinuating, her English heavily accented. "You are so clever with the fire. Without you I should freeze."

Vail rose but remained in the shadows on the other side of the fireplace, several feet from Prudencia. "It's my fault that you're in this predicament, Miss Cermeno. The weather was much too uncertain to go riding in an open surrey. If we hadn't found shelter, you might have drowned."

Prudencia was drenched but scarcely seemed to mind. She smoothed her hair and patted the place beside her. "Sit here by me, Vail, so we can talk." Her pout turned to a smile as coquettish as if she were in her brother's great house with hundreds of candles burning and huge fireplaces roaring.

Vail stayed where he was, maintaining a safe distance while Prudencia sent appealing glances above her fluted fan, and Marin remained behind the railing upstairs, an interested spectator. It was a potentially explosive situation. Spanish girls of good family did not—ever—entertain men alone. They did not ride, walk, dance, talk—they scarcely breathed unchaperoned. There was always a mother, an aunt, an older, married sister, or some other female relative to protect young ladies from ravishment by males presumed to be on the edge of uncontrollable passion the moment they were alone with a girl, any girl. And the fathers and brothers of those girls were ready to kill any man who by his unchaperoned presence cast a shadow on the honor of their women. Somehow Prudencia had escaped her solemn widowed sister, Beatriz, and her elderly Aunt Isabel, the dogged protectors of all the Cermeño girls, and inveigled Vail Severance into taking her riding. Nicolas wasn't going to like it, especially as the evening passed and she did not appear at the supper table. But Nicolas was an intelligent, cultivated man. Probably she thought she could manage him.

Vail went to the door and opened it. The rain had stopped. Marin tiptoed back into the room that had sheltered her all afternoon and looked out the narrow window. A sharp wind had blown the clouds to the east, and the stars were bright in a sky scrubbed clean, but the moon had not risen and the night was black. How late could it be? Mama must be frantic. A horse and surrey were standing in the derelict barn at the back of the house. She was familiar with the surrey. It had two wide seats with a generous space between them, the only such equipage in the district. Nicolas Cermeno had had it shipped from New York, and Marin and Sophy had been given a ride in it, a thrilling ride after the lumbering wooden-wheeled carretas they were used to. She regarded its shadowy outline thoughtfully. It was a long walk home.

She stuffed her belongings into her bag, bundled up the blanket, and slipped down the hall to the back staircase. Several steps were broken, and she drew up her skirt, climbed down carefully, and hopped across the muddy ground. Inside the barn she looked back. Vail and Prudencia had come out of the house, and Prudencia was exclaiming helplessly that she could not walk without ruining her satin slippers. Vail picked her up and stepped into the mud of the yard. Marin quickly tossed her bag and the blanket into the surrey, climbed into the space behind the front seat, and burrowed under the blanket. She heard Prudencia settle herself and Vail cluck to the horse.

It was uncomfortable wedged in behind the seat, and the surrey rocked and jolted on the rutted road. Marin's foot was twisted, and her bag poked sharply in her ribs. They were near the road leading to Little Mountain. A few yards on was the turnoff. She could ride along to Fontana and walk home; the fireworks that were sure to accompany Prudencia's arrival were a strong temptation. Still, it wasn't worth a long walk back in the dark through the sucking, slippery mud.

She threw off the blanket, leaned forward, and with pure deviltry dancing in her eyes said, "Good evening, sir and madam. Isn't this weather just grand?"

The occupants of the front seat turned. Prudencia looked stunned. Vail hauled on the reins and swore under his breath.

As the horse slowed, Marin jumped out, said, "Thanks for the ride," and raced up the road toward home.

Chapter 2

Lamplight streaming through the open door lit the path and reflected in puddles by the back step. She hopped up to the porch and moved quietly across the deserted kitchen, leaving muddy tracks with every step. Berta, the cook, came out of the pantry, saw her, and moaned, "Ai, Miss Marin, look what you done! I jus' washed that floor."

Marin put her finger to her lips and pulled off her damp, dirty slippers and stockings. "I'll come right back and clean it up," she whispered, scooting into the hallway before Berta could grab her and make her do it immediately.

From the front of the house voices rumbled—masculine voices rising, falling, interrupting each other. A stranger would have thought a heated quarrel was in progress, but Marin knew it was only an amiable political discussion between Papa and Uncle Cole, with her cousins, Dan and Harlan, making occasional contributions. When the Gentrys got together, it always sounded like a quarrel. Her problem was to get through the hallway, past the dining room door, and up the stairs to her bedroom before she was seen. Her blue dress with the pretty flounces was crushed and mud-stained, and her new kid slippers would never be the same. Why had she wasted her best clothes on John Wesley Morgan?

"Marin!"

She stopped in the shadows of the hall and shushed her cousin Harlan frantically.

"Where've you been?" he called from the dining room. "We looked for you half the afternoon."

Why don't you just run and tell Mama! she thought with deep resentment.

Harlan's brother, Dan, stuck his head around the door and added, "Your ma's real sore at you, Marin."

She liked her big, vigorous cousins—they had been her good friends since childhood—but right now she could have shot them both dead. She raced down the hall, but her mother's voice stopped her as she started up the stairs. "Where have you been? Gracious, child, I've been worried out of my mind."

Marin held the muddy slippers behind her and eased her bare toes back under her skirt, ignoring Dan, who was watching with a big grin. "I went down to the creek for a picnic, Mama, and the rain came on so sudden. I stayed in that empty house in the south meadow till it stopped." Basically true, except that it left a great deal unsaid. "I'm sorry I worried you." Her dark eyes were earnest, her expression sweet. Behind Rose, Dan doubled up in silent laughter.

Rose looked into Marin's face and felt her clothes. "You'll be lucky if you don't catch your death. Change that dress and come right downstairs. We will talk about this later."

Reckoning delayed, Marin hurried up the stairs, paused at the top to stick out her tongue at Dan, then swept out of his sight and ran to her room.

She sat on the floor so close to the fire that it kept her face comfortably hot, devouring leftovers from dinner and reflecting on the unfairness of life. Her mother had not even glanced at her when she slipped into the parlor, but she knew that this day's behavior would not be forgotten. Ethan, however, was still absent, and everyone knew perfectly well where he was. Yet when he finally did decide to wander home, not one reproachful word would be said. How unfair that he could come and go as he pleased with scarcely a frown from Rose, while she . . .

Beside her Sophy's head drooped, her fair skin pink with sleep and the warmth of the fire. This was the way Marin liked her sister best these days—asleep. In recent months, as Sophy moved toward her thirteenth birthday, she had changed. Gone was the gentle, sweet-natured little girl Marin had loved from babyhood, and in her place was a moody creature whose volatile spirits shot up or down for no apparent reason; who borrowed Marin's clothes, her jewelry, and her secret, hidden novels without permission; and who was in general a terrible nuisance. Where was her baby sister? Gone forever, Marin supposed gloomily.

The apple Sophy had been planning to eat rolled from her hand into the cup of her lap. Gently Marin removed it. It was tart and sweet, and she licked the juice from her lips as she leaned against the stone hearth.

She felt content in this room. It was without the refinements of wallpaper, fine woods, and carved moldings, but the adobe walls were whitewashed and the floor was made of good oak planks, hand-hewn and heavy. James had built solidly, and Rose had transformed the crude building into an echo of home with possessions from the white house, set on a green Maryland hill, that was already growing dim in Marin's memory. Almost everything in the room had been in that other parlor—the hooked rug she sat on, the black mahogany clock on the mantel murmuring its hushed tick-tick, the plush maroon sofa with the curving back, the walnut table and the oval mirror above it, the dozens of books on shelves that lined the fireplace wall. Only the rosewood piano, of all the things Rose valued most, had of necessity remained behind, and James had sworn faithfully several times that soon—by next year at the latest—he would order a new piano just like it from New York.

On the sofa beside the shadowed lamp, Rose and her sister Delphine talked as they worked on the family mending. The subject of their conversation was, as always, Maryland and the people and places left behind.

Rose Gentry was a sociable woman who delighted in setting her table with the fine china and silver brought with difficulty over so many miles of wild seas, yet she rarely invited neighbors, other than the Severances from Longridge, into her house. She did not feel at ease with the Spaniards, agreeable and open-hearted though they were; they were foreign, they were different, they were not her own kind. Sometimes Marin wondered if her mother could have survived the adventure James had led his family into if he had not been able to persuade his brother, Cole, to come, too, and if Delphine had not been widowed and afraid to be left behind. Rose needed her relatives to love, admonish, and minister to. Without them she might have shriveled and died, as Glenna and Michael and John Wesley's mother had died. Fear squeezed Marin's heart at the thought of her mother dead, and she got up and helped Rose serve more cake and coffee.

Delphine laid her sewing aside and greedily attacked the slice of cake Marin gave her, her third. The willowy slenderness of girlhood had gone, and Delphine's pretty face showed the beginnings of lines and puffiness. Her hair, once as blond as Rose's, had faded; everything about her had faded—her complexion, her blue eyes, even her voice. She had embraced widowhood, clutched it like a shawl held tight to keep out the cold wind of the outside world, and she clung hard to her sister and her sister's family. It was a situation that suited Rose, who loved to feel that everyone depended on her, but it irritated James, who wished to

God Delphine would find herself a man, before her good looks were completely gone, and establish a home somewhere else. Delphine, however, had no intention of remarrying, and made a virtue of it, saying with sad pleasure, "I have had my marriage."

Marin took her own cake and sat down beside the fire again, listening to the wind rattle the windows, wondering what had happened at Fontana when Prudencia Cermeno arrived with Vail after dark and unchaperoned. Sophy stirred from her doze and groped in her lap for the apple. She saw the core turning brown on the hearth beside Marin and pinched her sister vigorously. Marin started to pinch back, caught her mother's frown, and looked a threat at Sophy.

In the dining room the political discussion was mounting into argument. James waved his hands, his voice booming, and Marin settled back comfortably. She loved to listen to her father talk. As a child she had thought he was the strongest, wisest man in the world, and nothing had happened since then to change her mind. At fifty-six he was a vital man with a youthful face and a big, muscular body, a man who worked, played, and drank hard and loved to wrangle and debate. He seemed utterly sure of himself, and he was, for he came of a line of strong, able, adventurous men.

The Gentrys had always been a robust, headstrong people, tough, clannish, and obstinate, and their tendency to marry their own kind assured a constant and invigorating infusion of the same characteristics.

The first Gentry in America, Thomas, had crossed the water from London to Virginia in 1765, driven by the need for adventure that burned in all the men of the family, and with him, over the bitter protests of her parents, came his Scottish border lass, black-eyed, red-haired Catherine Elliott.

Catherine bore four sons in that wild Virginia country, helped Thomas clear the land for their farm, and, when the boys were still babies, saw him go off with a ragtag army to a war that seemed impossible to win. She listened for the rest of her life to his account of how General Washington accepted Cornwallis's surrender at Yorktown.

The lust for adventure passed on to Thomas's sons. When the eldest, Peter, was twenty, he traveled into unexplored Kentucky country and stayed for two years before coming home to marry the prettiest girl in the county, Maria Carey. It was Maria, with

Catherine Elliott, who gave Marin her name. She was the grandmother who, no matter what cosmic event afflicted mankind, would ask only, "Is it good or bad for the Gentrys?" Marin felt a deep affinity for Grandmother Maria.

Peter and Maria's daughters stayed quietly at home and never married, but their sons, James and Cole, were typical Gentry males. When, at nineteen, James took off on the first of his travels, he promised to come back for Cole within the year. But the year stretched to four, and war exploded again between the Americans and the British, for no reason except that politicians on both sides blundered into it.

Knowing the war was a fool's game, James nonetheless marched with General Andrew Jackson's army, but when peace was declared, he left New Orleans for Kentucky Territory, picking up Cole on the way west.

They had a fine time trapping on the rivers until they had built up a respectable fortune in furs. Then they headed home. Cole, always more cautious and habitually tidier than James, found a wife, and a farm in Maryland, and settled down to a carefully planned life.

James went north and, when the congestion and cussedness of the great northern cities became unbearable, returned to the rural peace of the South with the idea of buying a horse farm. Near Baltimore he found the land he wanted, and one summer afternoon in that leisurely city lying on the estuary of the Patapsco River, he was invited to a supper dance. That evening he was introduced to the lovely Landrini sisters.

Delphine was a famous belle with melting blue eyes and a flatteringly helpless manner when a man was around, but Rose was the one he could not stay away from. Her porcelain beauty bewitched him, her imperious manner charmed him. He loved to listen to her talk about the gracious home of her parents—so different from the small dwelling on the fringe of fashionable Baltimore that she and Delphine now occupied with one servant—and was amused that the house and the land surrounding it grew larger each time she told the story.

James's friends were happy to help him put together the background of the Landrini girls. Their father, Paolo Landrini, had arrived in Baltimore with nothing but gleaming blond hair, a smooth tongue, and a winning smile. He was no sooner off the boat than his name became Paul and the story circulated that he was the youngest son of a noble Italian family come to make his fortune in this grand new world. Within six months he was married to Jane Calvert, one of *the* Calverts of Baltimore, James was told, and so mismanaged his wife's inheritance that his daughters were left, after their parents' deaths, with unassailable social position and very little else.

James also heard that Delphine was as good as married to George Whitmore, a heavyset, red-faced, prosperous man on whom she appeared to dote. Surely Rose would not want to live on in the little house alone, with one elderly servant for company; surely the future looked very bright for James.

So it was a thunderbolt when she refused him. He loved her, and he knew she loved him, but he had reckoned without a quality in Rose that he was never to understand completely, to the end of his days. She feared change, even happy change, with a dread beyond the comprehension of a man as daring and zestful as he. Behind her gentleness was an inflexibility astonishing in one so young. Her parents' deaths had devastated her, but even more terrible was the loss of home and the way of life she had always known. Being young, she had survived and grudgingly adjusted, and now her life was Delphine and the little house on Laurel Street. The daily round of visits, the occasional parties, even the economies forced on her represented the comfortable security of the known. She would get married, of course, and it would probably be to James, but later, at some indefinite future time. Just now it was too disturbing.

Delphine had other ideas. Her vacillating nature contained a broad streak of selfishness that could harden into ruthlessness when her interests were threatened, and she hadn't the least fear of change. After many sleepless nights and a greater investment of energy than was natural to one of her indolent nature, she had finally brought Mr. Whitmore up to scratch. She was about to move into his beautiful new house, and she had no intention of sharing it with her sister.

Without the slightest intent to wound she said, "I am going to marry, and Mr. Whitmore rightfully expects to have me all to himself. Really, dearest, you can't move in with us."

She was viewing herself critically in her mirror, and Rose's reflection wavered into it, white, strained, frightened. Not unkindly Delphine said, "Why don't you marry that nice Mr. Gentry? He's a good-looking man. I vow, if I were not so devoted to Mr. Whitmore, I might glance his way myself." Delphine was convinced that she had only to glance a man's way to bring him hurrying to her side.

"Marry? Now?" Rose looked bewildered. "But I'm too young. I won't marry for years."

Delphine chuckled as she wound a shining yellow curl around her finger and let it fall against her smooth cheek. "Too young—at seventeen? I've noticed those little lines around your eyes, if you haven't. And Mr. Gentry doesn't look to me like a man who'll hang around forever. Don't come crying to me in another year when he's gone chasing after some other girl and you're on the shelf." She smiled inwardly as Rose's horrified gaze darted toward the mirror.

"Marry Mr. Gentry," Delphine repeated, dusting powder across her neck and bosom. "You can't afford to keep this house alone, and I've no intention of using Mr. Whitmore's money to help you stay an old maid." She snapped her powder box shut. "It's not as though you don't care for him, and he's mad for you . . . Oh, there's the doorbell. Put a bit of powder on your nose—there. And a dab of cologne on the bosom and wrists, honey, not just behind the ears."

James's deep voice floated up the stairwell, and Rose rolled her eyes in panic.

Delphine took a decanter of brandy from the table and filled a small glass. Brandy was her sovereign remedy for sniffles, coughs, and butterflies in the stomach. "Just drink this," she said. "It will buck you up nicely."

Rose wrinkled her nose. "I hate the stuff."

"Swallow it this instant."

Rose gulped it down and coughed until tears came to her eyes, but after a moment she decided Delphine was right; she did feel better. Obediently she chewed a mint, as Delphine instructed, and allowed the top of her dress to be tugged down until her small, shapely breasts were half revealed.

"You look lovely," Delphine said, satisfied. "Now go down there and let him look at you, and try not to be a fool tonight. I know he's going to propose again. Don't turn him down."

James did propose. He promised her a house as big as her old home and then said, "Horse breeding's a good business, and I'm going to make money at it. I swear you'll never want for anything. Rose, look at me."

She looked, and saw a powerful, self-confident man who was gazing at her as if she were his hope of life. All his vitality and certainty seemed to flow into her and make her certain, too.

Fear vanished, and her eyes glowed with the light he loved. "I'd marry you, James, if we had to live in a shanty."

• • •

Rose moved to the green, rolling land James had bought, expecting to make a home, build a family, and live there the rest of her life.

The baby, Sophy, was nine and Marin an energetic twelve when James decided he had to see California. Ethan Allen Gentry, born the first year of his marriage and named for the great hero of the Revolution, was now eighteen and so gifted with horses that he could be left with the running of the farm. James had stayed a long time in one place—at least, it was a long time for him. Domesticity smothered him, and dearly as he loved his family and his farm, he had to get away from them or die. Ten months later he was back, and he was a changed man. He had seen Elysium.

"It's Paradise," he told Cole. "Green pastures for cattle, wild horses by the thousands there for the taking, the most fertile land in the world, and the mountains! God never made grander mountains. The Spaniards live like kings, and they're generous with the land. The Mexican government has been granting— *granting,* mind you—thousands of acres to anyone who becomes a Catholic and a Mexican citizen."

Cole's head snapped up. "I'd never do that."

"Neither would I. We don't have to. We can buy land cheap from the men who hold the grants now. They have so much, they don't properly value it, and they'll sell cattle cheap, too. However"—James lowered his voice, although he and his brother sat alone in Cole's library with a bottle of bourbon between them—"we won't have to pay much, if anything. California is going to be American, and it will happen soon!"

Cole's conscience, never offended by a good business deal, was pacified, and he listened with interest rising as James went on, "Frèmont has been all over the territory, supposedly on a scientific expedition, but I know better. He's feeling out the ground for the president. James Polk wants to get hold of California before the English or the French do. There's always some of the English navy sneaking around with an eye on the bay at Yerba Buena—it's an ideal harbor, the best I've ever seen. We've tried to buy the territory, and we've tried to stir up the Californians into getting rid of Mexico themselves, which they would dearly like to do, but they're a lazy lot and there aren't many of them. They'll never do it alone. If our army can provoke Mexico into a war down on the Texas border, California will fall into our hands like a ripe peach at picking time."

Cole took a sip of whiskey and rolled it on his tongue, and James pressed on. "Those Spanish grandees live like feudal lords. The Indians have built their fortunes and given them leisure, like our Negroes here, but there's one big difference. No capital investment." He drew out the words. "Think of the money our people cost. These Indians will work for food and a place to sleep, and you don't have to buy them. We can make a killing, Cole! Think about that."

Cole thought, and he was convinced. It had been five years since his wife had died, and the old restlessness was upon him. He had turned the thought of Oregon over in his mind many times, but James made California sound like the place for him.

Rose was a different matter. The fear she had held off during the months James was gone burst over her in shattering reality. She looked at him with tear-filled, panicked eyes. "Leave my family and my friends? Leave home? James, I couldn't!" He tried to speak, and she rushed on, "And the children . . . it's so far . . . people die on journeys like that. We aren't pioneers, we weren't meant to live on a frontier . . ." She stopped for breath, and James patted her hand.

"It's not like that, darling. Listen, my queen, I wouldn't ask you to go if I didn't think it was best for you. I've done well here, but not well enough. I want to see you in a great house, with many servants, never lifting your hand if you choose not to. I can't do that for you here, but in California . . ." His eyes blazed with the look she knew so well. "In California there's no fever—hardly any sickness at all. You'll have a mansion surrounded by gardens—flowers and trees such as you've never seen, and it's always spring! There's a fruit called the pomegranate. You open it, and inside are bits of red fruit that shine like rubies. The ladies have dozens of servants, and as far as they can see the land is theirs, covered with their own cattle. They spend their time giving parties, riding, dancing, visiting . . ."

"But, James," she whispered miserably, "who would I visit *with*?"

That silenced him for a moment. Then he said, "Cole is willing to go."

Rose looked at him and turned away.

It was George Whitmore who settled the matter. Rotund, jovial George, who had been a kindly brother-in-law, sat down to an enormous meal of pork and port and sweet potato pie and afterward died abruptly of acute indigestion. And then, still numb with shock, Delphine sat in her elegant parlor after the funeral and

heard the family's lawyer explain that her husband had been
gambling in the stock market and though he would doubtless have
recouped his losses had he lived—the lawyer cleared his
throat—as things stood, the house, the matched horses in the
stable, the very chair Delphine sat on would have to be sold to
meet the debts George had left behind.

After a tormented night during which Delphine considered her
limited alternatives, she came to Rose. "I want to go to California.
Take me with you, Rose."

James seized his opportunity. In less than two months farm,
slaves, and horses were sold, and all the possessions the Gentrys
could take with them were on the dock in New York being loaded
onto the packet ship *New Haven*. They were on their way.

Chapter 3

The supper dishes had been cleared, and a jug of good
local wine sat on the table between James and Cole. Dan
and Harlan straddled straight-backed chairs, listening.

"We're going to be part of the Union, gentlemen. It's our
destiny."

"Not without a fight," said Cole as he took a swallow of the
dark red wine. He had become, in middle years, a tight-faced,
thrifty man, willing to gamble if the odds were right, but taking
nothing for granted. He was two years younger than James and
looked ten years older.

"Judas Priest, Cole," James thumped the table with a blunt
finger, "we've had control of all California since the first of the
year."

"Yeah, Pa," Dan said, his eyes shining with enthusiasm and a
drop too much wine. "We've got the Mexicans beat. The
Californians like us better anyway, and we'll never let the English
get the bay."

"Oh, we'll hold the territory, all right. God help anyone who
tries to take it from us." Cole laughed and shook his sandy head.
"But statehood? James, my lad, there'll be a battle over that one."

"The Free-Soilers, you mean? A tempest in a teapot." Casually
James brushed aside the monumental question of the extension of
slavery into new United States territories. He was heart and soul

a Southerner, but though he had owned slaves back East, he had never been dependent on slave labor as were the cotton planters farther south. Here in this lazy, sun-drenched country, he did not need slaves. His square, ruddy face lit with exhilaration. "We'll be part of the Union, and then Americans will pour in. We'll show these Californians how to make something of this country, by God!"

Beside the fire Marin shivered with excitement. As always when Papa talked like this, her imagination flared. The strategic importance of the bay escaped her, and the war with Mexico was so far away as to be on the moon. But James's exuberant words evoked a picture of her countrymen moving across the continent with the easy, free-swinging stride that was peculiarly their own—acquisitive, energetic, daring Americans descending from the mountains to sweep over this indolent land, shaking awake the arrogant, self-indulgent Spaniards. When they did, it would mean the end of the old barter system. There would be productive agriculture and factories, and that would mean money, Papa said, cash money to buy the kind of life they were meant to have. It was his promise to Rose, and Papa never lied. Now the Americans were coming to make his promise true.

A few American trappers had been spilling through the mountain passes for decades, and American sailors had left their ships and stayed, marrying local girls and taking Spanish names. John Baldwin, Celia's father, had been such a sailor. Twenty years ago he had jumped ship, married the daughter of a Spanish don and himself become Don Juan Baldwin, living in an imposing house, just he and his daughter now that his wife was dead, surrounded by enormous landholding and the trappings of great wealth. He was one of those about whom the New Englander Malcolm Severance said contemptuously, "He left his principles at Cape Horn," for John Baldwin had acquired free land by renouncing his American citizenship and becoming Mexican and a Catholic.

There were many such men scattered through the territory. Expedient men like Josiah Cutter, cold-eyed, thin-lipped, and grasping, but especially welcomed by the Californians because he was a doctor. Josiah expended most of his energy acquiring more land and overseeing his many business interests, and treated patients when he felt like it, not when they needed him.

In recent years there had been a few like the Gentrys and the Severances, who came with money, bought their land, and retained their principles, the land being cheap enough that the principles were not impossibly costly.

The Morgans were a different breed, the first trickle of a coming flood of hard-up people, desperate for a better life and willing to risk an overland crossing to get it. Michael and Glenna and John Wesley's father had died of cholera before the little family reached the Sierras, and Michael, then a boy of eighteen, had brought them through to Oregon and eventually down into California, taking the responsibility for his younger brother and sister, and his mother, whom Marin remembered as a haggard woman with hands like claws who had died quietly six months after they arrived. The brothers and their sister lived now on the small acreage James had given them, with a garden, a cow, and a few pigs and chickens. Rose treated them with the generous kindliness due hardworking people of a lower class and made extra efforts to help them because they were children and orphaned. But Glenna Morgan kept their adobe cabin scrupulously clean, and Marin harbored a sneaking admiration for what Michael had accomplished, and a disloyal suspicion that Ethan, in the same circumstances, might not have done half as well.

Over the rumble of James's voice came the sound of horses splashing up the muddy drive, and Marin raised her head. It was Ethan coming home, and someone was riding with him. She heard him give orders to the Indian boy who cared for his horse, then spurs jingled and boots thudded on the porch. Rose went to the door with a whisper of taffeta skirts and raised the latch, and Ethan strode into the light, a slender young man with narrow, intense blue eyes and a square jaw made squarer by his habit of clenching his teeth. His face glowed with the sting of the wind, and there was taut excitement in his movements as he pulled off his gloves and tossed his hat on a chair. Michael Morgan followed him into the room, ducking his head and looking embarrassed, as he always did when he came to Little Mountain.

Rose lifted her cheek for her son's kiss.

"You are late, Ethan. I've been worried." Her comfortable tone indicated that she had not given him more than a passing thought. She nodded pleasantly to Michael but did not offer her hand. "Good evening, Michael. Have you boys eaten?"

"I don't know about Mike, but I ate at the Victorias'," Ethan answered casually, and Marin gave him a bitter look. The whole neighborhood knew why he went to the Victorias' tumbledown shanty, and it wasn't for Mrs. Victoria's cooking.

"I'm not as lucky as Ethan, ma'am," said Michael in his slow, gentle voice. "I'd surely appreciate some of your good food."

Pleased, because feeding guests implied affluence and good

housewifery, Rose went to the table to heap high a plate. Michael bowed a little awkwardly to Delphine, sitting beside the lamp with skirts spreading decorously to the floor, her empty plate in her lap, and Marin smothered a smile as Sophy's eyes flicked quickly in his direction. Little Sophy was growing up fast. He bowed to the two girls sitting by the fire, managing it more gracefully this time, and followed Ethan into the dining room, where Cole and his sons bawled greetings and offers to share the jug of wine. James rose to pull up chairs for the latecomers.

Cole poured two more glasses of wine. Harlan refilled his own glass and tilted back in his chair.

"Come home with us tomorrow, Ethan. We're going after that marauder bear that's been raiding our stock." Harlan was a good-natured young man with eyes that seemed to be perpetually smiling. Since he last visited Little Mountain he had grown a short beard that he imagined lent him a dashing appearance.

Ethan helped himself to a piece of pie and answered with his mouth full. "Can't. You'd better not go either, laddie, or you'll miss the fun. Nicolas Cermeno's challenged Vail Severance to a duel."

Marin's head snapped around.

In the dining room voices exploded.

"What happened?" "Is Vail going to fight him?" And louder than the rest James boomed, "What did he do, boy?"

Michael grinned and went on eating, and Ethan said, "He took Prudencia out riding alone, and they didn't get home till after dark."

There was a whoop of laughter. They all knew Prudencia Cermeno. Then the laughter died, and into the silence Ethan said, "They got caught in the rain this afternoon and couldn't get home, but it didn't matter to Nicolas. Just taking her out alone was enough. Vail ought to have known better."

They all looked gravely at the floor or the tablecloth but not at each other.

Quietly James asked, "What will the weapons be?"

"Smoothbore pistols. At dawn day after tomorrow, on that high ground near the marsh. Vail asked Michael and me to be his seconds."

Listening in the parlor, Marin thought of what Ethan's offhand words actually meant. Although she had grown up around them, she was afraid of guns. Lying in her father's drawer or resting on the hooks on the wall, they seemed silently, latently deadly, ready to discharge and kill. For two grown men to stand a few feet apart in the dim light of dawn and deliberately attempt to shoot each other over the intangible question of honor was insane.

In this she thought more like her father than like her gentle mother, to whom dueling was an acceptable, even an admirable method of settling disagreements. The Spaniards' touchiness on points of honor, so like the Southerners', was one of the few characteristics of California that Rose could thoroughly understand and appreciate. James sometimes said, only half in jest, that the elaborate courtesy of which Southerners were so proud was actually a necessity of life. Without it, they would be involved in duels even more often than they were.

From where she sat Marin watched Ethan toss down a glass of wine and remembered Vail that afternoon, keeping a careful distance and fencing politely with Prudencia across a cold, empty room. He was a big man and physically strong, but a duel was not a contest of brute power or endurance, and Nicolas Cermeno was an experienced duelist and an excellent shot.

Outside, the wind whipped the trees to a lashing whistle, slipped under the wide oak door, and traveled across the floor. Marin still sat by the hearth, alone. The women had gracefully and properly retreated before a matter that was wholly masculine. But Marin leaned closer to the dying fire as a last tiny flame curled around a blackened log and strained to hear the men's voices in the next room as they talked on in lowered tones about the mechanics of the duel.

A strict ceremonial form had to be observed. There had already been a challenge and an acceptance—and if Vail was as smart as he was supposed to be, she thought in disgust, why hadn't he just told Nicolas to go tootle on his horn? Nicolas couldn't shoot a man who wouldn't fight. But Vail was a typically foolish male, so afraid someone would question his courage and, therefore, his manhood. They had already picked a location; riverbanks and meadows seemed to be preferred. Now all that remained was for news of the stupid affair to be spread, so as to have as large an audience as possible, and arrangements made for a surgeon to be in attendance. Ethan was wondering aloud if Josiah Cutter could be persuaded. Otherwise there would be a delay until that seedy fellow down in Monterey who called himself a doctor could come up.

"Cutter will be there," said James. "The old bastard never misses a fight, though I notice he's never one of the participants."

Harlan laughed. "He can't afford to be. Who'd he leave all his money to if he got killed?"

There was an uncomfortable silence, and Harlan's face reddened. He had committed the social gaffe of mentioning the possible end of the affair for Vail.

James placed his glass on the table, corked the almost empty jug, and rose. He gazed somberly at his son.

"Have you done your best to stop this? That's the first duty of a second. Will Vail apologize?"

"He apologized right off the bat for getting the baggage home late, but Nicolas wouldn't accept it. She's a bitch in heat, and he knows it, but it's Vail who'll have to pay for it. Damn fool." Ethan glowered into his empty glass.

There was nothing more to be said. The men went upstairs to bed, all but Ethan. He followed Michael into the parlor, and Marin shrank into the shadows. The blunt talk had interested more than shocked her, but her brother would not be pleased if he knew she'd overheard.

Her bedroom was cold, and wind seeped in around the closed window. In the dark she located her warmest nightgown and dived into it, climbed into the piled-up featherbed, and immediately jerked her knees up and wrapped the flannel gown around her feet. Josefina, the useless creature, had failed to put in the bed warmer, and the sheets were icy.

Slowly the eiderdown comforter overcame the chill of the bed, and she eased down her feet, imagining, as she always did before sleep, that the warmth came from Stuart's arms around her. After a long, dreaming time during which she fell half asleep, there slipped into her mind the memory of a splendid buck with branching antlers. It had leaped in the air as her father brought it down with one shot. A magnificent, wild, free creature, bursting with life, and in a moment a limp and twitching carcass. Vail Severance reminded her of the buck. Ridiculous thought. She yawned. She didn't especially like Vail, but he didn't deserve to be killed over a girl like Prudencia. The whole affair was unnecessary, foolish, and wicked, because, as she well knew, nothing improper had happened.

Her eyes flew open. *As she well knew.*

She could avert this needless tragedy! Tomorrow, directly after breakfast, she would go to Fontana dressed in her best and tell Nicolas that she had been present in the abandoned house and could vouch for Vail's gentlemanly behavior, the more impressive because he had not known anyone was watching. Stuart would be forever grateful, her parents would be proud that she had prevented an unjust killing, the story would probably spread all the way to Monterey and even San Diego. It was faintly reminiscent of an episode in one of Celia's novels—which one she could not now recall.

She lay for a while enjoying the prospect of celebrity and then drifted into sleep.

Chapter 4

Marin rode down Fontana's curving drive feeling foolish, wondering why she ever thought it was a good idea to come here. Nicolas Cermeno had listened to her story and believed every word, and it made no difference at all. Her presence in the little house had meant nothing, he said, for she was too young to be a chaperone. Prudencia knew the conduct required of her, and Vail knew what was required of him. Prudencia would be sent into a convent for her mistake, Vail would be shot for his. "If," Nicolas had said with a smile, "I can manage it." The smile confused her, for he was talking about killing a man who had been his friend.

She touched the horse lightly with her heel and trotted into the road toward home. To the east, over low green hills, lay Longridge, and ahead was the winding road that would take her to Malcolm Severance's sprawling adobe house. She would like to know what Vail was doing on the day before a duel he didn't want to fight and how old Malcolm was taking this latest scandal his elder son had gotten himself into. Then, too, Stuart would be there, helping his brother in whatever way he could. All things considered, it was a good idea to visit Longridge this morning.

She turned the mare into the Longridge road and, as she did, saw her brother coming from the direction of Little Mountain, riding, as always, at a dead gallop. Ethan pulled up beside her, his horse lathered and sweating in the mounting heat, yet she knew that no emergency had brought him roaring down that road. For an experienced horseman he was careless with his animals, riding them into the ground in a way that brought down James's fierce displeasure.

He grinned into her disapproving face, and annoyance slid away, replaced by pride, pride in the way he sat his horse, the silver blondness of his hair, the thick gold lashes around smiling blue eyes. The cast of his face bore a faint resemblance to James's, but his features were finer. And he was so much fun to be with, always good-humored and ready for any amusement. A perfect brother.

However, she could not resist a small, needling remark.

"Why the hurry?" She cocked an eye at the heaving horse. "Did Fermina send for you?"

The dart glanced off Ethan without leaving the slightest nick, and he fell into pace beside her.

"I'm heading up to Longridge. Michael went over first thing this morning to watch Vail target-shoot."

The significance of that hit home, and she was silent.

"And where have you been, little sister? You sure snuck off quietly enough this morning."

"I did not sneak off," she replied with a nice touch of injury, although it was exactly what she had done. "I had a visit with Nicolas Cermeno, that's all."

She had the satisfaction of seeing amazement leap into his face.

"You've seen Nicolas? What have you been up to?" He stopped his horse at the entrance to Malcolm Severance's private road and waited for her answer.

She turned her horse and moved up the drive at a walk so that he had to follow in order to hear her. "I was with Vail and Prudencia yesterday. I felt it was my duty to tell him."

Ethan grabbed her reins. "This is the devil's own business, Marin. Vail can't afford any of your tricks . . ."

"It's not a trick," she shouted, tugging at the reins. "Dammit, let go of my horse!"

He looked into her face and said slowly, "You really were with them." He threw back his head, let out a whoop, and leaped off with such a sharp thrust of spurs that she had to slam in her heels and lash the mare's flanks to catch up.

They pounded up the long drive and within sight of the house veered away and took the path down to the meadow. Some little way back they halted. Marin opened her mouth to speak, and Ethan lifted a hand in an abrupt signal for silence. In the meadow patches of lupine and mustard painted wide swaths of purple-blue and deep yellow across the green of new grass; brilliant dots of orange glowed where the poppies grew in profusion, and wild thorn spread in brambles. On the far side of the meadow dark oaks rose to the sky. One had a target nailed into its rough bark. A fence ran the length of the meadow, and Michael Morgan hunched over it, watching the man on the other side of the fence. Vail Severance stood with his arm outstretched and his pistol steady on the target as he sighted down the long barrel.

He was the tallest in a family where great height was characteristic even of the women—long-limbed and muscular, towering over Michael, who stood more than six feet himself. Watching him critically, Marin thought that everything about him was excessive—his size; his big, beaked nose; his deliberate pursuit of danger. He was facing combat tomorrow with an experienced duelist only because he had taken Prudencia out, knowing that the moment he left the house alone with her he was at risk. There was an intransigence in his face that begged for contention and dispute. If he really had apologized, it probably had been done in a style so provocative as to make Nicolas even angrier.

He squeezed the trigger and hit the bull's-eye squarely.

"On the money!" Michael cried out.

Vail shook his head and smiled. "The thing is, I won't be shooting at a piece of paper tomorrow."

He walked to the fence to lay the smoking pistol in its box, and Ethan dismounted. "My dear fellow," he called out with an expansive laugh, "your worries are over. Little sister went to see Nicolas this morning and told him she was with you and Prudencia. She's fixed everything."

Marin, sitting on her horse a few paces away, experienced a sinking sensation. Ethan had interpreted her wrongly, she had not meant him to think . . .

Vail said, "Has she, by God," and the expression on his face made her wish the earth would open and swallow her up. The last time she'd seen him was from the back of the surrey as she rose up behind him and Prudencia. It had seemed like a good joke at the time, but now she felt embarrassed and a little scared.

He swung his long legs over the fence, came up to the mare, and rested one hand on the bridle. "What did Nicolas say, Marin?"

His voice was so gentle that she raised her head. His eyes were a true, pale gray, and right now seemed to be drilling through her.

"What did he say?" he asked again, and she whispered miserably, "Well . . . he did believe I was with you, but . . . he said I wasn't old enough to be a chaperone."

He laughed, gave the horse a slap that sent it dancing sideways, and walked back to the fence. As he reloaded his gun, he said to Ethan, "If you can't control that girl, you'd better keep her home."

Marin battled her startled horse into quietness and exchanged glares with Ethan. Michael's face was turned, but his shoulders shook with silent laughter. Vail was once more taking careful aim at the target.

She jerked the horse around and thundered up the path, furious because she had been treated like a meddling child and humiliated because she knew she was one. They had laughed at her down there, Vail and Michael and Ethan. Her pride was injured and her dignity badly damaged, and she hoped Vail got his head shot off tomorrow so she wouldn't have to face him again.

At the head of the path she swerved away from the house, intending to ride for home, but a voice called, "Marin!" and Logan Severance ran down the front steps and waved.

"I'm so glad to see you, Marin. Have you been down to the meadow? They won't let me . . . oh, please stay and visit a while."

Marin considered returning a short reply and going on, but Vail's sister was plainly in sore distress. She unhooked her knee from the saddle and slid to the ground.

"Don't look so worried. Papa says Vail is an excellent shot, and from what I can see, he is. He's hitting the target every time."

The tightness in Logan's face eased a little, and they walked to the porch. The mare followed, prancing with excess energy and arching her shining neck.

"You've heard about this—this duel then," Logan said in a low voice.

"How could I help it?" Marin tied the reins to the porch rail and sat down on the step. "Ethan came home full of it last night. He's down there with Vail now."

Logan's face stained red, and Marin shifted her eyes. Unhappy Logan. Her feelings for Ethan showed in every word and gesture, though she didn't realize it and would die of mortification if she thought anyone guessed. Did she know about Fermina Victoria? Almost certainly not, and if told, she wouldn't believe it. Her eyes were swollen from tears shed during the night, and her hair had come loose from its net. Instead of softening her plain face, it only made her seem untidy.

She was nineteen, perilously close to spinsterhood, and looked as appealing now as she was ever likely to. Her skin was clear and her blue-gray eyes quite lovely, but unluckily she had inherited the large, aquiline Severance nose, so striking in Vail's masculine face and so calamitous in hers. She had the Severance height, as well, impressive in a man but awkward for a skinny girl who lacked the grace to carry it off. Men wanted dainty girls who looked up to them and made them feel big and strong, not towering young women who could look them straight in the eye. Then, too, her bosom didn't amount to much, and her chest bones showed through the fabric of her dress. She could stuff cotton wadding down her dress front, restrain her unruly hair, overcome her bashfulness, and still never be able to compete with Fermina's earthy, voluptuous charms.

Someone should tell her not to take seriously the flirtatious conversation and polite compliments Ethan tossed her way—but how to do it without crushing her completely? Liking her, pitying her, Marin decided that it could not be done.

Behind them the door opened, and Marin's heart flip-flopped and began to beat rapidly. She smiled offhandedly—so as not to expose her feelings the way Logan did—and looked up at Stuart. His face, so like his mother's in harmony of bone and line, was grim, but his expression brightened when he saw her, and he bent over her hand with a punctiliousness he had not lost for all the time spent in the wilderness.

"I'm glad you're here, Marin." He smiled, but his eyes remained sober.

"How is Mother?" Logan asked, her apprehension flooding back.

He lowered his long-limbed body to the steps beside the girls. "Still locked in her room."

"Father?"

Stuart grimaced. "Didn't you hear us? He isn't going to back down, Logan, not an inch. You know him."

Brother and sister exchanged looks, and Marin, thinking of Malcolm Severance, was glad she was not the one who had to deal with him: a big, humorless man with fierce eyes and an elegant sweep of white hair, who gave her the feeling he would destroy without compunction anyone who opposed him; an imperious man of rigid religious beliefs and demanding principles.

Considering Vail's truculent character, it was a miracle that he and his father had so far managed not to kill each other. No wonder Logan was so high-strung around her father, and her mother, Elizabeth, so retiring. Only Stuart, levelheaded, intelligent, never losing his temper, and always able to see both sides of an issue, could cope with the man undismayed. But he looked worried now.

"Dueling goes against Father's principles. He says if Vail goes through with this, he'll turn him out."

"Turn him out!" Logan went pale. "Where would he go? What would he do? Vail has worked as hard for Longridge as any of us. And he's his son."

Stuart laughed shortly. "Not if he fights this duel. Father told him this morning that while he's put up with all his other 'iniquities'—that was the word he used—if Vail does this, he'd better let himself be shot because he'll be dead anyway as far as Father's concerned."

"He couldn't have meant such a thing."

"Couldn't he?"

Logan's mouth straightened to a thin line, and she looked away. Marin thought, what a strange family, these Severances—without kindness, without closeness, without warmth, except for the love of the brothers for their sister. How could a father renounce his own son—no matter what he had done? Impossible to imagine James doing such a thing to Ethan. This was such a hazardous, lonely land for settlers like themselves. They must be able to depend on each other, or they were lost.

A short, sharp, crackling sound disturbed the quiet, and the three on the steps looked toward the oak grove that hid the flower-dotted meadow from their sight.

Stuart rose. "I'd better go down there—though there's nothing I can teach Vail about shooting. Stay here, Logan."

He walked with Marin to her horse, lifted her into the saddle, and stood, one hand on the horse's muzzle, looking up at her.

She was slim and straight-backed in her black riding habit, and the white plume of her tricorn hat curled prettily against her cheek, but for once she was not thinking of the impression she was making on Stuart. She was conscious only of an immense pity for the people at Longridge, all except that cold, self-righteous man who had passed such a brutal sentence on his elder son. No matter which way the dice fell tomorrow, nothing could ever be right for this family again.

There was another report from the direction of the meadow, quick, jarring, sinister. She touched her whip to her hat in a little salute, turned the chestnut's head, and trotted rapidly down the drive to the road, glad to get away from this unhappy house. Just before trees blocked her view, she looked back. Stuart was striding down the incline toward the grove of oaks, the sun shining on his brown hair. Logan still stood on the porch, her hands clasped in a hard grip, staring after her brother.

The night was as dark as though dawn were hours away, but the brightest stars had dimmed and the moon was almost down. The oak Marin sought was broad, its trunk at least four feet thick, a majestic tree whose gnarled branches were black against the sky. Near its base a great branch nearly as thick as the trunk angled upward, an easy path into a spreading crown of leaves. She pulled up her skirt, climbed to the natural seat formed by smaller branches, and huddled into her cloak. The days were growing hotter, but nights were still chilly in May. From here she commanded a good view of the river, the marsh, and the ground on which Vail and Nicolas would meet, but the foliage was thick enough to hide her. This was important, for she had no idea what her father would do if he caught her.

To the east, in the direction of the great Sierras, there was a lightening, a hint of less intense blackness. Along the rim of the sky a glow appeared, and the crest of Mount Diablo gleamed, luminous, faintly pink in the first light of the coming day. There were sounds: the jingling of caparisoned horses, the creak of leather as riders leaned in their saddles, the clink of harness and spurs, and the slap of a rein pulled taut. A horse snorted, and Marin saw the plume of his breath in the cool air. A team and wagon ground to a stop at the edge of the trees, and with a shock she realized its purpose. When it left, it would have at least one man in it, wounded or dead.

As dawn advanced, she could make out the burly form of her father. The thinner, shorter man beside him was Cole. Under the oaks at the far side of the meadow, her cousins Dan and Harlan were tethering their horses next to John Wesley Morgan, whose quick, jerky movements testified to his excitement. Probably he had never seen a duel before, Raimundo Galaz was there with his seven swarthy sons, all dressed in their best, the Solers from south of the bay had just arrived—they must have ridden half the night—the Costas, the Prietos, the Oliveras, even the Victorias, although they stayed at the back of the crowd, as befitted members of a lower class.

Nicolas Cermeno was the first of the combatants to arrive. He wore sumptuous black velvet breeches and a beautifully fitted, embroidered jacket, and laughed and talked as he walked to the high ground with his seconds. Armando Cermeno would not be there; he and Stuart were required to stay away while their brothers fought. The cause of it all, Prudencia, was locked up at home, presumably fearful for her brother or Vail—or perhaps for neither of them. Probably she was most worried about her own ultimate fate, not that her honor was sullied. Of course, no other women were present, for females could not be allowed at this utterly masculine affair, no anxious mother or worried sisters or even curious onlookers—except Marin, perched uncomfortably in the oak tree, frightened by what she was about to witness and beginning to wish that she had not come.

Three horsemen clattered up the hill. They dismounted beside James and Cole, and in the increasing light Marin saw the gleam of Ethan's hair and Michael Morgan's broad, stocky figure. The third man was Vail Severance, easy to identify because of his height. His head was bare, and his wide shoulders were covered by a cloak that swirled to his knees. He handed the cloak to James and walked with Ethan and Michael to the center of the meadow. The seconds stood with heads together, talking intently; then Ethan and Juan Estivez, Cermeno's second, walked off ten long paces—thirty feet—and hammered pegs into the ground as marks for the duelists. Each second had his own gun in his belt, insurance that the fight would be conducted properly. The two men opened a rosewood box, took out two guns—identical smoothbore pistols, nine inches long—and examined them carefully. The guns belonged to Nicolas, and they were beautiful weapons with gold and silver decorated barrels and carved Circassian walnut handles. Ethan was not happy that Vail had agreed to use one of them; it wasn't wise for a man to gamble his life on a gun he had never handled. But Vail owned no dueling pistols. The gun he had used to practice with was an old one, unsuitable for dueling.

The night before James, helping Ethan and Michael melt lead and pour it into bullet molds, had said that Vail was a good shot when hunting with a rifle and an excellent shot at a standing target, but that facing a man only thirty feet away who had his own gun, experience, and the intent to kill, could rattle even the steadiest nerves. Ethan had good reason for concern.

He and Juan tossed for position and the giving of the word. Vail stayed where he was, at the peg nearest the tree in which Marin was hidden. He wore black trousers tucked into knee-high boots, and a white shirt open at the neck, with sleeves rolled up for greater freedom of movement. His face was expressionless. Nicolas took the far side and stood at ease, one hand on his hip and a faint smile on his handsome face. They were waiting for the doctor, Josiah Cutter.

When he came, he did so slowly, allowing his horse to wander without urging, knowing nothing could happen until he arrived. He dismounted, untied his black bag from the horse's back, tossed his reins to the nearest onlooker, and walked to the meadow. He was a thin man, above medium height, dressed in a long, loose-fitting frock coat that flapped about him. Graying black hair straggled down to his collar, and his narrow-lipped turned-down mouth was grim, as always. He stalked across the field, and Ethan and Juan Estivez loaded the pistols and set the hair triggers—triggers so fine, Ethan had said, that the lightest brush of a finger, even a breath of air, could discharge them. It was this delicate trigger that worried him most, for a man inexperienced with hair triggers could barely handle one without firing it prematurely. He and Michael had delivered many lectures to Vail on the subject.

Nicolas and Vail each took a gun and held it muzzle down. They nodded to each other courteously, these two men who had been friends and now intended to kill one another. Beyond them the river shimmered in the early morning light, and ducks rose from the tule of the marsh, quacking and beating their wings. The sky had turned a tender blue, marked with cloud streaks, and beneath the blue a misty film of rose suffused the world.

Ethan said, "Gentlemen, are you ready?"

Not a sound, not a sigh from the crowd. Only a silent tensing and a hush.

Vail, still expressionless, his eyes narrowed slightly, his big body taut.

Nicolas, cool, slim, elegant, a much smaller target.

Ethan glanced quickly at each man. His golden head went up. "One . . ."

Nicolas raised his gun, there was a cracking sound on the crisp air, and a puff of dust blew up from the ground a foot in front of Vail. The crowd of watchers gasped, unable to believe what they had seen, and Juan Estivez reached for his gun. Ethan stepped forward quickly, his own pistol in his hand, and Juan moved back out of the line of fire. The impossible had happened, and in recountings that went on for months afterward, in arguments over jugs of wine that lasted far into the night, no one was ever able to understand or explain exactly how it had happened. Nicolas Cermeno, the seasoned duelist, using his own weapon, with which he was intimately acquainted, had accidentally discharged it before he could take aim. His pistol was empty, and he could not fire again until Vail had taken his turn. He was required to stand and wait to receive his opponent's shot.

The men on the sidelines were silent, waiting. Vail had a choice. He could make the magnanimous gesture, fire in the air, and hope Nicolas would accept the exchange of shots as sufficient to restore his honor. But if Nicolas's sensibilities were not yet soothed, he would have then the right to load his weapon and fire at Vail again. Nicolas waited, turned slightly, his gun at his side, his trim body tense.

Vail raised the classic gold and silver pistol that he had never used before, took deliberate aim, and fired. Nicolas reeled back, his gun falling to the ground as he clutched himself. Blood poured from the sleeve of his jacket, and he lifted his head, calling out to Juan to reload for him. Vail stood in his place, his hard-boned face still. Ethan ran toward Nicolas shouting, "Are you satisfied, sir?"

"No!" Nicolas cried out in pain and fury, and Dr. Cutter, bending over him, said, "You are in no condition to fire again, Señor," and shook his head at Juan.

"Your right hand is useless, Nicolas," Juan said calmly. "Let this be the end of it."

Nicolas struggled up, his jaw muscles clenched. "I'll fire with my left then," he said, and his head fell forward as a great gush of blood covered his hand. Juan slashed open the elaborately embroidered sleeve, and Dr. Cutter went to work.

Ethan picked up the rosewood pistol box, and Vail laid the gun on its velvet lining. He walked to the trees where James and Cole Gentry waited, and watched Ethan give the gun box to Cermeno's second, lean down to look at Nicolas and exchange a quick word with Dr. Cutter, then come swiftly back.

"I think the bleeding is slowing, but it's hard to tell."

Vail nodded, his face impossible to read. Not one person watching could guess what he felt.

Nicolas's seconds lifted him into the wagon and laid him gently on a pile of blankets. The gorgeous jacket, bloody and ripped by the knife, was put beside him. Slowly the creaking wagon moved away.

Under the trees James Gentry put his hand on Vail's shoulder. "It was a fair fight. I'm glad you're alive, boy."

Vail did not answer. His eyes followed the wagon, and when it disappeared into the trees, he vaulted onto his horse and galloped up the hill into the light of the rising sun.

• • •

Marin sat with Logan Severance and Celia Baldwin in the shady garden at La Gracia. It was cool here, for breezes seemed to be always gently trembling in the giant sycamores that rose above their heads. Fashion books that had come in on the last boat, more than a year old but eagerly awaited by the girls, lay neglected on the grass. Marin loved Celia's garden and coveted one like it for herself. It was a green haven of coolness on hot days, a treasured retreat of fine, soft grass and lacy ferns, palms and pomegranates and figs, and a thick, ancient grapevine that twisted over a long lattice, providing a cool corridor to the house.

From the sunny patio near the garden came the pleasant bubble of the fountain, and falling water splashed up prisms of color as it struck the quiet surface of the pool. A mockingbird that had nested all spring in the garden and could expertly imitate the cry of a cat called its haunting howl. Celia glanced about for her kitten, then looked up and smiled at the bird.

She was a remarkable-looking girl, slim, beautifully formed, deceptively fragile in appearance. Marin, torn between envy and admiration, thought her face perfect, for it greatly resembled the stylish, remote ladies in *Godey's Ladies Book*, faces that were the current ideal of beauty. Like theirs, Celia's face was oval, with a dainty chin and skin the color of rich, white milk. Her hair, which she allowed to hang loose below her shoulders, was so black that it seemed blue in some lights. The hair and creamy skin she owed to her Spanish mother, who had died giving birth to her, and her long, narrow, black-lashed eyes were the dark turquoise of her American father. But for all her perfection of feature and coloring, it was the aura of virginal unattainability that drove the young men mad.

Suitors came from as far away as San Diego and even Mexico City and Valparaiso, and she was known to turn down three and four proposals a week. In the last year the acquisition of Celia Baldwin had become a prize whose worth was beyond calculating. There had been many extravagant declarations and threats of duels, but to her great relief—for Celia abhorred violence—only three had actually been fought, and no one had died as a result. As she and Logan listened to Marin's account of the morning's bloody ceremony, there was concern in her blue-green eyes but nothing more, for Celia had one great deficiency not generally recognized—her flawless face held little vivacity and no fire at all.

Even now, moved as she was by Marin's description of the duel and Nicolas's wound, no one seeing her could have guessed that he was a man she had known since childhood.

"And what about Vail?" she asked after a pause. "Was he hurt?"

"Not a bit. Nicolas never touched him," Marin answered abruptly. Her own feelings were confused, and she had not yet sorted them out. For Stuart's sake and Logan's, too, she was glad Vail had not been killed. At the same time, the bloodied body of Nicolas Cermeno had shocked her profoundly. She was not at all sure Vail had done the manly thing. Her father called it a fair fight, but she knew that men's values were sometimes distorted and violent. It would have been a splendid gesture, firing into the air, yet Vail had deliberately chosen to gun Nicolas down. What would his high-principled father think of that?

What did Logan think? She looked as though she hadn't slept much. Bluish stains showed beneath her eyes, and her skin was sickly pale. She took a careful stitch on the embroidery panel in her lap, then raised her head and listened.

Celia's father was coming through the grape arbor, his head held forward in an oddly absorbed pose. He was talking to Vail Severance.

Marin thought, What's Vail doing here? And then, her pulse beginning to race, Is Nicolas dead?

John Baldwin had shrunk with the years, and he was no longer the big, dashing American sailor who had caught a wealthy señorita's eye. But he was a rich man. He had taken his wife's dowry and turned it into a fortune by smuggling in goods that the home government in Mexico City had declared contraband. The customs officials, all friends of Baldwin, became rich men, but none so rich as Don Juan Baldwin himself. In recent years his businesses had grown eminently respectable. Anyone allowed to acquire an interest in them was fortunate indeed, and whenever he was willing to talk business, men listened.

Vail was listening now, his dark head bent, his eyes down. He took the hand held out to him and shook it. Then John made what was, for him, a magnanimous gesture. He went back into the house, allowing Vail to proceed alone into the garden.

Logan jumped up, her eyes apprehensive. "Nicolas . . . ?"

Vail smiled. "He's alive. I've just come from Fontana. Joe Cutter says he'll live if the wound doesn't putrefy, but Armando's worried Nicolas won't be able to use his arm."

How peculiar men are, thought Marin. Nicolas's brother could talk in a civilized manner with the man who shot him, and then let him walk freely away because all had been done according to the rules. And yet the self-possessed man who in the dim light of dawn had waited to be shot and then taken careful aim and fired, the man who had watched, expressionless, as the doctor worked over Nicolas, did not look impassive now. Behind his smile he looked wretched.

He drew a deep breath and said softly, "Celia, I came to tell you that I'm going away."

Her fingers went to the cross at her throat.

"Because of Nicolas?"

"No. My father threw me out this morning."

There was a choked sound from Logan, and Celia turned on her. "You knew! You've known all morning! Why didn't you tell me?"

Logan answered with dignity. "It wasn't my place. Besides, I thought . . . I hoped Father might change his mind."

Vail's mouth twisted. "Father never changes his mind. He's found something in the Bible against dueling—don't ask me what—and he'd prefer me dead. I *am* dead to him. Nicolas had one idea of honor, and Father has another. So I'm going away."

Celia pulled her shawl close as though the day had suddenly turned cold, and color flushed and faded in her cheeks. In astonished revelation Marin thought, They love each other, and I never guessed. No wonder Celia's been turning down proposal after proposal.

John Baldwin had left them alone with the unspoken understanding that the girls would stay with Celia to preserve the proprieties. Without quite betraying his trust, Logan moved to the far side of the garden and stared out into the patio in order to give her brother some privacy. Marin followed her, but the low voices traveled clearly.

"Where will you go?" asked Celia.

"I'm riding down to Monterey. There's a ship sailing tomorrow that I have business with. I may be gone a long time." There was a pause. "Will you wait?"

"I'll wait. However long it is, I'll wait until you come." Celia lifted the gold cross that lay against her breast and kissed it, took it off, and put it in his hand. They stood like that, only their fingers touching, and Marin had to turn away from Vail's look of naked longing. A pain that was close to anger, a burning resentment seized her. Why should Celia have everything? Riches and beauty and a great love, too.

Someday, she thought, someday a man will look at me like that. Not Celia. Me!

And she watched Vail go swiftly down the long garden path.

Chapter 5

For some weeks the main subject of everyone's conversation was the duel and its aftermath, the most exciting event the quiet rural district had known since Altagracia Prieto ran away with the oldest Moraga boy. Altagracia's father and her discarded suitor found her in a state of undress in a house in Monterey and brought her home tied to the back of a mule.

There was general relief at the news that Nicolas was holding on, for he was well liked. On the day he was helped into his garden—his olive skin gray-tinged—to sit in a chair in the sun for half an hour, his neighbors were so gratified that they gave a party for him that lasted three days, although of course the guest of honor was unable to attend.

For Malcolm Severance there was nothing but condemnation. It was incomprehensible to the Spaniards that he had denied his elder son. In their view, Nicolas and Vail each had followed the only honorable course, Nicolas to challenge and Vail to respond. Sons were a precious commodity, elder sons even more so, and the Spaniards sat over their wine and shook their heads in commiseration for Vail, mystified that Malcolm based his actions upon his strange, heretical religion. They sighed, gave thanks to God that He had made them Catholics, and drank the health of both Nicolas and Vail.

Sympathy for Vail and condemnation of Malcolm were widespread among the Americans, too, although they criticized Elizabeth Severance almost as much as her husband. Used to strong-willed women who spoke their minds and greatly influenced their men, they thought Elizabeth should have taken her son's part. By her attitude, as reserved and cool as ever, she gave the impression of agreeing with Malcolm. If she felt any sorrow at Vail's sudden departure, she kept it hidden.

Stuart kept his feelings hidden, too. He continued to do his own work and Vail's as well, never referred even obliquely to the terrible moments on the riverbank that cool May morning, and no one quite dared bring up the subject of his absent brother or his unforgiving father. Logan bitterly denounced her parents to Marin, though she kept most of her anger for her father and hinted that her mother could not influence him if she tried. For the first time in her life she lied to her father, letting him believe she was at Little Mountain with Marin when both girls were with Celia in the fragrant garden at La Gracia.

Celia went about in a daze, hoping for a letter from Vail and spending much time before the prie-dieu in her private chapel, her lips moving as her beads slipped through her fingers. No letter came, but one day a rough, dirty man with tobacco stains in his brown beard and three fingers missing from his right hand appeared at her front door and convinced the doubting servant who answered that he must speak to the lady of the house. The news he gave Celia brought the color back to her face and the spring to her step, and she pressed food, a horse, and a small leather bag of gold coins upon the man before he left. Vail had sailed on the ship *Huntress* out of Monterey, bound for China; he was well and would write when he could; she was to pass on this message to Logan and his mother.

Glad as she was for the news, any news, Logan was disturbed by Celia's improved spirits. She failed to see what was cheering about her brother's traveling to the bottom of the world, as far away as he could be.

There was a message from Vail to John Baldwin, too, and word spread that he had not gone into the world penniless, as his father intended, but had been backed by Celia's father in some mysterious business venture. This heartened Vail's friends, for Don Juan had never yet lost money on an investment. Feeling comfortably assured that Vail's future was bright, and cheered by the spectacle of old Malcolm's cold fury when he found out, everyone went back to his customary pursuits, refreshed by the whole entertaining episode.

Spring of 1847 passed into summer, and the wildflowers died, the streams diminished, the hills turned yellow and then gold, weddings took place and births and deaths, and the endless parties continued.

All the previous year, as news trickled in about the war in Mexico, the Spanish Californians had wavered between dread and optimism. Neglected for decades by the home government, they had almost forgotten that they were technically Mexican and felt little patriotic fervor. They had long believed that they were destined to be taken over by some great power, possibly England or France. British warships had prowled hungrily up and down the coast for years, and even Russia had lusted after the great bay and the rich land around it. Now, although fighting continued in Mexico and the Baja California peninsula, the war had ended for Alta California at the beginning of the year, when the local residents' opposition collapsed. It was decided. God willed that they were to be American, and so far the change had made little difference.

James Gentry was in a splendid temper these days, slamming his fist into his palm and repeating that all his predictions were coming to pass, repeating it so loudly and frequently that his family began to wish the Americans would go quietly away. But American merchants and traders were arriving almost daily and were welcomed warmly into the busy social life of the district. American army detachments were present, and American navel ships were anchored in the harbor near the little settlement of San Francisco, as Yerba Buena was now officially called. The ships bore attractive young officers who came to all the parties—their primary purpose as far as Marin was concerned, for James encouraged her to attend any social events where Americans were present. There was a ball or supper or picnic by the river at least once a week. The incoming men, cut off from women for long periods of time and hungry for female company, passed the word among themselves as to where the prettiest girls could be found.

They all had heard of the fabled Celia Baldwin, but had recently discovered that another young lady of good family—American, too—with red-gold hair and quite extraordinary eyes, was worth searching out if one was stationed in the north.

Many of the young men who now came calling at Little Mountain had at various times in the past declared their undying love for Celia, but she seemed not to care about these defections. Instead she helped choose fabrics for Marin's new dresses and gave expert advice on the handling of men in every conceivable situation. It was as if she no longer cared about attracting men or accumulating proposals; her heart was with Vail in China, or whatever far-off place he had last written from.

There had been two letters, one following closely on the other, and Celia read freely from them to Marin and Logan, reserving only certain passages for herself. After that there were none, but she seemed content. She still spent much time in prayer, and it occurred to Marin that she might very well enter a convent if Vail did not return. Many a devout Spanish girl had done that very thing after the loss of a sweetheart. Meanwhile Celia attended parties, danced frequently, smiled her sweet smile, and told no one her innermost thoughts. She was charitable and kind to everyone in her gentle, detached way—no Indian who wandered into La Gracia left unfed, and no wayfarer went without shelter, food, and a fresh horse if he needed it. She took a special interest in Rodolfo Victoria's brood of twenty-three and passed on her old dresses to the daughters, who thanked her courteously, although the fabrics were usually so fragile that they were of little practical use.

Immediately after Vail's departure Celia had gone to see Nicolas Cermeno, and every few days she brought him delicacies from her own kitchen, as well as the local news and most interesting gossip, until he was recovered enough to mount his horse and ride out again. All summer his beautiful jackets hung loose over his shattered right arm, and when it healed, permanently stiff, all his jackets had to be adjusted. It was well known that each day he practiced target-shooting with his left hand in the field below his orchard, but whether he did it in anticipation of Vail's return no one knew, and no one, not even his brother Armando, dared ask.

He came often to La Gracia when Marin and Logan were there and escorted all three girls on carefully chaperoned picnics and long rides across open country, sometimes as far as the bay or to the edge of Josiah Cutter's property near Mount Diablo. Nicolas used his charm on Logan, enticing her to smiles and even laughter, and she ached to ask him if he meant to renew his quarrel when her brother came home, but kind as he was to her, she could not quite venture the question.

Autumn was golden and temperate, foreshadowing a mild winter. It had been a dreamlike summer for Marin, her first season as a young woman, and a triumph if one counted success in numbers of suitors and popularity at parties. More important than any of these trophies, Stuart Severance had become a frequent visitor to Little Mountain. Even under the pressure of his father's demands and the additional burden of Vail's work, he managed to find time for her. But her first actual proposal of marriage—the first notch on her gun, Ethan called it with brotherly disrespect—came from an unexpected and not too welcome source.

She had cut off John Wesley Morgan without a qualm when better prospects hove into view, and she saw him only occasionally, working with his brother, Michael, or sometimes talking to Sophy when he came to Little Mountain on an errand for his sister, Glenna. Michael was at the house often, ostensibly to see Ethan, but in reality, Marin was beginning to suspect, for other reasons. He seemed to have more to say to her than he did to Ethan.

One peerlessly beautiful October evening they sat together on the front veranda at Little Mountain, watching the sun set behind shimmering gold hills that hid the bay and the ocean beyond, she in the creaking, battered rocking chair that Rose had banished from the parlor and he on the steps at her feet. He wanted to take her small hand into his big, callused ones and feel the silky flesh and delicate bones beneath, but contented himself with fingering the end of her sash, which had come untied and lay over the arm of her chair, and watching the play of light across her face. Her skin glowed in the last rays of the dying sun, and little shadows lay at the corners of her eyes and beneath her cheekbones.

This summer had been a revelation to him. He had seen, really seen, Marin Gentry for the first time, and he wondered where his eyes and his head had been. Before this summer she had been Ethan's little sister, a girl who played with John Wesley or had to be rescued when she tried to ride horses not yet fully broken to the saddle. Without warning and in a manner destructive of his peace of mind, she had this summer developed qualities of womanhood that had a powerful effect on his emotions and—though he barely admitted it even to himself—his body. He thought about her constantly—had thought of little else for months. The compelling curve of her cheek and the firm little chin with the adorable dimple in it; her short upper lip and the way it met the sweet, full crescent of her lower lip; the shining mantle of hair, which seemed to give off its own light; her smile . . . it started in her eyes and slowly lit her face with warmth that suffused him. When he lay sleepless in the night, it was her eyes he remembered, dark mysteries he could not decipher. It was her eyes that kept him awake.

The sun dropped behind the hills and left the sky a welter of orange and coral and crimson; the small, white, puffy clouds carried no threat of rain, for wet weather was still at least a month away. When rain came, bringing back the wild green grass and tender oats, ducks and geese would appear again on the dinner table. Already a few early travelers, hardy brant and geese, beat across the brilliant sky on their way from Canada to their winter home in the south. Looking up, Marin followed their effortless movement and in imagination saw them adventuring bravely on into an unknown future—like her. The thought stirred her, and she trembled a little.

Michael said quickly in his flat Missouri accent, "Should I get your shawl?"

"I'm fine," she answered, and then wished she'd sent him for it as he went on, "I have something to say to you, Marin. I just hope I can get it right."

Judas Priest, she thought in a flurry, he's going to propose. How can I head him off?

He was a nice-looking man, and she did think of him as a man, although he was the same age as Ethan, who could still be boyishly irresponsible. Michael was a hard worker and looked it. His arms were heavy with muscles, and the tendency to weight suggested by his thick chest was held off by constant physical labor. There was a firm, settled expression to his square face, and he did not affect the beard and flowing mustache that so many young men wore to prove their manliness. His neatly trimmed, light brown hair rested on his collar, and his blue eyes held hers so earnestly that she could not look away.

"I have the farm," he began. Marin thought of the few acres James had given him and suddenly wished Papa had been more generous. "Wes will be going out on his own before long. There's Glenna . . ." He stopped, and they both thought of Glenna. Eighteen years old, not at all bad-looking if you discounted the fact that her brown eyes were slightly prominent, a good housekeeper, a good cook, a good Christian girl with a reputation for kindly deeds—and not a marriageable man in sight. None of the handsome young officers off the naval ships stopped at the Morgans' cabin. But more and more families were moving in over the mountains or down from Oregon the way Michael had come, poor farmers seeking land. Surely among them there would be a nice young man just right for Glenna. Perhaps, Marin thought, she should do something for the girl, invite her to some of the bigger parties and so free Michael for the time when he did find a girl suitable for him.

He went on, speaking his thoughts. "Glenna will marry someday, but of course I'm responsible for her until then. You couldn't share the house with her. It's small." Marin was silent, thinking of the tiny cottage Michael had built by himself for his family. "But, Marin . . ." he drew a breath and said quickly, as though his courage might fail if he hesitated, "if you would say you'd marry me someday, if you would wait . . ." He stopped. It was a long speech for a laconic man.

She waited for the indignation to come and was slightly surprised when it didn't. He was only a dirt farmer, even if he was her brother's friend. He had no education, no polish, no family background and was an object of her father's charity. It was impudent of him to suggest such a thing. Yet, in spite of the sophistication she thought she had acquired, she was still unhardened by life and essentially generous. It was, after all, her first proposal, and although she didn't intend to brag about it, he was a good man and it was an honorable offer. She looked into his unwavering blue eyes, and the cool, unequivocal refusal she meant to give him would not come.

"You do me a great honor, Michael," she began, falling back on Celia's old standby, and realized that it was true. It *was* an honor for a man to ask you to be his wife; what more could he do to show his regard? Silence. She ought to say something more. "Uh—you take my breath away." He looked heartened, and she groped for words that would clear up any possible misunderstanding. "However, I'm still very young and—and not prepared to take such an important step at this time."

He didn't look discouraged, he looked hopeful. But, good heavens, she had intended only to let him down gently. Now he'd hang around all the time, getting in the way and putting her through scenes like this until she gathered the resolution to hand him a flat and final no.

He grabbed her hand and before she could pull away kissed her fingers, just like a gentleman.

Oh, Celia, she wailed inwardly, now what do I do?

Gabriel Navarro was, with the exception of Ethan, the finest horseman in the district. There was intelligence in his narrow, sharp-featured face and a knowing expression in his dark eyes that made Marin uncomfortable. Although his manners were never less than correct—he was only James Gentry's head vaquero—there was always a suggestion of something else behind his eyes, as if his thoughts were very different from his polite behavior. She avoided him when she could. However, this afternoon he was training one of the wild mustang fillies the vaqueros had brought in last month, and she was drawn irresistibly to the corral to watch.

He dressed rather grandly for a working horseman, but then all the Spaniards, rich or poor, loved finery and wore as much as they could afford to buy. His jacket was plain dark brown cloth but heavily trimmed with thick braid, and the slashed sleeves showed a shirt beneath that was covered with fancy embroidery. His breeches were velvet, and a red sash was tied dashingly at his waist. So sure was he of his own ability that he was still wearing spurs, which chinked at every step, and brass bells on his leather leggings. The filly rolled her eyes at the twinkling sound, and Gabriel murmured quietly and stroked the soft muzzle. When he saw Marin, he bowed with the courtesy due the daughter of the house, but as he turned away, he was grinning, pleased that she had come.

She climbed to the top of the fence and watched him lay a blanket and then a light saddle on the horse's back. He had done this several times before, and the next step was to mount and see if the filly would willingly bear his weight. If Marin had not been there, he might have waited a few more days to try this, but he was an egotistical young man, sure of his horsemanship and his attractiveness to women, and he admired the señorita's eyes and bosom and the way her hips swayed. He decided to ride the filly today. He cinched the saddle, led the filly twice more around the ring, and mounted. The horse's ears twitched, but she did not move. Marin held her breath. This was the point where a recalcitrant animal usually began to buck. Of course Marin wouldn't want him hurt, but it would be funny to see Gabriel Navarro thrown for once and his self-satisfied face covered with mud.

He glanced across at her, winked, and touched one spur lightly against the animal's side. Marin was already climbing down from the fence, intending to march to the house and complain to James about the man's impertinence, but she stopped on the middle railing as the filly laid back her ears and rolled her eyes. A horseman was cantering down the hill from the house, probably Ethan or one of the vaqueros, but she remained on the fence, her eyes fixed on Gabriel, hoping he would be thrown. The filly shuddered, tossed her head, and stamped, as though deciding just what method she would use to rid herself of this unwelcome burden. Gabriel continued to murmur soothingly and nudged her with his knee. Reluctantly one dainty hoof went forward, then another. He flicked her neck lightly with the rope he was using as a halter, her speed increased, and docile as a lamb, she trotted around the ring. As he passed Marin, he lifted his sombrero in a boastful salute, and his sharp, dark eyes flashed an unmistakable message that brought the blood surging to her cheeks. She jumped to the ground. This time she would tell her father!

The horseman was down the hill and riding toward her. It might be Michael, and she did not want a renewal of last night's proposal. She shaded her eyes to see and immediately forgot Gabriel. It was Stuart. He had gone south four weeks ago on business that should have been Vail's, and she had not even known he was back. He must have debarked at San Francisco and come straight across the bay by one of the small boats, for he still wore the formal dress of a businessman. Her heart gave a queer little thump. Never had she seen him look so fine.

He halted beside her, and the late afternoon sun slanting through high oaks beyond the corral seemed to burn into his dark brown hair and leave a radiance around him. She looked up into his smiling eyes and thought, I love only him.

It was simple, it was true. It must have been true during all this long summer when she had danced and flirted with other men and found them attractive, knowing that none could compare with Stuart, but not knowing until this moment that she must have him and no other. Her feelings were plain in her face, and she turned to hide them, for Gabriel was watching behind the corral fence.

"I didn't know you were back, Stuart. Did you stop just to see me? My goodness, I'm flattered. I'm not used to seeing you so dressed up." Her mouth was dry. She was talking too much.

He dismounted and walked beside her, with the reins looped over one hand. The horse's hoofs clopped on the hard-packed earth and muffled as they reached a patch of matted grass under the long shadows of the trees. Down here Gabriel could not see them. They continued to the stream and walked out onto the little wooden bridge James had built.

What did he feel for her? Did she seem only a foolish, flighty girl who liked parties and flirted too much? He was so serious and worked so hard. If only his irresponsible brother had behaved himself, he would be here to help. Resentment of Vail flared briefly—Vail, who had caused so much trouble. It was hard to believe the two men were brothers, they were so different.

She glanced sideways at him—the high forehead and straight nose, the dark brows over hazel eyes that gleamed with flecks of gold if one looked closely, the mouth that was straight and firm without a hint of sensuality. He had not answered her lighthearted chatter. He had said nothing at all.

With new sensitivity to his moods she asked, "Is something wrong?"

He looked up, smiled, and shook his head. "I got some news today. I'm not sure what I think about it."

"Bad news?"

"Depends on your point of view, I suppose. Celia is going to marry Nicolas Cermeno next month."

"Celia . . . but she loves . . . oh, Stuart, you must be mistaken."

"There was a message from John Baldwin waiting for me in San Francisco. He wanted me to stop at La Gracia as soon as I got home. I've just come from there."

"He told you this?"

Stuart nodded, frowning down into the water. "He was sorry because he likes Vail—they even have some sort of business dealings, and he thought . . . but Celia has decided, and so it will be. It's an ideal match, of course, from John's standpoint. Nicolas is Catholic and has a great name, and when the land they hold is put together, it will be the greatest ranch in California." He laughed. "That can't help but appeal to John's business sense."

Slowly Marin said, "I've been with her all summer, and I never guessed. She's never even hinted . . . or Nicolas, either. That day, when Vail left, she said, 'However long it is, I'll wait until you come.' I heard her say it. And she looked, oh, she looked as if her heart were breaking."

"I guess hearts mend, after all. It's to be announced this week, but John told me now because he thought I might be able to get the news to Vail. He hasn't had word of him since he left the Sandwich Islands, and he wants him to have time to simmer down before he comes back. But I can't reach him. In San Diego I talked to a man who'd run into him in a bar in Sydney, but he could be in China by now."

Stuart leaned on the bridge railing, his chin jutting forward, his eyes intent on the dark, slow-flowing water. "There's a perversity in Vail, a streak of violence, and sometimes he takes things very hard—he brought that duel on himself and gunned down Nicolas deliberately. He did it with some pleasure, too. So there's no way of guessing what he'll do if he comes home and finds his girl is married, and to Nicolas, of all people." Stuart's hand was resting very close to Marin's on the railing, and he laid it over hers. "I came here as soon as I knew. I can't talk at home. Vail's name can't be mentioned around Father, and Logan will feel it very much. I wanted to tell you."

Warmth spread through Marin and settled around her heart. She stood in quiet contentment, her hand under his, watching the quivering eddies of dark water, thinking that she would remember this moment all her life. How incredible that Celia, who had stumbled, white-faced and tragic, through the days after Vail's departure, could so soon forget. How strange that a girl two years older than she and experienced in the ways of romance could have been so mistaken in her feelings. For mistaken Celia must have been. She could not have truly loved Vail and turned so soon to another man, not even one as appealing as Nicolas Cermeno. Or perhaps Celia was one of those who could not love deeply. If so, Marin pitied her.

She was sorry for Stuart in his concern for his brother, and sorry for the pain Logan would feel. She could even be a little sorry for Vail—unless he, like Celia, felt nothing permanently and had found someone else in the meantime. But for herself, she could only be triumphantly happy, for when he was troubled and alone, Stuart had come to her to be comforted. Thank God, she was one whose love would last forever. The hushed stillness of the golden afternoon came down around them, and she knew for a certainty that she would love Stuart Severance until she died.

Chapter 6

The party that Nicolas and Celia Cermeno gave for John Baldwin on the occasion of his fifty-ninth birthday was unforgettable for everyone who attended, for a variety of reasons. Some recalled it long afterward as simply the most riotous, foot-stamping good time they'd had in years, with enough local wine and imported champagne to float the English navy and enough food to sink it, with sufficient fiddles and guitars and dancing and good humor to last at least a decade, and one short but dramatic moment thrown in to make it even more memorable. For others who attended, it was a fateful night that changed their lives forever.

The spacious room at Fontana that was used only for entertaining had been cleared of its sparse furniture, and the tiled floor was polished for dancing. Not many Californians bothered to polish their floors, but it was a nicety that Nicolas insisted on. Banks of greenery and flowers filled the corners of the room—Celia's touch—and hundreds of thick tallow candles blazed at the tops of tall wrought iron and carved silver candelabra, illumining the dancers in a fountain of light. As the tallow burned, it trickled slowly down and hardened in pale yellow trails on the candlesticks.

Celia had been lucky in the weather for this, the first party she had given since her marriage three months earlier. The rains had stopped last week, and although it was only the first of March, the night was fine. John Baldwin's friends had traveled as far as five hundred miles, many covering the distance by ship up the long coastline, and the ballroom was jammed. People spilled over into the patios, the verandas that circled the house, and the broad sweep of grass rolling down to the orchard.

The Cermenos had invited everyone, not only their personal friends, but the American settlers who had come in recently over the mountains or down the long trail from Oregon. Though there was much goodwill and many smiles and pleasant greetings, the two groups had split almost unconsciously, and the newcomers were holding their own party outside the house. They had watched, bemused, as their hosts moved through the slow and stately measures of the fandango, shrugged, and were now dancing a round dance on the lawn.

A skinny, red-faced boy and an old man with a gray-streaked beard that reached to his belt were sawing furiously on fiddles, and longtime American residents were drawn from the formal party inside to listen to the familiar melodies of home. Wes Morgan had asked Sophy Gentry to dance, and she was pink with the excitement of attending her first grown-up party and the notice she was getting from a former beau of Marin's. Dan and Harlan Gentry were on the sidelines, watching. Their father and James stood farther back, near the house, drawn like the others by the music.

James, still infuriated by the unfortunate domestic incident that had occurred at home that afternoon and the unsettling quarrel with Rose, was mellowing under the influence of the fiddles and the merry dancers, and the angry lines were fading from his face. His fingers began to snap. The tune was catchy, a minstrel song that had swept the nation a few years back, with endless nonsensical lyrics and a rhythm made for dancing. All the onlookers were singing and clapping, and scarcely knowing he was doing it, James began to sing, too.

> Ol' Dan Tucker was a mighty man,
> Washed his face in a fryin' pan,
> Combed his head with a wagon wheel
> And died with a toothache in his heel.

Dr. Cutter, wearing the dour expression that always meant he was discussing business, stood inside the house near one of Celia's banks of flowers, talking to a slight, dapper, black-haired man with a trim mustache under his long, pointed nose. The man held himself with military erectness and kept his eyes on the crowd while listening to Joe. He was a lawyer by profession, and his mind was as agile as his features were sharp; it was easy for him to follow the doctor's conversation and make an affable comment from time to time while his real attention was on his fellow guests.

As the spirited music outside drifted through an open window, Dr. Cutter stopped talking, listened, and excused himself. A few minutes later he appeared on the lawn, fiddle in hand, and several men who knew him grinned in anticipation. Josiah Cutter was the best fiddler in the district, but could seldom be prevailed upon to play. He flexed his long fingers and tucked his instrument under his chin, and as he drew a fast tune out of the strings, his sour expression softened and his foot began to tap.

Inside, the spruce little lawyer with the neat mustache smiled at the spectacle of Joe Cutter enjoying himself and then returned to the task that had occupied him while the doctor talked—evaluating every pretty woman in the room. Although he had done considerable business with John Baldwin, he had never met the celebrated daughter, Celia. Her face was as exquisite as everyone said, but it lacked warmth and spontaneity. The chaste aloofness, the suggestion of an unknown country to be explored, which had enthralled so many men, struck him as merely cold. He had no desire to breach those fortress walls.

His eyes returned to the girl with the red hair and the marvelous smile who was now dancing with a young naval officer. He had noticed her the moment he came into the room and saw her walk across the floor. She was young, and ordinarily he did not fancy very young girls, but this one was unusual—she had to be to catch the eye of Gerald Crown. Her skin appeared to be flawless, her eyes were large, dark, and full of fun, she carried herself with confidence, and her figure was exactly to his taste—slim and small-waisted, but with the full breasts of a mature woman. There was about her an intense femaleness that contradicted the lack of experience in her face, a vital sexual quality she seemed completely unaware of—and that was exciting.

Others thought so, too. A number of young men had made it their business to capture her for at least one dance, and she obviously relished the attention without, he was sure, understanding the real reason for it. Her dress was pure white gauze, through which white silk shone, her only ornaments were a garnet necklace and long garnet earrings. After the ribbons, flowers, and bright-colored dresses, the inevitable high combs and lace mantillas of the Spanish women, this girl's restrained good taste was a pleasure. Gerald was now torn between watching the rise and

fall of the round flesh above her low-cut dress and an attempt to
decide at this distance whether her eyes were black or dark blue.
She was, by far, the most attractive girl on the floor, and for the
moment he was content simply to observe her.

Marin, unaware of the stranger's appraisal, was having a very
good time, a much better time than she had thought possible after
Logan sent word this morning that she could not be at the party
because her mother was ill, and mentioned in passing that Stuart
was not yet back from Monterey. This was to have been the night
he would propose—Marin had intended it to be. The words should
have been spoken at the Christmas party at Little Mountain, and
somehow they had not, but she'd been sure that tonight what she
wanted most would happen at last. And now he was not even here
to see her in her magnificent tulle and silk dress, the most
beautiful dress she had ever owned.

Her disappointment at Stuart's absence had ebbed a little when
she had seen herself in it, with Rose's garnet necklace circling her
throat and the garnet earrings in her ears. Unhappiness vanished
completely as she rode up the drive to Fontana and heard the
enticing sounds of violins and guitars and laughter coming from
the big house.

The crowd was dotted with the blue uniforms of United States
army men stationed in San Francisco and officers off American
warships in the harbor. The violins were playing waltzes, for
although Celia wasn't dancing, she preferred them, and Lieutenant Robert Shaw, off the warship *Powhatan,* was smiling in
triumph and ignoring the glares of his fellow officers on the
sidelines. He was a good-looking young man, the best dancer on
his ship, and he had captured Marin Gentry for two dances in
succession, which was reason enough to smile.

He spun her, pink and laughing, to the side of the room just as
the music stopped, and she sat down while he went to get her a cup
of punch from the refreshment table. As he went off, she snapped
open the white silk fan her father had bought for her, only last
week, off a ship from China. It was a charming little object, but
too frail to have much cooling effect, and she was warm and
thirsty. Bobby Shaw had disappeared into the crowd around the
punch table, and as a servant came by, she took a glass from the
tray he carried. It contained a pale, cool, bubbling liquid, most
refreshing, and she helped herself to another before he moved
away.

Across the rim of the glass she saw Michael Morgan coming
toward her, threading his way through the dancers with a

determined expression on his face. She gulped down her drink and prepared for flight. Tonight she did not want to be kind to Michael. Tonight she wanted to have fun. But his hand came down on her arm, respectfully yet firmly, and she had to stop.

Before he could accuse her of avoiding him, she said quickly, "Michael, where have you been? I've been looking for you all evening."

He looked uncertain but pleased, and his grip on her arm loosened and moved down to her hand. She closed her fan as her eyes passed over the crowd, and she murmured reproachfully, "Why, I'd just about decided you'd abandoned me."

"Marin, you know I'd never do that. I couldn't get near you." He scowled across the room. "Those fellows . . ."

But he never got to tell her what he thought of those fellows, for her eyes came to rest on Michael's sister, Glenna, standing at the top of the long flight of stairs that led up to the guest bedrooms.

"I must look after her, Michael. I'll come find you just as soon as I can." And before he could answer, she had freed her hand and was hurrying toward the staircase. A dirty trick on him, she thought as she skirted the edge of the dance floor. Glenna really didn't need her at all and would do nicely on her own.

Before Christmas Marin had, in an excessively charitable impulse and mostly to make it up to Michael for turning down his proposal, lowered the social bars, enlisted Logan's help, and taken on Michael's sister as a protégée. Glenna had been grateful and anxious to please. She was a modest, self-effacing girl, a trifle plump but pleasingly shaped and rather pretty when one got to know her. She was also devout, virtuous, morally upright, and unable to tell the smallest lie, even a social lie. As Marin frequently stretched the truth in the interest of safety or convenience, she felt some discomfort in the face of such high principles.

Even so, Glenna was pleasant to have around, for she admired the many attractive qualities of her young patronesses and mentioned them often in her light, high-pitched voice—Marin's vivacity and beauty, and Logan's pretty eyes and lovely singing voice—and she worked diligently at learning all the social graces they tried to teach her. Over her blushing protests they shook her brown hair from its tight knot and insisted she let it flow loosely, at least for parties. It was not at all improper, Marin had assured her as she tied the smooth hair with one of her own ribbons. This was not the States. In California ladies could wear their hair down in public without being denounced as fast or forward.

Tonight she looked very attractive in one of Marin's dresses, with a pink velvet ribbon in her hair and a pair of Logan's white lace gloves covering her hands, which were red and work-roughened in spite of the creams and lotions Marin had given her. Her prominent brown eyes moved slowly over the crowded dance floor, and to a stranger she might have seemed uncertain, but after three months of close association Marin knew better; it was Glenna's nature to observe carefully before moving into any new situation.

"How pretty you look!" she called as she came up the stairs, and Glenna blushed.

"Oh, do you think so? My hair . . . is it shocking . . . ?" Her hair was a slender brown column halfway down her back and looked especially shiny.

"No one will be shocked." Marin took her by the hand and searched the faces below for a suitable first partner. There was no use hunting for Ethan. Girls of stainless character and faultless morals were not what he was looking for. Cousin Harlan was standing in the open doorway, arms folded across his broad chest, watching the dancing on the lawn. Right now his brother, Dan, was out there, leaping into the air with outspread legs and touching his toes with his fingers. It was a difficult trick, one all the boys liked to try, and so far Dan had leaped higher than anyone.

Harlan, Marin decided with narrowed eyes, would be a good beginning.

They were on him before he saw them coming. He considered a dash for the outside, recognized that he was trapped, and bowed politely. Glenna's brown eyes shone with pleasure when he asked for the next dance.

With relief Marin watched them dance away and mentally dusted off her hands. She had done all she intended to do, and the rest was up to Glenna. Through the wide door leading into the next room she saw Nicolas's widowed sister, a slim shadow in her black silk dress. Beatriz Segura had handed over the keys and control of Fontana to her new sister-in-law with no apparent resentment; it was proper and necessary for Nicolas to marry, and he had married a girl both wealthy and Catholic. She had settled with grace into second place and applied herself diligently to aiding Celia. Even now she was supervising the refreshments . . .

Marin remembered guiltily that she had sent Lieutenant Shaw to the refreshment table. He must be searching for her with a glass of punch in his hand. She should make sure that he found her, but she wouldn't. This evening had been a triumph. She had danced with every attractive young man in the house and several not so young ones, and if she made herself visible on the floor, she would immediately be fought for—and yet for a moment she felt only desolation. Glenna, Michael, Lieutenant Shaw, this entire gathering of handsome people depressed her. It was all worth nothing without Stuart here to see her, popular and pretty in her glorious dress. How lucky Celia was. She had the husband and the home she wanted. As always, she had everything.

Celia was seated in a brocade chair on a platform at the end of the room, where she could sit above the crowd like a queen and comfortably oversee her guests without having to move among them—very nearly as content as Marin believed her to be. She looked beautiful in her tranquil way, but older, and that was as she intended. She was a married woman now and had recently passed her eighteenth birthday. No longer did she allow her blue-black hair to float down her back. It was piled, thick and lovely, on top of her head, with no comb or mantilla to hide it. Her milky skin was paler than usual, the result of illness a few weeks earlier. She had given everyone a fright, but had recovered quickly and now felt very well, although Nicolas had allowed the party only on the understanding that Beatriz would take all the responsibility for it and Celia would do nothing but look on.

So she rested quietly and smiled on her guests, an exquisite young woman in a wide-skirted, blue-green satin gown that fitted loosely at the waist in the uncorseted California style, with a shawl of Canton silk arranged gracefully over her shoulders. Only one who knew her very well could guess that she was pregnant, and with Nicolas's permission, she had told only a few. Her father knew, of course, as did Marin and Logan, and all had been sworn to secrecy. Beatriz had been told, as a matter of policy—it would not be wise to slight her when it came to the news of an heir to Fontana. But no one else knew, not even the younger Cermeno girls, who tonight were displaying the modesty and circumspection that had marked their behavior ever since Prudencia's downfall.

It pleased Celia, this keeping of an important secret, just as she had enjoyed her secret love affair with Vail. She thought of him frequently, although in no way that Nicolas could object to, had he known. She had loved Vail, but he was such a restless, passionate, disturbing man, complex in ways that she could not understand, demanding more of her than she could give. When he went away, she had thought her life was over—and then she had become aware of Nicolas Cermeno. He was everything Vail was not, calm, reflective, considerate, giving her the protection from life that she needed. With Nicolas there were no exhausting emotional scenes: no ardent reconciliations, but then, no quarrels to make them necessary.

She had decided without qualms to marry him. There had been no letter from Vail in months, no way of knowing if he would ever return, and she could not wait the rest of her life to tell him that she had changed her mind. Never once since her marriage had she doubted that it was right for her, and this evening she was very happy. There was only one rather urgent household matter on her mind, which had to be taken care of soon, she was thinking when she spotted Marin by the window, almost behind the draperies, and smiled. Her pretty friend had finally wearied of all the attention and was hiding from those young men. Celia herself knew how tiresome being a belle could become, especially when the man one really wanted was absent. She leaned forward until she caught Marin's eye and beckoned her over.

"Sit here by me," she said, and Marin climbed the steps of the platform and sank into the seat beside her, settling her skirts into graceful folds and smoothing back her hair in an unself-conscious manner.

Across the room Gerald Crown smiled to himself, decided it was time to arrange an introduction, and made his way through the crowd to Nicolas.

Celia was saying, with a little pucker on her smooth brow, "I wonder if your mama would do me a great favor. Petra Victoria needs work, and while I would gladly take her on here, I already have three of her sisters. She is very proud, and she thinks it would be charity."

"Oh, Celia, are you still worrying over the Victorias? It would be charity, wouldn't it—though I've never noticed that bothering those people before."

"Petra is different. Do you think your mama would hire her?"

"As it happens we do need a new maid, but . . ." Marin hesitated, considering the possible hazards of a Victoria girl in the house. Ethan was already deeply entangled with one of them and certainly liked the type. If he had one of Fermina's sisters at hand right in his own home, the Lord only knew what would happen. Rose Gentry, as a lady should, turned a blind eye on her son's activities away from home, but if he got involved with one of her own maids at Little Mountain, he would end up wishing he'd never been born.

"There she is," said Celia, and pointed out a slight, dark girl who had come in from the kitchen bearing a tray.

"Why, she's only a child," Marin exclaimed in surprise.

The girl moved with a swaying, boneless walk, but her body was thin, with small breasts and flat hips, lacking any trace of her sister's voluptuousness. Her face showed her mother's Spanish blood, narrow, straight-nosed and olive-skinned, but it was a plain little face, and she kept her almond-shaped eyes modestly down. Her hair was restrained in the manner Celia required of servants working with food, but Marin noted that the twisted knot on her slim neck was artistically done. After what had happened this afternoon at Little Mountain, Mama would need a girl who could arrange hair.

Someone had been at James's bourbon again, and this time had so diluted the bottle with water that he spat out the first mouthful and bounded upstairs, roaring that he would string up the servants by their toes until the culprit confessed. Unfortunately he had caught Consuela, the only maid who could do Rose's hair to her satisfaction, in the hall closet with the empty glass in her hand. Rose's wrathful intervention and a subsequent compromise had prevented James from putting the girl out in the road that very day, but she would have to go soon. It was hard to believe that plump, quiet little Consuela would be after James's whiskey, for the Mexican girls, if they drank at all, generally preferred wine. Rose's opinion was that the girl was covering up for Gabriel Navarro, who had both the opportunity and the taste to get into the liquor supply, but James would not hear of that explanation. Gabriel was too valuable to lose. Consuela was the guilty party, and she would have to go.

Celia listened to the story with laughter in her eyes, for she thought James's tempers were amusing, but she sympathized with Consuela's trouble.

"I'll take her, of course, although"—she glanced at her husband with wary affection, "if she does drink, Nicolas won't put up with it, either."

Nicolas was coming toward them in the company of a tall, haughty-faced, black-haired man. No one would guess from the way Nicolas held his right arm that he could move it only slightly, and no one knew if he still suffered pain. The thought crossed Marin's mind that Celia was quite right—Nicolas would not put up with much—and then she was extending her hand to the stranger, who bowed over it.

He was not so tall after all, not very much taller than she. The impression of height came from his slenderness and erect carriage. He was handsome though, in a sharp, angular way, and in his dark eyes was a knowing expression that reminded her unexpectedly of Gabriel. However, this man, so polished and smooth-mannered, was a gentleman. She tallied him as another admirer, and as he touched his lips to her fingers, she gave him her best smile.

The musicians had struck up another waltz, the violins sweet and lush above the rich strum of the guitars, and she was just rising to go onto the dance floor with Gerald Crown when the music faltered and stopped on a ragged, discordant note. There was a sharp intake of breath from someone nearby, and down the long room heads were turning.

In the doorway a man was removing his cloak and handing it to a servant. He seemed to displace a great deal of space, because of either his size or the way people moved back as he entered. He was wearing black evening dress and a white, frilled shirt, but his boots were dusty, as though he had ridden hard and just removed his spurs. He looked across the great hall directly at Celia and smiled. Vail Severance had come home after all.

The room hushed to a quiet so intense that the soft movement of draperies at the open windows seemed loud and the burning of the tallow candles was almost audible. Outside, the immigrants' party had moved down to the orchard, and the sound of their music and laughter drifted back on the night air. Of all the onlookers in the room only Marin and John Baldwin knew of the attachment between Vail and Celia and the promise she had given, but everyone knew about the duel. Nicolas could now shoot accurately with his left hand and was reputed never to forgive or forget an affront. Everyone was wondering what was going on in the mind behind the stern, aristocratic face and thinking that Vail was a brave man to come here.

Like leaves scattered by the first sharp wind of winter, the crowd parted, and Vail came straight across the floor to the little group at the end of the room—Nicolas, Gerald Crown, Marin, halted just as she had risen, and Celia, sitting in her brocade chair, her eyes enormous in her dead-white face and a rapid pulse beating noticeably in her throat. Out of nowhere John Baldwin had appeared. His well-manicured hands rested on the back of his daughter's chair, and his hair shone silver in the candlelight.

Vail stopped directly before Celia, ignoring everyone else. His eyes traveled over her, taking in every detail of her face and figure.

"So you are back, Vail," she said faintly.

"My ship docked in San Francisco this morning. I heard the happy news of your marriage and came directly here. My felicitations, señora." He bowed, and added, "I also came to return something." He dropped a small object into Celia's hand, and in the instant before her fingers closed over it Marin saw the dull gold gleam of the little cross.

Nicolas still wore the same pleasant half-smile that had been on his face when he introduced Gerald Crown, but surely he had guessed the truth from Celia's expression. Marin wanted to shake her, for her face revealed everything.

Vail turned to Nicolas, his distinctive, hawk face composed. "I congratulate you, señor. You are a fortunate man."

They eyed each other.

Nicolas's smile broadened, and his eyes crinkled, although the look in them did not change. "Thank you for your good wishes. I am indeed fortunate. Welcome home, sir."

There was a sigh like the rushing of a warm, easy breeze. Everyone smiled, and on the dance floor a pretty girl made a sally at her partner and tapped him lightly with her fan. John Baldwin signaled the musicians, and they started up a waltz. He came around Celia's chair and embraced Vail heartily.

"It's good to see you back, my boy. We have much to talk about. Was your trip successful?"

"I think so, sir. I'll call on you soon. Hello, Gerald."

Gerald Crown shook hands in a friendly way, his sharp face watchful, missing nothing.

Vail's eyes moved on and came to rest on Marin.

"Hello, Red." He looked impudent and interested, not at all like a man whose heart was broken. "My," he said, "how you've grown."

It was fundamental to her nature that she could not resist the admiration of a man. In spite of good intentions, something in her stirred.

"I told you never to call me that. My hair is not red."

"No, it's fire, I think."

He held out his hand, and she came down the steps into his arms, forgetting completely that she had promised this dance to Gerald.

"Have you been home yet?" She did not remember his being quite so large. She had to bend her head back to look up at him.

He seemed broader, heavier, older, and his face was burnt very dark by the sun, making his gray eyes paler.

"Home?" He laughed. "I don't have one. How is my mother?"

"She's ill tonight. Just a slight indisposition, I believe, but that's why Logan isn't here. Stuart is in Monterey."

"About his father's business, I suppose."

There was an undertone of bitterness in his voice that surprised her. "Why, yes. He does the work you used to do and his own, too."

He said nothing, and they swung around the room to the melody of Celia's favorite waltz, a Spanish one imported from Peru. He danced well, and she loved to dance. She closed her eyes and surrendered herself to the waltz.

Gaiety increased as the evening wore on. The fun-loving Californians had inexhaustible energy when it came to a good time and would dance and eat and drink until almost morning, sleep a short while, and be out the next day picnicking, riding, flirting discreetly, and gambling everything from a gold coin to a thousand acres on the outcome of a cockfight or a bear-bait. The foreigners in their midst were learning to keep up with them. Neither James nor Cole had been seen for some time; they were in the back of the house where the serious drinking was being done. Ethan had disappeared early, and Marin did not even want to think about what he was doing. Rose had become very friendly with Beatriz Segura during the evening and was helping her oversee the food that continued to arrive from the kitchen in endless variety. And Delphine was eating. The fat duennas sitting along the wall dressed in their inevitable black were concerned only for the behavior of their own charges. There was no one to observe or care what Marin did.

Most of the evening she danced with Vail and, when he periodically disappeared, with Gerald Crown. Between the two of them they eliminated the younger, less experienced men without seeming to try.

There was a tray of cool drinks on a small table against the wall. Marin drank one down and picked up another.

"You've been at that all evening," said Gerald. "Do you know what you're drinking?"

"Um. Some kind of sparkly punch. Delicious. I feel very good."

"I imagine you do. It's champagne, my child, and it's potent."

He took the glass from her hand and set it down. "No more or you'll be either very sick or very foolish."

"Nonsense. It's only wine. Ladies drink wine." She walked away from him and sat down on one of the leather benches that lined the wall.

"Ladies don't drink that much wine and remain ladies for long." He scowled at her. "And I'll give you another warning, since I see you are pitifully lacking in sense. Be careful with Vail. You are far beyond your depth with him."

"Pooh," she replied with dignity. "If you'd been paying attention, you would see that I'm very well able to take care of myself."

"If you are referring to those nice young gentlemen who were fussing over you earlier in the evening, you're comparing domestic pussycats to—" he paused, "to a leopard. You are a very tasty morsel, and if he chooses, he can swallow you in one bite."

"I thought you were a friend of his."

"I am. He's taken a hard blow tonight, and he's drinking heavily. Under such circumstances men can be mightily irresponsible."

"Well, I don't think much of a friend who says mean things behind one's back." This man with the condescending manner and the knowing eyes was beginning to annoy her. Vail had come back into the room and was searching the crowd for her. She turned and went to him with an enticing sway of skirts, leaving Gerald frowning after her. Silly, exasperating girl. Why had he wasted his time with her?

He plunged into the narrow hallway Vail had just emerged from and at its end found the room where the hard liquor was being served. Nicolas knew the tastes of his guests and had laid in a quantity of bourbon for the Americans. Gerald, normally an abstemious man, poured himself two glassfuls in quick succession and gazed with distaste on his countrymen, who were comfortably drunk and engaged in a boisterous political argument. He went back down the long, narrow hallway.

In the ballroom candles were spluttering low and servants were replacing them. A crowd had gathered around a girl who was dancing alone, whirling in a slow, rhythmic movement to the monotonous thump of a single guitar. Couples were seated on benches, eating, or were outside promenading on the wide veranda. Gerald swore softly. Marin and Vail were nowhere to be seen.

• • •

The tiny inner patio was enclosed by the house on all sides. A small fountain bubbled placidly, and in one corner an old fig tree sent heavy branches toward the sky. Somewhere among its thick, leathery leaves a nightbird called, and from far away a deep guitar thrummed steadily. Marin leaned back in Vail's arms, one hand resting on his shoulder, the other holding the glass of champagne she had brought with her. They turned slowly around the fountain, dancing to a private rhythm of their own.

Marin took a sip from her glass. How nasty of Gerald Crown to say that the champagne would make her sick when she had never felt more deliciously content and languourous. How small-minded and mean to imply that Vail was drunk. She had grown up around hard drinkers and knew a good deal about them. They got red-faced and loud and argumentative, like her father, or became absurdly silly and slurred their words, like Ethan. But Vail, who in the past had either been rude or ignored her altogether, had never been nicer or more charming. Instead of growing loud, his voice had become quieter as the night advanced, and his New England accent less noticeable. He had said a number of flattering things about her hair and her dress and the shape of her mouth in very clear-spoken words. She could not remember exactly what he'd said, but it was all lovely. He was not handsome like Stuart—she could not quite remember what Stuart looked like and must think about him again in a few minutes—but Vail was an immensely attractive man. In the thin moonlight his gray eyes were luminous in a face burnt darker than a Spaniard's and the curve of his nose was distinct and rather exciting. His arm around her waist was very firm and left her in no doubt as to where he wanted her to go as they danced. She hated the timid, hesitant way some men took hold of her, as if she might break under a solid grip; it was so hard to follow a timid man. He was smiling at her, too. Gerald had hinted that he was devastated about Celia, but he obviously didn't care two pins, not when he could smile at her like that. It was enormously pleasing, the idea of attracting Celia's lover.

She tossed the empty glass away, heard the tinkling shatter as it struck adobe brick, and, looking up, surprised an expression in his eyes that startled her. She shivered. The night had turned very cool, and she had lost her shawl somewhere.

He asked, "Are you cold?"

"Yes . . . I am." She looked around, uncertain, a little

muddled. Her hand fell away from his shoulder. "Maybe . . . we should go back inside?"

His arm went around her again, warm and protective, and he drew her along toward the house. The flames of a low wood fire reflected through the panes of a narrow window.

"Come. There's a fire in here." He opened the door.

It was a small room, a rich room, the tiny parlor that Celia used to entertain her friends when she wanted to escape Beatriz's ever-present shadow. A long sofa covered with velvet and trimmed with rosewood sat, dark and graceful, before the fireplace. There were inlaid tables at each end of the sofa and a comfortable brocade chair with a knit afghan tossed over it.

On the threshold Marin hesitated. From somewhere a voice told her that she should not be here. But Vail said, "Come along. Let's get you warm," and he said it in such a quiet tone that she forgot her fears and went in.

He found a poker in the rack on the hearth and pushed at the logs until the flames flared higher. Someplace she had seen him make that gesture before, in another room, with another girl, but her brain was not functioning well and she could not remember where. Oh, yes. In the little house near the woods on a rainy afternoon, and the girl—the girl had been Prudencia Cermeno. Prudencia, who had come to such a disastrous end.

He turned to her, and the firelight outlined his face—the straight, heavy brows above gray eyes, the cleanly carved lips. What would it be like to be kissed by a mouth like that? A pulse beat in her ears; she was no longer shivering, but warm and a little dizzy. Her eyelids drooped half shut, her lips parted as she leaned toward him, and her head tilted back.

Slowly he bent down and kissed her, a long kiss that sent the blood rushing to her head. In spite of her recent successes, in spite of fervent declarations on the porch at Little Mountain this summer and in the moonlight at various parties, she had had very little experience with kissing and none at all with the kind that made her feel like this. What was it Gerald had called this man? Some kind of large and ferocious animal. But he was not even touching her, except with his lips, though she could hear his breathing quicken.

Then his arms went around her. Somehow the two of them were on the sofa, and she was dizzy and happy and so comfortable. His lips moved over the soft flesh above her low-cut dress, and one tiny button came loose, then another; then there was a faint ripping sound, and her dress was down around her waist. No corset to get in the way, how nice that California girls did not wear corsets. She would help him get the dress the rest of the way off if her head weren't spinning so, but he had no trouble doing it alone. The cloth tore a little, but it didn't matter, for there was no past or future, only now. She was free and flying, and sensation was flaming through her. . . .

The light was gray, the wispy half-light of early morning. There was only blackened ash in the fireplace, and the room was cold. She pushed hair away from her eyes and raised her head. Immediately she lay back again and closed her eyes, trying to think. Her head felt swollen to an enormous size and ached miserably. Memory returned. She pulled herself up on one elbow and glanced quickly around the silent room. She was alone. Reluctantly she looked down at herself. The afghan that had been on the chair covered her, and beneath it she had nothing on but the garnet necklace, still clasped around her neck.

Slowly she sat up, her head throbbing, her mouth dry. From somewhere outside the room there came a soft scraping sound, and panic shook her. If she were found here like this . . . but it was only the heavy leaves of the fig tree in the patio, brushed against the house by a gentle wind. The vast house was silent, still sleeping after the party, which had finally ended just before dawn.

Now was the time to get out of this place, before the others woke. She must get home, home quickly, before she was found and ruined forever, like Prudencia. Moving slowly—sudden moves only made her head hurt worse—she got to her feet, the afghan wrapped around her. The room was still, giving no hint of what had taken place here—her mind veered away from the thought. On the floor were her petticoats and the magnificent tulle and silk dress. With fingers that shook she tied the petticoat tapes around her waist and slipped the dress on. It was worse than she thought; buttons were missing, and the fragile skirt was torn. How to explain if she was seen? And her feet were bare. Slippers . . . she had to find her dainty little flat-heeled slippers. They had to be here, she couldn't go home without them.

She felt almost superstitiously certain—if she found them, she would get home safely; if she didn't, she would be found out and life would be over. Ah, there they were, behind the sofa! How in the world had they gotten there? In triumph she snatched them up and slipped them on.

She peered out the door. The little patio was empty, but it was enclosed on all sides by the house. For the first time it occurred to her that she would have to pass through some part of the house to get out. This room was where? On the orchard side of the house, wasn't it? Across the hall was the library. Although sleeping guests would be scattered all over the house, surely no one would be sleeping in the library, and it opened—yes, it opened onto the orchard.

After glancing in both directions and seeing no one, she slipped across the hall and opened the door. Nicolas's library was quiet, peaceful, and empty. Like a ghost she drifted through the room, with only the book-lined walls to observe her, crossed the open space outside, and passed under the ancient twisted grapevine planted by Nicolas's grandfather. She gained the orchard. So far, no one.

In the stable were the horses, and a horse would get her home. They nickered softly, either pleased to see her or hoping for food. She selected one and thanked God that Californians were generous with horses. You could use what you needed and return the mount later without being considered a horse thief.

After much searching she found a plain sidesaddle, not one loaded with silver trimmings and thus extremely valuable. With hurried fingers she cinched the girth under the horse's belly and slipped a halter over its head. It tossed and stamped a little, but appeared willing enough. She mounted the block near the stable door and climbed onto the saddle. Then, speaking softly to the horse, she flicked the reins and rode toward home.

Chapter 7

The yard was peaceful under the climbing sun, the house deserted, her bedroom a sanctuary. Swiftly she changed clothes, hid the torn dress in the back of the wardrobe, and washed her face. Before the mirror she brushed her hair until it shone, tied it back with a ribbon, inspected her general appearance, and managed to do it without once looking directly into her own eyes.

Then she sat down on the bed, trying to compose herself, thankful that family and servants were still at Fontana sleeping off the effects of the party, for her hands had begun to shake again, and her thoughts darted about like wild things. There was no woman she could go to for comfort and advice. Her mother . . . she would rather die than confess to her mother. Rose's heart would break if she knew what her daughter had done. There was Logan, her closest friend, but Logan was as ignorant as she had been before last night. Celia was a married woman now and knowledgeable . . . Celia was the one Vail really wanted, and Marin only a substitute. How could she have been such a fool? Last night she had been out of her mind, some strange madness had taken over that she would never understand. The champagne—Gerald Crown had tried to warn her, and she would not listen. Why, oh, why hadn't she listened?

What she had done—she could not put a name to it—what she had done was absolutely prohibited by God and society. All girls knew the rule and broke it at their peril. If caught they became outcasts, unacceptable as marriage partners; their families were humiliated, their reputations destroyed; often they were most cruelly treated by girls whose reputations were untarnished or women who were safely married. That it was a terrible act for a woman but not for a man she did not question; it was the way things were. Even God turned His face away from such a woman. Marin had never felt herself to be especially religious, yet it shook her to her soul to think that God had turned His face from her. There were cases, whispers, rumors that some girls, hounded and ostracized, had been driven to suicide. And there was, of course, always the possibility . . . but that was a thought so horrifying that she forced it into a dark corner of her mind and slammed the door on it, never to be considered again. She would remain calm, keep her hands from twisting nervously as they were doing now, and no one would ever know. Fortunately a gentleman was allowed to do almost anything but was required never to talk about it. That was a rule, too. Men were required, in honor . . . She sat bolt upright as an entirely new thought occurred. In honor, there was only one thing Vail could do. Why, he must be searching for her even now, and eventually he would come here. She scrambled from the bed, inspected her appearance once more in the mirror, and went downstairs to the quiet parlor to wait.

Exactly how she felt about this new idea she was not sure. Marriage to Vail was not what she wanted or had ever dreamed of. She wanted Stuart. But no other course was open to either of them. The Severances were a fine family; her parents would be pleased. It could be worse. She sat in the parlor, alone, all day.

The sun had dropped below the grove of oaks that laced the

stream on the far side of the corral when a horse, one horse, came thundering up the drive. Her hands trembled in her lap, and her back was very straight. How could she face him in the light? How would he look? What would he say?

A fist pounded on the front door, and sick with nervousness, head held high, she crossed the room and lifted the bar. Ethan burst past her, his bright hair ruffled by the wind, his eyes giving off sparks of excitement.

"What are you doing here?" he demanded, and strode into the parlor without waiting for an answer. "God, I'm hungry! Have you seen Pa?"

"He's still at Fontana, I suppose. Sit down, Ethan. What ails you?"

But he continued to pace, his boots cracking on the polished floor.

"I've got to talk to Pa." He flung himself into a chair and grinned at her. "Heard you had a hell of a good time last night."

"What—whatever do you mean?"

"Why, all the men were wrangling over you, and you drank Nicolas's cellar dry." He threw back his head and laughed. "Wait till Mama hears!"

How could he know what she had done when he hadn't even been there? Who had tattled? She said, "That is ridiculous and untrue. Ethan, you wouldn't tell her, would you?"

His eyes danced wickedly. "Depends on how you behave in the future. You know what happens to girls who lose their reputation. Think of Prudencia!" He chuckled at the memory of Prudencia's tragedy, and fear shook her when he added, "A good thing you got away from Vail early last night. I'd hate to have to fight a duel over you." Luckily he did not look at her face, but pulled off his gloves and went on talking. "I didn't know he'd come back until this morning. The marriage hit him hard, but I heard he carried it off well in front of Nicolas and then got quietly drunk."

Marin picked up the needlepoint pillow cover Rose had been working, and searched through her mother's sewing basket for thread. She had some difficulty locating the exact color, finally discovered it, and threaded a needle.

"Was he really so drunk?" she inquired, and punched the needle through the heavy cloth.

"Armando said he'd never seen a man drink so much whiskey and still stand up. God, I wish I had a head like that! He looked fine this morning, but when I asked him where he'd been all night, he couldn't remember. Say, I'm starved, Marin. How about fixing me something, since you're here?"

She nodded, laid the needlepoint in the basket, closed the lid, and locked it with careful, precise movements. Then she walked to the window and looked down the drive to the empty road. Her hair swung forward like a curtain, hiding her face.

"Where is Vail now?"

"Oh, he took off early, back to San Francisco. He couldn't stay around here with Celia married to Nicolas. I'll bet he takes ship again—to China or wherever the hell he's been."

Above all things, she must keep her face hidden, for if Ethan saw her now, he would know, and that would mean his death. He would go after Vail and try to kill him, and Vail would gun him down as coldly and deliberately as he had gunned down Nicolas Cermeno, that experienced duelist. And Papa must never know, either, for the same reason. How strange, how incredible that a man could do with her what he had done and not remember. Yet she recalled her father's saying that men often could not remember where they had been or what they had done when profoundly drunk. Well, that was her good fortune. He did not remember, and he was going away. No one knew but she herself, and it was a secret she would take to the grave. Now she was free to build her life as she wished. She didn't love Vail. She could never have married him. She must have been crazy to think she could. Yesterday she had left this house a girl with no concerns more serious than her appearance and her popularity; today she was a woman who could cause the death of her brother or her father if she was not very, very careful. Vail had been drunk, and she had been both drunk and stupid. She could not afford ever to be stupid again. A child could afford to be careless, knowing some adult would resolve all difficulties; now her childhood was over. She could rely only on herself.

And the first step on this new road of responsibility was to appear unchanged. She smoothed back her hair and turned to face her brother. And Ethan saw only his little sister, shining black eyes free of any deep thoughts, red lips smiling the affectionate, derisive smile she often gave him.

"So I'm to be cook. Well, come into the kitchen then and keep me company. What is it you've got to talk to Papa about?"

She went down the hallway to the kitchen, and Ethan followed, saying nothing. She made coffee and set bacon frying, and as she began to beat the eggs, she glanced back and found him straddling a chair beside the table, his blue eyes gleaming with such unwonted brightness that she stopped, the beater in midair.

"What is it? What's got into you, Ethan?"

He looked down and laughed. Then, as though he might burst if he did not speak, he said one word. "Gold."

"What?"

"I said, 'Gold!' Marin, you've got to swear not to tell."

"Tell what? I don't know anything. What are you talking about?"

"Do you remember Jim Marshall, that fellow Michael brought to our Christmas party?"

"I remember him, the most peculiar young man I ever met."

"Peculiar or not, he works for Captain Sutter up at the fort. Last night at Fontana I talked to a man who's been working on the new mill at Coloma, and he says Marshall has found a gold mine, an enormously rich mine, right there on the river."

Ethan's voice remained low, but it was breathless and jerky. Clearly he was laboring under intense emotion.

Marin sat down, cradling the bowl of eggs in her lap, beginning to be very disquieted. When Ethan wore this look of barely controlled excitement, there was no telling what he might do.

"It sounds like piffle to me," she remarked calmly, hoping to defuse him. She went to the stove and dumped the eggs into the frying pan. "Somebody's always finding gold—you know that. There was a find down south a few years back that everyone thought would be El Dorado, and it came to nothing."

"This is different. It's a gigantic find. There's gold everywhere, just waiting to be picked up. Sutter's trying to keep it quiet until he gets title to all the land around there, but, Marin, he can't do it. Not many people know yet, I'm one of the few, but before long the whole world will know, and the whole world will be up there, getting rich. I aim to be there first!"

She set the plate of eggs and bacon on the table, cut a chunk of bread from one of Rose's long loaves, and poured two cups of coffee.

"Eat," she said, and sat down opposite him. The coffee was scalding hot. She sipped slowly, watching him shovel down his food and turn his head frequently to listen for sounds outside.

Finally she said, "Do you mean you're going up there?"

"I am. Marin, I've got to."

"Papa will never allow it."

"He can't stop me. I'm a man now, and I'll go where I please."

"How can you say such things?" she said anxiously. There were sounds outside now, she was sure of it. Sounds of horses and the creaking of the wagon. "You couldn't just—just abandon Papa with no one but Gabriel to help him. You couldn't, Ethan."

"But I wouldn't be abandoning him. Don't you see, it's for us, all of us, that I'll be going. Pa can run things fine with Gabriel, and when I get rich—and I will in no time—it'll be for all of us, I swear! I'll come home with my pockets dripping gold, and we'll be richer than we'd ever be with cattle and horses if we worked fifty years."

For a moment her mind took fire. Suppose, just suppose, this time it were true. Suppose there really were vast deposits of gold waiting to be found. The Spaniards had thought so once—that was the reason they had come to this distant, lonely land—but they had never found it. Perhaps it had been missed, left there expressly for people like the Gentrys to find. It could mean an easy life, a house grander than Celia's, endless lazy, indolent days . . .

She raised her head. Yes, there was the thunder of hoofs, which meant that the vaqueros were back and heading down to their quarters. The house servants would soon be coming into the kitchen. And that was Papa's voice outside, giving orders to Gabriel. Ethan heard it, too, for he bolted the rest of his coffee in one gulp, like a man taking whiskey neat, steeling himself for an ordeal. Marin rose without a word and went back down the hall, through the dining room, and into the parlor to face her family. It was Rose that she feared, Rose who had sharp eyes and knew her so well, Rose who would look once into her face and know everything.

She opened the door. Delphine greeted her in a faded, die-away voice and announced that she was exhausted and would have to lie down until supper. She drooped her way up the stairs, pulling off her cloak and bonnet, and Sophy bounced past her, intent on getting to her own room and trying out the piled-up hairdo that had looked so elegant on Celia Cermeno. Rose sailed into the parlor with a smooth swish of skirts and smiled absently at Marin.

"How nice you are home already, dear," was all she said as she pulled off her gloves and went into the kitchen, leaving behind a trace of lavender scent. The knot in Marin's stomach eased. Mama had scarcely glanced at her. Obviously yesterday's quarrel over the dismissal of Consuela still rankled, for James gave his wife's back an exasperated look. He went into the tiny cubicle off the dining room where he kept his account books and conducted the business of the ranch. Ethan, for all his truculent words, evidently was not ready yet to confront his father, for he did not appear until the supper bell rang. Supper was embarrassingly silent, for Rose and James confined themselves to only necessary courtesies, and after the meal Rose went into the parlor and picked up her needlepoint.

James returned to his office, muttering to himself as he worked over his accounts. Ethan, who had been lounging beside the fire, got up and walked into the little room. From where she sat, Marin could see her father seated behind his desk. The kerosene lamp flickered light over his heavy, handsome features and sent shadows chasing up the walls. Ethan sank into a chair across from his father, his slouch belying the tension he felt. At first their voices were muted, reaching the women in the parlor as only a soft murmur marked by frequent pauses. Then:

"By God, you won't!"

James was standing, leaning over his desk, fists resting on it. Ethan was out of his chair, and his tall, slender body cast a long shadow on the wall and ceiling. His jaw clenched into a hard line.

"Pa, you can't stop me."

Rose looked up, amazed, and Delphine sat with mouth slightly open, jolted out of her daydreams by the sudden intrusion of loud voices. Marin's hands tightened in her lap. It would be as she had feared, and there was nothing she could do to prevent it. Ethan came storming into the parlor, and James followed. The two men faced each other, Ethan reckless and defiant, James blindly furious. He pointed a finger at his son.

"You!" he said, and his voice shook with anger. "I've always known you were weak, always known you were not the son I hoped for, but I did believe that, selfish and unreliable as you are, you would be loyal."

"James!" Rose cried out. The needlepoint was in a heap at her feet, her hands were pressed against her white, shocked face. "James, please, what is it?"

But James, once fairly started, could not be stopped.

"It's exactly what I should have expected from you, knowing you as I do. You want everything the easy way, without work, without discipline."

"Work! My God, Pa, I've worked my tail off for Little Mountain. This is my chance . . ."

"If you go . . ." James drew a breath that trembled with his fury, "if you go off on this pipedream of yours, don't come back, with gold or without it."

Ethan's face, red with anger a few moments ago, went white.

"In heaven's name, James . . ." whispered Rose. She leaned against the chair to steady herself.

Ethan went to his mother and kissed her, shot one look at Marin, a burning glance that pierced her through, and went out, slamming the heavy oak door so that it crashed against the doorframe. They heard him call for his horse, heard other voices and then the rattle of hoofs fading down the drive.

"Gold!" muttered James. His face was dark, and a vein throbbed at his temple. "Gold, by God!" he roared. "I . . ." His face, his head, suffused with purple. He lifted a hand as though to ward off a blow, tried to speak, and went down like a great tree felled by lightning. The three women stood immobilized with shock. Then Rose was on her knees, lifting James's head, calling to him, her smooth blond hair gleaming in the lamplight, her wide skirt billowing around her like a dark cloud. Delphine's hand was pressed in horror against her mouth; she was unable this once to shut out reality. Marin, without conscious thought, made a choice. Instead of going to her father, as instinct demanded, she raced to the kitchen. The cook, big, well-fed Berta, was lifting a heavy pot from the stove. Josefina and Luz were cleaning dishes without speaking to each other. Gabriel sat at the table with his most able vaquero, Cosme, planning tomorrow's hunt for wild horses, and Mateo hovered nearby, his dark eyes shining, hoping to be included. None of them were disturbed by the noisy altercation at the front of the house for that was the way of the *patrón* and meant nothing.

As Marin ran in, they looked up with polite but casual interest, and the next instant they were galvanized into action.

"Mr. James is ill, very ill," she said. "Mateo, ride for Dr. Cutter and make him understand that it is urgent. Don't let him tell you no. Gabriel, you and Cosme come carry Mr. James upstairs." She gestured imperatively to Luz and Josefina. "You, too. You can help."

Mateo was already out the door and whistling for his horse. As she ran back down the hall, she heard the rapid hoofbeats on the hard-packed earth.

Joe Cutter came, examined James, and then, after a thoughtful look at Rose, beckoned Marin into the hall. Rose remained beside James's bed, stroking his hand and murmuring words no one could hear, her stricken face pale as a lily in the dim light. Delphine, energized temporarily by the emergency, wiped

James's perspiring face with a towel and occasionally patted her sister's shoulder.

In the hall Marin felt the doctor's cold gaze, heard his uncompromising words explaining her father's condition, and although later she realized it was odd that he had chosen to talk to her instead of Rose, at the time it seemed perfectly proper, in fact the only thing he could do.

"Your father has had a brain stroke," he said. "His right arm and leg do not respond to forceful stimulation, which indicates to me that his right side is paralyzed. His temperature is elevated, as is his pulse, and his breathing is stertorous."

"But—but he always snores when he's asleep, Doctor. Won't he be all right after a good rest?"

"He is in deep coma, not a normal sleep. Whether he lives or dies no one, least of all myself, can predict, for it is up to the patient. It is always up to the patient. Your father is a strong man, and his strength may bring him through, although sometimes the strong go under and the weak survive. He must be thoroughly purged. I've given him croton oil, and if there are no results soon, put another few drops on his tongue. Warm his feet and apply mustard poultices to his legs and thighs and between his shoulders. Keep his head raised and his clothing loose. If he wakes and can swallow, get some strong meat broth down him, for he must have nourishment. Remember, it is your father's own desire to live that will make the difference, that and good nursing. Your mother cannot do it, nor can your aunt. But"—his hard eyes brightened briefly, and he almost smiled, "I believe you can. Will you follow my instructions exactly?"

"I will." Her mouth was dry, but shock at his unsparing words had turned to determination. James would live. She was his daughter, and she would make him live.

It was Sophy who stepped in and helped, Sophy who carried and fetched and transmitted Marin's orders to the frightened maids. Delphine never left the room, but huddled in a chair in the corner under a blanket, and dozed and waked and commiserated with Rose and dozed again. Rose knelt unmoving beside James, and though Marin finally placed a chair next to the bed and got her into it, Rose never let go of his hand. Her sweet, stunned eyes saw only the subtle twitches of his face and the struggle for each shallow breath. Rose and Delphine kept the long vigil, each in her own way, but it was James's daughters who worked for him through the night and saw the sun rise above the Sierras and the day begin with their father still clinging precariously to life.

• • •

As soon as she heard the news, Logan came to help, bringing the quiet competence and steady nerves that always served her in a crisis. Her mother was still unwell, she said, but improved enough that the maids could care for her. At dusk Stuart came. He had just ridden in from Monterey and heard about James when he arrived home for supper. Marin sat with him on the porch in the tranquil light of early evening, listening to the chirrup of the nightbirds and feeling the fresh sweet air on her skin and in her nostrils. It was her first rest outside the sultry sickroom since the previous night, but she felt able to leave for a few minutes now that Logan was here, her gentle voice soothing Rose and her cool hands quieting James's restless movements in a way that no one else but Marin could do.

Stuart leaned against the post of the porch and lit a cheroot. Its tip glowed redly, and she could just see his face in the blue half-light of dusk, reassuring, strong, handsomer than she remembered. He was home, only one day late for Celia's party; only one day—and one night that would have made the difference in her life. It did not matter now, nothing mattered except James's life, yet in her numb, detached mood she recognized that had Stuart been there that night, she would never have spent five minutes with his brother, would never have drunk all that champagne, would never . . . .

From the upstairs window Logan called urgently, and her words wiped out remorse and brought soaring hope. "Marin, come quick! Your father is awake, and I think he's trying to talk."

Chapter 8

It was a very good sign that James had come out of his deep sleep so soon, Dr. Cutter said. The fact that he was alert and making determined efforts to speak was strongly in his favor as well. Immediately Marin sent word to Cole Gentry by one of the vaqueros, and the very act warmed her. It was good to know that her uncle and his sons would soon be here to take charge of the ranch until James was well, good to know that although they were strangers in a faraway land, there was loving family close at hand to help hold the world together. Neighbors would help very little, she knew that. Even Logan would have to go home eventually, and Stuart was already doing two men's jobs. Only family would stick with you to the end.

The next morning Cole, Dan, and Harlan rode up. She was out the front door before they had tethered their horses and embraced Cole gladly, something she had never done before. Uncle Cole was an undemonstrative man who, unlike James, kept his feelings well below the surface, but he was her father's brother, one who would feel this catastrophe as deeply as she did. He looked faintly embarrassed by her hug, patted her shoulder self-consciously, and they went into the house.

Cole stood by James's bed and looked down with an unreadable face, but the boys were too young and transparent to mask their dismay. They stood awkwardly, their hats in their hands, forcing smiles and mumbling that James looked fine and they were sure he would soon be well. They had always liked him and enjoyed his company, for he was a hearty, vigorous, utterly masculine man who could outride, outtalk, and outthink them and had a capacity for bourbon that they admired and hoped someday to emulate. It took a real man to keep up with Uncle James. But this gray, shrunken invalid lying helplessly in bed, his face distorted, making unintelligible sounds, was a stranger, someone they did not know and did not wish to know. Young, vigorous, and insensitive, they feared illness and wanted nothing to do with age or infirmity. So they shifted uneasily in their heavy boots, muttered something about letting him rest, and escaped from the room.

Cole said, "So, James," and cleared his throat. Marin offered a chair, but he shook his head. He touched James's hand. "Don't worry about anything." James attempted a grotesque smile and closed his eyes. Cole stood a moment longer, looking down, and then he, too, tiptoed from the room.

Downstairs he inquired, "What does the doctor say?"

Marin shook her head. "I'm not sure what he expects. He says that it's a good sign, Papa being awake and trying to talk. But I think—I'm afraid it will be a good while . . ." Her voice trailed away. There were so many things she needed to know about the ranch, yet right now she was too ignorant to know what questions to ask. Thank God Cole was here. Then she remembered her manners. "You must be starving. Come sit down, and I'll find something in the kitchen."

"No, we won't put you to the trouble. We'll eat on the trail."

Marin looked at him blankly. "On the trail?"

"We're in the middle of branding new stock. Really shouldn't have taken the time away, but that's all right."

"But . . ." Disbelief passed over her face, and then slow comprehension. Her head went up. "I'm sorry to have asked for you at an inconvenient time."

"Don't think of it. And you let me know if there's anything I can do." He walked out, followed by his burly sons.

On the veranda he stopped and gazed around. "This is a fine location. Better than my ranch." He looked back at Marin as he put on his hat and said in a not unkindly way, "You'll do fine here. Navarro is a good man. Let him run things until James is on his feet."

They untethered their horses and mounted. Cole looked up toward James's window, and a shadow of sorrow or regret or awareness of his own mortality passed over his sun-reddened face. He raised his hand in salute.

"Keep in touch," he said.

Dan leaned from the saddle and brushed her cheek with his lips. "I sure am sorry, Marin." He slapped his horse's neck with the reins and moved off.

She watched until they were out of sight and then turned back into the house, remembering with bitterness her reliance on family loyalty. What a naive fool she had been, believing there was anyone, anyone at all, who would set aside his own concerns to help. We are alone, she thought, and trembled slightly. Her sick father and her stunned mother and helpless Delphine were alone and dependent on two girls, one still a child and the other too stupid to recognize that it was a brutal world and you were lucky if there were two or three people in it who really cared for you. Most of the time you had to look out for yourself, no matter who you stepped on, for there was no one else to do it. It was a lesson she would never forget.

And now she would have to locate Ethan somehow, and tell him to come home. Hopes rising, she sent Cosme to Sutter's Fort—surely Ethan would come home at once when he knew. And yet, remembering the unforgivable words James had hurled at him, remembering the deathlike expression on his face and that last burning look at her, she was not sure. He might not come back. And if he didn't, what would they do? Against her will the thought occurred that James had done to Ethan very much the same awful thing Malcolm Severance had done to Vail. Both fathers had disowned their sons in an excess of righteous rage, although the act that had nearly killed her father had not disturbed Malcolm at all.

After supper she went into James's little office, sat down behind his desk, and flipped through the account books, which lay exactly where they had been when the quarrel with Ethan erupted. Her eyes ran down the pages; so much goods against so much credit, so much love and work against James's life. He had provided the necessities and luxuries for them all with his brains and muscle and determination. Now she knew how they had depended on his strength to provide for them. Now, when it was too late, she knew that he had not been a young man when they started out from Maryland and that neither he nor they had realized the toll this adventure would take.

Her lashes were wet, but she blinked back tears and read on. Duties exacted: twenty-five percent on imports, six percent by seller, six percent by buyer, three and one-half percent on coin exported—her head was beginning to swim. Little Mountain was a business whose complexities she could not fathom in one night. She closed the book, blew out the lamp, and slowly climbed the stairs.

In the clear morning light, with the arrival of another sunny day, the future seemed brighter. Papa was improving slowly but steadily, and she could surely keep the ranch going until Ethan got home. It was fatigue and worry that had made things seem so black last night. She was even more encouraged after she talked to Gabriel. He inquired after James with real concern in his dark eyes and commented soberly that the *patrón* was very much man, apparently the highest praise he could confer. He answered her questions intelligently and accepted suggestions—she did not yet know how to give orders—with goodwill and an obvious intent to be helpful, without one wayward glance or insinuating remark. As he rode off, she turned back into the house, pleased with both him and herself.

One worry continued to plague her, and that was Rose. All her short life her father had been her mainstay, the strong staff on which she leaned, but she had relied on her mother, too, in ways she did not realize until, suddenly, her mother was no longer there. Mama had always been wise and strong in the areas of Marin's life that no man, not even Papa, could really understand. She had met and surmounted so many difficulties—the illnesses and injuries when Marin and Ethan and Sophy were very small, the fateful decision to leave Maryland, the long, dangerous sea voyage when others were dying around them—Rose had faced them with courage and strength.

Now Marin wondered where her mother's brave heart had gone. More than a week had passed, and she still sat by James's side, pale, stricken, bewildered, and useless. But for his daughters and Logan Severance, James might have died, and Rose could have done nothing but sit helplessly and let it happen. All her strength had been drawn from the dynamic, self-confident man she had married, and now she was overmastered by fear—fear of his dying, fear of living without him to shield her from a dangerous world.

She became slipshod in her grooming, an unheard of thing. Her hair wisped untidily from its net and sometimes straggled down her back. She wore the same dress day after day, and grease spots appeared on the skirt. At times she would unbutton her basque at the neck with an impatient gesture, as if it choked her, and let it sag open carelessly. Rose had become slovenly, and that was the most frightening thing of all.

Marin understood only a little, but enough to watch her mother with anxious eyes and feel very much alone. Delphine was like a ghost, faded, wispy, unreliable. Sophy had come through in the emergency, but she was still a child and beginning to complain about the dullness of life. It was like living in a house filled with children and herself the only adult, for Elizabeth Severance needed her daughter, and Logan had had to go home.

Each morning Marin set the maids and cook to their work as she thought her mother would have done, and compelled Delphine and Sophy by sheer force of personality to perform the nursing tasks. Each morning Gabriel stood before the desk in the little office, his hat in his hand, and discussed plans for the running of the ranch, which were gradually becoming more his plans than hers. She was ignorant of tasks that must be done daily and completely incapable of making long-range decisions. She would listen to his suggestions with what she hoped was an intelligent expression, think them over, and then give gracious assent, as they both knew she must. He would go out with the courteously blank face he wore in her presence these days, leaving her scowling after him, certain that she should have done something differently and not knowing what. If only she could talk things over with Papa. If only Ethan would come home.

As often as he could Stuart came to Little Mountain, bringing loving messages and encouragement from Logan that only served to depress Marin. She needed Logan here, and it was most

inconsiderate of Elizabeth Severance to get sick herself at this
particular time. But she treasured Stuart's visits. There were so
many questions she would have liked to ask him. Branding and
butchering time was nearly here, and what on earth would she do
when it came? Should she require veterinary work on the cattle or
let it go, as Gabriel insisted? Should she allow the men to go off
wild-horse hunting this early in the spring when there were no
signs of drought? Horses were brought in primarily to save grass
for cattle. But she was reluctant to ask. These were decisions that
every rancher saw differently; if Stuart made them for her, he
would have to be here to enforce them, and he had burdens
enough. Now, if he were her husband . . . She put that thought
firmly away. For all his kindness and concern Stuart had never
once even hinted at a proposal, and she must not imagine that he
would. There were already too many romantic notions with Sophy
in the house. She could not afford them herself.

Michael Morgan was at the house frequently and was a
surprising source of comfort. He had lost his father and watched
his mother die of grief. He showed with very few words how well
he understood her fear for James and her anxiety over Rose. He
was a small farmer, not a rancher, and had no answers for her
problems with Gabriel and the cattle, yet somehow it was easier to
talk out her worries with him than with Stuart, much as she loved
him. Perhaps it was because with Stuart, she weighed every word,
wanting to appear before him in the best possible light; perhaps it
was simply Michael's kindness that made him so comfortable a
friend.

Weeks slid past, and the fear that had been hiding at the bottom
of her mind could no longer be ignored. She lay in bed early one
morning, reluctant to get up to face the day, going over yet again
the terrible possibility that plagued her through the days and
sleepless nights. If only she could go to her mother, cry in her
arms, and admit what she had done one night with a man she
barely knew; Rose would comfort her, perhaps assure her that it
was only the shock of James's illness, the strain and worry, that
caused her monthly period to be late. That is what the old Rose
would have done, but now she was gone somewhere deep inside
herself, and Marin could not reach her. There was no one to turn
to, for Delphine was a fool and Sophy a child. She pressed her
face against her pillow and thought, Oh, Mama, what am I going
to do?

Later that morning she came downstairs more despairing than
she had been since the night James first took sick, for now she

knew just how far away her mother was. Foolishly she had tried
to talk with Rose about Petra Victoria. Consuela still remained,
discreetly in the background, at Little Mountain, but she would
have to go before James became aware of her presence. Celia,
Marin explained to her mother, was willing to take Consuela,
provided she really was not a drinker, and asked only that the
Gentrys make a place for Petra, who was greatly in need.

Rose's beautiful eyes, always red-rimmed these days, filled
with tears. She waved one white hand vaguely and shook her head
as though gnats buzzed around it. It was all too much; she did not
know what to do; Marin must decide these little things and not
bother her when Papa was so sick.

Marin turned away, frightened by what she saw in her mother's
face. The decision itself was easy. Consuela would go to a kindly
mistress, and Petra, who looked like a good girl, would come
here, where, God knew, they could use another pair of willing
hands. It was her mother who terrified her, her mother who was
slowly slipping away.

In midmorning, as she worked in what she now thought of as
her own office, a messenger arrived with a letter, and her hopes
shot up. Ethan! He had gotten her message, she was certain, and
was coming home. But the letter was from James's agent in
Monterey with a series of impossible questions about credits and
debits and an urgent request that goods that had arrived a month
ago be picked up and the account settled.

She sat lost in her father's big leather chair, staring at the letter
as though it were a snake, filled with a strong desire to lay her
head on the desk and cry until there were no tears left in her. But
she had not cried once since disaster struck, and if she started now,
she would not stop until she was dead. She wished she were dead,
with no problems, no gnawing fears, no feelings at all. She put the
letter in the bottom drawer, out of sight. James's agent, with his
merchandise and his accounts to be settled, could rot as far as she
was concerned. She picked up her pen and resolutely copied
numbers into the unwieldy journal.

It was there that Gabriel found her in the early evening,
muttering over an account book, her long sleeves pushed up and
her hair skinned back ruthlessly from her face. She was hot and
tired and scowling, but his eyes moved appreciatively over her
bodice, and there was an old, familiar sparkle in them as he asked
politely if there were any orders.

At the sound of his voice she jumped and her head jerked up.
The man moved softly as a cat, and she had not heard him enter.

Her black eyes snapped fire, and she quickly pulled her sleeves over neat wrists and got up from the desk.

"In the future you will knock before you come in," she said coldly.

"A thousand pardons, lady. I did not mean to startle you."

A smile curled his lips, and she thought how odd it was that this Mexican vaquero spoke English as smoothly as a gentleman like Nicolas Cermeno.

"Yes. Well. What is it, Gabriel?" He usually reported to her in the morning. What did the man want now?

"I hope, if it is your wish, to discuss the matter of the wild horses. We should go out soon, this week if possible."

She came around the desk, still scowling. "Why? We have more than enough horses for our own use. As I understand it, we must bring in large numbers of horses only in times of drought. Since there is no drought, I do not see the need, although—" her tone sharpened, "I'm sure it's a diversion you enjoy more than working on the outbuildings or doctoring the stock."

"There will be drought this summer, it is to be depended on, so several hunts will be necessary before the hot weather." He moved ever so slightly nearer, his smile broadened and his voice lowered. "As to the diversions I most enjoy, let me assure you, lady, they do not include hunting wild horses."

He was very close now, his breath was hot on her cheek, his fingers brushed lightly over her arm. For a wild moment she was monstrously afraid. One step back, and he would have her locked in the space between the bookcase and the wall. All the family was upstairs, the servants were far back in the kitchen, and the adobe walls were three feet thick. She forced herself to look into his eyes, forced her face to quietness, and ignored her racing heart. Her brows met, and her voice, when she spoke, was commanding.

"Stand aside, Gabriel."

Black eyes stared into black eyes, and for a long moment neither wavered. But Gabriel Navarro, though as randy as a goat, was still in awe of his rich American employers. He had long lusted after this slim, fiery-haired girl who moved with such provocative grace and was the daughter of the *patrón*. The *patrón* was sick, paralyzed, and yet—she was his daughter. Slowly he moved aside. Marin walked past him to the door.

"You are a valuable man, Gabriel, especially now that my father is ill, but I promise you this. One more such mistake, and you will never work again at Little Mountain or for any ranchero who is my father's friend." The soft lines of her face had hardened perceptibly, and he knew she meant what she said. Every ranchero who was her father's friend. That meant every great ranch in the north. *Dios*.

He lowered his eyes, the challenge in them completely gone.

She said, "Never come into this house again. In the future I will speak to you only on the front porch. Now get out." Her voice was quiet and level, but something in her tone moved him swiftly through the door, with a slight dipping of his head and a murmured, "*Gracias, señorita*."

Outside on the veranda he remembered that the Gentrys did not allow Spanish titles. He should have said, "*Gracias*, Miss Marin." What else had he done wrong? The sun was nearly down, and a tangy wind caressed his cheek. In spite of the trouble he had very nearly gotten himself into, he felt invigorated, almost as if he had, in fact, had the girl. Jesus and María, what blazing eyes, what a magnificent chest! She was, as the Americans would say, one hell of a woman. He swung down the steps two at a time and went off toward his quarters, whistling.

Inside the house the victor in the test of nerves did not feel triumphant. Marin sat down on the edge of the leather chair and began to shudder spasmodically. Putting her face in her hands, she cried. It was a terrible kind of crying, great, racking sobs that came from the deepest part of her being.

She cried until she was gasping for breath and her sides ached and her swollen eyes burned. She cried until there were no tears left, and she lay with her head on the desk, breathing jerkily, her head throbbing. What fool had said tears did you good? When you were through, all the problems remained, and in addition you had a miserable headache. Her father was no better, and she had deluded herself in thinking he was. Probably he would never be well again. Rose was lost in some far country and might never find her way back. Marin had been a child, dependent on her strong, capable parents, as protected from life as ever a child had been. Overnight she had become a parent, and they were the children, and she could not manage. She had already failed. She could not run the ranch, she did not understand the business, she could not care for her helpless family.

In all this, she did herself less than justice. An impartial onlooker might have judged that for a sheltered sixteen-year-old girl suddenly burdened with the responsibilities and tribulations of an adult, she had done well. But it did not seem so to her. She had barely stood off Gabriel and was prey for any other man who came along and liked her looks. Only a man of her own to care for her and fend off the world could help her now. She fumbled for her handkerchief, wiped her eyes, blew her nose, and began thinking clearly for the first time in weeks. One fact stood out above all others. She must get a husband and get one soon.

So Josefina found her, still sitting behind the desk, frowning at the wall. Josefina tapped lightly, tilted her round brown face into the doorway, and her gentle heart was moved. The poor young mistress had been crying, and the good God knew that the situation above stairs gave her much to cry about. Her pretty face was swollen and blotchy, and she did not seem to hear the knock. Josefina hesitated, for she was reluctant to intrude on another's distress, then tapped again more loudly and cleared her throat.

"A visitor to see you, Miss Marin," she murmured softly, hoping to get her message across and still not disturb the sad lady. "Mr. Morgan."

Marin's eyes seemed to focus with difficulty as she applied her attention to the girl's words. Mr. Morgan. Michael. Comprehension flowed slowly into her face, and her jawline clenched so noticeably that Josefina was struck for the first time by her resemblance to the handsome brother who had gone away so suddenly. Marin did not speak, but stared at her with such a bright, hard expression that Josefina said uncomfortably, "He is waiting outside, Miss Marin, if you will see him?" She ended on a rising inflection, wanting nothing so much as to get out from under her mistress's curiously brilliant gaze.

"Yes, I'll see him. Tell him I will be out directly."

Marin went rapidly up to her room, washed her face, and brushed her hair. She looked awful. Well, it was dark outside. She went downstairs and walked out into the soft twilight. The sky was deep blue, and the first stars were out. The breeze brushed a cool hand across her hot eyes and cheeks.

He was waiting on the steps.

"How goes it, Marin?" he said, as he did every night when he called.

"Not good. I'm very worried."

"Is your father worse?"

"No. But he's no better, and my mother—she is not herself at all. As you know."

She sat down on the step, and he settled beside her, as close as he dared get.

She looked at his bulky silhouette in the dark and decided to gamble. In quick, plain words she told him what had happened that night with Gabriel.

"I'll kill the bastard," he said slowly, starting to rise. "Beg pardon, Marin, but I will."

She reached up and took his hand, something she had never done, and her touch stopped him.

"No." Her breath was uneven, and she swallowed. "Listen to me, Michael. I need Gabriel here, I truly do. Little Mountain needs him. Anyway, killing him won't help. There'll—there'll always be others."

The truth of this struck him forcibly, and he sat down, still holding firmly to her hand.

She swallowed again. This was the difficult part.

"Last fall you asked me to marry you, and I said I was too young. I'm not too young now. If you still feel the same way, Michael, I will marry you."

A tremor passed through the big hand that held hers. His whole body seemed to tremble, and her resolve almost failed. He loved her, and she did not love him. It was a wretched thing she was doing.

His voice came thinly, wonderingly out of the dark.

"Marin, do you mean it?"

"I—I do." Honesty forced her to add, "You know that I don't feel quite the same as you do, but," she went on quickly, taking away the sting, "I do like you and admire you, and I am very fond of you." The "very" was an exaggeration, but the rest was true, more or less.

His grip tightened on her hand. She wondered if he would pluck up the nerve to kiss her. He had never tried before.

He didn't try. He said, "One of the new settlers over on Piños Canyon is a Methodist preacher. He could marry us. Would you be willing to do it right away?"

"That was what I had in mind." He had a death grip on her hand. "There is one thing. You would have to come here to live. Glenna could come, too, if necessary." She hated making that offer, but knew she must.

"I know. You need me to help you here. Glenna—well, we'll see. I'm very lucky, Marin, and—and honored. You need a man here, and I'm glad it's going to be me. I'll do my best for the ranch, and I'll try to make you happy."

My God, he knew she was using him, and he didn't care. Or at least it wasn't stopping him. Gathering up her courage, she leaned toward him and lifted her face, wondering how it would feel now to be kissed by a man. His lips met hers gently, undemandingly, and he let her hand go. It was nothing at all. Well, she had paid her dues for the time being. In a day or so she would begin paying them for the rest of her life.

But in bed that night she began to have second thoughts. Why had she snapped up Michael without stopping to think? Probably because he had been there at a moment when she felt pushed to the wall.

A sense of self began to stir. She had given freely all these weeks, fought for her father's life, fought to hold her family together when there was no one else to do it. Could she not make one try for what she really wanted? She owed it to Michael as well to try, for if she didn't and married him, she would believe all her life that things might have been different; she would be miserable, and so would he. If she knew beyond doubt that Stuart did not want her, she could marry Michael more willingly. But if Stuart did love her—what exactly had she promised tonight? She had said, "I will marry you," no getting around that, and when Michael had asked if she meant it, she had answered, "I do," almost as if she were making her vows then. Why had she been so unequivocal? Well, no matter, she still must try. There was time, a little at least, for it would take a day or two to arrange for the preacher. Tomorrow she would go to Stuart.

Locating him was easier than she expected, for he could have been far out on the upper range and planning to be away for days. Logan met her at the door and, speaking softly so as not to disturb her sleeping mother, told her he was in the meadow below the house. Marin offered no explanation for wanting to see Stuart, and Logan was too well-bred to ask, but the large blue-gray eyes followed her thoughtfully as she rode down toward the meadow on the chestnut mare.

How like another day this was, another spring day almost a year ago. It was barely April, but the buds were bursting and the hills were the intense green that always followed the rainy season. She was wearing the same trim black riding habit with the trailing skirt and the hat with the curling white feather. With cold objectivity she had viewed herself in her mirror and decided that she was prettier now than she'd been a year ago. There was a subtle definition to her features that had been lacking then, a new maturity put there by fear and responsibility.

Ahead was the meadow where last May she had watched Vail carefully aim his pistol and hit the target square on, where Ethan had excitedly told of her futile expedition to see Nicolas, and Michael had stood with his back to her, his shoulders shaking with laughter. It was here that Vail had slapped her horse and told Ethan to keep her at home if he couldn't control her. Now Michael no longer laughed at her, Ethan was God knew where, and Vail . . . where was he?

She dismounted by the fence, looped the reins over a post, and climbed through. Across the field in the grove of oaks was Little Clear Creek, filled to overflowing by the winter rains and the spring runoff, a stream that meandered on for miles and eventually crossed the Gentry property just below the corral. It was on the bridge over that stream that she had stood with Stuart last fall when he told her of Celia's coming marriage and had known for certain that he was the man she loved. He was below her now; she could hear his smooth, well-modulated voice giving orders to the Indian laborers. On the bank she paused. The footbridge had been torn away by high water, and the workers were in the process of repairing it. Strange to think that by midsummer the full, rippling water would be reduced to a trickle that a child could jump across.

Stuart looked up, saw her, and smiled. She came to him, the tail of her skirt looped over one hand and the feather nodding against her cheek. He told the workmen to continue, took her hand, and drew her down the stream bank until the men were out of sight. She stepped up onto a rock that projected over the bank. In the water's clear depths silver fish darted, their shadows flittering over the sandy bottom. Below her was the beloved face, looking up and smiling.

With no answering smile she said, "I came to tell you something. I want you to be the first to know."

His smile faded a little. "Trouble at home?"

"More troubles every day, more than I can cope with." Her lashes swept down, casting shadows on her cheeks. "Last night I promised to marry Michael Morgan." The words echoed in her ears—*I promised . . . I promised . . .* Had Stuart said anything? She could not hear.

She raised her eyes and looked at him. His face was rigid, stern, like his father's.

"You don't—love him, surely?"

Would it sound unfeeling or cold if she said she didn't? But she had to admit it.

"No." She ducked her head like a little girl.

"Then in God's name, how can you do such a thing!"

He took her by the arms and dragged her off the rock. His hands hurt, and hope leaped in her. She moved back, her eyes huge. He still held her arms.

"I haven't any choice," she said quietly. "You know how things are at home. I'm alone. I don't know how to run the ranch or anything about the business. I can't even ask my father for advice. And last night I was very nearly . . ." she searched for the word, "assaulted by Gabriel Navarro." He reacted much as Michael had, although less profanely.

"I'll deal with Gabriel," he said simply, and his eyes glittered.

"That solves nothing. I will still be a woman and alone." On the last word her voice broke.

"But why Michael?"

"He's a decent man, and he loves me."

"I love you, and you know it. You've always known it."

Rage swept him. Rage at her for being so beautiful, rage at Michael and all other men for seeing her beauty. The thought of marriage had never crossed his mind until this moment, for he was young and absorbed in his work and the difficult task of keeping his father's approval, a requirement if his sick mother was to have peace in her home. But now the most desirable girl in the world was in his arms, and her eyes were shining with tears and her lips were very red. He had been blind and a fool not to see that other men would want her, too, and grab her if they could. He trembled to think what a near thing it had been, and his arms tightened around her. His chest and thighs felt every curve of her.

Against her mouth he muttered, "When you need help, you come to me. For the rest of your life you come to me."

The tears broke and ran down her face. The sun poured warmth through a break in the trees and shone upon her head. At last, at last she was home.

BOOK TWO

Chapter 9

Beatriz Segura had grown very fond of her sweet-tempered sister-in-law. She was also sensitive to Celia's moods and was quick to see that the child wished to visit alone with Marin Severance. She made certain that Celia was comfortable on her lounge, that the little cakes and pot of chocolate were within easy reach, and left the girls in the garden. Consuela, who was now Celia's personal maid, sat on the patio, within call if she was wanted.

Celia waited until Beatriz was out of sight and then beamed at Marin. "How good to see you. I thought she'd never go."

"Is she hard to live with?"

"She does take a bit of handling." Celia made a grimace at the doorway through which Beatriz had disappeared. She laid her hand over Marin's. "And are you very happy?"

Marin smiled. "Very."

"I never dreamed I wouldn't be with you when you married, but even then I wasn't well."

"I know. It was a quiet ceremony—because of Papa."

Marin and Stuart's wedding had been quiet indeed, nothing like the lavish affair that had joined Celia and Nicolas Cermeno forever. The ceremony had taken place in James's bedroom, performed by the preacher Michael had found for himself and Marin—the only Protestant minister in the district. The room had been crowded even though only the two families were present, and Marin wore her mother's wedding dress, for there was no time to make a new one.

Rose watched with the vague expression that had been on her face since James took sick, so vague that Marin wondered how much she understood. James, paralyzed and unable to speak clearly, seemed to understand everything. His alert, anxious eyes never left her face as she repeated her vows; his eyes asked, *Is this best for you, daughter? Do you love him?*

And her radiant smile answered, *Oh, yes, I've always loved him.*

He relaxed on his pillows, his mouth twisted into a lopsided smile. *Then you have all my blessings.*

Her eyes brimmed. *Thank you, Papa.*

The memory of that silent, loving moment with her father, the memory of the entire joyous day still brought Marin close to happy tears.

She said, "I thought of you that day, Celia, and very often since. I grieved for you."

A faint sadness entered Celia's eyes, and she looked away. Her cheeks were thin, and delicate bones protruded just above the low neckline of her gown, but illness had not destroyed her beauty. Much of her appeal had come from an air of gossamer fragility, which was only intensified now.

"Nicolas is disappointed, but he is so kind," she said. "He doesn't blame me."

"I should think not. He's lucky he still has you."

"Oh, it wasn't so bad. I'm stronger every day, but Dr. Cutter doubts I should try to have another child, and that is the real worry. We must have an heir."

"Nonsense. The name won't die. Armando will marry some strapping girl and she'll hatch a regiment, all boys. I believe less and less in dynasties, and I certainly wouldn't risk my life to preserve one. I hear enough of that piffle at home."

Celia's eyes warmed. "Stuart must be so pleased."

"Oh, indeed." Marin smiled, too, but an old irritation stirred. She had thought that her own blooming pregnancy might wound a woman who had so recently lost a baby. She had even hesitated to come at this particular time, for she honestly sorrowed over

Celia's loss. But as always, Celia was content. She had everything. Her choice of men—she had picked over her suitors as a
rich woman's hand hovers over a brimming jewel box until she
decides on the one that is exactly right. She had chosen Nicolas,
but she could have had Vail if she'd wanted him. She had this
huge, gracious house; lots of money; a husband who treated her
like a precious, fragile doll; a sister-in-law who was a nosy
nuisance, but who took all the responsibility of the household off
her shoulders and was easy to avoid in an establishment as big as
this. She had an army of servants to indulge her every whim, a
father who was strong and healthy and rich himself, no pompous
parents-in-law to bother her, and she wasn't even jealous of
Marin's coming baby. The prospect of at last having something
Celia wanted and couldn't get had cheered Marin on the mornings
when she felt the sickest.

She said, "Yes, everyone is delighted. Mr. Severance is certain
it will be a boy and won't hear of any other possibility. At the
moment I am his darling, which is a great change. He wasn't at all
pleased about our marriage, though he didn't forbid it. I think he
won't make that mistake again . . ."

She stopped, and Celia finished softly, "Or he might lose
another son."

After a little silence Celia asked, "Do you ever hear from
Vail?"

"He never comes to Little Mountain, but Stuart has run into him
twice, once in San Francisco and once in Monterey."

"Then he didn't go as far away as we thought."

"No."

In the sycamore above their heads a leaf trembled under the
light breeze, broke away, and drifted down onto Celia's dress. She
picked it up, looked it over intently, and let it fall to the ground.

"I wonder if he will ever forgive me. He was so angry the night
he came home."

"Yes," said Marin.

"His father hurt him badly, and then I did—what I did. I wish
him happy. He's such a good man, with a great capacity to love."

Marin said nothing. Was it possible that Celia regretted her
choice? You never could be sure what she really felt.

Celia dropped a crumb of cake to the kitten playing at her feet.
"Have you ever heard from Ethan?"

Some of the warmth went out of the day. Marin shook her head.
"Not a word. Sometimes I think he'll never come back."

"Poor Logan."

Marin made a wry face. Logan's gloom grated on her. The silly goose drooped desolately, seldom left Longridge, and made a servant of herself to her parents, particularly Elizabeth, whom Marin doubted was as sick as she made out. Who wouldn't be a little seedy, married to Malcolm Severance? The woman's languishing complaints were designed to keep her last child at her side and certainly had succeeded so far. If Logan wanted Ethan so desperately, why didn't she go after him, as Marin had gone after the man she wanted? Ethan was traipsing around the hills somewhere, and a determined woman would find him or at least make the attempt. Either that or get herself another man. Anything was better than being trampled on by her domineering father and used by her mother and dwindling into spinsterhood without a peep. But Logan would not launch an assault on life and willingly take the risks and hurts in exchange for being fully alive.

And it was such a waste. She wasn't pretty and never would be, but with a little effort she could become passably attractive. Her complexion was clear, her eyes were lovely, and something might be done about her hair. She had slim, long hands and a tiny waist and could sing in a soprano voice of pure gold. Many a girl less endowed and accomplished had married well. But she must have been behind the door when the boldness and the good looks were handed out; her brothers had gotten it all and left not a drop for her.

However, Marin wasn't about to express these thoughts to Celia. She agreed that Logan was much to be pitied, and the two girls sipped chocolate and talked of families and scandals, gossiping away the sunny afternoon. Marin went home feeling content with life.

She was usually content nowadays and went about with a complacent air that irritated those less satisfied with their lot. Her sister, Sophy, was one of these. She was bored, she was lonely, she hadn't been to a party since the one Celia Cermeno gave last March, and she was expected to do regular duty in her father's sickroom every day. Marin got to run the house and had a handsome new husband whom Sophy observed with envious eyes. She would have liked to have a beau, but so far the only one she had attracted was John Wesley Morgan. Wes had transferred his admiration for Marin to Sophy and now loathed Marin with the kind of passion that only rejected love could induce. Marin had dropped him flat when older men began to notice her, had promised to marry Michael and then coldly dropped him in favor of Stuart Severance. She was now a grand lady with her nose in the air and an attitude of kindly condescension that enraged him. Yet Michael, the fool, still cared for her and would not hear a word against her.

But Wes was wrong when he thought Marin had cast off Michael without feeling. She had gone down to the parlor to tell him she would not marry him, knowing he had come to tell her about the preacher and almost unable to face him. But she had done it and watched his square, solid face change from stunned disbelief to despair. In the end she was weeping, and he was comforting her. He was still her friend, probably the best friend she had, after her husband. Stuart was away more than she liked, for he still had responsibilities at Longridge, but the ranch was under control again, that was the main thing.

With Stuart at the helm, Little Mountain was indeed under control, and no one was more certain of that than Gabriel Navarro. He had been informed of his duties clearly and precisely, and there was a look in the new *patrón*'s eyes that he fully understood and did not care to challenge. Thereafter he adhered strictly to his job as chief vaquero and did not come near the house even to flirt with the maids. But he had many sources of information and knew most of what went on there. The old *patrón* had improved this spring to the point where he could now speak a halting word or two, but one arm and leg were paralyzed. Probably he would never walk again and Gabriel spared him a moment of pity, for he had been a man. The wife served only him, as a good wife should, and rarely came below stairs or spoke to the help. The young *patróna* ran the house.

Although maintaining a prudent distance, he was well aware of the young *patróna*'s activities, and he watched her when he could—her red hair now restrained in a matronly coil—as she swung down to the orchard or to the barn or to supervise the tending of the garden. As summer came on, his sharp eyes noted the thickening of her slender waist, and he sighed for his own deprivation and another man's good fortune. Out of necessity he was foraging farther afield in his conquests, for the housemaids Luz and Josefina no longer crept down to his quarters at night, and he had assessed the new maid and decided she was not enough woman for him.

However, the new maid suited Marin exactly. On the morning of her wedding Petra Victoria had come to Little Mountain with all her possessions in a small bundle and a fine shawl, a gift from Doña Celia, around her shoulders. She had helped Berta prepare the wedding dinner, tidied James's bedroom, where the ceremony was to take place, hooked Marin into Rose's wedding gown, and, since Rose's old veil was torn, wove a crown of flowers for Marin's hair. She had held a vinaigrette under Delphine's nose after Malcolm Severance spoke gruffly to her, bathed Rose's temples with cologne after the ceremony, and soothed her into sleep on the cot in James's room. Now Marin did not know how they ever had managed without her.

She was unlike any of the Victorias the family had known, a slight girl with a frail, childlike figure, considerably taller than her sisters. Her skin was pale olive; her wide-spaced eyes were almond-shaped and glossy black, almost oriental above high cheekbones; her straight, clean black hair was coiled neatly about her small head. She was attractive in a simple, unassuming way, and most important, she was intelligent. She could accomplish efficiently and with a minimum of fuss any task Marin set for her, and Marin, used to the emotional excesses of the other maids, marveled. At first glance Petra appeared very young, but in fact, she was eighteen and had for years carried many burdens for her constantly childbearing mother. In addition, she could dress hair. It was she who took down Rose's long blond hair, into which some gray had recently crept, brushed it until it glistened, and arranged it according to a style they had chosen together from a year-old *Godey's Ladies Book*. The result brought a smile from James. After that Rose allowed the girl to arrange her hair every morning. Petra also coaxed Rose into fresh clothes each day, and as a result Rose began to resemble her former self, at least on the surface.

July came, the hills turned brown, and there was no longer any doubt that that peculiar young man Jim Marshall had found gold. As Ethan had predicted, the secret had not remained secret for long. There had even been mention of it in a San Francisco newspaper as early as the end of March, but it was not until nearly June that gold fever struck in earnest. Most of the male population of Monterey went north with picks and shovels tied to the backs of mules; men were coming from settlements far to the south, and San Francisco was almost emptied. Every vessel that could float was pressed into service for the trip upriver, and the diggings were spreading rapidly north and south of the original find as miners sought their own private El Dorado. There were even prospectors coming down from Oregon and some from as far away as Hawaii and Mexico. Eventually the news would spread farther, and if the richness of the find held, the whole world would come thundering in.

There had still been no word of Ethan, which was strange, considering that in the gold fields were a number of men who knew him and knew of his family's desire to find him. Sometimes Marin thought he must be dead or he would have come home by now. At other times, usually in the middle of the night, she decided that he had heard of their trouble but was still too angry and hurt to forgive his father. To her intense relief Stuart had no wish to go gold hunting. He told her in his quiet, confident way that he still expected to get rich from cattle, not gold, and such was his hold over his men that while they murmured among themselves, only a few drifted off with their knives and spoons and shovels to chase after a dream. Little Mountain and Longridge maintained their usual working schedule while other ranches were steadily drained of workmen.

On the third of September—Marin always remembered the date—James spoke his first complete sentence, "I want . . . sup-per . . . now," and the event was far more important to her than finding all the gold in the world.

The sun was tipping the rim of the farthest hills when Marin stepped out onto the side porch. The days had become noticeably shorter, and Stuart would not be home until long after dark; he was working on Longridge's outer range today and had promised to stop and visit his mother before coming home. At noon the temperature had been high, but with the dropping of the sun it turned cool, and Marin wrapped her new wool shawl around her and breathed in the crisp, sharp air. Autumn at last. The baby was due any day if her secret calculations were correct. Back home in Maryland it would be autumn, too, and how different her life would be if she had never left there.

The vigorous neighing of a horse traveled on the cool air, and she looked down toward the corral. Gabriel was working with Valor, the magnificent wild mustang the vaqueros had finally captured after much strategic planning and months of effort. With the sound of that whinny she stepped off the porch, drawn irresistibly, for Valor had fascinated her ever since the day he had been brought in, and she intended one day, when she was again able, to ride him.

Mateo was at the corral. His dark eyes sparkled when he saw her coming.

"Good evening, missus," he said with a smile that lit his brown face. "Is he not splendid, that one?" He was sitting on the top rail of the fence, a dark, good-looking boy, tall and well muscled, who had grown up rapidly this summer, a nice boy whom Marin had learned to like.

"He is splendid," she agreed, and pulled her shawl forward. She was not so very large, considering her advanced stage of pregnancy, but she knew her condition was obvious and, thinking of Gabriel's keen, knowing eyes, tried to obscure her figure as much as possible before moving closer to the fence.

"How are you doing, missus?" inquired Mateo in an interested tone. "The little baby, it comes when?"

She could not take offense, for his face was so friendly. She must remember the different attitude the Spaniards and the Mexicans took toward such matters as childbirth and the intimate relations between men and women. They were strict about behavior, at least the behavior of their women, but they were utterly frank in their speech and never resorted to the euphemisms of American society. "In about a month," she replied, and wished it were true.

"You will be very glad, I think."

"Yes."

On the other side of the corral fence Gabriel was approaching the white mustang with a looped rope in his hand. Slowly, murmuring low, hypnotic sounds, he slipped the rope over the animal's beautifully formed head and led him around the ring. After weeks of work the rope was still as much as the horse would tolerate, but he followed Gabriel, deceptively docile, only an occasional toss of his head indicating that he was doing this on sufferance and might change his mind at any moment. After several circlings of the ring Gabriel laid a light blanket on Valor's back; he had gotten this far only once before and had not yet tried to add a saddle. But the *patróna*'s black eyes were on him. He slid a look in her direction. Ah, but she was a fine-looking woman, gloriously pregnant. He picked out a light, plain saddle, the kind of saddle used for training, and laid it gently on top of the blanket. A quiver passed through Valor's muscled body, but that was the only sign that he had noticed. He chose to ignore the indignity on his back and followed Gabriel around the ring, his head slowly bobbing, his tail flicking lightly.

Gabriel halted and, cooing soft endearments, carefully cinched the saddle under Valor's belly. This was a dangerous and precipitate move, and Marin held her breath, waiting for the horse to lash into a rage. But he stood quietly, head down, breathing slowly through flickering nostrils.

"Bravo," she whispered, and brought her hands together in silent applause.

Gabriel looked up, and the shine of admiration in her eyes was too much even for his experience and shrewdness. He winked, threw his brown cigarillo in the dirt, and eased up onto Valor's back. Once Marin would have been offended by the familiarity, would have left the corral immediately and perhaps even reported the incident to Stuart. But tonight she did not move. Tonight she remained at the fence, staring at the man and the horse. Valor had not twitched a muscle, and Gabriel sat quietly, waiting. Gently he touched his unspurred heels to the horse's sides and spoke softly, and Valor moved forward, almost clumsily, without his usual graceful, flicking step. They traveled past the two at the fence, who watched, scarcely breathing. Impossible as it seemed, Gabriel had done what no one else, not even Ethan, would have tried. He had skipped over weeks of work and had saddled and mounted Valor. He had broken the most dangerous horse ever seen at Little Mountain and was now fishing another cigarillo out of his shirt pocket and lighting it.

At that moment Valor gave a whinnying, high-pitched battle cry, leaped, and came down in a great, stiff-legged plunge. Gabriel flew in a curving arc and landed headfirst in the mud at the side of the corral.

For perhaps thirty seconds Marin and Mateo stared, rigid with horror. Gabriel might be dead. He lay unmoving, facedown in the mud. The infuriated stallion, instead of continuing to buck, had stopped and stood, head up, trembling slightly. If he stepped backward or kicked out, he would crush Gabriel's skull like a thin-shelled nut. Mateo tensed as he prepared to jump from the railing into the corral, and Marin's hand flew up and caught his arm.

"No!" she whispered fiercely. "You'll be killed."

"Let me go, missus. I can handle Valor."

"Cosme is in the barn. Get him." The boy wavered. "Mateo, I cannot run. You must go."

Her eyes were commanding. He cast an anguished glance at Gabriel, jumped from the railing, and tore off up the hill.

Gabriel lay still, his face submerged in mud. If his neck was not already broken, he would suffocate in that mud. Valor was standing quietly, at peace now that the alien thing was off his back. Cosme was still not in sight. Oh, she should have let Mateo go in. Maybe . . . if she entered slowly and stayed close to the fence, could she not reach Gabriel without alarming the horse? He was a good six feet from the unconscious man. Once more she cast an anguished look back toward the barn. No one. Her face ashen, her eyes enormous, she walked to the gate. A loud pulse pounded in her temples and her ears. She pushed open the gate, stepped inside, and moved toward Gabriel, her eyes always on the horse. Three yards. Two. Almost there. She bent, scooped a handful of wet earth away from Gabriel's nose, and looked up. High above her Valor's neck arched, and his forefeet went up. Clumsily she stumbled back, trying to get out of the path of the savage hoofs. Valor plunged, she felt the cold air of his passing, and as he leaped and plunged again, she fell over Gabriel's body and struck the fence. The horse reared once more, raced the length of the corral, and vaulted high over the fence. The last sound she heard was his hoofs, like distant thunder on the hard-packed earth.

Vaguely, through showers of light and darkness, she saw Cosme's horrified face above her, felt him lift her, carry her. The house was all lights and confusion, sharp exclamations and running feet. Cosme started up the stairs, and there was only darkness. Then consciousness returning and light beyond her eyelids. A rolling wave of pain and Petra's hands, exquisitely gentle, wiping her face with a cool, damp cloth, and Petra's voice soft in her ears.

The pains struck with increasing ferocity, and there was a throbbing hurt in her arm—but the arm was nothing compared with the other. Then a new voice, harsh, dry, peremptory. Bending over her in the lamplight's glow was the grim, immensely comforting face of Josiah Cutter.

There were times when she screamed. She tried not to, but she did. Later on there was another woman crying out monotonously. She pitied that other woman. And always the firm, sure touch of Joe Cutter; always Petra, gripping her hands, giving her courage. She began to babble in a rambling, disjointed way, and Petra bent close. "Yes, yes, it will be soon now," she murmured, and wiped the sweat from Marin's forehead.

Gray light edged the window. That other woman screamed, a long convulsive scream, and Dr. Cutter, sounding pleased, said, "I think it's a boy, yes, it's a boy," and then, sharp and commanding, "Wake up, Marin. Don't drift away yet."

She fought off the blackness into which she was sinking and opened her eyes. She saw the doctor's smile and the elation in

Petra's face and the red, scrawny baby lying across her stomach, waving his long thin arms and legs and yelling furiously.

"Hello, darling," she whispered, and the blackness came back and stayed.

When she woke again, the room was lighter. The sheets smelled sweet and fresh, and the pain was gone. Only her arm throbbed dully. It was wrapped and splinted.

"You broke it, m'dear," said Dr. Cutter.

Her gaze wavered around the room and finally located him, in shirtsleeves in the armchair next to the wardrobe, smoking a Mexican cigarillo, perfectly relaxed but somehow giving the impression that he had been waiting for her. Beside the bed was the cradle, a gift from Elizabeth Severance.

"Could I see him?"

The doctor rose, lifted a small bundle out of the cradle, and laid it in the circle of her uninjured arm. Awkwardly she fumbled open the blanket and examined her child, counting each finger and toe, looking over his skin and ears and every feature of his minute face.

"Isn't he awfully small?"

"They tend to be."

"Such skinny arms and legs." She looked up anxiously. "Is he healthy?"

"He seems sturdy enough. Early babies are always thin." He picked up some objects that she could not see from the table beneath the window, put them in a large leather bag, and shrugged into his long frock coat. The style was old-fashioned, reaching below his knees, and the black velvet collar was worn. He was, they said, one of the three or four richest men in California.

"I will be back in a day or so. Your arm is no worry because the break is simple and should mend without trouble, but I want to keep an eye on the baby for a while. I don't usually do that, you know. I don't usually come out for babies."

She sank back against the pillow, exhausted by the effort of examining the child. "Why did you come for me?"

He leaned on the bed, one hand on either side of her so that she was closed in by two long arms, and looked deep into her face as if he were interested in what lay behind it. His blue eyes were pale and cold. "I respect courage," he said.

"I'm not brave. I yelled a lot."

"You are brave—and foolhardy."

"How is—how is Gabriel?"

"Less damaged than you. His self-esteem is dented, and I think a couple of ribs are cracked."

"Thank God. I thought his neck was broken."

"It should have been." The doctor's eyes gleamed with curiosity. "What possessed him to try to ride that animal? He's too knowledgeable for such nonsense."

In a small voice she answered, "It was my fault. I was watching, and I could have told Stuart how well he did, you see, and so . . . I think he wanted to impress me."

"I'll wager he did." A light shone in his eyes, almost like laughter. He picked up his bag. "I'll tell your husband that I will be back soon, since prematures must be watched closely. And I'll leave instructions for Petra. She's a good nurse."

"Petra can do anything," Marin said, stroking the soft, dark down on the baby's head. She looked up. "Thank you, Doctor."

A smile formed on his cynical face, and he inclined his head.

"An honor, madam," he said, and went out.

Chapter 10

There was great happiness at Little Mountain and Longridge. Both families had lost a son needlessly, and the new child brought hope and enthusiasm and anticipation of a better future, in the way babies always did, no matter how unjustified the optimism.

Stuart not only was proud of his son but treasured Marin more than ever since the hideous night he had come home to a distracted house and raced upstairs to find her face distorted with pain and everyone despairing of her life. When it was over and it appeared that both she and the child would live, Dr. Cutter talked to him long and seriously and then allowed him into her room. She lay like a crushed flower, alarmingly pale, her body small and slight under the bedcovers.

"Have you see him?" she asked.

"They brought him out for just a moment. You were sleeping." He looked down at the cradle. "We'll have to decide now, you know."

She knew. She had managed to avoid a decision on a name

during all the long months of her pregnancy, knowing Malcolm's strong wish that a boy be named for him, knowing Stuart's desire to please his father, and determined that if the baby were a boy, he would not be named after that hard-eyed man she disliked so much. Well, there would never be a moment when she was more likely to get her way than now, when Stuart was still giving thanks for her life and inclined to grant her anything. Tired and weak as she was, now was the time to tackle it.

She took his hand, tears edging her dark eyes. The tears were easy, for she felt like crying with delayed shock over the risk she had run and her fear for the baby's health.

"Stuart," she said, "I know how your father feels, but there will be other babies—indulge me this time. I would like to call him Carey. It was the family name of Papa's mother, and that could be a tradition for our children, the way it is in your family. Your father is so strong and vigorous, but mine . . . I believe it would do him more good than any medicine in the world." Her lips trembled, and one tear spilled over and rolled down her pale cheek.

He picked up her hand, kissed it, and said, "I'll explain to Father."

She was right about James. He chortled with delight, a weak echo of his former bellow, pounded his chair with his good hand, and demanded to see Carey again. The baby was placed in his lap, with Petra's supporting hand there as insurance, and he looked deep into the tiny face. In his halting speech he informed them all that Carey had Marin's eyes and would surely have her brains, too.

Everyone agreed with him about the eyes, although in reality it was too soon to determine what shape they would be, and the color was still the blue of every newborn. Rose, dragged out of her lethargy into the mood of excitement around her, remarked mildly that Carey bore a distinct resemblance to the Landrini side of her family, and in that Delphine concurred.

Malcolm forbore saying in front of James that the child looked like himself, but he told everyone else. Marin smiled and agreed and could not imagine her treasured little boy ever resembling his fierce grandfather, at any age.

Elizabeth, too, quietly concurred with her husband's opinion. Her health seemed greatly improved, so much so that she was able to travel to Little Mountain for this great event. She even climbed the stairs, sat beside Marin's bed, and told her that Carey reminded her of her own children at birth—the greatest compliment she could give.

Logan didn't care who Carey looked like. She was an aunt, and was feeling the stirrings of happiness for the first time since Ethan had disappeared. She cuddled the baby, cleaned him, carried him when he cried, walking endlessly back and forth across the bedroom floor, and adored him uncritically. Watching her, Marin thought what a pity it was that she would probably never have a child of her own, for she was a natural mother.

So everyone discovered what he wished to find in Carey and got pleasure from it. Everyone but Sophy. She was sick to death of Marin and her precious baby and her heroism. It hadn't been brave to walk into that corral and save Gabriel, it had been just plain stupid, and if she hadn't done it, she wouldn't have been so sick and given everyone such a scare and gotten so much attention for herself. She sat up there in her bedroom with everyone running around waiting on her as if she were a queen, when all she'd done was have a baby, which millions of women did all the time without making such a fuss. Sophy herself could undoubtedly do it if she wanted to, and she would sometime, too. But first she would have to get a husband, and all the young men worth having had taken off for the gold fields. Even Wes Morgan had gone, promising to come back to her when he was rich, but she doubted gloomily that he would. Nothing had turned out the way she had expected, and sometimes she wished she had died on the long voyage around the Horn, like so many others.

Sophy was almost fifteen and for all practical purposes had lost her parents at the most needful period of her life. She missed them both in a way she did not recognize herself, and Marin, who might have helped, was too absorbed in her own problems to see the need. Sophy had not lived up to her early promise of great beauty, but she was very pretty in a mild, baby-faced way, with deep blue eyes and pale blond curls and a red, sulky mouth. She was also quite as precocious as Marin had been and as innocent, with no knowledge of the world as it really was, but a towering desire to go out and conquer it. At Little Mountain she was ignored by everyone, lived through each day, did her work, ate her meals, quietly hated Marin, and was a small, sputtering bomb, set to go off.

Contrary to Sophy's belief, Marin was not feeling any pleasure over what she had done. Her admiring looks had egged Gabriel into riding Valor too soon. But for sheer, blind luck he could be dead or maimed for life, and she would be to blame. So she refused praise and would not talk about the episode to anyone, which earned her more praise for modesty and made her feel a hypocrite. As for attention from the family, that was for Carey, not her. She chafed at being waited on in bed and would have been downstairs running the household but for her broken arm.

No one guessed that in the secret places of her heart, something else had happened to her, something astonishing and unexpected. She had become a mother in every fiber of her being. When Dr. Cutter laid Carey beside her and she felt his warmth and life and infinite smallness for the first time, she knew beyond any doubt that she could kill for him. During her pregnancy, fearfully counting the months, dealing with the demands of a new husband and ailing parents, of helping pull Little Mountain away from the chasm into which it had been sliding, she had never thought of the coming child as anything but one more burden.

And then, when she was handed her son, the burden became a miracle that awed and comforted her and made the agony that had gone before worthwhile. In the preceding hours, shattering emotions had gathered in quick succession—the dizzy fear in the corral as she walked toward Gabriel, the terror of Valor's sharp hoofs slashing above her head, the crushing impact as she hit the fence. Then pain, pain such as could not exist but did, pain that went on until she thought she must die of it, and then, suddenly, no pain, but a living child, soft, warm, helpless—her own.

Stuart would have smiled if someone had told him he was no longer first with Marin; he expected her to be devoted to the baby—that was a woman's calling, just as the ranch and the business were his. He did not know that after the birth she had looked at her baby and been filled with a fierce protectiveness. No harm was ever going to touch this child if she could prevent it. Because of the accident, the date of his birth would never be questioned. If the world ever guessed, if Stuart even suspected, this little boy's life would be destroyed; but only she knew the truth, and it was a secret she would keep as long as life lasted. Holding her son, so tiny, so vulnerable, she swore a vow to God: never, ever, would she speak the truth to anyone or even think the thought, for it might be revealed in her face. From this moment on, Carey was Stuart's child.

As the days went by and Carey's skinny body began to fill out, Marin exulted in every added ounce. Sometimes, in the dark watches of the night, he had seemed to be still incomplete, not quite arrived yet, carrying traces of some other world beyond her comprehension. But finally she came to believe that he had asserted his hold on life and was here to stay. Only a week after he was born—very early, Dr. Cutter said later—she noted that the clear blue of his eyes had turned muddy. After the first startled moment she smiled. Her father had been right. Carey's eyes were going to be black, like hers.

It was a happy Christmas for the family, the first with the new baby, a Christmas marred at day's end by stunning news. A rider from Fontana came roaring up the drive on a lathered horse, spoke briefly to Gabriel, who was coming down the front steps with a Christmas gift of brandy in his hand, and then galloped on to other ranches. Gabriel ran back into the house to announce, in a shocked voice, that Don Juan Baldwin was dead.

Marin sat down hard in her chair. Canny, kindly, supremely successful John Baldwin had seemed as invulnerable as the Sierras. How could he possibly be dead? Why hadn't they heard that he was ill? This would kill Celia, for she worshiped her father.

Stuart went out onto the porch, held a short, grim conversation with Gabriel, then strode down to the quarters where the servants' Christmas party was just getting started and talked to his vaqueros.

When he came back, Marin took one look at his forbidding face, handed Carey over to Petra, and followed him into the little office. He had thrown himself into the leather chair and was staring at the papers on his desk.

Frightening ideas tumbled through her head. It must be very bad for Stuart to look like that. Perhaps it was the cholera again, perhaps an epidemic was starting.

She sat down, afraid to ask and afraid not to. "What is it, Stuart? What did he die of?"

"A bullet."

Relief was so great that she almost laughed. Thank God, no ravaging disease, no epidemic to reach out and destroy her child. But—a bullet? Rich and powerful men like John Baldwin were never shot to death. They died peacefully in bed, in the fullness of their years. Only lesser men were destroyed by guns.

"I can't believe it," she said. "How could such a thing be? Mr. Baldwin couldn't . . . Stuart, who would dare?"

"Squatters." He said the word flatly.

She had heard of squatters, some of them poor folk, some farmers, some simply speculators looking for land, trying to take pieces here and there of the great ranches, the more audacious claiming that the Mexican grants by which the ranchers held their land were not valid. Whenever squatters were found, the vaqueros simply chased them away; they were not violent or dangerous—or so she had thought.

"Evidently John came across them unexpectedly, because he had only one man with him. He ordered them off, and they killed him and left his man for dead."

"But—*John Baldwin*? They must not have known who he was."

"They didn't care. I tell you, Marin, they're challenging us, and there are a lot of them. We'll have to fight to hold our land."

She stared at him. It had never occurred to her that the land, their land, could possibly be taken from them.

He saw the apprehension in her eyes, and his face softened. "It's nothing for you to concern yourself with. I've given orders to the men. From now on trespassers will be shot."

But with the new year came new trouble. In gradually increasing driblets, Little Mountain and Longridge were losing men to the gold fields. They usually departed just after payday, found a boat to take them across the bay to San Francisco, where business was flourishing and supplies could be bought, and then headed up river to the diggings and the easy riches to be found there.

Early in February Gabriel came to Stuart and, with much circumlocution and many flowery phrases, informed him that he, too, must now go find his fortune. Why the man had waited this long was a puzzle, and Stuart decided he must have felt some kind of loyalty to Marin for saving his life. It was unexpected in so self-seeking a man, and Stuart did not like the unexpected. He had never forgotten what Gabriel had tried with Marin before their marriage, and had never trusted him. He paid him off and watched him go with something like relief.

But Marin was not relieved. She knew the worth of Gabriel too well, and his departure brought home to her as nothing else could the dimensions of the blow they were reeling under. Without good vaqueros to run cattle, Little Mountain would go bankrupt. Without vaqueros to fend off squatters, the land itself would be lost. And gold was the most seductive of sirens, luring the men away.

All of Ethan's predictions of last spring were coming true. It had taken almost a year, but now thousands of men from all over the world were pouring in, coming to California for the gold the Spaniards had never found. Ever since his brother left, Michael Morgan had been chafing to go, too, afraid that all the gold would be gone before he got there. Typically, he said little, but Marin had come to know something of his mind during the past months when he spent so many evenings in her parlor, watching her face in the firelight, while she sewed, supposedly waiting for Stuart to finish work in James's little office. She knew quite well why he came; she enjoyed his company and would miss him if he left. But he appeared to be stuck, for Glenna was still at home, and he had too many scruples to abandon her. Then, in February, Logan gave him his opportunity. Her mother was sick again, and she invited Glenna to come to Longridge and help care for Elizabeth. Glenna leaped at the chance to escape from the Morgans' tiny cabin into a great rancher's home, and Michael was free.

Late in the evening, after Michael had said his farewells and left, Marin sat in her bedroom brushing her long, curling hair with vigorous strokes and scowling at her reflection in the mirror. Stuart came to stand behind her. Their eyes met in the mirror, and he said, "You're sorry he's going."

She ducked her head and smiled. "I'm selfish, I know, but I will miss him."

He bent and pressed his cheek against hers. His hands were on her shoulders under her wrapper, and his lips slid down her neck to the curve of her throat. "After all," he whispered, "I might go myself if I didn't have you."

He blew out the candle and picked her up, and as he cradled her against him, a thought occurred to her. She had meant to look in once more on Carey before sleep. Better not mention it now, with Stuart placing her on the bed and unbuttoning the neck of her nightgown. Oh, well, she'd check on Carey after Stuart was asleep.

At half past two the clock on the parlor mantel downstairs struck softly but resonantly, and Marin opened her eyes. She had been deeply asleep, but something, not the striking of the clock, had woken her. Stuart was sleeping with one arm over her, and she eased out of his embrace and padded barefoot into the hallway.

Carey's door was slightly ajar, as she always left it, and he was stirring in his crib, crying the subdued, sleepy whimper that had reached through her sleep. The room was not completely dark, for the sliver of a new moon hung low in the sky, and in its dim light she could see him rubbing his eyes and yawning. He was not a fussy, demanding child and had not required a night feeding in weeks. She knew quite well that she need only turn him on his stomach, pat his round, diapered bottom, and in moments he would be sound asleep again, but that would deprive her of her greatest pleasure.

She scooped him up, liking the soft, warm feel of him, murmuring silly, loving words, and sat down in the old wooden rocker that had traveled all the way from Maryland and had comforted three generations of Gentry babies.

Flesh of my flesh and bone of my bone, she thought with deep contentment. He snuggled against her with a drowsy cry that broke off as she began to rock and sing in a sweet, thin voice the old song Rose had sung to her and to Sophy and, before them, to Ethan, a song handed down, like the rocker, through the generations.

> Hushaby, don't you cry,
> Go to sleepy, little baby,
> When you wake you shall have
> All the pretty little horsies,
> Blackies and bays, dapples and grays,
> Go to sleepy, little baby.

It was almost suppertime, and Berta was removing roasted chickens from the big oven. Marin and Petra were at the dry sink, punching down bread dough on the floured wood surface and chattering as they worked.

They had discovered Carey's second tooth this afternoon, and it pleased Marin more than she would have dreamed possible a year earlier. His teeth were coming in early, for he was only six months old, but he was a precocious child and did everything early. He was sturdy and big for his age, his shiny dark hair lay close against his well-shaped head, and the great black eyes that dominated his baby face looked out in delight at a fascinating world. Everything intrigued him, the broken wheel that lay on its side in the barn and had such interesting spokes for him to poke at, the leaves that danced under a light breeze and scattered flitting shadows on the ground, the brilliant butterfly that he grabbed for but could not catch, the flower he picked when his mother placed him on the grass near the stream bank. Immediately he had tried to stuff it in his mouth and looked at her in puzzlement when she took it from him and said, "No, darling." He was a well-put-together child and was clearly going to have a strong, athletic body. Already he was up on hands and knees, rocking back and forth, trying to determine how one moved arms and legs in order to travel across the floor. He was a happy child, cooing and babbling and looking at his family perceptively, as though there was much he would say to them if only he could form the words.

On this particular evening Marin was pleased, too, because Michael was back, for a time at least. He was doing better than most on his claim, making eight dollars a day when the average now was only three or four dollars, but he had come home to see that all was well with his cottage and with Glenna and, Marin surmised, to see her as well.

Stuart had gone to San Francisco four days ago to buy parts for the water pump, and she expected him home for supper. There had been no more incidents with squatters, and her winter worries about the loss of workmen and imminent bankruptcy had vanished, for by late spring enough men had grown discouraged with the slender output of their claims and the bitterly hard work and miseries of mining to come back to cattle ranching. Stuart said that the ranchers were going to get rich now. With every week that passed, thousands of young, eager men from all over the world were arriving on ships at the port of San Francisco, and every man meant a mouth to be fed. Cattle were bringing five hundred dollars a head in some of the mining camps, and while Stuart said such thumping prices couldn't last, he was certain beef would bring in good money for years to come.

There were sounds of horses pounding past the side of the house and Stuart's voice calling to Mateo. Then boots on the wooden floor of the back porch and the kitchen door banging open. Marin swung around with flour still on her hands and a smile of greeting on her face. Coming in the door were Stuart, Michael, and, just behind them, Vail Severance.

She picked up a towel, wiped her hands, and moved to Stuart for a kiss of welcome. She said something to Michael, although she couldn't hear her own voice for the roaring in her ears.

What could she do? Where could she look? She must speak to him, look at him, smile at him. It would seem very odd if she didn't. But all the blood in her body seemed to have rushed into her head. Oh, God, how could she explain to Stuart why the sight of his brother upset her so? She forced herself to look into Vail's eyes, and the buzzing in her head made her think she was going to faint.

There was nothing at all in those clear gray eyes but friendliness and the mildest sort of interest, the kind of interest a man might show on greeting his brother's wife, a girl he had known slightly at some time in the distant past. She put out her hand because she had to, felt the corners of her mouth go up in a smile, and heard him say, "Hello, Red."

Somewhere she found the strength to say, "Welcome, Vail. Have you come home to stay?"

Supper went off smoothly, and by the time Luz served the cobbler and cream, Marin had decided that she was going to live after all. Stuart appeared to have noticed nothing odd about her behavior, perhaps because he had been pulling off his coat when she spoke to Vail and had his back turned. Michael had simply stood there and smiled as he always did when he saw her, and as for Vail—Papa and Ethan had clearly been right about the memory-destroying properties of alcohol, for he obviously recalled nothing about that night. He treated her just as he always had, perhaps a little more courteously because of her increased age and status, but that was all.

During supper he patiently answered Delphine's avid questions about San Francisco and the doings there and charmed her into an approval she hadn't expected to feel, considering his past, which she knew very little about but which shocked her nonetheless.

Sophy watched him with huge eyes, awed by this big man with the strong face who had done so many daring, dreadful things— gunned down a defenseless man, destroyed the reputation of Prudencia Cermeno, been thrown out—excommunicated, almost—by his father, traveled all over the world, and, some people hinted, had a tragic love affair with Celia Baldwin and lost her to the man he had shot. It was all marvelously thrilling and romantic, and she thought she was probably in love with him.

When the meal ended, Delphine left the table to the men, taking Sophy with her. Sophy went demurely, for she wanted to appear as grown-up as possible, and Marin gladly would have followed, but Stuart caught her hand and asked her to stay. She sat down, sipped a glass of wine she didn't want, and watched the men drink peach brandy.

Stuart smiled across the table at his brother. "How long can you stay?"

"Only the night. I have to be in Sacramento City tomorrow, and then I'm going on to Auburn."

Michael leaned forward. "Do you have more than one claim?" He had admired Vail in the old days, and anything Vail did interested him.

"My God, no, I don't have any. Digging ditches and standing

knee-deep in freezing water isn't my idea of pleasure. Believe me, Michael, the sure fortunes aren't in the mines. The real money is in supplying the miners with tools and clothes and liquor and . . ." He recalled Marin's presence. ". . . other necessities. There are more gambling saloons in San Francisco than hotels. Those poor idiots are stripped bare in town and have to go back to the diggings and work like slaves to find more gold. Then they come to town again and promptly lose it. If anyone forced them to work like that for so little return, they'd kill him. My advice is either stay out of San Francisco or come prepared to do real business."

Stuart's eyes were keen. "What is your real business?"

"Real estate, mostly. Are you interested? I might be able to put you in the way of several good things."

"Maybe. I'll let you know. Right now I'm more interested in Riley's proclamation."

Marin paid little attention to politics, accepting without question Rose's opinion, often stated in the past, that it was a crafty, demeaning, and exclusively male preoccupation, unsuitable for ladies. But even she knew that General Bennett Riley had arrived in San Francisco from Washington only two months ago to run the civil government. Before him there had been several blundering military governors, none of whom had the slightest idea how to handle the increasingly chaotic mixture of people pouring into California, and the grim and stubborn Riley was doing little better. For one thing, most of his brigade had deserted for the gold fields shortly after touching shore, and without soldiers to enforce the laws, he was helpless.

"He's a smart old bird," Stuart was saying. "He wants to get a constitution written and an assembly elected, and if we do, we'll be in the Union by next year."

That prodded an old memory, and Marin's interest picked up. How many times had she heard James say, "We'll be in the Union, by God!" She put down her wineglass and began to listen. Apparently there was to be a constitutional convention in Monterey in September, and state legislators were to be chosen, all with a view to pressing Washington for California's admission as a state. Characteristically Marin's first thought was, Papa will be pleased. To her, constitutions and legislatures and statehood were not nearly as momentous as Carey's attempts to crawl or the price of beef on the open market.

Vail said, "You're going to run for the legislature?"

"I've been asked. Whoever gets in at the beginning will have a part in controlling the state."

"Probably so." Vail poured himself another brandy. "How Father will admire that."

The old rivalry was still there in spite of their genuine good feeling at seeing each other again. And what was this about Stuart's running for the legislature? Marin could not quite take it in. It was not the future she had seen for him, for them.

There was a silence following Vail's jab, and into it Michael said with a grin, "I suppose you left the girls in San Francisco crying." He, like Ethan, had always envied Vail's popularity with women. "Why is it, Marin, that girls love a rake better than us steady fellows?"

Her face remained carefully blank. "I'm not sure they do. Some might be attracted to the idea of a . . . a dashing sort of man, but when it comes to living day by day—and that is the way we have to live . . . then I think a rake would be a most uncomfortable person to live with, and a woman of sense wouldn't do it."

"Very true," Vail said. He was smiling and observing her with heightened interest, as if he had caught sight of something he hadn't known was there. "And for your information, Michael, a rake is an immoral, dissolute fellow. That's a description I decline to accept."

Marin rose before anything more could be said.

"Luz will serve coffee in the parlor, if you care to join me."

They stood up politely, and she nodded to Luz, hoping the subject would be changed by the time they got to the other room. But Michael excused himself and asked Stuart to go with him to the barn. He wanted to buy a horse and also look at the broken water pump; mechanical work fascinated him, and he meant to help repair it before returning to his claim.

Marin sat down by the parlor fire in her favorite chair, the one Rose had used in the old days, and picked up a shirt of Stuart's to mend, thinking with relief that she now had a little time to compose herself. She looked up, and the thread snapped in her fingers. Vail had come into the room alone.

Damn the man! Why couldn't he go look at the horse or the pump, or tend to some other masculine matter? Why did he have to follow her in here, where there was no one else to share the burden of conversation? The business of rethreading the needle took her close attention, but she watched him covertly, noticing the way he moved, the vitality in his face.

He sat down opposite her and stretched his booted legs toward the flames, and she busied herself with the torn frill of Stuart's shirt, wondering how long she could maintain this domestic pose and make some kind of polite conversation.

Her mind fumbled, searching for something to say, and Petra came in with her gliding, boneless walk. She set the tray bearing coffeepot and cups on the table next to Marin and, as she bent forward, murmured, "Carey is still awake, Miss Marin. Should I bring him down?"

Marin snatched at the suggestion like a drowning man at a straw. Young as he was, Carey had a gift for drawing all eyes to him—in this case, away from her.

"Yes, bring him down," she said gratefully.

"How is my mother?" Vail asked suddenly. He was lighting a cigar and frowning into the fire.

It was a safe subject. "Not well," Marin answered, her eyes on her sewing. "Will you see her before you leave?"

"I can't."

She looked up, thinking of Ethan. It was such a sorry, stupid situation. "Surely your father wouldn't object? She's quite ill, I think."

"He would object—which would make it worse for her." A smile crossed his face, and Marin caught her breath at the bitterness in it. Without watching her hand, she shoved the needle through the cloth and jabbed her finger. A bright drop of blood appeared, and she scowled and put it to her mouth.

Vail's smile became genuine. "You looked like a child when you did that. I keep forgetting how young you are."

It was the first personal remark he'd made, and it unnerved her so much that she almost dropped the shirt. He must not have noticed though, for he went right on, "This is the first chance I've had to apologize for my conduct the night of Celia's party. I was very rude."

The finger remained in her mouth; her heart seemed to come to a standstill. He did remember, then, and he was apologizing for *rudeness*?

She was not thinking clearly, but she heard him say, "I had a bad case of hurt feelings that night, as you probably know, and I'm sorry to say I got very drunk. I seem to remember leaving you on the dance floor with Gerald Crown, which I certainly would never have done in my right mind. I hope you've forgiven me."

Her heart began to beat again. He thought he'd left her with Gerald.

"Oh, I forgave you immediately. Gerald is charming and a very good dancer." She picked up the coffeepot and began to pour with a steady hand.

He winced. "I deserved that. My brother married a quick-witted lady as well as a beautiful one. I wasn't so lucky."

He was thinking of Celia. Should she mention her? No, better not. Petra brought in Carey, and Marin took him on her lap with relief. Vail leaned forward and looked him over.

"A handsome boy," he said finally.

She warmed to the praise, as she always did to any kind words for Carey.

"Yes," she said, and laughed. "Forgive me, I can't be modest. I think he's handsome, too." She set the child on the floor, and he immediately went up on all fours and started to rock so vigorously that he tumbled over and lay there crowing. Then he struggled up and tried again to move forward.

Vail took his cup, watching with a smile.

"I suppose Father is delighted."

"Oh, yes. He was miffed at first when we didn't name the baby after him, but he got over it when he decided that Carey looked like him. At present he's very pleased with me."

"And with Stuart, too, I imagine. Well, Stuart always had the knack of pleasing him. I never did." He said it without self-pity, but Marin remembered Celia's words: "His father hurt him badly."

She picked up her own cup. "Except for your mother, no one agrees with him. My mother thinks Carey strongly resembles her family, the Landrinis, and my father says he looks like me."

Carey raised his head as if he knew he was being discussed, and Vail watched him, moved—even more than he had expected—by emotions hard to analyze. Shame at what he had done to this girl, so innocent and so drunk—it had all been his fault. Respect for her cool courage when she first saw him in the kitchen and her poker player's skill when she showed him her baby. Surprising sadness at the knowledge that, for the baby's sake and for hers, he could never claim the boy as his own. Wonder at the simple fact of the child. There might be other children in the world who were his, but none he knew of, none so certain as this little boy looking up at him with great black eyes shining.

He said, "Your father is right. At least he has his mother's wonderful eyes."

Carey spared her the necessity of a reply. He made a tremendous effort, lifted one tiny hand, brought it forward, and moved the knee behind it. Then he moved the other hand and knee, lifted his head, and chortled.

"Oh!" Marin breathed. "He's done it, he's crawling. Oh, he's been trying so hard!"

Carey began to move faster and faster now that he had figured out the difficult business, traveling in a circle with a triumphant gurgling laugh until he fell in a heap at Vail's feet. Immediately he got up and sat down again with a plop. The man above him extended a finger for him to tug, and the child examined it interestedly, talking to himself in a cooing babble.

Vail looked down at the soft, dark curls. "So now I am an uncle. God, it makes me feel old."

"Ethan is an uncle, too, but he doesn't know it."

"No word at all?"

"Nothing. I think about the knife fights and the hangings in the gold camps. Sometimes I'm afraid . . ."

"Don't be. Ethan can take care of himself. He's a good man in a fight, but he doesn't look for trouble."

"It need never have happened. Papa will never be well, and Mama—she is not herself at all. It was all so stupid . . ."

"Tragedies usually are, because people are stupid. I'm in the camps fairly often. I have business there at times. Ever since I heard about Ethan, I've kept an eye out for him, and I'll continue to."

With a rush of gratitude she said, "Oh, it would mean so much just to know that he's alive, even if he doesn't come home." Impulsively she added, "It's a shame Logan didn't know you were coming. Next time let us know, and I'll make sure she's here."

Why had she said that? Only minutes before she had been hoping never to see this man again, and now she had invited him to come back and to meet Logan in her home, which would make an enemy of Malcolm if he found out. No help for it now. She couldn't take back the invitation, not with him smiling at her like that and the warm light again in his eyes.

"That's very kind. I worry about Logan, trapped in that house."

"There's no place else she'd want to be, not now, with her mother sick. But—do come back. Seeing you will help her, I'm sure of that."

He did come back. Not as often as Marin feared after her first impetuous invitation, but twice during the rainless summer, once in July and once at the end of August, when the hills had turned to a sun-dried gold and the streams had shriveled to a trickle. Both times he sent messages before he arrived, and both times Logan was there. At the first meeting, in midsummer, Glenna was sworn to silence and left to tend Elizabeth Severance while Logan rode over to Little Mountain when the sun was barely up. All day she sat by the front window, playing with Carey, then pacing nervously, watching the empty road. In the late afternoon Marin heard a little cry and turned to see Logan staring down the drive, her hand at her mouth and tears starting in her eyes. The next instant she was out the door and flying down the steps, and the man just riding up leaned from his big horse, pulled her off her feet and hugged her. He swung to the ground, and laughing and crying, she threw her arms around his neck. Marin, watching from the house, thought what it would mean to her to see Ethan again. She went upstairs and left the two alone.

When he came back in August, the atmosphere was not so charged with emotion, and the visit was easier for everyone. He arrived in the early afternoon, bringing a gift for Carey, which he lifted from the depths of his saddlebag—a squirming puppy, so young that Vail could hold it in one big hand.

"The mother belongs to a sailor on an English ship that's leaving this week. He claims the pups are purebred Collie, and he has to find homes for them before he sails. This one looked too fine to drown."

"Drown!" Logan cried. "Poor little tyke. How can you say such a thing?"

"Better to drown him than turn him loose on the docks to starve." Vail set the puppy—a soft, pretty creature, helpless and therefore appealing—on the floor near Carey. The small dog staggered up onto short, slender legs, still frightened by the long jolting trip and the separation from his mother, but curious about his new surroundings. His black, silky coat was marked by a white-tipped tail, white legs, and a broad white band at the neck. His pointed infant face was intelligent and, at the moment, worried. He looked around, sat down again, and offered a small white paw to Carey, as though hoping earnestly that this gesture would solve all his problems.

Carey chuckled and reached out. There were hunting dogs on the ranch, but they were never allowed into the house. He climbed to his feet, took two wavering steps, and collapsed. The puppy squealed, scooted out of the way, then came back to Carey and licked his face until the child chortled with glee.

To Marin, Vail said, "I should have asked first. I hope you don't mind."

He'd done exactly as he wanted and deliberately hadn't asked permission. She answered politely, "I'm sure Carey will love him."

The day was sultry, and after Vail had paid a call on James in his room, they all walked down to the stream bank, where the servants were spreading cloths on the grass under the oaks and laying out a picnic lunch. Sophy had been flirting so blatantly and inexpertly with Vail that Marin wanted to slap her. Surprisingly, Delphine saw it, too, and took the girl in hand. She was marching her down the hill without allowing her a backward glance. The path was narrow, and Logan, with Carey riding on one hip, had fallen into step beside Stuart, leaving Marin to follow with Vail. She looked around for Petra, for Josefina, for somebody.

How did it happen that she was so often left alone with him? Now that she was certain he remembered nothing of that long-ago night, she felt less strained in his company, but never completely at ease. She always had to search for something to talk about.

Today she looked very pretty, and knew it, and that was a help. Her white lawn dress was lace-trimmed and sprinkled with tiny blue flowers, the most becoming day dress she owned, with an embroidered bodice that opened over a delicate chemisette and a flounced skirt held out by many stiffly starched petticoats. The breeze that had sprung up nudged her wide, flat-crowned straw hat, and she caught it just in time and tied the satin ribbons firmly under her chin.

"Tell me about San Francisco, Vail. Is it very exciting? I'm dying to go over, and Stuart simply refuses to take me."

"Stuart is quite right. It's no place for a lady. No place for anyone without a knife between his teeth and a gun in his belt. I never go to sleep without a gun beside me. The town is filthy, a ramshackle garbage dump. When it rains, the streets are rivers of mud so deep that mules have drowned in it, and they say that people have, too, and never been found. Then there's the hot, dry weather, when the sand blows off the dunes and sticks in your eyes and throat. The food is execrable, and the most attractive places in town are the saloons and gambling halls." He grinned cheerfully at her. "Still think you want to go there?"

She wrinkled her nose. "If you're not exaggerating, no. Why do you stay?"

"Because there's money to be made, lots of it, if you know how to go about it."

"And do you?"

"We'll see. By the way, I've talked to Ethan."

All the breath went out of her in a gasp. "But that's wonderful! Where is he? How is he? Why didn't you tell me before?"

His eyes were on Logan, watching her hand Carey to Stuart and climb down the bank. "This is my first chance to talk to you alone. I don't want to get her hopes up. Tell her yourself later, if you wish, after you hear what he said."

Marin followed his gaze. So he knew what Logan felt for Ethan. But of course he did, for he knew his sister so well.

"But why—if you've found him, why would it hurt to tell her? When is he coming home?"

"He isn't." She started to speak, and he went on. "I saw him in Coloma three weeks ago. He's well, although I think he's had a rough time of it. He claimed to have found a fifty-ounce nugget when he first went out last year, but it's gone now. Probably gambled away. He hinted at some immensely rich claim— naturally he wouldn't tell me where—but he's not coming home, not now anyway."

"You told him about Papa?"

"He heard last year."

She stopped dead on the path and stared at him, all embarrassment forgotten. "And he didn't come home?"

"By the time he knew about Mr. Gentry, you were married. You must admit, it let him off the hook. Now don't lose your temper, or they'll hear you down there."

Furiously she whispered, "How could he do such a thing! He could at least have let us know he was all right. When I think how I've worried . . ."

"He could have, but being Ethan, he wouldn't. Surely you know him by now. He didn't mean to be cruel, he just didn't realize how you would feel. Oh, and he said to tell you that he has complete confidence in Stuart's ability to run Little Mountain. He sends his felicitations, too."

"I could kill him, I could just kill him," she said through gritted teeth.

He laughed. "No, you couldn't. You may get mad at him, but you'll always be loyal to your impossible brother, just as Logan is to me."

They were at the top of the bank. Little Clear Creek had narrowed in the hot weather, but still contained enough cool water to chill the wine bottles suspended since yesterday just under the surface. Petra was supervising Mateo as he pulled them up and opened one for Stuart to sample. Logan was waiting below with Carey. Vail jumped down, and before she could find a way down for herself, he caught Marin under her arms, swung her off the bank, and set her on the ground.

"Thank you." She hurried to Stuart without appearing to hurry, settled on the grass, and spread her pretty skirts. The picnic feast she had planned so carefully was laid out, and she laughed and talked and passed plates to everyone, and beneath the thin fabric of her dress the skin where he had touched her continued to burn long afterward.

Chapter 11

On a warm September evening a week after the picnic Marin sat alone in the office making entries in Little Mountain's account ledger. It was work she liked doing, and Stuart seldom allowed it. Marriage, she had discovered, was not quite the partnership she had expected it to be. She had struggled alone to run the ranch, had learned a great deal, and had thought to have some say, at least to talk things over before Stuart made major decisions. But it was beginning to be clear that he expected his wife to run the house and bear and raise their children; he controlled everything else. She had tried to tell him what James taught her—she had a good mind, and it was important that she use it. "I love taking care of the baby and the house, but, dearest, they don't take all of my thoughts. I need to use my mind."

A stern expression settled over his face, and for the first time she saw a resemblance to his father. He said, "If using your mind is what you want, then do it. Read a book."

He wanted her obedient, submissive, like his mother, she thought gloomily. He ran the ranch with a harder hand than James ever had and expected perfect service from the house servants, who were unpredictable and volatile and often disappointed him; when he was disappointed, Marin heard about it. He had also decided to stand for the legislature and had been at Longridge most of the day talking politics with his father. She was glad she wasn't there listening to him agree with everything Malcolm said even when he didn't really believe it. It was strange how uncertain he was in the presence of his father. Somehow it seemed unmanly, and she did not want to think that about her husband.

One thing heartened her. James was better, so much better that today she had finally been able to tell him about Ethan. She did it carefully, making it appear that Ethan would have rushed home directly if Stuart had not been there to run the ranch. She also invented several loving messages and hoped no one would ask why he had not let them know months before that he was alive.

No one did ask. Sophy sat on the step, supposedly looking after Carey and in reality imagining herself as free as Ethan, free to travel the world and find gold, free to cross the bay on one of the boats that now made the trip regularly and go to San Francisco, where Vail lived. Rose, her wan face coming alive for an instant, only wanted to know how Ethan looked and when he would be home, and Marin improvised hastily, making up plans for Ethan's future that she thought sounded reasonable. It was a measure of James's illness, although she did not see it, that he accepted everything she said. In the old days he would have recognized the truth immediately, but today he smiled and nodded and questioned nothing, and she was relieved.

Tonight the house was quiet. Papa and Mama were fed and safely in their beds. Carey was sleeping the sleep of healthy exhaustion, Sophy was propped on her bed, immersed in one of her novels. The clock on the parlor mantel slowly struck ten, and afterward the only sound in the little office was that of Marin's pen scratching across the ledger page. There was a gentle tap on the open door, and she raised her head. Petra was standing in the doorway.

"I must speak to you, Miss Marin," she said with the musical, rising inflection that was one of the few holdovers from her native Spanish. She had worked very hard on her English, and it was almost accentless now.

"Come in, Petra." Marin laid down her pen. The girl's slanting eyes did not meet hers directly, and there was a faint rosy flush under the smooth olive skin. She looked embarrassed, and that was impossible, for nothing ever discomfited Petra. Good Lord. Surely she hadn't gotten involved with one of the men on the place. Surely—but such a thing could not be. Petra had too much sense.

"Well, what is it?"

Petra's flush deepened. "Miss Marin, I must go tomorrow."

"Go where? I'm sorry, Petra, I can't spare you just now."

"I mean go away, ma'am, to stay."

"What on earth are you talking about?"

"My brother came to see me this morning. He is taking me to San Francisco." Marin stared at her as if she had lost her mind, and Petra went on rapidly, "One of my sisters is there already, and she has found a job for me."

"You have a job. Aren't you happy here?"

"Oh, yes, ma'am, I am happy, but now I want to go . . ." Petra looked miserable. "Everybody goes to San Francisco now. There is much to do there."

"But it's a terrible place, not fit for decent women. Mr. Severance—Mr. Vail Severance—told me that it's filthy and dangerous and—" Marin's eyes narrowed suspiciously. "Which of your sisters is there, Petra?"

"Fermina, ma'am."

Fermina. She could imagine what Fermina was doing for a living. "And what kind of job has your sister found for you?"

"With a very respectable lady, the widow of Mr. Horace Fletcher. She needs someone to help run her husband's store, ma'am, someone who can keep figures and also can sew. I can do both," Petra finished with quiet pride.

Marin picked up her pen, tapped it against her thumbnail, put it down again. This was what she got for teaching Petra to keep books. She should have left her to mind the baby and mend clothes like any other maid. Stuart had done business with Horace Fletcher before the man died this spring, and undoubtedly his widow was very respectable. And the girl's brother was here to escort her, so there could be no complaint about that. And she said *everybody* was going to San Francisco. The truth was she was infected with the same disease as Ethan: she wanted to go adventuring, to make her fortune. Petra, a Mexican maid of no family and little education, whom she had treated generously, more as a friend than a servant. This would never have happened back home in Maryland.

Coolly she remarked, "You've been dealt with kindly in this house. You know nothing at all of the world outside, and I doubt you can manage in it. However . . ." Petra tried to speak, but Marin cut her off. "However, go if you wish, but understand that your place here will be filled."

"I wish you wouldn't be angry with me, Miss Marin," Petra said sorrowfully. "Tomorrow is very soon to leave, I know, but my brother . . ."

"It makes no difference, for I wouldn't want you to stay now," Marin replied with deliberate intent to wound. "And don't come crawling back to Little Mountain when you get into trouble, because there will be no place for you here. I do not keep disloyal servants." She picked up her pen and this time began to write busily.

Petra turned and fled, the tears spilling out of her dark eyes.

After a little while Marin closed the book, lifted it to the top shelf of the bookcase, and started up the stairs. Josefina, coming down, took one look at her face and ducked past quickly, preferring to keep safely out of the way when the mistress looked like that. But Marin did not even notice her, so great was her sense of injury. She depended on Petra in so many ways, large and small, and had counted on her help in the future. It had never occurred to her that the girl might harbor other ambitions than serving her.

She was still awake when Stuart came home at midnight, sitting on the bed, on top of the quilted coverlet, a book lying open and unread in her lap.

He shrugged when she told him the news. "I'm sorry because you're upset, but really, Marin, I think we can find another maid without difficulty."

"Not like Petra!" she cried, furious because he was taking it lightly. "You wouldn't be so unconcerned if it was Cosme leaving."

"True. Because Cosme is important to the ranch. Petra is a nice girl and intelligent, too, which is probably why she wants to leave. I suspect she'll do very well for herself. But the house won't fall down if she goes."

Always she tried to keep her temper with Stuart, for he never lost his and it made her look childish, but she couldn't suppress a bitter glance. This was not at all the moment or the mood in which she had planned to tell him, but now, angry and a little frightened at what lay ahead, she said flatly what she had known for several weeks—there would be another baby before spring.

The rain began on October 28, 1849, a gentle, persistent rain that was absorbed instantly by the parched, thirsty earth. It had come early, for the rainy season did not usually begin until mid-November, but everyone blessed it, for the summer had been hot and dry, and a wet winter meant lush pasturage for the cattle next spring. The wild oats began to sprout, and a faint green tinged the burnt gold stubble on the hills as though the reviving water had washed away a layer of yellow dust to reveal the true color beneath. Brant and ducks and geese marked the leaden skies, flying their eternal, mystical V formation south from Canada, descending to the watercourses to feed and rest. Men took their rifles out in the rain, and roasted wild goose appeared on supper tables. It continued to rain heavily for two weeks, only occasionally decreasing to a drizzle, until the soggy ground could not absorb it and ankle-deep puddles stood on the high land close to the house at Little Mountain. The corral, lying down the hill, became a lake, and it was messy, slippery work crossing from the house to the barn; the adobe soil, rock-hard in dry weather, became slick as ice when wet.

But despite constant, drenching rain interspersed with sudden wild storms, the campaign for election to office under the new constitution continued. Delegates had worked in Monterey from the beginning of September into October, and on October 13 it had been signed. Thirty guns were fired in proud celebration at the fort, and then one more for the state-to-be, California. Immediately copies of the constitution were dispersed to towns and mining camps and isolated ranches, and Stuart went to Sacramento City to stand as a candidate for the new legislature, attaching himself to no party, but making speeches and asking for votes just as candidates in a regular election did back East.

Marin privately thought he and all the other men were crazy, traveling about the district on horseback, slogging through the sucking mud of roads that had almost disappeared in the wettest, most miserable winter anyone could remember. On election day, November 13, a torrential storm struck, and sensible people stayed home, but enough hardy, politically minded souls struggled out to provide a light vote, and the constitution was ratified. Peter Burnett, that expert Southern politician and former slaveholder, became governor, two representatives to the United States Congress were chosen, and state legislators were elected, one of them a likable and talented young rancher, Stuart Severance.

The first session of the legislature was in San Jose, and Marin saw him off in early December with misgivings, for rain had washed out many of the roads, and the only way to get through was on horseback. All the discomforts of advancing pregnancy were with her, but she had a houseful of servants, the reliable Cosme at hand, and Dr. Cutter only two hours' ride away. And the baby was not due until March. The legislature would be adjourned and Stuart home long before then.

The steady downpour continued and by Christmas was at its height. It was a dismal, shut-in holiday with none of the usual visiting and parties. The only pleasant moment came when a messenger tramped into the house, dripping wet, sent by Celia with a fond message and presents for everyone, including a tortoiseshell comb trimmed with gold and pearls for Marin and a cunning pair of boots for Carey. Marin, who had not seen Celia since the rain began or even thought of her in weeks, was embarrassed that she had no gifts to send back. She sent the man to the kitchen to dry off and have a meal, and the instant he was out of sight hurried upstairs as quickly as her increasing size would allow.

In her drawer she found a lace shawl that she had not yet worn and that Celia did not need, and after hesitating, she took out a small package. In it was the fine gold stickpin with the tiny diamond she had ordered from New York for Stuart's Christmas present, a far more costly gift than she wished to give Nicolas. But she had nothing else to send, and anyway, Stuart was not here and would not be here soon. His last message had said he could not be home before the end of January. She had heard, too, that the gathering of elected officials was beginning to be called the "legislature of a thousand drinks" and that the people of San Jose were giving a Christmas ball in order to cheer up the hardworking legislators during the bad weather. Everyone who could get there between storms was invited.

She slammed the drawer shut and took her presents downstairs, thinking how splendid it was that Stuart was having a good time with a raft of pretty, slim-waisted señoritas down in San Jose while she sat here, lonely, sick, and enormous with child.

After Celia's messenger had plunged out into the storm again, she sat by the window watching him disappear down the drive, which was now a steady rivulet, and wishing she could visit with Celia or get over to Longridge to spend an afternoon with Logan.

But she could not get out, she could not go anywhere, and in spite of the many people sheltered under this roof, the house was always hushed. James never left his room through the dark, wet days, and Rose spent all her waking moments with him, took her sparse meals there, and never came downstairs. She had slipped backward in the last weeks. Often she did not even dress, but remained in her flannel wrapper all day, her pale blond hair straggling down her back now that Petra was not there to cajole her into arranging it. The one time Marin tried to get her into some semblance of order, she had pulled away like a petulant child, and Marin did not try again.

On New Year's Day another visitor arrived in the rain, trudging up the long drive, his boots sinking half a foot into the mud with each stride. He banged on the kitchen door, and Berta, after ordering him to pull off his slimy boots, allowed him into the warm room and gave him a chair by the fire while she ladled a plate of soup. He was a stranger, dirty, disreputable, with a wicked-looking face half hidden by a thick, damp beard and a soaked slouch hat, but he was mild-mannered and grateful for the food. Shivering slightly with the shock of the heat, he edged closer to the fire and greedily shoveled down the soup, then the meat and bread that followed. Regardless of his appearance or the gun on his hip, Berta would no more have thought of turning him away, even on a fine day, than she would have refused to care for a close relation. The stranger in need must never be denied food and shelter, however villainous or beggarly his appearance, for great would be her reward in Heaven, as the priest had said.

The correctness of this stricture was plain to Berta as soon as the man had eaten his fill and begun to talk. His words sent her huge bulk thundering down the long hall to the parlor and then back to the kitchen, where she hauled the stranger out of his chair and into Marin's presence.

Marin was sitting very close to the fire in an effort to avoid the draft that persisted in slipping under the front door. Sophy was curled on the sofa, knees drawn up for warmth, rereading a novel she knew almost by heart—she hadn't had a new book in so long.

The man came in, hesitant and abashed in his damp, dirty socks, his beard showing marks where he had tried to claw it into neatness with a hasty hand—a little man of thirty-five or forty, older than most miners, with the exhausted, worn appearance that grew on these men after months of backbreaking work and constant disappointment.

Marin gave Sophy a look, and she swung her feet to the floor and smoothed her skirt into modesty in a manner slow and in-solent enough to show her disdain for Marin's authority. The man kept his eyes politely averted.

Marin made a great effort, and smiled. "Berta says you have important news for me."

"If this be Little Mountain like this here lady says and you be Miss Gentry, I do, yes'm."

"This is Little Mountain, and I was Miss Gentry. Now I'm Mrs. Severance. May I ask your name, sir?" She gave him the courteous title despite his appearance. It was only civil treatment for a stranger.

"Willis Norton, ma'am."

"And what is your news, Mr. Norton?"

"I b'lieve I do know of yer brother, ma'am."

Sophy's head snapped up.

Marin, her heart pounding queerly, said, "Ethan?" in a faint voice.

"Ethan Gentry, yes'm. I do regret my news ain't the best, and I mean to break it easy as possible. He has joined the choir invisible, ma'am. He did ask for his mama before he died."

It was Sophy who fainted and had to be carried upstairs by Mateo. Marin sent Josefina to tend her and turned back to Willis Norton, her mind rejecting totally the words he had uttered. The man was mistaken, identities were so easily confused in the camps. He had heard of Ethan, perhaps met him once, and later seen someone who looked like him die. Or possibly his motives were as unsavory as his appearance; perhaps he hoped for money from the grieving family . . .

She questioned him like an attorney defending his client against a capital crime. Where had he met Ethan, what did Ethan look like, what had he said of his circumstances, his family? How had he died?

In his slow Midwestern accent Willis Norton answered. He had met up with Ethan on the American River last spring, a fine-looking young feller with yellow hair, best man on a horse he ever did see. Not a good gambler though, for he was a plunger at monte and when playing poker tended to draw to an inside straight. They had teamed up for a while, then Ethan had decided to head up to Nevada City, and they'd lost touch. That's the way it was with miners, everybody chasing after his own El Dorado. They'd run into each other again this autumn in Whiskey Slide. Ethan was down on his luck, temporarily, mind you. He'd struck pay dirt time and again, but had lost his stake each time and had to go back to digging. He said he and his pa had had a big fight that made his pa sick, and he had this idea stuck in his head that he couldn't go home till he was rich enough to make up for it. Then he came down with la grippe—you had to understand it was an awful hard life, digging gold, and lots of strong, young fellers couldn't stand the gaff. He just got worse, but there wasn't much around in the way of medicine. Talked about his ma, said he loved her. Said he had the two prettiest sisters in Christendom. Funny thing—while he was sick, he grew a long beard, and it came in a real pretty red, about the color of Mrs. Severance's hair. Now you wouldn't expect a red beard on such a blond feller. Well, after a while he died, very quiet, in the night.

Willis Norton stopped talking and looked at Marin.

She had listened to it all without feeling, rejecting, rejecting, until the part about the beard. Anyone who really knew Ethan intimately, someone who had cared for him when he was sick and had seen him unshaven, would know about that peculiarity. It struck her to the heart as nothing else had. No one thing this man said was especially convincing, yet bit by bit it piled up into the truth. She looked into his eyes, sad, embarrassed, filled with compassion, and knew that Ethan was dead.

"When—did it happen?"

"End of November, ma'am."

November, when they had celebrated Carey's first birthday so happily.

"Was he properly buried?"

"Yes'm. Six feet deep, with stones over. I'm by way of being a lay preacher, and I said a prayer. Carved out a cross with his name and 'Safe in the Bosom of the Lord' on it, but being wood, I don't know how long it'll last. He was a good boy, Ethan. A touch hasty, thoughtless-like at times, but he was a friend to me. That's why I figgered I'd come this way going back to Frisco. I did think you ought to know."

She told him he could sleep and eat with the vaqueros until he was ready to go on and offered him money and a horse. He accepted shelter for the night only, declined the money, and agreed to take the horse after she assured him that Little Mountain had more horses than it could sell at the moment. She told Berta to pack food for him when he left and took fifty dollars from Stuart's box in the office, to be secreted with the food. Mr. Norton, for all his pride, looked as though he could use it.

She climbed the stairs, slowly, as she did everything in these days of advanced pregnancy, went into her room, and sat down by the window without lighting the lamp. Rain beat against the glass and trickled down it like fast-flowing tears. She tried to summon up Ethan's face and bring it into focus in her mind. It glimmered and faded. Had she forgotten so soon? She searched for his voice and could not hear it. Was it possible for the sound of a loved voice to slip so easily from memory? Her handsome, laughing, rash, vibrant, errant brother, who had adored the girls, all of them, and had meant to make the Gentrys' fortune. Papa would have to be told—what would such news do to him? Mama—God only knew with Mama, but perhaps she would be comforted to know that prayers had been said. Logan must know of it, too, and finally, forever, give up her dreams. Mateo could take a letter to

Longridge—somewhere she must find the strength to write such a letter.

There was a tap at her door like a tiny bird pecking, and Sophy slipped into the room. She walked jerkily, as though uncertain of her step. Her face was wraithlike in the dim light.

"Oh, sister . . ." she said, and crumpled down with her head on Marin's knees, shaking with sobs. Absently Marin stroked her curls and remembered Ethan striding in the day after Celia's party, so vital, so confident, to tell her he was going off to find gold in the mountains and make the family rich. Her only thought then had been to preserve his life by preventing a duel with Vail over her, yet death had found him another way. She leaned her cheek against the cold window pane and continued stroking Sophy's hair.

When James was told, he turned his face to the window, stared out as though he saw something of significance beyond the opaque rain, and sighed, a deep, shuddering exhalation that was almost a groan. He did not weep, but then Marin had not wept, either. She gave quiet thanks that he had taken it stoically, almost as though the news was expected.

Rose cried soundlessly all day, cried until she slept, woke, and cried again. Gradually the tears slowed and stopped, but after that she slept a good deal more during the days, despite Delphine's efforts to divert her.

A note came from Logan, brief, correct in its condolence, carefully written in her neat hand. What anguish must have gone into its composition, how many false starts must there have been before this dignified message had been produced. It brought Marin closer to crying than all her mother's tears.

Sophy no longer went near her parents' room or talked much to anyone, but was a silent ghost, staring for hours at the gray, wet, desolate world outside her bedroom window, thinking dark thoughts, slipping so unobtrusively around the house that Marin almost forgot about her.

The dull, somber days went by. February arrived with another avalanche of water, and Stuart did not come home. Marin and Delphine began to make nervous jokes about building an ark in the backyard, and the servants crossed themselves, quarreled with each other, and obeyed orders slowly and sullenly. Below the hill, rising water licked at the footbridge over Little Clear Creek, and the word brought by rare visitors was that all the rivers were at flood stage and the roads almost impassable. Travel about the countryside was still possible, but no one tried it without a compelling reason. So it was with a feeling close to pleasure that Marin walked into the kitchen one evening and found Gabriel Navarro sitting at the round table in the center of the room, wolfing down a plate of stew.

His dark eyes warmed at the sight of her, and he was instantly on his feet, bowing, assuring her that his very soul was nourished by her enchanting presence and that his eyes feasted on her lovely face. He didn't mention her delightful figure, she noted sardonically. The florid phrases meant he had been told Stuart was not at home. When the *patrón* was around, he was a good deal more circumspect. Still, the man's zest and vitality were cheering in this gloomy house, and she sat down at the table and drank a cup of coffee with him, a thing she would never have done under normal circumstances. Out of real curiosity she asked him what he had been up to, and how he came to be at Little Mountain at this particular time, and he expanded under her interest.

"Ah, lady, I have been everywhere and done everything!"

Probably true, she thought, and grinned.

Encouraged, he went on. "I have a magnificent claim." His voice dropped. "Where it is I cannot, of course, mention. However, I have taken out much gold and have been to San Francisco many times."

"And left all your gold there?" inquired Marin, remembering what Vail had said about the expensive pitfalls of the town.

"Oh, ho! But what a time in exchange for it! The cost of everything, it is higher than the moon, and then one gambles—and so forth."

"Yes, indeed," she murmured, and sipped her coffee.

"But I have come back because"—he leaned forward and gazed soulfully into her eyes, "this is home to me, this fine rancho, where I have worked so devotedly and where the people"—he gave her a significant look, "are so dear to me. I grew lonely."

"And you grew hungry, too?"

He threw back his head and laughed, the first genuine laughter in the house in many weeks. "Ah, you have me, lady. I remember well the old *patrón* saying yours was the most clever brain in the family, and he was right! Yes, I was hungry, and the gold is at present all gone, but I will get more, never fear. In the meantime I may stay, yes?"

She looked into his dancing, impudent eyes and smiled back.

"You may stay, yes."

• • •

The morning began with a drenching storm and a wind that rattled the windows and slipped through cracks and under doors. Trees bent under the blustering gale, and even the evergreens were stripped bare. Mateo kept fires going in every room, and wet wood was stacked high in the kitchen, but the adobe walls were clammy and the house was cold only a few feet from the fireplaces. In early afternoon the wind died, the rain decreased to a fine drizzle and then stopped, but the skies remained pewter gray and threatening. After supper Josefina, sent by the other servants as the one most likely to wheedle what they wanted, came to Marin with a request. She came carefully, for the *patróna* was mostly not in a good mood, and one never knew whether she might bestow one of her unexpected, brilliant smiles, or hurl a handy object at one's head.

"Miss Marin," she began hesitantly, "tonight is it possible . . . it is so dark, so bad, we will all feel ver' much better if there could be some singing, perhaps a little dancing . . ."

"Dancing?" Marin raised her head from the parlor sofa, where she had been lying since supper. "In this house?" She dropped back with a groan. The roast pork was not sitting well. "Josefina, go away."

"No, ma'am, not here. In the men's quarters, down below the creek. It is so far away—nothing will be heard up here. A little food, a few guitars, perhaps a drink of wine . . . it would be"—she searched for the word, "cheerfully?"

Marin raised her head again and scowled.

"Who thought this up? Gabriel?"

Josefina lifted one plump shoulder in an eloquent shrug.

Slowly Marin sat up and put her hand to her back. A weight like a heavy flatiron had been resting there all afternoon. Cheerfully. They could all use some cheerfully in this dreary house. She would enjoy a party herself—but for the roast pork and this weight on her back.

"Oh, all right. Take what you want from the kitchen." She got up heavily and walked out of the room toward the stairs. On the bottom step she paused with one hand on the square newel post, turned, and smiled. "Have a good time," she said, and grasping the banister, pulled herself up, lifting each leaden foot with an effort.

From behind the dining room door Gabriel hissed, "What did she say?"

" 'ave a good time," replied Josefina, a crease between her straight black brows. With worried eyes she followed Marin's slow progress up the stairs.

Gabriel reached around the door, pulled her behind it and into his arms. "What a fine girl you are! I said you were the one to talk her into it."

Josefina pushed at him. "Let go, Gabriel. I am, I think, a little worried. She does not look so good." She peeked through the crack between door and wall and could just see Marin's skirt trailing over the top step as she reached the upper hall. "I think maybe I should go to her."

Gabriel nibbled at the top of her ear, and into it he whispered, "Don't be foolish, little one. The *patróna* can send for us if she needs us. I myself promise to see to her well-being, how is that? Come now." He nuzzled her neck and pulled her gently away from the door into the deeper shadows. One hand slipped inside the bodice of her dress and squeezed her soft, round breast. A brief battle took place in Josefina between duty and desire, and duty lost. She sank down, and forgot about Marin Severance.

It was completely dark when Marin woke. How long she had lain on the bed asleep she did not know, but she was still warm under the eiderdown quilt, although only small remnants of a log fire glowed in the fireplace, and the room was cold. In a few minutes, when she felt like getting up, she would call Mateo to lay a new fire. The afternoon respite had ended sometime while she slept, and outside the wind was hurling in from the sea, the front of a new storm out of the far Pacific. It prowled around the house, prying through cracks with cold fingers, tearing tiles from the roof and lashing the trees until they whistled. Rain came in sudden torrential bursts, pounding on the roof and windows as if trying to rip the house apart, subsiding to a quiet but steady beat, then volleying down again.

Suppose it never stops? she thought. Her mind veered back. Something had awakened her, but what? It could not have been a noise, for she could hear nothing above the tumult outside.

There, that was it. A niggling ache, almost like pain, a dull, snaky pain slowly turning, twisting low down inside her. She sat up, fear rising like nausea in her throat. The baby was not due yet—or was it? She could not think. Somehow she had lost track of days, of weeks, for each one was so much like the last. This was March. Yes, the first of March had passed last week, for she remembered thinking that it had been almost a month since Gabriel had come.

The slowly turning snake writhed again, and real fear struck. She must not send for Dr. Cutter on a night such as this, not if it was a false alarm, and yet how could she tell? The first time, with Carey, had been so different.

She struggled to a sitting position, braced her hands against the bed, and pushed herself onto her feet. After resting against the bedpost for a moment, she made her way to the door. The hallway was empty, the house silent.

"Mateo! Josefina!"

Down the corridors and through the vacant rooms of the house her own voice echoed and mocked her. No one was there—but how could it be? Fifty people worked at Little Mountain, and there were always at least half a dozen inside the house. She walked unsteadily back to the bed and eased down onto it. The pain had not come again, and her mind was clearer. Josefina had wanted something, a party, that was it, and she had said—what had she said? *"Have a good time."* They were all down in the long building where the vaqueros slept and ate, on the far side of Little Clear Creek, dancing and singing in the light of the tallow candles, in the flickering light of the kerosene lamps.

Sophy would have to go down there regardless of the storm and get help, for the pain was sneaking back like a devil, twisting, twisting, and fear was growing great.

"Sophy!"

Sophy, Sophy, Sophy, the empty house mocked.

Sophy was not there, she knew it now. Dim memory returned. Marin had stumbled upstairs and fallen on the bed, and Sophy had come in to ask if she could go to the party, too. She had been wearing her blue silk dress with the many flounces, and Marin's comb, the gold and pearl comb that had been Celia's Christmas gift, was perched like a crown on top of her high-piled, blond hair.

"To a servants' party? Don't be ridiculous, Sophy," Marin had said with finality. "And take off my comb." She had closed her eyes and turned her head away.

"Yes, to a servants' party, to anything just to get out of this house!" Sophy's voice came passionately out of the dark.

With an effort Marin had turned her head on the pillow and looked at her little sister. The lamp had not been lit, and the only light was from the fire, beginning to burn low on the hearth. Sophy's eyes glistened, close to tears, and her baby face was taut.

"I never heard of such a thing," Marin had said sternly. "Mama would faint. You go to your room and stay there, Sophy Gentry!"

Sophy had run from the room, and it had been too much effort to follow and make her give back the comb. She could be sulking in her room now, refusing to answer, but Marin knew she was not. Sophy was down below Little Clear Creek, too, dancing in her silk dress and singing and drinking wine, unreachable no matter how loudly Marin called. Marin was alone in this house with Carey asleep in the next room, Papa and Mama at the other end of the hall behind their heavy door, unable to hear her, unable to help if they did hear. Only Delphine remained, deep in her featherbed, contentedly asleep at this hour. Delphine slept like the dead. Marin could scream her throat raw, and Delphine would not hear.

The great thing was not to panic. The pain had not returned for a long time now. Probably it was a false alarm. Morning would come, the servants would return, and the house would pick up its normal rhythm. In the morning she would send Mateo for Dr. Cutter.

The clock in the hall ticked on, the rain slowed, the wind eased, and the steady, monotonous thud of a loose shutter lulled her to sleep.

When Delphine awoke, her room was dim in the gray light of another overcast day, but she was not fooled. The hour was late, the fire dead, and no warming, comforting pot of chocolate sat on her bedside table. Marin had let the servants get out of hand in recent weeks, and Delphine would have to speak to her about it. Of course the child was not well, but still, there was no excuse for sloppy service. How could she be expected to start the day without her chocolate? She opened her door. There was no sound from James's room, but down the hall Carey was talking contentedly to himself in his bed. From farther still there was another, faint noise that prickled her arms and drew her along the corridor in spite of a strong desire to retreat into her room and shut and bolt the door. What was that sound? A weak kitten crying?

She tapped at Marin's door and opened it. What she saw almost drove her back down the hall again. Marin was on the bed among the tangled bedclothes, and her face was the face of a stranger. No dainty, vivacious, pretty young girl this, but an old woman with gnarled, sweaty hair and a twisted face and a swollen body that jerked convulsively. The animal cries were coming from her.

Delphine was a soft woman and a selfish one, but not without pity. She mustered all the courage she had and went in.

"Marin, my dear!"

Marin opened eyes enormous with pain and fear. "Mateo," she whispered through dry lips. "Send Mateo for the doctor."

"Yes, dear, yes."

Delphine scuttled down the stairs, glad of a good reason for getting out of that dreadful room. She was not deserting, she was going for help. Distractedly she ran through each room, calling out for Mateo, for Luz, for Josefina, for Berta, and in the kitchen came to a hideous realization. There was not a single servant in the house. Back up the stairs she puffed as fast as her plump body could move, her skirts hiked, her loose hair falling about her face. Without ceremony she threw open Sophy's door. The room was empty, the bed undisturbed. But, heaven help us, where could the girl have gone?

She ran to Sophy's window and looked out on a drowned and devastated world. The grass that grew close to the house was washed away, and nothing was left but deep stands of water and thick mud. Trees that normally remained green all winter had been stripped of leaves by the great wind the night before, and their ragged branches were outlined against an iron gray sky. Below the hill on which the house stood, the gentle, wandering stream called Little Clear Creek was a muddy torrent risen far above its banks, its brown, boiling surface flecked with dirty foam. Fragments of the footbridge clung to the bank on the opposite side of the creek. The rest was gone as if it had never been. She ran to her own room, and from there she saw in the distance the broader water of Clear River, the boundary between Longridge and Fontana. It had become a wide, swift, deadly flood. Little Mountain was isolated, an island surrounded by spilling, rushing waters. They were cut off from the outside world.

She hesitated only a moment at the door across the hall and then pounded on it and called, "Rose, let me in!"

She tried the door, and it swung open.

James was asleep. She ignored him. He could not help her now. She went directly to the cot in the corner where Rose lay sleeping and shook her awake. Rose pulled fretfully away from the disturbing hands and slowly sat up, pushing her hair away from her face.

"Delphine? Is it morning?" She squeezed her eyes shut and yawned. "Please have Josefina bring hot water for James's bath and tell Berta to serve breakfast in half an hour."

"The servants are gone, all of them, there isn't one in the house, and Sophy is gone, too."

"Gone? Why, that won't do. Where are they?"

"I don't know, but listen, Rose. Marin's baby is coming, and I can't help her. I've never even had a baby. You must come and do what you can for her."

Rose leaned over the edge of the cot, searching in perplexity for her slippers. She found them and pulled them onto her bare feet with an air of having solved a great problem. "The doctor will have to come. I must not leave James."

Delphine sank to her knees, took Rose by the shoulders, and shook her. "Rose, pay attention! There is no one to go for the doctor, and he couldn't get here anyway. Your daughter needs help. You must go to her now. At least"—Delphine swallowed, "at least you can tell me what to do."

Very gravely Rose replied, "I would if I could, but I simply cannot." Her eyes moved to James's frightened face, and she smiled her sweet, vague smile.

He had come to full wakefulness in seconds and was tugging at the bedclothes, trying to push his paralyzed body out of bed. "Marin is in trouble, Rose! Go do something for her." He was half in, half out of bed.

Delphine said quickly, "Stop, James! In a minute you'll be on the floor, and I'll never get you up." Grunting, she shoved him back onto the bed, and he leaned around her and shouted, "Rose, I order you. Go to Marin."

Rose hugged her arms and began to rock. She did not seem to hear.

Despair rolled over Delphine. James understood perfectly and could do nothing. Rose could help but did not understand. She screwed up her courage and patted James's hand. "Don't worry, dear. I can manage."

Back down the stairs she went, a little slower now, and in the kitchen fixed a pot of chamomile tea, the only thing she could think of to do. Slower still, she carried it to that place upstairs and stopped outside. No sounds. Timorously she peeked inside. Marin lay very still on the bed, her head turned to one side. Our Father in Heaven, was she dead? If she was, there was nothing to be done, and yet . . . suppose she wasn't? How could Delphine face her Final Judgment when her time came if she left without knowing? She stepped inside, the teacup rattling on its saucer, wishing she did not have to look . . . The great black eyes opened, and Delphine breathed again. Thank God, she was not dead, thank God.

With shaking fingers she smoothed back her niece's tumbled

hair, dank and sticky with sweat, lifted the small head, and held the teacup to her lips.

"Swallow a little, dear. It's very strengthening."

Marin tried to swallow, coughed, strangled, and fell back on the pillow.

Delphine cleared her throat. "Your mother is not well this morning. She may be down to see you later. The servants are not in the house, and neither is Sophy. I can't imagine where they've got to."

"Not back yet?" Marin mumbled. "Hasn't Mateo gone for the doctor? There was a party down at the quarters last night . . . they should be back by now."

"How can I send Mateo when he isn't here?" inquired Delphine, a sense of grievance beginning to build. "If they're at the quarters, they can't get back. The bridge is washed out. Why on earth did you let them have a party?"

Marin looked up at her, dazed, confused. "The bridge out? But—I've got to have the doctor. Delphine, *this isn't like Carey.*"

Delphine reached into her meager store of knowledge. "The pains . . . are they close together, dear?"

"Sometimes. They start and stop." Marin closed her eyes, exhausted by the effort of speaking. Her hand stretched out, reaching for contact, for comfort.

But Delphine had spent the last of her courage. Quickly she said, "Rest, dear, while I go feed Carey. You needn't worry about a thing while I'm here."

She took the pitcher of water from the dresser, set it on the bedside table near Marin, and left the room, closing the door firmly behind her. Whatever took place in there, it had nothing to do with her. She had always ignored bodily functions, as a lady should, and the very thought of what was happening to Marin was repulsive. She could not be expected to witness such horrors; she would faint at the sight of blood. It was not her fault that they were here alone. Marin had let the servants go. And whose fault was it that the girl was in this fix anyway? Certainly *she* had never been so foolish. Delphine had done her best and could do no more. She would look out for Carey for as long as was necessary, and no one could ever say she had not done her best.

She took Carey out of his bed and carried him, along with a supply of diapers, to the kitchen. There she changed him, a distasteful job, fed him, and fixed a hearty breakfast for herself. Then she filled Angus's water bowl and took food to James and

Rose. She told them that Marin was coming along nicely and retreated with Carey to her room.

The party last night had begun very well for Gabriel. Josefina was a neat little package, and he had had a splendid time with her on the floor of the deserted, darkened dining room. So, it seemed, had Josefina, for she clung to him all evening, snuggled close as they danced, and refused the approaches of other men.

Marin's consent to a party had been interpreted generously, and trayloads of food and many gallon jugs of red wine from the *patrón's* cellar had been brought down to the quarters. The long trestle table at the end of the room was covered with great platters and huge pots of food. They had all eaten to the bursting point and drunk until the lighted tips of the candles danced and blurred before their eyes. The lull outside had ended, and a new storm had blown in, but they were cozy and happy inside, and the music of the guitars warmed their souls.

The men, who greatly outnumbered the women, eyed Gabriel resentfully and began snarling like dogs over the fat, homely girl who had taken Petra's place in the household. A few were already reluctantly dancing with each other for want of better partners. The little blond daughter of the old *patrón* had come, too, and Gabriel, although at the moment in love with his darling Josefina, considered going after her. Just in time he remembered the eyes of the young *patrón* when he had told him to stay away from the house, and decided he would leave the little Sophy to men less wise than he. With paternal interest he observed that she was now dancing with Mateo, a nice boy who could be trusted to behave well. He was beginning to be annoyed, however, with the way Cosme was conducting himself with Luz. Cosme had usurped too many of Gabriel's old prerogatives, and was much too full of himself. He was now chief vaquero, a position for which he had no talent; he ran the ranch in the absence of the young *patrón*, and with supreme insolence had replaced Gabriel in the affections of Luz. Or so it seemed. Luz hung on him, sang to him as they danced, flashed her big, dark eyes at him, and in general made an idiot of herself in a way that any woman of pride would never do. Now, if for just a little while, he could rid himself of Josefina, he would put Cosme in his place and teach Luz a lesson she badly needed.

His eyes slid sideways. Josefina was tippling at the wine again, and Luz was standing a foot or so, no more, away from Cosme, her smooth, creamy arms raised to adjust the ribbon in her black hair. What a charming line of neck she had. The guitars began again, and before Cosme could move, Gabriel had stepped in front of him with just a slight shove and had his hands on Luz's bare arms, whispering words no one could hear. A slow smile crossed her face. She looked up through ink black lashes and murmured a reply. She did not have the soft prettiness of Josefina—her features were sharper, and her small body less voluptuous—but, ah, there was something about the girl that drew him back!

They moved to the center of the room, and the floor cleared. Luz and Gabriel were the best dancers at Little Mountain and always a pleasure to watch. The guitars strummed a low, insistent beat, and the man and woman circled slowly, their lips and arms and bodies almost touching, but not quite, their hard heels stamping out the rhythm. The watchers began to clap and stamp, the tempo increased, and Luz came closer, arching her body backward as Gabriel bent over her, a half-smile on her lips, her eyes blazing into his. One arm slid sinuously around his neck, and then there was a shrill cry, a flash of red skirts, and Luz was hurled backward and went down with Josefina on top of her.

Everyone saw the blood at the same time. Sophy screamed and began to sob, and Cosme and Gabriel pulled Josefina off Luz and dragged her to the side of the room, kicking and screaming. Luz lay still, blood leaking onto the wooden floor boards, her white cotton blouse ripped and stained crimson. Cosme scooped her up and placed her on the table, which had been quickly cleared by the simple method of sweeping the platters of food to the floor.

The room was very quiet. Candles, burning low, cast grotesque moving shadows against the ceiling. Sophy lifted a kerosene lamp in her trembling hands, leaned over Luz, and whispered, "Dear Lord, she's dead!" There was a sighing expiration of breath from those who pressed near. Berta began to say her rosary on her fingers in soft Spanish, and the men still wearing hats took them off.

Gabriel's eyes darted over the room. Josefina was huddled against the wall, sobbing quietly and muttering in some dialect he did not understand. The others were clustered around the body on the table, stunned by the tragedy, their backs turned, their eyes down. The knife lay on the floor where Josefina had dropped it—a carving knife used earlier to cut the meat. The part of the blade not covered with blood gleamed in the candlelight. Quickly he picked it up, wiped the blade on his kerchief, slid on his poncho, and stuffed the knife under it. He looked longingly at the food on the floor. It was too near the table. *Bien,* they would not eat for a while. From a bench against the wall he took a wool shawl and a poncho from the pile, wrapped up Josefina, pulled her out the door, and closed it softly.

Under the wide, dripping eaves he stopped with her bundled against him and looked up toward the big adobe house on the hill. It was dark. All those beneath its roof must be peacefully asleep. The saints and angels were with him tonight, for the tranquil little creek had become a beast whose cold, dark waters had torn down the bridge, and that meant it would be a long time before anyone could get across and up to the house to report murder to the *patróna*. And the storm had died. Only a chill, fitful wind disturbed the quiet of the night.

He looked down at the girl. She drooped in his arms as though drugged or asleep. He dragged her down to the stables where the vaqueros' horses were kept, with an expert eye picked out the two best animals, and drove the others out into the dark. No one would follow them, not for a long time.

Chapter 12

Benicia, an ambitious, optimistic little town with expectations of greatness, sat on the north shore of the Carquinez Strait, a natural stopping point for vessels from San Francisco heading upriver to Sacramento City and the gold country. Its growth had been retarded by the previous year's exodus to the mines, but that was true of San Francisco, too, and its developers still believed that it was bound to outstrip its obnoxious rival sitting at the Golden Gate and become the great port city of the Pacific. At present it boasted only a few frame and adobe houses, a small hotel, a tavern, and a half-dozen stores, but the square was green with locust trees, wharf facilities were improving, and the Benicia ferry was the only way across the strait for anyone desiring to travel to the gold fields.

Gabriel had spent most of his tiny supply of cash to pay for ferry passage, but once on the Benicia side he headed directly for the tavern. Although there had been no more rain, the trip by night from Little Mountain to Benicia had been treacherous, with quagmire slopes and flooding streams. At the moment he did not even feel a sense of accomplishment but only a depressing suspicion that the money remaining in his pocket would not buy a meal for two, let alone riverboat passage to Sacramento City. The last time he had gone up to the gold fields, it cost twenty dollars just for space on the deck. Now it would be more.

He could see nothing of Josefina's face, buried as she was beneath the folds of the poncho, and she had not spoken once in all the hours just past, no words of thanks or loving admiration, not a sound. Even complaints would be more welcome than this unnatural silence, although if the ungrateful girl did begin to whine or snivel, he thought he would probably hit her. He had endured this miserable night, cold, wet, and hungry, he had cut himself off from Little Mountain and the comforts to be had there, all for her sake, yet he was not at all sure she was going to be worth it.

At the tavern he tied the horses, carried her over the mud to the porch, and took her inside. A delicious blast of warm air, redolent of whiskey and tobacco and frying eggs, struck his freezing face, and he sat Josefina on the floor against the wall and sidled up to the crowded bar. A man needed whiskey after a night like the one he had been through. It slipped down his throat raw and heartening. He ordered another and let his eyes wander over the group of miners playing monte, the men in flannel shirts and rough trousers standing around the stove eating from tin plates, the three well-dressed gentlemen talking at a table in the corner of the room. His eyes moved on and then came quickly back to the men at the table. Two of them he did not know, although he recognized the type immediately—hard, aggressive, self-assured Americans who would deal unkindly with any obstacles in their paths. The third man he did know, and from under his damp sombrero Gabriel searched the unwelcoming face for signs that he might get what he needed there.

He was big, that one, with an uncompromising set to his chin and a discouraging air of unapproachability. He was listening to the other men talk, his eyes down, his face indecipherable. One could not tell whether he was with good friends or men he detested. He was, by all accounts, a hard man to deal with, but he was also the only prospect presently in sight.

After a passage of time during which Gabriel had three more whiskeys, the unknown men at the table got up to take their leave, and he asked the bearded man leaning next to him at the bar, "Hey, my friend, who are those two over there?"

The man turned and looked at his face and poncho with an expression Gabriel was beginning to recognize.

"Who're you callin' 'friend,' Mex?" the man inquired, and went back to his drink.

Gabriel smiled ingratiatingly at the broad back and moved a little distance away.

"Them's businessmen, hardware dealers from Sacramento City," said the bartender, polishing the bar vigorously where Gabriel's drink had rested. "They got flooded out up there." He eyed the empty glass. "You can pay for that now."

"Oh, ho, but I am only started, señor. One more, if you please, which I will take over to that table."

The bartender followed his eyes and smirked. "If you're as sharp as you look, you won't bother him. He don't come here to be disturbed."

"But I am his employee, and he expects me." Gabriel gestured with the glass, and after a dubious glance across the room, the bartender filled it and watched him dodge around the men at the stove. At the table he bowed and took off his hat with a movement both graceful and appropriately deferential.

"May I sit with you, Señor Severance?" He inclined his head toward the line of men at the bar. "I am not popular over there just at present." *Dios,* but those gray eyes were cold. For an anxious moment Gabriel thought the bastard was going to refuse.

"Are you popular anywhere, Gabriel?" Vail asked, and shoved out the chair opposite with his boot.

Gabriel sank into it with relief and showed his teeth under his narrow black mustache. "Many thanks, señor. I am very glad to see you, as I am, you might say, in a great difficulty."

The bartender, an interested spectator, watched the Mexican talk rapidly with many gestures of his long-fingered hands, get up, and bring back to the table what appeared to be a small, walking bundle of old clothes. The oversize poncho came off, the shawl was unwrapped, and a small Mexican girl appeared, a downcast expression on her face and two long, shiny braids hanging down her back. He licked his lips appreciatively, for even though he didn't much like greasers there were very few women in these parts, even ugly ones, and this one was kind of pretty. Mr. Severance was standing up for her, just like he would for a lady.

Josefina sat down, her head still lowered, refusing to look at Vail.

"You have done something very bad, Josefina?" Vail asked,

and at the kindly note in his voice she raised her head, her dark eyes liquid with tears and defiance.

"Yes, but she was ver' bad first! So was he." She glared at Gabriel, who spread his hands wide as if to say, There you have the unreasonableness of women. Actually he was relieved to hear the aggravating girl speak at last. Perhaps there was nothing really wrong with her.

"The provocation was great," Vail agreed, and Gabriel remembered the old story of Prudencia and the duel. Señor Severance knew a good deal about exasperating women and the difficulties an innocent man could get into. He leaped into the conversation.

"Poor little Josefina has not eaten in many hours, for it was necessary to move rapidly and we brought no food." He smiled and looked hopefully at Vail.

"Then we certainly must get Josefina something to eat. And you, too, Gabriel."

It took the kitchen a remarkably short time to produce a meal when Señor Severance requested it. Gabriel thought he must have a great deal of money to command such respect; he would demand the same for himself as soon as he got rich. He talked expansively as he ate, describing the richness of his claim and suggesting that as soon as he got back up country and took out more gold, he might be willing to invest in a business venture, if Vail could recommend one.

Vail leaned back in his chair and dug in his pocket for a cigar. "It's nice to hear that an old friend is doing so well." He struck a match and drew on the cigar until it lit.

"Well . . ." Gabriel pushed his plate away and wiped his hand across his mouth, wishing the bartender could hear the señor call him an old friend. "Because we left so unexpectedly, there is one other small difficulty. All of my gold, which is of a very great amount, remains hidden at Little Mountain, so for the moment . . ."

". . . you are embarrassingly low on funds and you need a loan."

"In the long and short of it . . . yes. A trifling loan. Perhaps five hundred dollars?"

Vail's eyes rested on him thoughtfully, and under the table Gabriel's hands began to fidget. Jesus, he wished the man would look someplace else.

"What took you back to Little Mountain, Gabriel? Since you are doing so well? I thought you'd left the cattle business forever."

"I have, yes, by all means! But señor, Little Mountain is my home, and the people there are my family. One wishes to go home at times."

"Yes. One does. And how is your family?"

"As well as can be expected, considering they have only Cosme to run things now. Beef prices are up, though, so almost anyone can make money."

"I wasn't thinking of beef prices. How are the people?"

"Oh, very well. All except poor Luz, that is." Gabriel lowered his eyes in respectful memory of the dead.

Josefina had finished eating, and she interjected suddenly, "The *patróna* is not well; she is ver' sick, I think. I should 'ave stay with her, an' nothing bad would 'ave happen." Tears started in her eyes and rolled down her cheeks. She sniffed. "It's all your fault."

Gabriel could have struck her, and would have if they'd been alone. Before he could open his mouth to protest the unfairness of the accusation, Josefina had jumped up and looked about to stalk away.

Vail caught her wrist and pulled her back into her chair.

"What's wrong with the *patróna*?"

"The child comes soon, señor, an' she was not well las' night. I think it was coming then." She glared again at Gabriel.

"But my brother is there, and she has Dr. Cutter."

"The *patrón* is not home yet," said Gabriel. "He is gone since before Christmas, doing great things in San Jose. The doctor—" he and Josefina exchanged glances, "who would go for him? We were all at the party last night, and the bridge is out. No one can get back to the house, not until the water goes down."

Vail dropped his cigar on the floor and ground it out with a savage thrust of his boot heel that made Gabriel jump. "Suppose you tell me just who is with Mrs. Severance."

Josefina thought and began to count on her fingers. "The ol' *patrón*, Miss Rose, Miss Delphine, Miss Sophy . . . no, she was at the party, an' she was wearing Miss Marin's new comb, too."

Gabriel looked at Vail, hoping he was satisfied, and immediately wished he was someplace else, anyplace else.

"You left her alone with a paralyzed man, a sick woman, and Delphine Whitmore?"

"An' Carey," Josefina put in helpfully, and Gabriel wished he had struck her, in the mouth so she couldn't talk so much.

"Señor," he began, feeling sweat trickle down his armpits, "only think! Would I—*I*, who owe my life to the *patróna*'s bravery, I, who would have been trampled to death by that crazy stallion but for her—would I abandon her if I had any choice?" He paused dramatically. "Not even for Josefina—although she did have to be taken away. I would have jumped in the creek and tried to swim across. I would have drowned, of course—not that I care—but what could I do for the *patróna* if I drowned? Hey? Tell me that!"

Gabriel sat back, feeling as valorous, almost, as if he actually had tried to swim the creek, and in the next instant he was pulled out of his chair by the shirt front. All talk halted as everyone turned to look, and Vail said in a low voice, "Tell me exactly the way you came, every trail, every stream you crossed."

"You going to go there? You can't get across Little Clear Creek any more than me." These unfortunate words were barely out of Gabriel's mouth when he felt himself choked as the leather thong he wore as a cravat was twisted around his neck. He spluttered and turned dark red. Better to have drowned in the creek, because he was surely going to die a worse death now.

But the strangling thong loosened, and he breathed again. Vail said in a reasonable tone that his ferocious face belied, "What route did you take? Be very accurate."

Gabriel straightened his shoulders, adjusted his shirt, and described the trail as well as he could. It had been dark, and they had picked their way, but he could name major landmarks and the bridges that were still up, the streams still fordable. He talked quickly in a voice that rasped, and occasionally he rubbed his sore throat. The spectators, used to violence, had already lost interest and gone back to their drinks. Vail went to the table and counted out two hundred dollars.

At the sight of the gold coins Gabriel's pupils grew large. After nearly killing him, Señor Severance was giving him money. He was a crazy son of a bitch, all right.

Over his shoulder Vail said, "This is because Josefina is with you. Take good care of her, because if I hear of her wandering around the camps alone and in trouble, I'll find you, and next time I will kill you."

With one hand Gabriel took a loving hold on Josefina, with the other he scooped up the coins. He said with dignity, "Señor, there is no need to threaten me. I willingly guard Josefina with my life." But he was talking to himself. Vail had already gone out the door.

He strode so rapidly down the muddy street that dirty brown water splattered up onto his fawn-colored trousers and the tails of his coat. Several acquaintances started to speak, saw the expression on his face, and decided not to. He threw open the front door of the small, ramshackle hotel, the only hotel in town, passed by John Martin, the owner, without a word, and took the steps three at a time. John watched him go, the words of greeting stillborn in his open mouth.

In his room he changed to a flannel shirt and buckskin pants and stuffed the pants into knee-high boots. He packed a poncho in his saddlebag, put on a heavy wool coat, and went down the narrow hall to the last door.

Outside it he paused, as though in a short debate with himself, then knocked loudly. There was a silence of perhaps a minute, as he knew there would be. He pounded on the door with his fist.

A blurred voice said, "Who is it? Go away."

"Vail, Charles. Unlock the door."

A low, muttering rumble of profanity, a thud and a crash as some piece of furniture was bumped and some object knocked to the floor, more profanity, sharper and increasingly imaginative, and a key scraped in the lock.

The door slowly opened a grudging crack. A man, shockingly thin for his almost six feet of height, leaned out, blinking, wavering slightly, straw-colored hair straggling into red-rimmed eyes. His crumpled shirt and cotton pants hung like old rags on an emaciated body. His face was a skull covered by skin that was an unhealthy gray. A stranger might have decided that here stood a malnourished drunk suffering deservedly from a monumental hangover. Vail knew that Charles Towle was sick, perhaps unto death, and had probably just dropped off to sleep after a pain-filled night. He had disturbed him reluctantly and only because he could think of nothing else.

Gently he shoved Charles out of the way and came in.

"Go back to bed." His eyes traveled the room. "Where's your bag?"

"My bag?" Charles scowled and sat down in a chair by the tiny window. "In the wardrobe."

Vail located a black leather satchel under an Indian blanket on the floor of the wardrobe, set it on the table, fumbled in it, and laid out several objects, considered, then took out two more.

Watching, Charles said, "A lady in trouble?"

Vail grunted, bundled his selections in a cloth, and packed them in his saddlebag. "Oh, may I borrow these?"

"I was wondering if you'd ask. By all means." A gleam of

interest entered Charles's pale eyes, giving him the look of an alert cadaver. "I would like them back though. Who's the lady?"

"My sister-in-law. You'll get them back." Vail picked up the saddlebag and rested a hand on Charles's bony shoulder. "Promise me you'll take the steamer back to San Francisco as soon as the weather allows. Go to my room and wait for me there."

"Go to hell," said Charles.

"Probably. In the meantime I can arrange to have you carried on board, if you insist. And it's the only way to get these back." Vail gestured toward the saddlebag containing the medical instruments.

Charles's eyes shifted. He nodded.

"Go to bed and sleep if you can. I'll see you in San Francisco."

Vail went out, shutting the door quietly behind him. Charles sat for a while, gathering strength, looking at the closed door. After a while he shuffled back to bed.

Downstairs John Martin had his orders, and his son, an awkward, long-legged boy of sixteen, had his. Charles Towle's meals were to be brought in and his needs taken care of until the downstream steamer came. He was to be put on board, and the boy was to accompany him to San Francisco and stay until Vail arrived.

John watched Vail's horse pick its way up the soggy street to the ferry landing and thought about the odd friendship between the big, brawny man and the wispy fellow upstairs whose very appearance was enough to give you a queasy stomach. It was a peculiar world, and John had seen most of the peculiar types in it, a largish number of them having arrived in this tiny section of California during the last two years. Mr. Severance paid well for what he wanted, and John never turned away from a good business arrangement, but still he wondered what had caused Vail Severance, the embodiment of health and vitality, to choose as a particular friend dull, sickly Charles Towle, who already wore on his fleshless face the shadow of death.

If John Martin had known as much about Vail's character and desires and habits as he thought he did, he would have been bitterly let down, as would most of those who considered themselves Vail's close friends. That he had a fair amount of money was obvious. He wore fine clothes, rode high-quality horses, and was often seen in the company of women, always pretty and usually of doubtful reputation, since there were few ladies of refinement in San Francisco and none at all in the gold camps. As a result he was widely accepted as a fancier of good living, good times, and bad women—and yet he did not quite fit the mold. He had never been in a scrape over a woman; he rarely gambled for high stakes in a town where headlong plunging at cards or the dice table was a chief occupation of most men; he drank very little; and although he could be the soul of warm conviviality, he was a moody man, with an aloofness at the core of his nature that no one had ever broken through.

This puzzling reserve, combined with his commanding appearance and intense, driving personality, gave him glamour of a sort, and people loved to speculate about him. None of his newly come friends knew that he had a family living nearby or that he was estranged from his father. No one had heard of the scandal over Prudencia or the duel, and the rumors of a love affair with Celia Cermeno before her marriage had never traveled out of the tight-knit society on the other side of the bay. Men viewed him enviously as a hell of a fellow with women, and the women each decided in frustration that some other of their sex already had him and was not telling.

The conjecture about his private life appealed to his sense of the ridiculous when he thought about it, which was seldom. No one would have believed that there had not been a woman in his bed since the night he discovered Celia was lost to him forever, the night he also discovered Marin Gentry, unluckily for her; no one would have believed that he now found celibacy grimly satisfying, like a hair shirt worn so long it had become comfortable. He never had cared much for public opinion, and these days he cared even less. At present all he cared for was finding his way back along the trail Gabriel had come, riding as hard and fast as the horse could move over soaked, boggy ground, through wet grass so tall that it brushed the animal's neck, in a fine, chill rain that grew heavier as the afternoon wore on.

By the time he neared Little Clear Creek it was almost evening, and the slate-colored sky was turning darker. He was close to Longridge. Flecks of light from the house glowed distantly through filmy rain, but he could not cross here even if he wished. Below the high ground where he allowed his horse to pause and rest were the remnants of the footbridge Stuart had repaired on a long-ago afternoon when Marin came to tell him she was going to marry Michael Morgan. Like everything Stuart touched, the bridge had been solidly built—and had been swept away by the rushing waters exactly as had its counterpart at Little Mountain.

The quiet, meandering stream was a brown, frothing torrent, and boulders had washed down from the higher elevations to make it unfordable. But Vail did not want to go to Longridge and had never intended to cross here. He was heading downstream to the La Costa narrows, the place where Gabriel would have tried to cross had there been gold on the other side of the water instead of a sick and helpless woman. Rain dripped from the brim of his hat and ran off the poncho draped over his heavy coat. He turned the horse southwest.

Underbrush became a thicket tearing wetly at his clothes and slapping his face and legs. Higher up, the way would be clearer, but he dared not leave the stream, or he might never find it again in this dark night. Rain slackened and finally stopped, and although the breeze was stiff, the violent wind of the night before did not return. Smudged shapes of trees and rocks became sharp. He looked up. The cloud cover was thin over the curving bowl of the sky, and although no moon showed, a glow lightened the blackness. Ahead were the narrows where the small, swinging bridge once had been, a bridge built high enough above the water that it might have escaped the storm's destruction—if the wind had not torn it down. His eyes strained through the darkness, and he urged the horse up the slope, wondering for the first time what he would do if the bridge was gone.

It was there, creaking and complaining as gusts of wind shook it, a thin, writhing snake of a bridge, its pliancy the thing that had saved it.

Vail dismounted and pulled the reluctant horse forward. Boards groaned and gave under the weight of the animal, and its hoofs clacked sharply against wood. The man and the horse inched forward. Forty feet below them the water churned and leaped like a wild thing, and a sudden updraft snapped the swinging bridge in an up-and-down motion. The horse staggered. Vail clung to him as iron-shod hoofs struck dully on wet earth. They were across.

Below, the stream roared on its way to the sea. Vail rode out of the brush to the crest of the low hill. Miles to the northeast was Joe Cutter's ranch. The wind had increased, and clouds moved and changed and cracked apart. A patch of black sky appeared, and light from a cold, white moon shimmered over the main channel of Clear River, of which Little Clear Creek was only a small tributary. It was at this point that the river could be crossed in a normal winter, for here the banks were narrow and the streambed at its shallowest. Vail looked out and saw what he had expected to see: the river spread far beyond its banks, glinting darkly in the moonlight, a deep, broad, rapid, deceptively smooth swath of water, cutting off the two ranches nearest to Little Mountain and putting Dr. Cutter out of reach. It would be as he had feared, yet faced with it now, he was almost glad. Whatever waited for him at Little Mountain he would have to deal with alone.

It was a black pit of hell into which Marin descended and from which she rose at intervals. Petra had been in the room for a while, she was sure of it; she had talked to her and seen her face, but when she tried to touch the girl's hand, she vanished. After Petra left, it was very quiet and the cold came back. Somewhere in this house there were people, but they had left her alone, and although she begged them, they would not answer or come in or try to help. If Mama would only come, if Marin could see her sweet face and hold onto her hand—but Mama was not coming, she knew that now. And Delphine would not come back, not ever. She was abandoned and she was dying, for the baby would not be born. She had struggled alone through endless nights, and it would not be born. The great hand that seized her and squeezed intermittently was squeezing now. Monstrous assaults of pain had weakened her until her strength dwindled to nothingness, and she was tossed like flotsam in a moving sea, lifted up and slammed down under drowning waters. She would drown, that was the best way, let go and end this. But the hideous pain would not let her go; it seized again, and she screamed.

Dr. Cutter was in the room, lifting a lamp, talking in a quiet, reassuring voice, his sure, competent hands examining her. But she would not be fooled, she would be crafty this time and not speak to him. She had thought he was here before, and when she said his name, he disappeared; she had thought Petra had come, and when she reached out to her, she was gone. But her mouth was so dry. Just one swallow, one sip of water from the pitcher resting tantalizingly near on the table, the pitcher she could not move sideways to reach. She broke her own rule and begged for a drink and waited for Joe Cutter to vanish. But he did not vanish. He sponged her face and laid a wet cloth against her cracked lips, and a trickle of cool water ran into her mouth.

"That's all for now. Marin, can you hear me?"

He set the lamp on the table and leaned down, and the lamplight shone upon the heavy, dark brows, the forbidding lines around his mouth, the intent gray eyes.

"Can you hear me?" he asked again.

"Vail?" she whispered, puzzled. This was a new delusion.

"How long has this gone on? When did it start?"

Her hand lifted and fell weakly against his arm. The arm was solid, the cloth of his coat was damp and rough. He was not a vision, he was real, and she had never expected to see another human being again. She would not have to die alone. Tears slipped down her face, and she blinked and almost laughed.

"You're here," she whispered, and saw him close his eyes for a quick moment and heard him answer, "Yes."

Then his hands were pressing into her arms, and he was saying urgently, "How long, Marin?"

She struggled to think and remember, struggled to speak. "I don't . . . I don't know time. I've lost it."

"You sent the servants to a party last night. When did this start?"

"Only last night? I thought—days. Sometime—in the middle of the night."

"Twenty hours at least, then. Marin, will you let me take care of you?"

Old memories came back to her, the rumors, the idle talk.

"Are you a doctor, Vail?"

"You want my credentials?" He smiled, and she started to smile but, but pain tore the smile into a scream. Her sight blurred, and her nails dug into his hands. ". . . too late . . . I'm going to die."

"No, I won't let you die. The baby is presenting wrong. You'll be all right as soon as I turn it."

Pain receded, slow as the ebbing of a great tide, and she seized on his words.

"That's . . . what's wrong? Can you do it?"

"Oh, yes, I've done it before. I know it's been very hard on you, but the condition is not uncommon." His voice was matter-of-fact. Some of her terror slipped away. "I'm going to leave you—"

"No!" She clutched at him and dragged herself up.

"—for just a few moments. Be brave a little longer, and I promise I'll come back directly."

She eased down on her pillow. He meant what he said. He would come back.

"All right, all right," she whispered, and he started to rise. "Wait!" A new pain was mounting. "Please . . . stay till this one is over."

His arms went around her; he laid his cheek against hers and held her hard. It was a bestial pain, this one, rolling up and over her, ripping her with its violence. But he was holding her, putting his strength between her and the pain, and he had said he would not let her die. Fear retreated and, with it, some of the power of the pain to hurt. It was only pain and somehow more bearable now. She sighed and relaxed as the wave passed, and he laid her back on the bed and went swiftly out of the room.

He knew the door he wanted and opened it without knocking. James was lying on the floor halfway between the bed and the door. It had taken him hours to inch that far. Vail picked him up and carried him back to the bed, noting the lightness and frailness of this once powerful body. But James was not his patient; his patient was back in that other room, trusting in him.

"Marin," said James. "I couldn't get there . . ."

"I know, Mr. Gentry," Vail said, and pulled the covers high. The fire was long out, and the room was cold. A tray of food-encrusted dishes sat on the floor, testifying that someone had brought in a meal, but James's bed had not been made, the sheets were dirty, and the room smelled of old food and stale air. "Where is Mrs. Gentry?"

"Over there," James answered without meeting his eyes

Rose lay sleeping on the cot in the shadowy corner, her knees drawn up, her face delicately flushed. The agonized screams from down the hall that had tortured James into trying to reach his daughter had not penetrated Rose's sleep. She sighed and turned and settled into deeper oblivion.

Vail said, "Don't worry, Mr. Gentry. I'll take care of Marin."

James looked up into the face above his and saw something in it that reassured him. He lay back on his pillow and nodded.

"Now tell me quickly. Where is Mrs. Whitmore's room?"

"Across the hall, but she—"

"I said, don't worry." Vail smiled and went out, closing the door quietly.

The smile disappeared as he banged on the door directly across the hall. It opened just enough to reveal a frightened pink face and blue eyes wide and startled.

"Why, Vail, my gracious." The door opened a crack more. "What on earth are you doing here?"

"What are *you* doing here, Mrs. Whitmore? Why aren't you with Marin?"

"Oh, why, well, I've been watching Carey. My, what an active child! I haven't had a minute to call my own all day. He's finally fallen asleep." She swung the door wide to prove her words.

Carey lay sleeping on Delphine's bed, his round little arms thrown up, his hair dark against the white linen pillowcase.

"He looks fine." Vail pulled Delphine into the hall by a rigid, resisting arm.

"What is this? Let go of my arm. I shall speak to your father, young man."

"You are coming with me, Mrs. Whitmore. You're going to help me deliver Marin's bady."

"I? Oh, my God!" cried Delphine, forgetting herself completely. She leaped to the attack. "Have you been in her room? Oh, you have no business there. I *shall* speak to your father. A man in a lady's room—" She fluttered and was still. The eyes above her held an expression she did not want to identify. "I couldn't, really," she muttered miserably. "I'm not at all good with sick people . . ."

"Mrs. Whitmore," said Vail gently, "you are going to discover resources in yourself that you never dreamed you had." And he propelled her inexorably down the hall.

Delphine was unbearable. She had discovered that not only blood and pain, but splendor attended the birth of a child, and she preened around the house as if she, not Vail, had delivered the tiny living creature that mewled and slept in the cradle next to Marin's bed. She was also of great practical help, for having discovered, as Vail had promised, that she was not only competent and strong but very brave, she labored in the kitchen, produced edible meals, provided fresh-smelling sheets for Marin, cleaned James's room until it, too, smelled fresh, and dragged Rose from her cot and prodded her into changing her clothes and combing her hair. Her feelings of moral outrage had been soothed somewhat when Marin informed her that Vail truly was a physician, but she assured them both that she did not approve—and never had approved—of males' attending ladies in intimate matters, even though they were doctors. "However," she added unwillingly, "I suppose there are times when one really has no choice."

Marin recalled little about the actual birth, although she had a dreamlike memory of the exaltation in Delphine's face at the moment Vail held up the baby, and the smile in his eyes when he told her it was a girl. After that she slept through most of a day and a night and woke feeling stirrings of strength she had believed were gone forever. Able to examine the child thoroughly for the first time, she found the little face bruised and the head not yet rounded into shape. It was impossible to tell who her daughter would look like, but she was all in one piece, able to cry and nurse after the ordeal of birth, and Marin, who had feared toward the end that the baby might be born dead even if she herself survived, was satisfied.

She handed her back to Delphine and said, "We'll call her Belinda."

"Very pretty," said Vail. He had been watching without expression while she inspected her baby. "A family name?"

Marin looked abashed. "It's the name of a girl in a book I read once. I always liked it."

"A sensible reason for choosing a name."

She looked up quickly with a suspicion that he was laughing at her, but he seemed very sober.

She said, "I felt a bit guilty about not naming Carey after your father when he wanted it so, and now, with a girl—I can't call her Malcolm."

"Why feel guilty? You owe him nothing."

"I owe him the doctor who saved my life—and Belinda's."

An odd look came into his eyes, he muttered something that she could not hear, and after a few moments he left the room. Well, she was glad she had said it. She had to thank him even though it had accomplished what she'd thought was impossible—it had embarrassed him.

That afternoon she asked him if she couldn't please go downstairs, away from the room where she spent so many nightmarish hours, and he wrapped her in a blanket and carried her down, ignoring Delphine's protests that it was too soon, and placed her on the sofa close to the warmth of the parlor fire.

It had rained lightly but steadily every day since Belinda's birth, and the creek remained high. There was still no way across for the servants in the quarters on the other side, but they must have had plenty of firewood and food—and the body of Luz.

Marin shuddered when she heard the story. "Poor Luz. Poor Josefina. Papa always said someday they'd kill each other over Gabriel. What the great attraction is I'll never know."

Vail lounged opposite her in James's big chair, his boots crossed on Delphine's embroidered footstool. "Other people never understand why one chooses a particular person to love. Sometimes the one who does the loving doesn't understand, either."

Marin thought, he's thinking of Celia. She said, "Just the same, it is my strong opinion that if that horse had kicked his head in, it would have been a good job."

"Then why did you risk your life to save him? I've always wondered."

She looked down and rearranged her blanket. "I don't really know." A silence fell, and she searched for something else to talk about. "Poor Sophy . . . I hate to think of her down there with the . . . the body. It must be an awful experience."

"Perhaps a salutary one. Poor Sophy may decide that a dull life is not so bad after all."

"That's mean," she said, but she smiled. It would be a help if Sophy were willing to settle down to an ordinary existence.

Delphine brought in the afternoon snack that Vail said Marin must have every day. She ate, he smoked, and they sat watching the fire in a silence that had become companionable. It was so comfortable that curiosity overcame caution, and she asked, "Did you really go to Harvard, Vail? Back before your family moved West? There were all those rumors . . ."

"Were there indeed?" He looked as though he didn't intend to say more. Then suddenly: "Yes, I trained at Harvard Medical School under some of the best doctors I ever knew. They sent us into the poorest sections of Boston to learn our trade, and we did learn it."

"When you first came into my room that night, I thought you were Dr. Cutter. Then, when you told me what was wrong and what you were going to do, I wasn't afraid anymore."

"Good for you. I was scared to death."

"Scared? But you were so sure of yourself."

"That's the first lesson they teach in medical school. Never show how little you know or how worried you are. It makes the patient nervous."

"You said you'd done it before."

"I had—once. And I had seen it done a few times. But it had to be tried. Otherwise you both would have died."

She thought that over. "It seems to me that's exactly what any good doctor would do. Whatever has to be done. And you are good. Why do you keep it a secret? Why don't you work at it?"

"Why do you ask so many questions? I don't like working at it, that's why."

"It must have been very hard—the study and the training. Why did you go through it if you didn't like it?"

He was silent so long, staring into the flames, that she thought he wasn't going to answer, but finally he said in a musing voice, "I did it to please my father. He wanted his son to be a doctor. By the time I completed my training, I knew I could do it—but I didn't want to, not for the rest of my life. Watching people die and being unable to do anything for them, watching people get well and knowing I really had nothing to do with it. When you're a doctor, you realize how little you know. It's enough for some. Not for me." He smiled. "So I quit, and Father never forgave me. That was the real reason he turned me out—not the duel, not Prudencia, but because I would not run my life according to his wishes."

"But he loves you. Surely he'll get over it someday."

"Father doesn't love anyone. Don't look shocked, it's true. He only approves or disapproves. If you fulfill his expectations, if you bend to his will, he approves. If you don't, he destroys you if he can. If, as in my case, he can't, he simply cuts you off."

"What a horrible thing to say."

"Yes, it is. Stuart does as Father wishes, or has the happy faculty of appearing to. Logan bends, and he approves of them."

There was so much truth in this that she couldn't even argue over the implied criticism of Stuart. Instead she asked the question she had wondered so often. "Why doesn't Elizabeth stick up for you?"

"Mother was raised to be a lady, and a lady believes her husband is second only to God. In our house he is God. His judgments are always just, and his decisions always right. She loves me, but not enough to stand against Father. Maybe she can't stand against him."

On impulse she said, "You've been treated badly by the women you loved," and the moment the words were out of her mouth, she would have given her soul to recall them.

But he only laughed and shook his head. "I can't complain. I've been treated very generously by some women."

Delphine came in then, took away Marin's tray, and fussed over her with motherly fondness. She had not yet wearied of her new-found role as housewife and nurse, and chattered on in a self-satisfied way about her difficulties in the kitchen and the remarkable job she was doing. She would have liked to settle down by the fire and talk about herself for a while, for Vail was so understanding and appreciated so much everything she did. However, Marin said she was tired, and the little thing did look wan. She wanted to go back to her room, and Vail carried her up the stairs, with Delphine trotting ahead to smooth the sheets and fluff the pillows before he placed her on the bed.

Every afternoon Vail carried Marin down to the parlor and urged her to walk around the room. The prevailing wisdom was that after childbirth a woman should stay in bed for at least three weeks, but Vail believed it was wrong. He had seen poor women forced to get up and go about their work recover quickly, while ladies, encouraged to lie about and be waited on, remained sickly and drooping for months.

He developed the habit of spending the afternoon with Marin in the parlor, while the collie, Angus, slept on the hearth. They talked, and Carey climbed on and off their laps and toddled around the room, grasping at every object within reach of his exploring little fingers, knocking over two of Rose's porcelain figurines before Delphine put everything breakable on a high shelf.

Marin was having a hard time puzzling out her feelings. Once she had thought Vail was a man she could never like, but when she was alone and dying and the people who loved her best had failed her—yes, even Stuart, if she was honest about it—he had come out of the night and the storm like a miracle from God and pulled her back to life. She came to enjoy sitting by the fire bundled in her shawl and blanket during the wet, dreary afternoons, listening to his descriptions of that exciting boomtown, San Francisco, and his amusing, unbelievable tales of the gold camps, which he swore were true.

Late one afternoon, after Carey had been taken upstairs for his nap, she told Vail about Ethan. She had not meant to do it, it brought so much pain, yet suddenly she felt the need to talk about her brother, to grieve aloud and be comforted.

His first reaction was, like hers, disbelief. But after she repeated Willis Norton's story, he shook his head slowly. "It's hard to imagine Ethan dead, but . . ." he turned palms up in a gesture of reluctant acceptance, "it sounds like typical miner's disease, virulent, quick, and deadly."

"Miner's disease? I never heard of such a thing."

"Oh, it can be a lot of things—malaria, typhoid, scurvy, dysentery, cholera, influenza, pneumonia—all the ills of man. The real disease is a combination of man-killing work, food you wouldn't give to Angus, too much bad liquor, exposure—digging and sweating all day under a scorching sun while standing up to your hips in ice-cold water doesn't do you any good. Add to that the loneliness, the constant disappointment, the guilt, the home-sickness. I don't just mean Ethan and what happened between him and your father. Almost everybody out there is carrying some kind of private burden—don't we all. Even the lynchings and knifings and suicides—they're the result of miner's disease—men just break down."

Marin was silent, trying to reconcile this brutal picture of miners' lives with the entertaining, mildly risqué, always funny stories he'd told about the camps. In protest against such bitter truth she said, "But a young, strong man like Ethan . . ."

"They're all young and strong. Sometimes the strongest go under fastest while frailer men survive—no one knows why. I wish to God I'd made him come home when I saw him last summer, even if I'd had to boot him every step of the way. I'm sorry, Marin."

Through a constricted throat she said, "He was a grown man, and he made his choice. You couldn't have forced him to come home."

Only one other time did Vail say anything that went beyond the casual. It had rained lightly most of the day, and they were beginning to hope the unremitting storms were ending. Delphine brought in the tea tray, and after she left, he said, "There is something I must tell you, Marin, and I'll do it before Mrs. Whitmore comes back, since it's none of her business."

She looked up from her knitting. What could he intend to say? He looked very serious.

"Promise me that after the rain is over, you'll take Belinda to a good doctor and have her thoroughly examined. Sometimes after a long and difficult birth there are problems."

"What kinds of problems? You don't think . . ."

"I think she's all right, but it's much too early to be certain. She should be watched for the next couple of years. Don't look like that, Marin. It's just good practice. The probability is, she's as perfect as she looks." He hesitated. "There is one other thing. It's just possible—not certain, but possible—that you should not have more children, and when you are completely healed, I want you checked by someone with greater experience than I have."

He was telling her that perhaps she shouldn't sleep with her husband anymore. There was no other way to ensure not having children.

"Oh? Well, I can see Dr. Cutter, although I trust your judgment."

He had a cigar in his hand and was hunting through his pockets for a match. "Joe Cutter is a good doctor, but there is a man in San Francisco who is one of the best I've ever seen, as good as any you could find in Boston or New York. His name is Charles Towle. I wish you would see him when you can and be guided by his advice."

She nodded and continued to knit. "I'll see Dr. Towle as soon as I can get to San Francisco."

That day was the last day of the great rain. The next morning shadows appeared on the parlor carpet, and then squares of light. The sun burst through torn clouds, and the drenched trees sparkled as though diamonds had dropped out of the sky. Delphine called excitedly from the kitchen, and Marin left her couch and went down the hall. She was feeling well and had walked downstairs by herself this morning.

"Look!" Delphine, wrapped in Berta's huge apron, her face pink from the heat of the stove, was pointing out the back window.

Below the hill the creek was as high as ever, although it had lost some of its boiling froth, and a group of men were working at the narrow spot where the footbridge had been. They had lassoed a tree stump to serve as a support and were building a swinging walkway.

Vail came into the kitchen and looked out over Marin's head.

"They're going to get across!" she said. "Why don't you go help?"

"No, thank you. I'm not going down there and slide around in the mud with them. They could have built that bridge before this if they hadn't minded getting wet. My guess is they just ran out of food and wine."

"You mean they left us up here alone, when anything might have happened to us?"

"Anything did," he reminded her gently, and she flared, "Oh, just wait till I get hold of Cosme!"

"Contain yourself. It will take most of the day for them to get the thing built."

He was right. It was late afternoon, and shadows were lengthening before the first daring adventurers started across. The little bridge was a rickety structure that bounced with every step, but it held, and one by one the men came over and helped the women down. Marin went out onto the kitchen porch, less angry than interested now. An entire day of sunshine had cheered her immeasurably.

They struggled up the hill through mud that sucked off the women's slippers and tugged at the boots of the men, and Marin, watching, considered the element of chance in life. She had let them have their party against her better judgment, and now Luz was dead and Josefina a wanderer. Luz was dead, and because of it she, Marin, was alive. It was a bizarre chain of events, with an inevitability about it that struck her sharply. Cause and effect,

Papa would say. Chance was not chance at all, but was inherent in the character of people. Gabriel had behaved as Gabriel always would, Josefina had killed Luz as she was bound to do and then run away, with the result that Vail had learned of Marin's desperate situation at Little Mountain. Cause and effect, and yet . . . disease had struck down Ethan wantonly, while other men, no less impetuous and greedy, lived; John Baldwin, riding through his own woods, was dead from a squatter's bullet, while Malcolm Severance went his way unharmed; an unprecedented series of winter storms had drowned other people, while her life was spared. What did cause and effect have to do with any of it? No, it was chance that ruled life, not intelligence or calculation or innate character. If Gabriel had chosen a different direction, if he had arrived at the tavern in Benicia a few moments after Vail had left, if Josefina had not mentioned her mistress's illness, if Vail had not the sense to understand and the ability to do something about it . . . All blind chance.

Halfway up the hill Sophy was stepping gingerly through the muck. Her blond hair straggled down her back, and her blue silk dress was water-spotted and soiled and utterly unreclaimable. Her little chin was up, and her pretty face dirty but determined. Behind her came Cosme and—oh, God! Marin moved to the steps, her mouth open in consternation. Across Cosme's broad chest was flung a blanket that could contain nothing other than a body. Why hadn't they buried the pitiful creature days ago, even if it was raining? And it would take many more days for a priest to be located and brought here. She moved to the porch railing, torn between fascinated horror and a strong inclination to run into the house and hide.

Cosme strode across the muddy yard and mounted the steps.

"Good evening, señora. I 'ave here little Luz."

"Yes, yes," said Marin, drawing back. "Well, put her—put her in the barn, Cosme, and we'll decide what to do."

One hard, bright eye appeared between the folds of the blanket, and Luz announced, "I don't sleep in the barn, Miss Marin, ho, no. *Jesus, María*, what I 'ave suffer!"

Vail said the knife had slipped in neatly on top of the ribs and caused no damage to speak of.

Luz glared at him. "To speak of! Jesus, I am bled like a stuck pig."

"I don't doubt it. The pain must have been excruciating."

"Worse than that," Luz muttered sulkily.

Outside her door he told Marin, "That was a piece of luck. Josefina did a poor job."

"I never was so relieved. When I saw Cosme with that bundle—we've got to let Josefina know, somehow, that she isn't a murderess."

"My advice is to let it lie. She was feeling no great remorse when I saw her, and if Gabriel thinks it's safe, he'll come back here—you can count on it."

"Well, I don't want that—every time he shows up, something awful happens. But he is smart. Why do you suppose he ran away when Luz wasn't dead?"

Cosme had been standing with Sophy at the end of the hall, shifting from one big foot to the other, waiting for the verdict on Luz. His feelings at the moment were a mixture of relief for the girl, whom he more or less loved, and a violent desire to kill Gabriel, who deserved to die in some especially painful manner. Josefina he did not blame at all.

"Excuse, Miss Marin, but that bastard, he thought she was dead, an' he always runs from trouble. Miss Sophy says, 'Oh, poor Luz, she is dead' or somethin' like that, and Gabriel grabs Josefina an' runs out."

"Well, she looked dead to me," said Sophy defensively. "There was so much *blood*, Marin." Her full lower lip trembled with fatigue and self-pity. Her round eyes filled, and a tear ran down her dirty cheek. In another moment she would be howling.

Quickly Marin said, "Nobody blames you, Sophy. Go upstairs and take a bath. I'll send some hot water. Are you hungry?"

Sophy snuffled and nodded.

"I'll send supper, too. Go on now."

Slowly, feet dragging, Sophy passed down the hall and started up the stairs, combing her tangled hair with her fingers and sniffing. No questions about her parents' welfare, Marin thought, no notice of her sister's changed figure or the fact that the expected baby obviously had been born. It was not that she did not care for other people; she simply did not see them. Sophy was wrapped up in Sophy to the exclusion of all other things.

The three in the hall watched her go with a variety of emotions.

Observing the expression on Marin's face, Cosme said, "She's a good girl, Miss Marin, jus' a little . . ." He waggled his hand and shrugged expressively. "But she helped a lot down there and didn't faint till after we got Luz bandaged."

"That was considerate." Marin maintained her frown, but she did not look at Vail or she might have been forced to laugh.

The next morning Marin slept late and was finishing breakfast alone at the long table in the dining room when she heard Mateo outside the house, carrying on a low-voiced conversation. A stranger might have thought he was murmuring love words to his sweetheart, but she knew he was either grooming or saddling a horse. She rose, coffee cup in her hand, and looked out the window. Vail's big stallion was standing with its handsome head down, being readied for a trip.

She watched as Mateo cinched the saddle under the horse's powerful belly, smiling as he talked. The business part of her mind noted that the boy had even more understanding of animals than either Ethan or Gabriel and should someday, when he was older, be given Cosme's job. Another, deeper part of her said, Vail's going away . . .

Well, it was all to the good. He had helped her in a desperate time, and she was grateful, but it would be better now if he left.

She took a quick swallow of coffee to ease the hollow feeling in her stomach, set the cup on the table, and walked into the hall and out onto the side veranda. She leaned against the porch railing, watching Mateo, thinking that she must not be as fully recovered as she had thought, for her knees were weak. Heavy boots sounded on the porch behind her, riding boots.

He was ready for travel. His poncho was slung over one arm, and his spurs were no longer rusty but gleamed from Mateo's meticulous polishing. He handed loaded saddlebags to the boy and gazed, unsmiling, at Marin.

"I was looking for you."

"You're leaving?" A stupid thing to say, since clearly he was.

"It's time. Both my patients are doing very well. Keep your promise and see Charles Towle as soon as you can. If you don't, I'll tell Stuart, and he'll beat you for disobedience."

She smiled at the notion of Stuart's turning violent. "But why leave now? He'll be home soon—he'll want to thank you." Neither of them had mentioned Stuart's continued absence or the fact that if Vail had found a way to Little Mountain in spite of storms and swollen, raging rivers, Stuart could have done so, too. But the knowledge rankled, embarrassing Marin. Her marriage was happy, and her husband loved her. It was very important for

Vail to understand that, and how could he if Stuart didn't come home?

He started down the steps. "Oh, he won't have to thank me. I'll send him an enormous bill."

He placed a boot in the stirrup and swung into the saddle. The horse, mettlesome after its long lack of exercise, pranced back with a light dancing movement, fine head tossing, muscles rippling under its glossy coat. It was a big, powerful animal, impatient, venturesome, difficult to restrain, like its rider.

Her eyes went over her brother-in-law searchingly, as though it were a last look—eyes pale under the shadow of his brows; big, curving nose; finely carved lips; the russet lights in his dark hair. It was good he was going. Alone here, cut off from any company but Delphine's, she could become much too dependent on him.

She stood on the bottom step in the sunlight, feeling awkward, wondering how to say farewell. Delphine spared her the necessity. She came hustling out of the house and thrust a package into Vail's hand.

"My butternut cookies, dear boy. Take care, don't eat too many at one time, and don't get wet. I shall take all your messages to your mother."

He thanked her and tucked the cookies under the flap of his saddlebag, tossed a gold coin to Mateo, and flicked the reins lightly. The horse needed no other encouragement. With a squish and a splatter of mud they were off down the hill.

From the hallway came Sophy's light step and then the bang of the door. She stopped in the middle of the porch, her face a study in chagrin. She had brushed her blond hair until it shone and tied it with a velvet ribbon. Her dress was a pretty muslin covered with blue flowers that matched her eyes. "Oh, is he gone?" Her lower lip pushed forward. "But I didn't even get to say good-bye."

"He had to go, Sophy," Marin snapped rather more sharply than she intended. "The servants are back now, and he has a life of his own, you know." For some reason Sophy's disappointment and the pains she had taken with her appearance were mightily irritating.

Sophy came to the railing and leaned her little chin on one hand, looking at the top of the drive, where she glimpsed Vail before he passed out of sight. One long blond curl fell over her shoulder, and she twisted it around her finger and sighed.

"Well, I just think he's the nicest, smartest, most attractive man I've ever known. What a marvelous thing he did for you! Celia was crazy to let him go."

Delphine agreed heartily. "Yes, I sometimes think only we know what a fine man he is, for he does have an abrupt manner that puts people off." She had completely forgiven Vail's rough handling of her on the night of Belinda's birth and was now almost convinced that she had volunteered her help. "Wouldn't it be wonderful if the breach in that family could be healed? I shall speak to his father and point out how badly he has misjudged Vail."

Marin went inside, smiling at the picture of Delphine leading grim, pigheaded Malcolm Severance to a recognition of the error of his ways. Vail could certainly charm women, and in Sophy and Delphine he had two more devoted adherents, whether he wanted them or not.

Chapter 13

San Francisco was a noisy, boisterous town of scrub oaks and canvas tents on the sandy, windswept hills, old adobes and tumbledown shacks on the outskirts, changing to more substantial wood and brick buildings toward the center of business activity. Steamers and packets and fast, graceful clippers sailed around North Point and into the harbor every few days, carrying adventurers mad for gold and excitement. They usually found less gold than they hoped for and more excitement than they wanted. An invigorating recklessness raced through the brawling streets like a thin flame, touching every soul with a spirit of daring opportunism.

The disastrous rain of the previous winter had turned dusty thoroughfares into lakes of gooey mud in which animals and humans drowned. As a result the main streets had been planked, and now pedestrians and horses could proceed through the central district over uneven wooden boards. Business had leaped up overnight to serve every possible need and rake in miners' gold, and not only did the ubiquitous real estate offices sell small sections of mud and drifting sand to eager land speculators, but lots were marked off in the water at the bay's edge, and people lived on wharves and in the remains of old ships, waiting for the water lots to be filled in.

Liquor was available everywhere. There were saloons and brothels beyond counting, and gambling was the major diversion. Men whose whole life had become a gamble could easily be seduced by the click of dice or the slap of cards into making one more grab at fortune; games of chance continued through the nights and days in saloons and gaudy gambling houses.

Men were the overwhelming fact of San Francisco, a community of young, virile men, most of them under thirty, at the peak of their driving energy and physical power; men with few women, no civilizing forces, and unlimited opportunities to get into trouble.

The family from Little Mountain, stopping at the corner of Portsmouth Square, was a conspicuous group: Luz carrying Belinda—it had been decided that Luz, rather than one of the less volatile servants, should have this trip, as compensation for her suffering; Carey hanging over Mateo's shoulder, absorbing the noisy, exuberant surroundings with bright, intelligent eyes; Mrs. Victoria, Little Mountain's newest employee, with her most recent baby, Emelita; Marin, Sophy, and Delphine in demure bonnets and spreading skirts; Stuart, alert, narrow-eyed, and with two guns at his belt.

He has never looked more handsome, Marin thought, and carefully did not meet his eyes. Relations had been strained between them since he came home from San Jose and discovered what had happened in his absence. He was in the wrong and knew it, and he was angry because of it. She had not spoken a word of reproach, which did not help. His anger with himself made his words colder than he intended.

"You don't want me to go with you." He emphasized *want* in an accusing way.

"It's just not necessary, darling. Two more blocks down Clay Street and I'll be there. We're all together, with Mateo to protect us, and you can see how gentlemanly everyone is. Get your business taken care of while I visit Dr. Towle. There's nothing wrong with me, but I do think Belinda should be seen. Then tonight we'll go out to dinner and have a wonderful time."

She was right, of course. There was the matter of Belinda. He carried a burden of guilt over her hazardous birth that made it difficult to deny Marin anything. Yet how could he have been expected to come home in the middle of the convention when his future career—which would benefit his wife and children as much as himself—depended on his being one of the men taking control of the territory? He had every reason to believe Marin was being well cared for. Childbirth was a perfectly natural event that women had to go through. And yet he still felt guilty.

Belinda must be examined by a good, experienced doctor with

qualifications he was sure Vail did not have, although his brother evidently had done well enough in the emergency—a fact that still surprised Stuart. He could hardly believe that Charles Towle had such ability, either, for all Vail thought he was so fine. Stuart remembered Charles well, a skinny, studious, insignificant fellow who walked with a decided limp, his nose always in a book; just another young doctor starting his practice, who had come often to their house on Mount Vernon Street in Boston in the old days. It was hard to imagine that crippled, unimpressive Charlie Towle had acquired the learning, the skill, the masterful certainty of a top-rank physician, but at least he had had formal training at some European medical school and wasn't one of these eclectics or hydropaths or mail-order quacks with which San Francisco was infested. And since Marin was determined . . .

He frowned at the gambling dens that mixed with sober business houses on the square. The tinny tinkle of pianos and the thump of guitars were loud even at midday.

"I don't like this part of town. Go straight down Clay, and don't stop for anything. Mateo—" he reached under his coat and drew one of the pistols from his belt "—you don't know how to use this, and you must not try unless it's absolutely necessary. Just keep it where it can be seen and stay close to the ladies."

Mateo's dark eyes gleamed, and he ran his hand lovingly over the gun. "Yes, *patrón*. I shall take very good care."

So the little group continued down Clay Street at a rapid clip. On all sides was evidence of the devastating fires that had swept the city in May and June, but rebuilding was proceeding rapidly—it had started before the ashes were cold—and many buildings had already been replaced with bigger and better ones. San Francisco, with energetic defiance, was refusing to be downed.

Below the hill lay the harbor, the superb anchorage that the world's great powers had lusted after and that now would belong for all time to the United States. Although the Congress continued to debate, Californians knew they would soon be in the Union. A clipper was rounding Clark Point, a swooping, white-winged bird, reefing sail and heading toward the dense accumulation of slender masts that filled the harbor like a forest stripped of leaves. There were hundreds of ships riding at anchor, many of them abandoned by crews who deserted to the gold fields before the cargoes were even unloaded. Some of these empty ships had been pulled onto shore to be used for shelter, some were rotting into useless hulks that daily sank deeper into the bay.

On the streets were mustachioed Mexicans off the boats from
Mazatlán, Chileans and Peruvians from farther south, Indians with
feathers in their long hair, nattily dressed American businessmen,
huge, burly brown men whom Stuart had said were Kanakas—
Hawaiians—from the Sandwich Islands. There were Chinese men,
too, in baggy shirts and loose pantaloons and pigtails down their
backs long enough to sit on. It was said that they cherished their
queues more than their hands and feet, and that hundreds were
pouring off every ship that arrived from the Orient.

There was another oddity about the masses of people churning
through the streets. It was rare to see a female face, but even rarer
to see an old one. No white hair or stooped backs or wrinkled
faces—only eager youth came here, only youth could survive.

At the corner of Clay and Stockton Streets Marin stopped,
pulled money from her reticule, and turned to Sophy with a look
of mischief in her eyes.

"How would you like to go shopping?"

Sophy gasped and snatched the money. "We passed a dry goods
store in the last block!"

"Impossible," said Delphine flatly. "We cannot leave you,
Marin dear."

Inwardly Marin groaned. Was Delphine going to develop iron
in her soul today of all days?

"That is nonsense, Aunt Delphine. The doctor's house is in the
very next block—see, the one with the green trim. Luz and Mrs.
Victoria and the children will go with me, and Mateo will stay
with you and Sophy. I saw a bonnet in that window that was
perfect for you."

Delphine had seen the bonnet, too, and wavered, but Mateo
announced, "I 'ave to stay with you, Miss Marin. The *patrón*
expects—"

"The *patrón* expects you to obey my orders."

Their eyes met and locked. Marin was determined that no
member of her family talk to or even meet this doctor. She had
gotten rid of Stuart, and she meant to dispose of Delphine and
Sophy now. Mateo twisted uncomfortably, knowing what Stuart
expected of him and knowing, too, that he couldn't stand up to the
patróna, not when she looked like that.

"Go on, *estúpido*," said Luz with a scowl. "Do what you are
tol'." At the moment she doted on Marin for having brought her
along on this dazzling trip. She anchored Belinda firmly under one
arm and grabbed hold of Carey.

"But . . ." Mateo began, and Luz shouted, "But, but, but! Go on."

She thrust her sharp chin in the direction of the shop they had passed, and Sophy, who had been counting the money with large eyes and was now tucking it into her pocket, said grandly, "Don't dawdle, Mateo," and sailed off down the street with Delphine scurrying after her. Mateo, after coming to an agonized decision, raced to catch up.

Mrs. Victoria looked on with admiring interest. She was a buxom, creamy-skinned woman with alert, almond-shaped eyes—it was clear where Petra got her fine features and good mind—and she understood more English than she spoke. The *patróna* was a resourceful lady and governed her family with artistry.

"Give Belinda to me," said Marin.

Luz glowed at the approval, warmer than she was used to seeing, in her mistress's eyes. She felt conspiratorial in some way not entirely clear to her, and very clever. With a grin and an exaggerated groan she hitched Carey higher in her arms, for he was big for his age, and the two girls and the plump handsome woman walked on down the street.

If the directions in the letter Marin had received were right, the house they were looking for ought to be somewhere in the next block, although she had made up the part about the green trim. Four doors past the green-trimmed house she found a garden of straggling hollyhocks, a ramshackle house, and a small hand-painted sign that identified Mrs. Mear's boardinghouse: board and lodging one hundred seventy-five dollars a month, a moderate charge in these days of leaping prices and wild speculation.

She walked up the path of planks to the sagging door and rapped sharply. No answer came. She peered through the glass, adjusting her eyes to the dark interior, pounded loudly, and called, "Please, is anyone home?" Judas Priest, had she come this distance, with all the difficult logistics involved, just to discover that the doctor had forgotten, or was out drinking, or had gone back East?

There was a flap-flap of loose slippers against the floor, and a shape came slowly down the dim hallway. The door opened, and a squat, dark-haired woman with a freckled face said, "Whatcher want?"

"Are you Mrs. Mear?"

The woman squinted at Luz and gave a twitch of contempt.

"Depends. Whatcher want?"

"I am Mrs. Severance. I have an appointment with Dr. Towle."

The woman's surly expression was replaced by a relieved look. "Well, why didn't you say so? Come in. Doctor is expecting you, yes, all day. He said you might be here any time. Come a far distance, I b'lieve. Yes. Just this way, ma'am."

She led them up rickety steps, talking all the way. At the top of the stairs she turned and said in a penetrating whisper, "Can't be too careful, you know. People try to bother the doctor, but I don't let 'em."

Marin stepped inside the room that was offered, and Luz slipped past the landlady. Mrs. Victoria smiled, murmured, "*Gracias,*" and settled herself and her child on a straight wooden chair by the door. It was a dank, dusty cubicle with one small window, a table, and a sofa that had seen much service.

Across the room was a closed door. Beyond it must be the doctor's examining room. Marin sat down on the lumpy couch, holding Belinda well away from any possible contamination and wondering what she was doing in this place. The broken springs of the sofa back prodded and forced her to move forward.

"Sit down, Luz, and hold Carey on your lap. Don't let him touch anything. Get down from there, Carey!"

Carey, who was used to that note in his mother's voice and knew she meant business, slid down the back of the sofa, shoved his finger in his mouth, and gazed at her steadily with eyes as black as her own. In order to hide her smile, Marin busied herself with rearranging Belinda's blanket. Every time she looked at her little son, her love for him bubbled up. Before long he would guess that she could never be really angry with him. Perhaps he knew already.

Belinda had slept peacefully all through the rowdy streets of San Francisco, but now she blinked open her eyes and yawned enormously. The bruises resulting from her difficult birth had vanished, and her flattened nose had assumed a charming baby shape. Silky blond hair curled on her round little head, and more than anyone she resembled Sophy. Was she doing all the things she should be doing at her age? Was she developing as rapidly as Carey had? Marin reached back through her memory, so deeply absorbed that she did not hear the whispering shuffle in the other room. She did not see the man standing in the doorway, looking her over appraisingly.

His eyes lingered on the tender line of her half-turned cheek and moved on down the rich curves of her body, recalling Vail's face in the hotel room in Benicia as he fumbled swiftly through the bag of instruments. So this was the sister-in-law in trouble. No wonder he had been in such a hurry.

The sultry-looking Mexican girl who was wrestling with a small and determined boy saw the doctor and muttered to her mistress; Marin looked up. He drew in his breath at the sight of the startling black eyes and waited for revulsion to appear in them. None did. Instead, a smile that was like the sun coming out, and a hand held out to him.

"Dr. Towle, I am Marin Severance," she said, hiding her shock. This was the great physician she had come so far to see, this bony-faced man with pale, red-rimmed eyes, an emaciated body, a foot that twisted outward at an unnatural angle. A great doctor, Vail said, but one who evidently could not cure the ailments that racked his own body. Had she seen him in Benicia, she would have known that Charles Towle's health was now fine compared with his condition then. He had gained twenty-five pounds, and the tearing cough did not wake him so often in the night. She stepped into the examining room, and Charles closed the door.

"Sit down please." He offered her an unpadded wood chair. "I regret the amenities here are slight, but I can offer you tea."

"That would be very nice." She snatched at the chance to delay her unpleasant business, noticing the tray with teapot and cups and thinking that this homely fellow had the manners of a gentleman. She patted Belinda, who had begun to fuss, and the doctor set a steaming cup beside her and said, "May I?"

After a tiny hesitation that would have gone unnoticed by one less acute than Charles, Marin put the baby into his outstretched hands. He took the child with practiced ease and sat down with her against his chest; immediately she stopped her fitful wail and began to gurgle softly.

"And this is Belinda," he said with a slow, kind smile.

Warmth spread through Marin, warmth that did not come from the steaming tea. He was holding her baby, whom he did not know and could have no special feeling for, with the gentle hands of love—yet it was an impersonal, detached kind of love. It seemed to her that the pale eyes missed very little and that the examination of the baby was already well advanced. She would have to watch her step with this man.

"I think that by now Carey was a little farther along. I mean, doing more . . ." She could not keep anxiety out of her voice.

"Your son appears to be an exceedingly—ah—athletic boy." He placed Belinda on the table and stepped back. "Children's development, normal development, varies greatly. She holds her head erect and sits up well—that's good. And see," he said as Belinda turned her head, "She responds to my voice, don't you, my dear?" The baby began to rock in time to an inner rhythm, caught sight of her hand, and inspected her fingers with interested eyes.

Dr. Towle unbuttoned her pretty embroidered dress, embroidery done by Logan's devoted hands.

"You are not nursing her yourself." It was a statement, not an inquiry, and Marin felt suddenly apologetic.

"I've hired a wet nurse, Mrs. Victoria, whom you saw in the outer office. I was very tired after the birth—it was difficult, as you know, and I have many responsibilities . . . my son is so active, my parents are unwell."

"Um-hum," remarked the doctor noncommittally. He pressed his long fingers into Belinda's abdomen, listened to her little chest while she lay on her back and cooed and waved her hands. Finally he said in a pleased voice, "I think she is fine," and handed her back to Marin.

Relief rolled over her like soothing balm. There was infinite reassurance in the light blue eyes, in the smile that brightened his bony face.

He said, "Will you bring her back in two or three months? Not because I have any concern. It's just good practice."

"That's what Vail said."

"Vail knows what he's doing. I would leave her care to him with perfect confidence, but he feels differently."

"Yes." She had finished dressing Belinda. Her eyes were down. "There is one other matter. Vail suggested that I be examined again to determine the—the course of any future childbearing. Since I had such a difficult time." There, it was out. God, what an impossible business.

"A wise idea, if you have no objections. Would you like your maid to attend you?"

"No, no. Not at all necessary. She can watch the children."

Quickly she went into the outer room, deposited Belinda on Luz's lap, and then came back more slowly into the room where Charles Towle waited, and shut the door.

When she came out again she appeared exactly the same, only a faint flush betraying what might have been agitation. Luz, who had a good idea of what had gone on in there, made a grab for Carey—riding the back of the sofa like a horse—and thought that for a prissy American lady, the *patróna* looked very calm.

Marin turned back to Charles. He was a nice man, a good man, and she liked him in spite of what he had told her behind that closed door.

She asked, "Has Vail told you about my parents?"

"He said your father is partially paralyzed from a brain stroke, and your mother . . ."

"My mother is not herself, not since my father's illness. Could you—would you be willing to see them?"

"I can't hold out any promises. Paralysis of that kind is beyond our power to heal. The body does it on its own, if it happens at all. As for your mother . . ."

"Would you see them?"

"My health does not permit travel just now, but if you could bring them here . . ."

She gave a firm nod as if a compact had been sealed and went out into the hallway.

As they descended the creaking steps, Charles limped to the window of his office and waited. He had never been favored with the attentions of pretty gentlewomen, but he enjoyed looking at them as much as any man did. The consolation he derived from the kind of women available to him was joyless, impersonal, meaning little more than the scratching of an itch.

He scowled at his own self-pity and saw Marin appear and walk down the board path to the gate, followed by her entourage. The coil of hair beneath her bonnet took fire in the sun. A bewitching young woman—bewitching and puzzling.

Charles Towle was, above all, a superb diagnostician, for in addition to technical skill he possessed an intuitive sense that enabled him to go far beyond the superficial with his patients. With Marin he had not gotten beneath the surface, and he knew it. The dark eyes were like windows with the curtains drawn, windows he could not see through, but of one thing he was certain—underlying the lovely facade was a fiber surprising in one so young. Without doubt, Stuart had his hands full.

There were fewer passersby on this street than nearer the center of town, and his eye was caught by a group moving along the boarded sidewalk. A slim, swarthy boy loaded with parcels, a gun displayed prominently in his belt; an attractive, middle-aged woman walking sedately; a girl . . . He took a second look as the girl called out to Marin, waved, and began to run with a skipping step that jounced the hatbox swinging from her arm and afforded him a pleasant view of white ruffled petticoats. She arrived at the gate just as Marin opened it, tore off her plain bonnet, and dug into the box. Her spun-gold hair hung loose down her back and gleamed like sunlight itself. Reverently she held up a concoction of lace and ribbons and straw and tiny flowers, placed it on her head and turned around for Marin's benefit, laughing delightedly.

Charles leaned closer to the window and rubbed a clean circle on the dusty windowpane. Preening and posing, the girl raised her face. Hers was a pastel prettiness nothing like the dynamic beauty of Marin Severance. Her heart-shaped face was pink and white, her chin pointed, her eyes—blue, he thought—were round. She was slender and dainty and very, very young, and why was his heart thumping so alarmingly? He watched them walk off down the street. With every third or fourth step the girl gave an exuberant skip. Who was she? He sighed slightly. What difference did it make to him who she was? He stood watching the empty street long after they were gone.

Delmonico's was not only the finest restaurant in San Francisco, it was the finest west of the Mississippi and quite possibly (except for the temporary canvas walls, a result of the last fire) as fashionable, as tasteful, and as skilled as any establishment New York could boast. At least its customers thought so. It had good china and silver, tablecloths on the tables and upholstered chairs for the comfort of its patrons—astonishing elegance in a rough, frontier town. Prices were high, it was true, but those who could afford to eat in such magnificent surroundings thought it worth the fifteen or twenty dollars it cost them.

The clientele was elite. A roughly dressed but temporarily wealthy miner might show up on occasion, looking for a really good meal, but the men who came to Delmonico's regularly were the businessmen of the town, wearing frock coats of fine imported cloth, embroidered or brocaded vests, and heavy gold rings and watch chains. They were the men with fingers on the pulse of San Francisco, the men who intended to grow permanently rich while others, less farsighted, grubbed in the dirt for gold.

Vail sat at a table in the corner, watching the crowd with a sardonic eye. He knew most of the people in the room at least slightly. They all knew him, and many stopped to speak or waved from other tables. He impressed them—not an easy task in a community of free-swinging, self-seeking men—and they liked to be seen talking or drinking with him.

Just why he impressed them, most would have been hard put to say, except that he was an all-around good fellow. The real reason was the one that always made a man respected—Vail Severance gave the appearance of strength. None of them knew him well enough to accurately judge whether that strength was real or sham, but the appearance was enough. He was believed to have made considerable money in real estate and at this very moment owned several water lots that were bound to shoot up in value as soon as they were filled in. Financial strength was always a laudable attribute. He was also physically powerful, notably taller than most of his acquaintances and able to handle his body well, something other men admired as well as envied; there was a subtle intimidation when one had to look up at a man in order to talk to him. Never once had he been involved in a barroom brawl, let alone a serious fight, and his gun was kept out of sight, not openly displayed on his hip, yet even strangers sensed beneath the quiet surface of his personality a latent violence held under tight control. Such control was deemed to be strength of character. No one cared to cross him. Everyone wanted to be his friend.

Of real friends he had few. One of them, Gerald Crown, sat drinking with him for the first time in two years, waiting for their dinner companion, who was already half an hour late.

"I ran into a mutual friend on the ferry today," Gerald said, smiling across the top of his wineglass. "Marin Gentry—beg pardon, Severance. She looked good enough to eat. I was distressed to learn of her marriage."

"Don't tell me your heart is broken."

"Well, dented a trifle. It's hard to return after a long absence and find that the girl you intensely admire has been nabbed by someone else."

Not many people, knowing about Celia, would have made such a remark to Vail. Gerald watched him curiously, wondering what could have attracted him to that beautiful ice maiden in the first place and if he still imagined himself in love with her. Vail was not keeping a woman—an absurd way to live. The explanation must be some fancied loyalty to a lost love, and that was equally absurd.

Unfortunately for Gerald's curiosity, Vail had a countenance that was impossible to read. He said, "Of course you planned to marry her yourself."

Gerald screwed up his face. "Don't use that word. But if I were going to marry anyone, Marin would be first on the list."

"That ought to gratify her. Too bad she's already happily married to a most admirable man."

"You and Stuart on the outs again?"

"We see each other very seldom, so we're the best of friends. Ah, Charles! What kept you? Have you saved several lives this evening?"

Charles grinned imperturbably, shook hands with Gerald, and eased his long body onto the chair, maneuvering his twisted foot under the table. He picked up the glass of wine Vail poured for him, sniffed, sipped, rolled it on his tongue, and sighed, "Excellent. Is the selection of wines any better in New York, Gerald?"

"Not a bit. But the selection of women is *nulli secundus*." Gerald glanced sourly around the room. "What a gathering of gaudy hags you have here. The street sweepings of Paris."

It was true. The whores of San Francisco came not only from the United States, Mexico, and South America, but from England and Germany, too. But the most recent contingent had come, it was advertised, straight from Paris and were considered so desirable that they not only worked in the tonier bordellos but were paid simply to appear in gambling houses as an attraction for customers to look at. Respectable men not so nice in their requirements as Gerald routinely appeared in public with prostitutes, and if the whores wore a French label, so much the better. Prostitutes sat at almost every table in the room, expensively dressed, completely accepted, providing a good time for men who, back home, would have willingly died rather than admit they knew them.

"Oh, they're not so bad, once you get acquainted," said Vail.

Gerald considered a comment he could make and decided against it. Even he did not care to go too far with Vail.

They ordered supper.

Charles filled his glass again and said, "I saw two new patients today. Thank you for the referral."

Vail looked up quickly. Gerald caught the fleeting expression in his eyes and continued to assess the physical attributes of every woman in the room while keeping his ears open.

"What's your opinion?" Vail asked.

"The younger lady is bright, alert, has good motor reflexes and a sound heart. I'll watch her, but I'd say now that she's perfect. You did a splendid job."

They drank another glass of wine, and supper came: hard-to-get northern oysters, venison, a side dish of mountain trout, and potatoes, a rare delicacy, accompanied by a bottle of good Madeira.

Charles finished the oysters and began on the trout with an

appetite he hadn't shown in months. "The older lady," he said. "You didn't prepare me for the older lady."

"How the hell could I prepare you for her?"

Charles chuckled. "True. Well, she's in blooming health. I believe *blooming* is the appropriate word."

"No problems?"

"Not with her body. I can't speak for what is going on in her interesting mind, but I'll wager it's trouble."

Vail laughed and went back to his food, and Gerald's nimble brain went through several logical steps, arrived at a conclusion, and filed it away for possible future use. The old rumor was true. Vail was a physician. You never knew when information like that could come in handy. He wished he knew who the two lady patients were and listened for further enlightenment, but none was forthcoming. He gave up and switched his attention back to the woman he had noticed on first entering the room, a lovely, fair-haired woman who had given him a number of friendly glances. She sat a few tables away with two men and three other women. Four females for two men. That seemed rather piggish.

He said to Vail, "Since you're so well acquainted with the demimonde, will you introduce me to the blond over there?"

"I could, but she looks busy."

"Not so busy that I haven't received several invitations in the past hour. Come, old fellow, I'm sure you can manage it."

Vail rose with mock weariness and went over to the table. The men popped up, teeth flashing, and shook hands enthusiastically. After a few moments of amiable conversation the blond woman left the table and came back with him.

"Nothing to it," murmured Charles.

She was tall—she met Gerald's eyes squarely as he got up—with good bones, delicate features, and a superb figure. Her dress was stylish but restrained, of blue silk under lace, its décolletage no more daring than any lady of quality might wear, and she carried herself with an air of gentility. Only the boldness in her eyes confirmed that Gerald's assessment was correct—she was a member of the demimonde, but of the very highest order, and not French.

Vail said, "Annaliese, may I present Charles Towle, Gerald Crown. Gentlemen, Baroness von Helsdorf."

The men bowed over her hand, and she smiled on them with white, even teeth, greeted them by name—she had the slightest, most charming German accent—and graciously accepted a chair. They offered her exquisite courtesy, as they would have had she been only a common prostitute, and Annaliese was no prostitute but a courtesan of accomplishment. She chose her lovers as carefully as they chose her, and the selection process was now proceeding busily on both sides.

Vail and Charles, not being involved, looked on with interest while dessert came and was devoured, and Gerald and Annaliese went through the early stages of a possible connection as if dancing the stately measures of a minuet. Brandy was brought, and there was a murmuring near the entryway that traveled through the crowded room like a rushing wind.

A tall, good-looking young man was escorting to their table three ladies who were in fact *ladies*. Several prominent men of the town so far forgot themselves as to climb on chairs to get a better look. The ladies, too well aware of the sensation they were creating and unprepared for it, kept their eyes lowered until they were seated and some of the redness had faded from their cheeks.

"Merciful heavens, Stuart, why did you bring us here?" muttered Marin, and Stuart smiled, knowing every man in the room envied him.

"You wanted to come to San Francisco, and don't say you weren't warned. This is the finest place in town. Only the best people come here."

Marin peeked suspiciously at the woman at the next table, who was looking her over with unmannerly curiosity.

"Is that—is that a . . . a . . ."

"Indeed it is."

She peeked again, repelled and fascinated.

Delphine said faintly, "My gracious!" and began to fan herself.

Sophy's eyes slid to one side and returned hastily to her lap. It was the most horrifying, thrilling, overwhelmingly cosmopolitan night of her life, and she was close to tears from sheer excitement. Marin was the best sister in the world to bring her on this ravishing trip, and she would never again give her a moment's worry.

Charles poured another very small tot of brandy and said with elaborate casualness, "That young girl, the one with the long, blond hair. Do you know who she is?"

Vail's eyes grew sharp. "A relative, of sorts. Sophy Gentry. She's the younger sister of my brother's wife—I hope that doesn't make her my sister-in-law."

"You don't like her?"

"It's possible that I might someday if she ever grows up. Pretty, isn't she? Would you like to meet her?"

"Good God, no," mumbled Charles, sinking lower in his chair

as if hoping to disappear completely. He tossed the brandy down, grimaced, and kept his head down.

Vail and Gerald looked at each other. Neither had ever seen Charles so obviously attracted to a woman, and they liked him too much to joke about it. The banter another man could have taken and given back was impossible with Charles.

Gerald turned the subject. "So, Vail, you're going over to visit your brother?"

"I've already seen him three times this year. That's more than my limit."

At Stuart's table Marin was eyeing the bottle in the silver ice bucket. "Yes, you may have some champagne, Sophy. One glass. I think that's all right, don't you, Stuart?" She toyed with her own glass, not liking to remember the last time she had drunk this deceptive, delicate, bubbling wine.

"It's champagne, my child, and it's potent," Gerald had said. How right he was. He was over there, they all were. Some instinct for self-preservation had drawn her eyes that way as she came in, first seeing Vail's hawkish profile outlined against the canvas wall, and then Gerald, dark, dapper, elegantly dressed. What was Dr. Towle saying? He might not tell Stuart the advice he'd given her today, at least, not if Stuart didn't ask, and she would see to it that he didn't. But would he tell Vail? It would be perfectly ethical to discuss a case with a referring doctor. Judas Priest. Vail didn't talk much to Stuart, though, not if he could help it. Luckily. The blond lady was good-looking. Hard to tell which man she was with. This was an endless evening. God, how she hated champagne!

"I have an impulse to gamble," Gerald announced to his companions, and looked at Annaliese. "Would you like to go to the Empire and try your fortune, my dear?"

The Empire was the largest, fanciest gambling house in town, just opened in May, complete with mirrors, music, and crystal chandeliers.

Annaliese smiled. "My fortune is usually very good."

The decision was made in Gerald's favor. He retrieved her satin cloak, and with promises to see the others soon they said good-night and threaded their way past the close-packed tables to the door.

"Gerald's luck is in," Vail commented idly.

Charles shrugged. "She looks dangerous to me."

"Aren't they all?"

"Indeed. I got some details about your mother from Marin

today. She's been having incidents of dyspnea, even orthopnea, jugular distension, severe pain in the chest and jaw, running down the left arm, periodic improvement, though her ankles remain swollen."

"Has Joe Cutter seen her?"

"Your father won't call him."

"Son of a bitch," said Vail in a flat voice.

"Sal volatile might relieve her somewhat, but I wouldn't bleed her. I wish I could see her."

"I'll see her," said Vail. "If I have to break in the door, I'll see her."

The hotel Stuart had chosen was the best in town, which meant nothing. Buildings burned down and were rebuilt with such regularity that the "best" was always changing and seldom offered real comfort. The walls of the flimsy, two-story wooden building were paper-thin. One could hear with great clarity everything that went on in adjoining rooms, from bitter quarrels to violent lovemaking. What an education Sophy must be getting in the cubicle down the hall that she shared with Delphine, and what a struggle Delphine must be having, trying to answer her eager questions. Carey, Belinda, and Emelita were asleep across the hall, too young to know what they heard, and Mrs. Victoria and Luz presumably could not be shocked by anything. Mateo, who had been allotted a room over the hotel's stables, was out pursuing his first experiences with city life, and Marin's hope was that he would get back by morning without being knifed, or shanghaied, or contracting an unmentionable disease.

Walking down the streets of San Francisco at night had given her a different view of the place, and she did not feel so safe as in the daylight. Drunks staggered from curb to building, cursing or mumbling obscenely, shrieks echoed from gambling houses and saloons over the sounds of music, a brawl erupted in front of what was undoubtedly a brothel (Stuart said the fight was over a girl), and Marin had seen the flash of a knife before she, Sophy, and Delphine were hustled past by Stuart and a well-mannered, nicely dressed gentleman who had stopped to aid the ladies. There was more to this unique little city than the excitement of gold and ships arriving and vital, virile people finding their fortunes. There was also brutality, ugliness, disease, filth, and despair. There was life, but there was also death.

Marin looked into the mirror hanging on the thin wood wall, a fine mirror that would have been appropriate on the silk walls of an elegant hostelry. She pulled a brush through her hair, uneasy at the thought of what lay outside these insubstantial walls. For the present, at least, she was ready to go home.

Stuart lay on the bed, watching the light of one wavering candle trace the gleams and shadows of her hair. It fell down her back like a bright, undulating sea, gold at the edges, red at the crests of waves, dark auburn in the depths of shadows. He knew the feel of it so well, rich gold silk slipping through his fingers. Like Wes Morgan years ago, he wanted to put his hands in it, but for him it did not have to remain a fantasy. He could touch any part of her anytime he wished, a thought so pleasant that it was enjoyable to delay doing it. She wore a plain lawn wrapper. He would like sometime to buy her something finer. There was Brussels lace to be had in the city, and he would enjoy seeing her beautiful body under lace. Even beneath the lawn the whiteness of her skin shone through, the soft flesh rising at the front where the wrapper parted. His eyes moved down the slender line of neck, the curve of back, the roundness of her delightful little bottom where it met the padded stool.

He was not a lustful man. Rather, he was cool and controlled. He would never have agreed with Ethan that sex was the best thing about life, for there were too many other matters of great importance to him. But he was a normal man who desired his wife, and it had been a long time. During the many weeks that the legislature had sat in San Jose he had watched other men, deprived of their wives, unhesitatingly seek comfort among the available women of the town or the camp followers who appeared whenever there was a gathering of men without their own women. Those men would go home with no qualms and greet their wives without a twinge of conscience, but he was not like that and had contempt for those who were. He was a married man, a faithful husband, and he wanted only his wife. However, he did want her. It had been months since Belinda was born, a terrible experience for Marin, but it seemed to him that she had been well recovered for some time. There were times when he wondered if she put him off for reasons other than her health.

"Stuart."

Her face reflected in the mirror, small, pale, intent, framed by the flowing hair. Her eyes were shadows in the uncertain light. He came across the room and laid a hand on her soft upper arm, a pleasurable, possessive gesture.

Her hand came up and rested over his. "Stuart, there is something I must tell you. Not the best news, but . . ."

Cold fear rose up. "You said Belinda was fine."

"She is. I'm afraid it's me."

The fear took over, sweeping him. She moved under his hand and turned on the stool until she was facing him, and without knowing he was doing it, he knelt at her feet so that his eyes were on a level with hers.

She said, "We are going to have to be patient a while longer."

"What is it? What's wrong?" Fear drummed at him. She was so little, so frail beside his bigness.

"The doctor said it might be very dangerous for me to have another child and—and that I must not risk it."

Suddenly her meaning was clear. "But you're not ill, there's nothing . . ."

She smiled and touched his face. "No, no, I'm very well as long as I do not bear more children—for a while."

Her eyes seemed blacker than usual, opaque. He could not see into them.

"How long?" he said.

"Not forever, I'm sure. Just for a while. The body must adjust itself, he said."

"Why didn't you tell me this afternoon?"

Her hand cupped his lean jaw. "I didn't want to spoil our evening until I had to."

With the candle out the room was very dark, but noises from the street filtered in and the activities of the couple next door were unmistakable. He tried to shut his ears to those sounds. She had said, "*We* must be patient." That must mean she regretted this necessity as much as he. "For a while," she had said.

His breathing became deep and regular. She turned on her side, free to move now that he was asleep. How had she had the nerve? Disaster if he talked to Dr. Towle! She had told him "the doctor" said it might be dangerous, and so he had—Dr. Vail Severance. That had been last March, and Vail had emphasized his uncertainty, which she had not. It made so much difference how a thing was put.

Today Dr. Towle had concluded that she was in excellent health and quite able to bear children without more than the usual hazard. That was the sticker. The usual hazard. It was always there, looming over every woman every time she had sexual intercourse, the hazard of pregnancy, of ill health, of death, at the very least, of monstrous agony. She had tried to make Stuart understand the hideous pain, the fear, the looking into the face of death—a black, overwhelming tide that had almost engulfed her. The incomprehension in his face told her he could not, would not understand. He expected his wife to be available for him, to willingly take the constant risk of pregnancy, just as his mother had done for his father. Even kindly Dr. Towle saw childbearing as a woman's duty. Only Vail understood; he had been there and seen it. Those women she saw tonight, loose women engaging in every kind of profligacy, why weren't they constantly pregnant? Was there some biological difference between a good woman and a bad one?

She did not know the answer or how to find it out, but no matter, it was ended for her. Twice death had almost taken her in childbirth, and that was enough. She loved Stuart—of course she did. He was her darling; she had wanted him, and she had gotten him. It was not a question of love but of survival, and to survive was what she meant to do.

Chapter 14

Marin crossed Little Clear Creek at the bridge, sturdily rebuilt after last winter's devastating flood, and trotted across open pasture and up the hill on Little Mountain's prize horse, named, with fine irony, Dulzura. The animal was a classic cream-colored filly with a silver mane and tail and a disposition far from the sweetness her name implied. She was not to be ridden by anyone—Stuart's orders, for he wanted no accidents before he was ready to race her. That prohibition, along with her beauty and inclination to skittishness, made her irresistible to Marin.

At the top of the hill Marin halted and pushed back the sombrero that protected her face and tucked-up hair from the high, hot sun. Moving water glinted through the trees below the hill. She brushed the reins against the horse's neck, and they trotted down into the coolness of the woods. Today, since no one was with her to see, she was riding comfortably astride in a man's saddle, wearing a riding dress that she had made in secret. The white blouse was cool and flimsy, with short, loose sleeves, and the black broadcloth skirt was full enough to hide the fact that it was split into wide, graceful trousers.

She swung off Dulzura's back and climbed down the mossy bank to the edge of the stream. The water was no more than two feet deep, a limpid, glimmering treasure in an arid land, crystal mountain water flowing smoothly over the sandy creek bottom. She hiked up her skirts, pulled off boots and stockings, and let the cool water run over her bare toes.

Here, three years ago last May, she had sat in this very spot and believed, like a fool, that life was a ripe, rich plum ready to fall into her hand whenever she decided to reach out and pluck it. What a child she had been then, sheltered by her parents, ignorant of the world, expecting that life would be perfect if only she had a nice house and Stuart Severance. How could she have been so stupid?

The world was a brutal place, cold and without feeling for the weak—she had learned that long ago—and you could count on the fingers of one hand the few people in it who could be depended on. Until the day she died she would remember Cole Gentry looking down on his only brother, paralyzed and near to death, and saying what a damned shame, what a terrible pity, and do let me know if I can help. Cole had not been seen at Little Mountain since the morning he rode away with his two strong, healthy sons.

He had failed James just as Delphine and Mama, and Stuart, too, had failed her when Belinda was born. Papa had done his best to reach her—Vail had told her about finding him on the cold floor of his bedroom struggling feebly toward the door—and Mama could not help being the way she was. But only Vail had been there when she needed him, and who could tell what went on in his mind or why he did the things he did?

Her thoughts turned to Elizabeth Severance. Stuart's mother had died suddenly two months ago, only days after what seemed to be just a little flutter of the heart. Vail had come to Longridge and examined her in spite of her father's objections, and he had said there was nothing to be done. Every family in the district had been represented at the funeral. Celia, still in deep mourning for her father, had sent condolences and begged to be excused, but Nicolas came with his brother, Armando, elegant, aristocratic, magnificently courteous to everyone, his right arm held in such a way that no one who did not know would have guessed he could barely move it. Dr. Cutter, sardonic and shabby, stood with head bared at the back of the crowd and stayed after the service to talk business with Juan Estivez. Wes Morgan had turned up a few days earlier and was there with his sister, Glenna, trying to look sad and at the same time catch Sophy's eye.

Logan had looked pale but tranquil, defying the mighty efforts of the Methodist preacher, Mr. Daniels, to whip his listeners into a hysteria of grief. Several mourners mentioned afterward that Elizabeth's daughter had not shed a tear. During the funeral she stood with Vail and ignored her father, who, everyone commented, was bearing up well, His white, handsome head was bowed as Mr. Daniels read the Bible passages he had selected, but his bulky shoulders remained erect, and once he directed a gaze of corrosive hostility at Vail.

Marin had kept her eyes down all through the interminable prayers and avoided looking at the box about to be lowered into the earth. She had not loved Elizabeth as she loved her own parents, but she had grown fond of her mother-in-law, a kindly woman who had turned out to be simply shy, not aloof. This was Marin's first real facing of the ending of life, for Ethan's death had seemed only a tale told by a stranger. But she had seen Elizabeth gasp and tumble and become nothing, and it left her shaken. Glenna, Elizabeth's companion for many months, had said over and over that Elizabeth looked like she was sleeping, but she did not. She looked dead. Seeing her like that, Marin had made a promise to herself. It was not going to happen to James or Rose any sooner than it had to. They were going to get good medical care, and that meant moving to San Francisco. How she would get Stuart to do it she did not know, but do it she would, somehow.

Dulzura had wandered a little distance and was contentedly cropping the grass that clumped around the base of a tall oak. Marin took the reins, and the filly followed as docilely as though she had never known a wayward impulse. Just beyond these woods was the little adobe house where once Marin had hidden above stairs and watched Prudencia Cermeno try and fail to beguile Vail Severance. How silly and inherently innocent that flirtation had been, and how much disaster it had brought to so many lives.

She came out of the woods. There was the little house, falling quietly into disrepair. Curious, though. The bare earth around the house was marked with hoof prints, and a wagon sat before the barn, piled high with some sort of metal equipment. There was a smell in the warm air . . . She walked forward, and Dulzura stepped daintily after her.

"Ho, now, sweetheart."

She stopped dead. The man who had come around the side of

the house was of medium height and heavily built, with a rust-colored, tangled beard and small, greenish eyes under a dirty felt hat. His checkered shirt and brown homespun pants looked as though he had slept in them for months.

"That's a fine horse you got there." His red beard parted in an ingratiating smile. "Say, you're a pretty little Mex. I swear, you greaser gals been lookin' whiter every day I stay in Californy." He took a step toward her. "What's the matter? No speaka English, honey?"

The impudence! Her black eyes blazed.

"I am Mrs. Stuart Severance, and you are on my father's land."

He moved closer, still grinning. "Are you now? Well, you sure do talk English good."

"Severance. I've heard that name."

The man who spoke had come up quietly behind Redbeard and stood with arms folded, looking her over with eyes that were oddly empty. He wore the clothes of a gentleman, but his frock coat was creased and his frilled shirt unbuttoned, and a black cravat hung loose at the neck. There was something peculiar about his pale face, an absence of symmetry. His sharp features veered slightly to one side, and his nostrils were cut high, giving him a sneering expression at variance with his insinuating voice. There was an alien inflection in his speech, too, that told her he was not an American.

He pursed his thin lips. "Severance is an important name around here. And you say this is Longridge land, ma'am?"

"You are on James Gentry's land, sir. This is Little Mountain, and you are trespassing."

He laughed, a short, barking laugh, and her uneasiness increased. That ripe, warm smell she had first noticed at the edge of the woods . . . She tugged at Dulzura's reins and started around the men. Redbeard moved, blocking her path, but beyond him, at the far side of the dilapidated barn, she could see the bloody remains of slaughtered beef. Her face flamed, all fear forgotten.

"Squatters! Squatters, by God, taking our beef on our land. My husband will kill you."

"I doubt that, ma'am." The foreign-sounding man lifted an eyebrow. "Oh, we're quartering beefs, right enough, and they may be yours—in a manner speaking. But your land? How do you claim it? By Mexican grant? California is American now, and unused land—" he glanced around at the neglected adobe house, the barn, the open meadow beyond, "unused land is now available for the taking." His eyes returned to her. "For the taking—as is everything else."

He moved so swiftly and she was so stunned by his action that he had her by the wrist before she could move. He grappled for her and caught the collar of her blouse, then there was the sound of cloth tearing and the shocking feel of unfamiliar hands on her bare skin. In panic she hurled herself backward, wrenched her wrist free, and stumbled against the horse. From faraway she heard that foreign voice shouting for the other man to hold her horse. He was coming at her, his high-cut nostrils quivering, his eyes no longer empty but with an expression in them that mobilized all her instincts for survival.

She kicked out and, with strength made great by desperation, slashed the looped whip of her riding crop across his face. He screamed and fell back, his hands pressing his eyes, and she jumped for the horse, hampered by the yards of material in her skirt, her sombrero hanging by its cord, her long, bright hair tumbling over her shoulders. Redbeard released Dulzura's bridle, his mouth an open circle of astonishment in his hairy face.

A boot in the stirrup and a leap upward—no time now for niceties. She swung her leg over the horse's back, landed in the saddle with a thump as she'd seen Ethan do a thousand times, and looked down into Redbeard's face. With narrowed eyes he lunged for the bridle, missed, and grabbed her leg.

God help her, he was trying to pull her off. He would have her on the ground, and then . . .

Beneath her, Dulzura stood with head down, very still, a picture of the meek gentleness her Spanish name implied, but the fine-turned, muscled body trembled. With a shout Marin rammed her hard-heeled boot into the horse's belly, and Dulzura's taut nerves exploded. She rose with a clear, crying whinny, slashing the air with sharp hoofs, and Redbeard staggered backward. Down came the raging hoofs, and the man howled and rolled out of the way. Dulzura bucked twice, stiff-legged, while Marin clamped her knees in the way she had been taught and clung to the saddle. Then, for one moment, the horse stood without moving. Marin looked down and saw Redbeard groaning and holding his shoulder, saw that other, frightful man looking up at her from where he lay, the flesh around his eyes bleeding. She jerked the reins, and Dulzura took off in a flat-out run, ears back, tail out, slender neck straining forward, streaking like the champion she was toward home.

The man with the rusty beard sat up slowly.

"Well, she sure warn't no Mex," he said finally. "I think that damn horse broke my shoulder."

His companion dabbed at his wounded face with a soiled handkerchief.

"Of course she wasn't a Mex, you bloody fool. She said she was Stuart Severance's wife."

"You know him?"

"He's a state legislator. His father's a big rancher."

"You foolin' with a legislator's wife? Thunderation, Kemble, I allus wondered if you was crazy, and you are."

Kemble looked at the crimson blotches on his handkerchief, got to his feet with slow, deliberate movements, and stood upright, swaying slightly. "Not crazy, opportunistic. Which means, my ignorant friend, that I take advantage of opportunities. I haven't seen a woman like that in five years, maybe ten."

"But her husband's a legislator."

Kemble shrugged. "Her husband's a hard-nosed, narrow-minded, cold-blooded bastard, from what I've heard." He grinned crookedly. "I just thought I'd give her a treat."

Redbeard shuddered, groaned at the movement, and clutched his shoulder.

"Oh, you're crazy, all right." He stumbled to the porch, sat down, and stared disgustedly at the ground. "We'll have to get out of here. Sure would've liked to take that horse. I could win some races with that one. Long-flanked, just like a Thoroughbred."

"So was the woman," said Kemble.

Home was in sight before Marin dared slow the horse, and when she tried, it was a battle, for Dulzura had no intention of stopping until she was in her own stall.

Marin left the sweating, panting horse with a curt order to the Indian stableboy to rub her down well, and scooted into the house by the kitchen door and up the back stairs. What blessed privacy, to have one's own room. Thank God she and Stuart no longer shared one. It was late afternoon, and ordinarily he would not be home before evening, but at the breakfast table he had mentioned plans for a trip to San Francisco, which meant he might come home anytime to pack.

With hands still trembling she stripped off the torn blouse and divided skirt, shoved them into the farthest corner of her lower drawer, and at that moment heard Stuart's voice outside. He was home and calling to Mateo. He must not see her like this, flustered and hot and half dressed. She dived into a challis housedress, poured water from the pitcher into the basin on the washstand, and splashed her burning face. She was rolling her hair into a knot as his boots cracked sharply on the stairs. Lord, he sounded in a hurry. She pulled a net over her hair and was at the door as he pounded on it.

His face was set and his lips compressed, angrier than she had ever seen him. He must have discovered the squatters.

She put out her hand. "Come in, dear. I—"

"Marin, where is your sister?"

"Sophy?" It was so unexpected a question that her mind stumbled. "Why . . . in the house somewhere, I suppose. What do you want her for?"

"She is not in the house or anywhere near it." He came in and shut the door. "Did you know that Wes Morgan is back?"

"Of course I knew. He was at the funeral."

"Did you know Sophy has been meeting him?"

A nasty shaft of anxiety stabbed her. "Certainly she meets him. He was over here only two nights ago, and they sat on the porch for an hour. Delphine was with them. After all, they've known each other for years, and Sophy has so few diversions—"

"Sophy is more 'diverted' than you realize, and Delphine is not with her today. She met him in the orchard at noon. They haven't been seen since."

She felt out of breath, confused. "Well, then"—she swallowed—"where do you think they are?"

Sophy had been left alone at the lunch table that day. Delphine was lying down with one of her periodic stomach aches, brought on, she believed, by something she had eaten. Sophy giggled. It was something she'd eaten, all right—food, tons of it. Well, what was painful for Delphine was good fortune for her. There would be no censorious eyes to notice that she was wearing her new pink dress trimmed with eyelet lace and a dark pink satin sash.

She finished her meal quickly, went into the parlor, and examined herself in the mirror Mama had brought all the way from Maryland. There was a tiny network of cracks, delicate as a spider's web, and spots where the backing had worn thin, but it showed plainly that she was a pretty girl. Wes thought so, too. She smiled to bring the dimples into her cheeks.

With a last, self-conscious pat at her hair she went out the front door and started down the drive to the road. Once out of sight of the house she stepped off the drive and hurried to the orchard. He was waiting for her beside the peach tree, their peach tree. A few weeks ago he had kissed her under that tree—her first kiss—and it had been wonderful!

She ran to him, and his big, strong hands circled her little waist, swung her against him, and squeezed her until she squealed.

"Wes, stop! I can't breathe."

He set her down and kissed her long and hard. "Can you breathe now? Can you?" He laughed, his brown eyes gleaming, and she laughed, too, happy for the first time in so long, happy as she could be only with him. He took her hand and pulled her off through the trees.

Below the orchard, near the creek bank, Luz sat watching Carey play. Belinda slept in a basket nearby. Life was good for Luz now that she had made the children's nurse, and she was very content. Unseen, she had watched the *patróna's* little sister kissing that stallion of a young man and reflected that it was a good thing she was the one who had seen them and not that jealous Gustavo, who was only a vaquero and was in love with Miss Sophy's yellow hair and blue eyes. As if he could have her. But if he saw, he might tell in a fit of wicked envy, and many bad things could come of that. It was better if people's secret lives remained undisturbed and other people kept their lips shut.

But unknown to Luz and unluckily for Sophy, Gustavo had seen.

Sophy had no worries in the world. She rode happily in front of Wes—he had a fine horse now—but though she begged him to tell her where they were going, he only laughed and promised her a great surprise.

He rode up to the adobe cabin where he had lived with Glenna and Michael back when he was still a boy and had imagined himself in love with Marin Gentry. He dismounted and lifted Sophy down. She stood beside him, a little breathless, a little uncertain.

"What are we doing here, Wes?"

He smiled, and she loved his smile. "I told you. A surprise."

He drew her to the door and opened it.

"Oh, Wes!"

The house, empty for so long, was freshly swept and as neat as when Glenna had kept it, with clean dishes set on the table and a delicious odor drifting from the stove. There were flowers on the table, too, her favorite autumn wildflowers. He had done all this for her. "Oh, Wes!" she said again, and went inside.

"Sit down and eat," he ordered grandly, pulling out a chair. "I mean to show you what a fine cook I am. There's nothing like being on your own in a mining camp to teach you how to cook."

She wasn't hungry, but she ate, and the food did taste good. He dumped his gold dust on the table to show her how rich he was, and when her eyes grew enormous, he let her run it through her fingers before he carefully scooped it back into its small leather bag and tucked it deep in his pocket, satisfied that she was impressed. He told her stories of the camp—the miserable weather and the icy streams and the excitement when you saw "color" glinting in the rocks. He told her about a knife fight he had been in and won, and when she asked if he had ever killed anyone, he replied, "Oh, sure," in such an offhand manner that she was reduced to total silence.

He was so big and strong and good-looking, and such a *man*. And he thought she was pretty. He was the best-looking man she'd ever seen, better looking than Stuart, whom Marin was so stuck-up about. It was grand, having a man who admired and respected you, as Wes did. It was grand, being loved.

The sun sank lower, and she did not notice. He pulled her out of her chair and across the small room to the bed, the only other place there was to sit. It was covered with one of Glenna's quilts, made with her tiny stitches. The wedding ring pattern, Sophy remembered later.

"Wes, I don't think . . ." she began, and he closed her lips with his own.

He unbuttoned her basque, and she made feeble efforts to stop him. In her ear he whispered, "Don't you love me? Don't you trust me?" He sounded hurt, and she wouldn't hurt him for the world because he was the only one in it who loved her. He was taking off her dress and caressing her bare body, and the sensations that were sweeping her were sinful and wrong, and she was drowning in the wonder of it. Even so, some memory of moral precepts taught her by her mother, some scrap of religious scruples, deeply ingrained, caused her to push away the groping hands and protest, "We can't do this, it's wrong."

Wes looked into her pretty, heart-shaped face and saw another girl, a girl with hair the color of wild honey in the sun and white, white skin and a peach-bloom mouth that curled at the corners, a girl with shining black eyes who did not love him and never had. Against Sophy's throat he murmured, "That gold dust, that's for us. I love you, Sophy, and they'll never let me have you. Run away and marry me, and we'll be happy for the rest of our lives."

The magic words had been spoken—"I love you" and "marry me"—words that had vanquished many a more experienced, less lonely girl than Sophy. She sighed and smiled and yielded herself.

Horses outside and the faint slap of a bridle. Footsteps on the hard-packed earth, the bang of a door flying open, and the late afternoon light streaming in.

Sophy screamed. Wes grabbed his pants and boots and in one leap was out the window and running barefoot and naked, over the rough ground to his horse.

Stuart's gun was out of its holster. He fired through the window, and Sophy screamed again, wrapped in the quilt Marin had thrown over her.

"You've killed him, oh God, you've killed him! I'll hate you as long as I live!"

Stuart turned from the window. "No. I missed. But I will kill him if I ever see him again. As for you, you trollop—"

"Shut your mouth, Stuart."

Marin sat on the bed, holding the quilt tightly about Sophy, who sobbed against her shoulder. Never in Marin's married life had she spoken to her husband like that, and it gave him pause. Their eyes met, and he was the first to look away.

In an altogether different, reasonable tone she said, "Be so kind as to step outside while Sophy gets dressed."

She waited, looking up at him while he thought this over.

"Very well. Yes, of course." He went out, closing the door behind him and wondering why he was suddenly at a disadvantage.

"Marin—"

She looked into Sophy's tear-marked face, shook her head, and laid her finger lightly against her sister's lips. She was having a hard time with her own emotions. The blood on the rough cotton mattress left no doubt as to what had happened here. She was so furious with the little fool that she could have strangled her, and at the same time she pitied her with all her heart. If she ever saw Wes Morgan again, she would kill him before Stuart had a chance to.

"Come," she said as calmly as though they were preparing to go to dinner, "let me help you dress."

• • •

Stuart packed his bag methodically, as he did everything, taking nothing he would not absolutely need.

"I'll be gone two weeks, perhaps three."

At the window Marin nodded. The sun was down, but an afterglow still lit the earth, and the first star was already bright in the eastern sky. Late to begin a journey, but he was going, and she would not ask him to wait until morning. He had locked Sophy in her room without supper, a child's punishment for an adult misdeed, and Sophy, in a wild excess of emotion, had raged and stormed and finally cried herself to sleep.

Stuart looked at his wife's rigid back and wondered what else he could possibly have done. Gustavo was no unbiased witness, as Stuart knew well, but he had been proven utterly right. The girl was lonely, as Marin had said. They should have watched her more closely and provided her with a suitable, satisfying social life, as Marin had also said. But loneliness, boredom, and youthful spirits did not excuse blatant immorality. Everyone had frustrations—God knew he did himself—but you lived with them, controlled yourself, and made the best of things. Not all men believed, as he did, that abstinence was required if you could not have your wife. A good many men had both their wives and as many other women as they could manage. Not admirable, but not really wrong—for a man. For a woman, however, especially a young girl of good family, such behavior was not to be tolerated, and he would not tolerate it. He had left neither Marin nor Sophy in any doubt of that. He had a career to think of and an increasingly prominent social position to maintain. Suppose people found out?

Marin was looking down, running her fingers absently over the soft material of the draperies, and he felt a surge of love and sympathy for her, the softest emotions he had felt all day. The humiliation of this must be even worse for her than for him. It was her sister who had ruined herself—and with Wes Morgan, of all men.

He came across the room and laid his hands on her shoulders, liking the feel of soft flesh under cotton. When she did not move, he leaned down and kissed her cheek.

"I understand your feelings, Marin. Have Sophy settled down by the time I come home, and we need never speak of this again." It was magnanimous of him, but he felt magnanimous, for he loved her. He had put up with living in her father's house, with her peculiar mother, her garrulous aunt, her foolish, flighty sister, all for love of her.

She turned, put up her arms, and kissed him.

"Good-bye, dear. I hope your meetings are successful."

He picked up his bag and went out, encouraged by her smile and wondering why her black eyes were sometimes so curiously hard to see into.

Chapter 15

Marin rose early, dressed, and braced herself for the conversation she must have with her sister, knowing she would have to comfort more than condemn. Stuart had provided all the necessary castigation last night after they arrived home. Strange that the cruelest, most devastating judgments could be made without using one word of profanity.

She had known for some time that he was not the man she thought she had married—his constant currying of favor with his powerful father lessened him in her eyes; his desire for an obedient, submissive wife, not a partner, lessened him even more—but until last night she had believed they could work out a good life together. Last night his concern had been not for the harm done to Sophy but for what people would say if they found out. Watching him demolish a young girl too frightened to defend herself, the word *bully* had come into Marin's mind, and feelings she had had for him from the day they met had died.

Now Sophy thought her heart was broken. What could she have seen in that horrible boy with the long, awkward arms and legs and the brown pop eyes so much like Glenna's, a boy with nothing to recommend him, certainly not the kindliness and intelligence of his brother, Michael. Marin had a brief memory of Wes, long ago, trying to paw her, and wondered what disgusting blandishments he had used on her gullible sister.

To settle her nerves she drank the cup of China tea Luz had brought, steadied herself for the ordeal ahead, and went down the hall to Sophy's room. She hesitated, then unlocked the door and went in. Sophy slept much as Carey did, bottom up, and the bedclothes were piled high. Why not let her sleep? But that was the coward's way. Better to listen to the tears and the wailing now than to have it hanging over her all day.

She moved the coverlet just a trifle in order to wake Sophy gently, and then tore the covers back from pillows that had been carefully placed to produce the semblance of a human form. A note was pinned on one of the pillows.

"God in Heaven," she said, and sat down on the bed because her legs would not support her. With a hand that shook she unpinned the note, read it, and read it again. It was tear-blotched and stained with candle wax and covered with jiggly lines.

Dear Sister,
I am leaving this house forever. I am going to find Wes, and we will get married, because he loves me and I love him. I will hate Stuart and curse him till I die. I will die if I stay here, and I wish the ship had sunk and I had drowned when we came around the Horn, because I am a bad person and will never be good. I hate you and Mama and Papa and Aunt Delphine, too.

Love from your sister,
Sophy Gentry

Marin sat with her hand over her eyes. Damn Stuart and his self-righteous, moralizing, cruel words. Damn all men. Damn . . . oh, what was the use? And how had the girl gotten out of the room? Long, white curtains fluttered at the wide-open window. Marin flew across the room and leaned out. Not a ridge or a handhold or a fragile vine marred the adobe wall of the house. The big oak was there, spreading its gnarled branches, at a distance that would make it a dangerous leap. Yet that was the way Sophy must have gone, for there was no other.

She sat down on the windowsill, trying to compose herself, trying to think. Money. Did Sophy have any money? She went to the big walnut dresser and scrabbled through every drawer. There had been ten dollars that Sophy had saved from her birthday money, and it was gone. So was the jade ring Papa had bought off a China trader, the gold locket trimmed with three small pearls, and every other trinket she owned, everything that could be turned into money. It was pitifully little.

In a rage of frustration Marin slammed the top drawer shut. And gradually rage faded as it was borne in on her that her pretty, naive, fifteen-year-old sister, who had never been on her own in her life and knew absolutely nothing of the world, was wandering alone, hunting for the man who had seduced her, through a

country almost devoid of women and filled with young, vigorous
men, many of them rapacious and dangerous, all of them recently
released from the tight restrictions of the societies they had left.
She must be found and brought back, and there was no one but
Marin to do it. Delphine would have to know, and nothing could
keep it from the servants—they always knew everything almost
before it happened. But Papa and Mama must be spared. She
would tell them Sophy was spending the week with Logan at
Longridge.

Unaware that she was doing it, she squared her shoulders. This
was going to be a very different day from the one she had planned.

San Francisco had been a hustling, booming place when Marin
was there in August, and it had since grown bigger and lustier.
Alongside the hundreds of canvas tents straggling up the hills were
many more buildings of wood and brick, giving an air of such
solid permanence, it was hard to believe that much of the town had
been destroyed repeatedly by fire. Disastrous fires were a commonplace because so many of the structures were as flimsy and
combustible as straw, and the persistent west wind could fan the
tiniest flame into a conflagration so fierce that supposedly
fireproof buildings of corrugated iron twisted into molten metal in
the intense heat. And there was another reason for the frequent
fires—the looting afterward was so safe and profitable that many
unregenerate characters preferred arson to digging gold.

Yet the town was bold and brassy, and to Marin the very air
seemed invigorating. She had left home with only a crammed
carpetbag, as much money as she could find in the house—which
meant all the cash Stuart kept in the iron box in his office
desk—and no male to protect her. She had not wanted anyone
with her, for God alone knew where and in what condition she
would find Sophy or what new and horrible contretemps would
have to be kept secret from the world. She did not even know
where to start her search, but headed instinctively for San
Francisco. Now, as she walked along Broadway, jostled by men
much less respectful than they had been in August, she wondered
if, as Delphine had tartly suggested, she was touched in the head
to go off to this overwhelming city without even Mateo to guard
her.

As she walked, she became aware of a tension in the streets
unusual even in this rowdy town. Men stood in groups and
chattered and waved their hands. They darted out of buildings,

strained their necks toward Signal Hill, the high ground rising steeply above Clark Point, and then hurried back inside, only to return moments later and stare upward again.

"Hello there, honey," said a voice, and for a sinking instant she thought it was the foreign-sounding squatter who had frightened her to death the day before; the indefinably odd accent was the same. But it was a different face, and the man was neatly dressed, with a diamond the size of a pea winking in his shirt bosom. Although she did not know it, he was, like the squatter yesterday, one of the town's multitude of professional gamblers, with the white skin of one who spent most of his time indoors hunched over a gaming table. This man was a successful gambler, too; the large diamond proved that.

As he removed his tall hat and bowed, a surge of the crowd pushed her against him, and he grabbed at her enthusiastically. She sucked in a startled breath and jerked away, and he came after her, smiling.

"Get away from me, you hound!" She swung the carpetbag, caught him in the chin, and, losing her balance, fell backward off the boardwalk into the dusty street.

He looked down at her in offended surprise and rubbed his smooth-shaven chin where the carpetbag had hit him. "No need to get huffy, girly. There's plenty of others."

He sauntered off down the sidewalk, leaving her sitting, humiliated, among the horse droppings in the street as wagons and carriages rumbled past. Other men were staring and laughing, and as she struggled up a strong hand grasped her arm.

"Let me help, lady-madam. Here, I take the bag."

She was lifted to her feet by a huge brown man who smiled all over his square dark face and made clucking sounds of sympathy as he brushed off her skirt with enormous hands.

"Bring her here, Kaui. Quickly!"

Poised for flight, Marin glanced back at the fine landau with its top down that had drawn up just as she landed in the dirt. The lady in it leaned on an elegant elbow and nodded graciously from under a silk parasol. It was the handsome lady who had been in the company of Vail and Gerald and Dr. Towle at Delmonico's on that memorable night last August. She was smiling with white, even teeth and extending a gloved hand.

"Do allow my servant to assist you, ma'am. I shall be only too glad to drive you wherever you wish to go."

Marin was lifted onto the black leather seat by that great, brown, smiling fellow—he must weigh three hundred pounds, she guessed—who then hoisted himself onto the driver's seat with surprising agility and clucked to the horses.

The lady leaned forward, her face shaded by her parasol. "But where is your maid, my dear, and some male member of your family? It is shocking that you should be on these dreadful streets alone." She spoke English with the exquisite precision of the well-educated foreigner, with almost a British accent but something else underlying it. Another alien in this polyglot city, but this time a woman and one of gentility.

Marin straightened her bonnet, feeling the comfortable security of the padded seat against her back. "The streets are rough, quite different from the last time I was here. My husband was with me then. Is something out of the ordinary happening today?"

"But don't you know? We are expecting the mail steamer. There is a very good chance that the news of statehood will be on it."

"I had no idea. I suppose everyone will go wild if we're admitted. My father will be happy, and my husband—"

She stopped and thought. Statehood. That must be why Stuart had come to San Francisco, yet he hadn't said a word to her. She hid sudden anger at him behind a pleasant smile and offered her hand. "My husband is a state legislator. I am Mrs. Stuart Severance."

The lady's eyes were bright blue, and they seemed to turn brighter at the mention of the name Severance. She clasped Marin's hand. "I am so glad to meet you. I have heard of your husband—so very prominent a man." She looked deeply into Marin's face. "I am the Baroness Annaliese von Helsdorf—here, where we are democratic, simply Mrs. von Helsdorf. Oh, but that is such a mouthful! You must call me Anna."

So German was the tiny touch of something else behind the British accent. And she was a baroness.

Marin inquired, "Your husband is here on business?" It must be important business for him to come so far from home, and he must be an important man, a baron with a *von* before his name.

Anna von Helsdorf sighed and bit her lip. "My husband is dead. No, don't apologize. You could not know. I have left our home in Bavaria and traveled here—such a long voyage—in the hope of easing my grief. Here it seems everyone is happy and full of hope and energy. Here I try to find a new life." With an effort that was plain to see, she banished sadness from her face.

"There, I am better now." She smiled brilliantly. "But your gown is soiled, and your slippers, they are covered with dust. You must come home with me, and we will get all in order before you go on. Kaui is a fine boot polisher."

"Oh, I couldn't impose. I can walk from here."

"I beg you will not," Anna entreated in alarm. "This part of town is particularly unsafe. For instance, that place . . ." She pointed at an abandoned ship planted on the street and being used as a building. "It is not a place a lady should even be near."

Marin stared at the ship's hull, which seemed to grow right out of the dusty ground instead of resting on water, where it belonged. It must be a house of ill fame. Were there nothing but bawdy houses and gambling halls and drinking establishments in this benighted town? "Why is it especially dangerous here? The whole town is past praying for," she said.

Anna rolled her eyes. "The town could be worse, though not by much. Already we have our better residential sections. But"—Anna's voice dropped, "just north of here is Sydney Town, a dreadful place filled with convicts from Australia—Sydney ducks, they are called, criminals of the lowest sort, robbers and murderers. That awful man who accosted you was Australian—one always knows them by the so uncouth accent. You must never be in this part of town alone."

Timidly, Marin looked back down the street at the spot where she had fallen in the dirt. Delphine was right. She had been touched in the head to come here alone.

Anna continued, "I myself never venture out without Kaui. With him, of course, I am perfectly safe."

"He certainly is formidable. Is he, ah . . ." She paused.

"Kaui is a Kanaka," said Anna.

"From the Sandwich Islands?"

Kaui chuckled deep in his chest. "From Hawaii, lady-madam."

"Hawaii." Marin tasted the soft vowels on her tongue. Hawaii, the far-off Sandwich Islands, where she had once planned to sail on a raft made out of an old barn door. Stuart had pointed out Kanakas on the street when they were here in August.

"Turn here," ordered Anna, and Kaui headed the horses into Kearney Street. "My hotel is not far. After your gown is cleaned, we shall take you—what is your destination, my dear?"

Marin looked away from Anna's inquiring eyes. What was her destination? Where could she go to get help for Sophy in this wild town? Not to Stuart—never—even if she could find him. But for his harsh words and unrelenting judgment, Sophy would be sulking safely at home right now. Well, she could not search this town herself, she knew that now. The hazards for a woman alone

were too great. And what if Sophy had not come here at all, what
if Wes was heading for his claim somewhere in the mountains and
Sophy was blindly struggling after him? No matter how brave and
determined Marin was, she could not fight her way alone across
endless miles of rugged country, through the roaring, wide-open
mining camps, asking strange men if a small, blond girl with blue
eyes and a besotted expression on her pretty face had passed their
way. She did not like to think of the answers she would get.

Almost unseeing, she gazed out of the rocking carriage. They
were passing the Parker House, rebuilt again after it had burned to
the ground for the second time last May. Across the street men
were jostling each other, looking up, straining their eyes northward. A small, dark woman in a dress of spangled red satin
climbed on a box for a better view, and Marin turned to discover
what everyone was staring at.

To the north on Signal Hill, the rocky height that overlooked
both harbor and seaward coast, the wooden arms of the semaphore
announced that a ship of the steamer class was coming in. A low,
growling rumble grew in the crowd and built to a frenzied roar that
caused Anna's horses to start in sudden fright and toss the two
women forward. For a terrifying moment it seemed that Kaui had
lost control, but then he was standing up, cracking the reins and
shouting enthusiastically, and Anna, her eyes glistening, was
urging him on with silk parasol waving and a small gloved fist
raised. They swooped around the corner in a mad, careering turn
that threatened to topple them into the dusty street and dashed
headlong back toward the waterfront without concern for anyone
who might be trampled by flying hoofs. From the heights
commanding the harbor, entrance cannon boomed in ragged
volleys, and somewhere bells were pealing ecstatically, echoing
across the flatland to the hills and resounding out over the water.

Anna cried, "Look!"

Ahead, chugging steadily across the wrinkled surface of the
water toward the wharves was the mail packet *Oregon,* side-wheel
churning, pennants whipping in the wind, the flag of the United
States fluttering in the bright sun, and a banner proclaiming
"California Is a State" flying triumphantly from the rigging.

Marin, who had never had real interest in the political destiny
of the territory or cared about any world-shaking events, except as
they directly affected herself and her family, felt her stomach
quiver and tears wet her eyes. For the first time she understood a
little of what statehood meant to James. There was an intangible
worth in being part of the Union, which transcended politics or

tariffs or economic gain. The Gentrys had left home for a far place, and now they were home again, for it had followed them.

Anna was weeping openly, smiling and shaking her head. "Wonderful, is it not?" she whispered.

On the docks was pandemonium. Men jumped in the air, climbed poles for a better view of the *Oregon*'s banner, shouted and danced and thumped each other on the back in vociferous congratulation. Girls hung precariously out of windows, waved and called and tossed ribbons and fancy undergarments. There was a steady crack of small arms and rifle fire, and the bells continued to peal joyously.

Daintily Anna blew her nose and poked at Kaui's broad back with the tip of her parasol.

"Go on, go on! Push through, Kaui. We must get down to the ship."

Kaui nodded. The reins lashed the horses' backs like whips, and the animals leaped forward, straight into the exuberant mob. Men stumbled in all directions, hustling to get out of the way, and at least three unlucky fellows were knocked flying. The mood of the crowd changed abruptly from hysterical good humor to indignation, and the least wounded and dazed of the victims launched himself furiously at the landau. Several companions joined him in an attempt to tip over the offending carriage, regardless of the large man on the driver's seat and the two frightened young women in the back.

The carriage began to tilt, Kaui roared out several threats, on which he could not at the moment make good, and the two women shrieked.

Diagonally across the street, on the balcony of Harry L. Callendar & Co., a tall man watched the landau dash recklessly into the milling mass of people, stop, list to port, shiver, and capsize in a jumbled confusion of frantic, whinnying horses, screaming women, and a lacy white froth of ruffled petticoats turned up to the view of the mob.

The horses struggled up immediately, unhurt but terrified, intent on plunging straight ahead. They would have spread real devastation if they could have detached themselves from the overturned carriage. As it was, they leaped futilely, pawing the air and becoming more entangled in the harness with each lunge. A tawny-skinned giant rose from the ground, calling down bizarre evils on the men responsible in a thunderous bellow that carried clearly above the shouts and ringing bells and booming cannon.

He lurched toward the maddened horses, trying to soothe them and at the same time get possession of the reins.

On the balcony, Harry Callendar himself had come out and was grinning with delight caused partly by the good news on the *Oregon* and partly by the entertainment in the street below.

To the tall man beside him he said, "Think we ought to rescue the lady?"

Vail laughed. "I never saw anyone less in need of rescuing. Kaui is as dangerous as a bull elephant. He sounds like one, too."

There was a sudden scuffle at the edge of the crowd. The other woman in the landau, who had been tossed farther than Anna and whom Kaui seemed to feel no responsibility for, was attempting in a dazed manner to walk past a line of men who were snatching at her and at the same time struggling to hold off the men behind them.

"Now that other lady may need . . ." Vail paused. Her face was hidden by a wide-brimmed green bonnet, but there was the unmistakable, slim roundness of body, the familiar, unstudied grace of movement. He swore under his breath, and as though she had heard, she turned toward him just enough to reveal a well-known curve of cheek and slender throat. Without another word he was inside and racing down the stairs.

Harry Callendar looked down into the street. The mood of the crowd had veered wildly in the past few minutes from good humor to violent indignation to good humor again, and he knew from long experience that any trivial happening could cause it to swing just as wildly and violently once more. The scuffle below was going on among a few men a little drunker, a little more undisciplined than the rest. They had surrounded the woman in the green bonnet and were disputing possession of her like dogs snarling over a juicy bone. She was backed into a corner where the corrugated iron wall of Sargent's warehouse met the brick of the bank next door. Her cloak had been pulled from one shoulder, her bonnet dangled by its ribbons, and a long strand of red hair hung over one shoulder. Harry turned and ran down the stairs after Vail.

The scuffle had progressed to an all-out fight between a hulking creature with a scar that cut a white slash through his ragged black beard and a short, stocky man with arm muscles like hams and a face red with liquor and fury. A knife flashed out, and the bearded man bellowed as a crimson stream ran down his arm. Like a bull he lowered his head, charged, and crashed straight into the ring of shouting spectators, for the knife wielder had leaped out of his path with astonishing agility for one so stout, grabbed Marin around the waist, and was attempting to lift her off her feet as she kicked at him. The wounded man on the ground shook his head to clear it and looked up with a face full of hate.

At the back of the crowd there was another, separate commotion. A large man in a fine gray coat slammed through the close-packed onlookers with brutal force. Marin was wrenched free, and a fist smashed into the startled face of the man who had tried to carry her off. She heard the crunch of bone on flesh, someone groaned and went down. The bearded man with the bloody arm launched himself forward to aid the friend who had recently tried to kill him. Marin stumbled backward with a confused notion of slipping away while these maniacs were engaged with each other, and she never saw the blow coming. Her head exploded with bright light, and she pitched down into the encompassing dark.

He was bending over her with a sharp line between his brows, an intent expression in his eyes. Something wet and cool was on her face, and in her jaw was a throbbing ache that sharpened into pain when she tried to speak.

"Don't talk," he said. "I don't think your jaw is broken, but it's going to be sore for a while."

"Perhaps a little sherry . . ." said another voice.

Her eyes opened again. Sunlight poured in through a broad, open door. There was soft salt air and the sounds of tooting whistles and bells and distant booming. Something marvelous had happened—oh, yes, they were in the Union, and never, never would she forget the day she heard the news.

She raised a shaky hand and poked gingerly at her jaw and chin. "What hit me?"

"One of your admirers, by mistake. He meant to hit me. What are you doing here by yourself, Marin? Where is Stuart?"

"I have no idea." She sat up slowly, holding the wet cloth against her jaw with one hand and bracing herself with the other. "Anyway, I wasn't alone. I was with Baroness von Helsdorf and her bodyguard, only . . . somehow we got separated."

"Yes, well, the baroness had her own problems. Do you realize the risk you took—"

Marin closed her eyes. "Don't lecture me, Vail. My face aches too much."

"Perhaps just a small sip of this sherry," said the other voice again, and a round pink face dotted with brown button eyes swam into her line of vision, a little man with quick, fussy gestures. His brows were thick tufts of gray, but the hair fringing his shiny, bald head and the side-whiskers down his face were thick and dark, his expression youthful, his eyes filled with solicitude and the kind of gentlemanly admiration that she was used to seeing in men's eyes.

With an inexplicable feeling that she had just met a friend, she smiled, and the movement sent a stab of pain through her jaw. "Thank you," she said, lips stiff, and took a careful swallow of amber liquid. The sweet wine slipped down her throat, warming and soothing, without the fiery blast of brandy. She drank it all and stretched her lips tentatively into a smile. "I believe we have met . . ."

"Yes, indeed, Mrs. Severance. We met on the street one evening last summer when you were here with your husband. I was fortunate enough to assist you and the other ladies of your family in a small—uh—misadventure. I am Harry Callendar, very much at your service, ma'am."

She remembered. They had been walking with Stuart back to the hotel after dinner at Delmonico's, she and Sophy and Delphine, and a knife fight had erupted in front of a fancy house. This was the kindly, well-dressed gentleman who had stopped to help Stuart conduct them safely away from the brawl. He looked as though he had recently been in a brawl himself, silk cravat askew, broadcloth coat ripped open under the arms, velvet collar hanging by a thread. The angry red swelling around his eyes would probably turn black by tomorrow.

She looked back at Vail. His gray coat was smeared with dirt, a frill had been torn loose and dangled from his ruffled shirtbosom, his brocade waistcoat was missing two buttons, and the knuckles of his right hand were wrapped with a handkerchief that bore a tinge of blood.

She said, "I fear I've caused a deal of trouble."

"Not at all!" Harry Callendar looked with satisfaction at his damaged clothes. "It was a grand fight."

Marin expressed her everlasting gratitude, thinking that although she abhorred violence, she could have borne with equanimity seeing those menacing thugs beaten to a bloody pulp.

"What do you mean, you have no idea where Stuart is? Didn't you come with him? Marin?"

She looked up reluctantly. Vail was scowling, deep suspicion in his eyes.

She took the cloth from her face and sat up. The throbbing pain in her jaw had settled down to a dull ache, and she rubbed it tenderly.

"Don't use that tone with me, Vail. I'm neither incompetent nor a child." A new thought crossed her mind and, with it, hope. "There's been rather a . . . a calamity at home, and Stuart is away."

"Oh, my. Oh, dear," said Harry Callendar primly, clicking his tongue. "Family troubles. Well. We are inventorying a shipment of tools and machinery just unloaded this morning, and I must get downstairs, but do me the honor, dear ma'am, of resting here as long as need be." He darted a thoughtful look at Vail, said, "I'll be in the warehouse," and tactfully retired.

Vail leaned against the table, folded his arms across his chest, and waited while Marin grappled with the problem of how to enlist his aid without betraying Sophy or revealing Stuart's devastating judgment of her. Suppose Vail thought Stuart was right. Suppose he, too, believed Sophy had proven herself hopelessly depraved. God help us, suppose he told? Everything depended upon this being kept quiet forever.

She looked up into his eyes, and her agitation lessened. She fumbled in her lap. "My reticule. Have I lost it?"

"You dropped it in the street."

On the table lay the expensive, woven-silk purse that had been Stuart's gift on her birthday. Vail handed it to her. One of the cords was broken, and it would never be clean again, but the contents were intact: her money, her comb, her linen handkerchief. She drew out a piece of paper, folded many times. Vail watched. Her mouth was open slightly, her upper lip caught by the edge of her teeth in an anxious manner. The delicate, heightened color in her face reminded him of the porcelain skin of the Dresden shepherdess he had recently bought, which now rested on the mantelpiece in his new brick house. The figurine was a costly piece, like the girl who sat there struggling with her uncomfortable thoughts. He waited while she came to a decision.

"Here." She unfolded the paper and held it out. "You'd better read this. I found it on Sophy's pillow this morning."

He read the note through and handed it back to her.

"Tell me about it."

She told as much as she decently could, not quite looking at him, picking her way warily through the mine field of yesterday's events as though the wrong word would explode in her face.

His expression, when she peeked at him, showed no shock or

even mild surprise, but when she got to Stuart calling Sophy a trollop his face hardened noticeably.

However he said only, "Did he hit Wes?"

"No, Wes was moving very fast." She had a sudden, awful desire to laugh at the memory of that big young man, with his sunburned neck and arms and his body white as a woman's where clothes normally covered it, hopping barefoot over the rough, stony ground and throwing himself, stark naked, onto his startled horse. She must not laugh, but still it would have been funny—if the girl in the bed had not been Sophy.

"Stuart is in San Francisco, at least he said he was coming here. I probably could find him if I tried, and he might be willing to go after her, though I'm not altogether sure of that. But—oh, Vail, if he did go and he did find her, especially if he found her with Wes, there's no telling what he'd say or do. I must find her and bring her back myself before something dreadful happens to her or Stuart finds out she's gone. He might tell Papa, too, thinking it his duty, and it would just kill Mama."

She was twisting her handkerchief nervously, half wishing she had said nothing. What could Vail do, after all? Why should he disturb himself for her?

But he said, "Does she have any money? Did Wes tell her where his claim is?"

"Ten dollars and a bit of jewelry, not very valuable. He might have told her what camp, because he meant to impress her. He had an enormous amount of gold, she said, although Heaven only knows what would seem enormous to Sophy."

Vail walked to the open doorway of the little balcony and looked down into the street, his back to her, his height and breadth of shoulder outlined against the bright daylight. He was always larger in life than she remembered him. Outside, boats in the harbor still hooted gaily, bells continued to echo against the hills, the sharp, dry crack of handguns and rifles sounded at irregular intervals, and the noise of the jubilant crowd welled upward, along with a band that had set up on the wharf and was tootling disjointedly but with great enthusiasm.

Without turning, Vail said, "Has it occurred to you . . ." He looked back at her and continued in a reflective way, "Has it occurred to you that Sophy may not want to come back, that she may be better off away from your home than in it?"

All the air went out of her in a shocked explosion. "Not want to come back? She must come back. She's a young girl, not a man like you who can just—just go off and rattle around the world.

Why, even if she finds Wes and he does marry her, she could never depend on him or trust him or know what he'd be up to next. He's not worth the powder to blow him up with . . ." She jumped up and began to pace. "Oh, I take your meaning, all right. Stuart has been ungenerous, and I haven't looked out for her as I should. She needed parties and beaux and a normal life, and instead she's been stuck out at Little Mountain with no one but Wes to turn to. But all that's going to change, I swear it."

The last words were ground out in such a low, grim, passionate tone that Vail's eyebrows lifted and the corners of his lips turned down. "That sounds ominous for Stuart. What are your plans?"

"Never you mind. Just help me find Sophy and keep this mess quiet, and you'll see the feathers fly. Stuart Severance won't know what hit him."

"Unlucky Stuart. Well, it won't be the first time, will it?"

She fumbled with the strand of hair that had come loose in the tussle downstairs and tucked it back into its net. The satin ribbons of her bonnet were tangled, and as she unknotted them, she shot a glance at him. He looked just as he always did, his gray eyes holding nothing more than teasing laughter. He was only baiting her, only taking a brotherly cut at Stuart.

She tied the bonnet ribbons under her chin. "Will you help me?"

"I think I can find out where Wes's claim is—that is, if I can locate Michael. This town will be bedlam tonight."

"Is Michael here?"

"I saw him yesterday."

"You mustn't tell him why you need to know."

"Don't you trust him? Men generally keep their mouths shut, especially men like Michael."

"I don't trust anyone, not with this. I wouldn't have told *you* if I could have thought what else to do. Oh, Vail, you know what it would mean for Sophy if this got out. Wes wouldn't be hurt. People would just nudge each other and wink and say what a devil of a fellow he is, but Sophy would be destroyed. I'd rather see her dead."

"Would you? Yes, I see that you would. And you're right, the world is a hypocrite, brutal to women." Almost as an afterthought he added, "It can be brutal to men, too." He slung his battered coat over his arm and picked up the tall hat that had been left on the table during the fight and so escaped destruction. "Come along. I'll have to stash you somewhere while I look for Michael."

Marin still stood in the middle of the room, watching him with a pucker between her brows.

"Don't look so worried, Marin. We'll find her and bring her home, and no one will ever be the wiser." He grinned. "And then I shall sit back and watch while you tie Stuart into knots."

Harry Callendar's house was large by San Francisco standards—two stories high with eight good-sized rooms—and prefabricated, Harry told Marin with pride; it had been brought round the Horn in pieces and put together by the best craftsmen.

Mrs. Callendar, half a head taller than her husband, was as comfortable and substantial as her house, enveloping in motherly solicitude the young lady with the rose-petal skin and immense, anxious eyes whom her husband had brought home.

Marin ate dinner with them and chatted pleasantly and wondered where Vail was and if he could possibly find Michael in the swirling crowds, around the bonfires in the streets, or in some saloon or gambling hall or brothel—her mind balked at the thought of Michael in a brothel, then moved quickly on. Vail would find him, never mind where.

She sat by the fire in the cozy parlor and sipped a thimbleful of Madeira. Her head sagged, and Mrs. Harry raised her brows at her husband. Together they urged her up the stairs. Into the deep featherbed in Mrs. Harry's commodious nightgown. Marin's carpetbag with all her belongings had been lost in the melee at the dock. She would have to shop tomorrow. But there was no time for such nonsense, and the stores might be closed for an impromptu holiday. Her eyelids drooped and closed.

At half past two, the heart of the night, a rapping, soft yet clear, sounded at her door. As if she had been waiting, she was instantly awake, throwing on her hostess's flannel wrapper, lighting the candle with a hurrying hand, crossing the floor. Vail was there, one hand braced negligently against the doorjamb, triumphant beneath his casual manner, her carpetbag in his hand.

"Anna sends this, along with her regrets for today's happenings, her fondest love, and her hope that you will meet again at some more convenient time. I explained that you were about to depart on a journey and couldn't visit her tomorrow. Or, rather, today." He handed her the carpetbag. "Kaui found it beside the carriage. Good man, Kaui."

She set the candle on the little table by the door and accepted the bag as the treasure it was. "But how . . . do you know the baroness well?"

"I know all our more distinguished citizens, and she certainly is distinguished. She lives at the Union Hotel, a most elegant hostelry. I thought it worth checking, and sure enough, she had it."

He was in the best of spirits, his eyes dancing, his face a trifle flushed. In Ethan such symptoms would have meant a liberal hand with the bottle, but she did not think Vail was drunk.

Her lips began to curve. "You found Michael."

"Wes's claim is at Dead Man Bar on the Middle Fork of the American River."

"Oh, Vail!" She threw her arms around him, still clutching the carpetbag, her head whirling with the news. He must have changed his broadcloth coat, for the rough cloth of a heavy jacket scratched her cheek. His heart beat strong and steady under her ear. Slowly his arms came around her, and she moved back, holding the bulky carpetbag like a shield between them, keeping her face turned away from the fluttering light of the candle.

"What is it?" he asked. "That jaw hurting? Let me see."

"No! No, it doesn't hurt a bit. It's just amazing you found Michael so fast. Thank you, Vail."

"Don't thank me yet. Wait until we find her. Go back to bed and sleep in tomorrow. The steamer doesn't leave until late afternoon."

She nodded, her head down, said good-night, and closed the door. On the table the candle was only a stub from which a small, moving column of flame reached upward, transformed itself into smoke, and disappeared in darkness. She took it up, climbed onto the high featherbed, blew out the frail light, and sat, arms clasped around her knees, thinking. Sophy was as good as found, thank God, and once she was found, everything would speedily be made right. Wes wouldn't give any trouble. He was a white-livered skunk. Many a bolder man than he had refused to stand up to Vail.

She scooted under the comforter and pulled it up to her chin. Not since Papa got sick had she felt so warm and safe and sheltered by a man's strength. She lay for a long time smiling into the dark until quietly, gently, sleep closed her eyes.

Chapter 16

✦ "Mrs. Severance, come in!"

Charles Towle appeared genuinely glad to see her, and that was a relief, for she had no appointment. She had disobeyed Vail's instructions and risen as soon as the Callendar household began to stir, hoping to arrive before the doctor's office hours started, get the advice she needed, and be back before Vail discovered she was gone. There were no patients waiting on the sagging couch in the outer room. She was early enough.

She went into the little office—with, Charles noted, a touch less than her usual assurance—and accepted the chair offered her.

"I apologize for appearing on your doorstep so early . . ."

"A visit from you is a pleasure at any time, ma'am," he answered, and meant it. Along with being enjoyable to look at, Mrs. Severance presented an interesting challenge, as he tried to deduce what she was up to. On a man's jaw that purple shadow would probably mean participation in a barroom brawl. Unthinkable, of course, for a lady, but with Marin Severance, who could tell?

She smiled and hurried on, "I must leave on the afternoon steamer for Sacramento, and I have to speak to you before I go." Slowly, finger by finger, she pulled off her gloves, giving herself time to think. She smoothed them in her lap, looked up, and met his eyes straight on. "I am correct in my belief that when one speaks in confidence to a medical man, one speaks as to a priest?"

Charles was hard put not to laugh. Although she was as feminine a woman as he'd ever seen, that last had been spoken as by a man arranging the terms of a tough business deal. He allowed himself a wager as to what she would say next, but his expression remained professionally benevolent.

"No physician worthy of the name would ever speak of things that ought to remain private."

"Would that apply if the confidence concerns someone who is not your patient?"

He inclined his head, thinking that he had probably just lost his bet.

Her eyes were on the gloves in her lap. "There is one who is very close to me, a young girl—exceedingly young—who is at present in serious trouble." Dr. Towle's eyes grew alert. "She has been—has been seduced by a young man of her acquaintance. My husband caught them." She looked up. "You know Stuart, of course."

He nodded composedly, but his complexion, never a very healthy color, had gone gray. Marin wondered why she had not noticed when she came in that he looked quite ill this morning.

"Well, since you do know Stuart, how strict and scrupulous he is, you can imagine . . . he was very shocked and harsh with her and made no allowance for the circumstances or her extreme youth, and, well, the long and the short of it is . . . she's run away."

Silence fell in the room. Dr. Towle said nothing, and Marin thought unhappily that he must be too repelled to speak. Oh, she should never have come, should never have told him.

But he lifted his head and, although he was still alarmingly pale, asked calmly, "Where is the man?"

"Oh, Wes jumped out the window and ran. Stuart tried to shoot him, but he missed." The doctor said something under his breath which Marin did not catch. "We know Soph—we know the girl has run away to find Wes. He has a claim up country, and Vail is going to help me get there."

Dr. Towle put a finger to his chin, rubbed it, and clasped his hands before him on the desk. "How can I help?"

"There is something I need to know, something I couldn't bring myself to ask Vail, though I'm sure he could tell me." She stopped twisting her gloves and looked at Charles, formality gone, leaving only the pleading in her eyes that he had seen so often in other women's eyes as they sat across the desk from him. "Is there anything, anything at all, some drug or medicine to prevent . . . she's just a child herself."

"When did this episode occur?"

"The day before yesterday—in the afternoon, the late afternoon."

"Ah, the late afternoon," he repeated, as though it had some significance. He seemed oddly moved. Then he nodded. Whatever emotion had gripped him was gone.

"Mrs. Severance, if I could answer yes to your question, I not only would be a happy man, I would be a wealthy one. It would be a blessing if conception itself could be prevented after the fact, so to speak, but it cannot. There is only abortion, a procedure immeasurably dangerous if performed by some ignorant midwife.

But may I point out, the human body is not a machine turned out by a factory. A woman's fertile period is limited and can vary greatly from month to month. Conception is always a random chance, depending on exact timing and the flawless meshing of many mechanisms. It does not take place easily." In spite of emotions rioting just behind his professional veneer, Charles very nearly smiled at the skeptical expression that came onto Marin's face. "It sometimes may not seem so, I realize, but it is quite true. Often many months of frequent and regular exposure are necessary before all the elements happen to conjoin, and since the lady you speak of has not had such exposure . . ." He let the implied inquiry hang delicately.

"No, no, I'm certain she has not. This was the first, the only time."

"Then be comforted. For the present we can only wait and see, but the probability is that random chance will not strike this time."

She was comforted, more than she would have believed possible considering that Charles Towle had given her only words, not some potent herb or magic elixir to save Sophy from catastrophe. But the words were so reassuring that she walked away from Mrs. Mear's ramshackle boardinghouse with all her natural resoluteness reinforced. They would find Sophy—of course they would, Sophy well and unpregnant and sulking just a bit—and once they got her back, things would change. Exactly how things would change was not yet entirely clear to her, but ideas that up until now had been only a formless blob of feelings were hardening into a plan of action.

So absorbed was she that when she saw a stylish lady coming toward her, picking her dainty way along the uneven planked sidewalk of Clay Street, she was conscious only of faint envy of the lady's hat, a sweet concoction of straw and ribbons and lacy veils, the ingredients no different from those of most bonnets but put together in a cunning way and worn with great panache. In its indefinable quality of style it was reminiscent of the dashing bonnet worn by Anna von Helsdorf, and this lady had the same kind of simple elegance in dress, but she was dark as Anna was fair—black hair, clear olive skin, delicate Spanish features with a hint of Indian about the mouth and oblique dark eyes . . .

"Petra Victoria!" Marin stopped dead in astonishment, and her eyes ran over the other girl.

Petra stopped, too, smiled hesitantly, and stepped forward until they were only a pace apart.

"Miss Marin." Her teeth were a flash of pearl against dark skin, and her cheeks flushed dusky pink; she was unsure of her welcome. Marin recalled that they had parted less than friends, with some high and heated comments on her side. The girl had deserved every word, deserting her for no good reason at a time when she most needed her—but that was a long time ago; it was always better to be generous and return good for evil, and certainly she was not one to hold a grudge. Besides, it appeared that Petra was not going to come crawling back to Little Mountain begging for help, as Marin had predicted. She looked much too prosperous.

"How nice to see you again. Your job with Mrs. Fletcher has gone well?"

"Yes, thank you, ma'am. Very well."

It had to be true. Petra was blooming, still willow-slim but with a bosom that was considerably more substantial, a face that was more mature and, it must be admitted, almost pretty. The girlish diffidence was gone. This was what came of freedom and democracy on a frontier.

"Your bonnet is charming," she commented coolly. "If Fletcher's Emporium is carrying Paris fashions, I may stop by one day."

"Oh, thank you. Mrs. Fletcher does have some dresses from Paris, but this dress and bonnet, I made them myself."

"Indeed. Yes, you did copy one or two nice gowns for me out of *Godey's*."

"But I don't copy anymore." Petra touched her little hat. "I make it up myself."

"Make it up? Do you mean you design bonnets?"

"Yes, ma'am, and dresses, too. I am a modiste now, Mrs. Fletcher says, but mostly I am a milliner. My clientele is very good. I have, as the saying goes, struck a rich vein! I'd be proud to make a bonnet for you, Miss Marin, the best one I can, because you are so beautiful, you would be a good advertisement." Petra laughed. "See what a good businesswoman I have become."

It was said with eager delight and the clear intent to please, but Marin had to choke back rising envy. She assumed an amiable expression.

"Very kind. Perhaps one day." All the forgiving words she had planned to speak about Petra coming to her anytime she was in need were ridiculous now. "Good-bye, Petra. Do extend my regards to Mrs. Fletcher."

She walked on down the street, feeling dowdy and drab and only a little mollified by the knowledge that her coldness had gotten through to the upstart girl.

Petra watched until Marin had passed out of view. She had not inquired about the crippled *patrón* and poor, confused Miss Rose, or Carey, darling Carey, and the new baby girl whom she had never seen. She had learned nothing at all about the people who had been so dear to her, nothing but that Miss Marin had not changed much and yet was very different in some indefinable way. Miss Marin would never come to Fletcher's Emporium, and perhaps it was just as well. She might not like what she would find out if she talked to Mrs. Fletcher.

On any ordinary afternoon the waterfront was the most frenetic, boisterous place in town, the best place to go for a thrill if the delights of saloon, gambling hall, and bawdy house had begun to pall, for here, faithfully each afternoon at four o'clock, the steamers bound upriver departed.

Vail had arranged cabin passage on the *Senator* early that morning, not easy to get on this day of all days, when the news from the East had sent the entire population into a frenzy of movement. However, it seemed that the captain was a particular friend of his. Everyone seemed to be a particular friend of his, and a valuable asset it was, Marin reflected as she struggled through a welter of people toward the big steamer's mooring, as close behind Vail as possible. He shouldered his way with impersonal callousness, using his body and the bags he carried as battering rams, opening a path for her. No one appeared to take offense. They were doing the same with equal ruthlessness, and only Vail's greater height and weight and the protective shield he offered Marin prevented her being knocked down and trampled.

The calliope was tootling, and a little distance ahead Chinese laborers were being herded like livestock onto the steamers, where they would be put down into holds, far away from the regular passengers. They were freight to be hauled to the gold fields, along with other merchandise, odd beings from half a world away.

A bell was pealing urgently. Somewhere a resonant whistle hooted. It was departure time, and people hurried to get aboard. Inside the steamer's saloon were comfortable chairs and couches, but Marin and Vail stayed on deck and pushed their way to the rail.

The great paddle wheel began to turn, dip down, lift a foaming gush of water, and dip down again in a rhythmic, throbbing beat. The boat trembled delicately, like a high-bred filly daintily pawing the earth before a race. The wheel thrashed the water faster as the boat backed and turned. There were the cries of officers and crew, of passengers arrived too late and left shouting in frustration on the dock, and "Good-bye! Good-bye!" echoing more and more faintly.

The expanse of bright water between the wharf and the boat increased, and the afternoon sun slanted low, dazzling Marin.

Vail was watching her and smiling.

"You look like a little girl let out to play."

The blood was in her cheeks all right, and her breath coming fast with excitement. She lowered her eyes to hide the sparkle in them and said primly, "It's all most interesting. I haven't been on a big boat like this since we left New York. I haven't gone anywhere, really, since New York."

He leaned on the railing and looked out at the water. "It seems to me you haven't had any fun in a long, long time."

"What a thing to say! I have—I have a wonderful life."

"Do you? I'm glad to hear it. I might suspect that country life couldn't offer quite the opportunities a girl like you needs. I might even wonder that you don't go crazy with boredom—that is, if you hadn't set me straight."

"How could I possibly be bored? I'm always busy with the house and the children and Mama and Papa and the horses . . ."

"Don't forget Delphine and the chickens and the ducks."

"That is not one bit funny, and you are very rude. Stuart was in the wrong with Sophy, I know it as well as you, but that doesn't mean that he isn't a good man or that we aren't happy, because we are—marvelously happy, and I am not bored!"

He turned and looked at her directly. "You misunderstand me. Stuart is a very good man indeed, and I'm delighted that you are happy and not bored." He sounded perfectly sincere, and whether or not he really was, it gave her a chance to retreat with some dignity.

"Just so you do understand," she answered loftily, accepting the apology he had not made, and became very interested in activities on the lower deck.

The *Senator* was away, trailing a feathery plume of smoke, heading for San Pablo Bay. There was a light, fresh tingle of autumn in the air, and the great island sea was as blue as the sky. Alcatraz slipped past and was left behind, the steamer's big paddle wheel beating resolutely, inland bound toward the winding Sacramento, the broad water road that would surely lead them to Sophy.

Vail left Marin to buy the tickets for their evening meal. The high ridge of the Sierras glowed into fiery crimson to the east, and the delicious odor of well-cooked food drifted up from the dining room. People were beginning to move toward the stairs even before the dinner bell sounded, and Vail was coming down from the hurricane deck, swiftly, the way he always moved. She picked up the heavy bags and went to meet him.

Sacramento City had leaped into life at the natural landing site on the river's east bank, just below the old fort built by Captain Sutter, and was now a booming town of ten thousand.

Vail and Marin pushed through the crush of people on the embarcadero to Front Street, where clouds of gritty powder churned up by the constant passage of horses and pack mules and heavy wagons were rising into the warm October air. The town had gone as mad over statehood as San Francisco had, and unless great care was taken, it was worth a pedestrian's life to try to cross between the rumbling, overloaded wagons and the impromptu horse race presently being held in the middle of Front Street.

As the race finished, Vail took Marin by the arm. "Now's the time." He hustled her across the rutted, dusty road to the entry of the Jewel Saloon. She halted in the doorway.

"Vail, I can't go into a drinking house. Take me someplace respectable."

"The Jewel is as respectable as you're likely to get in this town, and it's safer than the street. Come on."

Inside he rolled a drunk miner off a chair. "Sit down, Marin, and I'll bring you something to drink."

The miner, who seemed to bear no ill will for being swept off his seat, smiled up at her with drowsy good nature.

"Shur an' yer a darlin' girl," he remarked in a thick Irish accent from his position on the floor. His head lay between the heavy boots of a man leaning against the bar, but he appeared gloriously unworried. He contemplated her face, said, "Prettiesh shing I ever shaw," and went quietly to sleep.

Vail was back, and surprisingly he had a cup of hot chocolate for her and a plate of pastries. She had supposed nothing but hard liquor was served in these dens. The cries of men caught up in gambling fever were plain over the low buzz of the room, and through an open passageway she saw the glint of gold on tables covered with green baize, glimpsed the flash of cards, and heard the click of a roulette wheel. The fools were gambling away in minutes gold acquired painfully in months of brutally hard labor.

Had Ethan done the same thing—built up a stake so that he could come victoriously home and then lost it over and over again in some gaming hell like this? Probably he had, and now he was dead and would never come home at all.

She took a swallow of the chocolate, and a cultivated voice behind her said, "Vail, my dear fellow. May I join you?"

He was a square, broad man with chest muscles as heavy as a wrestler's. His brown hair was brushed carefully across the thin spot on top, his brown beard was full but neatly trimmed, and he was dressed in the fashion of a young man-about-town, a trifle pompous but gentlemanly. It had been a long time since she'd had her hand kissed. His name was Dr. Thomas Anderson.

"If you're going up the American," he was saying in the manner of a man used to command, "do it today, that's my advice. This morning, if you can obtain passage. Get Mrs. Severance out of town."

Vail's expression had gone from one of pleasure at meeting a friend to an intense, alert look that made Marin uneasy. Dr. Anderson's naturally stentorian voice lowered to a forceful whisper.

"Yesterday morning a body was found on the levee. It looked questionable to me, but last night the coroner's jury brought in a verdict of cholera morbus, not Asiatic cholera."

"Cholera . . ."

"Keep your voice down please, Mrs. Severance. If this gets out, there'll be a general panic, which will not help the situation. So far word has not spread, and if it *is* cholera morbus, it won't be such a threat from the standpoint of epidemic."

"If it is?" Vail's eyes were on the cigar he was lighting, and he seemed perfectly calm, but Marin felt like jumping up and screaming. Oh, if only she could find Sophy today and go home to Little Mountain, where it was safe.

Dr. Anderson said, "I'm a peculiar fellow, you know, always nosing about where I'm not wanted. The coroner wants it hushed up, but I've already found at least one sure case of malignant cholera in the town, no doubt about it, and there are several other possibles. As I say, get Mrs. Severance upriver as soon as you can."

The riverbank glided by like a cool, green dream: tangled wild grapevine, cottonwoods, willows bending to the water, sycamores, gnarled oaks with great branches arching fifty feet high and then drooping down until the tips almost touched the moist, brown earth. The little flat-bottomed steamer *Aetna* putted cautiously past submerged tangles of branches and tree stumps, sandbars and rushing rapids, its stern wheel thrashing rhythmically. But for its slender beam and its wheel on the stern instead of the side, it could never had made passage, for the beautiful American River was little more than a hundred yards wide at this point, and the uncertain channel even narrower.

In the stern the two horses and the pack mule Vail had bought in Sacramento City were corraled along with those belonging to other passengers. Marin, as a horse breeder, approved of them.

The first wild panic she had felt when she heard the word *cholera* had diminished in proportion to the steamer's distance from the town. Cholera was such a horrifying, baffling, deadly disease, coming from God only knew what source. When it struck, it sent whole populations into a hysteria of fear. You could wake in the morning in apparent perfect health, and in a few hours would come the raging fever, the vomiting, cramping, and unquenchable thirst, the bowels turned molten. By nightfall you could go into convulsions and die. The swiftness of the disease was the only good thing that could be said for it, considering the anguish of the sufferers. Although Marin, along with most of the citizens of San Francisco, did not yet know it, cholera had in fact arrived in the city in early October on a boat from New Orleans and had been spreading stealthily since then. It had ridden the riverboats up to Sacramento City and had been lying in wait for many days.

But here on the tranquil river, with mountain birds singing in the tall trees along the bank and the air sharp with the clean scent of pine, Marin felt safe from the disease of the cities. The sun beat down, high and hot. Her bonnet brim spread a little patch of shade over her face, and she leaned into the cool wind stirred by the boat's steady movement.

"Vail, if it's true that cholera is mostly brought on by intemperance and immoral living, why was Dr. Anderson worried about me?"

"Who says it's true?"

"Why, the ministers say so. Depravity lowers the resistance, and that's why the poor get such awful diseases. I've read newspaper editorials that said the same thing."

"Which shows how much attention you should pay to ministers and newspaper editors. The churches frighten their flocks into rectitude since they can't persuade them into it, and the editors print what their respectable readers want to believe."

"You think they're wrong?"

He shrugged. "I think if the garbage and filth were cleaned up, Sacramento City might not be facing an epidemic right now. Except that someone would bring it in from San Francisco, where it's just as filthy."

"The doctors say cholera isn't catching."

"Some doctors say it's not." He grinned. "Which shows how much attention you should pay to doctors. Wouldn't *you* rather believe you couldn't catch it, if you had to take care of people who are down with it?"

"But that's stupid. If it is contagious, believing it isn't won't make any difference."

"I told you most doctors aren't worth shooting. They slap on mustard plasters, drain a few quarts of blood, and poison patients with calomel or strychnine. Once in a while one of the poor wretches recovers in spite of them, and the medical profession pats itself on the back." He laughed shortly. "My father should have been the doctor in the family. He's pigheaded enough."

"Dr. Towle isn't pigheaded."

"That's why he's good. An open mind and close attention to what's happening right under your eyes can go a long way even when you don't have all the answers. Of course cholera is contagious. It is passed between people somehow, but most doctors won't admit it. Anyone with common sense can see that there is a connection between squalor and some of the worst diseases, but look at the outcry whenever it's suggested that we clean things up. As for the depraved poor, they not only drink whiskey and do other naughty things, but they also live in pestholes. A rich man out in the country, safely removed from city filth, can get drunk every day and sleep with his slaves every night and never get cholera. So much for wickedness as a cause."

"That is a snide, ugly, Yankee thing to say, and it's so untrue! My father never touched a female slave in his life, and never, never would—no, nor any of the gentlemen I knew back home."

"No doubt. I was only pointing out the illogic of relating virtue and cholera. I meant nothing personal. Mr. Gentry is a fine man, and as for insulting Southern honor, God forbid. You might challenge me to a duel."

"I'm surprised you'd care to mention the subject, considering your past performance." She was frightened that he might be right about the contagiousness of cholera, uneasy at being once more drawn into a conversation about intimate matters when she had promised herself it would never happen again.

"I thought my past performance was rather good."

"How can you be so unfeeling? Nicolas will always be crippled, for all the job he does of hiding it."

"Better him than me. Nicolas would have shot me dead if he could have managed it. It was my good luck that his gun went off early and his good luck that I'm such a bad shot. Otherwise he'd be dead."

She looked up at him, shading her eyes from the sun. "You meant to kill him? You didn't aim for his arm?"

"I meant to kill him, and I would have if I'd been more familiar with the gun."

"But to deliberately shoot a defenseless man . . ."

He leaned against the rail and shook his head. "You've read too many romances. If I'd only tried to wound him, I might have missed altogether. And if he'd had a second chance, he would have killed me. Anyone who knows guns will tell you never pick one up if you don't intend to use it, and never pull the trigger unless you mean to kill. Keep that in mind if you ever have to shoot someone."

She stared out at the green, rapid-flowing water, wondering whether to believe him. He might be teasing, deliberately intending to shock her, or he might be telling the God's truth. If he had killed Nicolas that day, so many things would have fallen out differently—he'd be married to Celia right now. Did he often think of that, or was it merely a sad, lost love, mostly forgotten? Whatever he really felt he'd never show it, not to her or anyone, but it would be nice to know, purely as a matter of curiosity.

There was a halloo from somewhere ahead. The beating of the stern wheel on this isolated stretch of the river announced the *Aetna*'s coming even before its bell rang out on the warm, still air. Miners working at scattered locations on the stream bank dropped their tools and came running. There might be mail from home aboard, and if not that, a new supply of whiskey to help them forget that no letter had come.

They danced and shouted on the bank, waving bandanas and dirty hats, and as the engine slowed and the boat drifted close to shore, they splashed hip deep into the water, eager to speed up the unloading, making loud, enthusiastic offers to help Marin, the only female passenger, onto dry land.

Vail declined for her, and when the ramp had dropped into shallow water, he swung her up and waded ashore with the

murmured comment that close proximity to her charming person
would be too cruel a strain on the lads, starved as they were for the
company of ladies.

Without giving her a chance to answer he set her down on high
ground and went to retrieve their bags. All the passengers had
waded ashore, and the livestock were being urged down the ramp
into the rapid stream.

Marin turned her back on the activity in the water and looked up
the main street—the only street of the camp. Rattlesnake Bar,
they called it, an ugly, flea-ridden place. Down the dusty street,
only a little higher than the river and always flooded during the
rainy season, were crude structures that might generously be
called buildings. A few were made entirely of wood, but many
were canvas tents. Several were simply stakes planted close
together in the dirt, roofed with pine branches, and open to the
street. Men about to strike a vein of pure gold that would make
them millionaires would not take time away from prospecting to
build a real house or a permanent town.

There were numerous rickety saloons with liquors prominently
displayed, a blacksmith shop, a livery stable, several stores
containing odd conglomerations of merchandise. The sturdiest
building on the street, constructed of pine logs and sporting a
shiny tin roof, gave equal space to liquors, pharmaceuticals, and
hospital facilities, for the bartender acted as surgeon and dentist.

On the northern border of the camp, a clump of low-growing
bushes bore colorful fruit—newly washed shirts, pants, socks,
and undergarments spread out to dry. Near the laundry, under the
sheltering branches of Rattlesnake Bar's one oak tree, the inevitable monte tables were beginning to draw players.

Those who had received letters from home or merchandise
ordered months before were in fine spirits and crowded around to
get the latest news from San Francisco and the East. They cheered
and pounded on each other at word of statehood; one fellow did an
Irish jig in time to his own singing, pirouetted on the bank, and
fell headfirst into the water. But Marin had the feeling that their
joy was more dutiful than deep-felt. They wanted in the Union—it
was proper, right, inevitable—but the thrust of their lives was to
get rich quick, then go back home as wealthy men to the settled
states where life was ordered, calm, and familiar. In the long view
of things what did it matter whether or not California became a
state when they meant to stay just long enough to make their pile?

But they hopped joyfully through the main street, the banjos
and guitars and harmonicas came out, and Marin followed,

sticking close to Vail, looking from side to side in mild shock at
the oddities of dress and behavior around her. Most miners wore
the clothing that had become almost a uniform in the gold
fields—slouched, dirty felt hat, bright flannel shirt, heavy trousers
tucked into muddy boots—and all were a walking arsenal of
knives and pistols stuck into leather belts or boot tops. A few
nonconformists dressed in buckskins like the mountain men or
wore natty straw hats from Panama or fancy embroidered vests
and dancing pumps. The one Frenchman in camp kept his
treasured beret on his head at all times but jammed a sombrero
over it when digging in the broiling sun. Indians, who had come
out of the wilderness to trade for flour, were presently haggling
over price with a top-hatted storekeeper. They were in a state of
nature, except for one with a cravat around his neck and another
wearing a derby hat with a turkey feather in the band.

Covertly Marin peeked at them, remembering stories of brutal
raids descending in the night and women and children slaughtered
in lonely camps, and wondered if they were as friendly as they
seemed. Their fellows populated the rugged country through
which she and Vail would have to travel, and some were known
not to take kindly to the intrusion of whites into land they
considered theirs alone. No white man passed through the Sierras
without going well armed, and Marin noticed that in addition to
the carbine and the shotgun strapped to his pack, Vail now had a
long-sheathed knife stuck in his belt and two pistols in holsters on
his hips, weapons that had not been in evidence on the boat.

The Rattlesnake Hotel was an airy hovel with walls and roof
consisting mostly of branches with the leaves still on. It adjoined
the Bon Ton Saloon, an open space with a canvas roof tied to four
stakes. Inside the hotel they sat down at a rough table with a long
crosscut log for a bench, and eager young men crowded nearby to
watch the pretty lady eat.

Supper was unexpectedly good—fried oysters, roast pork, and,
wonder of wonders, fresh green peas—but it was growing so late,
that they might have to stay here tonight. Behind her nods and
smiles, she was wild to get out of this squalid shantytown and on
to Dead Man Bar, wherever that was. She heard Vail say, "That's
right, Mike's younger brother. An obnoxious type, but then you
fellows would hardly notice that, being the same kind." Everyone
chuckled, as though he had just made a grand joke, and as the
laughter settled down, he added, "But you might remember the
girl who was with him, very young, very pretty, long, blond
hair . . ."

There was a collective sigh. Yes, they remembered the girl. She had come in overland by mule yesterday morning and had kept very much to herself, but she certainly was blond, they remembered that. So the bearded boy with her was Mike Morgan's kid brother. Not the man Mike was, they agreed. In fact there had been some question of cheating in a poker game, and the couple had left camp hastily last night. As for Dead Man Bar, there were a couple of diggings that went by that name on the Middle Fork, and at least one on the South Fork. No one had any idea which one Wes had been heading for.

The hotel owner, Sam Canty, who was also the cook and waiter, stopped on his way to the open-air kitchen in the back. "You might talk to Flora, down at the shack. The girl was pretty tired, and Flora felt sorry for her. Let her rest down there all afternoon. She seemed like a nice little girl, too. What in hell was she doing out here with trash like Wes Morgan?"

What, indeed, thought Marin wearily. That was the question everyone would ask if this got out. Luckily none of these men knew Sophy's name. And there was a woman in camp. Flora. Probably the wife of one of these miners. Sometimes especially intrepid women did follow husbands out here, although Marin was convinced they must be crazy rather than brave.

She tugged at Vail's sleeve. "Please, let's go talk to this lady now."

He eyed her speculatively. "You sure you want to? I can find out what she knows, if anything, while you wait here. You'll be quite safe."

"Of course I want to. She might tell me something she wouldn't tell you, or . . . anyway, I want to thank her."

"Come along then."

She trotted behind him in the gathering twilight, down the deeply rutted road, past tethered mules and horses, past the isolated campfire of the few Mexicans still allowed in camp. At the outskirts, where the level land run out and the river lapped against the abrupt escarpment of the hill, was a lone wooden shack built on stilts. Marin thought they had left the entire population of the camp eating, drinking, and gaming in the main part of town, but there were a number of men down here, lined up in the gloom, shadows of men waiting patiently outside the shack.

Vail walked up and said something quietly, and there were murmurs of agreement as the line parted to allow them through.

His hand was on her arm, and he kept her close beside him as he said courteously, "Pardon us. We'll only take a moment, gentlemen."

There were replies, equally courteous, coming out of the dark, New England accents as flat as Vail's, an Englishman's voice, various foreign accents she could not identify, soft, slurring Southern tones—the accent of home. But what on earth were these men doing down here in the dark?

They were at the door.

"Well," she said urgently, "go on. Knock."

"That would be impolite," Vail said. "We'll wait."

Pinpricks and thin shafts of light showed through cracks where the boards of the shack did not meet. A lamp had been lit. There were sounds of boots scuffing over rough flooring. The door creaked open and hung sagging on leather hinges. In the light of a kerosene lamp held high, a man, his young face obscured by the usual scraggly beard, was tucking his shirt into his pants. He said, "Thanks, Flora," and dropped a small bag into the hand of the woman who held the lamp. She weighed it on her flat palm, nodded, and peered out into the night.

"Next?" she inquired, and saw Vail at the head of the line. Slowly, in some surprise, her eyes traveled over his face, his body, down to the polished knee boots, and back to his face.

"Well, howdy do," she remarked after a moment of silence. "Step right in."

"Thank you, ma'am. Another time. Just now this lady"—he indicated Marin, who was standing behind him wondering if she was going to swoon or possibly die of humiliation on the spot, "this lady and I would appreciate a moment's conversation with you. It would be worth a considerable amount in gold to us, and we'd take very little of your time."

Flora looked at Marin, back at Vail, then gestured them inside with the hand that held the lamp. The moving circle of yellow light swooped through the blue light of evening like a huge, fluttering moth. She closed the door, set the lamp on a rickety table, and turned to them with hands on hips and questions in her eyes.

Later, thinking over the awful few minutes in that dank little shack, Marin could not recall the room itself, for she had not seen it. She saw only the woman's face, dark-eyed, heavy-boned, deep-lined, not old but with immeasurable hard experience in it, a body that was heavy and graceless under a dirty silk wrapper, broad hands, splayed bare feet. Her hair was black, lank, and none too clean, her homely face was bare of artifice. Where was the paint, the gaudy dress, the jangling jewelry and cheap perfume that women who sold their bodies to men always used? This woman looked like a tired, canny washerwoman.

In silence she listened to Vail and studied Marin ruminantly.

"You the little girl's sister?"

Marin nodded numbly. "I want to thank you . . . my parents will be so grateful . . . for taking care of her, that is."

Flora shrugged. "I didn't do much. She was tired, poor little thing, and more scared than tired, I b'lieve. She don't belong with that young feller. He's not her kind."

She scowled reminiscently at the thought of Wes Morgan, and gently Vail brought her back to the point. "His claim is at Dead Man Bar, but unfortunately there are several camps by that name hereabouts. Did she say anything that would give an idea of where they were headed?"

Flora let go of her kimono, which she had been clutching tightly, and gnawed thoughtfully at her thumb knuckle. Marin looked quickly away. The woman didn't have so much as a shimmy on underneath.

"She talked about all the gold the boy was goin' to get, the kind of blather you always hear from fool miners. Said she'd go back home and show everybody, especially Stuart, whoever he may be." Flora looked at Marin with frank curiosity. "Her other man friend?"

"No, not quite," Marin answered in a muffled voice, not wanting to see the expression on Vail's face at that moment.

"Well, she said nothin' about where they was headed. I doubt she knew."

Vail counted out a number of gold coins. In the dim light Marin could not see how much, but Flora's eyes lit. Evidently it was a lot of money to her, and real minted coin was scarce in the hills. He bent over Flora's hand and brushed it with his lips as if she were the grandest of ladies; she flushed a deep, dark red. He opened the door and handed Marin down the steps.

Behind them Flora said, "She did ask about Tragedy Creek, if it was as bad a place as it sounded, and I said no, it was a fine, pretty spot and don't be put off by the name, though the truth is, I never heard of it."

She stood a little inside the door, the kimono clutched tight again, her hard, dark eyes asking hopefully if this bit of information was of any use.

Vail looked up at her with the endearing smile that had captivated Delphine and Sophy and so many other women, and Flora looked almost flustered. "I think perhaps you just told us where to find her, ma'am," he said.

Chapter 17

It took three days of hard riding to come upon Tragedy Creek, three long, exhausting days over formidably rugged terrain—narrow, deep ravines somber with low-lying fog, dangerously cragged and depressing to the spirits; streams of pure crystal water that were often difficult to cross because of submerged hollows dug out of the streambed by the swift current; secluded little valleys darkened by trees so thick that sunlight never touched the damp, moss-grown earth; forests of buckeye and ash turned gold, orange, and crimson, a flaming autumn mantle spread against the evergreen oaks and towering pines.

It was a forest sublimely still, deserted or apparently deserted. At times Marin heard the distant, chilling yelp of Indians, but they remained invisible and no arrows came whistling out of the screen of leaves. The only living creatures that showed themselves were fat elk and black-tailed deer and shaggy, lumbering grizzlies made corpulent and lazy on a rich diet of acorns and buckeye nuts.

At the end of the first day Vail picked as a stopping place a spot near a stream that was well concealed by a brambled thicket. In the early hours of the night Marin sat on a pile of buckeye leaves near the small fire he had built, warming her feet and listening to the whoops and hoots that could be nightbirds or could be Indians. With her back to the dark she felt exceedingly vulnerable and moved so that she was propped against the rough bark of a ponderosa pine. There was a long, drawn-out, quavering howl, and she jumped as though struck.

"A wolf," Vail said.

Her skin crawled. Earlier there had been coyotes, which could howl disconcertingly, too, but were not nearly so frightening to think about. The night was damp. Moisture dripped from the pine needles, and the pungent odor of incense cedar tickled her nose. At sunset a wedge-shaped flight of southbound black brant had passed, flying high, honking their curious, mournful cry, and now the stars of Orion were rising in the night sky. The winter stars, the call of the wild geese, the vivid colors of the autumn leaves all proclaimed the turning of yet another year, and for some reason, hard to define, the thought was melancholy. It should not be. Bleak dreariness was for the old, not for one who was young and pretty and had a fine life ahead of her. To shake off depression she ate another piece of the heavy, sweet cake Vail had bought at Mr. Canty's hotel and licked sugary icing from her fingers.

"If you eat like that every time you have the dismals, you'll end up fatter than Delphine Whitmore," said Vail. He was sitting on the other side of the fire, resting against his saddle and pack.

She sat up straighter. "What makes you think I have the dismals?"

"Did you really expect to find Ethan in one of the camps?"

How had he known? At every camp, every scratched-out gully or river bar, she had searched each bearded face for Ethan—hope leaping up each time she imagined his familiar walk and shape in some shaggy, rough-clothed miner; hope dying as the man came closer and was not Ethan, did not even faintly resemble Ethan.

She said, "Did I ever tell you that I never cried for him, not once? I decided not to, when I first heard. I couldn't spare the strength. I felt sad, but I didn't grieve, and I was glad I had that much control over myself. But—it's strange—this summer, when I thought it was all behind me, I dreamed of him. In my dream I was standing somewhere, on a street corner, I think, and far down the street came Ethan, striding along with his head thrown back in that way he had, full of life and health, looking so well, Vail. And I thought, Oh, why didn't somebody tell me it was all a mistake? He isn't dead, and he's come home. In my dream he walked right past without seeing me, but I could see the color of his eyes and his long, gold eyelashes and his hair blowing a little in the wind. He wasn't coming to me, he was going to see somebody else first, but my feelings weren't hurt a bit, and I was so happy he was alive that the tears were streaming down my face. I woke up with my face all wet, and I knew it was only a dream. Then I cried from pain. Every once in a while I dream that dream again."

"How often? Is it always the same?"

"Sometimes little things are different, but mostly the same. It's come, I guess, three or four times since summer. Do you know what I think it means?" The fire had burned low, and its inconstant shadows changed and moved on her face.

"What does it mean?"

"That you can't cheat on—on life. You can't hold back your feelings and get away with it, no matter how much you want to.

It's like a debt come due, and if you don't pay one way, you'll be made to pay in another. Do you think that's true?"

He stirred restlessly, almost irritably. "Yes, I think so." He threw the stub of his cigar in the fire.

She drew up her knees and rested her chin on them, her thoughts turned inward. "Riding along today I was counting up all the people I really care about, and it's scary how few there are. Papa, Mama, Carey, Sophy, Belinda. Out of all the people in the world only five, like a special inner circle that I would do anything for. Outside the circle there's Delphine. She's silly and selfish and she drives me crazy sometimes, but she's family, so I have to look out for her. And there's you and Logan. You're family, too, so you're special but not quite so close. I hope you don't mind."

"Not at all. I'm flattered to be mentioned, and Logan would be, too, if she knew. But haven't you forgotten someone?"

"Who?"

"Your loving husband, ma'am. Doesn't Stuart belong in that special inner circle?"

"I said Stuart."

"No. You didn't."

"Well, I meant to. Right now I am a bit put out with him, but . . ."

"*Put out* isn't the word for it. You're mad as hell, and you intend to make him pay. And pay and pay."

In vast annoyance she snapped, "You surprise me, so busy looking after his interests. You never were his particular friend."

"Believe me," he answered softly, "I have no intention of looking after his interests. He'll have to do that himself—if he can."

She wiped her hands on her handkerchief, carefully cleaned off the cake crumbs and icing from each finger, got to her feet, and dug a blanket out of her pack. She stood aside while he demonstrated how to make a bed of leaves as a buffer against the hard ground; she packed away the food and politely agreed that they should wait till morning to wash out the plates rather than stumble down to the stream in the dark. Then she rolled up in her blanket without saying good-night and turned her back to show her displeasure at his uncalled-for remarks. With eyes shut she listened while he piled more wood on the fire and made his own bed. After a while she opened her eyes and saw his shadow lean toward the fire as he lit another cigar.

• • •

In the late afternoon of the third day they drew rein at the crest of a ravine and looked down on Dead Man Bar. At least, Vail believed it was Dead Man Bar. There were no signposts to guide them. The stream that might be Tragedy Creek tumbled down a wild, rocky gorge past a collection of tents and hovels spread out on a level space tucked between hills, and lost itself in the waters of the big river. The sun had dropped below the rim of the western peaks, but men still worked in the lingering yellow afterglow.

Marin and Vail urged their horses forward and clattered down a slope of sliding gravel, splashed across the creek, and dismounted before a log structure that appeared to be the camp's bakery, general store, shoe shop, and smithy. Marin smiled at the proprietor, who was at this moment completing the repair of a broken shovel, but stayed by her horse and watched Vail walk up to the forge.

He came back with word that made her heart leap with hope.

"Wes's claim is on the hill outside of camp. He rode in with Sophy night before last, bought some supplies, and went up there. Nobody's seen them since."

"Oh, Vail!" She was delighted and nervous at the same time. There might be a knock-down-drag-out fight before they were through, but she could manage Sophy, and ornery as Wes was, he had a healthy respect for Vail Severance's ability with guns and his willingness to use them. Wes had been a spectator at that long-ago, early morning duel, too. Now that the moment was almost here, she decided she really didn't want Wes shot to death but wouldn't mind Vail's beating him to a pulp if he tried to defy them.

Vail put out a hand to help her onto her horse, but her boot was already in the stirrup and she bounced up without aid. She grinned at him. "I'll race you."

"You'll walk your horse and follow me. The animal is tired, and when we get there, I'm going in first."

He took the mule by its leading rope, nudged his horse in the flank, and rode slowly toward the edge of camp. She followed, subdued by the sternness in his face. What was the matter with him? He couldn't be worried about confronting Wes Morgan.

They clopped through the camp, and miners put down picks, shovels, and pans and gazed at the unexpected sight of a young woman with fiery red hair and the straight back of the born horsewoman. She was the second pretty girl they had seen in as many days, and they stared after her until she and the big, scowling man were out of sight.

Wes's cabin was a log shanty on high ground a mile up Tragedy Creek. It sat alone a few yards from the woods, hurriedly built and ramshackle but a substantial shelter compared with the tents and flea-ridden communal sleeping quarters most miners settled for.

At present, however, the cabin looked uninhabited. No trail of smoke told of a supper fire, and no lamp showed through the tiny window, although day had faded into dusk. There was a tightening sensation in Marin's midsection, and a shiver crawled up her back. Someone walked over my grave, she thought.

Vail said, "Wait here." He swung to the ground and pushed open the cabin door. "Sophy?" he said softly, and disappeared into the dark interior.

An animal groan and a sob compelled Marin off her horse and into the cabin. Her eyes adjusted to the darkness. She cried out, "Sophy!" and went down on her knees beside her sister. Vail fumbled in his pocket, a match flared, and the wick of a kerosene lamp took fire and settled to a steady glow.

Sophy lay on a bed that was nothing but a shelf of rough boards nailed to the wall. Only one who loved her would have known her. Her face was sunk against its delicate bones, all round prettiness gone. The skin below her great, staring eyes was purple, her long, fair hair was soaked with sweat. She jerked upward in a shuddering spasm, retched violently, and gagged. Vail turned her so that she would not choke on vomit and, when the seizure passed, laid her down gently. She lay so still, eyes open and staring, that Marin, terror-stricken, whispered, "Is she dead?"

"Not yet. Come here, Marin."

He pulled her to the open door, and the sweet smell of outdoors was perfume after the fetid cabin.

"Is it cholera?" she asked, and saw the confirmation in his eyes. She swallowed. "What—what can we do?"

"Not very damn much," he answered, and she threw out her hands in wild appeal. "—but we'll do what we can." He stripped off his coat and rolled up his shirtsleeves. "Give her some water from your canteen. I'm going to take all the pots I can find and fill them down at the creek."

Sophy's face was blue, cold to the touch, and bathed in sweat, her pulse was feeble, and the thin, reedy voice that issued from her lips did not sound like her own. The fingers of the small hand

Marin held were wrinkled and spongy, as if they had been soaked in water. Vail bundled her blanket around her and told Marin that this was the collapse stage of the disease. "If she makes it through this, the fever will come on."

If she makes it, Marin thought, and clung harder to her sister's hand, willing her not to slip away.

Again and again Sophy vomited, and after each violent attack Vail coaxed her into swallowing more water.

"What's the use?" cried Marin in despair. "It just comes back up again."

"It puts something in her to come up. Dry retching would be much harder on her, and she does retain a little."

Kneeling beside the bed, Marin looked up at him. How calm he was, and how patient. There was not a sign of disgust in his face as he took away the blanket fouled by the savage purging that tore Sophy, no hesitance as his hands, such gentle hands, cleaned her thin, childlike body. No mother could be kinder, Marin thought, and tears came to her eyes, tears of gratitude, fear, and fatigue. *Even if—if Sophy doesn't live, I will owe him for this forever*.

He said, "Her fever is rising," and she realized that the hand she held had grown hot.

"Does that mean . . ."

"It means she's come through one stage and is entering another. Sponge her off and keep her as cool as possible. Get water down her as often as you can. I'm going to take these clothes and the blanket and burn them."

As fever mounted, Sophy began to babble, not recognizing Marin, never once calling for Mama or Papa or even Wes, but moaning what sounded like "Jemmy, Jemmy, Jemmy," endlessly, monotonously, swallowing the water Marin held to her lips and then moaning "Jemmy" again.

Marin put her hand to her back. There was a spot just below her waist that ached viciously.

Vail took the wet cloth from her. "Let me do this for a while."

"I'm all right, I'm fine," she mumbled, but sat down gratefully on the floor. The rough boards of the cabin wall against her back felt as comfortable as any cushion.

As the night passed, Sophy's ravings dwindled. Vail laid his hand against her damp forehead, and at the sight of his smile Marin began to hope again.

She touched Sophy's cheek and whispered, "She's cooler. Oh, thank God!"

Sophy sank into restless sleep, and for the first time since she entered the cabin, Marin took time to look around. The evidence was plain. Wes had abandoned Sophy. In the beginning he must have made some attempt to take care of her, for clothing had been washed and laid out to dry, and a half-full can of water and a tin cup had been left on the floor near her bed—much good it could have done, since she had been too sick to reach it or even know she needed it. And when he realized what was wrong with her and decided to run, he had ransacked the place. There was not a tin of lard or a bag of flour left, not a stick of firewood cut or an extra blanket to comfort her. He had left her to die.

Marin muttered a favorite oath of James's and went outside. Vail had tethered the horses and the mule in the woods, far enough away that their soft nickering and shuffling movements would not disturb Sophy. The baggage and saddles had been piled under a tree, and the light of the campfire reflected from the long barrels of the carbine and shotgun propped near the cabin's open door. It had been decided that they would sleep just outside the door, where the night air was fresh and breathable but the tiniest sound from within could be heard.

Marin washed her hands until the skin was raw, sat down by the fire and nibbled on a piece of hardtack, hating to bring anything to her lips. She had been terrified for Sophy, but now that the worst of the crisis was subsiding, she was beginning to feel terror for herself, too. There was a niggling pain in her stomach. Was it the start of the dreaded cramping? She felt a trifle nauseated and very warm. Was her face hot from the flames of the fire or the onset of fever? Oh, she did not want to die out here in the wilderness. She did not want to die at all.

"You might as well eat," Vail said. "You're thoroughly exposed already, and you'll need your strength."

"I'm not hungry. I don't see how you can swallow that." She had been watching with revulsion while he downed beans and dried beef with apparent relish.

He finished the plate without answering.

After a while she said, "It isn't right for you to be here. She's not your sister. Why don't you go down into town, and I'll let you know if I need anything." If he left her here alone tonight, she would die on the spot without waiting for cholera to kill her.

"A selfless suggestion, but it's too late. I'm just as exposed as you are. Anyway, I'd rather be up here with cholera than down there with the drunks and the fleas."

"You knew she was sick before we got here, didn't you?"

"It's what I was afraid of. The blacksmith said she looked sick to him when they came through camp, and Flora said she was very tired when she took her in. I wonder how Flora is feeling right now."

Marin shuddered. Sophy had brought the disease with her, unknowing, and might have spread it through every camp in the region.

"That rotten Wes," she spat out bitterly. "Leaving her without even food. If only Stuart had killed him, this wouldn't have happened. He deserted her as soon as he figured out what was wrong."

"Yes, but any contagion he got from her is traveling with him. He can't outrun it."

It was a satisfactory picture, Wes dying horribly, wretched and alone, abandoned by decent people, but the thought of his possible suffering brought her back to Sophy and herself.

"Shouldn't we be doing something more for her? Some medicine or something?"

"*Primum non nosere.*"

"Beg pardon?"

"First rule of medicine. Make sure the remedy isn't worse than the disease."

"What could be worse? I remember Aunt Delphine's butler getting sick with cholera when I was visiting her in Baltimore years ago. The doctor did all sorts of things."

"Did he recover?"

"Well, no, he died."

He chuckled, and she snapped, "How can you laugh!" God knew there was nothing funny about this situation.

"I was just thinking how lucky it is that I don't have any strychnine or calomel or ipecac with me. I might be tempted to use some."

"Couldn't you bleed her?"

"I could, but I won't. If I leave her alone, she may get well."

"Do you really think she will?"

"She's quieter and the fever is down, both good signs. She's still alive. That's the best sign of all."

"We thought Elizabeth was getting better, and she up and died."

"You thought she was better, I didn't. Mother's heart was worn out, but cholera can be fought off if the body decides to do it. I told you once that most of doctoring is standing around waiting while the body does the job, which it will sometimes if it isn't interfered with too much. So I won't do a thing but take the credit when she gets well."

He spoke lightly, but she knew he was trying to comfort her. He had said "when" not "if" she gets well. Gratitude welled up once more.

She wrapped up in her blanket and lay down on the pad of leaves that was her bed. The night air was noticeably chilly—it got so cold in the mountains once the sun was gone—but the fire was warm and cheerful. Perhaps she didn't have a fever, but, oh, she was saddle sore, not being accustomed to days of constant riding. In a little while she would get up and check on Sophy. Her eyes drooped and closed. In a little while . . .

Sophy was getting well. Two days of care and constant watching, and the worst symptoms had passed. Braced by Marin's arm she swallowed a small quantity of broth made from boiled dried beef, sank back, and smiled. She was weak as a newborn, her face gaunt, her eyes sunken, her body stripped of its appealing curves, but she was getting well.

Their supply of food was low. Only dried beef and beans were left, and a convalescent needed strengthening, easy-to-digest victuals. On the sixth day Vail went down into camp for provisions, being careful to buy nothing that could reveal the presence of cholera in the little cabin on the hill. If they guessed, if they even suspected, he would be driven from the camp, he told Marin, and no one would sell him food.

"They wouldn't be so inhuman."

"Wouldn't they? My dear, you don't know people. They'd panic. I'll wager there have been some edifying sights in Sacramento City this past week."

An encounter with a new arrival in camp confirmed this. Vail was in the general store bargaining for eggs and two of the chickens that Jim Hopwell, the enterprising blacksmith-storekeeper, nurtured in a pen behind the store and guarded with a gun. Everyone wanted the chickens as well as the eggs, and how could he produce eggs if he killed all his chickens?

"Not all, Jim. Only two, as a special treat for the ladies. I'm sure they'll want to come down and thank you themselves."

That was an attractive thought. "You think so? Well, I might spare a couple—but only two, and don't come back askin' for more. You got to come down with the dust, too. No credit."

"I wouldn't think of it." Vail produced a leather bag. "Weigh it out, and figure in a bag of flour and a bag of rice, two of those tins of oysters, and any vegetables you've got."

"Got some potatoes and punkins. Onions a dollar apiece. Got grapes, but I have to charge four dollars a pound. They're awful hard to come by."

"That'll be fine. And a bottle of your best brandy."

Jim shook the dust into the pan with an expert flick of his wrist and watched closely as the scale swayed into balance. He looked up. Vail was leaning on the counter, watching just as closely. They smiled at each other.

"How's the blond dolly? She looked mighty tired when she rode through here."

"She was. The man she tied up with hadn't the sense to let her rest, but she's fine now."

"Wouldn't let her rest, huh? Why, that's shameful. He shouldn't have a nice girl like that if he don't know how to take care of her." Jim grinned dreamily. "*I* could sure take care of her."

He was about to expand on exactly how he would do it when there were shouts and hallooing, and a rider trotted briskly down the main street and dismounted in front of the store, closely followed by a mob of miners.

"All right, boys, stand back," the newcomer shouted. "You'll all get yours, but if you crowd me, I swear I'll make you wait."

He came stalking in, slammed his saddlebag on the counter, and said, "Gimme a drink, Jim. I'm dry as a Eyegyptian mummy."

He was a dashing figure, brandishing a whip and wearing a cape that swirled to his boot tops. Under his broad-brimmed hat his bearded face looked like well-tanned leather, and a cavalryman's mustache swooped under his long nose. He actually had been in the cavalry and had taken the expressman's job when he was mustered out a year ago. Letters and newspapers from the East came upriver from San Francisco, he picked them up at the post office in Sacramento City and then visited nearly every ravine and gully and river camp in the northern mines, delivering mail to his subscribers.

The men outside were shouting out their names hopefully, and he shoved the bag over to Jim. "Hand 'em out. I got to have another drink." He picked up the whiskey bottle and noticed a big man, a stranger to him but friendly-looking, lounging against the counter. He waggled the bottle. "Buy you one?"

Vail nodded agreeably and moved over. "Any news from town?"

"Yeah. They've gone crazy downriver. If you're heading that way, take my advice and don't."

Vail swallowed the whiskey neat. "Trouble?"

The expressman's eyes slid sideways. In an undertone he said, "Cholera. Half the town's got it, and the other half thinks they have. Anybody gets a hangover or gas on the belly, he's scared he's dyin'. The riverboats is bustin' at the seams, everybody clawin' and scratchin' to get down to Frisco, and it ain't gonna do 'em no good. It's there, too, so I hear."

"A bad business."

"Yessir. Don't nothin' bring out the meanness in a man like cholera. The Indians now, they let a pore sick bastard freeze up to his neck in the river till he can't stand it no more, stick him out in the sun, then back in the river till he dies or gets well. For me, I take a good bleedin' ever spring and a largish dose of whiskey ever day, and I ain't never had the cholera. It's the whiskey does it. Keeps the blood clean between bleedin's." He filled both glasses generously and lifted his own. "Here's to you."

Sophy was sleeping. For the past week she had slept heavily at night and a large part of every day, waking long enough to drowsily gulp down spoonfuls of broth, then dropping off again. With each waking she seemed a little stronger, a little more with the world.

Marin tiptoed to the open door. For all the cleaning she had done, the cabin, with only one tiny window, was a dank, cheerless cubicle. Outside was pine-fragrant mountain air and the mellow sun of early November. She stepped out. The woods were a jewel box of color—autumn leaves of topaz, amethyst, and ruby against dark emerald pines. Ahead lay an open field, a pale gold sea of dry grass, flattening, billowing, shimmering under the pressure of an amiable breeze. Oh, how fine the day, how good to be alive and striding swiftly through the aromatic, crackling wild grass, for one stolen moment free of all responsibility.

The open field ended in an abrupt precipice, and she dropped down into the grass, broke a strand, sniffed it, tilted her head, and looked up to the limitless blue sky.

I am happy, she thought. Right now, in this moment, with insects buzzing in the grass near her ear and the sun hot on her hair and butterflies with iridescent wings chasing each other across the tops of the bending reeds and somewhere a mockingbird calling liquidly. She would say to life, Stop right here, if she could, before the sun sank a fraction in the sky or the shadows lengthened an inch, while she lay on her back with eyes closed, knowing Sophy was sleeping her way back to health in the cabin, knowing Vail was down in town getting the precious, strengthening food and would be coming back soon. He would get eggs and chickens and vegetables, too, impossible as they were to find. He could do anything he set out to do. And tonight beside the campfire he would tell her stories about the nonsensical doings down below in Dead Man Bar and make her laugh, and overhead battalions of wild geese flying south would darken the moon.

Her back itched. The stiff, dry grass was poking through her dress. She rolled over, scratched vigorously, parted the weedy growth, and peeked through.

In the river below she could see dozens of men squatting in the icy water, patiently washing pans of sand, hoping that when the lighter debris was gone, a grain or two of shining yellow might remain. It was backbreaking work that often brought on heat stroke from the intense sun or rheumatism or pneumonia from the constant immersion in frigid water, this in young, hardy, healthy men.

Fools, all of them were fools, she thought, and Ethan had been the biggest fool of all, leaving the slow but comparatively sure rewards of cattle ranching to follow the will-o'-the-wisp of gold. She could see for herself, even if Vail had not pointed it out, that the merchant at the general store was getting far richer, far faster than any of the miners, and was doing it almost effortlessly on their hardworking backs. Well, hadn't it always been so? Anyone with brains lived off the work of others, and Ethan ought to have known it.

Still, she had some understanding of the passion that was driving these men. While passing through mining camps, she, too, had seen the exultation in the eyes of a man who found a fair-size lump; she, too, had seen the seductive gleam of yellow metal glittering among the rocks and had had to fight the desire to leap from her horse, grab the knife from Vail's belt, and start scratching in the earth like a madwoman. It was a disease as old as man, this craving for quick wealth.

She sat up. The sun was beginning to burn. She could feel the freckles popping out on her nose, and her arms itched from the scratchy grass. Across the field the woods were dim, deep, and inviting. She ought to go to the cabin and see if Sophy needed anything, but . . .

She skipped across the field, jumping over rocks with her skirts up like a child. It was cool, almost chill in the woods, and so dark after the brilliant sun that for a moment she was blind. Somewhere water bubbled lightheartedly as it homed toward the big river, and the very sound was cool.

Noisy mountain jays quarreled overhead and darted insolently close to her, big, bright blue birds, fat with acorns, wearing their long black crests like crowns. The sound of the creek was nearer. She climbed down a short incline.

> Ol' Miss, she prommis me
> Dat when she die she set me free,
> But she bin daid many a year ago
> An' yer Ah'm hoein' de same ol' row.

A soft, true tenor voice was rising up from the creek bottom. Marin stood posed, half scared, half curious, ready to run if need be.

The voice subsided to a vibrant hum. It came from under what appeared to be a careless heap of brush piled against a tree. She stepped back, intending to retreat quietly, skidded on the slippery pine needles, and went to her knees with a startled, "Damnation!"

The brush pile exploded, and greenery flew past her. A man rose up, tall, skinny, and shining black, with clothing that was nothing but tattered rags and a glare so ferocious that it pinned her where she sat.

But his voice, when he spoke, was as soft as the song. "Whut you doin', missy? You kin git hu't, runnin' round disyere fores' alone."

His accent was of the deep South, familiar and steadying, but what on earth was he doing in the California mountains? She got to her feet, brushed the clinging pine needles from her skirt, and pulled from dim memory the manner she had used back home in Maryland.

"What is your name, boy?"

"Jeremy, missy."

"Well, Jeremy." What to do now? He might be a freedman, since he was out here by himself, but she had heard of Southern gold seekers' bringing their slaves west to do their digging for them. Was his owner somewhere about? Back home she would not have hesitated to ask—indeed, it would have been her duty—but years away from the South had worked a subtle change in her that she was not aware of and would have disapproved of if she had recognized, and delicacy stopped her tongue. You did not inquire closely into a man's circumstances or background, not even a black man's, in California. It would be a violation of good manners, for there was no telling what embarrassments he had shed coming west. The unspoken agreement was that past difficulties were best left in the past.

"Well, Jeremy . . . why, you're hurt."

He was leaning on a stripped branch that served as a cane, and below his ragged pants his right ankle was swollen. He looked down at it with disgust.

"Stepped in a rabbit hole, missy. It do hu't some since den. Busted mah haid open, too."

"Let me see it. Sit down."

He looked doubtful but folded his long frame down onto the heap of brush. There was a deep laceration in his scalp, but it was drawing together nicely. She poked at his swollen ankle.

"Does that hurt?"

"No'm."

She took his bare foot in her hands and gently turned it.

"Dat hu'ts!"

"I think it's a sprain. I'd wrap it if I had . . ." She looked around. "Is this your camp? Where are your food and equipment?"

"Food." His sigh was almost a groan. "Ain' got none. I made a rabbit trap, but the li'l dickens was too smart."

"How long since you've eaten?"

"Foah, fi' days, mebbe. You and the gentman was here."

"Have you been spying on us?" She thought of the nights she and Vail had sat beside the campfire, outlined in the light. It was creepy, being watched, unknowing, from the silent, shadowy forest.

"Lawd, no," he answered quickly, taken aback by the sudden accusation. "Not me, missy. I was seein' to dat li'l gal wid yaller hair, and when I falls in de hole an' hits mah haid, I did'n think so good fer a while. Den when I gits mah cane made and comes hobblin' back, you is dere, and I is glad you is. She was shore a sick chile, pore birdy. How is she doin'?"

The water by Sophy's bed, the clothes washed and laid out to dry—she should have known Wes hadn't done any of that, the skunk. In an altogether different, somewhat abashed tone she said, "My sister is getting well. Did you—were you taking care of her before we came?"

"Yo sistuh, huh? Well, I ain' surprised. I been thinkin' mebbe you was relatives. Yes'm, I brung in water and sech after dat man run away, but I did'n do much else. Not much you kain do 'bout de cholera. You jest gits well or you doesn't."

His medical philosophy was in sympathy with Vail's, she thought wryly. And he hadn't done just a kindly deed, but a brave one, for he'd known it was cholera and had taken care of Sophy anyway. He was the "Jemmy" she had cried out for in her delirium.

She looked at him directly, and his eyes faltered and dropped. In her own mind she was certain. He was no freedman, he was a runaway, and her obligation was to return him to his owner if she could. But he had cared for Sophy and then had stayed nearby to watch when he could have slipped deeper into the forest. She was beholden to him. Ethics never had been Marin's long suit, and this was a fine point. Well, it would all come clear in her mind at some future time. For now she would do the obvious, which was to feed him and bind up his ankle.

They sat by the fire after feasting on a delicious, heartening stew of chicken, onions, and potatoes, with juicy purple grapes for dessert. The brandy bottle was now being passed from Vail to Jeremy. Marin was dubious about this, as she had never before seen liquor allowed a colored man except at Christmastime, but it cheered Jeremy so much that she decided not to object.

Sophy had cried out in delight when he hobbled in, clung to his hand and wept tears of weakness and pleasure, and generally carried on so that Marin was a trifle testy as she fed her the good chicken broth and rice she had made. It was all very well to show gratitude, but effusiveness was in poor taste, and, besides, what about the many days and nights of hard labor she had put in—and Vail, too. Sophy hadn't thanked him yet.

But now Marin was fed and feeling content, and Vail jarred her peaceful mood when he said, "The expressman came into camp today. Shouldn't you send a letter home by him? It will be weeks before we can get Sophy on a horse."

Home. It had been far in the back of her mind. She missed Carey, but he was safe in his accustomed routine, and Luz had, surprisingly, turned into a responsible nursemaid. Getting a wet nurse for Belinda had been a stroke of genius. If Marin were tied down in that department, she would have missed out on this adventure. True, it had been more than a week since the morning she'd found Sophy's bed empty and had said good-bye and "I'll let you know" to a frantic Delphine. Her aunt would be in a frenzy of anxiety by now, and so would Papa and Mama if they realized she was gone. It was up to Delphine to invent some lie that would keep them calm.

And there was Stuart to consider. If she wrote home, if he had any idea where she was, he would buckle on his guns and come roaring after her, spoiling everything. It shocked her to realize that she didn't want him here. Once she had believed that she could not face life without him, but right now she was marvelously content with things as they were, and she intended to be back in San Francisco and have her plans for the future well advanced before he got to her.

She twisted a grape from its stem, chewed it, and answered, "No, I don't think I'll write. Aunt Delphine knew I'd probably be gone for a while, and Stuart won't be home for ages. I'll explain everything when we get back."

Vail said nothing. She took a quick look at his face, wondering how her speech had gone down.

He was watching her across the fire, and she had the uneasy feeling that he could see every one of her hidden thoughts. She muttered something about hearing Sophy call and went inside the cabin—anything to get away from his eyes.

Chapter 18

It was a raw, blustery December day. Far out in the Pacific a storm snarled at the ships caught in its path, snapped stout oak masts, ripped heavy canvas sails, ravaged and sank one unlucky vessel of the China trade with all hands lost, and let San Francisco, a thousand miles away, know of its passing with a bitter, biting wind that churned the dark gray surface of the bay.

Inside Dennis Timothy's office at the corner of Montgomery and Clay streets, an iron stove was producing a pleasurable warmth in the room that matched the satisfaction in Marin's heart. Everything was working out exactly as she had hoped. Mr. Timothy was an Irishman, with little blue eyes bright in a whiskey-red face, and a mind as tough and cagey as her own. Gerald Crown said he was the best building contractor in the city, hard-driving, a terror to his workmen, but the best, exactly what she wanted. She included Gerald in her smile. He was being very much the lawyer today, his face bland, his eyes missing nothing. So far he had let her do most of the talking.

"Speed is essential," she said. "One day soon I shall want a larger house, a fine brick house with all the elegancies my family is accustomed to, and if your work is satisfactory, I'll employ you to build it. But my parents must move to the city immediately, and a hotel will not do for them. Can you really have a decent, comfortable house ready before Christmas?"

Mr. Timothy whistled and puffed out his words as though working past some great obstruction in his bulbous nose. "Indeed, ma'am, I can. New York and Philadelphia are shipping wood houses in sections, thousands of 'em. Prefabrications are arriving from all over Europe and even from China, though I don't use them because the assembly crews come with the houses, straight from Canton. All my gangs are good, honest Irish workmen who can put up a prefabricated wood house with plate glass windows, wallpapered, and painted to your taste in a week, week and a half at the outside. If you're in a real hurry, I can be providing you with a corrugated iron house complete in half a day."

"Corrugated iron?"

"Or sheet metal. They do get hot as a pistol in the summertime, and while 'tis true they'll never burn, I've seen 'em melt down to a puddle in some of these fires we've had."

Marin had a brief, unhappy picture of her family living in an iron box that melted down around them like ice cream during one of San Francisco's periodic conflagrations. "No, wood is what I want. A nice, two-story colonial, painted white, and a portico with pillars."

"Pillars," Mr. Timothy wheezed, looking nonplussed. "Well, I don't know that we could manage pillars. They'd cost."

"Money is not a problem."

A crafty expression entered and left his eyes, followed by a wide, guileless look.

"Not a problem. My, 'tis a clever position to be in, is it not, Gerald? And on that subject, ma'am, will your fine husband come here to sign the contract, or must I go to him, busy man that he is?"

"This is not Mr. Severance's house. I am arranging for it myself."

Dennis Timothy leaned back in his swivel chair until only his fingertips remained on the edge of his new oak desk. The affability in his eyes was replaced by dawning comprehension combined with wary curiosity.

" 'Tis your house, not your husband's? You'll be the one who's paying for it? You'll be the owner?"

"I shall."

His face closed in disapproval. "Meaning no offense, ma'am, but you can't do that. The home is the lady's bailiwick—'tis a thing every proper thinking gentleman will agree—but the paying and the owning, now that's the man's."

Although Gerald had done his best to prepare her for this, Marin's temper began to rise. This coarse man with his red face and stupid opinions and complacent assumption of superiority, presuming to tell her what she could and could not do, because she was a woman. Here she sat with money in her pocket—or, at least, within her reach—and he said she couldn't buy what she wanted with it. He wouldn't be so condescending to a man who didn't have two nickels to rub together. "Would you approve if I planned to buy a bonnet or a new dress?" she inquired with a pleasantness that caused Dennis Timothy to relax too soon.

"That's the ticket. You trot out and buy yourself some fripperies and let Mr. Severance and me worry about the house. And you looking so pretty and genteel, he'll consider his money well spent."

"It is my money," she said in a steely tone.

He sighed and folded his hands in a firm, final gesture. "Beg pardon, ma'am. You're a woman and a married one. 'Tis your husband's money, and 'tis he who must sign the contract. I can't start work without it." At the expression on her face he appealed almost plaintively, "Would you explain to her, Gerald? There's a good lad."

With a sparkle in his eyes Gerald said smoothly, "We have no problem here at all, Dennis. Mrs. Severance didn't mean that the property is legally hers. She is acting for her father, who is an invalid. It is his money—hers only in the sense that she is his dutiful and loving daughter, carrying out his wishes. It is he who will sign the contract as soon as she presents it to him."

During these remarks Marin kept her eyes down, knowing the fury they would reveal should she raise them. If what Gerald had told her in his office this morning was correct, she stood little chance of achieving her aims except through men and by their tolerance. "They have tradition and the law behind them, you see, and most important, they have the power," Gerald had said. Galling as it was, she knew he was right.

By an exercise of will her reasoning mind took control of her mutinous heart. The corners of her mouth turned up, her lashes trembled, and an expression of vapid stupidity settled over her features. Enormous, velvet black eyes implored the man behind the desk to understand, and Dennis Timothy suddenly discovered that he did. She was a dainty thing, confused-like, but very pretty. He must have imagined that hard stare a few moments before, for her eyes were soft as dewdrops.

"Mr. Crown has the contract all ready—you do, don't you, Gerald? I don't rightly understand it, but my father will. Would you be willing . . . it would mean so much if you could begin work immediately, and I will have it signed and back in your hands just as quickly as I can."

"Well . . . I'm not one to work without a contract. I'll have to be laying out money . . ."

Gerald interposed genially, "Now, Denny, I've seen you take jobs on nothing more than a handshake, and Mrs. Severance can advance a limited amount for expenses before she sees her father. She does have a problem, with her young sister unwell here in the hotel and unable to travel, but I guarantee the contract will be on your desk within the week."

Marin leaned forward, timid but hopeful, the basque of her dress pulled taut, and Dennis Timothy, like many a man before him, wondered what she would look like without it. He looked at the dark, slender man beside her, and under his gaze Gerald's face became stern and reliable. "Well . . . if you'll be guaranteeing it, Gerald . . . where is this lot you have in mind, Mrs. Severance?"

Gerald arranged for her letter to be delivered to Little Mountain. The messenger boarded the ferry at noon, an hour after the deal had been closed for the lot on Stockton Street. At ten o'clock that evening Stuart was in her hotel room, angry, relieved, meaning well, and saying all the wrong things.

"How could you do such a thing!" he shouted, while she tried to hush him. "Two months, *two months* without a word. I've been out of my mind with worry."

"Seven weeks."

"What?"

"Seven weeks, not two months."

"Don't make game of me, Marin," he said bitterly. "To disappear off the face of the earth for two months, to stay away . . . Don't tell me you couldn't send word. Abandoning your children . . ."

"How are the children?"

". . . They're fine . . . and your poor, sick parents. Do you have any idea what such anxiety could do to them?"

"Delphine wasn't stupid enough to tell them?"

"She told them you and Sophy had gone with me, and when I came home alone, you were supposed to be visiting Logan."

"There, you see? I knew she'd manage."

"And what about me? Don't you think that I—"

"The less said about your part in all this the better, Stuart, and please lower your voice. Sophy is just next door, and she needs her rest. I don't know what it would do to her if she heard your voice like that, all angry and unreasonable . . ."

"Unreasonable, by God!"

"Lower your voice."

"Unreasonable, by God," he repeated sullenly, but in a softer tone. He felt guilty about Sophy, although he didn't really see why he should. She had committed the unforgivable. He had reacted the way any decent man would, the way her own father would, had he been able, and yet somehow it had all ended up with him in the wrong, and Sophy—who had been wickedly rebellious and unrepentant and had run away from home, of all things—was coddled and forgiven because she had nearly died of cholera. She would never have gotten cholera if she'd behaved herself and stayed home, and yet . . . he had spoken to her harshly, for her own good, but harshly, and now Marin blamed him.

He sank down in the chair next to the window, weary, but not with a physical tiredness. From under scowling brows he looked up at her. She must have been starting to get ready for bed when he came, for her hair was free of its net and lying loose and shining on her shoulders. Oh, but she was lovely with her hair like that. A thought rose to the surface of his mind, a nagging, nasty, uncomfortable idea that he had been ignoring.

"I don't care for Vail's part in this," he said, very low.

She had begun to brush her hair, dragging a slow, even stroke through the tangled curls, and she stopped in midswipe and gazed at him over her shoulder.

"Well, I don't," he said doggedly, not quite meeting her eyes and veering away from his real suspicions. "I know he's wild, he's irresponsible—always has been—but to go along with you on this . . ."

"If he hadn't gone along with me, I don't know what would have happened to me or to Sophy."

"You're playing with words again! You know what I mean. He shouldn't have encouraged you in such a harebrained scheme. He ought to have packed you home with a flea in your ear and gone after Sophy himself. He ought to have got hold of me. I was right here in San Francisco, and he knew it."

She turned on her stool and look at him very straight. "First of all, he was exceedingly responsible in this instance. He found out where Wes's claim was and got me there safely; he took care of Sophy through a messy, dangerous illness; he got us back over hundreds of miles, through all kinds of hazards and crazy miners and I don't know what all. Second, if he had told you anything, I would have gone by myself. Stuart, I couldn't have you chasing after her. I didn't know what . . . kind of situation she would be in or what you might do, after the way you acted. I couldn't have her upset again."

"Upset! Oh, God. *I* was upset!"

"You're shouting again." She resumed brushing her hair. "You ought to be grateful to Vail for pulling your chestnuts out of the fire. We have her back and no one the wiser, which was what worried you most." She sank that sword thrust swiftly, to the hilt, and went right on, "Suppose she had died up there, then you'd have something on your conscience. She could have died, alone in that miserable hut with no one who loved her, no one to even bury her. I could cry just thinking about it."

He eyed her uneasily, hoping she wouldn't cry. He couldn't cope with tears right now. It was a new idea, Vail stepping in, upright and staunch, to repair his, Stuart's, blunder and save the family name. Stuart tried very hard to do the right thing, and usually he succeeded. Always it had been Vail who was the sinner, Vail who was the disappointment and despair of their parents.

He stared at his dusty, scarred boots, feeling large and out of place in the little room. These hotels were all rickety and jerry-built. The whole damn town was jerry-built.

"What's this nonsense about a house?" he asked sulkily, and her face transformed. She whirled across the room and plopped down on his knee.

"Oh, Stuart, it's not nonsense. It's going to be the very thing. I've found a lot on Stockton Street, which is the finest residential section, near several churches, with an option to buy the lots on either side. Mr. Timothy, who is the best contractor in town, will build the house—a prefabricated house, imagine!—in only a week. The family can be settled in before Christmas."

He straightened in shock, almost dumped her on the floor, and grabbed for her. Disturbed as he was, he didn't want her off his lap. It had been too long since they had sat cozily together, and she felt deliciously soft and warm pressed against his thighs like this. He frowned but kept his hands firmly on her waist. "What in hell are you talking about? I can't leave Little Mountain. I can't live over here."

She laid a finger over his lips and felt him relax. "Dearest, I am persuaded that without proper treatment Papa and Mama will just fade away and die. We can't sit by and let that happen when a fine physician like Dr. Towle is right here in town. Why, if your mother had had the right care, she might be alive today. There's Belinda, too. She needs constant watching, just in case. We came so near losing her."

He moved uncomfortably, not liking to remember the circumstances of Belinda's birth. It had been Vail then who—oh, hell.

"So you propose to move your parents and the children to San Francisco."

"And Delphine. She loves the city. And Sophy, of course. She can't possibly go home, not for a while. She needs medical care, too, and she's so unstrung and nervous . . ." She hesitated.

"Nervous around me, you mean."

She said nothing.

Stuart drew a breath. "It's all very interesting. The best lot in the finest residential section, the best contractor, the best doctor, a house practically built . . . You haven't mentioned how much this is going to cost."

"That's the best part. We can do the whole thing for not more than thirty-five thousand."

"Dollars?"

She beamed.

He rose so suddenly that had she not been very quick, she would have landed on the floor. "Thirty-five thousand—Marin, you have gone stark, staring mad."

"Now, Stuart, before you say another word, listen to me. The lot itself I got for seventeen thousand. On Stockton Street, so near to Portsmouth Square, you can almost spit on it. Two years ago the same lot sold for fifteen dollars. What do you think it will sell for next year or the year after? That's why I took an option on the neighboring lots. Stuart, lots on the Square are going right now for over fifty thousand dollars! If only we'd bought last year when I said we should, we would have made a load of money. As it is, I got a tremendous bargain."

"A few more bargains like that and I'll go bankrupt." In anger and exasperation he ran a hand through his hair, leaving it uncharacteristically ruffled and untidy. "What am I doing? Listening to you talk about lots and options and thousands of dollars, just as if you knew . . . just as if you could decide . . . It's out of the question, Marin. That's final."

"It's already done."

"Then undo it. You know I'd never deny you anything you wanted that I could manage, but this is beyond me. I don't have thirty-five thousand dollars to spend on a house."

"Papa does."

He turned. "Your father?"

"He wants to invest in land over here; he's told me so many times. And he has the money." She sat down on the edge of the bed and talked on quietly, selecting her words with as great care and precision as she ever had in her life. "Naturally I would never think of committing you to such a debt without your consent and approval. I couldn't, since I'm only a woman." His tense pose eased a little. "But Papa is a gambler, always has been. This is his kind of adventure, the only kind he can have now. You're so different from him, Stuart, strong and steady and conservative. You and Papa are a perfect combination. He can take a flier over here and probably do very well, but only because he has you building up the ranch slowly and surely, taking no risks, backing him up. Between the two of you, you'll be the wealthiest men in California."

As she talked, the rigidity left his face and his color became less dangerously red. She said, "I think we will never regret this move, dearest. No matter what the outcome, even if Dr. Towle can't help Papa and Mama, even if Belinda . . . We'll always know we held back nothing. And we can get Sophy launched on a life of her own. We don't want her a spinster in our home for the rest of our days, do we? It will be perfect for your political career, too. You're an important man in California, and you're going to be more important, I just know it. We need a town house to properly entertain your friends, and this way we can have it without laying out a penny ourselves."

At the bar downstairs a few minutes later, Stuart faced his reflection in the gilt-framed, plate glass mirror that had come direct from France and had been installed only recently. He laid his hat on the polished mahogany wood and ordered whiskey, wishing he were back upstairs with her, in that bed, in the dark, with the moonlight silver on her skin—but as she had said, it was not possible yet. He drank the whiskey straight and ordered another. Everything she had said was true. If he agreed to this, he could never be reproached for having failed his child, his parents-in-law, his sister-in-law—the silly chit. Surprising how much Marin knew about business matters. She'd never talked so knowledgeably before, not to him. Probably because James encouraged her to read books, talked politics with her and business, too. James thought she was so smart. Well, she was smart, and there was nothing to be ashamed of in that, so long as she didn't flaunt it. He told the bartender to leave the bottle.

The whole thing would collapse without him, steady as a rock at the heart of the scheme. A town house. It had a nice ring. He did need a place here to entertain, and it would be a pleasure to have her as his hostess and show her off to his friends. And there was the comforting fact that it would be James's money at risk, not his. It might all work out very well. He poured another drink.

As soon as the door closed behind Stuart, Marin pulled off her clothes and scrambled into her nightdress. It had been a day of hard, sharp bargaining right through the last few minutes, and she was tired in mind as well as body. She sat on the edge of the bed and stared at the floor, discontent and wondering why. Stuart had responded to her arguments exactly as she intended, and yet she felt nothing but irritation. He hadn't wanted the new house or the move, he'd had no say at all in the far-reaching agreements she had made. Why had he let her get away with it? He had started out very well, justifiably furious over her long absence without a word, and all his indignation had dwindled away with a few firm words from her. Why hadn't he told her to sit down and shut up? Why hadn't he stuck to his guns about the house? Why hadn't he simply picked her up and carried her home without further debate? She would have fought him on all counts, and blood would have spilled, but she would have respected him more.

The floorboards creaked. This hotel, the Union, opened just this fall, was four and a half stories high, built of brick, containing a hundred rooms, gilt-framed mirrors, chandeliers, and fashionable furniture, the first really nice hotel in San Francisco; but still the floorboards creaked. She looked around. Sophy was standing in the open doorway between their rooms, wan, thin, childlike in her plain flannel nightgown, her big eyes clouded with anxiety.

"Is he gone?"

"What are you doing out of bed? And you've got nothing on your feet! Yes, he's gone. Come, get in with me."

Marin pulled back the blankets, and Sophy crawled in, snuggled down on the pillow, and drew the blankets up to her chin.

"He was mad, wasn't he?"

"He got over it."

The dimple appeared in Sophy's cheek. Her smiles were rare these days, and this one, twinkling, knowledgeable, made her look more like the old Sophy. "I'll bet he did."

Marin couldn't suppress a responding grin. It was so good to see that smile, so good to know with vast relief that Dr. Towle's optimism had been justified and that random chance had not struck. Sophy finally had had her monthly period, its regularity probably upset, Vail said, by the violent assault of the cholera on her system. "Settle down now. You may stay if you go right to sleep."

"Don't turn the light out, Marin. Not just yet."

There was a note in the soft voice that made Marin hesitate, her hand on the lamp.

Sophy was looking down, her fingers rubbing the edge of the blanket. "I want to thank you for what you did for me. I have to thank Vail, too, the next time I see him."

All the sharp words Marin had considered saying in the past about gratitude were forgotten. Indulgently she replied, "You don't have to thank us, honey. That's what family is for."

Sophy was silent. Then suddenly she burst out, "Oh, Marin, do you despise me? Do you think I'm a fallen woman?"

The anguish and humiliation in her face were painful to see. Marin answered swiftly, "Of course you're not a fallen woman, of course I don't despise you. What a thing to ask."

Sophy's hands went over her face. "I was such a fool! Oh, what can Vail think of me? How can I look decent people in the eye?"

"Vail thinks nothing at all except that you've been a very sick girl who needs a lot of love and care. He'd never judge you, because—well, because he wouldn't. He isn't that kind. As for decent people, you have a lot to learn, Sophy. Everybody has something to hide, usually quite a few things."

"But, sister, I'm not a . . . a . . . you know . . . anymore."

"You're not a virgin," said Marin flatly, and Sophy gasped at

the word being said right out like that. "Neither are any of the men
you know, not one, unless there's something wrong with him—
not Gerald or Michael or Vail, not any of them."

"But that's different. It's all right for men."

"It's all right for women, too, so long as they don't get caught;
you just remember that. Good heavens, Sophy, God isn't going to
hold it against you on the Day of Judgment, and that's all that
matters."

"You don't think so?"

"Of course not, and neither will anyone else as long as they
don't find out—" her voice hardened, ". . . and no one will.
Ever. We're going to live here from now on, where there are
parties to go to and lots of other interesting things to do. You'll be
Miss Gentry of Baltimore and San Francisco, and men will line up
all the way down the street just for the chance of calling on you."

Sophy's teeth bit into her pale underlip. One large tear rolled
down her cheek. "You are the best sister any girl ever had. I'll
never borrow your clothes or tell stories again, I promise."

"Go to sleep," Marin said, and turned out the lamp.

James Gentry had come a long way from the time he could not sit
upright without being held, could not feed himself or use the
chamber pot alone, could not even speak. Now he could hoist
himself out of his chair with his one good arm, pull on a shirt,
walk several steps as long as there was a railing or some support
for his left hand to hold on to. The grip of that hand was strong,
and he had learned to write with it in a slanting scrawl. But the
man he had been was forever gone, and he recognized it with a
clearsighted honesty that refused to despair.

That was not to say he wasn't bitterly frustrated at times or that
he never railed at fate; he did. Then he thrust the useless anger
aside and struggled on. As infuriating to him, almost, as his loss
of physical power was his inability at times to express his thoughts
as precisely as he intended. His mind, as agile as ever, formulated
ideas incisively, and his tongue, the traitor, sometimes failed to
relay them properly. Somewhere in nerve paths and muscles and
the convolutions of his brain, the impulse turned upside down,
and the words came out wrong. James, the word spinner, the
eloquent debater who loved to dispute and discuss and argue
endlessly, James was sometimes rendered inarticulate. Conse-
quently, he listened to Marin's story with great attention and
formed his words with even greater care.

"You told Stuart this new house is—my desire?"

"It is, isn't it, Papa?"

He looked from under an ironical eyebrow at the daughter he loved so much and sometimes felt he knew so little. How did a parent judge a child cherished from infancy through so many difficult years? How did a father see past the familiar features into the mind behind it? He could almost laugh at the way she had nailed Stuart into a box with a few well-driven strokes—and yet it wasn't funny. Never had he genuinely warmed to that young man, try as he might, but Marin loved him, and a wife should be honest with her husband. Stuart ought to blister her bottom. He would regret it if he didn't.

The property, now, she was right about that. This was the time to buy, although thirty-five thousand dollars would take some juggling of accounts and drawing on funds from the bank in New York, maybe even a loan. But it was the right move. He would go mad if he stayed immobile at Little Mountain much longer. Not for a moment did he believe that this Dr. Towle could help him, but Rose, dear Rose, his love . . . she was sitting across from them on the porch, working indifferently at the needlework Marin had placed in her hands, a sweet, absent smile on her face . . . maybe Dr. Towle could help Rose. There was nothing to lose, and it would be exhilarating, living in the hustling city across the bay, in the heart of the whirlwind.

"Not only your desire, Papa," Marin was saying. "I said you told me to do it. Please back me up in that. And Mr. Timothy wants your signature on the contract. Will you sign it?"

He rubbed his chin in the old way, nodded agreement slowly, his eyes sharp and worried on her face. He saw her smile in relief.

"Daughter," he began, sorting his thoughts out carefully, "daughter, don't . . . manipulate those who love you, because . . ." he hesitated, struggling for expression, "because . . . it is their love, their trust in you that makes manipulation possible. Deceive the rest of the world if you must, but never . . . never those you love."

Her eyes were startled. "Papa, I've done this for those I love. It's for all of us. You and Mama . . . Sophy . . . Stuart, too."

He patted her hand and held it. "I know, chicken. You mean it for the best, but . . . Marin, always deal the cards faceup with those you love. You'll pay dearly someday if you don't."

"Yes, Papa," she answered automatically, her hand still in his, her eyes on Stuart, who was coming up from the corral without his usual springy stride.

Stuart was not normally a heavy drinker, and the amount of

whiskey he had drunk at the Union Hotel last night had left him with a headache of monumental proportions. He saw Marin walking down to meet him, looking happy. Thank God she was in a good frame of mind. He couldn't take any stormy confrontations today.

From the porch James waved and smiled his lopsided smile, a shrunken figure, and Stuart recalled with peculiar force the dynamic, youthful man he once had been. He thought he would rather kill himself than be like that, chained to a chair, without power, without future, without sex—Stuart thought a lot about sex these days, which was not his habit. It would be intolerable to be like James, cut off from all hope of such good things. But the man was nearly sixty. Perhaps you didn't care much when you reached so great an age.

"Darling," Marin called gaily. "Papa is so pleased! And Mama and Delphine are just delighted."

Undoubtedly Delphine was, thought Stuart. Rose didn't look as though she'd heard a word that had been said.

"That's good, Marin, that's fine." He put his arm around her waist, and they walked up to the porch together.

Dennis Timothy's word was good. His honest Irish workmen had the house on Stockton Street assembled, painted, and wallpapered in seven days. It stood on a stretch of almost barren ground that ascended from gentle hillocks into a series of steep barricades. Marin planted small trees behind the house to complement the two wind-bent oaks in the front, trees that made the lot more valuable because they were rare on these desolate slopes, and put lilac bushes beside the front porch. She also cast acquisitive eyes on the nearby hilly but buildable land, wishing she had taken more options. With Delphine to help she spent two long, arduous, thoroughly satisfying days buying furniture, curtains, carpets, linens, a mammoth kitchen stove, cooking utensils, a moderately good set of china as well as a set for every day—the really fine china and crystal could be bought later, perhaps by next year.

On the day the largest pieces of furniture were to be delivered, she left the hotel and walked to Stockton Street as soon as the sun was up, long enough before deliveries could be expected, to pace off the rooms again, to think and to plan. Early as it was, the town was humming with activity, and the streets were busy. One man made an admiring but indelicate suggestion as she passed, and Jeremy, stalking along beside her, halted in midstride with such an

intimidating glare on his bony black face that the fellow immediately realized his error and faded into the crowd. They walked on,
the vicious expression on Jeremy's face being replaced by one of
amusement.

Marin suppressed her own smile. What luck it had been to find
Jeremy. What even greater good fortune that he had accepted her
offer of employment, for in the long run, his presence, more than
anything else, would mean her freedom. She had made the offer
tentatively, on the steamer before they had arrived back in town
with Sophy, not wanting to be turned down, not knowing what
plans he might have for the future. In him she recognized a spirit
kindred to her own, a tactician in the war of life who figured the
long odds and looked far ahead. It would have to be a tempting
proposition, well worth his while, for him to stay on with the
family. So Marin offered him a comfortable home in the stimu-
lating environs of the most exciting, packed-with-opportunity
town in the world, time off for his own pursuits, wages high
enough to build a stake yet not so high that he would build it too
soon. He accepted with a surface hesitancy and an underlying glee
that made her wish she'd set the wages somewhat lower.

But the thing was done, and she could not regret it. Not on this
day, with the sun glittering on the bay and the stiff salt breeze
fluttering her skirt as she walked in safety through the streets
toward her wonderful house.

Dennis Timothy was already on the site, watching the crew lay
the last shingles on the stable behind the house. It was to be a
good, roomy stable (no jerry-built barns for Mrs. Severance), with
space for four horses and two carriages (Mrs. Severance thought
big and planned for the future), and a weathertight, comfortable,
commodious room above it for that ornery-looking black servant
who was always just a step behind her.

There they came, on the crack of morn as usual, and Jeremy had
a picnic basket over his arm, which meant that herself intended to
stay most of the day. She always brought food when settling in for
a siege of harassment. He smiled winningly and lifted his brown
felt hat. "And the best o' the day to ye, ma'am." Maybe it was her
father's money making the payments, but it was her house. Every
day she came by and, more often than not, stayed to watch each
nail go in, find fault with his boys' craftsmanship, double-check
his decisions, disparage the quality of his materials, run her
fingers over the edges of cabinets and complain about the fit,
announce after a cursory glance at the structure that it was out of
plumb. What did a girl know about plumb?

She had rejected out of hand the fine front door he'd acquired for her and insisted on a larger, heavier door of solid oak with a big brass knob and lock, a door never intended for a prefabricated house. It had meant cutting a larger doorway, and this had led to other difficulties, none of which she appreciated or thanked him for. She hadn't been willing to pay extra, either, claiming he had contracted for an impressive front door and the one he offered did not impress her.

She inclined her head at his greeting, the feather on her bonnet bobbing saucily, her red lips curling upward at the corners. It was a new dress she was wearing—at least he hadn't seen it before—of a rich, blue, slithery material that whispered and rustled when she walked, and that fitted as trim and snug as all her gowns. His dour mood lifted. Doing business with women was always difficult, irrational creatures that they were, but when the woman was as young and pretty as this one, there were compensations.

It had rained in the night, and the yard was muddy. She crossed it gingerly, lifting her skirts. The lanky black man slouched toward the stables with the grin on his face that Mr. Timothy never quite trusted and an appraising, possessive look upward at the room he would occupy.

Inside Marin set the picnic basket on the hearth and paced off the parlor, mentally placing sofas and chairs and tables, then reversing everything, trying each piece in a different spot. The long velvet sofa should face the hearth—Lord, she hoped the chimney drew properly. You never knew until you lit the first fire. Or perhaps the sofa should sit before the big window. No, two comfortable chairs there, with the new drum table between, chairs turned slightly to take advantage of the view—the spreading town below, the white-winged ships, the blue, shining bay, the road leading straight up the hill, where every visitor could be seen long before he arrived . . .

She leaned forward to peer at the rider who had escaped her notice and was already turning in at the place where the gate would be once the picket fence was built. Heavens, it was Vail. He was dismounting by the thin, young magnolia tree she had planted as soon as the land became hers and tying his reins to its slender trunk. Unconsciously she patted her smooth hair, went out onto the porch, and waved.

"Good morning. What are you doing here?"

He walked up the muddy trail where the brick path soon would be, looking the house over with interest. "I came to see the marvel."

"It's hardly a marvel—" She scowled in Dennis Timothy's direction. "There are several matters I have to take up with him."

Mr. Timothy, seeing the scowl, came stumping over with the intent of heading her off. "Vail, how are ye this fine morning, and how do you like the results o' me handiwork? Splendid, ain't she?" He waved an encompassing hand at the house.

Marin's frown deepened. "Mr. Timothy, the kitchen walls are the color of old mustard. If you recall, I said daffodil yellow with just a touch of lemon. The kitchen is on the shady side of the house, and I want it to seem sunny all day long. Servants cannot be happy if they must work in a dingy hole. Also, three bedrooms remain to be papered, and the beds and wardrobes are arriving today. I can't have paste dripping on my new furniture, so you must have it all done before noon. Come on in, Vail."

She turned and sailed into the house.

"Dingy hole! It's a beautiful kitchen," Mr. Timothy said indignantly. "Just you look at it, Vail, and see if you don't agree." But he said it in a low mutter that Marin wouldn't hear.

"Dennis, lad, don't involve me in your squabbles. I advise you to repaint her kitchen."

"She's fanatic about keeping domestics happy. Spoils that black boy rotten." Dennis sent a resentful glance in Jeremy's direction. "Seems she lost a servant she valued once because the girl was dissatisfied, and she ain't going to let it happen again."

"Yes, I know about the servant she lost. You should honor her for it, Dennis. You've thrown off your old world shackles and got yourself an employer who cares about the problems of the working man."

"Not this workingman she don't, by God!" Dennis jammed on his hat and went down the steps. At the bottom he shouted at Jeremy, "Here now, no need to go up there just yet. We're not finished, you know."

Marin came back to the door. "What is he hollering about? I won't have him plaguing Jeremy."

"Don't worry about Jeremy. I'll back him against Dennis anytime, and you against them both. Do you really want me to come in with this mud on my boots?"

"Oh, scrape them on the step. I must get some bootscrapers the next time I'm in town. What did you mean, you'd back me? Mr. Timothy would hear no complaints from me if only he'd do what I want."

"Exactly. Ah, this is very nice. A fine view, too." He walked to the window to look down to the sea, and her look of annoyance was replaced by pleasure.

"Come, see. I'll show you all around!"

She danced ahead of him through each room, up the stairs and down the hall, throwing open doors and holding up rolls of wallpaper in the rooms as yet undone so he could see the effect, and finally back to the parlor.

"Now here . . ." She spun around, her eyes shining. "Here I've saved the best for last. My parlor will be perhaps not elegant like yours—" She waited hopefully for him to talk about his house, but he said nothing. "But it will be cozy and homelike, and that's good for a start, don't you think?"

"What could be better? Tell me what you've bought."

She moved through the room, marking out exactly where the plum velvet sofa, the settee, the occasional tables, the lamps and footstools would be placed, pleased that he was interested and wishing he hadn't fobbed her off again about the big brick house he had built for himself up on Rincon Hill, a house that was, so people said, the biggest and finest residence in San Francisco.

He pointed to the end of the room opposite the stairs. "And is nothing to go there? Or have I forgotten?"

"That's for the piano."

"You've bought a piano, too? Little Mountain must be doing well."

She tried hard not to look embarrassed. She hadn't meant to mention the piano. "Little Mountain is doing well enough, but I haven't bought it yet. Maybe next year. I'm afraid to put anything where it belongs because if I filled the space, I might never get it—that's superstitious, isn't it? But we must have one—a Chickering like we had back home, or maybe a Baldwin, a big grand made of inlaid rosewood. So you see why I need the space."

"And you're going to get it next year, after all this? Marin, do you have any idea what a piano would cost in New York, let alone shipped out here?"

She sat on the stone hearth, rummaged in her basket of food, and took out a piece of chicken. "Five or six thousand dollars? Have a chicken leg."

"No, thank you, not at nine o'clock in the morning. I see you do know the cost. How are you going to manage it by next year?"

"I'm not exactly sure, but I will somehow."

He sat down beside her. "I didn't know you were musically inclined."

She polished an apple and took a bite. "You don't know

everything about me. Mama made us all learn because you can't be a cultured person if you don't appreciate music, and besides, it's good discipline. But I was the only one who took to it. Sophy's tone deaf, and Ethan liked horses better. Mama inherited our Chickering from *her* mama, and we couldn't bring it with us. Papa promised he would get her another, and he was never quite able to. I think it might help her get well if she had it. She had to leave behind so much that mattered to her." Her voice softened. "And I miss it, too. If I'm upset, it soothes me. If I'm blue, it cheers me up. I can put all the feelings inside me into the music, and then I feel better. Can you understand that?"

"I think so."

"Anyway, when I say next year, I say *maybe* first. It's what Papa always says. It means that's what I'm going to do sometime and, God willing, maybe soon. It's like a promise to myself, and it always comes true eventually. Of course it has to be something that could happen, not an impossible wish, like Ethan walking through that door or Papa being the way he used to be. But Papa getting better or buying a rosewood piano, now that's possible and not really superstitious, do you see?"

"Yes, I see."

A voice came booming through the open window. Dennis Timothy was engaged in a loud argument with someone.

Marin sighed in exasperation. "That man is always in the vilest temper and usually over nothing at all." She hopped up and leaned out the window. "Yes, there he is up on the roof bullyragging Jeremy." She called out, "Jeremy, will you step down here for a minute, please?" and came back and settled on the hearth again. "I certainly would pick another contractor if I had it to do over. Why Gerald recommended him is beyond me. I was planning to ask for the loan of one of his men to help Jeremy with the furniture moving, but he'll probably refuse outright or else try to charge extra. He is the most difficult man."

Vail was tapping his riding crop against his boot with a sparkle in his eyes, but he said only, "I'm going down to Monterey for a few days or I'd help you myself, but I could ask Usual to come over."

"Oh?" She had heard about Vail's household help from Gerald. He had an Irish housekeeper-cook, Mrs. Moon, and Usual MacIntyre, a derelict he had picked up on his travels and who served, whenever the mood struck him, as valet or gardener or steward, take your pick. Her eyes were bright with curiosity.

"Would Usual do it? Gerald says he's very much the prima donna."

"Gerald talks too much. Usual is just as susceptible as the next man to a pretty girl. He'd probably do it for one of your very nice smiles."

"Where did he ever get such a nickname?" she asked, pleased at the compliment.

"He swears it's his baptismal name. I asked him once how he got it, and he said, 'Well, sir, your mother named you Vail, and my mother named me Usual,' which shut me up. However, another time he told me that he was the twelfth of fifteen children and his father was a traveling man. Whenever his father came home, another child arrived nine months later, so when he was born, his mother named him Usual. For the usual thing, you see."

"Oh," said Marin.

"He had a brother named Reluctant, so you can see how his mother's mind was running."

He picked up the hat he had dropped on the hearth. She followed him onto the porch and said tentatively, "There is something else you could do for me, if you would."

"If it's back to the gold country in pursuit of another relative . . ."

She laughed. "No, not that. But I do wish you would stop by the hotel and see Sophy. Just a casual visit. She's been in a funny frame of mind since we got back, and she worries."

"What about?"

"About your—your opinion of her, Vail. You're the only one who knows about Wes and—everything. Stuart knows, of course, but she doesn't care what he thinks. She does value your good opinion; she values it highly. If you would assure her of your continued respect, in a roundabout way, it would do her a world of good." It had been a difficult speech to make, for it brought up too many subjects that had to be ignored between ladies and gentlemen, things the two of them had discussed only with extreme circumlocution even when washing Sophy's naked body in that cabin in the mountains. She could never have brought herself to say a word of it for anyone but Sophy, not with his eyes watching every change in her face.

He said, "That's the cholera. It leaves people with peculiar moods. I'll drop by before I leave today and tell her we'll go to Mrs. Tierney's new ice cream parlor when she's back on her feet. That ought to cheer her up. I never saw anyone enjoy ice cream like Sophy."

"Oh, she would love that." Her discomfiture washed away in a tide of gratitude. He had put all the blame for Sophy's unhappiness on the cholera.

They said their farewells, and Marin watched Vail walk back through the mud to his horse.

"Send Usual over today, if he'll come," she called, then, with narrowed eyes, turned her attention back toward Dennis Timothy.

By Christmas Day, 1850, the family was settled in comfortably enough that guests could be invited for Christmas dinner.

Vail's friends Mr. and Mrs. Harry Callendar arrived—he friendly, talkative, pleased to meet the Gentry and Severance families; she plump, overdressed, beaming, carrying two rum fruitcakes to add to the feast. Baroness von Helsdorf arrived in a cloud of furs and expensive French perfume, wearing a bonnet of roses and delicate veiling that made Marin's heart turn over with envy. Anna devoted herself most of the afternoon to James and Rose, managing with ladylike charm and vivacity to bring a light to James's eyes and a spark of interest to Rose. Gerald Crown came bearing six bottles of French champagne, and just as the two fat geese were coming out of the oven, Vail walked in with gifts for the children, a smile and a cordial word for everyone, including Stuart, and a vitality so cheering that to Marin the new parlor seemed prettier and the china faces of the angels on the mantel more benign. Only Charles Towle of all those invited had regretfully declined, pleading a prior engagement. So almost everyone she was fond of was there, everyone except Ethan, dead these many months and buried in a grave they would never see.

She offered a steadying hand to Carey, who was agilely clambering onto his new rocking horse and needed no help from anyone, and then sat down by the fire. This was the sort of thing she'd had in mind in moving to the city. Stuart hadn't scowled all evening, and Papa and Mama had even joined in the carol singing. Sophy, who had slipped into the room with an uncertain, almost frightened look in her eyes, was now giggling at a story Vail was telling her, and a delicate, becoming flush had appeared in her thin cheeks. The collie, Angus, had made a fool of himself greeting each guest and was now sleeping the sleep of the well-fed and pure of heart on the warm stone hearth.

A most successful party, a truly splendid Christmas, all the guests agreed as they took their leave. At midnight the family went up to bed, everyone but Marin, who stayed behind to see Vail to the door.

The night air was moist and salty, and fog clung to the tops of the two precious oaks in the front yard. Vail said, "Come outside. I have a favor to ask."

She stepped out onto the porch and closed the door. The only pillars Dennis Timothy had been able to supply were six white-painted two-by-fours, which supported the overhang of the roof. Even so, it was a most satisfactory veranda, broad and long and suitable for sitting on during warm summer evenings. But as yet there were no chairs or porch swing, and Vail sat on the top step and pulled her down beside him. The night air was damp, and she wished she had her shawl.

He said, "You're crowded here. Could you make room for Logan?"

"Why would she want to come over here?"

"For the same reason you did. She's cut off from the world at Longridge, she has nothing in her life but work, and she's lonely."

With a wry little laugh Marin said, "It's true, we are crowded. She might go crazy with the hubbub."

"Hubbub is what she needs. More than anything she needs a home."

"But, Vail, she has a home. She was cross with Malcolm when Elizabeth died, but . . ."

"Cross is one way to put it. There's a more urgent reason, however. My father is getting married again."

She stared at him.

"With Elizabeth hardly cold? Who to?"

"Glenna Morgan."

"Glenna? Merciful heavens." Her mind ran rapidly back over the last two years at Longridge. Glenna, dutiful and indispensable at Elizabeth's side all during her illness, Glenna supporting Malcolm Severance in his grief, Glenna and her Bible reading and her high-toned, genteel ways.

"The viper," she said slowly.

He shrugged. "She does take advantage of opportunities."

"Just like Wes. They're all of a piece, those two. And I always thought she was so religious."

"Nothing irreligious about getting married. Maybe it's her piety that appeals to him—though I doubt it."

Glenna, plump and bosomy as a pouter pigeon in her tight basques, widening her prominent brown eyes innocently. "It's disgusting. She's as young as his daughter."

"Younger. Logan will be twenty-three in February."

"And all the time she was taking care of Elizabeth she must have been . . . when I think how Logan and I helped her, taught her how to behave in polite society . . ."

"She would have learned anyway."

"And your father, why he's old!"

"A man is never too old for a pretty girl. Even Father. Maybe he found something in the Bible that said it was the righteous thing to do."

"How can you laugh about it? I'd think you'd feel so bad. Stuart will."

"Why should I feel bad? Mother's dead, and maybe it's just as well. Sometimes I think she died just to get away from him. And he may have found his match in Glenna. I hope so."

"Stuart hasn't heard a whisper of this. How did you find out?"

"Michael told me before he went back upriver. He had a letter from her. I didn't want to spoil Stuart's holiday by telling him, and I wouldn't have mentioned it to you except for Logan. Things have been difficult for her at home in the past, but it will be hell from now on."

Glenna, the mistress of Longridge, ruling the home that had been Logan's. How Glenna would lord it over her, once she was in control. What a future for Logan.

She is my sister-in-law, and I love her, Marin thought. Besides, Vail had rescued her sister at some jeopardy to himself when he owed Sophy nothing. She couldn't refuse to extend a hand now that his sister was in need. But—where to put her? It would be hard cramming another person into a house already bursting at the seams.

"Let's see. We have seven bedrooms, none of them very big. Mine is in front over the parlor, and Papa and Mama are next door. Then Sophy—she needs her privacy right now, so I wouldn't want to put Logan with her. There's Delphine. Even Logan couldn't live in peace with Delphine. The children and Luz have the largest room, and they need every bit of it because it's the playroom, too. I guess I could give her the back bedroom and move Mrs. Victoria and her baby into the little cubbyhole behind the kitchen, but it's so tiny, and I want it for my office."

"That's six rooms," Vail pointed out.

There was a silence while Marin scrambled for something to say. She had stepped into the pit without seeing it gaping before her, and now Vail knew something she'd just as soon he didn't know.

"Uh, yes. There's Stuart's bedroom. He can't leave the ranch too often, but it must be ready for him when he does come over."

"Naturally." The half-light hid any expression that might be on his face. "I talked to Mrs. Victoria this evening. She seems happy here."

Marin snatched at the change of subject. "Oh, yes. She loves the city, and we're lucky to have her. Belinda still needs her, of course, and she's a better cook than Berta. I was afraid she wouldn't leave home, but she just told her older girls to mind the little ones and left Rodolfo to his siestas. She goes downtown every day, scours the markets for the best seafood and vegetables, and bullies the shopkeepers into giving her good prices. It's amazing what a business head she has."

"There are brains in that family. She tells me Fermina has a good job and Petra is making money in the millinery business."

"So I heard," replied Marin shortly. Every time she thought of Petra and her successful business, she felt annoyed. Was he grinning? She closed her lips on her opinion of Petra's money-making abilities. Already she had revealed too much of herself tonight.

The front door opened behind them, and yellow lamplight fell on the painted floorboards of the porch.

"'Scuse me, Miss Marin. You bettuh come upstairs, Mistuh Stuart say, 'cause Mistuh Carey ain't goin' ter bed widout he takes his rockin' hawse."

"Oh dear, he does love that horse, Vail. You couldn't have brought him anything nicer. Tell Mr. Stuart I'll be up directly, Jeremy."

From above there was a loud, furious, "I won't have it, by God!" followed by a howl of rage. Stuart and Carey. The three on the porch looked up, and Jeremy said, "You bettuh come right now, missy. Mistuh Stuart don' have de patience ob Job."

He left the door ajar, and Marin could see his long, limber body folding down as he moved the fire screen and banked the fire. "I know what I'll do," she said. "It's simple, Vail. Jeremy's room is over the stables, and he's very satisfied. I'll have Mr. Timothy build on another room—I'll bet he can do it in a day—and put Mrs. Victoria out there. Tell Logan to come just as soon as she can pack. We'll have such fun! Oh, dear life, I wish I could see your father's face when he finds out she's leaving."

"I'm going to enjoy that myself," he said.

BOOK THREE

Chapter 19

February arrived in San Francisco with gossamer breezes that ruffled the calm surface of the bay and transparent morning mists that dissolved quickly under a gentle sun. The terror of the previous fall's cholera epidemic was only a nightmare remembered. Pervasive filth was a constant anxiety to the Board of Health, but most citizens were too busy working, manipulating, buying, selling, and having one hell of a good time to worry.

Fortune hunters, drifters, criminals, hopeful entrepreneurs endowed with widely differing portions of honor and uprightness continued to pour through the Golden Gate, although the volume was down from the tidal waves of the last two years. Businessmen scooped up profits in every kind of speculative venture. City officials were deep in corruption, law officers and judges sold themselves routinely, and the riffraff of the city flourished.

Men carried guns as matter-of-factly as they pulled on their boots every morning and used them without hesitation when they felt threatened or insulted or were too angry to think or too drunk to care. Murder was commonplace and seldom punished—as long as it was committed openly and not in an unmanly sneak attack—and viewed with considerably less disfavor than larceny. An armed man should be able to protect himself, everyone felt, and if he couldn't, he'd better go someplace where life was softer and safer. But property was sacred, the be-all and end-all of existence. Wasn't the accumulation of property the reason everyone was here?

For the family in the new house on Stockton Street life was very good. Logan had fit into their routine gracefully, making herself quietly useful, happily helping Luz care for her adored nephew and niece, taking dozens of small household tasks from Marin's shoulders.

Marin was in the best of humors most of the time, for everything was turning out as she had hoped. Her first act after the New Year was to take James and Rose to Charles Towle. The doctor talked frankly to James, explained as much as medical science understood of what had happened to his brain—why the right side of his body was partially paralyzed, why his tongue did not always work as his mind instructed it—and assured him that he did not believe the brain to be softened in the slightest. He prescribed immersion of the affected limbs in a tub of warm water, along with certain exercises, a bland and nourishing diet, a single glass of light wine with his evening meal but no spirits, short daily rides in the open air, and, above all, strict avoidance of situations likely to bring on a fit of passion. Any violent emotion, particularly anger, Charles warned soberly, could kill him.

In the small parlor of Dr. Towle's living quarters Rose waited with Marin on a new plush sofa that made its shabby surroundings seem even shabbier. Poor dear, he certainly needs a woman, Marin thought, looking around the room. Somehow a way must be found to bring him and Logan together; it would be the best thing for both of them. Then the doctor walked in, friendly, mild, pleased to see her. She had fully intended to stay and listen to everything that passed between her mother and Charles Towle, but she found herself making a polite excuse and leaving the room promptly.

After the door closed behind her, Charles sat down beside Rose and explained James's condition and the reasons for optimism. He asked a few casual questions as he held her wrist and searched her eyes, and some of the pervasive fear Rose lived with diminished. An inner pressure eased under the gaze of this restful, pale young man, and she found herself doing something she had never intended to do—she allowed this stranger to see a little way into her mind.

Some time later, as they were preparing to leave, Charles suggested to Marin that the heartening diet required by her father would benefit her mother, too, as would long walks in the brisk air to improve circulation and bring the roses back to her "lovely cheeks."

Rose preened with some of her old coquettishness. "I vow, Dr. Towle, you are the one to make a lady blush!"

James smiled at the rare sparkle in her eyes, and a grin spread over Dr. Towle's bony face. "And you remember, Mrs. Gentry, I depend on you to supervise your husband's exercises and watch what he eats. He is to have a small glass of wine, only one, with dinner. I advise you to remove all spiritous liquors from the house in order to spare him temptation."

They all laughed, but Marin thought, He means it, and promised herself that she would lock up the whiskey, brandy, and the wine, too, and keep the key. Papa would try to follow the doctor's orders, but he did like his liquor.

Stuart, visiting a few weeks later, had to admit that Charlie Towle must have learned something in medical school, for his treatment had brought undeniable improvement. James had gained weight, his color was improved, he even spoke more smoothly. Like Marin, he loved San Francisco, ignoring the ugly side when he could, and when he couldn't, declaring it to be deplorable but invigorating. The carriage ride was the highlight of each day, and Rose went with him, brighter and more aware than she had been since he took sick. On these outings, they were accompanied by Jeremy, walking a pace behind, long, lean, alert, and armed with a new Colt revolver, which Stuart had paid forty dollars for.

The gun and Jeremy's presence in the household had been a point of sharp contention between Stuart and Marin. When he first agreed to the setting up of a house in town, Stuart had, with great reluctance and a sense of considerable sacrifice, offered Mateo as the man Marin would need on the premises to help with James and serve as the male protector of the house in Stuart's absence.

"I don't like losing him—he's the best horseman on the ranch—but he's a good boy, dependable, and I know you like him."

"Oh, dearest, that is so kind, but Little Mountain needs him, and anyway, I've already arranged for a man."

When she told him who the man was and how she had met him, Stuart was thunderstruck.

"Marin, what are you thinking of? I can't leave you with no one to protect you but some black boy you ran into out in the bush."

"Why ever not? Jeremy is intelligent, strong, and reliable, and he needs the job. I'd think you'd be glad you can keep Mateo."

"He'd have to take care of your father's personal needs, he'd be in and out of the house, serving your food, handling the children—I don't see how you could do it."

Marin's jaw hardened. "Well, you Yankees do take the cake. You rave on about the evils of slavery and weep over the plight of the downtrodden colored people, but when it comes to letting one come close and share your life, it's oh, dear me, and touch me not, and I'm just too dainty to let one serve my food. I thought you were a diehard abolitionist, Stuart."

He had the grace to look embarrassed. "I'm opposed to slavery, morally opposed to it, yes. It's wrong, and that's all there is to it. However, I'm not used to having them around, and I don't feel comfortable with them. They're different. They're strange. I never know what's going on in their minds. Sometimes I think Governor Burnett is right. They shouldn't be allowed into the state, slave or free. Dammit, Marin, you don't even know this Jeremy. I want someone in the house you can trust."

"You forget, I was raised by colored people. It was a colored woman who washed me, made my bed, cleaned my clothes, fed me—yes, and before that nursed me, just as Mrs. Victoria nurses Belinda." The mention of Belinda's wet nurse revealed the depth of her anger, for Stuart strongly deplored a mother's not nursing her own child and there had been several stiff quarrels on the subject. "As for trust, just you recall that Sophy was a total stranger to Jeremy, but he risked his life to go into that pestilential cabin and care for her after a white man left her flat. How many people, white or black, would have done that?"

Outgunned on one front, Stuart shifted his fire. "Has it occurred to you that he's probably a runaway slave? What will you do if his owner shows up on your doorstep?"

"I'll tell him kindly get off it, that's what. As it happens, Jeremy is free, but even if he weren't, this is a free state. Nobody can hold slaves here. You sound like a Chivalry Democrat instead of a good northern Whig. What would your father say?"

Stuart stared at his exasperating wife, considered turning her upside down and beating her bottom, and was immediately shocked at the thought. A gentleman could not lay violent hands on a woman and remain a gentleman, but by God, she could be infuriating.

"Sarcasm doesn't become you, Marin," he replied moodily. "I know a lot of the blacks in town are free, but some are runaways.

They're being retaken all the time, and the courts are backing up the owners. I don't care to have my family involved in a fugitive slave case."

Marin didn't care for it, either, and the possibility shut her up for a moment. Jeremy had never volunteered information as to his legal status, and she had not inquired for fear of learning something she didn't want to hear—always assuming he would tell her the truth. Southern to the core, she had accepted slavery as reasonable and right back home and would have found it convenient in California—as, for instance, the time Petra abandoned her for greener fields. But she had no deep feelings about it. Back home slavery had not been essential to the Gentrys' economic well-being, as it was on the great plantations farther south.

The interminable discussions between Stuart and his father about the evils of the slave system and the iniquities of Southern politicians had been to her only typical Yankee talk, all of it highly theoretical on this far frontier. Now, with Jeremy a member of the household, it was not abstract but might, as Stuart put it, sit down right on her doorstep and cause trouble. Most of the better class in San Francisco was Southern, with more coming every day, and the Chivalry wing of the Democratic party possessed a number of hotheaded but effective debaters who were determined to "do something" about the blacks coming into town claiming to be free, competing with whites for jobs, and behaving in much too cocky a manner for a white gentleman to swallow.

But Marin shrugged at the talk. Politicians, especially Southerners, were given to high-flown rhetoric. Last year in Washington City politicians had huffed and puffed and declared that the Union would break apart if California were admitted free or admitted slave, depending on which side the politician stood. The state had come in free, and nothing dreadful had happened. The Union still stood. Here in San Francisco the occasional fugitive was returned to his master, but in general the blacks were left alone. What a shame it would be to deny herself a good servant because of something that probably would never happen. Her momentary doubts dissolved, and she smiled into Stuart's scowling face. "It will work out fine, I promise. And buy a good pistol for him, Stuart. I wouldn't know what to pick out myself."

"You want to give him a gun?"

"How can he protect us if he doesn't have one?"

In this frontier town it was a reasonable question, and Stuart saw the sense of it, although unrecognized feelings buried deep in him made the arming of a black man a disturbing idea. For Marin it should have been unthinkable; fear of slave uprisings and black reprisals simmered just beneath the skin of every white Southerner. But she thought of Jeremy only as a good, strong man who, with his presence and protection, could free her from dependence on Stuart and Little Mountain. Jeremy must have his gun.

She bought him livery to wear while driving the carriage, too, and was most pleased with the result. He was just as impressive in his long, loose-limbed way as Anna von Helsdorf's Kaui, and did far more justice to the uniform, for Kaui was growing decidedly fat with good living. He and Jeremy hit it off well and were, Marin suspected, involved in a number of business deals on the side that she hoped never to learn the nature of. If Jeremy could turn a profit on his own initiative, more power to him as long as it didn't interfere with his working for her. He had plenty of opportunities to meet with Kaui and discuss the best methods of exploiting the cupidity of the human race; not only did they have the same day off, but they were required to spend long hours waiting outside stores while their mistresses shopped together.

Anna had quickly become Marin's closest woman friend outside the family, and they got along famously, for each had something the other wanted. Marin knew, or thought she knew, what she had to offer the glamorous baroness—a place for a lonely woman far from home in the loving warmth of her family circle. And Anna could offer her one of the things she wanted most—the fashion expertise of a sophisticated European. After years of relying on outdated *Godey's Ladies Books*, going from childhood to young womanhood on a wild frontier with no chance to develop taste in dress or discover how to make the most of her face and figure, she hungered for skilled instruction in the latest styles. She did not dream that Anna received a percentage of the sale for every customer she brought to a shop.

However, for no other reason than goodness of heart, Anna told Gerald Crown during one of their private meetings, she also had taken on the beautification of Marin's little sister, Sophy, and that gawky sister-in-law, Logan Severance. As a beginning she bullied the three women into wearing corsets for the first time in their lives and took them to a shop to be fitted for dresses according to their new measurements. It had been Anna's plan to take them to her milliner as well, for the girls all admired her bonnets, but when she mentioned that Mlle. Petra was the artist who had designed them, she was astonished to see Marin's lips straighten into a thin line.

"She does your hats? I might have known. No thank you, Anna, I'll go elsewhere."

"But you like them so much, and Mlle. Petra . . ."

" 'Mademoiselle' my foot. Did she tell you she was French? She's Mexican—my former maid."

"Petra made that darling thing?" exclaimed Sophy, gazing appreciatively at the confection of tulle and feathers on Anna's blond head. "My goodness, how clever of her."

And to Marin's irritation, Logan said, "I'm not a bit surprised. She always was smart as a whip. Don't you think we ought to patronize her, Marin? She's an old friend, and her work is simply lovely."

"Patronize whomever you wish," Marin replied loftily, miffed that neither Logan nor Sophy saw the matter of Petra her way. "I would never presume to tell you what to do, but Petra was my maid, not my friend. People like that have to know their place and not pretend to be what they aren't. I'll go elsewhere for my bonnets, and so will you, Sophy."

Anna's eyes narrowed in shrewd amusement, but she said, "To be sure, I completely understand. We shall buy adorable hats in some other shop, but you will find that all milliners are 'mademoiselle' or 'madame' even if the name is O'Toole. It means nothing. And," she added, almost as an afterthought, "here so many people find a new name, a new life. That is the style of the place, is it not?"

Marin needed the new clothes because at last she had a social life. There was so much to do in town, and Vail saw to it that the ladies of the family did it all. There were theatricals, good restaurants, Sunday horse races out near the old mission, all perfectly proper for ladies to attend as long as at least one gentleman was with them. And Rincon Hill, overlooking the bay, was a delightful place for picnics. The children were always taken along, and on one especially pleasant afternoon Rose and James were prevailed upon to come. Blankets were spread on the wild, stubby grass, and everyone ate and talked and watched the fog below move in across the city and drift out to sea again on the changeable wind. Carey whirled exuberantly from Grandpa to Grandma, plopped down beside Vail, got up, and chased a butterfly that had rested briefly on a weed near his hand. Logan was kept popping up constantly, pursuing him up the hill or retrieving him from the fascinating spot where the cliff sheared off precipitously.

Belinda watched for a while, crawled off her mother's lap, and halted, her attention caught by the sparkle of sunlight on the gold watch chain that looped across Vail's waistcoat. She grabbed his sleeve while he watched with a smile, struggled to her feet, and stood unsteadily, one chubby hand resting on his shoulder for support, looking at the blowing grass, the glittering bay, the world—a plump, pink, pretty child, all pale spun-gold ringlets, pink and white skin, enormous dark blue eyes. There was no longer any doubt that Vail's early fears for her were unfounded. She was developing normally, as bright and beautiful a daughter as any woman could wish. Solemnly she shoved her thumb in her mouth and hooked her fingers firmly over her little tilted nose.

Marin frowned maternal disapproval and pulled her hand away from her face. The thumb came out with a pop. "Stop that, my pet. You'll mash your nose, and no one will marry you."

The wet thumb returned instantly to Belinda's rosy mouth, and her fingers clamped her nose flat again. She stared at her mother, wide-eyed, unblinking, mutinous.

Marin was forced to look away quickly to preserve her countenance. Oh, it was a lovely day for a picnic, and this was the very best place for one, high and breezy, warm with sun, far away from the stink and dust and hurly-burly of the town. Somewhere, not too far from this spot, was Vail's big, elegant house, but she still had not been invited there. None of them had, not even Logan.

Why he had to make such a mystery of that house and, indeed, all his life away from family gatherings . . .

Not that she really cared what he did, but it rankled, hearing vague stories about him from people who were scarcely more than strangers and having to admit that she knew less about her own brother-in-law's activities than they did. Today, on their way home, she would suggest stopping by his house. Everyone would beg to see it, and it would be hard for him to refuse.

But when the time came, her nerve failed and they traveled back down into town with the house still unseen.

On the occasion of Logan's twenty-third birthday Vail and Gerald escorted her, Marin, Sophy, and Delphine to a lobster dinner at Delmonico's and then to the new Adelphi Theater to watch magicians and listen to a German violinist and a statuesque lady from Naples with an astonishing bosom and a clear soprano voice. Afterward they went to Mrs. Tierney's Shamrock Ice Cream

Parlor and Candy Shoppe to eat ice cream and discuss the marvelous entertainment they had just seen.

Mrs. Tierney, a woman of aggressive respectability despite her hennaed hair, had become a widow when her husband died in a barroom, not from the usual cause, a gunshot wound, but from acute alcohol poisoning brought on when he bet the entire house he could drink more red-eye whiskey in a shorter time than any man in the El Dorado Saloon and then won the bet. As a result of this tragedy his wife was left with an abiding hatred of drink and an urgent need to earn her living. Her shop was one of the few places in town where edibles were sold but no liquor was allowed.

Logan was still in mourning for her mother, and black did not become her, yet she looked prettier this evening than Marin had ever seen her. If only Charles Towle had come with them tonight, he surely would have noticed. What was the matter with him? Why did he invariably refuse invitations? Although he was now their family doctor, he had declined Sophy as a patient and recommended Tom Anderson as much more experienced with cholera and its aftermath. This puzzled Marin and worried her a little. Perhaps she had misjudged his largeness of heart, perhaps he despised Sophy for her indiscretion as the world would despise her if it found out. But surely not—he was too kind. Yet what, for instance, would Gerald Crown think if he knew? Would he be so gallantly respectful to Sophy as he was being at this moment?

Marin snapped open her new silk fan with the mother-of-pearl trim, fanned herself briskly, and said in a low voice, "I am about to expire from the heat. Please take me outside, Vail."

As soon as they were safely out of Logan's hearing, she asked in an accusatory way, "Did you invite Charles Towle to come tonight?"

He smiled. "As you instructed."

"Why didn't he come?"

"He had a previous engagement."

"He always has a previous engagement. What's wrong with him? He should be glad to accept invitations from a respectable family. There are few enough in this villainous town."

"I thought you liked it here."

"Don't change the subject. Why won't he come to dinner or to my little musicales? Why does he always turn me down?"

"Why don't you stop trying to manage other people's lives? Really, Marin, you'd be much more charming if you weren't so bossy. Maybe Charles doesn't want to be pushed at Logan. Maybe Logan doesn't want it, either—have you thought of that?"

She sat down on the bench under the tree, careless of the dampness seeping through her new dress. How had he known what was in her mind when she'd been careful never to mention Logan and Charles together? "Is he shy because of his affliction? What caused it?"

"You mean, why does he limp? He had a paralytic illness when he was a child, and he very nearly died. It left one leg deformed, and he's accepted it far better than I could've."

"Is that what causes his ill health? When I first met him, he looked dreadful, but he seems much better lately."

"In Boston he was told to get his affairs in order because he had consumption and wouldn't last out the year. He decided that if he was going to die, he'd rather do it in California. As you've observed, he seems to be getting well." He spoke reluctantly, as though already regretting what he had said.

"Consumption," she murmured, horrified. "No wonder you don't want him for Logan."

"I've told you before, doctors are often wrong. Charles was overworked and exhausted, he has asthma and chronic bronchitis, but he isn't consumptive. Anything else you're curious about?"

That was sarcasm, and she decided to ignore it. "Does he have—that is, are his affections engaged anywhere?"

"How would I know? Men don't whisper their heart's confidences to each other like giggling schoolgirls."

"Oh, you'd know, all right. I'm sure men talk all the time, a good deal more than they should. So, if there's no one else . . . he likes Logan, he said he does. Couldn't you point out her good qualities and such in a tactful way? She needs somebody, Vail."

"I know what Logan needs. I can't give it to her, and neither can you. Leave them alone, Marin."

"Another thing," she went on as if he hadn't spoken, "he won't accept Sophy as a patient. He said Dr. Anderson had more experience with cholera patients, but Charles has had lots of experience. Now why do you suppose he did that?"

"I haven't the slightest idea," said Vail.

Tom Anderson's attitudes about life and death and the human needs of his patients were as different from Charles's as were their body types. He was a stocky, athletic man, he rode well, ate heartily, prided himself on his shooting eye and his head for liquor. His natty clothes, his luxuriant beard, the brown hair carefully arranged to cover a small bald spot, the aggressive set of his muscular shoulders all spoke of a man dedicated to the appearance of youthful vigor in the face of middle age. It had been a determination to prove himself right and others wrong as much as medical insight that had led to his discovery of the incipient cholera epidemic in Sacramento City. He believed that robust action was the solution for most ills, physical or spiritual, and tended toward strenuous methods in the treatment of his patients. But because Sophy was already nearly recovered when he first saw her, he bled her only once, prescribed daily cold baths, a heartening diet, a cup of beef tea with every meal, and a wineglass of egg beaten in sherry at bedtime.

His regimen must have been the right one, for she quickly came back to health. Her dimpled cheeks turned rosy, her thin body became round again, and although there were at times shadows in her eyes that troubled Marin, most of her old vivacity returned, along with a new touch of maturity in her face that could only be a good sign for the future.

Within a week of his first seeing Sophy, Tom Anderson got himself invited to dinner at the house on Stockton Street. Although he was not the kind of suitor Marin had in mind for her sister, he was a gentleman, affluent, well educated, presentable, and, all things considered, quite a good beginning. Being a gentleman, he did not devote himself exclusively to Sophy, but paid equally flattering attention to Logan, so much so that as Vail was leaving after a Friday night dinner, Marin followed him out onto the porch and said, "You'd better tell your friend Charles to stop dawdling and get over here, or I'll marry Logan off to Tom Anderson right under his nose." She said it lightly, hoping he would sense the seriousness beneath and, just maybe, do something.

But he said only, "Marin, you never cease to entertain me," and rode off, chuckling.

She stood on the top step, watching him go with a line between her brows, wondering, as she so often did, where he went and what he did away from these sedate family parties.

If she had asked, he would have told her, for he had nothing more disreputable in view for the evening than a poker game with Charles, Gerald, and Harry Callendar, if Harry could escape the domestic embrace of his wife. Charles was late, as usual, and Harry had not yet arrived, but Gerald was waiting for him in the saloon attached to the Restaurant Rondeau, an elegant French restaurant where Vail's female relatives had eaten several times, unaware of the little private dining rooms upstairs that one might enter as a lady but never leave as one.

The saloon was new, the most glamorous drinking establishment in town, at least this week; competition was stiff, and there was never any knowing what refinements a rival saloon might bring forth next week. The brutality, vulgarity, and danger of the frontier were banished from this establishment. Yet along with respectable citizens was a tougher element, acceptable as long as they had money and did not tear up the place too much. They crowded together at the long mahogany bar, the best people in town, the riffraff, and every degree between.

Harry Callendar trotted in, apologized for his tardiness, sank into a chair, and poured himself a drink from the bottle on the table. The bottle was mostly window dressing; in San Francisco it was considered peculiar not to drink heavily, but Gerald was careful with liquor and Vail was known for nursing one glass through an evening.

The altercation that had begun at the bar a few moments earlier was growing loud and there was a sudden scuffle and a parting of the crowd as bystanders moved prudently away.

A thickset man with a dirty rust-colored beard growled in a twang that carried clearly, "What I said is, I ain't drinkin' next to no greaser, not even a dainty thing like you."

The man standing next to him at the bar was gorgeously attired in a brilliant red jacket of embroidered silk and blue velvet breeches decorated with tinkling bells, a startling sight among the workaday miners and sober, broadcloth-suited business men. It was as if an exotic tropic bird had settled among a group of peahens. Costly worked-silver spurs—of the type Marin had once coveted for Ethan—were attached to his soft deerskin shoes. Obviously he had dressed in his best for a visit to the city.

He smiled and bowed with formal courtesy, his left hand over his heart, his right arm held stiffly at his side.

"I humbly beg your pardon, señor, for any offense my presence may have caused. This is a public drinking house, not a private club?" His contempt was the more insulting because it was so controlled.

The red-bearded man slammed down his glass and made the usual response to any annoyance, a move for his gun, but his companion at the bar put out a hand to stop him. "Put up your gun, my friend. Mr. Cermeno is just nervous about that land he stole, and he's apologized for being a popish Mex. Can't do more, now can he?"

Nicolas's head went up, and his dark face flushed. In that moment he looked all that he was—the aristocratic descendant of a proud race, the absolute master of a feudal kingdom.

"My seconds will meet with you, señor," he said, and there was a guffaw from Redbeard.

"D'you hear that, Kemble?" he shouted, and then events moved very fast. Harry Callendar, who had remained at the table in the corner, tried afterward to recount the affair to his wife exactly as it happened and couldn't quite do it.

He saw Redbeard pull a long-barreled pistol out of his belt, but the peculiar-looking man called Kemble already was pointing a small handgun at Nicolas. There was an explosion as his arm flew upward, and then somehow he was on his back with Vail's big boot planted squarely on his throat.

Gerald, who was perhaps half as broad as Redbeard, brought an unopened bottle of whiskey down on the man's hand and picked up the pistol as it hit the floor.

At the sound of gunfire Frank Maguire, who owned the Rondeau, had run out of his office with the gold he had been weighing still in his hand. He quickly estimated that the cost of replacing the shattered mirror would be less than the cost of the undamaged crystal chandelier directly above it, gave thanks, took in Nicolas in all his rage and his finery, and noted it was Vail Severance who had Kemble under his boot. Kemble was a clever and useful friend, but Vail Severance owned the land on both sides of the Rondeau, land Maguire hoped to buy to accommodate his growing business. He silently damned all high-nosed Spanish peacocks to perdition, ordered Kemble and Redbeard thrown out, and expressed his regrets to Nicolas.

"I can't tell you how sorry I am, sir. Take any table you care to, and accept a bottle of champagne with my apologies."

The Spaniard's face was rigid, and he was staring at Vail so hard and haughtily that Mr. Maguire wondered if he had misjudged the situation; maybe the two were not friends after all.

"Keep your champagne, señor. I am leaving."

"Not yet, Nick," Gerald said amiably, and his hand came casually to rest on Nicolas's shoulder. "Come over to our table and catch us up on the news. I haven't been across the bay in six months. You won't refuse to drink with me?"

Some of the stiffness slid out of Nicolas's face. "It was to see you that I came to this unspeakable town." He smiled sourly at Gerald and allowed himself to be led across the room.

They had the ritual drink of whiskey, which no one enjoyed but which had to be drunk, and Gerald inquired, "So you're bringing me business, Nick?"

Nicolas stared into his empty glass and laughed.

"I was pro-American, did you know that? I despised the Mexican government, and I thought, We are going to be taken by someone. Better the Americans than the English or the French. That is what I thought." He reached for the bottle, filled his glass to the top, and drank as swiftly as if the bourbon were cool water on a hot day, then grimaced. "*Dios,* you people are barbarians, to invent a drink like that." He filled the glass again, drank half, and set it down. "The English are overbearing bastards, and the French are almost as cruel to their colonies as we Spaniards. I thought maybe the Americans wouldn't be as bad, eh? I'll never know, but I know this—you are a people to be feared, not for brutality or arrogance or greed—we all share those—but for your damnable energy. Yes, your damnable energy." He finished his drink in a gulp. "You are eating us up with the best will in the world, and we, poor fools, opened the door and invited you in."

Gerald borrowed a cigar from Vail and took his time lighting it. When he was finished, he asked, "Is it squatters?"

"Yes, *por Dios,* squatters!" Nicolas roared so loudly that despite the din of the room, men at nearby tables turned their heads. "I find them on my land every day. Those two at the bar, I caught them last week. They've built a shanty, and they've got a crew slaughtering my beef. I ran them off, and Kemble—" Nicolas choked on the name, "Kemble came to my door, my *front* door yesterday. He claims my title to Fontana is not good, that the American government will take our land and give it to their settlers, and native Californians will own nothing five years from now. But what about the peace treaty, what about justice? My great-great grandfather was a captain of King Charles! He was here at the beginning. My grandfather received our grant from the Spanish governor fifty years ago." He passed a hand over his sweating face. He was used to good red wine, not whiskey. "Gerald, can they do this?"

"Do you have the grant itself, the piece of paper?"

"I searched most of last night and found it in an old trunk. I have it . . ." Nicolas fumbled under his jacket with a jerky, uncharacteristically nervous movement, "right here." He pulled out a brown paper folded many times, and Gerald took it and smoothed it on the table.

"Good, good. This is what we must have." He smiled so

encouragingly that Nicolas smiled, too, for the first time. "This is best kept in my safe. Will you trust me with it?"

"If not you, who then? I must trust someone, so it will have to be you. Everything is all right, *verdad*?"

"Come to my office tomorrow, and we will talk." Gerald folded the paper, following each original crease carefully, and tucked it into his big wallet. "But for now, forget it, Nick. Give me a chance to take you at poker."

Nicolas got to his feet in the cautiously dignified manner of a man who knows he is almost drunk. "Tomorrow, perhaps, after we talk." He looked directly at Vail. "I thank you for my life tonight. He would have been glad to kill me, that Kemble." His flushed face came close to Vail's. "But I care for myself and mine, as you well know. Don't interfere with me, not ever again."

He made a formal bow and walked across the crowded floor, silver spurs jingling, and passed through the open door into the night, a creature out of his time and place, lost and about to be swept away by a tidal wave of change.

Vail watched until he was out of sight and then looked at Gerald. "What are his chances?"

"Lord God, I don't know. We had possession of the territory by forty-six, and we made a lot of promises about recognizing existing property rights. The Guadalupe Hidalgo treaty confirmed the promises, it's all down on paper, but back East they imagine the state is one solid gold mine. Do you think we'll worry about 'existing rights' when that kind of wealth is at stake? The squatters claim that the American takeover invalidated all titles and the land is now up for grabs, with the present owners sitting on what doesn't belong to them. That's what the bastard meant when he said Nicolas stole Fontana. Congress will pass some kind of bill to settle the claims, but God only knows what they'll come up with."

"Not fair, not fair," murmured Harry.

Vail shrugged. "How fair were the Spaniards when they moved in on the Indians? Not being satisfied with just the land, they took their souls as well because they were stronger and meaner. Then, after a while, they got soft. Look at Nicolas. He's a smart man, yet he never saw this coming. We're stronger and meaner than men like him—right now, that is. Someday someone else may do the same to us. Personally I don't give a damn, except for Celia and the Cermeno girls. I'd hate to see them tossed out in the road. Will the grant do them any good?"

Gerald gnawed at his lower lip. "Mexican land titles are a

mare's nest, and it's all their own fault. I'll bet every dollar I've got that the Cermeno grant was never recorded. They're casual about details like that. Did you notice he had no idea where it was, although his entire fortune hangs on it? Where did he find it? In an old trunk. Probably the land was never surveyed, or if it was, not accurately."

He pulled the grant out of his wallet, glanced over it, and snorted. "Listen to this. '. . . four leagues, more or less, south to the great oak and thence to the water . . .' I'll have to get this translated. My Spanish isn't good enough. 'More or less.' Try to clear that up in a court of law. 'The great oak.' This was fifty years ago. Which great oak? Is it still standing, or was it knocked down by lightning before Nicolas was born? 'To the water.' In this country it could have been a major stream at the time and only a trickle now, the streambed could have changed, it could have disappeared altogether. What the hell kind of boundaries are those? But they were gentlemen then, and everything was understood. How easy to be a gentleman when land is cheap, and how unpleasant everyone gets when the price goes up." He put the paper down in disgust, and then his eyes sparkled. "I'll tell you one thing. These title fights will go on forever, and the chief beneficiaries will be the lawyers. My grandson will inherit this case."

An hour later a message came from Charles saying that he was with a patient and couldn't leave, and Vail, Harry, and Gerald settled down to play serious poker. It was nearing dawn when Harry, who had drunk more than he was used to, said good night outside the saloon's door and rolled off down Dupont Street to explain to his wife.

A chill, biting wind had come up, and the smell of rain was in the air. Vail and Gerald turned up their collars and took the shortcut down the narrow, shadowed alley behind the Rondeau to the stables where they had left their horses. It was a dangerous way, which neither would have walked alone even though Gerald had a small gun in his vest and a knife hidden in his boot as well as the massive pistol he had taken from the man with the red beard.

Vail had shoved his own gun in his belt and carried in his pocket the tiny derringer Kemble had tried to use on Nicolas. Near the end of the street he stumbled in the dark, swore, dug for a match, and struck it on his boot sole. It flared in the wind and went out. He struck another, and sheltered it with his hand; its shifting light

spread over the scarlet silk jacket of Nicolas Cermeno, wet now
with a darker crimson. He knelt down.

"What can we do?" breathed Gerald.

"Nothing," said Vail. "He's dead. Light another match."

Chapter 20

Nicolas was buried in the family graveyard at Fontana
near his father, his mother, two sisters and a brother who
had died in infancy, and three generations of ancestors.
Despite the crowd of relatives and friends assembled on the matted
grass near the grape arbor, it was a quiet funeral, the hush of the
sunny afternoon broken only by the breeze ruffling the tops of
the tall sycamores, the subdued sobbing of the Cermeno girls, the
tinkling of bells as the Mass proceeded, and the low, rapid Latin
of the priest as he assisted Nicolas Cermeno's soul on its journey.

Armando Cermeno stood alone as he became the new head of
the family, a stern expression on his narrow, boyish face and fear
in his eyes. He had recently grown a mustache to emphasize his
manliness, and it succeeded only in making him look younger.

He's lost without Nicolas, like all the rest of them, thought
Marin. He was only twenty-three, and his life up to two days ago
had been horses, hunting, and girls. Now he was required to
change instantly from an irresponsible boy to a man, run Fontana,
care for its dependent women, face the threat of squatters—for
some reason Ethan came into her mind. He and Armando had been
great friends. Ethan would have looked scared, too.

Finally it was over. Together Marin, Stuart, and Logan walked
up the path to the house, where a funeral collation awaited. There,
in the crowd on the patio, was Glenna Severance, spreading
herself like the green bay tree, pretty, smug, and dressed to kill.
Malcolm doesn't mind spending money on his new young wife,
thought Marin. Something nice would have to be said to her,
something to welcome her into the family, seeing that it was the
first time they had met since the ridiculous marriage. Malcolm
looked vigorous—and lowering. He must have caught sight of
Vail. Yes, there was Vail talking to Gerald Crown. The two of
them had brought Nicolas's body home and were here by Celia's
special invitation.

It was on this patio one long-ago, sunny day that she had begged Nicolas to call off his duel with Vail. Here he had kissed her hand, sat with her on the bench beside the morning glories, and explained why honor demanded that he try to kill Vail. Now he was dead by an assassin's hand, and it was as if death, which had so narrowly missed him four years ago, had now arrived to claim its own. Could he have fought off his murderer if his right arm, his gun arm, had not been destroyed by that duel? Stuart said he probably could have. Speculation, of course, and useless, but had the same thought occurred to Vail? Stuart said Nicolas should never have been allowed to leave the saloon alone that night, anyone who knew San Francisco knew that. Did Vail feel culpable? He looked somber, as was fitting at such a time, but not in the depths of self-reproach.

Celia moved among the guests with an individual word for each, poised, composed, every inch the great lady she was born to be. She came to Marin and Logan with the fond look she reserved for old friends and kissed them, a brush of soft lips against their cheeks.

"Come visit me soon," she said, and only the slight trembling of her hand in Marin's betrayed emotion. "I've missed you since you went off to the city," and Marin assured her, "I will, oh, I will."

As it happened, she did not go. March was miserably wet, with lead gray, depressing skies and cutting winds even on the days it did not rain. Belinda caught a cold that settled in her chest, and Marin and Logan were up through the long nights trying to comfort her and putting on mustard plasters, which only made her cry louder.

Marin was in a bad humor because the rain had revealed deficiencies in her beloved house: the plaster had cracked; the roof leaked; and cold, damp air seeped in around the poorly sealed windows. April brought pleasanter weather, but the perpetual wind off the water was still cold, and it took all her charm, combined with astute bullying, to get Dennis Timothy and his sterling Irish workmen to make the necessary repairs. It took them a month to do it, too, considerably longer than the time spent building the entire house—probably the reason for the problems, she told Vail gloomily. These days Vail did not come by the house as often—the press of business, he explained—and it was precisely this business that Marin wanted to question him about. But it had to be done indirectly. He was so touchy about personal inquiries.

"I ran into Harry Callendar the other day," she began. They were sitting in the parlor after dinner, and she knew he was eager to leave. Rose had been poorly all day and had not appeared at the supper table, but James drowsed in his chair very close to the fireplace, occasionally opening his eyes to draw on the one after-dinner cigar allowed him and stare into the flames with the pensive, abstracted expression that was often on his face when he thought he was unobserved. Logan creaked back and forth in the big rocker, cuddling Belinda, who fussed and coughed and was having a hard time falling asleep. Carey sat on the rug taking apart an old clock that had been given to him because it no longer worked. So far it had occupied him for almost an hour. Delphine was peering at her knitting and muttering to herself over what had gone wrong with the stitch.

Marin picked up her own knitting. "Harry says nothing much is going to be done about catching the men who killed Nicolas because he was a Mexican and nobody really cares. Do you think that's true? I could hardly believe it, especially after the to-do last month over Mr. McKinstry being robbed." The armed assault on Mr. McKinstry's goods, the latest in a series of bold robberies, had so inflamed a mob of law-abiding citizens that they had nearly beaten to death a man caught nearby who had an Australian accent and appeared to fit the description given by the victim.

"McKinstry is a prominent merchant and an American, one of our own. All the shopkeepers are nervous," Vail said.

"Then it's true? Nobody cares about Nicolas because he was Mexican?"

"Oh, there was a good deal of outrage when it happened. If Kemble and his friend were handy, they'd be given a fair trial and hanged in half an hour. But they've disappeared, and they won't be found easily. No one is going to take time off from business to chase after them."

"It's all so sad. How are they over at Fontana?"

"About as you'd expect. Armando is a weak reed, terrified of the responsibility, which is mostly Nicolas's fault. He never gave the boy a chance to learn. I haven't been out there myself, but Gerald has had to go several times, since he has the job of untangling the title to the ranch. He says Celia is taking it bravely."

"Of course she is," Marin replied, pleased that Vail hadn't rushed over to comfort the new widow.

Logan, who had been too busy struggling with Belinda to attend the conversation closely, said, "Vail, tell us your news. Marin says you are now enormously rich."

"She does? Where did she get that idea?"

"Why, Mr. Callendar told her just the other day. Didn't he, Marin?"

"Papa, watch your cigar," said Marin, pleased with Logan. Now she wouldn't have to bring up the subject herself. She leaned forward to catch the long ash that was about to fall on the carpet and in the process managed to avoid the look Vail was giving her. "Wake up, Papa. Vail is going to tell us about that property he sold down on Montgomery Street."

James snorted, coughed, and opened his eyes. She slipped an ashtray onto his lap and said brightly over her shoulder, "Harry told me you made almost half a million dollars on that deal."

Vail was regarding her with a frown.

"I don't know who is the worse gossip, you or Harry."

"Why should you mind telling your own family news like that? I'd think you'd be proud of it."

James drew on his smoldering cigar until the tip glowed red again, thoroughly awake now and remembering what Marin had told him. Only a year ago Vail had bought land on the waterfront for a few thousand dollars, and he'd just realized a profit in the hundreds of thousands. The thought made James's blood race with some of the old adventurous excitement. "I have a little money to speculate with." He spoke slowly, pronouncing each syllable distinctly, and Vail waited courteously until he got the words out, knowing exactly what was in this wan, half-paralyzed man's mind and who had put it there.

"Sir, don't guide your actions by tales you hear about me. Harry exaggerated greatly. I did buy land that was relatively cheap last year, and I've sold it at a gain because of the location, but I had partners who helped me buy it and who also take part of the profit. Several warehouses are going to be built on it, and I don't know yet if I've been wise or foolish to sell now. If I had the capital, I'd build on the land myself, but I don't, not for a venture like that. My advice, if you want it, is never gamble except with money you can afford to lose. Right now land speculation is the wildest crap game in town."

James's eyes sparked, and he trembled with the effort of sorting out the thoughts in his mind. "I c-can . . . I c-can . . . God damn it!" He went white with anger at his infirmity.

Marin was off the sofa and on her knees beside him, soothing, caressing. "There, Papa, there. Slowly now, and it will come." She could have explained what he wanted to say, but knew she must not. It was important that he express himself and also that he stay calm while doing it.

He took a breath. "I can . . . get the money. The town is booming. Must not let it . . . pass me by." He sighed with the exertion, and Marin laid her cheek against his hand.

Vail said, "This house is a good investment, and it's appreciating while you live in it. Isn't your excess cash pretty well tied up right here?"

"I can borrow against Little Mountain."

"Not at the rates the banks are charging, not for a long-term loan. You must be able to hold out until the price is right."

"No banks." James brushed away the objection with a jerky, impatient gesture. "I'd borrow from Malcolm."

"My father? He's the worst usurer of all. Don't indebt yourself to him, and don't use Little Mountain as collateral. He'll steal the soles off your shoes, quoting scripture all the time."

Even Logan looked shocked at that, and Marin said, "Oh, Vail, don't be so bitter. He's not the kindest man in the world, but we're family, after all."

"I'm not bitter, just realistic. I know that man."

The door chimes rang, preventing the hasty reply that was on the tip of her tongue. It had taken some time to work James around to his present point of view, and all she wanted from Vail this evening was information as to how he'd made his killing, not opinions on how she and James should conduct their business.

Jeremy loped out of the kitchen to open the front door, and Sophy whirled in, her eyes bright with laughter. She was wearing a new dress with a wide satin sash and tiers of lace, and the veil of misty drops on her blond hair sparkled in the lamplight. Tom Anderson followed her into the parlor, vigorous, hearty, immensely pleased at having captured the popular Miss Sophy Gentry for an entire evening. The Winfields, whose dinner party they had attended, were new in town, had connections with some of the best families in Virginia, were already quite rich (having arrived with considerable capital), and had a pretty daughter, Kitty, who was just Sophy's age. Tom didn't care if they had ten pretty, eligible daughters. He was never a man to turn away from a good thing, but he was in love with Sophy and teetering on the brink of asking James for her hand.

Sophy kissed her father and then plopped down in the sofa next to Vail and kissed him, too. His kindness to her had swept away all her early notions of romantic infatuation and mixed him up in her mind as a magnificent combination of her handsome, laughing, long-dead brother and her once-strong, protective father. Quite simply and unaffectedly, she loved him.

She chattered on, describing Mrs. Winfield's china and silver and table decorations, the other girls' dresses, the several narrow escapes coming home through the fog in Tom's carriage. Vail noted the fatuous expression on Tom's face. As soon as he courteously could, he made his excuses, shrugged into his greatcoat, and kissed Logan good-bye at the door before going out into the blindness of a San Francisco fog.

Marin watched him go and wondered if anyone else had noticed the cold, impersonal way he had referred to his father only as "that man."

Chapter 21

On the afternoon of May 3, 1851, Logan rushed in the front door with an armload of packages and started upstairs, hurrying because she was late and would need all of the remaining day to sew the lace found at Fletcher's Emporium to the neck of her lavender silk gown, bathe, do up her hair, and be ready by six o'clock for the dinner and theater party planned for that evening.

The social spin of city life had revealed new facets of her personality. Quiet, undemanding girl that she'd always been, no one, including herself, had suspected that she so longed for pretty clothes and male attention and the excitement of getting dressed up to go out. Tom Anderson would be in the party this evening, and while she knew quite well that he preferred Sophy—and she didn't mind, since he was not her heart's ideal—he was a man, good company, and flatteringly attentive. She wanted him to think she looked pretty.

On the landing she tripped on a toy soldier Carey had dropped and fell forward onto the steps. A few minutes later she was in her bed with a badly wrenched ankle and the depressing knowledge that she would not be going anywhere for several days.

At the Tyler Winfield residence, Mrs. Winfield, a fragile-looking woman with gracious manners, an elegant Virginia accent, and the iron-willed ambition of a Napoleon, had taken to her bed, too. Her head ached painfully as it often did from overtight lacing, and she had just reluctantly informed her miserable daughter that under no circumstances could Kitty attend the theater tonight without her mother's chaperonage. The thought made her headache worse, for tonight was to have been another brick in the friendship she was building with the Gentrys and the Severances. Marin Gentry's grandmother had been a Calvert of Maryland, her husband, Stuart Severance, was a state legislator; and her brother-in-law, Vail Severance, was by far the most attractive bachelor in town. Also, Tom Anderson would be in attendance tonight, and he was a man of substance, a good catch if it came to that. Kitty's sobs only brought her spirits lower.

"I am as sorry as you are, my dear, but it is impossible. Young ladies of good family do not appear alone in public with gentlemen, no matter how innocent and respectable the occasion. Yes, Marin is a matron, but of tender years herself. I make no doubt her mother, who is a Calvert, will agree with me completely and cancel the outing since I cannot accompany you." She opened her aching eyes long enough to gaze fondly at her pretty, sniffling daughter. "Never forget, Kitty, that young ladies are as cities set upon a hill, and society does not forgive those who allow even a shred of doubt to attach to their reputations. Now, my poppet, stop crying. Your nose will be red all week."

Mrs. Winfield was mistaken about Rose. She would have scotched her daughters' plans if she had known about them, but she didn't know because she had not come out of her room all day. Delphine disapproved and said so, but promptly gave up when she saw the expression in Marin's eyes. The girl was obstinate, intractable, stubborn as a mule, and quite exhausting, and Delphine was not going to volunteer as substitute chaperone when all she wanted for the evening was her bed, the new novel by Mrs. Fitch, and her box of French chocolates.

So it happened that Marin and Sophy ate dinner alone with two unmarried men in the public room of a restaurant and then went to the theater, giggling like schoolgirls, enjoying a situation that was great fun because it was slightly improper yet not at all dangerous.

The play was a soul-wrenching melodrama, *Camilla, or the Battered Heart,* and at intermission the girls wiped their wet eyes and apologized charmingly for their foolishness. They struggled through the crowd to a window while Tom and Vail went to the saloon next door to find them refreshments. Far across the mob milling in the theater aisles they saw Gerald and Baroness Anna chatting together. They waved and smiled, but it was impossible to get close enough to speak. Marin leaned on the windowsill and listened to the mildly ribald ditty that was drifting from the saloon.

She sneezed, wrinkled her nose, and sneezed again. "Sophy, what . . . oh, my God!"

After that first startled gasp she did not try to explain her purpose but simply took action. Once glance at the door told her that there was no escape in that direction. A solid mass of people barred their way, a mob already beginning to murmur and look around nervously as the smell of smoke drifted up the stairwell. In moments they would become a maddened, trampling beast.

"Quick! Out here." She grabbed Sophy's arm and shoved her through the window and onto the roof, over the main entrance to the theater. The building was a simple, boxlike structure two stories high; the sloping roof they stood on extended from just below the window to the street and was supported by posts at each corner. It was a wooden roof; the entire building was wood, as were most of the surrounding buildings, as was most of the town—matchsticks all of them, fuel for the flames already crackling up the walls of the theater.

There was screaming from inside. Every San Franciscan knew instantly what fire meant. There had been countless minor burnings, and great conflagrations had wiped out large parts of town four times in the last year and a half. The city was a tinderbox, a pile of dry straw ready to explode into flame at the toss of a match.

Sophy was rigid with fright, terrified almost as much by this high, unprotected place as by the fire. She quavered, "How . . . how do we get down?"

"Follow me," Marin commanded as if she knew where she was going, and they teetered downward toward the corner of the roof.

Smoke rose, stinging their eyes. The night was hotter than noon in midsummer, and the roof was already blistering to the touch. Fire had leaped onward, and all the structures around Portsmouth Square were blazing. People poured out of buildings, bawling, screeching, stampeding through the streets like beings driven suddenly mad.

There were shrieks and shouts from behind. Other people were spilling out the window from the fiery interior of the theater, and the roof buckled and shook under their weight.

Sophy cried, "Look out, I'm sliding!" bumped toward the edge of the roof, and stopped as the tiny heels of her flat slippers caught the ridge of a shingle. "Oh, Marin, we're going to fall!"

"I'd rather break my neck than burn to death." Marin rubbed her smarting eyes and got down on her knees, feeling for the post that ran from the roof to the porch below. "It's not so far, Sophy. We can do it."

"No!"

Marin glared at her. "Any girl who can jump out a second-story window into a tree and get to the ground with a suitcase in her hand can slide down this post."

Sophy screwed up her face and moaned, "I was desperate then."

"You're desperate now, you silly thing. Look behind you."

Flames filled the window they had crawled through, and a wave of panicked humans was rolling toward them down the roof.

Marin hiked up her skirt and petticoats, lowered her bottom half gingerly over the edge, and felt for the post with her pantaletted legs. The hot shingles cut into her waist, and she damned Anna and her whalebone corsets. Through the smoke she could see Sophy's white face tortured with indecision. God in heaven, she might not follow, she might stay up there until the whole structure burned and collapsed and brought her crashing down with it.

Marin's hands dug into the roof's edge, her legs were wrapped tight around the increasingly hot post. "I'm going down," she gasped, "and if you don't come down after me, Sophy Gentry, I'll never speak to you again!" With that final intimidation she slid slowly out of sight.

Sophy clamped her tongue between her teeth, biting hard to keep from crying, and with stern concentration lowered her little body off the roof in the manner Marin had. Her legs swung in space, she almost let go of the roof, and then her thrashing legs found the post and closed around it. She hung there, afraid to go down, unable to go up, and from the ground Marin screamed, "Sophy, you get down here this instant!" With a hopeless prayer Sophy squeezed her eyes shut and plummeted to the ground. Fire had engulfed the porch and was very close to the spot where she landed. Instinctively she rolled away from it, amazed to be still alive, staggered up, and threw her arms around her big sister. They huddled together in the road, paralyzed by the deluge of noise and confusion, clutching each other in a frantic embrace.

Around them was bedlam. Men and women darted through the streets, searching for escape. A girl in a vivid crimson dress hurtled out of the Union Hotel with her hair on fire and ran screaming toward the waterfront. Horses tied to hitching rails bucked and plunged, tore free, and charged by with empty stirrups flying. Two mules harnessed to a beer wagon careered, driverless, in the direction of the two girls, and a rocketing barrel skimmed over their heads. It smashed open with a squashing sound, and beer gurgled, dark and frothy, down the gutter.

The sight galvanized Marin. "Come!" she shouted, and pulled Sophy to the safety of the boardwalk beside a man who was loading long bolts of cloth into a wagon with insane energy. His horse, ears flattened, eyes rolling, reared with a whinny as a burning two-by-four landed in the wagon, and plunged down the street with the bolts of cloth afire and the man racing after it.

A blustery wind that had been blowing out of the north and west when the blaze began now swerved, and the fire shifted with it, greedily assailing sections of town only recently rebuilt after the conflagration of last September. The center of town was walled in by flames. Fire was on all sides, creating its own sweeping wind, thundering with a noise not of this world, noise that bludgeoned and pounded, making reasoned thought impossible.

The dry boards of the sidewalk were growing hot, and a tiny arrow of bright fire flickered up in a gap where the planks did not meet. The wooden planks of the streets and sidewalks were not fitted flat to the ground, and the space beneath drew like a fireplace flue, hauling sparks and hot air to new sources of fuel as yet unburned. On Clay Street flame burst up in the middle of the street as though generated in the depths of the earth, and another block kindled.

Bells of the volunteer fire companies were clanging all over town. At the end of the street an engine pumped furiously, but the feeble stream of water it produced was powerless against the strength of such a fire.

Marin held on tight to Sophy's hand, trying to organize her frantic thoughts. Through all the noise, the smarting haze of smoke, the pandemonium in the streets, the intense heat and blinding glare, a vague but important worry had been gnawing at her, a restless anxiety caused by something other than concern for her own skin.

"Vail!" she cried. "He was going to the El Dorado . . ." As she said it, she looked up. The El Dorado Saloon, solid brick, not flimsy wood, was enveloped by fire. Bricks couldn't burn, but they seemed to be burning now, easy prey for the solid sheet of flame that shot up the walls and attacked every doorjamb and windowframe, every bit of wood it could find. As she watched, dumb with horror, the roof appeared to billow as if forced upward by an internal explosion—she could see wooden fragments flying in the light—and then grandly, slowly, it fell inward and collapsed with a deep, rumbling crash and anguished screams from inside.

With a harsh cry she began to run toward the shivering building, and as its walls broke apart with a thunderous cracking sound, she appealed to a man with a singed coat and blood on his face who was dragging an unconscious woman off the blazing sidewalk, "Oh, sir, can you tell me . . . have you seen Vail Severance?"

He looked at her as if she were crazy and continued dragging the woman with his good arm. His other arm dangled uselessly. Rage brought on by great fear rolled over her. She snatched up a smoldering piece of timber and, eyes glittering, went after him, prepared to beat information out of him whether he knew anything or not. From somewhere beyond the uproar of bells and falling walls and horses and people screaming, Vail's voice called her name.

She stopped, looked back, and dropped the stick without knowing it had seared her hand. He was coming from the direction of the theater. It had burned so completely that it was now only a smoking ruin over which a low, languid flame flickered. He ran flat out with the look on his face of a man just reprieved from death. She stood with her hand held out, unable to move, bricks from the crumbling El Dorado crashing near her, tears washing white, twisting paths down her sooty face. Then she was in his arms in a rib-crushing embrace that swung her off her feet and knocked the breath out of her. She heard Tom Anderson cry, "Sophy, oh, Sophy," in a voice that broke, and Vail set her down, his hands clamped hard on her arms.

In an accusing, angry way he said, "I thought you were still inside," and they stared at each other, he with that furious scowl and she blinking, tears dripping off her chin.

She gulped and wiped her wet face with the back of a dirty hand, which further smeared the soot. "Are you *mad* at me?"

He laughed exultantly and hugged her again, and the last wall of the Union Hotel, next door to the El Dorado, went down with a crash that resounded to the water and far out across the bay.

Without a word the men took off, dragging the girls with them down a street that was a gauntlet of scorching heat and choking, smothering smoke but offered darkness at the end, darkness that meant no fire yet. There was no moon, but the night sky was lit by a moving mass of fire such as had never been seen in this wild land before man arrived in marauding numbers. Geese, awakened by the false dawn, rose from their boggy resting places and beat across the sky in confusion, searching for the subtle signals of natural light to help them navigate.

The volunteer firemen, who loved to sing and parade and dress up in fancy uniforms between fires, were fighting as well as they could with the equipment at hand, but water was scanty, and had it been available in quantity, the hose to transport it was in short supply. It had been months since the last fire, and in the invigorating chase after profits everyone had forgotten about the need for humdrum things like axes, ladders, and hose. They directed the one hose they had toward flames now so fierce that the thin flow sizzled into steam as it struck. There were cries of "It's falling! Get back, get back!" and the high front wall of a store, its heavy timbers red-hot, crashed outward into the center of the street. Blazing chunks of wood exploded in all directions like Roman candles on the Fourth of July. Instantly new buildings kindled, and the open end of the street was cut off. Onlookers who moments before had been watching in relative safety surged forward, stampeding toward the little group who had stopped dead in their flight as the wall roared down before them.

Vail shouted something and, without waiting for an answer, pulled Marin out of the path of the mob and into a twisting alley lined with buildings so tall and close together that the heat was less intense and the glare of the fire was blotted out. It was so black down the long, narrow way, and yet her dazzled eyes still saw leaping yellow flames printed on the blanketing darkness. From far down the alley there came the sound of shattering glass. Vail pulled her to a stop and Sophy and Tom, right behind, bumped into them.

Marin looked apprehensively at Vail. She could not see him, but she could hear his quick breathing. They were all gasping from the long run, the heat, the fear.

"What is it?" she whispered. Despite the surrounding uproar, it seemed necessary to whisper in this darkness.

"Looters, I'll bet on it."

Looters! Oh, they were devils—arsonists, murderers, criminals of the worst kind who started these fires for the looting that was easy and lucrative in the anarchy that always followed. Looters would do anything. She clutched his sleeve. "We can't go out there."

"We have to." As if to prove his words there was a rumbling crash behind them as another wall came down and fire shot into the sky, lighting the alley enough for them to see each other's faces. "Tom, are you ready?"

Tom grunted assent, and metal gleamed dully as he transferred a pistol from his inside coat pocket to his belt. Vail had a gun, too; she heard the click-click as he checked it, and in the dim light his face was strangely calm, considering the peril they were in. Tom wore the same cool, set expression. How did men face up to terrors with such ready courage? Her own insides were turned to water.

At the end of the alley Vail raised his hand in a warning gesture, and they halted. Fire had not yet arrived here, but the street was washed in red light, as though by a hellish sunset, and demons were raging through it, tearing the city apart. Store windows disintegrated with a shivering, tinkling sound, smashed in by lengths of timber or hammers or pistol butts. Doors and shaky walls burst open under ax blows, and triumphant looters swarmed through the rifts like ants and staggered out with armloads of treasure: shovels, hunting rifles and dueling pistols, furniture, barrels of whiskey, clothing—anything portable.

At Moore and Dunker's, the best jewelry store in town, looters had struck paydirt. Not only did they have bags stuffed with gold brooches, rings, chains, and watches, but they had dragged the fireproof safe into the boardwalk and were pounding at the lock with a sledgehammer. Vail veered into the center of the street, and Marin, her instinct for survival working in high gear, understood his purpose and followed, hoping to make clear to the heavily armed looters that she hadn't the slightest interest in the fate of Moore and Dunker's property. Unfortunately Sophy, her own survival reflexes less finely tuned, saw what was happening. In shocked tones, she cried, "Tom, those men are opening that safe!" and Tom, torn between getting out of this madhouse and appearing heroic in Sophy's eyes, made a move toward the gun at his belt. One of the looters let loose a stream of profane warnings and fired at the same time. In less than three quick heartbeats Vail had shot the man point-blank, and the looter was lying still in the gutter, his gun in the dirt at his feet.

The two remaining looters, automatically reaching for their weapons, gazed at Vail in astonishment, aggrieved that anyone should take their companion's action in bad part, uncertain whether they wanted to fight about it. Then above the clamor of bells, the grumbling roar as weakened walls collapsed on other streets, the whistle of the fire itself, there came a different sound, an ear-shattering, earth-rattling boom followed by another and then another. High over the buildings in the direction of California Street, the brilliant flashes exploded against the gray-red sky. The looters glanced up involuntarily even as their hands began to move toward their guns, and Vail grabbed Marin and propelled her onward as she looked wildly over her shoulder and screamed, "Sophy!" But Sophy was taken care of, for Tom was with her.

Even in the panic of the moment some part of Marin remarked on how comforting it was to have men around when the world turned savage.

Down Montgomery Street they ran, avoiding looters, who in turn ignored them. They plunged through the glare and heat of Pine Street into the comparative darkness of the open field beyond.

Sophy slowed and called out, "Sister, stop! I can't run anymore." She sank to her knees in the weeds, her hands pressed against her heaving sides. Tom was trying to lift her.

"You can't just quit now," Marin shouted, and raced back. "Help us with Sophy, Vail!"

He walked back slowly and sat down.

"It's safe here. Let her rest."

Safe here. Vail said it was safe. Creakily Marin lowered herself to the ground. Around them in the field were clumps of people flung out like rag dolls or sitting up, looking back at the heart of town. Beyond the mantle of smoke the sky was a dark, oppressive purple-red. Below, the fire raged, gobbling up the city like a voracious giant, flames ascending in bright yellow columns, dying away, then vaulting again, higher and hotter into the sky. It was the end of San Francisco, the end of the world.

Fresh gusts of wind swirled ash in little storms; ash covered the rough ground and settled on hair and clothes. A bitter, stinging, caustic smell rode the breeze, the smell of many things burning— pitch, chemicals, wood, tobacco, textiles, grain, flesh. From somewhere came the odor of roast chicken. Mrs. Tierney's ice cream parlor was burning, and her chickens were trapped in the pen behind the house. They were roasting alive.

Sophy had thrown herself down and lay with arms across her eyes. Beside her Tom sat with knees drawn up and head bowed, breathing hard. He was a strong man, but he carried twenty pounds too much above his belt, and the night's exertions had taxed him past his limit.

Without warning another explosion, stunning in intensity, ripped the night, and Marin was on her feet, ready to run.

"Don't be scared," Vail said. "It's not the fire. They're blowing up buildings to make a firebreak."

Slowly she knelt down, still poised to leap and run. "You mean they're blowing up perfectly good buildings? Somebody's property?"

"What else can they do? On one side there's the water, but on three sides there's nothing to stop the fire until it burns itself out in the hills. If that happens, everything will be gone."

She looked at him in fright. That last explosion had been very near Dupont Street, close, much too close to Stockton. "Vail, we've got to get home."

The house on Stockton Street was safe. With thankful tears Marin saw it as she hurried up the road, standing unscathed, lights glowing in the front windows. The horses had been harnessed to the carriage, but were locked in the stable to prevent their running off in a fit of terror.

Within the house all was in readiness for emergency flight. Logan, Jeremy, and Mrs. Victoria, the only adults both able and sensible, had essentials packed and the other members of the household dressed. They sat together in the parlor with coats and blankets at hand, watching through the window the fiery display below, shuddering at each explosion, darting apprehensive glances at each other. Logan sat next to the window with Carey on her lap, compressing her nervous hands into stillness, straining her eyes toward the glare, as if by force of will she could see into the flames, see the fate of Vail and Marin and Sophy. Tom was down there, too, and somewhere, Luz. As soon as Luz had seen Marin leave early in the evening, she had asked permission to attend a dance in the Little Chile section, where citizens of Latin descent congregated. Logan, her injured foot resting on a pillow and her spirits depressed over her own lost night on the town, had granted the request and was now regretting it.

Delphine looked out the window and moaned for the twentieth time in a tone of bitter reproach, "If only those wrongheaded girls had stayed home tonight," and Logan, at the end of her rope, replied coldly, "Delphine, do shut up." Delphine gasped, mumbled something about respect for one's elders, and subsided.

Logan was the first to see them turning in at the gate. She set Carey on the floor, hobbled onto the porch, and with a glad cry, hurled herself into Vail's arms as he came up the stairs.

"My dear, are you all right?" She ran her hands over his face and chest, looking for wounds. "Oh, your face, Vail. You're filthy! Marin, Sophy, dear Tom!" Her laughter rippled as she hugged each of them enthusiastically, and Carey, his face pressed against the window, heard her laugh and raced out the door straight to his mother. He was exhilarated by the commotion and the noisy booms, the sudden flashes of light and the tension among the grown-ups; he had no awareness of danger, but only a strong desire to be at the center of the excitement.

As Logan started back into the house, she stumbled and almost fell. All through the frantic evening she had limped up and down stairs, giving Jeremy orders he didn't need, overseeing the packing and organizing the family, and her injured ankle finally cried out for rest. Vail carried her to a chair while Sophy and Marin hugged their parents and assured them that at no time had they been in any real danger.

Tom turned Logan's foot this way and that, announced that despite the poultice he had applied before leaving for the theater, the swelling had greatly increased, and scolded her for walking on it contrary to orders.

"But, Tom, I couldn't stay in bed when the town was burning down."

"I wish I had my bag," he muttered. "Well, we shall bind it, and if there is any aggravation of symptoms by morning, we shall apply leeches and follow with a thorough purge. Have you any Seidlitz powders in the house?"

"No, I don't think so," answered Logan in some alarm. "Truly, Tom, it doesn't hurt a bit, and I promise not to walk at all."

"Ah, thank you, Miss Delphine." Tom took the hastily gathered strips of linen and began to wrap Logan's long, narrow foot, ignoring her protestations. "No Dover's powder or calomel? Every well-run household should have Dover's powder. Six or eight grains along with a couple of grains of calomel would do wonders for the pain. If I can find any left in town after this night, I'll bring some over tomorrow."

"It feels wonderful," Logan assured him, looking down at her white-bound foot. "I'm sure I won't need another thing."

He pushed his lips forward and frowned. "And stay off your feet, young lady, until I allow you to get up. Now, Miss Marin, let me see your hand."

As the tumult of homecoming subsided, Marin had become aware of a sharp throb in her singed hand and was holding it in the fold of her skirt, hoping no one would notice.

"Come now, let me see," Tom commanded, and reluctantly she held out her hand, unable to withstand the magisterial authority that so impressed his growing list of patients.

"It's nothing, really."

"To the contrary, it could be most unpleasant if not treated. How did it happen?"

A blush stole into her face as she recalled her ruthless intention. "I can't remember," she said.

"Cotton wool is what we need. You do have cotton wool?"

"I'm sure we do." She didn't want to fail again in housewifery, as she had failed with all the other medical supplies Tom had asked for. "Aunt Delphine?"

"Oh, yes. Of course." Delphine skittered off, hoping there were sheets of cotton wadding in the linen closet.

Tom lifted Marin's chin and turned her to the light. "Ma'am, you are alarmingly flushed. Do you think a bleeding and a purge are in order, Vail?"

Vail laid the back of his hand against her forehead and her cheek, then pressed his fingers lightly just below her jaw. She stared at the floor, wishing both men would go away and not come back for several months.

"Rapid pulse," he murmured, and her flush deepened. "It must be the heat and the fright, Tom. Let her rest tonight. You can always bleed her in the morning."

"Well . . . yes, Miss Delphine, this will do nicely."

By three o'clock it was decided that the family could safely go upstairs and endeavor to sleep, although the explosions downtown continued. Vail, Tom, and Jeremy sat downstairs and smoked and talked until dawn. Somewhere above the cloaking smoke the sun must have been shining, but for miles in all directions around the great bay May 4, 1851, was a bleak, gray day of loss and desolation. The fire burned into the morning, and when it finally dwindled and died, it left a city utterly destroyed except for scattered buildings outside the center of town.

In the late morning Vail left to see to his own house, which was almost certainly safe up on Rincon Hill, and Tom returned to town, to his hotel, which had undoubtedly burned with all his possessions in it.

All the rest of the day Delphine and Sophy, Jeremy and Mrs. Victoria flew about under Marin's energetic direction, sweeping, dusting, polishing, taking down sooty curtains to be laundered when the air cleared, cleaning off the thick layer of ash that had settled on windowsills, veranda, and steps, and covered the ground around the house like a crumbling gray blanket.

Considering the devastation, Marin could have been expected to be in a bitter mood, for she regarded all calamities as personal affronts. But Vail had been frantic to find her last night; she would never forget the look on his face when he saw she was safe. So today, in spite of the damage to her possessions and the soreness of her burned hand, she was in a humor so buoyantly cheerful that Logan, watching her whirlwind activities from the parlor sofa, noticed it and wondered. Logan had little direct experience of the world, but behind her diffident manner was a perceptive and subtle intelligence, and her insight into the character and motives of others had sharpened with the years. She observed, she recorded, she held her peace. Marin would have been mortified to the bone had she guessed Logan's thoughts.

Just before suppertime, Luz wandered in, disheveled, which was understandable enough, but also vague as to where she had been since the fire ended. Marin, who had pictured her dying a horrible death in one of Little Chile's tumbledown shanties, was so relieved to see the girl healthy and in one piece that she sent her off to clean up without a word of reproach. Luz had her own secret life. She also had more lives than a cat.

Only two others, of those few people important to Marin, remained unaccounted for. Gerald and Anna had been in that theater, too, and in the middle of the crowd, far away from any exit. Tom had been all over town and had heard no word of them. Perhaps it wasn't possible that everybody she cared about could come safely through such catastrophe. She went to bed that night grateful that those few who made up her inmost special circle were safe.

Chapter 22

In the morning Jeremy drove Marin into town. They saw a ruined city. Every building from Portsmouth Square to the water was leveled, with only a few scattered, scorched exceptions. Not only those built of wood, but scores of iron and brick structures, supposedly fireproof, were consumed. The enterprises that were the lifeblood of the community—the customhouse, the U.S. assayer's office, the quartermaster's office, banks, stores, warehouses, gambling halls, every newspaper except the *Alta California*, restaurants, including Delmonico's, even store ships in the harbor—all were gone. The town was flattened, quiet after the madness of the night before last, but a pulse was still beating. People were poking through broken bricks and partly burned heaps of wood, dragging out odd bits and pieces of possessions not completely destroyed. Already some lots had been cleared and building materials were in place for the new structures that would rise on the sites.

Several times Marin stopped to speak to people she knew, to commiserate and to ask for news of Gerald Crown. Each time there was sorrowful shaking of heads followed by the heartening words that, after all, who could tell in such a disaster, he might yet turn up, things often looked worse than they were. It was a familiar refrain, typical of this place and time, and it lifted her heart. Somewhere an optimist was hammering, the quick thudding sounds loud on the smoky air. On the lot where the Midlin Steam Navigation Co. had been, wood was being measured and sawed.

As she passed the blackened remains of McAffrey's Bank, she heard, "Marin! Halloo!" in a full-throated bellow.

She cried out, "Stop, Jeremy!" and hopped from the carriage before Jeremy could descend to assist her. She scrambled over piles of charred bricks and joyfully embraced a slight, wiry man in a rumpled suit with a bandage wrapped around his dark head. "Gerald, I've been so worried! What happened to your head?" The whiteness of the bandage made his skin look very brown, his dark eyes very bright.

He grinned and squeezed her hard. "This is most pleasant. Oh, the head, that's nothing. Some enterprising ruffian wanted my wallet and cracked me with a pistol butt. He ought to have used the other end, the fool."

"Did you . . ."

"I surely did. He's dead as nits, and no loss to the world. So you got out safely. I thought you would. My, but you look delectable." He squeezed her tighter, and she made a little moue of mock reproach and removed herself from his arms.

"I was truly anxious for you, Gerald. You and Anna were in the middle of that awful mob so far from the door. Is she all right, too?"

"Anna is fine—a slight burn on one arm, but nothing serious. We got off the roof just before it collapsed, which is how Anna got singed. What's the matter with your hand?"

"The same thing—a little burn." She slid her bandaged hand into her muff. "Does Anna have someplace to stay? She and Logan could share, and you could have Stuart's—that is, we do have space if you are in need."

"Why, that's more than kind, Marin, more than kind." Genuine warmth replaced his habitual, half-mocking smile. "I have found a place to roost, and Anna is with friends, but I will tell her of your generous offer the next time I run into her. Good morning, Jeremy."

Jeremy, who had remained discreetly near the carriage to allow them private conversation, tipped his tall hat in salute.

They climbed off the ruins of the bank to what had been the sidewalk, and Gerald looked back. "McAffrey's Bank. It's not so high and mighty now. I hear they got their gold out, but most people's stock in trade was not rescued so easily. There are a good many men in this town today who are brought as low as that building."

"But I see signs of rebuilding everywhere, and everyone is so hopeful. Tom Anderson says we're going to bounce right back, bigger and better than before."

"We are—some of us. Tom carries what he sells in his head, like me. Specialized knowledge, training, for whatever it's worth. And others, like your esteemed brother-in-law, own the land itself. But men with every cent sunk into merchandise that went up in smoke the other night, they are in a bad way, and it's worse for those who bought stock on credit." He grinned jauntily. "Which makes the situation ripe for a fellow with a little ready cash and an eye for a good thing."

It was exactly what James had said. Last night, just before she went to bed she had made her usual visit to her parents' room to kiss them good-night and assure herself that all their needs had been seen to. Rose was in her bed, already half asleep. The excitement of the past day and night had left her enervated. She smiled when Marin kissed her, and her eyelids drooped shut.

Marin tiptoed across the room to James. He had been reading, his book propped on a small stand that straddled his legs—Jeremy's invention. Against the white, high-piled pillows his skin looked ruddy and healthy, for he sat in the sun much of each day, but he was so thin! It tugged at her heart, the flaccid shoulders that once had been so powerful, the wasted body, the haggard face. But vitality was still there in his eyes, in his expression. As flesh had fallen away, his forceful spirit had become more visible, and the very gauntness of his face emphasized the strong bones beneath. James, like his daughter, was a survivor, and he wasn't licked yet.

"Time to shut up shop, Papa, time for sleep."

He let her take away the book and the stand, but when she bent to turn down the flame of the lamp, he took her hand and held it.

"Sit beside me, chicken."

His blue eyes were bright with a dancing light that piqued her curiosity. He'd looked like this when he told the family they were going to California. It was something similar he was mulling over now, although the only trip he had in mind for her was a sortie into town with Jeremy.

This morning she had ridden through the streets alert to each sign of activity, trying to be her father's eyes and ears and legs, recording everything in the brain James had so much faith in, wondering how to overcome her ignorance of the real ways in which money was made and accomplish the mission he had given her. "This fire is a true disaster, Marin," he had said. "I can't guess all the repercussions, but I'm dead certain one man's bad luck can be another man's chance." That's what he had said last night, and now Gerald was saying much the same thing, with the same roguish gleam in his eyes. The best thing to do was part company with him now, for clearly Gerald was on the lookout for a good speculation too. He was the dearest of friends, but she would not care to tussle with him if they both stumbled onto the same opportunity. It was much too likely that she would come out the loser.

She held out her hand, the unburned one. "Every one of your clients must be searching for you this very minute, Gerald, so I won't keep you." Instantly he took his cue, bowed, kissed her fingers in that lingering way he had, and sauntered off.

"Do come by the house anytime," she called after him, and Jeremy helped her into the carriage. They proceeded slowly down the street, picking their way around heaps of debris, carefully skirting chuckholes big enough for a horse to fall into. They turned the corner, and safely out of Gerald's sight she said, "Hurry up, Jeremy. Let's go down to Montgomery Street. I want to find Mr. Callendar."

Near what had been the corner of Montgomery and Jackson the fireproof warehouse of Harry L. Callendar & Co., eighteen-inch-thick brick walls with shutters and reinforcements of iron, lay tumbled like one of Carey's toy houses. When the test came, iron and brick had proved no safer against the flames than wood. Although it was the familiar sight she had been seeing all morning—blackened, broken bricks, melted, twisted metal—she had not expected this. She had thought that although all of the city collapsed, Harry L. Callendar & Co. would somehow still be standing, with Harry bustling about, taking an honorable entrepreneur's advantage of other men's bad luck.

Harry sat alone beside the rubble on a small folding camp stool, surveying the devastation with an expression Marin could not read. At sight of her he jumped up, overflowing with greetings and goodwill, dusting off his little stool, hiding his private thoughts well.

"No, thank you, Harry. I've not the slightest need to sit. Oh, this is terrible."

She poked at a brick with the tip of her closed parasol. It toppled over and slid to the bottom of the pile accompanied by a puff of ash that made Harry sneeze.

He pulled out a large handkerchief and blew his nose. "There it is, my fortune in a pile of dust. I have gone down with a sneeze, dear ma'am, and I would have preferred, if I must go at all, to do it with more style."

"Go down? Harry, what do you mean? This is an awful loss, but . . ." She looked over the charred remains of Harry's warehouseful of goods—heavy machinery, whiskey, furniture, no telling what had been in there, for he had his finger in so many pies.

He sat down again on the stool with such a groan of genuine woe that she looked at him in alarm. "Harry Callendar is a warm man," James had often said in respectful admiration, and indeed he was, with that solid financial well-being that is the best foundation on which to build a fortune. She had come to see him in the expectation that he could show her how to put this catastrophe to good use. And here he was, making no move to set things right as others were doing all over town, but sitting, staring, looking as if he'd lost his best friend.

"Good heavens, Mrs. Harry isn't . . ."

"She is well, and I should be grateful. Indeed, I am grateful when I think of the fate of others. I give thanks to God that none of my crew worked late the other night." He nudged a hunk of metal with a dusty brown boot. "This damnable iron. Pardon my language, ma'am. This iron, which was supposed to protect us from fire, caused the deaths of five men that I know of. The heat locked the iron shutters tight, and the men inside were cooked alive. Cooked alive," he repeated somberly. "We couldn't reach them, couldn't help them. I shall hear those screams until I die. Others were crushed by falling walls, no one knows where or how many, but bodies are being found every time a lot is cleared. John Gibb's entire family died. I heard he shot himself yesterday. It was arson again. Something must be done, something will be done to stop it, and I tremble to think what."

"Arson? I thought it was an accident."

"It was an incendiary gang, we are certain. It started in the paint store on Portsmouth Square, and they picked a good night for it with the wind high as it was." He looked up with a sudden frown. "Forgive me. I haven't asked how all is with you."

"We came through very well, and our house is safe. We were lucky, too."

He shook his head worriedly, and his long side-whiskers quivered. "I'm happy to hear it. Shameful not to have asked at once, shocking self-concern—my only excuse is the prospect of starting from scratch at my age. It fair overwhelms me."

"From scratch? With your resources?"

He barked a short, bitter laugh, got up, paced to the crumbled wall, and stared at it with face averted, a little man who with shoulders slumped looked even smaller. Was it possible that he was one of those ruined men Gerald had talked about—cautious, conservative, well-to-do Harry? Could such a thing be?

"Is it . . . are you embarrassed for funds at the moment?" A tentative probe, easily withdrawn.

His gray tufts of eyebrows drew together. He turned to look back at her.

He said, "I am wiped out. My upholstery shop was one of the first buildings to burn, and my home is a heap of rubble. My restaurant on Sacramento Street no longer exists, my smaller warehouses on Clay and Sansome are gone, a steamer I had a half interest in burned at the dock, several other buildings that I owned in whole or in part were blown up in an effort to stop the fire, and this . . ." He glanced at the devastation before them. ". . . this represents my greatest reversal."

It was stunning, the quiet, undramatic listing of such over-whelming loss.

"Did you . . ." She paused, trying to think of some delicate way to put it. "Are you indebted for the goods that were here?"

"Two thousand bags of Chilean flour, five hundred chests of tea, twelve hundred barrels of pork, four thousand cases of tobacco—most was paid for, a great mistake. I could have dumped the gold I paid for that merchandise in the bay for all its use to me now. The machinery, that's the pickle. I signed a note on it to Adams and Sons, New York—twenty-two thousand dollars for what are now globs of melted metal."

"There is no insurance?"

"I'll wager that not above two buildings in town were insured, neither of them mine. We do not present an attractive risk to Eastern insurers. I planned to pay the note with cash received for the food-stuffs and tobacco. Another day, two days at the most, and it all would have been transferred and the gold in my hands.

Some other man would have taken the loss. Those ashes you see before you are what I have left to sell. With credit I could get hold of some sort of salable merchandise and come up with a profit to pay off the note and relaunch, but no credit will be extended with such a debt on the books." He smiled, a pinched, tight smile. "So I am at a stand."

"You have friends—"

"Not in a muddle like this. Besides, nearly everyone is as hard-pressed."

"Some people have money. Why, only a couple of months ago Vail made a killing on his land—you told me so yourself."

"And he promptly reinvested it in waterfront property. Money must work for its keep, don't you see, and Vail is not the man to put it in a sock and hide it under the mattress." He chuckled at the picture. "I never wanted my money in land, wanted it more liquid, available for quick action, a decision I have recently come to regret. Even the land my warehouses stand on—stood on—is leased. Oh, Vail is worth a packet, I expect. He has a cargo due in on the *Matilda,* but she is late. If she makes port soon, he can command a fancy price, but she may be long delayed or even lost. Ships are more of a gamble than faro. No, he will not be flush of cash just now. I would not embarrass him by asking."

Marin ran her tongue over dry lips. What would Papa do if he were here? What would he have her do? She was far beyond her depth, intimidated by the magnitude of her ignorance. It unsettled her certainties to see Harry Callendar, of all people in the world, brought so low. Looking at the blackened remains of his fortune, she wondered if perhaps luck was not the crucial element in making money.

A wagon rumbled past, bearing lumber and new bricks just unloaded off an unscathed ship in the harbor. There was an example of luck—anyone who happened to own a supply of building materials conveniently near the city but unburned was in clover now.

She smiled. "Here we stand in this dusty street when my carriage is right at hand. Come sit with me, Harry."

They climbed in, and she settled her skirts prettily. "I am so interested in your present situation, and my father will be, too. I'd like to be able to explain it to him when I go home. You need twenty-two thousand dollars, is that right?"

"Fifteen would do it. I swear I would stand a good chance with fifteen, for the city will be starved for goods, and any merchandise I can lay hands on will sell."

"I'm sorry, I don't follow. How can fifteen be enough when your debt alone is twenty-two thousand?"

He looked deep into her eyes and saw the intelligence there and the earnest struggle to comprehend.

"The note is not due for two months," he said, and the pieces of the puzzle fell into place.

She swallowed. "My father has some money available for a good investment."

Harry's button eyes grew sharp. "How much?"

"I believe he would consider fifteen thousand."

"Ready cash?" asked Harry.

"As you say, money must work for its keep." Glibly she picked up the phrase he had used. "But it can be—can be made liquid reasonably quick. Papa is willing to mortgage Little Mountain."

The light of hope died in Harry's face. "Ranches are a long-term investment, and they build slowly. Mr. Gentry will not find such a lender in a year."

"We have a lender already interested. My father-in-law."

"Malcolm?" Harry turned this new information around in his mind. "If Malcolm has such an amount available, I would expect him to put it down over here rather than loan on a ranch when he already has so many acres. The rewards would be greater and much faster."

"Yes, I suppose, ordinarily. But in this case there are special circumstances."

Harry leaned back on the comfortable seat, took out his handkerchief again, and mopped his face. He was sweating, he could feel the moisture trickling down his armpits, sweating and trembling at the vision of salvation when all had looked so black.

"Your husband—is he in town? Will he approve?"

"Stuart is in San Diego, or he was last week. He thinks it's a good idea to borrow against Little Mountain for investment purposes. I know he'll approve going into business with you."

"He will surely be home in a hurry when he hears of our fire, and we can talk it over."

She nodded, her eyes down, and Harry decided to say no more about Stuart. It had been obvious to him for some time that Marin Severance and her husband were in fact separated, although they kept up the public facade of marriage. It was a not uncommon solution for a failed marriage, since divorce was almost impossible.

"Marin, this offer is tempting to me, as you must realize, but I am bound to point out—indeed I shall point out to your father—

that he will be running considerable risk. I believe given the sum we've discussed that I will come out with a whole skin, but having lost everything already, it is no gamble for me. If Mr. Gentry is unable to pay back his loan, it would mean losing Little Mountain." He softened what he said by adding quickly, "Of course within the family there may be agreements I am not privy to."

She touched his arm lightly. "Come by this evening, and talk to Papa. Come about six, for supper, and bring Mrs. Harry."

The horses were growing more restive. Harry climbed out of the carriage and brushed at his side-whiskers. All the fussy little mannerisms, gone completely during his talk of money, were back. "We shall be there. You've given me hope on a very dark day."

"May I also give you a ride somewhere?"

"Thank you, no. I'm going to round up a crew and start clearing the land. Can't wait for Christmas, can we?" Vigorous, aggressive words from a man so recently ruined. He lifted his hat in farewell, and Jeremy clucked to the horses.

They trotted down Montgomery to Washington and turned right. Marin huddled in the back with her thoughts, exhilarated, frightened, feeling she had taken the first step on a tightrope over a gaping chasm, knowing she could still turn back if the drop looked too fearful.

"Circle around the square and drive me to Rincon Hill, Jeremy."

"What you want to go up dere for?"

She scowled at his back. "To look at the view. I want to talk over my plans with Mr. Vail, that's what for."

"He ain' gonna be home this day, he gonna be out scratchin' up big money deals like Missus Cornelius Vanderbilt heah. Oh, my Lawd, on'y fifteen thousand, Mistuh Callendar, suh? Is you shore you don' want twenny-two? Them's dollahs you was talkin' 'bout, not titbugs. Wait till yo' Daddy heahs."

"That's how much you know. Papa told me to look for a good proposition. You take me up to Rincon Hill."

"Nobody s'pose to go dere less they's invited, an' you ain' been invited. Besides, I don' know de way."

"Oh, what a lie! You think I don't know you go there all the time? You think I don't know you and Kaui have roped Usual McIntyre in on your schemes, you Machiavelli."

"What's dat Machiavelli?"

"A slyboots, that's what."

He chuckled. "Don' do no good callin' me names. You already

knows what Mistuh Vail gonna' say 'bout mortgagin' yo' Daddy's land. He gonna' say lie down an' put lavenduh watuh on yo' haid till de fevuh drops."

She gazed resentfully at his nattily uniformed back. It wasn't his arguing back that bothered her, it was the casual way he used words like *mortgage*. Why, for all she knew he might even hold some mortgages himself, and while she didn't mind his making money, it wasn't right that he had a clear grasp of matters she barely comprehended herself.

"You drive me up Rincon Hill, and no more back sass!"

Slowly he turned the horses, and she settled more comfortably. He was going to take her. He might have refused outright, and it would have done no good to threaten to fire him, for he knew perfectly well she couldn't do without him. Still, beneath his acquiescence she sensed a lack of enthusiasm for the trip. He didn't want to take her, and later, when she had time to apply her mind to it, she would figure out why.

The house was every bit as impressive as she had heard, commanding a sweeping view of town and bay and magnificent mountains to the east, built of substantial, dark red brick, and so large! The ornate, wrought iron fence and gate were fine, much nicer than her own wood picket fence, and within the spacious grounds there were young trees, well-trimmed grass, and a rose garden.

She walked up to the varnished front door with the ornamental fanlight of leaded glass above it and tugged the bellpull. Chimes rang distantly. From inside the house a flutelike melody wandered, soft, elusive, muffled by heavy door and thick walls. Footsteps, then a rattle of the brass knob. The door swung open, and her smile brightened.

"Usual, how nice to see you. Is Vail at home?" She was walking in as she talked, glancing swiftly around the elegant vestibule. Usual was still at the door, a burly man of forty-five or so, attractive in a rough-hewn way, or he would have been if he hadn't had his nose smashed repeatedly in barroom brawls and hadn't lost half his right ear in a knife fight with a justifiably indignant husband. But she was used to lusty, forceful, trouble-seeking males and preferred their company to any other so long as they treated her with proper respect. Usual had helped her move into her house, had done a number of chores and favors for different members of the family out of the goodness of his heart and a liking for them, and had refused all offers of recompense other than a Sunday dinner upon occasion. She had developed a fondness for him and an admiration for his prickly, independent character.

He looked out the door at Jeremy and raised his hand, and Jeremy responded with a touch of his whip to his hat and a movement of shoulders that was almost a helpless shrug. Usual closed the door.

"Good day to you, Miss Marin. Heard you and Miss Sophy had a bit of adventure the other night."

She shuddered delicately. "More than we wanted." The music had begun again. It was a violin being played with an expert touch. Surprised, she asked, "Is that Vail?"

"Yes'm. Come sit in the parlor, and I'll tell him you're here."

The music curled and trembled though the quiet house, mellow, deep, then soaring, sweet and true, a rich complexity of sound coming from across the hall behind closed double doors. She stood still, listening to the emotion in that sound, remembering that she had once lectured him on the importance of music to the inmost self.

"He's very good."

"Sounds pretty to me. I don't know about music as such, but I like to hear it. Means he's in a good mood."

"Why does he keep such a talent hidden?"

Usual shrugged. "Don't ask me why he does things. You just step in here—Miss Marin!"

She had opened the double doors and gone in before Usual could stop her, wanting to hear the music more clearly, wanting Vail to know that she heard. The doors closed behind her, and the melody broke off in midflight. Later she recalled that it was a small but beautiful room, heavily draped, thickly carpeted, the flames of a low fire moving and flickering behind a marble hearth, giving a cozy, homelike atmosphere of great intimacy.

This was where he lived. On a table was spread the remains of a late breakfast, and he was standing with his violin under his chin, just lowering his bow, staring at her with, at first, nothing more than surprise in his eyes. Curled languorously on the sofa before the fireplace, black hair flowing loose about her fine-boned, creamy face, an exquisite lace peignoir covering her slender body, and a stricken expression in her dark, slanting eyes, was Petra Victoria.

Marin stood with hands pressed to her lips. She saw Vail lay the violin on the table, saw Petra straighten and draw the peignoir close across her breasts. Thoughts and images tumbled in confusion in her mind. His face in the lamplight on a hellish night when she was abandoned and alone and trying to have a baby that would not come . . . his eyes watching her night after night in the campfire's light in the high mountains . . . and only two nights ago, in the heat and glare of a great conflagration, in the terrifying din, with the world collapsing around them, his face as he ran to her, looking as if he'd been given back his life . . . How could she have been wrong? Memories returned. The evening he came back to Little Mountain for the first time . . . Petra so unobtrusive in the room; Petra leaving for the city such a short time later; the family never invited to this house; Jeremy trying to keep her from coming today; Usual hustling her toward the parlor with that odd look on his face. God, they had all known, everyone had known except her. He had taken her to parties and plays and picnics, had eaten at her table and smiled at her with those gray eyes, and teased and scolded and helped her and cared about what she did. And every night when he left her, he had come home to Petra.

I've got to get out of here, she thought. Out, with dignity and pride intact. She struggled, and found her voice.

"I beg your pardon. Usual tried to put me in the parlor, but I heard the music . . . you play beautifully. I had no idea . . . I fear I am *de trop*."

"Not at all, Marin. Come in." His face, his voice gave her no guidance.

She forced the muscles of her mouth into a smile. "Jeremy told me not to come without an invitation. I did have a little business matter to discuss, but it can wait for another time." That was better. She had herself in hand.

Petra glanced at Vail, and the look that passed between them was the communication of two people who know each other very well. At sight of it a gust of jealous anger such as she had never known swamped Marin, demolishing her hard-won control. She could have clawed out those anguished, slanting dark eyes and enjoyed doing it, torn apart that slender, voluptuous body and ground the pieces into the dirt.

Color flooded her face. "You slut. You sneaking trollop."

Once Petra had wept at far softer condemnation from Marin, but she had matured in mind as well as body, and while the words wounded, they did not crush. She went even paler, but her head came up.

"I'm sorry, Miss Marin. I wouldn't hurt you for the world." She walked out of the room and closed the door quietly.

In the silence the fire snapped softly. A log burned through and fell with a shower of sparks. She could not decipher the expression on his face.

"I regret your finding out this way, Marin," he said slowly, "but you should not have said that to Petra. Blame me, if you wish, but she's done nothing wrong."

"I do blame you. Coming out to Little Mountain as a friend, spotting a servant girl you like the look of, and—and getting her to come over here to you. And she told me she was going to work for Mrs. Fletcher. Mrs. Fletcher—what a joke! Did you plan that story together? Did you tell her just how to say it?"

"I suppose you won't believe this, but I didn't ask Petra to come, I scarcely noticed her at Little Mountain. There was no plan. She worked for Mrs. Fletcher for several months, and we met by accident."

"You're right, I don't believe you. How can you stand there and lie like that? Why do you even bother when it doesn't matter to you what I think."

"It matters. The last thing I want is to injure you, the last thing . . . What the hell do you expect of me, Marin? To live all my life as a monk?"

"Do you mean to marry her?"

"No. Not that it's any of your business."

None of her business. It was cold, and it was true. Nothing he did was her business or ever would be. He was Petra's business, Petra, with the gliding walk and the dark, provocative eyes and the woman's body that he must know so well. She was upstairs now, in his bedroom, waiting while he got rid of the foolish, unwelcome intruder as gracefully as possible, waiting until he came up . . . They would talk about her and smile or feel sorry for her and then do a number of things that must not be thought about or she would begin to scream.

Anger had sustained her thus far, held off the bitter hurt and crushed pride and the fear that everyone had been laughing at her, but that last remark struck home as nothing else that had happened in this room. The tendency to towering, unbridled passions—kept carefully repressed for years but deep in her—the temper James had always cautioned would someday do great harm, took over, annihilating every restraint. Without a thought beyond the desire to savage him, she reached for the most hurtful weapons she could find.

"How I despise you." Her voice was low and distinct. "You take that foolish, ignorant girl who has no understanding of what she's doing, you use her as you wish, and when you're through, you'll leave her all alone with no one to help her, no one to turn to, with only her own little strength and wit to pull her through. Your father is hard and cruel, but he's right about one thing. You are a contemptible man."

His face went still. It was the way he had looked when Elizabeth died.

She fumbled for the doorknob, found it, walked into the hall, not seeing Usual, not seeing anything. She opened the front door and went out into the sun. It was barely past noon, and she blinked in the light. Somehow it seemed that the world should be dark with lowering clouds.

On the steps she stopped and leaned against the iron railing, her breathing ragged as that of a runner who has just lost a grueling race. Her heart pounded in her throat so loudly that it frightened her, her body shook, her mouth and lips were dry, and now that the first rage was subsiding, she was clammy with cold sweat and a hideous sense of loss. She had left her life back there in that room, and now it would never be right again. For one instant some kind of apology, some partial retraction had been possible, but not now. The bond between them, the friendship built slowly with care and commitment over the long months, had been hacked apart with a few swift strokes, and never again would she have the certain knowledge that there was one person in the world who would never let her down. Never, never, never. The word beat in her mind and made her sick.

A figure moved up the path from the street, a small person, all in black even to the shawl over her head.

"Miss Marin? Señora? It is so long that I 'ave not see you."

"Consuela?" Marin said numbly.

"Sí, Consuela. Miss Rose, she is well?"

"Very well, thank you. I'll tell her you asked." The girl was smiling, nodding. What was she doing so far from Fontana? What did it matter what she was doing? "Buenos días, Consuela." Marin ran down the path to the waiting carriage. She climbed in, avoiding Jeremy's knowing, compassionate eyes.

No word passed between them. He snapped the reins and headed the horses toward home.

There was no fire in the grate. Understandable, for the day had grown warm as the sun rose and dipped, yet she was cold. She hugged her arms and shivered. No amount of wool shawls or comforting fires could warm the cold places in her heart.

The house was quiet. Jeremy had let her off at the front door, and she had come into the parlor instead of going upstairs. Delphine was out, but Sophy and Logan were home, and she could not face either of them just now. What had she said to make him look like that, what had she done? Her confused mind could not remember.

The doorbell rang a single note. Oh, please, not a visitor now. There was no way to get to her room except by the front hallway. She remained by the empty fireplace, trapped, and heard Logan's light feet on the stairs, heard her say, "Gerald, how nice. Yes, I do believe she came in."

Silence, then the opening of the parlor door. No way to hide swollen eyes and red nose. She turned her back, taking deep breaths to steady herself.

"Gerald is here, Marin." Logan was in the doorway.

"Tell him I can't see him now, tell him to go away." As she spoke, he walked in.

Or, rather, he bounced in, in the best of moods, smiling broadly. "I have news of the finest sort. I've found an investment . . . Marin, honey, what is it?"

Logan took in Marin's averted face and tense figure in one quick glance and backed out tactfully.

"What's the trouble?" His hand was on her arm.

"Don't touch me, I can't stand it. Oh, Gerald, I've ruined my life!"

His hand dropped away. He didn't say "Nonsense" or "Don't be a silly child." He said simply, "Tell me," in the reasonable, reassuring tone that had led clients to confide all sorts of crimes up to and including murder.

She turned and he looked into a tormented face, puffy with crying.

"I went to see Vail today at his house. I walked in on him and Petra." Something moved in his eyes. She said, "You knew, didn't you."

"As a matter of fact . . . yes."

"Everyone knew, except me."

"Hardly everyone. It isn't a subject of general gossip."

"Why didn't you tell me?"

His lips turned down. He led her to the sofa, made her sit down, and sat beside her. "It had nothing to do with you . . . No, don't get mad, it didn't. And a gentleman couldn't mention such a thing to a lady."

He couldn't, of course. Her nose was runny. She dug a wisp of lace-trimmed linen out of her pocket, wiped her face, and stuffed the handkerchief back. "How long has it been going on?"

He considered the code of honor among gentlemen, and decided there was no harm in the truth.

"Since late last summer, right after his mother died."

After Elizabeth died. Perhaps that meant they hadn't planned it after all. She sniffed and rubbed at her damp cheeks. "I said awful things to him, bad things about Petra, too. He'll never forgive me."

"Really lost your temper, eh?"

She squeezed her eyes shut and nodded.

"I'd like to have seen that."

"No, you wouldn't. It was . . . Gerald, the whole room turned kind of reddish purple . . . horrible. I think I could have committed murder."

"A killing rage," he murmured.

"What?"

"Tell me what you said."

She shook her head. "I'm not even sure. I remember saying he'd lured Petra over here for—for immoral purposes, and he said they met by accident. I guess they liked each other," she added forlornly.

He smiled, but she didn't see it. "That part is true. I was with him when they were introduced. He recalled her only faintly as one of your servants, but they did become good friends rather quickly. So as not to mislead you I must confess I was happy to see it. Things had not been well with him for some time. Oh, on the surface he was a pleasant companion, a good friend, busy all the time, but there were black moods, times when he couldn't bear to be around anyone. The cause I don't know, estrangement from his family perhaps, but he was an unhappy man. He indulged in none of the usual vices—he didn't drink, never really gambled, and there were no women, none. You won't understand, but believe me, for a man like Vail it was not a healthy state of affairs. Since he met Petra, it's been much better."

"Then he loves her?"

He took her hand and smoothed it in his, liking the feel of soft skin and small, fine bones beneath. "Honey, I've given up trying to guess what people really feel inside. We humans are complicated, mixed-up animals. But in this case I venture to doubt that he does—in the way you mean. And I can't believe that such words as you've told me, spoken in haste, could cause a permanent breach between the two of you."

"There was more. I said he used young girls and then deserted them. I said I despised him."

"You covered the ground thoroughly."

"I said he was contemptible."

"Ah, that as well. And what did he say?"

"Nothing. But his face—oh, Gerald, you didn't see his face. He won't forgive me, not for this, and I feel so bad about it. He saved my life and Belinda's—have I ever told you that he saved my life?"

"Yes, you have told me, several times."

"He saved Sophy—well, that's another story. But he didn't have to, he just did it. He's done so much for me, so many kindnesses. I hurt him, and I wish I hadn't."

"Now, lamb, don't look so tragic. It's nothing irretrievable. We all say things and do things in the heat of the moment that we have to be forgiven for. If nobody ever forgave, we'd all be in deep trouble, wouldn't we? Innocently you walked into a situation that was understandably shocking to a lady, and you spoke sharply, in a manner you now regret."

"You do make things so clear and reasonable, Gerald."

"That's my business."

She pushed back a curl that had fallen forward on her cheek, tucked it carefully into the coil on her back, and said primly, "He is Stuart's brother, so we have to make it up. I couldn't be the cause of another break in the family. You do see that?"

"Yes," he said gently, "I see. In case I can arrange it, would you like him to come over tonight?"

"Oh, that would be wonderful! But—what shall I say?"

"Say you're sorry in your own charming way."

Silently she contemplated the painfulness of apologies. "I won't take back what I said about Petra. Not one word."

"Naturally. But if you can, refrain from adding to what you've already said. Men are peculiar creatures—they have a distaste for hearing one woman comment unfavorably on another woman."

"It was true!"

"If it was, that makes it worse. Take my advice, don't mention her. Now go upstairs, wash your face, and tidy your hair while I go see what I can do."

She shook her head, smiled, brushed his cheek with her lips. "Dear Gerald, how can I thank you?"

"I shall give the question profound thought and let you know."

• • •

Gerald rode away from the house, sorting out a number of speculations, wondering what humor he would find Vail in, but confident of his ability to bring about a satisfactory conclusion. Negotiation was his business, too. Ahead came a horseman, but Gerald's mind was turned inward and he scarcely noticed. At the corner of Stockton and Pine they came abreast.

"Good afternoon, Gerald. Have you been to see my family?"

Gerald looked up, drew rein, smiled the friendliest of greetings. "Stuart, good to see you. Everyone is safe, and the house still standing. You must have had a dash for home."

"We touched port at Monterey last evening and heard about it then. They said the flames could be seen from there and the sky was lit up like day. It looks like the city is finished. There wasn't even a wharf to dock at, we had to anchor in the bay and row in."

"Yes, it's bad, but did you notice the rebuilding as you rode through town? We shall rise from the ashes yet again."

Stuart's horse tossed its head and stamped skittishly, a nervous animal, short in the flanks, not the quality he was used to riding. He brought it quickly into line, nodding agreement with Gerald's optimistic words, hiding his irritation at coming home after a long absence and a night and day of severe anxiety to find Gerald Crown coming down the road after what was obviously a social call on his wife. He had never liked this oily, dapper little man with the foreign-looking, pencil-thin mustache—he had much too smooth and facile a tongue and could convince you that black was white if you listened to him long enough. He didn't like Gerald's perpetual snuffling around his home and his wife, and he didn't see why Marin allowed it or enjoyed the fellow's company. Not that he believed there was a thing between them, it was all most platonic, but with a teasing, flirting edge that was much too European for his taste. And he couldn't say a word of criticism without her getting that stubborn look on her face and refusing to discuss it. More than once he'd been mightily tempted to tell her about Gerald and her other fine friend, Anna von Helsdorf, and see if she could countenance such an immoral connection or feel so flattered by Gerald Crown's admiration. So far, good judgment had kept him quiet.

He lifted his hat and rode on. Gerald grinned to himself and headed for the climb up Rincon Hill, ruminating on what effect this new fly in the ointment would have on the reconciliation he had planned to stage-manage this evening.

Usual McIntyre was nowhere in sight, but Mrs. Moon let him in, Viona Moon, forty years old, round as her name, Vail's voluble Irish cook and housekeeper, whom Gerald envied almost as much as he did Vail's other women. On a chair in the entry hall a plump Mexican girl garbed in deep mourning sat brooding.

"Consuela, what are you doing here?" For once Gerald was surprised. Consuela was Celia Cermeno's personal maid and close confident, a shy little person who was not comfortable with the English language and had not left Fontana's grounds in years.

"I wait, Señor Crown. Mr. Vail, first he say go home, then he say sit, wait. So I wait."

A movement like the flutter of a soft bird in the gloom at the top of the stairs. Petra. "Come up, Gerald," she said.

The upstairs sitting room was familiar to him. He and Anna had eaten a number of fine dinners here, played cards, chatted comfortably with Vail and Petra, like two married couples, but with the added piquancy of knowing they were not. She was wearing a simple white muslin dress, long-sleeved, high-necked, her black hair drawn into a modest knot. He had seen her when she looked less sedate. Strange how mood could affect a woman's comeliness. When happy, Petra came very close to what Americans saw as beauty. Now her face was tight, her olive skin sallow in the fading light. She was in deep misery.

"I just saw Marin," he said. She looked at him swiftly and then away. "Where is Vail?"

"Out. Oh, it was terrible, Gerald. When Miss Marin is mad, she usually yells, but today I couldn't hear a thing. She ran out the front door—I saw her out the window—and he came upstairs. I never thought I could be afraid of him, but I was then."

"Why is Consuela here?"

"Miss Celia sent for him. Some squatters, something. She wants to see him."

"Squatters on her land? That's my business. Why didn't she send for me?"

Petra looked directly at him, one black eyebrow raised in irony. "Miss Celia's never been without a man, not in her life."

"Oh, for God's sake." Gerald shoved his fists into his pockets. "He's not going to be a damn fool and go, is he?"

She laughed, a dry, mirthless sound in the quiet room.

"When Consuela told him Miss Celia wanted him, he said, 'Oh, she does, does she.' That was all. First he told her to go home, then he decided Usual better take her. It's a long trip. I don't know what Miss Celia was thinking of, sending her alone."

"Miss Celia was thinking of Miss Celia. Where is he now?"

"He shouted around for Usual and couldn't find him. Then he put on his coat and flung out of here all . . . all . . . When he comes back, I won't be here."

For the first time he noticed the trunk sitting beside the door. He said quickly, "Do you think it's wise to have him come home and find you gone? I've seen him like this before, and it passes."

"He'll mind a little, but not much. Miss Marin—I was afraid she'd find out someday. She hates me, you know. Yes, she does. But she was very good to me once, and I loved that family, poor Miss Rose and darling Carey . . . I never saw the new little girl, but Vail says she looks like Miss Sophy. Oh, Gerald, I don't want to hurt Miss Marin. She's been hurt so much." In her distress a touch of her old accent crept back. "Well, I learned from her—how to sew good an' keep figures an' act like a lady. My clientele is very devoted an'—and I'm not like Miss Celia. I don't have to have a man."

Gerald patted her arm. "You are an independent, astute businesswoman, and I'm sure your clientele venerates your work but, Petra, you should not leave him now. He will need you."

She moved away from his hand. "I have to think of myself. If I stay, I will be sorry someday. It isn't me he needs."

Gerald shrugged and put on his hat. "Well, I tried. I'll tell him he owes me for that."

"Oh, Gerald, sit down. I haven't even offered you refreshment."

At her sudden recollection of a hostess's duties, he laughed. "Never mind, my dear. When I locate our mutual friend, I'll get my refreshment there."

The Restaurant Rondeau had not been built in the heart of town for Frank Maguire couldn't afford the high prices of the very best land, a circumstance for which he was giving thanks today. The roof of the restaurant had been set afire by windblown sparks and was partially burned, but canvas had been spread over the hole and business was going on as usual—better, in fact, for most of the town was dependent on restaurants for meals, and not many remained in operation. He was working the bar himself, for business was brisk and his regular bartender had foolishly allowed a large timber to fall on him during the excitement and would be on his back for some weeks.

He smiled ingratiatingly at the new customer.

"Good evening to you, Mr. Crown. A fine evening, is it not—that is, considering the terrible disaster, it could have been worse."

Gerald looked around. "It surely could have been worse for you. My congratulations, Maguire. A short whiskey—ah, thank you. And could you tell me, have you seen Vail Severance in the past few hours?"

"That I have," Maguire answered, and Gerald sighed. This had been his last hope, for Vail had not been sighted in any of the other few saloons still open and dishing out the booze. "He came in shortly after noontide, looking like he'd lost every penny he owned. Sure 'tis a look I've been seeing all yesterday and today." Maguire considered pleasurably the picture of Vail Severance, who'd had so much greater financial luck than himself, pinched and tatty with poverty. The thought warmed him. "But when I offer me condolences like a Christian, does he say, ''Tis good to know I've fast friends'? Does he say, 'Thank you, Maguire, for your kind thoughts,' as you might expect such a pleasant, soft-spoken gentleman to do? No, he says, 'Mind your own goddamn business,' takes a bottle off to that table in the corner, and doesn't speak another word all afternoon."

"He was drinking heavily?"

Maguire leaned on the bar. "Mr. Crown, fourteen years I kept bar in Dublin City, and never did I see a man down the drink like Vail Severance and not slide off his seat unconscious, not even an Irishman."

"Jesus."

"Well you may say it," said Maguire. "I watched in wonder and amazement meself. Then he walked out o' here and got on his horse, steady as a rock, with me expecting him to fall off the other side. But he didn't."

"Better for him if he passed out like a gentleman."

"Now how can you say such a thing, and him sober as a judge. The man's a phenomenon."

"When drunk the man's a peril to himself and anyone in his path. Believe me, he was as drunk as you or I would be with that much liquor in us. Was he headed home, do you know?"

"I doubt it. Just before he went out, he asked if the ferry to the Contra Costa was still running."

Vail looked out into the little enclosed patio where the fountain bubbled on, although the way of life it represented was torn and bloodied and almost as dead as the master of Fontana. He hated this house and had avoided being in it except for the few painful moments when he and Gerald brought Nicolas's body home.

He had been in it only two other times—the night he came home to find Celia married and pregnant and irrevocably lost, and the night long ago when he saw her for the first time at a grand ball given shortly after he came to live in the district. All through that first luminous evening he had watched her, talked with her, danced with her whenever the other young men gave him the chance, stunned by her beauty as was every male in the room. How experienced and cosmopolitan he had thought himself then; how young and unbelievably stupid in reality. John Baldwin had smiled on his suit, had regretted the unfortunate events that drove him away from home, and even helped give him his financial start in friendship and compensation for his loss. A crafty one, Don Juan. It had fallen out exactly as he intended; things usually did for him. He had meant all along for Celia to marry the great Cermeno kingdom; never opposing the impetuous American, relying on the young fool's own character flaws to destroy him.

The windy trip across the bay had cleared some of the alcohol from his brain. He was at the moment intensely aware in all his senses—of the balmy air moving in the sycamores, the slight crackle of leaves brushing each other, the odor of fragrant flowers blooming somewhere in the night. Spanish houses were withdrawn, stern, like the people who lived in them, cold with echoing tile floors and hard, leather-thonged chairs. The mellowness and apparent warmth of a people who liked to sing and dance and welcome strangers with kindness hid an austere, self-flagellating core. Well, didn't he know about self-flagellation, and wasn't it sometimes a requirement, if you were to save your soul?

She was in the room, he knew it before he turned. It was late. Somewhere a clock chimed eleven, and the room was shadowed where the candlelight did not reach. Time and tragedies had only increased her beauty. The severe black of mourning turned her skin to ivory. Her dark hair was not bound into a chignon, but fell to her waist as it had the night they met. Her blue-green eyes were jewels in the dim light, long, narrow, turning down slightly at the corners as though weighted by her heavy lashes—how was it that he'd never noticed that downward tilt before, he who knew her face by heart.

She said, "I am so glad to see you, I needed to see you." There was tense emotion underlying the words, although her hands were clasped quietly and she remained where she was. Celia would never run to you with a cry and a joyous embrace if she was glad to see you, or hurl dagger-sharp, wounding words if she was not. Celia never lost control of her feelings.

He didn't say he almost had not come. He said, "More troubles, Celia? Something Gerald can't handle?"

Her breviary lay on the table. She moved to it, her skirt whispering against the floor, and turned a page absently. It should not be here, it should have been left in the little chapel where she worshiped daily. She had dressed carefully for this interview, but not with a wholly conscious intent to captivate. She had always been a beauty, she had a normal degree of vanity, and it was impossible for her to appear before anyone at less than her best. It was natural to wear her hair the way he remembered it, to dab on the scent he had liked, because those were the things one did for a man. She was an intelligent woman with much of her father's shrewdness. With belief in herself she could have run Fontana as well as Nicolas had ever done. But men had always been the powers, the providers, the problem solvers—first her father, then her husband—and now she must find another man to save her. Who could it be but Vail?

She noted his suggestion that she should have sent for her lawyer and moved until the space between them was very slight, until he could smell her perfume and see the pulse beneath the translucent skin of her throat. She said, "I don't understand the legalities except that it is all very slow, it will take years, and even then we may lose. But, Vail, in the meantime we lose anyway. These squatters stake off land they say is not theirs, cut our timber to build houses, slaughter our beef. Today Armando caught them building fences, fences on our land so that our cattle couldn't get to the creek. He went after them in a frenzy, and they shot him in the leg. Oh, he will be all right, Dr. Cutter says, though they could as easily have killed him. He is in a terrible state of mind, for he feels that he failed, poor boy, and what can I say? He is just a boy, rash and ineffectual. We are quite alone and will go under without a man to protect us." Her eyes revised the statement to, I am alone, and you are the man to protect me.

She was too astute to even imply that the riches of Fontana and La Gracia would be his if he could hold them, a goodly dowry to bring to a husband. With intuitiveness similar to her father's she knew that for this man the prize would have to be her, not the land.

So it had been said. She had offered herself, and she waited, lovely, passive, knowing he had wanted her desperately once,

never considering the possibility that he might not want her now.
As for her own feelings, she had loved him, too, in her fashion,
had continued throughout her marriage to think of him as hers if
ever she wanted him. She could find it easy to love him again.

Unused to heavy drinkers, she had no suspicion of the amount
of liquor he had recently consumed, no thought that he might not
be entirely accountable for his actions on this night. His face was
darker and more flushed than usual, which she ascribed to
overwhelming emotion on hearing her words. He was still
profoundly attractive to her—the strong face, the driving energy,
the formidable physical power, the intense maleness that had
fascinated and then alarmed her into taking Nicolas instead—all
were qualities that made him just the man she needed now.

If she could have known his thoughts, she would have been
stunned and bitterly offended, for he was laughing inwardly, at
himself more than her, and congratulating himself for learning
something about women in the intervening years. The loose,
luxuriant hair, the perfume, the low bodice revealing more
curving white breast than was usual in deep mourning, all were
signals he had frequently received from interested women and not
much subtler than the tawdriest of them.

He watched with appreciation the rise and fall of white skin
above stiff black taffeta and was amused at himself for enjoying
it—his taste in women having undergone a sea change since he
had loved her. Strange how whiskey increased the clarity and
quickness of his mind. He must remember to drink heavily more
often. And since he was feeling so clever, what should he say to
her proposition? Darling, I am yours? Or perhaps, This has come
so unexpected that I cannot think what to say?

Then, unknowing, Celia did something that penetrated the haze
of whiskey and laughter and made the world not a joke but a
tragedy. She moved a little farther into the light.

Her face was thin, the fragile bones at the base of her throat
showed plainly, and her eyes were weary and defeated. In a low
voice she said, "I made a wrong choice a long time ago, but if
Nicolas had not died, we would have lived out our lives in peace
here at Fontana. With him gone . . ." She blinked back tears
without guile and turned her head so he would not see. She had too
much dignity to plead.

Tears he could withstand, the hint that she wished she had
chosen him meant nothing now, but the words "if Nicolas had not
died" struck deep. If he had stopped Nicolas from going alone into

the murderous streets that night, he would not be dead; if Nicolas could have used his right hand, he would not be dead.

It was true, as Maguire of the Rondeau had observed—Vail had an astonishing capacity for liquor in that he could not only stand up and walk straight when most men would have been on the floor, but also be aware of nuances and think logically to some extent. But Gerald was right, too, for he drank only under stress, and then the part of his brain that looked ahead to consequences and restrained destructive impulses shut down completely.

On this occasion the bitter regret he had hoped whiskey would blot out came flooding back. Marin . . . and Carey. It was all his fault. Everything in the goddamn world was his fault. He was a contemptible man, a contemptible man. Too many things he could never make right, but this he would.

Chapter 23

That evening Harry Callendar and his wife were guests at dinner, and afterward they had a conference with James, Stuart, and Marin, during which it was decided that James would try to borrow fifteen thousand dollars from Malcolm Severance and go into partnership with Harry—James to supply the capital; Harry the contacts, experience, and business acumen. At the close of the conference they toasted the new enterprise with small glasses of Madeira, and the Callendars left with expressions of great optimism for the future and regret for Marin's increasingly severe headache.

She had grown edgy as the evening progressed, flicking little glances at the mantel clock every time it chimed the quarter hour. She refused to go to bed until after midnight, and when she finally went upstairs, her face was so haggard that Delphine remarked with doleful relish that she was probably coming down with the grippe.

Stuart thought Marin looked ill, too, and it worried him, but not enough to suppress completely a sense of quiet gratification at James's entry into business. He had counseled that a short-term mortgage on Little Mountain was the best way to raise the necessary capital even at the twenty-one percent per month rate of interest that Malcolm felt compelled to charge. The standard bank rate was currently ten to twelve percent, and twenty percent the highest Stuart had heard of, but the present uncertainties of land titles made a bank loan unobtainable and justified the twenty-one percent Malcolm wanted, he assured James. There was no doubt in Stuart's mind that the loan would be repaid handily out of quick and easy profits. There was also no doubt—although he did not analyze the idea closely—that he himself could not lose either way the cat jumped.

Marin, as it happened, did not have the grippe. No fever or sniffles developed, but she stalked around the house, losing her temper over trifles, and after a week of silences alternating with sharp tiffs Stuart took the steamer across the bay, glad to return to his horses, cattle, and vaqueros.

On Sunday, Delphine attended church and afterward stopped to chat with Mrs. Tyler Winfield and her daughter, Kitty. From them she heard news of such a stupefying nature that instead of proceeding to the tiny recreation hall for cake and coffee, she trotted straight to her waiting carriage and ordered Jeremy to head for home at full gallop.

Marin was in the garden at the side of the house, and Logan was standing on the steps with arms folded. They had been discussing whether it was too late in the spring to plant hollyhocks against the fence, and both looked up in amazement as the carriage bounced down the lane from the street and halted with a jolt only a few feet from them. Delphine never allowed more than a sedate trot when she was in the carriage, especially on a Sunday, and here she was rocketing into the yard and attempting to scramble down while the spirited horses were still blowing and stamping.

"Girls," she cried, "you will not believe . . ." She picked up her skirt and hurried toward them. "I have just heard the most astounding news!"

Marin was brushing dirt off her hands, smiling in amusement, squinting a little in the sun. "What is it, Auntie? Have they discovered diamonds in Portsmouth Square?"

Delphine arrived in the middle of the patch of cabbages, pressed her hand to the stays that pinched painfully into her stomach, and took a long breath. "Vail and Celia Cermeno were married last Thursday afternoon."

Logan, who had started down the stairs, stopped on the bottom step, overwhelmed by a welter of feelings: shock, astonishment, a tingle of jealous resentment that her favorite brother had not told her this—disbelieving, yet knowing it was true.

Marin said, "I'm sorry, Auntie, you're mistaken." She took a step, just one, toward Delphine. "You should not spread silly stories."

Delphine, put off by the flat rejection in Marin's voice, replied indignantly, "I have not told a soul except you, and it is not a silly story, though it may have been a silly thing for him to do. It was told to me on the best authority by Charlotte Winfield, who heard it from her cook, whose brother is keeping company with Beatriz Segura's personal maid, and it has certainly set Charlotte's nose out of joint, for she had her eye on him for Kitty. They were married on Thursday at Fontana—by a priest, mind you, which means their children will be Catholics, Logan, and I can't imagine what your father will say to that." She puffed into the house to find Sophy and, possibly, a more satisfactory audience.

Logan followed slowly in her wake, leaving Marin alone in the quiet garden with the sun warming her arms and the limpid May breeze stirring her hair, in a world gone desolate and cold.

In the weeks following the fire the city fulfilled the hopes of the most optimistic with vigor, and as always, the demands of commerce came before the needs of people. At least two thousand dwellings had been destroyed, but the first shelters thrown up were only canvas tents or wood shacks. All available labor, brick, and stone were gobbled up in the construction of better commercial buildings.

The new firm of Gentry and Callendar was one of the successes of the reconstructed business community. The first move Harry made was to buy with James's money a percentage of the cargo of a ship still in port in Hawaii. He sold the goods on arrival at a profit exorbitant enough to permit him to purchase more merchandise and allow James to meet the first payment on the debt to Malcolm Severance. When that thousand dollars—most of it interest—had been transferred, they all breathed easier.

The new two-story office building on Montgomery Street was utilitarian, businesslike, and immensely satisfying to Marin, for it was the tangible evidence of James's enterprise. She could look up at the sign with the firm's name in impressive black and gold lettering, touch the dark red brick, climb solid wooden stairs to an office furnished with oak chairs and tables and a huge rolltop desk with dozens of cubbyholes, look out across low rooftops to the busy harbor and the ships at the wharves. In this room she worked most of each morning with Harry, absorbing almost without realizing it his methods of operation and habits of mind.

It was a new world, this balancing of money you could not see against goods you did not have, betting that there was somewhere, moving toward you, a customer for those goods, anticipating with a fine eye the moment at which merchandise and purchaser must be brought together to ensure a happy outcome. It was a frightening world, too, for the more she learned, the more clearly she saw what a tumultuous venture she and James had plunged into, a gamble more reckless and uncertain than playing monte or vingt-et-un for high stakes in the gambling saloons. And the stakes were high indeed, for Little Mountain was the family's only substantial asset, and Marin knew in her heart that Malcolm would foreclose with pleasure if given the chance. She watched the rise and fall on the balance sheets; she listened to Harry tell of a firm saved by the arrival of a small shipment of tacks, an item greatly in demand just after the fire, and of another company wiped out when forced to sell a cargo of flour dirt-cheap, the price of flour having dropped suddenly and disastrously after the unexpected arrival of a huge shipment from Chile. It was, as Vail had said of land speculation, "the wildest crap game in town." He had also said, "Never gamble except with money you can afford to lose." Sometimes at night, after a long day spent hunched over a ledger while watching through the window for a ship that was overdue, Marin twisted in her bed, fighting off nightmares of the company wiped out, Little Mountain lost, and all of them—James, Rose, Sophy, and her children—in the street.

She remembered other words of Vail's. "My father? He's the worst usurer . . . He'll steal the soles off your shoes . . ."

She wished she could talk it over with him; that was exactly what she had meant to do the day she walked in on him and Petra and lost her temper and ruined her life. And now he was married to Celia. Just how that had come about when the problem had seemed to be Petra, she couldn't quite figure out. It had all happened so fast. But she ought to have expected it, now that Nicolas was dead—he had always loved Celia.

She turned over again, threw off the quilt, heard the faint, mellow chime of the clock in the parlor signal half past two. She must get to sleep, she must, in order to face yet another empty day.

As for Vail and his bride, only Stuart, Glenna, and Logan had seen them. Logan went out to Fontana without waiting for an invitation, wanting to see Vail and assure herself that all was well with him, feeling that some seal of acceptance must be set on the match regardless of the disintegration of the Severance family.

Her father, she knew, would ignore the event. Stuart went, also without an invitation, and over Malcolm's objections Glenna insisted on going with him. So brother and sister and young stepmother visited at Fontana, drank cups of hot chocolate, chatted, smiled, congratulated, and scrutinized the happy couple, each harboring separate thoughts and speculations and motives for being there.

Logan brought back the information that everyone was fine and bore affectionate messages from them. She managed this without once mentioning Vail and Celia in the same sentence. Stuart reported that Fontana was responding well to American efficiency after years of Spanish indolence, though he doubted Vail would for long be willing to pour his energy into Armando's ranch when his own economic interest lay in Celia's inheritance, La Gracia. The creekline squatters had been cleared out, but it was a never-ending battle, and Vail was probably carrying it on only to please his bride, who, by the way, was blooming like a peach. Celia sent her dear love to all, along with an invitation to a party.

Delphine, her curiosity at white heat since she had first heard of the marriage, would have bartered her soul to get out to Fontana on any excuse, and Sophy at first was all for it. But Logan hemmed and hawed and felt unable to undertake the long trip again so soon, and Marin was noticeably unenthusiastic. In fact she said nothing at all. Sophy looked at them both and, although puzzled, agreed that on second thought the trip might be a trifle beyond her, too.

All through the summer the firm of Gentry and Callendar engaged in a seesaw battle for survival. There were nights when Marin went to bed certain that the end had come and woke in the morning to find that a ship believed lost was riding at anchor at Broadway wharf and they were saved for at least another month. The anxiety was constant, and she bore it alone. She and Harry had agreed that James must be spared the strain of the daily crises. He would be told of disaster only if it was total and there was no way to hide it. Two more payments on the loan had been made to Malcolm by the end of August, and though the major portion was still interest, the principal was being slowly reduced. It was possible, if one looked through a very rosy glass, to see success and security in the distant future.

One morning while Marin worked at the rolltop desk in the second-floor office, absorbed in figures that were beginning to tell a story she wanted to see, there were quick, light footsteps on the stairs outside her closed door and then a rattle as the door opened. Anna von Helsdorf floated in with Sophy in tow. Since the fire Marin had visited Anna once in her rooms at the new hotel on Battery Street, but had been too busy recently to engage in shopping tours, Anna's principal daytime activity.

"Close that horrid, dull book, dear child. You must come with us this morning."

Marin laid down her pen, swung around, and rubbed her eyes. "It's not dull, it's quite interesting. I've worked for two days trying to balance these accounts, and I think I've found my mistake. I can't quit now."

"Your mistake is huddling over a desk all day. You will end up with bleary eyes and a humpback. Look at her eyes, Sophy. Are they not red? And to find account books interesting—that proves we are almost too late. Come, we shall have our luncheon in some elegant restaurant and then shop all afternoon and spend a great deal of money. Now, no arguments. Here is your jacket—Sophy, help her on with her jacket. And your bonnet—oh, dear. Well, we must find you a new one."

In the end, Marin allowed herself to be seduced from duty, for the fog had lifted and the air was limpid and sweet, the sun shone, Anna exuded energy and enthusiasm and revived memories of other, better days, and besides, she did need a new hat.

After lunch and the finding of the perfect bonnet, the three ladies traveled to Taffin's glove shop to find long white gloves for Sophy to wear to the fancy ball to be given the following Saturday by the fire department. Firemen's balls were always great fun, and to Tom Anderson's dismay, Sophy had agreed that George Winfield could be her escort. George was Kitty Winfield's older brother, possessed a handsome, flowing mustache, cut a fine figure on the dance floor, and had a pleasant disposition. Tom despised him.

Across the counter Sophy spied Mrs. Winfield with two other matrons of good Southern families, Mrs. Parrish and Mrs. Venable. Charlotte Winfield and Harriet Venable were women of fashion who both aspired to social leadership. Margaret Parrish was of a different cut. Her family was as prominent in Virginia as the Winfields and the Venables, but she was a little brown wren of a woman who dressed in simple gowns of pale lavender and dove gray. She was a devout communicant of the Episcopal church, known for her good works, especially on behalf of the orphan asylum, the insane asylum, and the Fund for Stranded Seamen.

Her friends sometimes avoided her if they could manage it discreetly, for Margaret was forever soliciting donations. At the same time they recognized her social power, greater already than Charlotte Winfield could ever hope for. Everyone knew that if Margaret backed a charity, it must be a worthy one and it would be wise to contribute.

These three ladies expressed themselves charmed to meet the Baroness von Helsdorf. Mrs. Winfield was so charmed that she invited Anna to a dinner for twenty of her most intimate friends that she was planning for a week from Friday, and Anna, after reflecting on her social engagements, was pleased to accept. After they parted, Anna, in great good humor, suggested that she and Sophy and Marin now proceed to Taylor and Spencer's, where a new shipment of silk from Lyon, France, was on display. As Marin started up the steps of the shop, the box containing her new bonnet swinging on her arm, the door opened, and she looked directly into the faces of Vail and Celia Severance. There was no way to avoid them. To turn and run was impossible. She stopped, her face up, and behind her Sophy cried out a delighted greeting, rushed to hug Vail and press her cheek against Celia's. Then Anna and Celia had to be introduced, and Marin found it almost easy to murmur congratulations without quite looking into Vail's eyes, to squeeze Celia, to nod and say meaningless words and smile until her lips hurt and her face felt stiff.

He looked very well, he said all the right things; no one could have guessed what had passed between them when they last met. Celia was, as Stuart had said, blooming.

"This is my first trip to town in so long," she said, "but there was shopping I simply had to do."

"And this is the place for it," sighed Anna, rolling her expressive eyes. "Since you are not familiar with the town, do call on me if you require guidance to the best shops."

"If only we'd met earlier, Celia certainly could have used your advice, but the ferry leaves in an hour," Vail said with a hint of amusement in his voice.

Anna's chin lifted, and one eyebrow went up. "Then keep it in mind for the future."

Sophy took in the exchange with interest and tucked it away in her mind to be thought over later, but Marin did not even notice, so burdened was she with the effort of keeping her expression pleasant and saying anything but her real thoughts.

There were good-byes and promises to meet again soon, and Celia and Vail went off down the street.

Anna watched them go.

"So that is Celia Baldwin."

"You've heard of her?" inquired Sophy.

"Oh, indeed. The exquisite Celia whom all men desired, the princess of a great kingdom before we Americans took over." (No one knew if Anna was now legally an American, and no one asked, but she always referred to herself as such.) She tilted her head consideringly at Celia's retreating back. "She is beautiful enough, but . . ."

"But what? Don't you admire her?" Sophy pressed.

"I am difficult to please, I admit, but as one who has made a study of female beauty—one must, you know, if one aspires to it—I believe there is more required than perfection of feature or fine coloring or clear skin. There must be animation in the face, the soul must shine forth. Celia Baldwin does not have that." Anna laughed. "As we do, my dears!"

She marched them into the shop on a search for the ideal dress fabric, with Marin less than interested in the project and Sophy amazed that there was someone in the world who did not think Celia faultless. She wondered if there was anything in what Anna said.

On a translucent October afternoon when the shimmer of autumn and the snap of the invigorating air were lifting hearts and causing people to smile at strangers as they walked down the breezy streets, Marin sat propped on her bed, deep in Mr. Dickens's new novel, *David Copperfield*, which had come in just that morning. Harry had brought it directly to her, knowing her love of books and how seldom she read for pleasure these days. She had come home, eaten lunch, and retreated to her bedroom with this new treasure, trying to savor it slowly. Novels such as this came too rarely to be raced through without thought. Just as she got to the part where David bit Mr. Murdstone's hand, there was a quick knock on her door and Logan peeked in.

"Guess who just appeared on our doorstep dressed to the nines. My beloved stepmother."

"Glenna?" Marin put down the book and sat up. "What does she want?"

"A good look around our house, I suspect. On your feet, my love. You must help me entertain her."

Marin lay back against the pillows. "Beg her to excuse me. I have a most dreadful headache."

"Get off that bed and come downstairs. I'm not going to be stuck alone with her all afternoon."

"Malcolm isn't with her?"

"You know he wouldn't come here. He's too mad at me."

Marin rolled off the bed with a groan, smoothed her hair, straightened her skirt, and said, "You do have the most disgusting relatives." But she grinned when she said it, and they went downstairs together.

Glenna was seated in the parlor on the settee, but she rose when Marin entered and glided to her with glad cries of greeting. They touched cheeks, and she arranged herself again on the settee. She looked in the pink of good health, slightly more rounded in the bosom and upper arms, but with a waist neatly pinched by whale-bone. She wore demure dove gray silk that proclaimed her matronly status as well as the fact that her husband could afford to dress her well. Elizabeth's fine cameo pin with the gold filigree was at her neck, Elizabeth's chased gold bracelet was on her wrist. By rights both should have been Logan's; she had nothing that had been her mother's. Marin wondered if she saw and if it pained her.

Mrs. Victoria came in with the tea things she had hurriedly put together, and Glenna exclaimed over the tray, tossing her head back so that the tiny diamond earrings Malcolm had just bought her flashed fire.

"Um, the tea is delicious. So unusual. Is it China?"

"India," said Marin. "A new shipment. You must let me give you some to take home."

"So kind." Glenna took a dainty bite of cake. "We came over on the same boat with Stuart. What is this division matter he's so upset about, Marin? He and Mr. Severance ran on and on discussing it, and I could not make head or tail of their talk."

"Oh, it seems that our southern counties are agitating to secede and form a separate state, and some of the legislators are going along with it to the point of holding a convention down in Santa Barbara. The people down south say they pay more taxes, which I guess is true, while we run the state up here. Stuart says it's all a scheme of the proslavers to cut us in two and start up the old fight for another slave state. He's fit to be tied about it."

"I should think so. Gracious, we must oppose such wickedness with all our strength. As Mr. Severance says, 'Evil shall slay the wicked, and they that hate the righteous shall be desolate.' "

With a snap in her voice Marin replied, "Yes, and 'Woe unto them that call evil good, and good evil.' " She could quote scripture, too, when she had a mind to, and Glenna's affected way of referring to Malcolm only as "Mr. Severance" irritated her beyond endurance.

Glenna looked confused, unsure of exactly what had been meant by that last remark. "Yes, indeed," she said finally, and moved on to more secure ground. "I've been visiting at Fontana often lately. Celia will have me over every few days. Poor child, with mother and father gone she does need another woman to lean on, and as I told her, I am Vail's stepmother, and she must let me be a mother to her, too."

Logan said drily, "Yes, you're all of twenty-two."

"But so much older in experience. I was a mother to my brothers, you know, and being married to an older man ages one—matures one, I mean to say."

Logan looked down at her hands, and Marin took a hasty swallow of tea.

"I haven't seen as much of Vail as I would like," Glenna went on, "for he always seems to be busy elsewhere when I visit, but I hope to bring about a reconciliation between father and son one day. 'He, being full of compassion, forgave their iniquity,' as I tell Mr. Severance. Vail was once quite out of hand, but his marriage has had such a settling effect, especially now that Celia is"— Glenna lowered her voice to a discreet but distinct whisper, "in the family way." She sat back comfortably to enjoy the effect of her bombshell. Neither Logan nor Marin spoke. She looked from one to the other. "I hope I haven't talked out of turn, but I assumed you knew, you and Vail always being so close, Logan."

Logan said, "We hadn't heard. How is Celia? When . . . uh . . ."

"February. The first few months were a touchy time, and Dr. Towle was quite concerned. But since August she has been very well, able to do anything she wants, and the doctor thinks she is out of the woods."

"I saw Charles only last week," Logan murmured. "He didn't say a word."

"Well, he wouldn't. Doctors don't, you know. He travels over there regularly, which generally he won't do, but he's such a good friend, and Vail simply won't have anybody else. Nothing but the best for Celia!"

Marin put down the teacup lest she drop it. During the long, lonely months she had clung to the belief that there was nothing, could be nothing, between Celia and Vail, for Celia was not strong enough to bear children. He had married her only to take care of her, because she had no one else. What a ridiculous idea that had been, something that happened only in fairy tales. He had married her because he wanted her, and they went to bed together just as people always did when they got married, and they had made a baby the same way everyone else did. She had been a fool to think it could be otherwise.

A horseman was trotting past the side of the house, heading for the stable. Marin stood up and smiled. "There's Stuart. Now we shall hear what the wicked secessionists are up to. Must you meet Father Severance, Glenna, or will you stay to supper?"

It was the day before Christmas, warm and golden, the kind of day when transplanted Easterners nostalgically bemoaned the lack of sleigh bells, drifting snow, and icy roads, while they picked flowers and reveled, bare-armed, in a soft sun. Berries and pine branches decorated the house, and the silver punch bowl waited in polished splendor on the sideboard in the dining room for the party that night. Logan had chased everyone from the house, even the children, and ordered them to occupy themselves downtown until midafternoon. She had a tremendous surprise planned, which she had shared with no one but the servants. Jeremy and Luz and Mrs. Victoria went about with sparkling eyes and self-conscious grins and would not have revealed her secret under torture.

What Logan could possibly have thought up that was so monumental no one could imagine. As Delphine said in a not unkindly way, the dear girl meant for the best, but she had only the allowance Vail gave her, she always sewed gifts for the family, and what could she sew that was so large, she couldn't hide it? But because they loved her, they did as she asked and stayed away until almost three o'clock.

When they walked in the front door, she met them with bright spots of color in her cheeks and her blue-gray eyes shining the way they did when she was happy. The parlor doors were shut tight, and she forbade anyone to open them on pain of instant death.

Guests arrived promptly at seven. Harry Callendar and Mrs. Harry, Tom Anderson, Usual McIntyre, and Gerald Crown. Gerald had had the good sense not to apologize for his failure to bring Marin and Vail together last May, allowing her to pretend she had never cried on his shoulder or said things that could be misinterpreted. Gerald always took a lady's words in the best possible light so she could give him a Christmas kiss without reservations and be genuinely glad to see him.

"French champagne! Gerald, you are spoiling us. We'll come

to expect it every Christmas. Jeremy, take Mr. Crown's coat."
Marin slipped her arm through his. "Anna is dining with the Tyler
Winfields this evening, what do you think of that? But she
promised to be with us for New Year's. No, not in there. The
parlor is out of bounds till after we eat. Logan has some splendid
surprise and won't let us go in, which is a great nuisance, but she's
so pleased with herself that we have to humor her."

Dinner was not a large, formal affair such as Charlotte Winfield
was staging, but a family party including only relatives and close
friends. Looking around the table Marin thought that Tom and
Usual were the only new faces since the last Christmas, the first
spent in this house. And of all those who had gathered here last
year, only Anna was missing—and Vail.

The last of the champagne was finished, and Logan led the way
to the parlor, lips pressed tight and eyes shining, for the moment
had come for her surprise. She stationed Rose at the front of the
assembled group and flung open the double doors. Tall candles
had been placed on the mantel; their twin gold flames bent and
wavered in the mirror, and the lamps cast a warm, rosy glow over
dark carpets and plush sofas. The parlor was the largest room in
the house, but it seemed smaller since this morning, diminished in
some undefinable way.

Rose said, "Oh!" her hands pressed to her cheeks, and the
group crowding around the doorway for a better look gasped.

At the far end of the room sat a rosewood piano, polished until
it shone like a dark, gleaming mirror, filling all the space that had
been waiting for it. With her hand in Logan's, Rose dazedly
crossed the room, ran her fingers along the fine inlaid wood,
instinctively struck a chord, and produced a single rich and
complex sound. "Oh!" she said again, her face flaming, and
looked at James.

"Not I," he said hastily, and shook his head, pleased for Rose
and a little stunned.

On the music stand was a square, creamy envelope with "Mrs.
Rose Gentry" written on it. Rose fumbled it open with shaking
fingers and read it silently. She handed it to Sophy, who read
aloud: " 'To a gallant lady who was obliged to leave too much
behind, my respect and admiration. Vail Severance.' "

There was another collective gasp and sigh. It was indeed a
monumental surprise, a prodigious gift, so much so that ordinarily
a gentleman could not have given it to a lady. But this gift was
from a young gentleman who could afford it to an older lady who
was a kind of relative by marriage. Not only was this gift

allowable, but it had been handled so smoothly that a lady of refinement could do nothing but graciously accept.

Still, no one moved, no one quite knew what to do, and Logan said, "Notice, please, the bench pad. That is my contribution." The cushion was done in intricate needlepoint, a large cushion, for the piano seat was a bench long enough for three ladies to sit on together if they crushed their skirts. Logan must have labored over it for weeks in the privacy of her room.

"It is excellently done. Quite lovely, Logan," quavered Rose, on the edge of tears, and Logan said briskly, "Then you must sit on it right now. Sit down and play for us, ma'am."

Rose seated herself, arranged her skirt, said, "I doubt I can remember," and "My fingers are so stiff." She struck a chord experimentally in bass and then in treble, flexed her hands, and asked, "What shall I play?"

Someone suggested "Drink to Me Only With Thine Eyes," and Rose began, tentative at first, stumbling once or twice, then gaining authority as long-ago training asserted itself and memory began to flow from brain to fingers. Gerald had a fine tenor voice, and he and Stuart carried the melody while Logan sang the harmony in her lush soprano and everyone else chimed in with varying vocal qualities but equal enthusiasm. They sang "The Bluebells of Scotland" and "Long, Long Ago." Delphine wanted the new song by Mr. Foster, "Old Folks at Home," but Marin looked at her mother and suggested that it was time for something livelier. They sang a loud, lusty rendition of "Buffalo Gals," and the dangerous moment passed.

Then Rose passed her hand across her eyes, smiled, and said that she was tired. Marin took her place on the piano bench and gently rested her fingertips on the deliciously hard, smooth ivory keys.

Gerald leaned forward. "Nothing would make my Christmas happier than to hear Logan sing 'Bendemere's Stream.'"

Marin played the opening chords and raised the key; Logan, always surprisingly lacking in shyness when she sang, stood alone beside Marin and lifted her head, and her lovely voice poured out, rich, pure, true. The servants, who had been just outside the parlor door, drifted in and moved closer, listening with the same expression of pensive pleasure that was on the faces of those gathered near the piano. Charades and the other games that had been planned were forgotten, and every person in the room sang the evening away—the sentimental songs, the happy songs, the rollicking, joyous, dancing songs, each well-remembered tune calling up old memories and associations and emotions that could only be felt, never explained.

Marin, glancing up from the keyboard, saw the expression on Tom's face as he gazed at Sophy and thought what fools humans were. Tom had fallen in love with the outside Sophy, not just her pretty face but what he thought he knew of her mind and heart, never dreaming that the real Sophy was buried deep, known to no one, perhaps not even to herself. Each person fell in love with a mask, as Marin herself had with Stuart, as Stuart had with her, not realizing that far beneath that surface was a very different human being whom only life, lived day by day, might gradually reveal. People were like onions, layer upon thin layer peeled away to expose only another layer, with the true self found—perhaps never?

At midnight they sang "Silent Night." Jeremy bore in the silver punch bowl, and Christmas was toasted with a powerful punch made by a recipe handed down from Grandmother Maria Carey. Marin promised Rose that she would help her compose a note of thanks to Vail in the morning. Rose said good-night to her guests, kissed her daughters, and sleepily climbed the stairs holding on to Logan's arm. The rest of the family followed, and Marin and Stuart were left to see their guests out into the night. On the porch Sophy was saying good-night to Tom. She went past them into the house, humming to herself.

When everyone was gone and the door was shut, Stuart followed Marin into the parlor and watched her move slowly around the room, straightening the antimacassars on the chair arms and emptying the gentlemen's cigar butts into the fireplace.

He said, "That was an astonishing thing for Vail to do. He never once mentioned it to me. On the edge of being excessive, don't you think?"

"It was immensely thoughtful and generous. Did you see Mama's face?"

"Generous yes, but . . . he's never been close to your mother. I'll wager they haven't exchanged a dozen words beyond the courtesies. Why do you suppose he did it?"

"I can't imagine."

"Odd of him to sign only his own name, not Celia's, too. Did you notice that?"

"I noticed."

"Marin." She had been snuffing out the candles on the mantel, her back to him, and he turned her around. "Are you coming down with a cold? You sound . . ."

"You and Delphine are a pair, both of you forever determined that I'm coming down with something when I never felt so well. Go to bed, dear. I'm almost finished tidying up." She kissed his cheek and watched him climb the stairs.

In her bed Logan snuggled down, happy over the success of the surprise, drowsily planning the letter she would write to Vail tomorrow, describing in detail every remark and exclamation of delight, the expressions on each face, the songs sung, re-creating as best she could the mood of the evening for him to experience as if he had been there. Just as she was moving into sleep, there came to her the faraway sound of a melody they had sung that night, picked out slowly on the piano by one finger, and Marin's light voice softly singing the sweet, yearning words.

> Now you are come, all my grief is removed,
> Let me forget that so long you have roved.
> Let me believe that you love as you loved
> Long, long ago, long ago.

Chapter 24

Celia's child was a girl, an exceptionally pretty baby, who, everyone said, would surely grow up to look like her mother. A month after she was born, Gerald presented to the U.S. Board of Land Commissioners claims for confirmation of title to Fontana and La Gracia ranches. The claims were made separately, for Fontana, he explained to Celia and Armando, like most Spanish ranches, had never been surveyed, and the boundaries in Nicolas's grant were vague. However, John Baldwin, with Yankee canniness, had had his ranch surveyed in 1845, and La Gracia's boundaries had been duly recorded.

Armando stomped to the window, looked out at the land he felt slipping through his fingers, and strode back, glowering at Gerald. Behind the glower was fear.

"Surveys!" he snorted. "What do I know of surveys?"

"Exactly," replied Gerald with gentle sarcasm.

Celia looked up quickly, not liking the implication in that one

quiet word. The night before last she had had a mild disagreement
with Vail over this, mild because Celia could not quarrel and Vail
would not. But she had let him know in her soft-voiced way that
she expected him to retain both ranches and to exert equal efforts
to save them. He then had made it clear that he would do what he
reasonably could to help Armando, but that he would neither invest
his money nor jeopardize her inheritance to do it. And that was how
it had been left. She could pressure Vail just so far and no farther, and
she was beginning to discover what the limits were.

Just why it was so important to her to keep not only La Gracia
but Fontana as well, she was not sure, since she did not realize
how much of her father's plans for the future she had absorbed as
she was growing up. In her heart she had always known that John
Baldwin meant her to marry Nicolas, acquire the far greater
Fontana ranch, and expand La Gracia into a kingdom. In that deep
part of her she had never intended to fail her father for all the
girlish promises she had made to Vail in the days before a hard,
cold decision had to be made. Now she had the ranches, and she
had the man. She had given him her lovely person and borne his
child, and now she wanted what she had bargained for.

"Do you think we can win?" Armando demanded.

Gerald drew on his thin cigar. Yesterday he and Vail had
thrashed this out thoroughly and privately. He knew Vail's
feelings on the matter.

They had walked together down through the orchard, climbed a
rise of ground to a spot where the land dropped off and the valley
rolled away, green and lush from the rains of the winter just past.

"Magnificent!" Gerald exclaimed. In all his visits to Fontana he
had never seen this vista before. To the east rose the great
mountains, their scarf of snow hanging low. Winter had been
remorseless, and many a miner had died up there, feverish or
starving or frozen, believing his bonanza was near at hand and that
he would find it tomorrow or next week. A mighty monument,
those mountains, for so many graves.

Vail said, "Never mind the view. Spell it out for me, Gerald."

Gerald sat on the stone seat and grinned at him. "I think we
have La Gracia sewed up. The survey is professional, it's
accurate, the grant is properly recorded, all neat as a pin. If we file
now, I venture to say the claim will be confirmed before the end
of summer. Fontana, however, is another story."

"What is Celia's position in all this?"

"La Gracia became hers when John Baldwin died. He left it to her in a will that couldn't have been better drafted if I'd done it myself."

"She was married to Nicolas at the time."

"Aha. That could be the rub. We recognize community property rights in this state, based on Spanish law, did you know that? If Nicolas and Celia did not maintain her inheritance separately, community property would apply, and he could bequeath his half of both ranches elsewhere if he chose."

"Which he did. Armando has the will."

"Indeed he has." Gerald fumbled in his inside coat pocket and drew out a single sheet of paper. "Signed by Nicolas, every word in his own handwriting. It leaves no doubt in my mind that he considered Celia amply provided for, and as he had no child, he intended his interest in the properties to go to Armando and the sisters. In all modesty I believe most courts would agree, which means that the Cermenos get half of both ranches."

Vail took the paper, which he had already read twice, read it again, and handed it back. "You look very content, Gerald. What's wrong with it?"

Gerald cocked his head to one side and gazed at the will. "I don't know what possessed him to write this, for he wasn't one for legal niceties or getting things down on paper. He must have felt strongly about it. He wrote out his wishes in plain language and signed it. Nicolas Vicente Cermeno y Morelos. The thing is, he didn't date it. Therefore, it is invalid. He died intestate, Vail. If the ranches are community property, Celia, as his widow, takes them both in toto. Even if they were ruled separate property, she would keep all of La Gracia and still be entitled to half of Fontana."

"Hells afire, I don't want Fontana, and Celia doesn't need it. Nicolas was right."

"That's not what Celia's father would say. He wanted her to have it all."

"John can twirl in his grave."

"Don't say that to your bride."

"I already have. La Gracia is a fine inheritance for her and the baby. Let it end there."

Gerald's lips curled up under his narrow mustache. "Very generous of you. Sensible, too, since La Gracia is the ranch with solid title. You going to become a rancher and rusticate out here?"

A sparkle came into Vail's eyes. "I've given it some thought." He looked out across the broad, quiet, oak-covered valley, spacious and unspoiled, slumbering in the late afternoon sun.

"Pretty, isn't it? Take a good look, because it won't last long. The vultures have arrived, and the pickings are good. Over near the bay, streets have already been laid out and a few buildings put up with timber right off the land, some of it Fontana land. They're going to build a town, Gerald, and without clear title there's not a thing I can do to stop them. La Gracia hasn't been hit as hard, probably because it's farther south, but the squatters are coming, I can smell it. If title to La Gracia can be confirmed before they get a toehold, Celia will have her inheritance—not a ranch, but the most valuable chunk of real estate owned by one family on the coast."

"Gonna sell it by the inch, eh?" Gerald remarked with admiring envy. "John would approve of that. He was always one to move with the times."

"I don't give a damn for his approval. It's what I'm going to do."

Gerald stood up, stretching, staring out at the green, virgin land, and seeing dollar signs. "God, but I'm jealous! With that kind of coin at stake it might pay you to make a fight for Fontana, though I fear it would be money down a rat hole." He said this cheerfully. He felt little sympathy for the beleaguered former grandees and even less for Celia; he had never liked her and had a shrewd idea of her motives in marrying Vail so suddenly. As for Vail, he didn't have the smug, contented look of one who had just fallen into a fortune. He looked like a man who had dealt the cards himself and was playing out a losing hand with stubborn patience and a complete absence of self-pity. Now if he, Gerald, had the opportunity to sell off La Gracia bit by bit, he believed he could confront the prospect with equanimity, even with that frozen-faced beauty a part of the deal. He would use the money as he pleased and let Celia fend for herself. Celia was good at fending. But Armando was pitiable, a victim of his older brother's fecklessness, bullheadedly determined to hang onto his birthright.

And so, he had set aside his private opinions and must now assume his best bedside manner. He put out his cigar and said encouragingly, "We must not try to solve everything in one gulp, Armando. We must take a step at a time, deal with each problem in turn. Then it will not seem so overwhelming, and we can see where we are going."

Armando sat on the edge of the hard leather chair, ready to leap up and begin pacing, but with the tension in his face easing as hope rekindled.

"Gerald, tell me what you really think. Do we have a chance?"

"My boy," Gerald answered comfortingly, "there is always a

chance," and sent up a request for forgiveness, in case there was a God and he happened to be listening.

During the spring and summer the firm of Gentry and Callendar prospered mightily. Harry whirled through each day, bustling and gingery, fired with energetic devotion to the business, whistling perpetually under his breath. Marin was in improved spirits herself, a fact noted with relief by those close to her. Not only did they care about her well-being, but Marin, in her black and brooding moods, had been almost impossible to live with.

She herself recognized the change and did not know the reason for it. Nothing in her life had altered for the better, and yet she felt better. She was too young, too healthily optimistic, and, at the core of her nature, too demanding of life to remain forever sunk in despair. Vail was married, as he should be at his age, and if she did not approve of the person he'd chosen, if she thought it was a stupid, mischievous, wicked mistake, if he foolishly doted on a woman not nearly good enough for him, a woman who would doubtless make him miserable—well, it was his disaster, not hers, and she would not let it crush her.

In the end it was her fundamental optimism that saved her. She refused to go through life like Mama, with misery as her companion, and so she bundled it up determinedly and set it aside. She was not happy, but she tried to be cheerful. She learned not to look too far ahead, not to plan or worry or think too much. She learned the inestimable value of keeping busy, of getting through each day, of finding pleasure and even, on rare occasions, joy in the ordinary events of life.

One day as she was circling around a mud hole on Sansome Street formed by the collision and subsequent deluge of two wagonloads of beer, she had an unexpected encounter that lightened her heart for many days.

A burly man in a well-cut frock coat, elegant checked pants, and a high beaver hat on his trim brown head, saw her coming, stepped aside to let her pass, then took a second look.

"Marin!" he boomed in a voice that caused passersby to stare, and she glanced up from the careful path she was treading around the muck.

"Oh, my stars, Michael!" She dropped her skirts, forgetting the beery mud, and ran to him. "Michael, how good to see you. Michael, you're scrunching my ribs."

"Beg pardon, Marin." He eased up a little, grinning down into her face, a square-built man with brown side-whiskers and carrying more weight than when last they met, a prosperous-looking man with a touch of authority in his manner.

She stepped back. "If you aren't the grand sight!" He flushed, self-conscious but pleased. "What have you done, Michael, found the biggest gold mine in California?"

"I found *some* gold. Enough to start me off in business. Let me help you to the sidewalk." He picked her up, lifted her past the mud, and set her down on the planking at the edge of the road.

She brushed at her damp, dirty hem with the handkerchief he offered.

"I smell like a brewery. Oh, never mind." She looked him up and down. "It must be quite a business, to deck you out so fine."

He suddenly remembered the hat still on his head, snatched it off, and fidgeted with it. This woman could always fluster him just by her presence. Either his memory was failing or she had grown even more beautiful. He couldn't go on standing here staring like a puppy with its tongue hanging out. What the hell question had she asked?

"Uh—a hardware store. Not a big store, but a damn—a first rate business to be in nowadays. I bought a load of nails right after the fire and opened up in a tent, but I have a brick building now."

Another bright fellow with a bit of cash who had struck, so to speak, while the iron was hot. Imagine Michael, that overgrown farm boy, having enough brains to go into business and prosper at it. But why not? Everyone in the city was an opportunist. She slipped her arm through his.

"Walk me down to Montgomery, Michael, and I'll show you the business my father has gone into. You must come to dinner this Friday, no excuses now. I'll give you directions to our house."

He did come on Friday, and most Fridays thereafter. And on one such evening Vail rang the doorbell just as they were sitting down to eat and was pressed into staying, too.

Vail was often in town alone. Celia did not like the clangor of city life. Her tiny daughter, named Alida Elizabetha, after her two dead grandmothers, and baptized into the Holy Catholic Church, was growing rapidly, and Celia preferred to stay home with her.

Vail stopped by regularly to visit Logan and the children, almost always during the midday hours, when Marin was away.

Their few meetings had been brief and accidental, she arriving home just as he was leaving.

Tonight, after the supper dishes had been cleared away, Rose smiled down the table and said, "Vail, my dear, this is my first opportunity to thank you properly for your marvelous gift."

"I had your very gracious note and the knowledge that you were pleased, Mrs. Gentry. That's thanks enough."

It was a tasteful, urbane reply and could have ended the matter, but Rose would not have it.

"You must not call me Mrs. Gentry, you must call me Rose from this moment on. After all, we are more or less related, although, I vow, I cannot exactly explain the connection."

They all laughed, and James said, "If Rose can't explain it, no one can, for she can follow the most tangled relationships, out to the seventh kissing cousin twice removed." He beamed lovingly at his wife, happy that she was in such high spirits tonight.

"Be that as it may," she replied, "I still have my thanks to give, and it shall take the form of a small concert—quite impromptu—if you care to stay, Vail?"

"It would be a great pleasure."

So they gathered in the parlor, and Luz served coffee while Rose, who had spent months practicing intensively for this opportunity, arranged herself at the piano and looked over her music.

Belinda went directly to Vail, climbed onto his lap, stuck her thumb in her mouth, and looked around as if daring anyone to dislodge her. Carey sat on the floor taking the wheels off a toy wagon, aware of his baby sister's challenging stare and unperturbed by it. He was almost four and had a clear and confident idea of his place in the world. He regarded Vail as his personal property, he knew he could climb up on his lap anytime and be welcome, and he was content for the time being to sit nearby and dismember the wagon.

Logan moved her chair closer. She did not often have the chance for a private chat with Vail, for when he called, Delphine or Sophy unfailingly joined them without a thought that brother and sister might like to talk alone.

She handed him a package tied with bright ribbon and, under the buzz of talk and clatter of china, said, "This is a dress for Alida. Don't forget it when you go home."

Belinda tugged Vail's watch from his pocket, put it to her ear, and then, with blue eyes dancing, began to twirl it on its long chain. He watched with a smile, kissed her blond curls, and took the watch away. It was a game they played regularly, the only question being how long he would let her get away with it.

"Ornery brat," he said, and she chuckled and snuggled against his chest, her eyelids drooping. It was long past her bedtime.

Logan watched with a pucker between her brows. "I do worry about her. Carey, too."

"You worry too much. They are fine."

"Now, yes, but what about the future? How can children grow up well when their parents . . ."

"More trouble there?"

Logan grimaced. "On the surface things are better. Marin doesn't lose her temper so much, and Stuart isn't as grouchy, but you know how she is. She won't put up with a thing, and he . . . He is my own brother, and I hate to say it, but Stuart is an awful prig. Don't laugh; it isn't funny."

"You can't fix things for them, Logan. They picked each other."

"It's not them I worry about, it's the children. Not this little pill, so much." She ran a hand lightly over Belinda's curls, and the child stirred drowsily. "Already she can wrap Stuart around her finger, but Carey . . . there's a fundamental clash of temperament there. Stuart doesn't come over as often as he should, and when he does, he expects Carey to do as he's told, speak when he's spoken to,—yes, sir; no, sir,—that's Stuart's idea of how a son should be with his father."

"I wonder who he got it from."

"It just isn't in Carey to knuckle under, and if he won't do it at four, what will it be like when he's fifteen or twenty? I fear—oh, Vail, I can see the same thing happening all over again, bitterness and estrangement and the family split. Life's too short to make such dreadful mistakes."

"Yes, it is. But we keep making them, don't we."

There was a clearing of throats, and conversation died as Delphine, who had appointed herself mistress of ceremonies, tapped her spoon lightly against her coffee cup. Rose was ready to begin.

She sat on the long piano bench, back straight, head bent gracefully, elbows floating and fingers curved over the keyboard as she had been taught in childhood, and under her firm and confident touch sound began to flow out of the fine instrument, deep, mellow chords rippling up to clear, bell-like tones, melodies interweaving, separating, and returning. It was Schubert, and she played with a fire and passion that moved even the listeners who thought they cared little about music. At the end there was an instant of silence and then enthusiastic applause.

She stood, flushed with triumph, a little breathless, and while she was bowing and smiling, Vail asked Logan in a low voice, "Is she often like this?"

"Not usually this lively," Logan whispered back, "but she's been ever so much better since the piano came. It's been the very thing, Vail."

"You watch her closely?"

"Like a hawk, although I wouldn't swear but what there are times when she gets away from me."

"Don't let it wear you down."

"Oh, it gives me a mission in life. Only sometimes I wonder . . ."

"You mustn't fret. You can't do more than you are doing." He looked across at Marin, who was setting up the music for her mother's next selection. "Does she play often?"

"Every day when she comes home from the office. Sometimes late at night after I'm in bed I hear her down here. When I fall asleep, she's still playing. Oh, my, I believe you have acquired a permanent fixture there." She smiled at Belinda, rosy and contented and sound asleep, thumb in mouth and fingers hooked over her nose.

Vail moved his arm to settle the little girl more comfortably, and she sighed, turned, and sank into deeper sleep. He said, "Well, you know my power over women."

From the sofa, Delphine frowned, wondering what had tickled Logan into such a fit of giggles. Rose, oblivious now of anything but her music, began to play.

Chapter 25

Sunday in Malcolm Severance's home had always been a day devoted to Bible reading, prayer, and quiet, presumably pious reflections. Stuart was not a religious man in the profoundest sense, but he could not remember a time when the unexpected intrusion of a worldly thought on Sunday did not give him a sense of unease, and he ordinarily observed the outward forms meticulously. So his father would have been astonished as well as disapproving to see his younger son making his way through a crowd of fashionable people at the Pioneer racetrack near the mission one Sunday afternoon. The slender, handsome boy Marin had fallen in love with almost seven years ago had been replaced by a large, handsome man, with a quality of unbending sternness settled firmly on his patrician features, a tall man walking with his head held very high, as if he wished to appear even taller.

Compared with most of the crowd he was soberly dressed, but to him a coat perfectly tailored to show off his broad shoulders, an embroidered waistcoat, and a very wide cravat represented flamboyance. He was self-consciously and guiltily pleased with his appearance.

It pleased him, too, that so many men of consequence went out of their way to speak, to inquire of his opinion on various subjects, even in some instances to curry a little favor, and there was a look in the eyes of the many ladies who smiled and bowed that was especially comforting considering the beating his vanity had taken at home in the last few years. But his mind was primarily on the business that had brought him to the track, and although he bowed and smiled in return and stopped once or twice to chat briefly, he kept moving at a fairly steady pace toward the point where both the start and the finish of the race could be observed.

Near the rail he saw Charles Towle, and knew that this was the moment, before Charles's gaze met his, to decide whether to stop and speak or to pretend not to see him and move rapidly on. The sight of the young doctor disturbed thoughts that had been resting quietly in a far corner of his mind for years, thoughts that had been roused again only that morning by remarks Marin had made at the breakfast table. More than once it had occurred to him to talk to Charles if he could do it in a casual, roundabout way, and this was a heaven-sent opportunity. Yes, he would speak.

"Charlie!" He approached with a big grin and a friendly hand held out. "I didn't know you had a taste for the turf. Any luck?"

Charles shook hands and smiled. "Oh, yes, all of it bad so far. But I like to see the ponies run."

Stuart pushed into a place beside him. "There's no dandier sight than a good nag coming up from behind to take the lead, especially if I have money on it."

A gun cracked, the horses broke, and conversation halted as they thundered down the track. Charles stared tensely toward the finish line, sighed, and turned away before the outcome was announced.

"Well, lucky in love, eh?" said Stuart heartily. "When I send out my filly, you can put everything you own on her and make up for all your losses."

"You going into the racing business?"

Stuart lowered his voice. "I've got the fastest horse in Christendom, sweetest filly you ever saw. There's nothing here today that can come within a mile of her. Temperamental as all hell, but a honey if you handle her right." He lifted his hat to two approaching gentlemen and turned to speak more earnestly to Charles, thus presenting them with his broad back and discouraging the beginning of a conversation. They were important men, a state legislator and a judge, and they were two of the unlucky fools who had run out the front door instead of scrambling out the window into the dark alley behind Madame Colette's parlor house when that elegant establishment burned in the last big fire. They had been caught, literally, with their pants off. Many a prominent pillar of the community had been found out that night—not too great a disaster in a town that gave no more than a wink and considerable laughter to such doings; the only men who really suffered were those who had hurt, infuriated wives at home—but it did not pay in the long run to have such a blot on one's record. One had one's family to account to, and anyway, appearance was everything in this world. Stuart still broke out in a sweat when he recalled what a near thing it had been that night.

"Like all women," said Charles.

"What?"

"Your filly. What's her name? I'll watch for her."

"Dulzura. Yes, she's female, all right. Sometimes reminds me of Marin—stubborn as a mule and twice as headstrong. I tell you, Marin gets an idea in her head, and nothing will get it out until she's had her way. The plans she has for Sophy . . . have you met my sister-in-law, Charles?"

"I haven't had that pleasure."

Stuart grunted. "It might not be much pleasure. Marin has decided Sophy must make a great marriage, so she dolls her up in much too expensive clothes and sends her on a constant round of parties and balls, hoping to attract a string of suitors."

"It sounds like a pleasant life for a young girl. With such beauty I imagine she's had no trouble attracting the string."

"I thought you didn't know her."

"We have not met, but I've seen her. At a distance. A charming girl with intelligence and strength of character to boot."

"Oh, she's pretty enough if you like the style, and apparently the young bucks do. I fall over three or four every time I go into the parlor. As for strong character—where did you get that idea?"

"From Vail. He says she has developed into a remarkable young woman since her illness. 'A valiant spirit' was the way he put it."

"He would," replied Stuart with a touch of contempt. "Fact is"—Stuart's voice dropped to a confidential murmur, "Sophy is a great anxiety to me. She's bound to marry someone soon, with Marin pushing her the way she is. Tom Anderson would take up permanent residence if we let him, but George Winfield is the current favorite. Marin was saying at breakfast this morning that she expects George to come up to scratch any day."

The horses broke again, and after the race was run and the shouting died, Charles said, "George is an agreeable chap. Money, good family, good-looking. A desirable connection."

"Yes, and if it comes off there may be hell to pay."

Charles's pale brows rose. "Why so? Does Sophy—not care for him?"

"He's a good catch, so I suppose she does. That's not the worry." Stuart stared out at the track. "Charles, may I confide in you? As a doctor, that is, on a private matter?"

If Stuart had been looking, he might have noticed Charles's narrow shoulders slump as if an invisible weight had just descended.

"I do not repeat confidences."

"Of course not. I don't for a moment suggest it. Charles, between you and me, that illness of Sophy's—she wasn't on a trip to Sacramento with Marin when she got cholera. That was a prevarication, a necessary one, to hide the fact that she had run off to the gold camps with a worthless young man just a cut above white trash, a man I caught her with in a state of . . . in flagrante delicto. She came down with cholera out in the hills, and the man abandoned her. Marin and Vail found her in some dung-heap gold camp, at death's door so they say, and when she recovered enough to travel, they brought her home and put out the story about her being with Marin all the time." Stuart darted a glance at Charles. He was listening thoughtfully, as he might to the recitation of any ordinary set of symptoms, without a sign of shock on his thin, angular face. "If she marries, especially into a prominent family like the Winfields, what will be the outcome?"

Charles tilted his tall hat to guard his eyes from the sun. "I'm sorry, I don't follow. If she cares for George and she has fully recovered from the cholera, which she appears to have done, what's the problem?"

Stuart rested his elbows on the rail, clasped his hands, and looked down at them. Charles was being annoyingly obtuse. "There is one thing she cannot recover from, and no telling what a proud man like George would do if he believed he'd been diddled. You get my meaning?"

"I can't say that I do."

Stuart, pushed into a corner where he had to put into words what he was loath even to think of, said unwillingly, "He would wonder, wouldn't he, that she did not have, that is . . . is lacking . . ." He paused, groping for an acceptably delicate word.

"A hymen?" Charles supplied helpfully.

"Just so," said Stuart, thinking that doctors were a peculiar lot. "After all, a man expects his wife to be pure. George certainly would."

"If he's at all knowledgeable, the question would not arise."

"What d'you mean, knowledgeable?"

"As I have had occasion to explain to patients in the past, the body is not a machine, it is not stamped out, each one exactly the same as the last. Were it so, the practice of medicine would be considerably simpler—and duller. 'Male and female created He them,' but not identically, not by a long shot. This myth—this cult, I would call it—of the hymen as incontrovertible proof of virginity or the lack of it is a beastly one, invented by men, a cult that has caused the ruin, even the death of many a chaste and virtuous woman."

Stuart blinked at the sudden passion in the doctor's quiet voice. Charles seldom spoke so forcefully about anything. He said, "I haven't the least idea what you're talking about."

"I'm saying what every student of anatomy knows. We are all the same, yet we are creatures of infinite variety. Doubtless you're aware of the many differences among males—we are by no means exact copies of each other. It is the same with females. The hymen is simply mucous membrane, and I doubt seriously that it was put there by God to allow the male to determine if his mate is virginal. It may be relatively tough and wide or very thin, flexible, even vestigial. Some women are born without it, yet in primitive societies such women, perfectly chaste, have been killed for their supposed lack of virtue. Our society, being more civilized, does not kill them, it merely casts them out. Does it occur to you that for all we know, your own little daughter may be without this organ—and she is certainly, as you put it, pure."

"Belinda?" Stuart thought that over. "Is it possible that such a deficiency can be passed on?"

"An inherited trait? I shouldn't wonder. And what a monstrous injustice if someday some arrogant man were to doubt her and she suffered thereby."

"Monstrous indeed!" Stuart contemplated with detestation that unknown, unreasonable man in Belinda's future. "I'm indebted to you, Charles. I always thought such must be the case, and yet I did not know . . . As you say, any knowledgeable man would know or could find out from one such as yourself." His smile was so warmly grateful, so genuine, that Charles was moved by a feeling of friendship. Stuart had his limitations, but he was, on the whole, a decent man.

"Of course," Stuart went on, "in Sophy's case we know her to have fallen. Isn't it something of a cheat to pretend otherwise?"

"What would you have her do? Never marry?"

"Oh, she could take some ordinary fellow, but Marin sets her sights high. Nothing is too good for Sophy, she says, but under the circumstances . . ."

Charles's cordiality vanished. "Marin is quite right. There is another aspect of the matter, which, being a man of sensitivity, you will have given thought to. When all's said and done, what difference does it make?"

"You aren't serious."

"Never more so. One error does not determine the worth of a person. Surely we must be allowed at least one stumble. If I loved a woman—I'm human, and I might be a thought jealous, but if I loved her at all, I could not love her less whatever she had done. Even a woman who lacks the beauty and accomplishments of your young sister-in-law, if that woman brings loyalty, love, and tenderness to a marriage she brings very great gifts, gifts any man should treasure." Charles turned, and his narrowed eyes passed coolly over the crowd. "Look at them, all these people from every walk of life, the cream and the dregs of society and all alike in their frailties. Whited sepulchers, every one of them. How many nasty secrets do they carry, how many could afford to have their every thought and action printed in tomorrow's newspaper? Not one, I'll wager. I certainly couldn't, any more than you or the next fellow. What dirty little hypocrites we are, hiding our own taints and vices, often failing even to recognize them, but clucking and tutting and covertly rejoicing when our neighbor falls publicly from grace. And do you know why we rejoice? Because we can join our fellows in pointing the unforgiving finger while telling ourselves we are better than that. It makes us feel virtuous and safe, though it ought to terrify us. If our own flaws come to light, the pack will as easily turn and rend us."

Stuart's face had slowly hardened as Charles spoke. He was a man of sharp, if narrow, intelligence, the narrowness being caused not by lack of mental ability but by a tight and inflexible personality. One followed the rules carefully and was rewarded; one broke the rules and was rightfully and severely punished. He believed this precept, judged others by it, and was deeply disturbed to hear it attacked. Although he did not realize it, it was his rigid, righteous view of life more than any other thing that had caused his problems with Marin. Her quick, agile mind twisted, trimmed, adjusted, risked, while he marched straight ahead with blinders firmly in place.

But he was not stupid. He understood very well what Charles had said, and he did not like it. That good, respectable people without a stain that anybody knew about had ugly things in them? That bad people, caught out in full view of the world, could be worthwhile? A dangerous theory, one that assaulted the very fabric of civilized society.

He replied coldly, "I do not share your unhappy view of humanity. There are many good people in our midst, and I earnestly endeavor to be one of them. Perhaps you couldn't afford to have your activities appear in the newspaper, but let me assure you that I have nothing to conceal and do not expect to."

The passion died out of Charles's face. "My apologies. I intended nothing personal. But except for the few living saints among us we are all sinners, are we not? For myself, I fear to judge others, for 'with what measure we mete, it shall be measured to us again.' I still hope for mercy when my time of judgment comes."

"Quite right, we all pray for mercy. Thank you for your enlightening medical advice. Perhaps all will work out well for Sophy." Stuart tipped his hat and walked off, angry, uncomfortable, relieved, meditating on Charles's anatomy lesson. It always struck him as odd, the way the man quoted scripture with such ease and apparent approval. It was odd, considering . . .

With contemplative eyes Charles watched him go, thinking over the information that had just come his way and hoping he had snuffed out a slow-burning fuse.

Chapter 26

All afternoon a fierce wind had roared in off the sea, whirling the dirt on the bare hills into little cyclones and kicking gritty sandstorms through the streets, but toward evening it gentled to an intermittent breeze and the streets became habitable again, the April air clean and tangy-sweet. Stuart had tickets to the premiere performance of young Edwin Booth in the role of Hamlet, prince of Denmark, and the women of his household were going, all but Delphine, who faithfully attended her Ladies' Aid Society on Monday nights.

Shortly after Delphine left, Rose sent word by way of Luz that she had a sick headache and would not be able to join the party.

Marin said only, "What a shame. Thank you, Luz," but as soon as the girl slid out of the room, she sat down at her dressing table and stared at her worried face in the mirror. The day had been a long one, filled with small annoyances—friction among employees at the warehouse, books that would not balance, and at the end of the day a major decision to be made. But for her father's stubborn attitude about keeping his fingers on the books she would insist they hire a bookkeeper. They could afford one now, and she had grown to hate the job. The idea Harry had presented to her just before she left the office was exciting, a daring, dangerous suggestion that made her nervous even to think about, and she wanted it settled in her own mind before she broached the subject to James.

Harry proposed expanding the business in an entirely new direction. He wanted to open a shop featuring costly Chinese art treasures imported by Gentry and Callendar. No one else had ventured in such a direction yet, but some imaginative entrepreneurs were sure to see the possibilities soon, because both taste and money were present in the city. Harry believed that the farsighted entrepreneurs should be himself and James Gentry. He even had a name for the store, The Golden Cathay. It was mostly Mrs. Harry's idea, and what did Marin think?

Marin didn't know what she thought except that it was an enticing proposition that would cost a mint to put into operation. It would take every penny of reserve they had built, and that was frightening. Even now that the loan from Malcolm was fully repaid, expansion, especially such innovative expansion, was a big risk for a company as undercapitalized as theirs. Harry was already in love with the idea; his opinions had to be taken with a wheelbarrowful of salt when that gambling light was in his eyes. Papa was just as bad. He would laugh and say, "What the hell, chicken, shoot the works!" Stuart—she didn't want to talk it over with him. The one person she did want to talk to she had not seen for months.

She rubbed her right shoulder, the one that always ached after long hours of struggle with the account books. This afternoon she had felt anxious and fatigued, as she often did on days of unremitting wind. The children had been restless and excitable all day, Luz had said, and were cranky when Marin went in to kiss them good-night. The hubbub of a constant wind always disquieted them. Probably the gustiness of the day had put Rose off, too, and she would have to be jollied into gathering herself for the excursion tonight.

Marin opened her bedroom door and looked out. Luz had gone back to the nursery, and the hallway was empty. She went to her parents' door, but outside it she hesitated. No one in the household respected James's and Rose's privacy more scrupulously than she. She never entered their room without first knocking and being invited in. No telling what, if anything, went on in there, for James had never completely recovered from the paralysis, but there was another, even more important reason for circumspection.

James's money had paid for the house, and Rose was the lady of the house, although in practical fact Marin was in charge. She gave the orders to the servants, and made the day-to-day decisions, and her will was obeyed. Instinct prompted her to step very carefully with her parents, to consult with them, listen to their opinions, and give at least the semblance of being guided by them. Never must those two strong-willed people be forced to acknowledge that they were now the children, for it would crush their pride to bits.

However, this evening she knew that James was downstairs by the fire, reading the newspaper and smoking his daily cigar. Rose was in there alone. Marin raised her hand to knock, changed her mind, and gently turned the knob. The door was not locked. She eased it open a fraction and peeked in. Only one small lamp had been lit, and the circle of light was too pale to lift the shadows in the corners. Rose lay on the new chaise longue that James had proudly bought for her out of the firm's last shipment of furniture from New York. Her wrapper trailed on the floor, a damp cloth covered her forehead and eyes. Marin crossed the floor quietly and knelt on the thick carpet beside her.

"Mama?" she said softly.

"Oh!" Rose snatched off the cloth and sat bolt upright, her hand at her throat. Her eyes darted around the room and came to rest on Marin, and the wild look faded. "Gracious, Marin, you startled me near to death." She sank back on the little couch and closed her eyes. "Didn't Luz tell you I have a headache? I declare, it was almost gone, and now it's started again."

"I'm so sorry. Perhaps it will be better soon and you can go with us, Mama. We needn't leave for over an hour yet. Papa is so looking forward to seeing you in your new dress. Ten yards in the skirt! Anna says velvet is *the* fabric this year."

But the appeal to vanity, so often successful, got nowhere with Rose tonight. She laid the cloth on her forehead again and said wearily, "I am not well enough. I'd rather be here at home with Papa." She looked up at her frowning daughter, and an affectionate smile erased the shadows in her eyes. She ran a caressing hand over Marin's cheek. "My pretty, pretty baby. You're the one who will look lovely tonight. Smile for me, and be sure you stop by before you leave and let me see you."

Marin turned her face into the soft palm and kissed it. She smiled obediently, got to her feet, and left the room. Tomorrow, she thought as she went back down the hall, tomorrow she would not go to the office, she would take the day off, a number of days, and devote them to Rose, get her dressed and groomed and back on her schedule of daily outings. Logan had been very good to Rose, but she was not her daughter and could not care as much as she, Marin, would. Tomorrow things were going to change.

Thus fortified by the prospect of a new cause to devote herself to, she called Luz for help with her stays, then sent the girl to help Logan and Sophy, and finished dressing by herself. She was only a trifle annoyed when Mrs. Victoria came to her door with a message from Stuart saying that he was unavoidably detained by business but that Michael was coming in his stead.

She tossed Stuart's note on the dresser.

"Is Mr. Morgan here?"

"Yes, Miss Marin. Downstairs talking with Mr. James. He's a fine caballero these days, *verdad*?"

"Oh, *verdad*. Mr. Morgan dresses splendidly as a king, which day I never expected to see. Come hook this locket for me, please."

Mrs. Victoria slipped the thin gold clasps together, chuckling deep in her large bosom. "He's got on this long black cape an' almos' tripped over it when he came in the door."

Marin giggled. "I shall admire it extravagantly. Are the other ladies ready?"

"Miss Logan, she's gone downstairs, but Miss Sophy says she cannot go."

"Can't go! At this late date? Mr. Winfield will be here any minute."

Mrs. Victoria lifted her shoulders expressively. "Miss Logan, she tried an' gave up. Miss Sophy's just sitting there in her underdrawers, won't get dressed, won't let me brush her hair."

"We'll see about that."

Marin marched to Sophy's door and flung it open. Sophy sat on her bed in chemise and drawers, her head lowered, her hands clasped between her knees.

"If you aren't a picture," Marin began ominously, and Sophy groaned, "Oh, Marin, don't scold. I can't go tonight, truly, so don't try to make me. Oh, dear life, I have got myself in the most awful mess!"

Scorching words died on Marin's lips. She came in swiftly and shut the door.

"What do you mean, mess?" The fear that leaped to her mind was an ugly reminder of things best forgotten. But stars above, Sophy had learned her lesson, and anyway, she hadn't been out of sight of a chaperone for more than a moment or two since they had come to San Francisco. At least, Marin did not think she had. She sat on the bed, afraid to ask the necessary question.

"Sophy?"

Sophy's head remained down, her face averted.

"What have you done, Sophy?"

There was a silence, during which Marin's chest tightened nervously.

Sophy gulped and gasped out, "I did the stupidest thing. I promised to go with George tonight, but I promised Tom, too. Oh, how could I have done it? They're both going to appear any minute, and George is so stiff-necked, and you know how high and mighty Tom can be. They're going to insult each other, I know it, and end up shooting each other, and it will be all my fault. Oh, what am I going to do?"

Relief was so great that Marin almost laughed aloud. Sophy

wasn't in a fix, thank God, and almost anything else could be
smoothed over somehow. But Sophy wasn't laughing. Her heart-
shaped face was tragic, and tears dripped off her little chin. So
Marin hid her amusement, found a handkerchief, and wiped her
sister's face.

Sophy took it and blew her nose vigorously. The door chimes
rang, and her head snapped up. "It's them, I know it's them." She
shuddered. "I will not go down there and face them, no, not if I'm
beat for it."

"Who's going to beat you? Certainly not me, and neither Tom
nor George would injure your little finger. Oh, stop snuffling. You
can stay up here. I'll think of something to defuse them."

"Would you, Marin? Do you think you can? Of course you can,
you always think of something. You are the best, dearest sister in
the whole world!"

"Thank you. How did you come to do such a dumb thing? You
can't expect to juggle men if you don't keep your dates straight."

"I can't juggle men at all. I'm not even sure I want to. I'm not
like you, Marin. I don't have the brains for it."

"Nonsense. All it takes is a little attention to detail. What do
you mean, you're not sure you want to? Every girl wants a lot of
beaux."

"Not me," said Sophy glumly. "I like the idea of it—who
doesn't? Heaps of men flocking around, desperately in love with
me. But real-life men, the men who like me anyway, they're so
pushy—sweet as pie, but underneath always demanding, always
wanting to be the only one."

"They're all like that, every one of them, no matter how nice
they seem. You have to get used to it and outthink them without
letting them know you're doing it. Now wash your face, and I'll
go smooth their feathers. I guess you'll have to miss Mr. Booth."

Smoothing their feathers wasn't easy even for Marin. On the
surface Tom Anderson and George Winfield were well-bred
gentlemen whose only concern was for Miss Sophy's sudden
indisposition, but just beneath the courtesy they were two fighting
cocks, longing to tear into each other with sharp spurs and beaks.
Men! thought Marin in disgust. What a paper-thin coating of
civilization covered their violence, and for all their good manners
how hard it was for them to hide and control it. Best to get out of
the house and on to the theater. It would be a good job if this night
was gotten through without words that led to serious trouble.

But to her immense relief Tom declined the invitation to
accompany the two remaining ladies as soon as George accepted,

and the evening passed off pleasantly. They came out after the play agreeing that dark, brooding Mr. Booth, although a mere boy, showed signs of striking talent and was sure to be almost as great a star as his father, the great Junius Booth. Marin and Logan sent their fondest regards to George's mother and his sister, Kitty, then he bowed over their hands and took himself into the night.

Michael's carriage rolled off toward home, and Marin leaned her head against the damask cushion, thinking that men were, without doubt, the unsolvable problem of the universe and a great nuisance, too. Even kind, gentle Harry Callendar, with his enthusiasm and optimism and his Golden Cathay store, was a problem. He would press for an answer soon, and what could she tell him? She wished she hadn't come tonight, she wished she'd had a headache and stayed home with Mama and Sophy.

"Michael, what is that funny light—"

She sat upright, horror-stricken. Quiet, placid Stockton Street was lit by a sinister, yellow-orange glow. A fire company thundered past them, bells clanging madly, horses racing at a flat-out gallop. Down the street of occasional buildings interspersed with wide vacant lots, James Gentry's house was burning.

Michael stood up and brought his whip down on the horses' backs with a mighty whack, and the carriage leaped forward, hurling the girls back against the seat cushions. They careened down the street, Michael lashing the horses mercilessly all the way, lurched into the side yard, and jerked to a stop just beyond the water cart. Firemen were scurrying like dark, busy ants, shouting, cursing the equipment and each other as they jockeyed the pump into position. Flames licked around the frame of an upstairs window. The white curtains caught, flared, and shriveled instantly into black rags.

Before Michael could turn to help her down, Marin leaped over the carriage wheel, heedless of billowing satin skirts, and ran across the yard screaming, "My children! Where are my children!"

In the savage glare that lit the drive a small figure came hurrying, hurrying, as fast as his short legs could move, flying to her with dark head up and arms held out, his little face anguished but determined. They met in the middle of the drive, and he jumped into her arms, his fingers digging desperately into her shoulders, his legs wrapping tightly around her waist.

He buried his face in her neck, and she whispered, "Carey! Oh, baby, baby!" kissed his soft cheek, and hugged him passionately. Her son, her vibrant, obstinate, energetic, exasperating, deeply loved little son. Beyond his head she saw Luz coming, running lightly with Belinda in her arms. Luz had done her duty, God bless her; she had saved the children. Something must be done for Luz, some reward given for this night's work.

Belinda's plump arms reached out, went round Marin's neck in a strangling grip, and she had them both safe, their sweet, warm, infinitely precious bodies tight in her grasp. She shifted Carey to one hip to make space for Belinda, and the little girl raised her tear-streaked face. The light of the flames reflected in her wide, frightened eyes, and she hid her face against Marin's shoulder.

Carey, now safe from all harm in his mother's arms, gazed at the mad scene on the lawn and cried out, "Mama, where's Grandpa?"

Marin looked at Luz. The girl spread her palms wide. "We was in the stable-room with Señora Victoria. I don' know where Mr. James is, or Miss Rose neither."

Marin shoved the children at Luz and clutched the arm of the nearest fireman. "Please! My parents are up there!"

"Yes, ma'am," the young man shouted back. "The hook and ladder company is on its way."

"You don't understand! They're sick, my father is paralyzed."

He nodded. "We'll get 'em out, don't you worry," and went on uncoiling hose.

In the side yard Jeremy hurtled up the path with a bucket of well water in each hand. She ran to him.

"Jeremy, Mama and Papa are still in the house!"

He looked upward. Sweat rolled down his face.

"Jeremy!"

"Yes'm, I heerd you." He continued to stare upward at flames that were curling the shingles off the south end of the roof.

A rough hand came down on her arm. "Marin, for God's sake, get back!"

"Michael, they didn't get out, Mama and Papa and—has anybody seen Sophy? Oh, God, Sophy must be in there, too. Michael, help me!"

There was a cheer from the firemen as the hook and ladder company rolled in. Michael and Jeremy exchanged a look, and over the uproar Michael shouted, "Marin, go to the carriage and stay there. Let's try the back, Jeremy."

They ran for the kitchen door and disappeared into the house. The fire ladders went up, and brave men climbed the front of the house, hauling hose toward the flames. Then, as Marin and Logan watched, horrified, the blazing roof came down. All the blood seemed to leave Marin's head in a rush. She fell against Logan as she went down.

There was a babble of voices, many people chattering at once; the collie, Angus, was licking her face. Weights seemed to rest on her eyelids and she struggled to lift them and raise herself onto her elbows.

"Stay down a while longer, Marin. You'll go dizzy if you get up too quick."

It hadn't been only a nightmare that would vanish with the morning light. She was on the lawn, and although there had been no rain, muddy water stood in puddles. It seeped through her dress to her skin. Logan was standing beside her, looking upward at the house, and she looked up, too. The upper floor was gutted, and most of the roof had collapsed, but the rest of the house still stood, scorched and wet and splattered with mud but still there, outlined in the white light of the half-moon. There was no breeze, and the air was heavy with stinging smoke.

She rubbed her smarting eyes. "They put the fire out."

Logan smiled. "The fire laddies did a grand job. I shall write a letter to the newspaper about it."

Everything must be all right for Logan to stand there so calmly, talking about writing letters to the editor, yet fear drove Marin's heart to race.

"Did Michael . . ."

"They got them out, Michael and Jeremy and the fire captain together. They got everybody out just as the beams came down. My, they were so brave!"

Marin glanced around. A few yards away Mrs. Victoria and Luz were sitting on the ground with the children. Firemen were rolling up hoses. The equipment of the hook and ladder company was spread all over the yard. But James and Rose and Sophy . . . anxiety rose like spreading fire itself. "Where are they?"

"Dear, they'll be all right . . ."

She jumped to her feet, grabbed Logan, and shook her in a frenzy of fear.

"Where are they?"

"Michael used our carriage because it's bigger and left his for us to follow in as soon as you are feeling like it. Your papa's hands were burned, just a little, and your mother and Sophy were overcome by the smoke—but they got out, that's the main thing. We decided to take them to Vail's house. I don't think he's in town, but that won't matter. Almost everyone else we know either lives in a hotel or has too small a house. Anyway, I thought Vail's was best because the hospital . . ."

Marin thought of the dingy pesthole on Clay Street and shivered. "No, not the hospital." Her mind spun and darted. "We must get Charles. I want Charles to see them."

"I've already sent for him."

Vail's big house shone through the night. There seemed to be a lamp lit in every room. The front door was unlatched, and far down the hall, in the passageway leading to the kitchen, Mrs. Moon came hurrying, carrying a basin of steaming water in her hands and a wad of towels stuffed under one arm. She nodded a quick greeting and started up the stairs, balancing the basin carefully. Marin followed her, taking the steps two at a time, and passed her on the landing.

Logan was wrong. Vail had not left town, for he was in the upper hallway, talking with Charles outside a closed bedroom door.

She rushed forward. "Charles, how are they?"

With the warm smile that always reassured he said, "Sophy is sleeping. She has a bump on the head . . ."

"Logan said they were overcome by smoke."

"That is what we thought at first, but actually the ceiling came down as Sophy was trying to reach your parents. I believe she will recover well, given a few weeks."

"A few weeks!"

"Well, I am conservative, as you know. Perhaps sooner. With good care."

Marin looked from him to Vail. It seemed to her that neither man quite met her eyes. A lump of fear rose in her throat.

She said, "Papa? Mama?"

"Mr. Gentry tried to move some hot bricks and burned his hands, not severely. Otherwise he's unhurt. Your mother is resting. You can go in if you wish."

Charles opened the door, and she walked into the room. James sat beside a tall bed with a canopied top. In it Rose lay sleeping.

She went to him, knelt down, and put her arms around him.

"Papa, how are you? Let me see your hands."

"It's nothing." He looked at the bandages. "Dr. Towle put these on, but I don't need them."

Rose was deep in sleep, her breathing a light flutter. Her face had been washed, and her long blond hair brushed. A small bruise on one cheek was the only sign that she had been through an ordeal.

"Why don't you get to bed, Papa," Marin whispered. "She'll be fine in the morning."

"No. No, she won't. I think we've lost her, daughter."

"What a thing to say! That shows how overwrought you are, and no wonder with such a shock. Now you are to come . . . oh, thank you, Mrs. Moon." She watched the housekeeper set basin and towels on the marble-topped washstand. "Would you find a bed for Mr. Gentry . . ."

"I can't leave her, daughter." James raised his head. There was a long, raw scrape running across his forehead and down one cheek. His eyes were red-rimmed and without hope. A chill crept over Marin, as if cold wind blew suddenly through the warm room.

Mrs. Moon said, "There's beds ready anytime you need them, Mrs. Severance," but she said it with eyes down and ducked quietly out the door.

A moment later Charles and Vail were in the room, Vail at the foot of the bed, Charles on the other side, bending, his hand on Rose's wrist, his eyes traveling over her sleeping face.

In a trembling voice Marin asked, "Charles, will you reassure my father? He thinks Mama is hurt seriously."

Charles dug his stethoscope out of his bag. "This is a dandy, brand new from New York." He laid the small, flat ivory bell on Rose's chest. Marin opened her mouth to speak, and he held up his hand for silence. Cold swept her again, a sickening cold that nauseated her and left her legs quivering. Who cared about his stethoscope? Why didn't he encourage Papa? He knew worry wasn't good for him.

Charles stowed the instrument in his bag. "Mrs. Gentry was caught under the chimney when it collapsed, Marin. She has suffered internal injuries."

"Big pile of bricks," James murmured, "big pile."

"But . . . she'll be all right, won't she?"

"I don't know. Internal injuries are hard to predict."

That was Charles for you. *I don't know.* What kind of a thing was that to say? What kind of a doctor was he? Why didn't he do something, there must be lots of things he could do.

She rose, her hands clenched into fists. "I want another doctor. I want Tom to see my mother."

"Of course. I'll be happy to have another opinion."

When Tom came, shocked, anxious for Sophy, he examined

Rose in much the same way Charles had, agreed that the pulse was thready and the extremities cold, took out a fine brass box containing several knives of varying shape and size, opened a vein in Rose's earlobe, and let a small amount of blood drain into a cup.

"Rest is what she needs," he said heartily. "Come, Mr. Gentry, let's get you to bed."

Slowly James shook his head, and Tom forbore to say more.

Through the long night Marin sat on a hassock beside her father. Logan put the children into hastily made up beds, then tiptoed into the silent room and kept the vigil with them. She whispered to Marin that Delphine had been driven up the hill by Mrs. Parrish's coachman after arriving home to find it halfburned.

At Rincon Hill she had debarked from the carriage, in tears over the ruined house, tears that escalated into hysterics when she learned that Rose was injured. Charles had given her a strong dose of chloral hydrate and put her to bed.

The whispered words rolled over Marin. She nodded, her eyes fastened on her mother's face, scarcely able to take in what Logan had said.

Across the room the clock on the mantel measured off the slow hours before dawn, and one or both of the doctors came in at intervals, looked grave, murmured a few words, nothing that meant anything. Marin had long since given up hope of help from either of them. She prayed silently, an intense stream of bargaining, promises, debates with God designed to make Him see the reasonableness of her propositions.

Let Mama live through this, let her live just—just ten years more, ten years that she and James would have together, a lot of living could be done in ten years. It was such a small amount of time that was needed, time that would mean so much to them and so little to God. What did ten years mean to Him when He had all eternity? Let her live, let her live, and there would be no more bad temper, no more estrangement from Stuart. Over and over she promised that she, Marin, would be a very good girl, kind, gentle, tolerant, soft-spoken, utterly upright at all times. Only let Mama live!

Through it all some part of her was dimly aware of the comings and goings in the room. At times Vail was there; she knew it without looking around. He never talked to the two doctors, but only listened and watched and kept silent.

Shortly after two o'clock Rose woke and complained that her feet were cold and her chest hurt most dreadfully. A hot brick was put to her feet, and Charles measured out drops of laudanum. She slept.

At some time during the next hour Stuart walked in. Somehow he had been located and told of the disaster. He patted Marin's shoulder and slumped into a chair.

At half past five Rose woke again, but this time her eyes were clear. She smiled her old, sweet smile and moved her fingers to touch Marin's hand.

"Are you warm enough, my queen?" asked James.

Her head turned toward him. Her cheeks had color in them, her expression was bright and aware. "Yes, dear, I'm warm. James—" Her voice was low but strong.

He leaned closer.

"James, it is so beautiful. You must not grieve. Promise me you will not grieve, or it will spoil everything."

"I promise, Rose."

She sighed, satisfied, and closed her eyes. Outside the sky grew lighter, and birds sang their morning song in the scrub oak in the garden. Her breathing became a rattling snore. It grew more ragged, hesitated, and, with James holding tight to one slim white hand and Marin kneeling on the floor holding the other, it stopped.

Marin walked down the stairs, heading for the parlor. There were decisions that had to be made, and her mind must remain firmly on them. It was important to keep command of oneself, she must not forget that.

They were in the parlor, as Mrs. Moon had said: Vail by a fire that was almost out, standing in that characteristic manner, dark head down, hands thrust deep in his trouser pockets; Jeremy slouched in a chair; Michael pacing slowly down the room, flexing his big hands as though he would like to strangle someone if only he could identify his opponent.

Jeremy leaped to his feet as she entered, and Michael came directly to her, put his arms around her, and kissed her in a manner so affectionate, so brotherly that she thought, Oh, Ethan, why aren't you here . . . , and shunted the memory of him away before it had time to take root and grow.

"Michael, will you do something for me?"

"Anything, Marin, you know that."

She drew a breath and began to speak all the unspeakable things. "I've decided that Mama will be—will be buried in the cemetery here in town, not at Little Mountain. Papa will want to

visit her, and it should be someplace near, so he can go every day
if he wants to. Do whatever needs doing to arrange it, and have the
bills sent to me. I want a good, strong coffin, the finest you can
get. Watertight. When it rains—I don't want Mama out in the rain.
Find out what kind of stone stands up to the weather best, granite
or marble. Back home there were so many monuments in the
graveyards that you couldn't read at all. The lettering on the wood
went in no time, I don't see why anyone would have wood—but
so often the carving on the stone gravemarkers was almost worn
away, too, even stone only fifty, seventy years old. We used to
make a game of piecing together the stories on the stones, and the
ones that we couldn't read—it was as if those people never lived,
because you couldn't figure out their names or when they were
born or when they died or who they married. The carving must be
very deep on Mama's stone."

The rush of words halted, and Michael asked gently, "What
should be on the stone?"

"'Amalia Rose Gentry.' A-m-a, not A-m-e—make sure it's
spelled right. You'd best write it down."

Michael patted his pockets. "I don't seem to have any paper . . .
I'll remember, Marin."

"Under her name say 'Beloved wife of James Elliott Gentry.
Born June 5, 1809. Died April . . . April . . .'"

"Twenty-six."

"'April 26, 1853.'"

"Anything else? Something from the Bible?"

"No Bible verses. Just say, 'She was all the world.'"

Michael's eyes dropped away.

Marin said, "You risked your life for Mama and Papa and
Sophy last night. I know what I owe you."

"No debts between us, Marin." He bent, kissed her again,
pulled down his hat as if he were going out into a storm. Cool
morning air swept in as he opened the front door, and in moments
the wheels of his carriage crunched on the drive as it rolled out to
the road.

"Jeremy." She went to the lanky man, waiting politely, watching,
his dark brown face stern with grief. She put her hands into his. "I
know what I owe you, too."

"Don' owe me nuthin' neither, Miss Marin," he muttered.

She was reminded of the first time she saw him, that day when
she surprised him in his hideaway in the woods up above Dead
Man Bar. He had looked then as he looked now, startled, wary,

unsure how to deal with this white lady, a white lady who at the moment was holding onto his hands like a friend.

"I am beholden to you, we are beholden to you, Jeremy. This family doesn't forget its debts."

He shrugged. "You done for me in times past, I does for you as de case happens," and seemed easier when he had retrieved his hands.

"Have you a place to sleep?"

"Yes, missy."

"Miss Logan is busy right now"—she shut her mind against the picture of what Logan and Mrs. Moon were doing upstairs—"but later on we'll want you to drive us back home to look for personal items. If everything is ruined, we'll have to do some shopping to tide us over."

"Yes'm. I's glad ter do dat." He edged toward the door. "Anytime you is ready, jis' call." He slid out as though he had done something wrong and were escaping a scolding. It was not that he minded appreciation and kind words. He knew Miss Marin valued him. He had, strangely enough, received more real respect from that feisty white lady, Southern though she was, than from any of several Northerners he had briefly worked for. But he recalled other times when, under the immediate press of emotion, some of his former employers had expressed something more than the appreciation of a good master for a good servant, something close to genuine friendship, and invariably the moment passed and only embarrassment remained, embarrassment that led to dislike and thence to trouble. There was nothing but trouble to be found in friendship with white folks. Jeremy preferred to work hard, step cautiously, and keep his powder dry. He didn't want Miss Marin to have any cause for embarrassment.

In the parlor Marin sat down on the sofa, abruptly aware of every muscle in her back and legs. Why was she so tired, so shaky in the knees? She felt pleased with the way she had handled things—strong, dignified, composed, not flinching from the difficult decisions, which meant she had made the right ones. Or had she? Was it right not to bury Mama at Little Mountain when Papa had meant it to be their home forever? Was it right, what she had told Michael to put on the tombstone, or had she left out something important, should she have said something different? It would be engraved in stone, unchanging, immutable, so it had to be right. But she must not begin to doubt herself or she would break and start to cry, and then where would she be?

The world had gone mad last night, everything was slipping

away, out of control. If Mama could die, anything could happen, and she was lost and terrified. Her hands were twisting in her lap, and with an effort she stilled them, conscious of Vail, standing before the fireplace, his eyes on her. He hadn't kissed her or said the usual consoling words, but he was there, and his solid presence made the events of the past hours a little less hideous.

She looked up at him. "Those words for Mama's stone, it was what Papa said just after she died. 'She was all the world.' Oh, what will he do? They've been like two parts of the same person ever since I can remember. They loved each other best; we children knew it, and we didn't mind because it seemed right that they should. We knew they loved us, too, that they'd do anything for us, but they always came first with each other. In a way it was better. It left us free. Maybe it wasn't so good for them though, maybe they needed each other too much. Oh, what will Papa do? I'm afraid for him, Vail."

"Don't be. Your father is a strong man, stronger than you know. He won't sink in despair no matter what the loss. It isn't in him to give up." He sat down beside her, smoothed out her fingers, which had begun to twist again, and held them until they were quiet. "As for being too close, they were lucky. They had the best for—what was it—almost thirty years? Most people don't have thirty months before the magic goes and they get disillusioned, and just plain bored."

"Oh, that's true, that's true. Why does it happen that way? Why is it that you think you have just what you want, and then that person turns out so different than you thought?"

"We expect too much. Most people are lonely most of the time, that can't be news to you. We get desperate to wipe out the loneliness, so we convince ourselves we've found the one perfect person—not because we really have, but because our need is so great. It's a bitter pill when the disillusionment sets in. For your parents it never did. They were lucky."

"Does it have to be like that—all regrets and sadness?"

"Not if our hopes aren't too high. My philosophy is never expect anything, and you won't be disappointed."

She stared at his hand over hers, darkly tanned skin against white, and she thought of James and Rose, of herself and Stuart and the muddle of her life. Her hair was coming loose from the chignon she had worn to the theater last night; she could feel the strands on her neck. Was it only last night that she had struggled with that hairdo, had been upset because her satin dress was a trifle tight? Was it only last night that Rose had caressed her cheek and smiled and told her how pretty she was?

"Vail, do you suppose we go on living after we die?"

He hesitated, thinking that the white column of her neck would be easy to circle with one hand, wondering what answer would hurt her least.

"I don't know, Marin. Your religion teaches that we do."

She shrugged. "I've found out religion works only when nothing is wrong. It doesn't help me now. I guess that means I'm bad. But, Vail, something happened this morning. You see, Mama wasn't one to suffer silently—not that she was weak or cowardly, she was immensely brave in her own way—but she always made sure Papa knew when she was sick; she wanted him to be concerned and worry for her. But this morning just before—before she died, she came back to herself, she knew us all, she knew she was dying, and she said, 'James, it is so beautiful. You must not grieve. Promise me you will not grieve, or it will spoil everything.' Papa promised, and she was satisfied. That's not like her at all. And the look on her face. She was happy. You must have watched a lot of people die. What do you think it meant?"

"Yes, I've watched people die, and I've seen that look on some faces."

"Don't you think she saw something so beautiful that she didn't mind dying?"

"Marin, I'm not the one to say. If there is anything more, we are not meant to know it for certain, and we never will, not in this world. We are required to believe without having seen, so the Bible tells us. One thing I do know—each of us has his own road to travel. We come together for a while, but eventually we must go on our way alone. Your mother has gone on her way, and you must let her go. I believe that is what she was telling James."

She nodded, clinging to his hand, clinging to hope, and neither of them heard Stuart coming down the stairs.

The past twenty-four hours had been unpleasant for Stuart for a number of reasons. He had lost a committee appointment he coveted to a man he detested. He had been forced by unforeseen circumstance to miss Edwin Booth's performance as well as an evening out with his wife, who was sure to be in a good mood and looking her best. He had had to endure a distasteful scene and then work very hard to erase any ill feelings harbored by the other party. He had been found in an awkward situation when hunted down by Michael and informed of the disaster at home—not that Michael would talk. His wife and children were dispossessed, their house in ruins. And, of course, his mother-in-law had died.

Having just lost the committee appointment, his mood had been already dark when the hysterical, accusing note from Francine Briand arrived, forcing him to cancel his evening at the theater and send Michael in his stead. He had made Francine's acquaintance shortly after the fiasco at Madame Colette's parlor house almost two years ago, when fire and panic had brought the transgressions of so many prominent men into the open. Only his presence of mind, which led him out the back window instead of the front door, had saved him from the public ridicule others had had to endure. The close call convinced him that other arrangements would have to be made.

For many months Francine had filled the bill wonderfully. She was available, ardent, easily satisfied, attractive in a high-nosed, thin-lipped, French way, and she regarded him with a respectful admiration that verged upon awe. She was none of your offscourings of the Paris streets, either, but a delightful young woman of culture, refinement, and discretion. But Francine, like all her sex, was subject to many-sided moods that he could not fathom, and over the months she had changed.

The compliant girl who used to receive him gladly whenever he chose to come to the comfortable hotel room he paid for now insisted he make an appointment and complained when he did not appear on the dot. The undemanding girl who used to tease him for little gifts that it was his pleasure to bestow now told him in no uncertain terms exactly what she wanted. And what she wanted was out of the question. He was not a stingy man, but as he told her, he had a family to provide for. He could not afford expensive jewelry, and he would not pay for the three-room suite she was pressing for, not at the rates charged by the Union Hotel. Her discretion was open to doubt as well, for last night she had hinted that she might be forced to discuss her distress with others if her needs were not promptly met.

If she talked to Marin (and she had the nerve to do it!), life would not be worth living. If she talked to his father . . .

He would negotiate some compromise with Francine, but it infuriated him to have to pay to keep her quiet. He felt humiliated, imposed upon, harassed and pressured from all sides, and it was in this frame of mind that he came into the parlor and saw his wife sitting on the sofa with a faraway, musing, untypically subdued

expression on her delicate face; saw his brother, close enough to
breathe down her bosom, lift a stray curl from her neck and tuck
it into its net in a manner so intimate and tender that all the old
antagonism, the resentment, the jealousy of Vail that had rankled
in his heart since boyhood rose up and swept away restraint.

Marin heard only a muffled sound, but it was enough to bring
her out of her abstraction. She looked up at Vail and then past him.
In the wide double doorway stood her husband, rigid with rage,
eyes glittering, lips straightened into a thin, hard line. But it was
a cold rage, still under control, and he was staring not at her, but
at Vail.

"What in hell are you doing with my wife?"

She jumped to her feet, snatching away the hand Vail held, and
Vail rose, too.

He said, "Don't be a fool, Stuart."

"Goddamn you! *Goddamn* you!" Stuart took a step toward him,
then turned furious, accusing eyes on Marin. "And you! Playing
pattycake with him while your mother lies dead upstairs. What
kind of woman are you?"

Marin, stunned and off balance for one instant, regained her
footing and came back fighting.

"A woman who has just lost her mother, as you point out." Her
words dripped ice. "How can you, how dare you speak to me like
that."

"Vail . . ."

"Vail has done nothing but offer some little comfort in
innocence and kindness when I was near to breaking. And where
were you? Why weren't you down here with me when I needed
you? I expect an apology, Stuart, to me and, more important, to
Vail."

"An apology, by Almighty God!" he shouted, but her quick
counterthrust, aided by his knowledge of his own secret guilt, had
hit its mark. In all honesty he did not suspect them of actual
wrongdoing—not that he put anything past Vail, but he knew that
Marin, like most women of breeding and gentility, had little
interest in the physical side of love. Still, he was not unaware of
the other, more significant side, the side that might never be
consummated by more than a look in the eyes, a touch of hands,
a deep interest and a caring heart, and it was that subtle and
unchallengeable love that he feared and was jealous of. He had felt
nothing but relief when Vail married Celia so unexpectedly; it
wiped away all his suspicions and left him thankful that he had
never hinted them to Marin. So now his certainty wavered, and he

might have backed down but for the sudden sparkle of amusement in Vail's eyes at her demand for an apology. Rage rose again, and this time it exploded like a burst of light in Stuart's head. He could hurt her, hurt them both, and he would.

His lips curved down, and his eyes went cold. Instead of shouting, his voice became deadly quiet.

"You're a clever woman, I'll give you that, but not so clever that you don't miss what's going on in your own household, under your own pretty nose. Do you know why your demented mother is dead, your sister and father hurt, your children endangered? Do you know how that fire started?"

Vail said, "Stuart, don't," in a hard, warning voice, but Stuart was beyond caring what he did. He plunged on. "I'll tell you how. That woman was cracked, crazy as a loon, with her babble about the Landrinis and the Italian nobility . . ."

"It's true! My grandfather was . . ."

"Your grandfather was a smooth-talking dago with an eye for the main chance and a way of turning a bad break to good account, just like you. There's bad blood there somewhere because that grand, fine lady, your mother, was a drunk and everybody knew it. She toped all night and all day if she could sneak it. Tonight, in her drunkenness, she knocked over a lamp and set the house on fire."

He had the satisfaction of seeing her flinch and her eyes grow huge with shock. Her hand went up as if to ward off a physical blow.

"It isn't true, it can't be true. It's a vicious, horrible lie."

"Is it? Ask Charles Towle. Ask your father. Ask *him*." Stuart pointed a finger trembling with fury, and Vail said, almost laconically, "I should have let you drown."

In the next moment Stuart found himself hard against the doorjamb from a blow so swift, he hadn't seen it coming. Vail was inches from him, wearing the most lethal expression he had ever seen in another man's face. Stuart was no physical coward. He was a strong man, in good shape, and at this moment he hated his brother as he had never hated anyone before. But the air was knocked out of him; he had lost his balance and also any tactical advantage. And beneath his hate and anger was a nasty sense of having made an irreparable mistake.

Slowly Vail loosed his hold. "Get out before I kill you where you stand."

Stuart straightened his cravat, shrugged his coat back onto his shoulders, gave Vail a look that was a promise, and walked into the hallway and out the front door, carrying with him the memory of Marin's stricken face and the knowledge that he had hurt her at last.

Vail watched him go and said again, this time to himself, "I should have let him drown."

"Is it true?" He turned, and she saw his face. "You did know, you knew all the time. Why didn't you tell me? Oh, how could it be?" Rose—a secret drinker? It was an idea impossible to take in. Beyond a cup of wine punch at a party or a small quantity of champagne to toast a newly married couple, ladies did not drink—certainly great ladies did not. Only the lowest of common women did that. Marin's mind shuddered away from the memory of women she had been unlucky enough to come across on the street, rough, shrieking women, silly with drink, staggering and giggling and hiccuping obscenely, bottles in their hands, staring at her with bleary eyes and tilting the bottles so the fiery liquor could trickle down their painted throats. How could she associate such a repulsive thing with Rose?

Vail said, "I suspected a long time ago. All the signs were there, the seclusion, the stupors, the secretiveness. And, eventually, the physical signs in the eyes and the nervous complaints. Charles found an enlarged liver when he first examined her. That's why he told you to lock up the liquor, because of her, not James. Your father was adamant that you and Sophy not be told. He was afraid you might think less of her if you knew."

"I could never think less of Mama. Why didn't he trust me?"

"Try to understand him. He'd already lost so much, his son and to an extent his wife. He was determined no one would look down on her. He said that even when they were first married, she drank brandy for Dutch courage. He used to tease her about it. The move out here was beyond her, he knows that now. She drank to ease the homesickness and the fear, and he closed his eyes and blamed the servants for the disappearing liquor. When he had his stroke, her mind simply shut down and the drinking took over completely."

Marin sat down and put her head in her hands. "How could I have been so blind? How could she fool Delphine and Sophy?"

"She had to have liquor. When it's that important, people become very clever about getting it. She learned the uses of cologne, she hid out a good deal of the time, and then—you weren't looking for it, were you?"

"Who else knows?"

"Only Logan. She watched over her as best she could. It wasn't enough."

"Is it true about—the lamp?"

"James said she was in a happy mood last night. She put on the dress she had planned to wear to the theater, she sang a song he liked and danced for him. She bumped into a table, and the lamp went over."

Her face was ghostly white. "Poor little Mama, so frightened and so far from home."

Her voice broke. Up until now she had kept control over her feelings in the face of James's anguish and Logan's tears, Michael's kind kiss and the ugly scene with Stuart. But now she remembered beautiful, snobbish, warm, loving, frightened Rose, whose voice she would never hear, whose gentle touch she would never feel again in this world, no matter where she looked or how long she lived.

She dug her knuckles into her cheek. "I said I wouldn't cry."

His arms went around her, and he held her head against his shoulder.

"Cry for her, Marin, but just for a little while. She lived with such pain, and now it's over." He laid his cheek on her hair. "My honey, my baby, go ahead and cry."

The tears welled, spilled over, and she cried, for her mother, her father, herself, cried until she was spent and languid and resting quietly against his chest.

Chapter 27

 Stuart rode into town, accepted the commiseration of acquaintances, sent a note by messenger to Longridge informing his father of the night's events and assuring him that his grandchildren were safe, and spent the afternoon consulting with two close political allies; then, on impulse, he rode down to the waterfront and caught the cross-bay steamer just before it pulled away from the wharf. He was disembarking on the Contra Costa side when he remembered Francine. She was expecting him that evening and would be upset and angry if he didn't show. Let her stew, and to hell with her. He wouldn't even send a message.

It was almost nine o'clock when he pounded on his father's front door. The house was dark and silent, but there were immediate scurrying footsteps, and a plump Mexican girl opened it a crack and peeked out.

"Señor Stuart!" The door opened wider.

"Who did you expect, Teresa, your lover with a guitar over his shoulder?"

Teresa blushed and giggled. "Oh, señor, it would not be him. He is off in the great Sierras looking for gold."

"Aren't they all. Why, good evening, Glenna. I hope I'm not an inopportune guest."

Glenna had come into the entrance hall, and the lamp she held cast soft light over her smooth hair and modest gray dress. She looked as fresh and well-groomed as if she were just beginning the day.

She came toward him with her quick, light laugh. "What nonsense. You are always welcome in your own home, as you well know, but after your note we weren't expecting you. Oh, it is all so dreadful. Come in, come in. Your father has a slight cold and retired early, but he will be so happy to see you in the morning. Have you eaten? Good! You shall finish up the shepherd's pie and have a nice, cold quail. How lucky I made raspberry tarts this morning. Teresa, run and get Mr. Stuart's supper on the table, there's a good girl."

Stuart ate hugely and after dinner settled into a comfortable chair in the parlor with coffee cup in hand and a warm, expansive feeling around his heart. It was good to be here in the home of his parents, in this room, which had been changed not at all since his mother's death. Perhaps a touch here and there, a new chair, a bright cushion to make it even more homelike and reposeful, but essentially the same. The miniature of Elizabeth, painted before the family left Boston, still rested in a place of honor on the mantel. Not many second wives would be so generous. For all her humble beginnings and the trashiness of her two brothers there must be good blood in Glenna, and he took off his hat to his father for recognizing what everyone else had been too blind to see.

She expressed grief for Rose and sympathy for the bereaved husband and daughters, she recounted Rose's many sterling virtues and conveyed the certain hope that the good lady, believing Christian that she had been, would wake to find herself in the land of the blessed. Then she said, "Sad as it all is, we must give thanks that the babies were spared. It makes one's blood run cold to think what could have happened." She added sugar to her coffee and stirred it with one of Elizabeth's thin silver spoons, her little finger held outward in excessive gentility. Stuart found her lack of polish rather endearing. She asked, "And where is the family staying?"

"At Vail's." In spite of himself he flushed deeply.

Quietly she remarked, "I have always admired your forbearance toward your brother. Indeed, I have been amazed by it, considering the grief he brought his parents, considering—so many things. Such a willful, self-indulgent man. I am never quite at ease in his presence, for one never knows what he will do. And you have had to bear with him since childhood. I think you have shown the patience of a saint."

Stuart looked up, startled at her words and the subdued passion in them.

She went on, "Although we must leave judgment to Heaven, I cannot help but form an opinion. Mr. Severance and I speak of it often." The seriousness left her face. She smiled and leaned forward to touch his hand in an unconscious manner. "But then you know you are your father's favorite."

Unbidden, his mind traveled back down the years. He hadn't always been his father's favorite, but he couldn't recall a time when there had not been ill feeling between him and Vail.

There was a bare year's difference in their ages; Elizabeth had been happily absorbed in her first son when the second came along much too soon. Vail had always had the advantage of that year; not only a little older, he was always a little taller, quicker of mind, more adept at everything. This morning he had said, "I should have let you drown," and only the two of them knew what he meant.

Stuart's forbidden excursion onto the ice, the fall into the Charles River on a frosty, long-ago morning when he was eleven and Vail was twelve, the sudden terror, the numbing cold, the frigid water closing over his head. Then hands grasping his hair, tugging at his clothing, pulling him free of the deadly water; his strong, quick-witted older brother lying flat on the treacherous ice, hauling him, dripping wet and blue with cold, to safety, and then half dragging, half carrying him home, bawling him out every step of the way; his frightened mother toweling him dry before a blazing fire while his father praised Vail.

And then Father had turned on Stuart, small, skinny, shivering, stripped of clothes and dignity. Father, as mighty and righteous and powerful as God (when he was very little, Stuart had believed he might *be* God), had stood with his hand on Vail's shoulder, his eyes hard as flint, and scourged Stuart with the tongue-lashing of his young life. From that moment his chief fear became the sight of scorn in Malcolm's eyes; his first goal became winning Malcolm's regard. His second goal was to outdo Vail. Approval from Malcolm turned out to be easy to get; all that was required was complete submission, or at least the appearance of it. Surpassing Vail proved more difficult.

By the time he reached twenty, Stuart was two inches over six feet, a splendid, satisfactory height for a man, allowing him to tower over most of his friends, except Vail. Vail was three inches taller, and there was absolutely nothing to be done about it. So Stuart worked hard developing his body, in particular his shoulder and arm muscles. Unluckily, Vail had grown into an exceptionally powerful man without seeming to do much to achieve it. In every battle they had—and the fights were countless—Vail won. When the two boys matured enough to duel with words instead of fists, Vail inevitably came out ahead, for his was the keener mind. He excelled in school, he excelled in every area of their lives. And then he made his great error; he became an adult, chose his own path instead of his father's and handed the triumph to Stuart. To retain it, Stuart had only to become the person Father wanted.

An introspective man might have pondered the fate of his own soul in such an exchange, but self-analysis had never been one of Stuart's strong points. Tonight he thought only how soothing it was to be welcomed by this gentle, pious, attractive woman; how touching was her understanding; how pleasant the knowledge that Father would be glad to see him in the morning. He did not need Marin; he did not need Francine—he would buy her silence and pass her on to one of his friends. And in the future he would live the life he had always thought best, the life of self-denial.

He leaned back in the tall chair that suited his large frame so well, put his boots on the pretty footstool with Glenna's smiling permission, and accepted a second cup of coffee.

The calamity that had fallen on the family was so complete that in the days following, Marin had no time or strength to reflect on it. She responded to each need as it occurred, fell into bed late each night, and slept without dreaming. The closest friends came by with condolences, Gerald and Harry together and, a little later, Anna von Helsdorf. She arrived subdued in dress and manner, kissed Marin with warm affection, and promised practical help. She had already talked with the dressmaker, who had the measurements of every lady in the family, and suitable black mourning dresses would be delivered in time for the funeral. "I am of no use at all with the pots and the cooking," she said, "but dresses—that I know."

Tom had confidently expected that Sophy would be well enough to go to the funeral, but at the last moment, buttoned into the black dress that had been delivered that morning, she felt weak and dizzy and was hustled back to bed. "It's those heathenish stays," Tom muttered, and ordered her to unlace at once, but the dress had been made to fit her waist with a corset, and there was no time for alterations.

She wept a little, lying on her bed looking like a pale, grief-stricken angel. She insisted that she felt much better, tried to sit up, and lay down again swiftly. Ever since regaining consciousness, she had been in a state of profound inner turmoil. Her last memory was of her father's voice calling frantically, of herself running to her parents' room and finding James struggling to get out of bed and Rose crouched on the floor across the room, staring at flames that had already licked up the wall and were eating rapidly through the roof. She remembered helping her father out of bed and then rushing to her mother, using all her strength to lift Rose. But Rose did not want to move; she hung in Sophy's arms, a deadweight, and wildly Sophy turned to James, stumbling toward them. Then the roar as the chimney fell in. Then nothing.

She had waked with a hideously aching head to find her home gone and her mother dead. It was not real to her, nothing was real, yet she knew she must be at her mother's funeral or regret it all her life. Only her hurting head and the weakness in her legs persuaded her that she could not. Tom promised that within a week at the most she could visit Rose's grave and say her prayers then. He patted her hand and left her in the care of Mrs. Moon.

In midafternoon the mourners returned to Vail's house on Rincon Hill, speaking little, separated from each other by private thoughts and emotions, the nature of which depended on each one's feelings for the woman they had buried and whatever memories of past losses this day's ceremony had disturbed. Tom, his mind chiefly on Sophy, went directly upstairs. After a brief time he hurried down and drew Marin out of the room where a cold collation was being served to guests.

"I don't wish to speak of this to your father, Marin. He should be in bed himself. But I do not like Sophy's condition. Her head pains her more severely, and she has had chills and fever all afternoon."

An ominous, familiar cold crept over Marin's skin. "What is it, Tom?"

He cleared his throat. "The pulse is quickened, there has been some vomiting, the pupils are contracted, she is very near complete unconsciousness." He looked at her directly for the first time. "I fear an inflammation of the brain."

The room seemed to tilt. She floundered. "But—but she was getting well . . ." And then, as it always did under pressure, her mind began to work with clarity and precision. "This is too much for you to handle, Tom—no, I beg you. You are too close to her, much too close. No man . . ."—she groped for a way to push him in the direction she wanted, and words she had once heard Charles speak returned and fitted themselves onto her tongue, "no man should ever have to take care of his own if there is anyone else to do the job." That implication should appeal to his vanity. "And how fortunate that there is someone else. You trust Charles . . ."

"He is an excellent man, yes, but—"

"I'm so glad you agree, for he would never take the case without your consent. Thank you, Tom. I'll send Jeremy for him at once."

When Charles arrived, huddled into his greatcoat against the late afternoon wind, she met him outside Sophy's door and asked him into the upstairs sitting room. He had stood at her mother's graveside that day, a little apart from the others, withdrawn, frowning slightly. He had not come back to the house for the food, gossip, and socializing that always followed a funeral, the feeble method by which those left alive shook off the sudden clear vision of their own mortality. Charles did not seem to need that.

She said, "Please don't be angry with me, Charles. I behaved like a fool the other night, calling Tom for Mama. You must think I have no head at all."

"Did I look angry? I'm not, only concerned." He smiled bleakly into Marin's anxious eyes. "Dear girl, I don't blame you for wanting more for your mother than I could give. I would have done exactly the same had I stood in your shoes. But this . . . it wouldn't be ethical for me to take over Sophy's care if Tom isn't willing, and he won't be. He loves her, I think. And Sophy was Tom's patient from the beginning. I sent her to him."

"Oh, he's all over her like a broody hen, but he has already agreed that it's up to you. I pointed out that a physician should never take care of his own if it can be avoided. A dirty trick, I know, since Sophy doesn't feel that way about him, but I couldn't think of anything else, and—oh, Charles, I've lost Mama and I've lost Ethan. I can't—I won't lose my sister, too, not without a fight."

Charles's eyes rested on her briefly, and for an instant she felt as transparent as glass. "In a really tough fight I'd want you on my side," he said. He picked up his bag and went into Sophy's room to begin his own battle.

Marin was left alone in the quiet sitting room. She had had her way; Charles would do all that he could. She walked to the window, leaned her head against the pane, and looked down on the dust blowing in the road. How odd men were with their talk about ethics, protocol, rules, honor. All high-flown nonsense that was swept aside without ceremony when the chips were really down. It had been plain dishonest to let Tom think he was almost engaged to Sophy, and he would have a painful letdown later, but she didn't regret her tactics for one moment. If Sophy died because of his bumbling, he couldn't have her anyway, but if Charles pulled her through, Tom still had a fighting chance. He wasn't nearly good enough for her, and Marin planned to undercut him at every opportunity, but that was for the future. She thought that perhaps only women looked straight at life, kept their eyes fastened on the important goals, and were not deflected by technicalities like ethics. Men, for all their vaunted hardheadedness, could be sentimental fools. You had to be ruthless when life was at stake—or love.

Cold wind crept in at the point where window met sash, and she shivered. Even this well-built house had leaks. She left the window and sat down to wait.

Charles ordered the room darkened and Sophy's head shaved. Logan cut the long gold curls at the scalp, laid the fine hair in a scarf and folded it into a neat package. The wigmaker could make a beautiful switch of that hair, if Sophy lived to wear it. Towels were filled with ice and packed around the shorn, vulnerable little head. Good nursing was the primary thing, Charles said, good nursing and absolute quiet. Marin and Logan spelled each other, piling blankets over the sick girl when she shivered violently and bathing her limp arms and legs with cool, wet cloths when her skin turned hot to the touch. She complained bitterly of thirst and of intolerable pain in her head. The dimmest lamplight stabbed her eyes. At times she thought she was in the high mountains again, alone in a tiny cabin, deserted by Wes and dying. In her delirium she thought Charles was Vail; she dug her fingers into his hand

and begged him to hold her, then opened her eyes and screamed. "You're not Vail, you're not Vail, go away!" She moaned, and pressed her hands against her eyes to shut out the sight of him.

Gently he laid her on the pillow. "Where is Vail?"

"He went to see Dennis Timothy about starting work on the house," Marin whispered.

"When he comes in, let me know. I want him nearby in case she asks for him again. It may help keep her quiet."

Downstairs Tom paced restlessly, glowering at the situation and at George Winfield, who sat staring helplessly at the floor. Shortly after leaving the funeral meal, George had heard the news of Sophy's turn for the worse, and had rushed back, entrenched himself in a chair in the parlor, and refused to budge, let alone consider going home, even though Tom assured him he would be notified instantly of any developments. Once Tom took advantage of his professional status to enter the sickroom. He gazed silently at the girl in the bed, asleep at the moment, her thick, dark lashes a shadowy crescent against white skin.

He whispered loudly, "Some leeches, Charles, and an active purgative—calomel and colocynth or jalap . . ."

Charles laid a hand on his shoulder. "Yes, Tom, I will consider it. Shall we let her sleep for a while?" and ushered him out of the room.

They kept up the iced applications through the night, and Jeremy made another trip to the ice cream shop, the nearest source of ice brought from the mountains and packed in insulating straw through the summer months.

Toward noon of the next day Sophy began to move and twitch violently despite the frantic efforts of Marin and Logan to soothe her. Such amounts of laudanum as Charles dared give were powerless against the pain, and she cried out and tried to push away the ice. James caught her hands, and she opened her eyes. The wildness faded from them as his face swam into focus; she clung to him and begged, "Papa, don't let me die. Papa, please don't let me die!"

James's mouth jerked. "I'll never do that, baby. You just hang on to me, that's right. I won't let you go," and the tears streamed down his face.

Through the week Sophy's temperature would rise dangerously high, then fall abruptly. Delirium took over for long intervals, then she would come to herself and talk weakly but with comprehension. Toward week's end her temperature settled to a more tolerable level and never again rose to alarming levels. And there were other signs of improvement—the periods of lucidity were longer, and the dim lamplight no longer hurt her eyes. By the beginning of the following week Charles said that the worst was over.

Rejoicing, Marin drove to Stockton Street for the first time since Sophy's collapse to see how Dennis Timothy was progressing with the house. It had been a desolate sight after the fire. Miraculously the first floor still stood, but its glistening white paint was scorched and blistered, most of the windows were broken, and it looked strangely flat-headed with only the ceiling for a roof.

The repairs were going well, but in the back of Marin's mind was an uneasiness that the clean new rooms could not dispel.

For all its pretty wallpaper and fancy trim this hastily built wooden house was a firetrap; she knew that now. She would not rest until the family was into something safer. It must be a brick house this time, well designed and solidly built, with larger rooms and a better location. Planning it would give James something to think about. Money would have to be found for this rebuilding and for the new brick house, which must not be long delayed, and a daring gamble was the only way she could see to do it. Although she had sworn a silent vow never to speak to Stuart again, she would have to break it and talk him into negotiating another loan from Malcolm. Then she would tell Harry Callendar to go ahead with his plans for the Golden Cathay.

After Sophy's temperature had remained normal for three days, days through which she slept deeply and restfully, Charles examined her in the quiet, darkened room, confirmed his opinion of her condition, and came downstairs. He pushed open the screen door and sat down on the steps of the side porch.

It was pleasant up here on the hill in the cool breeze of afternoon with the scent of roses sweet in his nostrils, with the noise and busyness of town far removed and the sweeping view of blue, sparkling bay and distant mountains to delight the eye.

Vail came up the path that bordered the rose garden and sat down beside him. "I just saw the suitors off. We'll be plagued with them underfoot every day until Sophy is well, but you have made a friend for life. George says he plans to advertise your medical genius to the entire town."

"And how does Tom feel?"

"Grateful, I think."

Charles lifted an eyebrow and rubbed his lower lip, his eyes on the busy shipping in the harbor. "I've been sitting here thinking of the day I first saw Sophy. It was the day I met Marin, the day she brought Belinda to me. Marin fascinated me, she—well, you can imagine. She was wonderfully attractive. I'd never known a young woman with such verve, such a quality of the unexpected. I was intrigued."

"She does have that effect on men."

"When she left, I watched her out the window, feeling a little like a snoop, and Sophy came running up the street. She had a bonnet that she must have just bought, a charming thing." Charles smiled at the memory. "She held it up for Marin to see, put it on, and whirled around. Then she looked up. I didn't know who she was, but—Vail, is it possible that we can see, only see, someone we know? Or is that romantic nonsense, not fit for sensible men?"

"Having shown myself to be occasionally fallible, I've given up telling others what to believe. Anything is possible in this world. I'll even admit to a similar experience. Once I saw a girl—she had been kneading dough and was wearing an old faded apron miles too big; there was flour on her hands and her arms—I looked at her and felt overwhelming admiration, a need to know her much, much better, a need . . . I never was able to stay away from her after that."

Charles thought of Celia and could not imagine her kneading dough. "How did it work out?"

"I don't know yet. Why haven't you gone after Sophy? Why let the other fellows have a free run?"

"How could I? Look at her. Look at me. I'm not just a homely, plain-looking man—if I were, I might have tried. But I am ugly."

"Charles, how you underestimate yourself. You underestimate Sophy, too."

Charles looked out at the shining bay. "It is ironic. I avoided meeting her, refused her as a patient, offended Marin by declining invitations I wanted to accept, all because I didn't want Sophy to see me. I worshiped her at a safe distance and imagined all the things I would say to her if only she couldn't see me. Oh, God, Vail, I have my wish. I examined her a few minutes ago, and it is what I have feared all week. The optic nerve has been damaged. She can barely see the outline of my face. I believe within another week she will be completely blind."

Chapter 28

After a businesslike session during which Marin and Stuart behaved with the utmost civility, Stuart agreed to approach his father about another loan to Gentry and Callendar. Malcolm ruminated over the proposition for three days and then notified James that he was willing to lend forty thousand dollars at twenty-one percent interest, repayable in ten months.

When asked to draw up the papers, Gerald frowned over the terms and presented a rational, lawyerlike argument against taking on such indebtedness; Marin listened with a stony face.

She had come to Gerald's office directly after a run-in with Vail on the same subject. Immediately after breakfast that morning she had shown him the offer from Malcolm. He read it through and stared out the dining room window, thinking rapidly through the state of his finances. His only assets easily convertible to cash were the waterfront lots he had been holding for a peak price in partnership with Hadley Davis, the former hardware store owner from Sacramento City who was now one of the richest men in the state. Hadley was a tightfisted man who intended to be richer still and wasn't likely to agree to sell those lots before the time was right just because of the Gentry family's misfortune or Marin's desire to expand Gentry and Callendar into the world of fine art. Which she was hell-bent to do; one glance at her hopeful, obstinate face told him that. As for the La Gracia property, last spring Gerald had said the fight for title clearance would be over and forgotten about by fall, but it was spring of another year, and confirmation was still hanging fire. And if it were clear, he would not sell any part of Celia's land in order to help Marin. Any loan to the Gentrys would have to come out of his pocket, not his wife's, and at present his pocket was empty.

Outside under the windblown oak, one of the many stray cats resident in the stable because Mrs. Moon fed them regularly was creeping with stealthy patience toward an unwary jay pecking at the damp ground. The cat leaped, and the jay shot upward with a wild flapping of wings and a raucous, taunting squawk.

"One of these days the cat is going to nail that bird. And one of these days Father is going to nail you if you go on giving him opportunities like this."

He tossed Malcolm's letter on the table, and, nettled, Marin picked it up and folded it. She didn't want any critical nitpicking from him, she wanted approval and encouragement and advice on how best to tackle her new business venture.

In exasperation she asked, "And what do you think I should do?"

"Wait. I expect to sell my lots by summer. If you're still determined to go ahead with this, you can have the cash then."

"I couldn't take your money."

"I'm not offering a gift. James would have to pay a healthy rate, but not twenty-one percent and not in ten months, God in heaven."

"We did it before."

"You were damn lucky before. Everything went right, but think back and remember what it was like. The sleepless nights when a ship was late, the nightmares when Harry guessed wrong about what would sell and a payment was due on the loan. You got through by the skin of your teeth and paid Father off, which must have disappointed him. I notice he wants Little Mountain as collateral, not the company or the house in town. That land will be a bonanza one day."

"He says he's taking a big risk because our title is shaky."

"Father never intentionally took a risk in his life. If he can get hold of Little Mountain, he expects Stuart can slip the title through the land commission without a fight."

That surprised her. If Stuart really had such influence, it meant his political reach was far greater than she had dreamed. She said, "Stuart never told me he could do that."

"He told me once in one of his expansive moods, and it may be the God's truth. Father must believe it. You asked for my advice, and here it is. Tell Harry to forget his Golden Cathay for the time being. It's a fine idea for someone with a lot of loose change and the taste for a long gamble. All you've got is the taste."

"Harry is a smart man. Anyway, nobody ever got anything without taking a chance."

"He's smart, and he also likes to sail too near the wind. This is a chance you don't have to take."

"I do if we build a new house."

"Forget the damn house. By fall I can probably build it for you myself."

Her lips straightened. He didn't understand. It wasn't only a house she wanted . . .

With hands that shook she tied her bonnet strings. "I am going to Gerald's office and get the papers for Papa to sign. What do you say to that?"

He shrugged and smiled. "I wish you luck. You'll need it."

She had gone to Gerald and heard much the same objections voiced in smoother, more dispassionate words. Well, he was entitled to his opinion. She met his disapproving eyes squarely. "Don't frown at me, Gerald, and don't lecture. Just fix up those papers quick. Papa will sign them right away so Stuart can take them to his father tonight."

But when she left his office, she did not climb in the carriage and take the papers directly to James. Instead she shoved them into her net purse, a fragile object meant to hold lace handkerchiefs and smelling salts, not documents that could make or break a family, and with Jeremy following, walked down to the waterfront. Near Broadway wharf she leaned against a low railing and stared moodily at a harbor littered with abandoned, rotting ships yet alive with other vessels underway or riding at anchor. With much shouting and swearing by dockhands the clipper *Victorious*, out of Boston, was being unloaded at the wharf, its dashing, gracious lines a rakish contrast to the chunky side-wheel steamers lumbering past.

It was a hopeful, invigorating sight. Every wagonload of merchandise off a newly arrived ship, every departure for a far port bespoke vitality and ever-increasing wealth. In such good times, how could her plan fail? Yet she knew well that the booming prosperity did not mean success for everyone. Businesses failed every week, the market was chaotic and unreliable, faraway events sent prices skyrocketing or tumbling with no warning. Only a month ago a close friend of Harry's, Joseph Bowes, a prominent man with what every one thought was a solid real estate and importing business, had gone broke and hanged himself from a beam in the warehouse he had just lost to the bank. In itself it was not an unusual event—suicide was a leading cause of death in San Francisco—but it struck home to Marin. Joseph Bowes was someone she knew, and that meant his tragedy could happen to anyone; it could happen to her. Even more daunting was the fact that both Vail and Gerald were dead set against what she planned. They believed she was tempting fate and begging for ruin.

Before the fire such disapproval by the two men whose

judgment she trusted most would have been enough to dissuade her, and even now resolution faltered. But neither of them understood the pain and the need that drove her.

Before the fire—oh, before the fire the world was sane. Not always to her liking, but sane. People did die, she had seen it close up, but it happened only to people like Elizabeth, like Nicolas, people she could spare. Ethan's death she had never completely taken in. She had not watched the light go out of his eyes or looked on his dead face, and it was possible to pretend that although she would never see him again, he was alive somewhere, chasing girls and playing absurd jokes. As for the rest of life, most of it was either distasteful, infuriating, or bitterly disappointing, but some pleasure could be found along the way, and there was always the hope that things would improve. As long as life lasted, there was hope.

But then Mama died, and nothing in Marin's life had prepared her for the destructive, slashing pain. It was not a simple arithmetical progression—greater loss than those other, lesser deaths causing greater grief. It was anguish of a different order entirely, devastating, beyond bearing. And along with grief came fright at the violence and wild irrationality of the thoughts that tumbled around in her head, thoughts she could admit to no one.

She hated Rose for dying, for leaving her when Marin needed her. She was ashamed of Rose for being weak and a drunk and for setting the fire that killed her. She wished Rose were alive so she could shake her and demand to know how she could do such a thing, how she could be not a great lady after all but a foolish, frightened, flawed human being like everybody else. She wept burning tears for having such cruel, crazy thoughts about the mother she loved so much; then in her mind she turned on her father, whom she had always believed even more necessary to her than Rose, and raged at him for daring to be alive while Mama lay in that cemetery. She turned the rage against herself and decided she must be going mad, for both her parents were unutterably dear, there could be no choice between them, she could not do without either of them. Then she wept again, out of love, out of loss, out of bitter grief.

All through this tumult of emotion she got dressed each day, ate, spoke softly when she wanted to scream, made difficult decisions, prepared to move her family back into their rebuilt house, and bled inside from gaping internal wounds. And then Charles, his eyes pain-filled, told her that Sophy would soon be blind.

Her first inclination had been to laugh, for such a thing could not be. Then she argued with Charles, trying to make him acknowledge his error. Finally she accepted the unbelievable truth—Sophy could barely distinguish noontime from midnight, and with every day that passed her sight grew dimmer.

Pretty, delicate, wayward, loving Sophy would never dance or flirt or flash her great blue eyes at her importuning admirers. The admirers would creep away, regretful, guilty, embarrassed at abandoning the girl for whom they had declared undying love, but creep away they would. Slowly Sophy would age into a sightless spinster, dependent in the house of her father for as long as she lived. And James's life was balanced on a knife edge. It was a miracle that he had survived these turbulent days; one fierce outburst of temper, and he would be dead, too. He was like a sleepwalker most of the time, sitting and staring, blaming himself for dragging Rose out West, for ignoring her drinking in the early days and then concealing it when it took final hold, accusing himself of causing her death, his son's death, his little blond baby's blindness. James would never again be the bulwark of the family. That left Carey and Belinda, too young, thank God, to understand what had happened, and Delphine, the depth and extent of her grief made plain by the fact that she could not eat but only sat and wept and tore her handkerchief into shreds and moaned that she did not know what was to become of them.

Marin wondered, too, what would become of them. A tumbling lamp, a vagrant spark, and the world had turned upside down. If Mama could die, anything could happen; there was no security anywhere, nothing and no one to rely on. The realization shook her to her soul. Home was not absolute refuge from the cold winds of the world, but only a building of wood and plaster, fragile and easily demolished. Build it of brick, build it of solid stone, and the truth remained—it was a material object and could be destroyed as could all things physical. Nothing you built with your hands could be relied upon to last, nor anything else you possessed, not health or sight or life itself. Yet as long as life did last, you had to sustain yourself somehow, rebuild houses, replace furniture, buy food and clothes, care for Sophy and James, shelter Carey and Belinda and Delphine.

Little Mountain had not been doing well in the last few years, just why, Marin did not understand, for beef prices were up, but Stuart's account books backed up his words. In recent times most of the support of the household on Stockton Street had come from Gentry and Callendar profits. The burden was hers, to hold the family together and provide a secure future for the weaker members. And she was mortal and could die; if ever she had doubted it, she knew it now. What would happen to all these helpless ones if she died? The only protection was to build a fortress of money, the one real security if you had enough of it. And to acquire such a quantity a gamble was needed. She would bet on Harry Callendar's business acumen and Mrs. Harry's instinctive sense that this rich frontier town was ready to spend some of its wealth on the finest objects civilization could produce.

Unconsciously she clenched her fist as if grasping at a handful of real gold coins and said, "Let's go home, Jeremy."

After the first spasm of hysteria Sophy slipped into a depression that was even more worrisome and heartbreaking. She lay with eyes closed or staring at walls she could not see in the upstairs bedroom in Vail's house. In this room she had waked after the fire and learned of her mother's death, here she had been desperately ill and come close to death herself for the second time in her short life, and here, her heart thumping queerly, she had asked Charles why everyone and everything around her was strangely shadowed even when the heavy draperies were pulled back from the windows.

She guessed the answer before she heard his quiet words, and after the first shock and terror had worn itself out, she simply lay with silent tears trickling from the sides of her eyes.

In her suffering she would not talk to Marin or James or even Vail. She endured Charles when she had to and then turned her face to the wall. Marin had been wrong about the fickleness of her suitors, however. Both Tom and George came every day, bringing flowers and loving messages, waiting patiently to be allowed into her room, but she would receive no one and responded to nothing.

Oddly it was Celia who chipped out the first crack in the wall she had erected around herself. Celia had not come to the funeral, because Alida had been teething and feverish, but now she came, bringing Alida and Consuela and her own distinctive personality to the wounded family that had taken refuge in her husband's house. No one but Celia could sit so quietly, undisturbed by silence, her innate tranquillity coming down over Sophy's damaged soul like balm.

The afternoon she arrived, she and Marin had hugged each other and pressed cheeks, but that night Marin announced that the family would move home the next day, a decision made the moment Celia had walked in the front door. Sophy was left behind until such time as Charles decided she was well enough to be moved. Logan stayed, too, to take care of Sophy, but it was understood that she would come back to Stockton Street when Sophy came.

Marin threw herself, mind, body, and spirit, into preparations for the opening of the store. She intended to be in business before the end of June, and with energy and dedication she worked into the nights and through weekends to bring it about. The original idea had been Mrs. Harry's, and Harry Callendar had pressed the matter, but once Marin was committed, she took over in her usual highhanded style. Harry negotiated for the lease of a small brick building in a good location on Washington Street near Portsmouth Square, and nearly every penny they had went into inventory. She did allocate money for two other purposes—a spectacular sign for the front of the store and interior decoration of a lavishness presently found only in the finest of saloons. She had the bare wood floor carpeted and the walls hung with silk out of Gentry and Callendar's own warehouse and then in businesslike fashion paid the company back out of the decorating fund. Gilt-framed, floor-to-ceiling mirrors on the side walls made the space seem twice as wide. Glass-topped display cases and glass shelves were expensive innovations but made the merchandise seem even more glittering and seductive. It was her theory that the more you intended to charge for an item, the more luxurious must be its presentation.

Mrs. Harry made the first selection of merchandise, but submitted every piece to Marin for her approval. There were cunningly carved pieces of jade and delicate china vases in both subtle and brilliant colors, but although the motif of the store was Chinese, they also bought a few pieces of marble sculpture from Italy, three French oil paintings, and a small but magnificent German clock with a jeweled pendulum. It was Marin's idea to hire a Chinese man—the tallest and most imposing she could find—to dress in embroidered satin robes and bow as each customer entered.

The sign with the words *The Golden Cathay* inscribed in flowing gold script went up, and the next morning, on schedule, two days before the end of June the doors opened.

Marin watched from the rear of the store with rising optimism. The fliers on buildings all over town, the newspaper announcement, the gossip in parlors and saloons had had the desired effect.

Fashionable, affluent people were coming in, as well as the merely curious, but it remained to be seen if anyone would buy.

With a tautness in her stomach that she did not recognize as nerves, she went forward to speak to Charlotte Winfield and her daughter, just entering the store, and caught the glint of disapproval in that worthy lady's eye. Probably everyone disapproved, probably everyone thought she ought to be weeping at home with Delphine, sitting with her father, making daily trips to her mother's grave, instead of being here greeting customers with a smile and keeping a sharp eye on every transaction. But she would go crazy at home. Work was a blessing that filled her days and offered a battle that could be won with shrewdness, effort, and a bit of luck. She had to have an attainable goal, something to work toward. If the world disapproved, that was just too bad.

"Good morning, ma'am," she said with a brilliant smile. "Kitty, how pretty you look."

Kitty Winfield blushed at the compliment. She was a comely girl with a slender figure set off by stylish clothes, the fresh skin of youth, and the thin nose and narrow eyes of her father. She was also a vapid, giddy girl whose chief concerns were her complexion, her clothes, and her popularity. Now that Sophy Gentry was out of contention forever, she reigned as the princess of the younger set in San Francisco society.

All earnest solicitude, she inquired, "How is dear Sophy, Marin?"

Marin looked into the bland blue eyes, the *seeing* eyes, and steeled herself to answer calmly, "Better every day. We expect to have her back to full health soon."

"Good health is indeed more precious than jewels," remarked Mrs. Winfield with a satisfied glance at her robust daughter. She had heard that Sophy Gentry was permanently blind; so sad, but there it was. "Has she come home yet? My George is devoted to her, but we seldom get any information from him."

"Yes, ma'am. She came home yesterday. Now do look over our little displays, feel free to browse, but first let me show you this figurine from Dresden. Isn't she adorable? The moment I saw her, I was reminded of Kitty . . ."

Marin left them exclaiming pleasedly over the figurine, and as she moved away, Mrs. Winfield's eyes followed her. Something about that young woman rubbed her the wrong way, although she couldn't put her finger on exactly what it was. Certainly she had no business to be here bustling and smiling with her mother hardly cold and her sister a blind invalid. Her father, by all accounts, had gone round the bend with grief, but she had a perfectly competent husband to earn a living for her. There was something about her—flamboyant, that was it—flamboyant both in actions and appearance. Even covered in somber black from head to toe she looked overdone, her skin too white, her hair under its black veil too red for good taste. The girl couldn't help the color of her hair, but how to account for the burning glitter of her eyes and the bright flush in her cheeks when she should be pale and drooping with grief?

Kitty exclaimed over a gilt-trimmed clock with a tiny bird that came out and cheeped on the quarter hour, and Mrs. Winfield agreed, "Yes, my love, charming," before turning her attention to the crowd, her main reason for being here.

By midafternoon three large sales had been negotiated, as well as a number of smaller transactions. Kitty went to her papa's office and dragged him back with her, and in the end Tyler Winfield bought the Dresden figurine. Vail bought a jade god for Celia and paid the full price in gold despite Harry's low-voiced explanation that the store discounted to relatives. Without doubt the opening had been a triumph. Now all that remained was for business to hold on and build over the next months after the novelty had worn off.

Business did continue reasonably brisk through the summer. There was a drop-off at the end of August when a mild panic in the east sent shock waves rippling west, but recovery was swift, and Marin and Harry continued the agreed-upon policy of plunging most of the profits into more and ever costlier merchandise. In typical fashion other businessmen took note of their success, and two stores similar to the Golden Cathay soon opened. As Marin saw it, the only way for her and Harry to combat such competition was to provide superior goods, to become accepted as the only place to go when one wanted the best and still not price themselves out of the market. To this end she devoted all her energy, time, and attention. Most particularly, her attention. For this reason she was not fully aware of developments taking place at home.

By the time Sophy was brought home, she had passed the stage of tears and withdrawn silence. She answered when spoken to, thanked Mrs. Victoria when she brought her tray at mealtimes, allowed Logan to button her into her dress and put on her shoes. But she would not leave her room and would not allow the curtains to be opened. However, when Charles walked in on his first visit since she came back to Stockton Street, he snapped back the velvet draperies and raised the window.

Sophy threw her hands over her face and cried out, "Please! Close them, close them!"

Charles looked at her, sitting forlornly in a chair beside her bed. "Why? It's a lovely day. Smell that sea air. If you sit over here, you can feel the sun on your face."

"I don't want to feel the sun. Close the draperies, please. It makes no difference to me if the room is light or dark."

"It does to me. I can't see to examine you in the dark."

She drew in a quick, anguished breath. No one talked to her like that, so curt and unfeeling, no one even used the word *see* or mentioned the dark in her presence; certainly no one ever called attention to the fact that he could see and she couldn't.

"Walk over here," he commanded. "I want you on the window seat, where I have good light."

"By myself? I—I can't."

"Of course you can. You walk around this room all the time, and you know it very well. Now come here."

An unkind man, a heartless, insensitive man. A wave of anger passed through her, anger that for the moment overmastered hopelessness. She got up with a sharp sense of injury and, arms out, feeling forward cautiously, walked to him, found the window seat, and sat down.

Without any comment on her accomplishment, he listened to her heart, pressed the stethoscope on different parts of her back while instructing her to breathe deeply, lifted her eyelids, pressed firm fingers into the soft flesh under her chin and down her neck to her collarbone, told her to open her mouth and say "ah."

"Well. You are coming along nicely."

She made a bitter remark under her breath, but he ignored it. She could hear him folding his stethoscope, tucking it into his bag, snapping the bag shut.

"You are to come downstairs today."

"No."

"Indeed you are, if you have to be carried."

"You wouldn't dare. I'll kick and scream."

"Will you? You'll look very silly, like Belinda having a tantrum, but if you don't mind that . . ."

"Oh!" she gasped, and burst into sobs. "I don't like you at all. Tom would never treat me so."

"Probably not, but it is my prescription, and you must take it if

I am to continue as your doctor. If you wish to make a change, that is your privilege, and I'll certainly understand."

She started to answer him, to say she did prefer Tom and right now, too, but the words died on her lips. This man's manner of speech was so bald, so unadorned with the flourishes and circumlocutions she was accustomed to that she hardly knew how to take him. He was cold and cruel and completely unsympathetic, but she knew she didn't want to change doctors.

She sniffed and rubbed her hand against her damp nose. It was hard to back down when she had already refused absolutely. "Very well . . . I will try . . . but only this once and only if you hold tight to my arm."

"I'll hold tight," he said.

He led her down the first flight of stairs, holding her left arm, requiring that she place her right hand on the banister and count each step.

"Now we are at the landing. Slide your foot forward and note how far it is to the next step."

"I . . . I can't. I feel like I'm falling out into space. Oh, please, take me back to my room."

"No. Before we are through, you are going to come down these stairs alone and walk out of the house anytime you wish. Now put your foot forward."

She came down, frightened, wobbling, weak in the knees, but she came. At the foot of the stairs he put the cane he had brought for her into her right hand and instructed her to reach out with it and feel her way across the parlor to the window. "Touch the window and the wall, notice the chair that sits here. This is the west side of the house. You face in the same direction when you look out your bedroom window. Smell the breeze off the bay and notice the sun on your face. Now tell me, which way is east?"

"That's easy." She turned, holding onto the windowsill, until her back was against the window and she was facing in the opposite direction.

"It wasn't easy at all. You are doing very well."

"Oh, do you think so?"

"Yes, indeed. You have lost one of your senses, and the remaining four must work harder, but after a while you'll find that they tell you much more than they ever have before. Now point yourself toward the north and then the south."

Sophy hesitated, thought a moment, and edged around until she faced the front door. She waited for his approval and then turned to face the back of the house.

"Now you know the points of the compass. You are oriented." His voice had an enthusiastic lilt that had not been there before. "Let's investigate this room."

In this way they explored every room downstairs. Sophy discovered the hazards of the kitchen and learned that by paying close attention, she could feel the heat of the stove before coming close enough to burn herself. She walked down the porch steps, felt the points of the picket fence that enclosed the front yard, caressed the tissue-thin, velvety petals of the roses lining the fence, and pricked her finger on a thorn even as her nostrils drew in the sweet scent of the blossom. At Charles's urging she walked around to the side of the house, her cane tap-tapping on the path, stooped down, and ran her palm lightly over the plants in Mrs. Victoria's herb garden. She picked a sprig and crushed it in her hand. "It's . . . it's . . . oh, I don't know what it is. Charles, it's too hard. I am so tired."

"I know you are, and we'll go back in the house in a moment." He closed his eyes, picked another sprig, crushed it, and sniffed. "Don't be discouraged. With my eyes closed I can't tell what it is, either."

She said, "Let me try again," and he held it to her nose. "It's . . . rosemary."

"You see? You have one sense that is far better developed than mine already."

"Ah, yes, I am a marvel. But is the rose that pricked my finger white or red or something in between? Is the bay green or dark blue today? Is it covered with diamonds or flat and smooth? I'll never know. Oh, Charles, my world is so dark."

If she could have seen his face at that moment, she would have known everything, but she could only hear his voice, and it was matter-of-fact, with only a hint of sympathy in it. "You are deprived of all those things, it's true, but listen to what you just said. In your mind's eye you can see the water sparkle and you know what light is as those who were born blind never can. You have it stored in your memory to be taken out and enjoyed and used. It's tiring for you now, but before long you'll be using the senses you still have much more efficiently. I promise you it's true, for I've seen it happen. Sit down here on the bench for a while, and then we'll go back inside."

After that day she came downstairs every morning and tapped around the house with the cane that was already a part of her. Sometimes Charles stayed for dinner after a professional visit if his call was late in the day, but he didn't count as company. She still would not receive Tom or George, and one evening sitting on the bench in the garden, Charles taxed her about it.

"They care very much for your welfare. You are unkind not to see them."

"I, unkind? How can you say such a thing when I . . ."

"When you have suffered so much? Yes, you have. That's why they're so concerned. You, in turn, are obligated by their concern, whether you like it or not."

"And you," she replied, "are a perpetual scold. Sophy, do this. Sophy, do that. Can't you understand how I feel? They won't love me if they see me like this."

"Is that what you're afraid of? That they'll go away if they don't like your looks? Then why not find out now instead of keeping them dangling? If they care for you, they won't change."

"That's easy for you to say, but you're not the one who has to show yourself. You don't understand what it's like to know people think you're hideous even if they are polite. You don't understand that I just want to hide."

"I understand better than you think. And I also know that you must do it. See each of them separately, accept their regard. If they draw away, you will have lost nothing of value—but I rather fancy they won't. As a matter of fact Tom is in the parlor now, waiting for you."

"Here? Oh, dear life, is that what this lecture is all about? You got him here, didn't you."

"He came on his own, as he always does. He's been very faithful, Sophy. You owe it to him to see him, and if you don't, I fear I shall have to mark you down as a coward."

"How can you say such a thing to me. To *me*!"

"Yes," he went on quietly, "a coward. All has not gone as you wished in your life, I don't minimize your tragedies, but I have seen too many whose condition was vastly worse, so bad that I couldn't even describe it for fear of nauseating you. I have seen courage and fortitude of such dimensions as to bring tears to my eyes, hard-hearted as I am. I expected better of you, Sophy, than to hide like a rabbit trembling in a hole."

She jumped to her feet, her cheeks flaming. "I'll show you fortitude! I'll show you courage!" She pressed shaking hands against her eyes, and then her head came up. In an altogether different voice she asked, "Is my collar straight? Do I look—passable?"

He had risen, too, and was standing beside her. Her sightless eyes were wide, her skin was pearly in the evening light, her hair lay close to her head in short ringlets, a shining cap of gold. "You look . . . very lovely. Come, let us go into the house."

As Charles predicted, Tom did not run. He kissed Sophy's hand fervently, chatted for a brief while, then muttered that he must not tire her and left. For all the abruptness of his departure he rode back to his hotel slowly, with tears trickling down his face in the concealing shadows of the night. The next evening he was back, and he came thereafter whenever Sophy would allow.

George Winfield had not been at the house for three days, but bravely she sent a message, and he came. George had yearned to see her, but he was not a physician like Tom, he did not know what to expect, and he feared, not her, but his reaction to her. He feared he would find her unlovable now and knew he would be dishonored if he did. To his intense relief the girl who waited for him on the parlor sofa was the same adorable Sophy, a little thinner, a little quieter, but her eyes were the same, not deformed or strange, her smile was as heart-lifting as ever, and her short hair was charming, certain, he assured her, to start a new vogue. All the girls would be cutting off their hair when they saw her, and he hated to think what his sister, Kitty, would look like if she tried it! That sent her into a spasm of giggles, which amazed him. How could she laugh in the face of such misfortune? How brave she was, how wholly admirable. He departed that night more deeply in love than ever.

So Sophy began to see her two suitors regularly and by the end of summer was agreeable to carriage rides and picnics out of town. She even went into the city to visit Marin's new store. As Charles had promised, she was far more aware of the tang of salt air, of spices, of all odors; she felt the tiniest shift of a light breeze, was intensely conscious of the hardness of jade, the smooth curve of a china vase, the threads in the fabric on the walls; her ears registered the click as Marin set the vase on the counter, she felt the rush of air as the front door opened, heard the quiet brush of slippers on the carpet and the whisper of silk skirts, smelled the attar of roses perfume.

She turned. "Good morning, Mrs. Winfield."

Charlotte Winfield came as close to stammering as she had since she was fourteen years old and had been caught helping herself to her mother's diamond earrings, for Sophy had learned the trick of orienting herself in relation to other people and appeared to be gazing directly into her eyes. But stars above, they had said the girl was blind.

"Ah—uh—my dear child. You look—look marvelously well."

"Thank you, ma'am. I feel very well."

Charlotte's eyes grew narrow; she had seen Sophy come in here and had followed her deliberately. Her son, George, instead of returning to his senses, was more infatuated with this girl than ever, and she was profoundly worried. Before Sophy's illness she had had no objections at all, in fact strongly favored the match. She treasured her own impeccable lineage and loved to recount the fine names attaching to her family tree like rich fruit. Sophy Gentry also had a splendid pedigree, she was beautiful, and marriage to George would remove her from competition with Kitty. But now! The boy was feverish, infatuated beyond all reason, and she did not intend to stand by helplessly while he attached himself to a blind wife who would drag him down for the rest of his life. There must be something wrong with the girl that would cure him if only she could find it out.

Sophy's smile widened, and her head turned slightly. "Is it . . . Mrs. Parrish?"

"My gracious, yes." Margaret Parrish had entered quietly, and no one in the shop had noticed—no one but Sophy. The older woman put out her arms and enveloped Sophy in a soft embrace. "I had heard you were doing well, but I am astonished at how well. Tell me, what is your secret, how did you know me?" and she drew Sophy along with her down the row of glittering counters and away from Charlotte's probing eyes.

One evening in late September, Sophy sat with Charles in the new porch swing that Marin had had installed only that week. She had asked him to stay after supper to talk over a problem, and he watched her, wondering what was coming. Physically she was well, her ability to compensate for her handicap grew daily, and he knew he had little excuse for coming here so often; soon he would have to stop coming altogether. He knew it and dreaded it. She had become such an integral part of his life, more essential to him than he had dreamed possible. Now she was going to tell him that she had made up her mind and had accepted one or the other of those two clowns—he thought the word bitterly and then berated himself. They were perfectly decent men, and he loathed them both.

"Charles, you are a blunt man and at times have said some very hard things to me."

He sat with hands between his knees, his head down. "I regretted the necessity, but I hoped to help you."

"You did help. Look at me. I see people—did you hear what I just said—I *see* people. I go to town, dress myself, feed myself . . ."

"Your progress is gratifying."

". . . and it's all due to my wonderful doctor."

He raised his head. "It was your body, your will, your spirit. I only pointed the way."

"You did more than that. You taught me to say things that have to be said, even delicate, embarrassing things." She turned and, with that trick of appearing to look directly, said, "I love you, Charles, and admire you more than any man in the world, more than Papa, more than Vail. You are the dearest, strongest, kindest, best man, and I wish you would have me for your wife." She took a quick breath, for she had completely run out.

He stared at her, and the expression on his face, instead of happiness, was one of great pain.

"Well," she gave a small, abashed laugh, "have I shocked you? You are the shiest man in the world, too, so I was afraid you would never ask me."

"Sophy . . ." He fumbled, stopped, began again. "Dear, dear Sophy, let me explain something about illness. When a patient has been very sick, especially sick for a long time, she becomes dependent on her doctor, like a little child upon her father. She credits him for her recovery when nine times out of ten it is due more to her own recuperative powers than anything he has done. She leans on him, ascribes to him all kinds of splendid qualities he doesn't have, and sometimes she comes to believe that she loves him."

"You think my feeling isn't genuine?"

"I think you mistake gratitude for something more. You can't love me, for you don't know me. You know only that little part that I let you see, the professional facade, not the man behind it."

"Oh, Charles, you are wrong. Let me be the judge of my feelings, and take me at my word."

"Don't tempt me," he muttered.

"What?"

"Nothing. Sophy, what you feel now is a normal reaction. Every doctor is aware of the phenomenon, but it passes. In a few weeks you will laugh at yourself and wonder how you ever thought such a thing."

There was a long silence. Sophy's face was averted. Upstairs Carey could be heard presenting his usual vigorous protest against bedtime. Jeremy was gently urging James to put away his cigar and come to bed. In the kitchen dishes clicked, and Mrs. Victoria was singing in soft Spanish about a girl who died when her lover went away and the roses of Castile twined over her grave.

Muffled, humiliated, Sophy said, "Forgive me for embarrassing you. I thought you cared for me, but I see now it was only duty."

"I do care."

"As a doctor for a patient."

"As one human being for another. You are valuable to me. I want you to be happy. Someday you will marry, perhaps George or Tom . . ."

"Oh, them." She made a gesture of dismissive contempt.

"They are both good men. But if you can't care for either of them, there will be someone else, someone you haven't even met yet. The world is so full—I want you to go to parties . . ."

"Parties? I couldn't."

"Parties and balls—there's no reason not to. You can do anything if you try. It's my prescription. You must take up a full life again, and when you do, you will find someone you can truly love."

She faced him, and in the moonlight falling through the lattice of the porch he saw that her eyes shone with tears.

"Will you still be my doctor?"

"Of course I will."

"And my friend?"

"And your friend." He laid his hand on her short gold curls and then went swiftly down the path to his waiting horse without saying good-bye to anyone.

Chapter 29

For a time after Charles's kind but firm rejection Sophy was crushed with humiliation, but hers was a hardy soul. Despite loss of mother and loss of love she wanted to be happy more than she enjoyed being miserable, so she drew on anger for support, lifted her chin, and, as much as a recently bereaved young lady could, went out into society.

In the weeks that followed she was a primary attraction at social events. There were elements of altruism and kindness in this attention. Everyone was shocked by her tragedy and honestly sorry for her, but sympathy could wear out, and generosity had limits. The kind young men would have gradually drifted away to girls without distressing afflictions but for the fact that black mourning greatly enhanced Sophy's blond beauty, misfortune had not quenched her bubbly personality, and her courage appealed to the sentimentality of lonely men far from home.

James was not doing as well. He sat and stared and sometimes wept quietly and showed none of the resilience Vail had predicted. He was not interested in the new store, although twice Marin took time from her harried day to show him around it.

Then Vail discovered that he needed James's counsel about the waterfront lots that still had not been sold. James limped slowly over the valuable land, expounding his theories of real estate development, explaining that the lots must not be sold until spring, when there was sure to be another sudden jump in prices. Vail seemed to value the advice. When the long-delayed confirmation of La Gracia's title was finally handed down, Vail took James on his first trip back across the bay so that he could see Celia's inheritance and suggest how best to handle it. He came home with more color in his face and spontaneity in his voice than had been seen in him since Rose died.

Marin quietly gave thanks and thought how strange it was that Vail understood her father better than Ethan ever had, better than she, herself, did. She wished she could tell him how grateful she was and how much she regretted her awful words the day she walked in on him and Petra; she wished she could tell him so many things. Since the night Rose died, when he had held her in his arms and let her cry, all had been well between them again without anything being said, yet she wished . . . She pushed the thought away. He was married. All her mind and spirit had to go into the business now, for the months had swept by with lightning speed, and March, the due date on Malcolm's loan, was looming like a rapidly swelling storm cloud.

It was after nine in the evening when Vail entered the offices of Gentry and Callendar, but the street was bright with the light of the modern, newly installed gas street lamps. He took the narrow wooden stairs lightly, two at a time, tapped on the door at the top, and went in as he heard Marin answer.

She looked up, and pleasure at seeing him lifted the grim expression from her face. "Why, Vail, I thought you were at Fontana."

He shoved a chair away from the worktable with his boot and straddled it. "Where are those new clerks of yours? Where's Harry? You shouldn't be here by yourself at this time of night. Get your coat, and I'll drive you home."

"Jeremy's coming for me later on. How did you know I was here?"

"I went by the house, and they told me you left before six this morning and hadn't been home since. What's wrong?"

He knew, he always knew when things were not well with her, just how, she had never figured out.

"I needed to think by myself, that's all." She shook her head. "You were right, utterly, absolutely right. I was a fool, and now it's all coming home to roost. That infernal loan is due Friday, and we haven't got forty thousand dollars or anywhere near it. Oh, I thought having it all fall due at once was a better deal, but if we'd had to make installment payments, like last time, most of it would be paid. This way, Malcolm is going to take everything."

"The store has been a grand success—what's happened to the money you've been raking in?"

She took a ring of keys from the desk drawer, unlocked the safe, and brought out a small oil painting. In it a ship floated in diffused pink and gold and lavender light, and the city of Venice glimmered dimly in the background.

"It's by an English artist called Turner. I don't know one thing about art, but Harry says it's good, and it *is* pretty. He says if the Golden Cathay is going to establish a reputation, we've got to offer art as fine as the best shops in any great city in the world. It took almost all our cash, but he thought he had a sure buyer. Yesterday he told me the man had gone broke and we're stuck with it, and I exploded and said such mean things when he already felt so bad. He went home and didn't even send word that he wasn't coming in today. Oh, what gets into me? It's not as though he bought the thing behind my back." She looked with disgust at the painting. "I've been here all day figuring. The firm has about seventy-five hundred dollars in the bank, and Harry said he can scrape up a thousand. I don't have a single piece of jewelry to sell. The house is all we have that might turn over really quick, but we could never get the cash by Friday."

Vail set the painting up so that the shifting lamplight fell across it, and Marin, who had stared at it all afternoon, meditating on what she would be willing to do to get hold of the money it represented, turned away and put out her hands to the potbellied stove. It had been hours since she had bothered to stoke the fire. Now she felt the cold, and Vail saw her shiver. Fatigue had washed the color from her face, and the fine bones stood out. She seemed thinner than when he last saw her, frail and tired and vulnerable.

"Marin, how old are you?"

"Almost twenty-two. Why?"

"Almost twenty-two. Many a case-hardened, experienced man has gone under in a gamble like this." He put the painting back in the safe. "I wish to God I'd sold those lots last fall when I had the chance. I have no assets that can be converted to cash in three days."

"Don't speak of it. I'd never take money from you."

He paced restlessly to the window. Down at the wharf, ships were preparing to leave on the early tide; there was busyness and energy everywhere. Here in this room where she spent most of her waking hours, there was despair and defeat. The weaker ones in the house on Stockton Street rested on her slender shoulders like a lead weight.

He came to her, took her hand, and spread the long, slim fingers wide, running his thumb over each in a careful, intent way. He turned the hand over and looked at the palm.

"No scar," he said. "The burn healed a long time ago. Do you remember the night you got it?"

The night San Francisco burned down. The night she and Sophy nearly perished in that inferno of a theater. The night she thought Vail was dead.

"I remember. I couldn't find you, and then I saw you come running . . ."

"You knew then that I loved you. You know it now."

Strange how the heart could seem to stop and then suddenly start again. She said, "I never . . ." her voice faltered. ". . . I never thought I'd hear you say that, not ever in my life."

She reached out, needing to touch him, and his arms went around her, banishing fear and loneliness. It was sweet, so sweet to be held by him, safe, supported, loved. She whispered, "Why, *why* did you marry Celia?"

His mind went back to the night Celia summoned him to

Fontana, the night a mood of guilt and black despair had sent him into her arms. He smiled a little.

"At the time it seemed like a good idea—like all my mistakes."

"Was it because of those terrible things I said that day about you and Petra? I've wanted to apologize so many times. I didn't mean it. It wasn't true."

He kissed her forehead and then her lips. "Forget the past. It's now that matters."

She smiled, a loving, dazzling smile. The gray little room no longer seemed cold, the light no longer bleak. It was as if a cozy fire were burning there for just the two of them. After a while she said, "I have a mad feeling. I want to run outside and tell everybody."

"I know what I want. To live with you any way I can."

It was a shining thought, and for a moment she pretended it was possible. "I could come live in your beautiful house, and we'd be together every day and every night . . ." And then, with a chill, "What would Stuart do? No divorce, not ever. He'd take the children. Celia . . . she'd never forgive us. She wouldn't let you even see Alida."

He held her closer in a sheltering way, one hand stroking her hair. "I think I could talk you into it if I tried, but I love you too much to do that to you. More than anything, more even than loving you, I want to protect you. I don't want you hurt. Do you understand?"

It was, to her, a more powerful declaration of real caring than any fervent lovemaking could have been. They were caught by choices made long before, and nothing would change, she would still be yoked to Stuart and he to Celia, the business was going down, the ranch was lost and it didn't matter. She was loved, truly loved.

"I don't care about Little Mountain. Let it go. Just so you love me."

A smile came into his eyes. "I have a thought, a hope that I can do more for you than just love you. Tell me something. If you've been putting everything into the store, what have you been living on?"

"We take a little out of the profits, enough to get by, and put the rest into inventory."

"That's all you have?"

"Darling, you know our circumstances as well as I do."

"If I do, then there's something that puzzles me. Little Mountain is a going ranch, and Stuart is a fine manager. He sells horses and beef on the open market and has a contract to supply the army."

"The army? I didn't know that. But the market has been bad, and he's had to put every dime into the ranch."

"When was the last time you saw the books?"

Her eyes widened. "He wouldn't do that."

"When did you see the books?"

"Not since we moved to town."

"Then it's time someone looked them over."

"He won't show you, not in a million years. Now don't look like that. You'll get into a fight and get hurt."

"Not me. I'm a peaceable man, slow to anger, as you know. We won't fight, but I think he'll be over here with an accounting for James before Friday."

Mateo was in the barn examining the injured hoof of a bay gelding that had been ridden in limping that morning. He saw the horseman riding up the hill past the house, wiped his hands on his pants, and walked into the yard.

"Hola, señor!" he called. "How goes it?"

Vail swung to the ground. "Very well. How goes it with you?"

Mateo grinned, and his hand went automatically to the horse's soft muzzle. He liked Señor Vail, and he liked the horses he rode. Nothing but the best horseflesh. He murmured a few love-words to the horse, inquired after the señor's health, his exquisite señora's health, the charming little niña's health. Vail sent messages of esteem to Mateo's mother and army of brothers and sisters, and when these courtesies were disposed of, he asked if it would be possible to locate Señor Stuart sometime today.

Mateo looked down at his boots, picked up a stone, and began to scrape off the mud and manure.

"Well, señor, that is a good question. The patrón was here this morning, but he rode off," Mateo gestured vaguely, "somewhere."

"Did he go to Longridge?"

"No, not to Longridge. His father—your father, señor," he added politely, "he wen' down to Monterey town las' week, so the patrón isn't over there. He'll be back, oh, by suppertime. He always is."

"Thank you, Mateo. I'll drop by at suppertime."

From the rise of Little Mountain the land dropped away in long, undulating curves to the wide valley. Southeast was Fontana and

Celia. He would not go there today. East was Longridge, that boundary he had not crossed since his mother was buried. He turned his horse east.

Little Clear Creek was full and flowing fast, but not raging over its banks as it had been during one other March not so many years ago. He crossed at the bridge. From here he could not see the house and with luck would not be seen. His forbearance, never unlimited, was at low ebb today, and the last thing he wanted was a conversation with his prim stepmother.

He rode through the oaks and crossed the meadow, where he had once practiced with an old dueling pistol, to the higher ground, the family burial place. There he stood for a few moments beside his mother's grave, then remounted. He cut back toward Little Mountain and turned down into the flat land that James Gentry had given years ago to a desperate widow and her three children. The evidence of Michael Morgan's hard work were wiped out, the once productive acres gone back to wild brush. Young trees were already sprouting and would grow great unless squatters took possession and cut them down. The cottage looked in surprisingly good repair; Michael had built it well.

As Vail prepared to spur past, the back door flew open and a girl with flying, waist-length hair dashed out, her bare legs flashing beneath what appeared to be a strip of white cloth. She raced through the dust of the yard, around the pump, and back into the house with a large, barefooted, long-legged man wearing only underdrawers and making odd, half-snorting, half-bellowing noises in close pursuit. As the girl ran inside, he leaped for the door, caught it before it banged shut, and plunged in after her. Vail trotted into the yard. From inside the house came more braying sounds followed by happy screeches and rippling female laughter. He left his horse in front of the small, tumbledown barn, opened the unlatched cottage door, and stood in the doorway, watching with interest.

They were wrestling on the floor, rolling over and over in breathless, giggling abandon. She was making halfhearted attempts to keep the sheet around her, and he was desperately trying to kick off his drawers without letting go of her. A chair toppled, bare legs and table legs tangled, and the table and dishes on it went over with a resounding crash. They stopped abruptly, twisting around to stare at the damage, and Vail, his eyes dancing and diabolical, said, "I feel the awkwardness of this and humbly beg your pardon, but I've been looking everywhere for you, Stuart, and haven't much time. Could you spare me a moment to talk business?" He took off his hat politely as the girl struggled under Stuart's heavy, suddenly immobile body. "Please don't trouble to get up, Glenna. This won't take long."

Stuart was on his feet and snatching his drawers up at the same time, his broad, hairy chest heaving with exertion. Glenna still lay on the floor, the sheet pulled up to her chin, gazing at Vail with dilated, dumbfounded eyes. Slowly, those wide, staring eyes never leaving his face, she got onto hands and knees and, her sheet held before her, backed into the farthest corner of the room. Her breath came in loud, terrified gasps. Her face had gone gray.

Hoarsely Stuart said, "I know this looks odd . . ."

Vail righted the overturned chair, sat down, and smiled; Glenna squeezed her eyes shut, murmuring, "Oh God. Oh, God," in a quiet litany.

The room was sparkling clean and freshly painted and, at the moment, in as much disarray as its occupants. Articles of clothing, stripped off in furious haste, had been flung in all directions. Embroidered petticoats, silk dress, rough flannel shirt, heavy leather boots, dainty slippers lay mingled on furniture and floor. Glenna's lace-trimmed pantalettes and one cobwebby silk stocking had somehow hooked over the small iron chandelier that hung from the ceiling in the center of the room and now dangled there, silent, damning, exactly at eye level and impossible to ignore.

Stuart located his trousers at the foot of the rumpled bed, scrambled into them, and, with his back to Vail, struggled with the buttons. "I suppose you're wondering what we were doing here . . ."

"Not really."

Stuart swung around. "Damn it, Vail, you've got to understand . . ."

"Let me assure you, I do, and I envy you. A comfortable, quiet, out-of-the-way retreat. An enchanting lady companion"—he smiled a compliment at Glenna, who shuddered and withdrew further into the corner, "an ideal situation, which only the luckiest of men can arrange. Popular, too. I hear this little cottage has been used for tête-à-têtes before—by your brother, John Wesley, ma'am." Under the sheet Glenna's bosom quivered. Vail grinned cheerfully at Stuart. "And you very nearly shot Wes on the wing. Death has always seemed to me an overly severe punishment for adultery, considering the weakness of human flesh, but my moral tone is notoriously low, so probably I'm wrong."

Stuart's jaw worked. "All right, have your fun and then get the hell out. What difference does it make to you?"

"None at all. As I said, I came to talk business. After we've tidied up a few matters, I'll be on my way and leave you to meditate on the amazing effect of happenstance in our lives."

"What business do you have with me?"

"Oh, several little things—now let me see, I have the list here somewhere. Well, no matter, I'll try to recall them. First, the loan Father made to Gentry and Callendar is due Friday."

"I know that."

"They don't have the money."

"Why not? That store is the mother lode."

"Not quite. Harry overinvested in inventory, leaving them temporarily embarrassed."

"Harry is a plunger and a damn fool. I knew that when Marin took the loan."

"But you didn't refuse to get her the loan. I wonder why?"

"If you're suggesting that I had any motive other than to help . . ."

"Now how could I think such a thing when I know your nobility of character so well? To see James lose Little Mountain—it's the last thing you'd want. That's why I know you'll get Father to extend the repayment period to—oh, say, another year? That ought to give them a fair chance."

Stuart stared at him grimly. "He'll never do it. I couldn't make him do it."

Idly, Vail flicked a chunk of mud from his boot. "Maybe you can't. Well, I don't believe adultery ought to be a capital crime, not even when one's own father is being cuckolded, but he may not see it that way."

Glenna sucked in her breath in a hiss, and Stuart shouted, "He'd try to kill me, and you wouldn't mind if he did. But"—he waved a shaking hand at Glenna, who had managed to get to her feet with the sheet swathed around her while still huddling against the wall like a terrified animal caught in a trap—"he would kill her, sure as fate. Not even you would want to be responsible for getting a woman murdered!"

Vail rubbed his thumb over his chin and mused, "I don't know. I'm an unprincipled bastard with very little of the finer feelings, and I can be unpleasant when I don't get my way."

Glenna's voice, scarcely recognizable, whispered harshly, "For pity's sake, Stuart, don't argue. Do what he says."

Stuart's lips went thin, he burned with the desire to smash his fist into his brother's sardonic face, but he said tightly, "All right, I'll—I'll point out the accumulating interest. Also, it would look bad to foreclose on a relative. I'll talk him around."

"Good. That takes care of our first item. Now, regarding Little Mountain, be in Gerald's office by ten o'clock tomorrow morning with the account books, the set you keep for yourself."

"Are you insinuating . . ."

"No, I'm stating a fact. You are going to be there tomorrow, books in hand, ready to turn over James's money to him. You're going to disgorge, Stuart. I don't know where you've stashed the cash, but you'd better dig it out fast."

Stuart opened his mouth to speak, changed his mind, slumped into a chair, and stared at his feet, extending, white and bare, beneath his pants. "I run a good ship and I'm entitled to live well, but I haven't cheated anybody. That ranch is a lot more valuable today than it was when I took it over."

"Sure it is. Like every other property in the state. Oh, I grant you've worked hard. But you've also lied to Marin about the profits and kept her on a short lead financially."

"A short lead is what she needs. A good beating is what she needs."

"Why don't you try it? Or better yet, do something for her, give her what she wants most."

Suspicion leaped into Stuart's eyes. "What does she want now?"

"A house. A big, brick house in a better part of town—you know the sort of thing a woman would like."

"She's got a house, a damn expensive house, too . . ."

"Built with James's money. It didn't cost you a penny, and you haven't contributed much to the upkeep. But it's too small, and she worries about fire." Vail stood, picked up his hat from the floor where he had dropped it. "You build her that house, Stuart, with your own money. It will make her happy and be good for your soul."

"I haven't got that kind of money!"

"Then find it somewhere. Take out a loan with Father." He bowed. "Good-bye, Glenna."

Glenna had the sheet wrapped so tightly that her legs could barely move, but she called out, "Wait!" and shuffled slowly yet determinedly across the room. She circled wide around Stuart as if she had never seen him before in her life and wanted nothing to do with him, came close to Vail, and looked up at him from her little height. Tentatively she touched his sleeve, then drew her hand away; real terror lurked in her eyes.

"You won't tell him, Vail?"

He watched her with a sensation closer to pity than he would have believed possible and nodded toward Stuart. "Not if he keeps his end of the bargain."

"Oh, he will, he will!" She looked down and whispered, "Vail, please don't think I'm wicked. You don't know how hard it is for—for a young woman married to an old man."

In the yard shadows were lengthening. The horse Mateo admired so much had strayed to the edge of the wood and was contentedly cropping the juicy spring grass. Overhead a pair of cormorants, too far inland, were swooping back toward the sea. Vail said, "Glenna, I'm not particularly proud of my life. I've broken all the commandments. Coveted, fornicated"—her eyes batted rapidly—"stolen, killed . . . well, you know the list. But one sin I'm not guilty of. I don't judge others, not being in a position to, you see." His eyes were thoughtful. "Spiritual pride, that's the great sin, they say, the one that makes the others child's play, the one God can't forgive." He put on his hat. "Don't bother to come to the door. I'll see myself out."

He walked across the dusty yard to his horse, swung into the saddle, and rode up the slight rise of ground into woods that were growing dark, to the trail leading out to the main road. He rode quietly for a while, but as he emerged into open meadowland, his wide shoulders began to shake, and then laughter exploded and he laughed most of the way back to the ferry.

BOOK FOUR

Chapter 30

To Carey Severance the best thing about the new house his father had built on Rincon Hill was the broad staircase that swept from the second floor down to the spacious entrance hall. The best thing about the staircase was the banister, a softly rounded mahogany railing that Mother kept highly polished—it gave you a thrilling ride ending in a swooping curve. However, he indulged in this pleasure only when Belinda wasn't around. She was too little, her legs were too short, and she insisted on trying to do everything he did; Carey was careful not to throw temptation in her path.

At six he was a loving and lovable child with a temperament more equable than either of his parents', a quick, keen intelligence, and a God-given ability to get along well with all the widely differing people who were important in his life. He had grown from a pretty baby into a handsome, dark-haired boy with the startling black eyes of his mother in a face still childishly round, a strong, well-developed body, and legs that seemed to have stretched to a great length in the last year.

Today Father was coming, and Carey looked forward to that event with excitement, laced with the anxiety that was always present on such occasions. Father was big and handsome and full of energy. He smiled a lot when you pleased him and meted out blistering disapproval when you didn't. Now that Carey was old enough to ride ponies and had learned not to be insubordinate, he was frequently taken across the bay on a large boat to visit Little Mountain, the ranch where he had been born, a ranch he had heard about all his life but could not remember. Father lived and worked there most of the time.

On these visits across the bay Carey was always allowed to take his dog with him. Angus had grown into a superb, larger-than-average collie with a shining black coat and a leonine white shawl circling his long, slim-nosed, intelligent face. Carey would dig his heels into his pony's sides, and off the three would go with Angus racing ahead, circling, returning to his young master, then leaping forward again, belly down, plumed tail and full white shawl streaming, front legs reaching for distance, powerful haunches driving like pistons. Little Mountain was a wonderful place for Angus and for Carey.

But as with all good things there was a price, for on these visits Carey was always taken to see Grandfather Severance, a large, awe-inspiring man with eyes that pierced through you and a voice that struck notes like the bass tones on the organ in church. Aunt Glenna would squeeze him against her soft, lavender-scented bosom, whisper that she wished she had a boy just like him, and offer him fudge that she had made just for him. Yet, with all the treats and pleasures and approval, Carey was never entirely comfortable at either Little Mountain or Longridge. With maturity beyond his years he recognized that he was the favored grandchild and resented it for Belinda's sake. He loved his bright, mercurial, strong-minded sister very much; he was unfailingly protective of her and saw no reason she should be valued less because she was a baby and a girl. And there was another element that kept him uneasy. He craved Father's approval and sensed that he would have it only so long as he never crossed him and always measured up to his high expectations. Vacations across the bay became work sessions during which he tried very hard to master every task set for him, guarded his tongue, and then came home with relief to his real life where he could be simply Carey, a child who could make mistakes and be loved anyway.

At home were the people who did not come and go like Father but were always there, as certain as the rising of the sun. The center of his world was Mother, but there was also Grandpa, who had trouble walking and was sometimes ill but who defended him when he was naughty, told wonderful stories, and never boomed at him in a loud voice or expected more than he could deliver. And there was Sophy—she could not see anymore, but she smiled often and played games with him like another child; there was Logan, who took care of him and Belinda while Mother was at work and sang songs to him when he could not sleep; there was Vail, who could fix anything and was his best friend. It was Vail who put him up on a pony and taught him to ride so that he would do well out at Little Mountain. Father had been very pleased at the amazingly quick way he caught on, had called him a crackerjack, and the truth was a secret known only to Carey and Vail.

The responsibility in his life was Belinda. He watched over her, scolded her and showed her how to do things right; in return she followed him everywhere, an adoring, playful nuisance.

She raced in now, letting the heavy front door bang behind her, and he abandoned plans for another trip down the banister. Instead he took her hand, and they went off to inspect the enormous room, created by opening the double doors between the two large parlors, where Jeremy and Usual McIntyre had worked all morning, moving furniture, rolling up rugs, and polishing the floor until it shone like a mirror, in preparation for the many people who would be coming to the party tonight.

"Walk across to the bed and then back to me." Marin watched with a critical eye as Logan obediently walked, turned, and came toward her. Deep rose was Logan's color. It imparted a glow to her fine-textured skin and brightened her blue-gray eyes. The wide, ruffled lace bertha had solved the dilemma of her unimpressive bosom without resorting to pads, which Logan considered dishonest and refused to wear. It also emphasized her minuscule waist and showed off her smooth shoulders to advantage.

"Don't slump," Marin said. "You have lovely shoulders—stand up straight and show them off."

Logan flushed with pleasure and looked down at her shoulders, rising silky and white from the encircling lace. "Do I? I never thought so."

"That's your worst fault, underestimating yourself—but that's going to change. Now sit down and let me get at your hair."

Logan watched doubtfully in her mirror as Marin went to work undoing a high knot of soft brown hair, brushing, combing, using the curling iron with an expert touch, humming under her breath, her mood expectant and happy. Tonight everybody who was anybody in San Francisco was coming—several important bankers and businessmen and almost every influential politician in town.

There was a tap at the door. Marin muttered, "Drat!" for she was just maneuvering a recalcitrant curl into position, and called, "Come."

Luz slipped in and handed over a small, square envelope.

Marin read the brief note, and her heart lifted, but she said, "Oh, what a shame. Celia can't come."

Logan peered up through the strands of hair that hung over her eyes. "Why not? Vail was expecting her only this morning."

"Corona's young man has run off—couldn't face the wedding, I guess—so she's in a state, and Celia can't leave her. Here, read it yourself."

Logan fumbled for her spectacles, slipped them on, and read the note. "How sad. Corona must be so unhappy."

"Yes. Aren't men disgusting," Marin agreed good-humoredly. Celia wasn't coming. She reheated the curling iron, lifted a strand of hair, and wrapped it carefully. "Speaking of men, you'll never guess who I ran into in the bank yesterday. Dan Gentry."

"Dan? Heavens, how many years has it been?"

She said, "Since Papa first took sick. We haven't seen hide nor hair of them in almost seven years. I didn't even know if Uncle Cole was alive." She restrained herself from adding, And I didn't care. Logan would have been shocked. "But he's doing fine, Dan says, making money selling cattle. Dan and Harlan were just like Ethan. Ran off to the gold fields to make their fortune and left Uncle Cole flat, only he didn't have a stroke over it like Papa. Harlan is still up there digging, but Dan's got a job as a teller at Douglas and Hartley's Bank. I always did think he had the brains in that family." Deftly she divided the long brown curls she had created into two clusters and tied them above Logan's ears with ribbons of rose velvet; suddenly Logan's face appeared fuller, softer, closer to the ideal oval. "There. Now stand up and walk for me again."

She watched as Logan walked and turned, her wide rose taffeta skirt swinging. "You look perfect—except for those spectacles." She whipped them off, and Logan wailed, "But I can't see."

"You see well enough. That shortsighted, helpless look is very appealing."

Marin gathered her own fan and gloves and as an afterthought remarked, "By the way, will you do me a favor? I invited Dan to come tonight. He's a shy boy and doesn't know a soul in town."

She thought of that good-looking man with the laughing eyes and bounding self-confidence and almost smiled. "He may be overwhelmed tonight. Be a dear and give him special attention, will you? Just to help him along."

Marin and Stuart stood in the entrance hall under the crystal chandelier, which was her pride, and greeted their guests together. They made a handsome couple. The house was handsome too, red brick and white shutters outside, spacious and impressive inside, with the subtle richness that only large amounts of money could produce. The floors gleamed, the spanking new French wallpaper was lush, banks of evergreen boughs trimmed with red ribbons gave off a pungent, piny odor and added the Christmasy touch she wanted, for her party marked the opening of the season. Many such parties would be given before the great day arrived, and hers must be the best. Everyone had been waiting with anticipation to see the house, and to be a success it must create massive envy in every matron's heart. After assessing the expressions on faces, the comments and muttered asides as to Stuart's surprising affluence, she decided that it did.

Stuart's affluence had surprised her, too. Never would she forget that morning in Gerald's office with the account books from Little Mountain spread out. It had come home to her that they were very well off indeed. Anger at Stuart's methods, as Gerald smoothly referred to her husband's—well, duplicity was not too strong a word—such anger as she had felt was minimized by the fact of so much money suddenly in hand, money that was rightfully Papa's, as well as having Malcolm's loan extended for an entire year. Then, too, Stuart had behaved very well. What magic Vail had used to achieve such results she could neither guess nor find out from him. He would say only that once the matter had been put to Stuart in the right way, he had been more than happy to straighten things out. And then there was Stuart's offer to build the new house—the last thing she had expected and quite out of character. Again Vail steadfastly denied any duress, and she was left with unvoiced but lingering suspicion.

The lot she made Stuart buy was exactly where she should have built her first house—in the best section of Rincon Hill, only three blocks from Vail's house. Much of her time was spent savoring the location and happily assisting Mr. Timothy with suggestions and advice. This house went up much more slowly than a prefabricated building; it was laid brick by brick, the cabinetwork

was finely done, and often work had to wait on special materials
ordered from the East.

In August one lamentable event occurred that brought her down
to earth for a time. The weather had been mild, and the constant
illnesses that plagued the city took only a light toll. In the entire
year there had been only two dozen cases of pneumonia, and of
those stricken only five had died. One of the five was Mrs. Harry
Callendar.

They were all shocked, and Charles Towle was especially hard
hit, for he took his losses greatly to heart. But Harry Callendar
was brought near to death by grief. He had no child, no other kin.
He and Mrs. Harry had been everything to each other. Now he had
only his friends.

They did their best. Marin left Dennis Timothy to struggle alone
with the building of the house and took over completely the
running of Gentry and Callendar. James spent every evening in
Harry's company, talking or sitting in silence if Harry wished it,
two widowers seeking solace in each other's understanding.
Everyone helped with whatever strengths he had to offer, but as
with all mourners, in the end Harry had to find his way back to life
himself. He began coming into the office for part of a day and
staying longer as the weeks went by. One late afternoon when
Marin was absent, an emergency developed at the warehouse;
Harry dealt with it speedily and efficiently, and after that he was
back at work full-time.

He came in the front door, the last guest to arrive, and Marin's
formal hostess's smile warmed into real pleasure. Although he had
promised to come, she had feared he might back out at the last
minute. But here he was in black evening dress, removing his high
silk hat, laying down his greatcoat, a small man with side-
whiskers a little grayer than before but his brown button eyes
darting approvingly about the bright room and a genuine smile on
his round, youthful face.

"How grand you look, Harry." She kissed him and, as her
receiving duties were over, slipped her arm through his and took
him off to greet other guests.

Stuart watched her progress through the crowd with a certain
enjoyment. She was a stunning girl, no use denying it, and tonight
she was running in high gear. The enormous bell skirt of her green
watered-silk dress swayed with her swaying walk and made her
trim waist disappear. There must be a dozen yards of cloth below
that tiny waist and practically none above it. What little there was
clung lovingly to her breasts, soft, round, white breasts rising,

falling quickly with excitement—God, no wonder he'd married her. Perfumed white skin with the faint, healthy tinge of pink, she was all skin above her dress, creamy shoulders, soft, slender neck, every bit of her so well known to him . . .

But she was a story long over, and he could look at her as any stranger would, relishing what he saw in a detached way. He liked what she'd done with her hair, hair he had once buried his hands in. It was smooth over her head, and long curls were drawn to one side by a black velvet ribbon and fell, vivid, glowing, onto her bare shoulder. She wore no jewelry but small swinging gold earrings that hung near her soft cheeks and glittered and danced as she turned her head. Probably he should have bought her something—a necklace, maybe—in celebration of tonight, but she had said she didn't want anything. The men, he could see, were respectful, admiring, murmuring gallant, impeccably proper compliments, hiding their real thoughts well. He could laugh at what they were thinking when they looked at her; how shocked she would be if she knew. She always brought out that side in a man and always seemed surprised when she realized it. It was more than beauty—there were other pretty women in the room—more than walk or manner or a look in the eye. It was an allure, a subtle suggestion of something more beneath the surface, a quality of mystery, of sexuality, of promises, of—but he'd never been able to put his finger on it. She slipped away like quicksilver. He'd been a fool to think he could hang on to her.

Well, no matter. His own love was across the bay, perhaps sewing quietly, undoubtedly thinking of him; meanwhile Marin was his wife for all public purposes, a credit to him, as was the house. He was glad he had built the house, it was worth the cost, for everyone was impressed. He would start circulating now through the buzzing crowd, work his way down to the end of the room, where he could smile at his brother, that bastard, and interrupt his conversation with the banker Bill Sherman.

As with the men, the ladies in the room were doing their share of assessing, and a good many, like Marin, were cheered by the fact that Celia Severance had not come tonight, leaving her interesting husband free for the evening. Feminine eyes strayed constantly toward the corner where those two noticeable men stood talking. Redheaded Mr. Sherman, with a well-known nervous temperament and the hard, aware look of a man who has no illusions, had been in California in the early days as a young army officer and had come back, like so many others, to make his mark in this city of endless opportunity. Now he was a rising banker with many influential friends and a great future in the world of finance. He had left his wife, Ellen, with the ladies and was at the moment absorbed in discussion with another man much like him in many ways.

Certainly Vail Severance looked as if he had no illusions left, a piquant quality to young ladies with nothing but illusions. Several of them, trying to reason out what it was about him that they liked, decided that he wasn't the handsomest man in the room. His face was too harsh and unaccommodating; evening clothes looked out of place on him—he was too big and took up too much space, and the decorum and conformity of fine black suit and ruffled white shirt were in too sharp contrast with his unconforming personality. But they connected him in their minds with freedom, action, dissent, all the things they didn't have and mustn't dare; they sensed in him a contained violence, were pleasantly frightened by it, and wondered secretly if they could set it off.

Hearts rose with the sound of violins' tuning up, for it meant that the dancing would soon begin. It was Dennis Timothy's band, a heterogeneous group of Irishmen who earned their living at a variety of jobs but played for the sheer joy of it.

Men bowed and requested the honor of a dance, ladies graciously accepted and they were released, whirling, swaying, swinging around the big room, candlelight soft on smiling faces and sparkling, flirtatious eyes. They were a young group for the most part, rambunctious, vigorous, less stiff than their eastern counterparts would have been in a gathering of equally high society. The waltz gave way to a reel, then a round dance, then back to a fast waltz.

Charlotte Winfield, having gone breathless during the reel, sat against the wall fanning herself and smiling approval as Baroness von Helsdorf circled the floor with Tyler Winfield, a delicate butterfly caught by a solemn frog. Behind her fan she murmured to Harriet Venable, "I see Mr. Crown is after my Kitty again. Charming man." And Mrs. Venable responded, "He has his work cut out for him. Kitty looks delightful tonight."

They smiled at each other and accepted glasses of punch from Jeremy, who bowed before them in his new livery, a model of expressionless courtesy.

As he moved away, Mrs. Winfield remarked, "Grand, I must say. Do you know, he can read and write. Marin says she has no idea how he learned and has never asked, as it was before she employed him. She shrugged off my warnings, but I know an uppity colored when I see one. Have you noticed his speech isn't near so thick? He's working at it—aping us. I can tell you."

"It does make him easier to understand," Mrs. Venable replied mildly.

"If that were all. But it's a sign of the times and not a healthy one." Mrs. Winfield lowered her voice. "Let me tell you what else he's done. Taken a last name and expects to be called by it! My maid, Bridie, met him in the street the other day, he lifted his hat and she said, 'Good morning, Jeremy.' Well, he stopped and informed her that he was Mr. O'Connell and she must address him as such from now on. Naturally I spoke to Marin"—she frowned in her hostess's direction—"and you will not believe what she said. 'He is called Jeremy when he serves the family, but on his own time he can call himself Mr. Bonaparte for all I care.'"

Mrs. Venable pursed her lips. "Both the girls suffered by their mother's illness. She was the dearest woman in the world, but she did not guide them properly through their formative years. Did you hear the rumor about the real cause of that fire?"

"It was told to me in the strictest confidence, and I simply refuse to believe it. She was a Calvert, you know. Look at Sophy—she's talking to Dr. Towle. If I didn't know better, I'd say she was flirting, and he looks as if she's the only person in the room."

"Well, he is her doctor. No doubt he has keen interest in her progress."

"No doubt. But Marin ought to keep an eye out since her mother isn't here to do it, or she'll end up with him in her family . . . Ah, good evening, Margaret." She paused to greet Margaret Parrish. "Isn't this a lovely party?"

The musicians had taken breaks throughout the evening, sampled the lavish buffet, and drunk more than they ate. Dennis Timothy was inspired to do a jig and danced in the Irish manner, upper body stiff and straight, arms at his sides, feet flying, while the pipes tootled and the drums beat fast time. There was wild applause at the end, and then someone asked for another waltz. They struck up "The Black Velvet Band," a lilting, romantic melody, and for the first time Vail came to Marin and drew her onto the floor, smiling down into her eyes.

"The last time we danced I left you with Gerald. I won't make that mistake again."

"I'll see you don't by keeping you away from the punch bowl. Papa says it has a kick like an army mule."

"What's in it?"

She wrinkled her nose. "Only Aunt Delphine knows. She mixes it from a recipe handed down by my great-grandmama."

They laughed as they swept past the matrons sitting against the wall, and Mrs. Venable's interested gaze turned toward Stuart. He was watching his wife and his brother with a blank face, and he bowed and smiled genially when he saw her eyes on him.

Dennis, having regained his breath, laid down his violin and began to sing, his voice harsh but sweet, his face red as a crimson moon.

> Oh, her eyes they shone like the diamonds,
> And I thought her the queen o' the land,
> Her hair hung down over her shoulder,
> Tied back with a black velvet band.

Vail said, "He must have made up that song for you."

The glow she always felt with him suffused her. God, it must be obvious to anyone who looked. "Maybe. I hope you've noticed your sister tonight. I had to wrestle her to the floor to accomplish that hairstyle, but isn't she pretty?"

"Yes. You're good to her. Does she know you dragooned your charming cousin for her?"

His voice was low, but she darted a guilty glance in Logan's direction. "Lord, don't let her hear you. If she knew, she'd freeze up and not say two more words all night."

Logan was having an excellent time. Her appearance gratified her more than she was willing to admit, and because she felt attractive, she relaxed, talked easily, and did not lack for dance partners. She was comfortable with Dan, having known him as a boy, and they danced together frequently. When supper was served at midnight, they sat on the stairs eating and talking and, as always when she was happy, her fine eyes darkened and glowed and her cheeks went pink. She was a graceful dancer, and when she and Dan took to the floor again after supper, several gentlemen watching her agreed that they hadn't realized before how attractive Logan Severance was.

Dan, to his surprise, was having a good time, too. In the old days he had seen Logan much as she saw herself, a tall, homely girl with an overlarge nose and a reticent manner. Tonight she sparkled, she had ideas about things girls seldom even mentioned but that were important to him, and he was drawn to her. Late in the evening they danced all the dances together, and when, toward two o'clock, the crowd finally tired and gave up the floor, they joined hands and gathered with the others as Marin sat down at the piano.

Mr. Foster's new songs were sung first, for everyone loved them, sung with great verve and some good voices among the loud ones. And then came the old songs, the sad or happy songs that took them back to other places, other days. All were strangers in this land, come from somewhere else, and these were the songs that bore them home again.

Carey and Belinda in their nightgowns came to sit sleepily at the top of the stairs and peer through the railing. Their mother saw them and did not send them back to bed. Instead she smiled and played on.

Finally, because it would show Logan to advantage, Marin asked her to sing, and she took her place beside the piano and sang the first melody the remarkable Mr. Foster ever wrote, "Open Thy Lattice, Love." Then for an encore the old, melancholy, "Oft in the Stilly Night." It was tremblingly sad and haunting and spoke of friends and loved ones gone, hearts broken, past happiness, and present loneliness. Eyes were wet as her rich, clear voice died on the last quiet note.

Gentlemen produced handkerchiefs to dry ladies' eyes, there was a search for wraps, many compliments and expressions of pleasure in the evening, and promises to meet again soon. Then all were gone, and the big house was still.

So quiet, Marin thought, lying in her bed with the lamp out. Empty now that everyone had gone. But that was foolish, for with Stuart occupying the front bedroom, decorated especially for him, there were eight family members sheltered under this fine roof tonight, as well as Luz, Mrs. Victoria and her little Emelita, and Jeremy in his private quarters over the stable. A houseful of people, all silent, all sleeping. The party had been a triumph, the men important, the women pretty, the food, drink, and music excellent, the new house marvelously impressive, the other aspiring hostesses envious. And there had been shining moments when she thought she would explode with quiet happiness. She had been in his arms many times tonight, they had swept rhythmically around the room together in full view of a world that could do nothing but approve, and his eyes had been only for her. He knew her through and through, her strengths and her failings, and loved her anyway. It was what she had dreamed of once when she was very young. A great love. But there was something the child she had been hadn't realized. A great love brought great happiness but also great pain. What if you couldn't be together? What if you lost the love?

Maybe the evening had been too successful and this was a normal letdown, a bleakness of spirit that would pass with the morning sun, but in the dark of the night it seemed to her that every triumph turned sour, every achievement proved hollow, every longed-for prize was vanity. For what was the use of striving and succeeding if there was no one to reach out to in the night, no one even to talk to.

She turned in her lonely bed, buried her head in her pillow, and whispered, "Oh, Mama, things haven't turned out a bit good. Oh, I do miss you so."

The evening had been a triumph for Logan, too, and she was feeling no letdown at all. Of all the rooms in the sprawling house only hers showed a light. She sat on the edge of her bed, smiling to herself, humming the tune of a waltz she had danced with Dan, giving her well-brushed hair an occasional swipe. She felt like a wealthy lady now with the allowance Vail gave her, and out of it she had bought a pretty nightgown and lacy peignoir. She ran her fingers over it lovingly. Tonight had been a revelation. No wonder girls worked so hard at being attractive to men; the rewards were so gratifying.

Dan was the same as ever, yet different. Marin had certainly misread him, for he wasn't at all shy. Quieter, more thoughtful, yes—he had faced many hardships in the gold camps—but full of confidence and fun. He had truly liked her, she was sure of it. He had actually asked to call on her. She would have to consult Marin and Sophy about what to wear.

Absently she dragged the brush through her hair. All that curl Marin had labored over was gone. Logan would ask her to curl it again tomorrow . . .

There came a sound, soft and unidentifiable. The single candle on her bedside table was very low, fluttering as wax ran slowly onto the pewter candle holder, casting odd, dancing lights and shadows on the wall and into corners. Another thump, very soft, and then a faint sound, as of wood rubbing against wood.

Logan was not a timorous girl, but that muffled thud made her heart bump in her chest and a quiver rush through her stomach. It was not timorous to be frightened of sounds in the night, not in a town filled to overflowing with the offscourings of the world, violent men who would be attracted to a home of such obvious wealth as this one; there had been so many robberies of late and witnesses killed to protect the robbers, so many women raped and murdered. Jeremy had painted the window trim this afternoon. Had he left the ladder out?

Get up, up onto shaking feet, run to the fireplace, grab the poker. No use to shout for Jeremy; he could not hear out there above the stable. No use to shout for anyone. Stuart's bedroom was far to the front of the house; nearby there were only women and babies. The candle still guttered. Too far to go back and put it out. Lean close to the window, lift the poker with cold, stiff hands, and pray for courage to bring it down hard.

Blood pounded in her ears, drowning out the telltale rubbing noises, but she saw a brown, slouch hat, a full red beard, and heard distinctly an unmistakable Australian accent—"Open thy lattice, love"—and then low laughter.

Oh, God, if only the candle were out! Why had she not screamed and run out of this room? Her muscles tensed, she raised the poker high—and he saw her above him.

His hands gripped the sill and he whispered hoarsely, "Lord love you, darlin', put that thing down and help me in. This damn ladder doesn't quite reach."

She lowered the poker and said in a flat voice, "Dear God." Then the poker fell from her fingers, and she was laughing, crying, hauling him over the sill. "Oh, my dear, my blessed, blessed dear, how beautiful you are! Oh, Ethan, we thought you were dead."

She let go of him and sank to the floor, shaking with great choking sobs. Tears ran down her cheeks, dripped on her long hair. She struggled up, found a handkerchief, and sat down on the bed, still crying helplessly, her eyes locked on him.

He dropped his hat and came to her. His blond hair fell below his collar in dull, dirty curls; the huge, bristly mustache and beard were bright red in his sun-browned face. His body was gaunt under his rags, yet he moved heavily, with none of the quick, easy grace she remembered. But it was Ethan, alive and breathing, concern for her showing in his dark blue eyes.

"Calm down, love, I didn't mean to scare you. Logan, will you stop it? I guess it is a shock, but I didn't know you thought I was dead."

"What did—what did you think then?" she cried in sudden rage. "All these years, these *years* without a word! Besides, he said you were dead!"

"Who?"

She blew her nose furiously. "That—that man who came. It was just before Christmas in forty-nine. He said you had died in the fall of the grippe."

"What did he look like?"

"I don't know. I wasn't there. Marin said he looked—pretty disreputable, but miners always do. You're a trifle ratty yourself."

He grinned, scratched in an impolite place, and remembered himself. "I'm not so pretty, am I? Well, why did Marin believe him? She's too smart for that."

"She didn't want to, Ethan, as you must know." The jumble of emotions in Logan made her voice irritable. She saw no reason to criticize Marin for a perfectly reasonable assumption. "He knew all about you, your home, your family, your—disagreement with Uncle James. He knew you had two pretty sisters and—well—a lot about your personal habits." Another thought struck. "Yes, and he knew about your red beard, too! That convinced Marin more than anything else. I should have remembered your beard, although I don't believe I ever saw you unshaven."

"Everyone and his dog knew about my beard. I've taken enough razzing over it. You sure you don't know what he looked like?"

Logan's mind went back. How many times she had repeated to herself Marin's description of the man and what he had told her. Slowly she said, "He was about forty, bearded, talked like a Middle Westerner. He said he buried you himself. Oh, yes, and his name was Willis Norton."

"You know his name, Jesus God! Why didn't you say so? Willis, the son of a bitch!"

"But he wasn't. He must have been mistaken, that's all, it must have been someone else he buried. Why, he came through that miserable rain all the way to Little Mountain just to tell us."

"He's a son of a bitch all right," said Ethan with unqualified conviction. "How much did he take the family for?"

"Not a thing, though Marin offered. He did take a horse finally, because he was walking and a horse, after all . . ."

"It might not have meant much to Little Mountain, but a hell of a lot to him. What else?"

"Nothing," answered Logan, wondering why she felt so defensive of Mr. Norton. "Marin gave him some food when he left, and . . . she did slip fifty dollars inside the package, but he didn't know about that."

"Didn't know but was sure as hell counting on it. The son—"

Logan laid her fingers firmly over his lips. "Don't say that again, I don't want to hear it. Your language is disgraceful, Ethan."

He looked down sheepishly, his grin a gash in the red of his beard, and she saw how thin was the face above it, saw the trembling of the hands that rested on shabby knees. Love and pity swept her. "Oh, I must be crazy, scolding you. What are we quarreling about? Dear Ethan, you look so tired. Are you hungry?"

"More tired than hungry. I wouldn't mind lying down."

"Of course! Lie down right here. Don't mind the coverlet, I don't care. Let me pull off your boots. I'm quite good at it because I used to do it for Father."

Ethan sank down on the bed with a groan and extended a dusty boot. "How is the old son—how is your father?"

"Very well," Logan answered briefly, tugging at the boot. It came off abruptly. She staggered, regained her balance, and began to pull the other one.

Ethan's eyes glinted up at her. "And you're living here." He glanced around the room. "Fancy, I must say. Did Stuart strike gold?"

"Not exactly. A lot has happened, Ethan. A lot to catch you up on. Oh, why didn't you write—a note, anything—to let us know you were alive? Why on earth did you climb in my window instead of walking in the front door like a normal human being?"

" 'Cause I ain't normal, sweetie, you know that." He passed a hand across his eyes as though they pained him. "Ah, Logan, how could I walk in here tonight looking like this? I've been in town three days, living down in Little Chile . . ." She gasped at the thought of that wild, dirty, dangerous section of town. ". . . I asked around, scouted out this place, watched you all coming and going. My, what a to-do tonight. Marin is Mrs. High-and-Mighty, and how she must love it. She looks wonderful though. So do you." He grinned up at her and played with the end of her sash. "I heard you tonight. 'Open thy lattice, love, listen to me/In the voyage of life love our pilot will be!' " He sang it softly, watching her face. "You sing prettier than ever."

"Thank you, but why didn't you come straight here three days ago if that's when you got in? You're not telling it all, Ethan."

"See, I said you knew me. There were a couple of fellers who didn't like me much, so I hid during the day and looked in on you all at night. You never saw me. They've taken off now, so I heard. Anyhow, this seemed like the safest way." A little of the old sparkle entered his eyes. "I figured out which room was yours. I always wanted to climb in a lady's window at night and find her all dressed in lace and her hair down her back. Should have sung you a serenade first, but I didn't want to wake up the rest of them."

She swallowed. "Why didn't you write? Even without Mr. Norton you must have known what we'd think. Where have you been all these years?"

"Oh, China, Hawaii. Australia most of the time. I talk good Aussie—have an ear for accents. They've got gold down there, too, did you know? Lots of it, only I never found much, and when I did find it . . . I didn't want to write and tell lies. I always figured tomorrow or the next day I'd strike something big, come home rich, fix things up with Pa . . ." His voice was grinding slowly down. "How is Pa? How's Mother?"

"We'll talk in the morning. Rest now, close your eyes."

He was asleep. She pinched out the light, crawled onto the bed beside him, and, because he was asleep, kissed him tenderly on the lips. Tomorrow would come the cries, the disbelief, the gladness, the years to be relived for him, the deaths, births, marriages, all the painful or wonderful vital statistics that told only the surface facts, not the deep-down changes in people he had once known and now did not know so well. Nor did they—or she—know him anymore. But it didn't matter. The core was the same, the heart did not change. At least, hers hadn't. Brave in the darkness, she slid down, drew his shaggy head close and cradled it against her thin breast. In his sleep he turned, his lips touched soft skin where her nightgown had fallen aside. She closed her eyes, leaned back against the pillow, and let him rest on that forbidden, untouchable part of her, for these few hours wife, lover, mother. Tomorrow he would become theirs, but for now he was hers alone.

Chapter 31

On a cool Sunday morning in January, Ethan sat on the railing in the stable and smoked while Vail examined the right front leg of Carey's pony. Carey squatted, hands clasped between his knees, watching anxiously.

"How is it?"

"You tell me. Put your fingers here." Vail placed Carey's hands on either side of the affected joint. "Can you feel the tendons? Like little ropes moving over the knee?" Carey, felt, thought, and nodded. "Now press down easily on the fleshy part. Is it still swollen?"

"I don't think so."

"Feel the other knee." Small fingers poked delicately at the pony's uninjured knee. "Now feel the right knee again."

Carey pressed on the sore joint, his black eyes intent. "Maybe it's a little puffier."

Vail knelt beside him. "Some edema, not much, right along here. Always compare. It gives you something to measure by. What do you think we ought to do?"

"Um—how about another poultice?"

"All right, we'll try it. Run up to the house and ask Mrs. Victoria for some flaxseed."

Ethan took a long drag on his Spanish cigarillo and dropped it in the dirt. "While you're there, Carey, go up to my room and get me my knife, the one with the ivory handle. Look on my dresser or the table, but mind you don't go digging through my drawers."

"Yes, sir." Carey took off up the path to the house. There was a loud bang of the kitchen door as Carey disappeared inside, followed immediately by Mrs. Victoria's shrill, scolding Spanish.

Ethan looked at the house. "Nice boy. Hard to believe he's my little sister's kid; hard to believe any of this." He scuffed the dirt absently. Six weeks of good food, restful nights, and safety had put ten pounds on him, and the wildness in his eyes had calmed, but years of danger, arduous labor, deprivations, and dissipation had battered a good-looking, impetuous, decent boy into a wary man with a lined, hard, handsome face from which all youthful idealism and good humor had been stripped. "Pa looks like hell, like a shriveled-up little old man. I have a tough time looking straight at him, not because I feel guilty. I don't. But he was always so strong . . . The worst was Mother. Somehow I thought she'd be waiting there in the parlor at Little Mountain. I'd walk in the door, and she'd hug me and kiss me and then feed me. That's what she always did when I'd been away. And she'd look just the same, gold and pink and pretty. I never imagined her looking different, getting older . . ."

"She got older."

"Is it true about the fire? Had she been—was there liquor involved?"

"Who told you that?"

"I was downtown with Charles the other day. We ran into a lady patient of his—a dreadnought with a daughter that comes on strong."

"Kitty Winfield."

"Yeah, Kitty. Mrs. Winfield hinted, she more than hinted . . . How could it be? Mother never tippled."

"She drank, and drank heavily, anything she could lay hands on. Mrs. Victoria caught her once with the vanilla out of the kitchen cupboard."

"But why . . ."

"Why do you drink? For the fun of it? Or because you hope it will stop the pain for a while? She drank to stop the pain."

"But she wasn't unhappy."

"You know better than that."

Ethan was silent, remembering. "Why wasn't she watched?"

"She was, for all the good it did. Don't bring it up around the house. It's a sore subject."

Ethan lit another cigarillo and smoked for a while in silence. "And Sophy, blind. God, what a waste." His eyes narrowed in the stream of rising smoke. "Marin seems just fine, sassier than ever."

"She has her troubles."

"Who wouldn't with that little tin Jesus she married."

Vail smiled faintly. "Stuart has problems, too. It isn't always fair weather with Marin."

Ethan laughed, and the laughter turned into a hard, barking cough. When he got his breath, he said, "Pa used to say the man who got her had to be strong enough to stand up to her and love her enough to make it worth his while."

"Your pa's a smart man."

Vail backed the pony into the stall and closed the gate, and

Ethan watched him with keen-eyed interest. Once, long ago, Vail had been a paragon of audacity to him, the ideal of all a reckless, free-swinging man should be. On first meeting after his return he found his model much changed, like everyone else. Older—well, it had been seven years. With a wife and child—God knew that had clipped the wings of many a high-flying fellow. Quieter, his real thoughts even harder to read than before. And his mother was dead, too, the inevitable break with his father complete. Where was all the fine fury, the old perverse contempt for the norms? Discipline, that was the new thing in Vail's face. What had caused the man to change himself so much? Responsibility, obligations, all the dull, depressing virtues, probably.

He said, probing, "Too bad about Nicolas, but it worked out well for you," and was startled by the expression that flashed through Vail's eyes in the second before he looked away. "What I mean to say is it must be great to finally get exactly what you want out of life. I wish to God I could be so lucky."

Vail leaned against the fence rail, arms folded, and the old dancing gleam came back. "Be careful what you wish for. You might get it."

"What's that supposed to mean? You've got a rich, beautiful wife—something I sure could use. You're happy, aren't you?"

"Oh, sure, but I'm unusual. Marin and Stuart got what they wanted, and look at them. James insisted on having his big adventure, and it cost him everything."

The obdurate, lowering look that had become Ethan's natural expression intensified. "Prosperity hasn't been healthy for you, Vail. You've gone cautious, which day I never expected to see. Just let me get hold of some money and a set future, and I'll show you how by God happy I can be."

"Will you? When you are, tell me, and I'll take it all back."

Except for George Winfield, only family was in attendance for Sunday dinner that afternoon at Marin's house, a family complete now that Celia Severance had moved to town. Rumormongers were engaged in enjoyable speculation, but no one guessed what had caused her to enter San Francisco society after so many years of aloofness. No one but Celia knew that the reason was Glenna Severance.

At Marin's Christmas party a number of onlookers had noted that Marin and Vail not only made a striking couple on the dance floor but also appeared to enjoy themselves hugely. With the

incredible speed that only a good piece of tittle-tattle could
generate, this intelligence flashed across the bay to Glenna, who
then descended on Fontana, dressed in her best, to take tea with
Celia and express admiration for her wisdom and forbearance.
Within the week Celia had moved into Vail's house on Rincon Hill
with her child and three maids and the intention of staying
indefinitely.

After dinner the usual division took place, the ladies to the
parlor, the men remaining at the table with brandy and port and
weighty conversation. They were in agreement that the proposed
transcontinental railroad across the Rockies to San Francisco
would be miraculous for California and possibly great trouble for
the nation. The railroad would pass through Kansas, where the
battle between the proslavery people and the Free-Soilers had
already resulted in bloodshed. The men gathered around the table
watched George Winfield with interest; he was a Southerner, hot
for slavery, and known for shooting off his mouth around town.
But George was also in pursuit of Sophy. Rather than offend the
man he hoped would be his father-in-law, he agreed with James
that the railroad would be a great thing no matter which faction
won in Kansas, and they all decided it was time to join the ladies.

Immediately Ethan leaped up as if he had been waiting for the
moment, muttered, "Excuse me, Pa," and left before James could
utter a word. When he came downstairs again, he had his new
stovepipe hat in hand and his fine wool greatcoat over his arm.
Marin caught him in the entrance hall.

"Just where do you think you're going?" Her lost brother had
been home for weeks. Shock and joy and overflowing gratitude to
God could last only so long, and as always after peaks of emotion,
there had followed valleys of dullness, depression, and, unbelievably, annoyance with some of his more irritating ways. Suffering
had not honed his finer qualities. In some respects he was more
feckless, more boyish than ever.

But he wasn't a boy, and she could no longer manipulate him
easily. His blue eyes were cool, and one golden brow went up.

"I'm going out, little sister."

He had the look he used to wear when going off to see Fermina
Victoria, but she didn't think he was headed for that kind of visit
now, at least not during the shank of the evening. She shut the
door to the parlor and whispered furiously, "You can't go out now.
We've all just settled down to talk." He pulled on his coat and
opened the front door. Cold air swept in, fluttering her skirt and

causing the crystal drops of the chandelier over their heads to tinkle sweetly. "Ethan, where are you going?"

He looked back at her. "On a perfectly respectable mission. I have been graciously granted permission to call on Miss Kitty Winfield, and that's what I propose to do. Good night, Marin."

She stood for a long time looking at the closed door and thinking of Logan with her shining eyes and her pretty rose dress, waiting in the parlor for him to come back. Dan had not called at the house in weeks. He had tried, you had to give him that, but he had soon realized how the land lay. Logan was a fool, and what could you do with a fool but close your eyes and stop your ears against the inevitable crash that was coming.

As the mild, pleasant days of February began, most people would have agreed with James that the future looked sunny. San Franciscans were more interested in the booming prosperity of local business than in slavery troubles back East.

In midmonth Mr. and Mrs. Tyler Winfield hosted a dinner dance for several dozen of their most intimate friends, the most important social event since Christmas, and all the best families attended.

Logan, who had planned to stay home with a book, stood on the sidelines, tapping her feet in time with the music and watching the whirling dancers with a sense of unexpected pleasure. She had glimpsed Ethan once when she first entered the room and then lost him in the crowd, but Dan had danced with her twice and was now bringing her a cup of punch. She was beginning to be glad Marin had bullied her into coming. The musicians played a rippling chord to draw everyone's attention, and Tyler Winfield, graceful in his black tailcoat and black satin waistcoat, climbed onto the orchestra platform. His mild gaze passed over the assembled guests, and when all were silent, he smilingly announced the engagement of his beloved daughter, Kitty, to Mr. Ethan Allen Gentry.

There was a general gasp, exclamations of amazement and delight, and people began to collect around the betrothed couple. Marin stood thunderstruck, a variety of thoughts careering through her mind. Ethan had been giving Kitty a tremendous rush, but matrimony? He hardly knew the girl. What could have possessed him to do such a brainless thing? He didn't want to marry anybody. And—oh, God—Logan! There she was, next to Dan, her eyes very wide, her face utterly still.

Across the room Kitty glowed and giggled while being hugged by several excited young ladies. Next to her Ethan shook hands and accepted the congratulations of the men. How striking he was, a tall, golden god in his severe black evening dress. And Logan—but the place where she had been was empty. Dan was alone.

Marin made her way forward, kissed Kitty's cheek, and expressed pleasure that they would soon be sisters. She moved on. Behind her a young man gallantly declared that his heart was forever broken, and Kitty laughed and hid her blushes behind her fan.

The twit, Marin thought in disgust, and looked up into her brother's handsome, lined face.

She tiptoed, he bent, and their lips brushed.

"What a surprise, Ethan. Couldn't you even share it with me?"

"We just decided the other night." His smiling eyes ignored the question in her face. He looked very satisfied.

She left him, wondering if he'd gotten the little fool pregnant and deciding he hadn't, for Charlotte Winfield was greeting her with open arms and looking like the cat that got into the cream.

Ethan observed them from the side of his eye and then gazed down fondly on his beloved, his mind ranging back over the past busy month.

Kitty had fallen in love with him almost immediately. She had many beaux, but she took one look at Ethan, newly arrived from the other side of the world, dressed in the finest of new clothes and cutting a wide swath in society, and quickly decided he was the most delectable man she had ever laid eyes on. The faintly disreputable mystery about his recent past, the hint of the dissolute in his face frightened and fascinated her. When he touched her hand, she went hot and cold; when his arm decorously circled her waist at a dance, she was shaken by feelings she did not clearly understand because no one had ever explained them to her. She knew only one thing—she wanted him and was going to have him.

Kitty's mother surrendered almost as easily. She viewed importunate young men as a natural hazard for pretty, innocent girls and guarded her treasure with the gimlet-eyed ferocity of a shopkeeper protecting his merchandise. So far, she had dismissed every suitor as unworthy. But Ethan Gentry's lineage was impeccable— almost; his family was prosperous, he was connected by marriage with the powerful Severances. Had she known how much his golden good looks, smooth compliments, and rakish charm resembled those of his grandfather Landrini, she might have found strength to resist him. But she did not know, and within a week of first meeting him on the street with Dr. Towle, she was looking forward to his calls almost as much as Kitty.

Kitty's father was another matter entirely. He viewed Ethan with the distaste and contempt he would accord a man with no collateral asking for a hundred-thousand-dollar loan, and for a while Ethan feared his suit might smash up on the rock of Tyler Winfield's skepticism. He had to be gotten around, and Ethan set about searching for his vulnerabilities.

He appeared to have none. He looked every inch the patrician—fine-drawn, inbred. His reputation was that of an aristocratic Virginia gentleman, a man of affairs with a small, solid private bank, hard but fair in business, gracious and kindly in private life. He was, in fact, grasping, unprincipled, thick-skinned, possessive of his daughter, and a shrewd judge of other men, especially men whose ethics were as questionable as his own. As he told his shocked wife, he had seen that Gentry boy coming a mile away.

"Young Mr. Gentry is a fortune hunter, my dear."

"Why, he brought home a fortune, Ty, and you said yourself the Gentrys are mining gold in their store."

" 'The Gentrys' meaning James and that daughter of his. Not the daughter George is mooning after. The other one. In my opinion, there is not a soft bone in that young woman's body. I'll wager she won't allow her brother near the business. As for his fortune, I don't believe he has a plugged nickel."

"But Marin dotes on him, she was quite beside herself with joy when he came home. Ty, have you heard something?"

"Not at all. I speak from experience and observation. I have had reason, you will grant, to observe the Gentrys closely since that scapegrace came sniffing around Kitty. The redheaded girl rules James, a sorry state of affairs. His illness must have weakened his mind. She does not bank with me, but those who have had dealings with her say she is hard as a man. She and Harry Callendar built that company, and, mark my words, she will not give her brother a crumb no matter how much she dotes on him. If his fortune is the lie I believe it to be, then he is penniless. Don't expect I will hand my daughter over to a ne'er-do-well adventurer, for it shall not be."

Charlotte had heard that note in her husband's voice too often not to know what it meant. He was dead set against Ethan, and her heart quailed at the thought of Kitty's hysterics when she found out. It was all very well for Ty. He would issue his edict and then go off to his peaceful bank. *She* was the one who would bear the brunt of the storm.

But the storm did not materialize or at any rate, it was a very quiet storm. Kitty did not collapse. She cried only a few tears, dried them, and turned coldly away from her father. She refused to sit on his knee and let him cuddle and pet her as he liked to do, she refused him so much as a smile. For two days it was all-out war.

In the early evening of the second day, at the time Kitty usually sat with him and told him all about her day's activities, Tyler paced alone in his small study. Finally he went upstairs and tapped on his daughter's bedroom door with a timidity that would have astonished his business colleagues.

"Kitty, dear?"

Silence.

"Kitty, it's Papa. I have a package for you, dearest. Don't you want to see what it is?"

Not a sound. But he knew she was in there, punishing him with her coldness. He looked around quickly. No servants in sight, no Charlotte to see him humbled, a mendicant at his twenty-year-old daughter's door. Damn Kitty! She knew he loved her more than anyone in the world.

Deliberately he unclenched his hands and inhaled slowly to calm the anger and the fear, and his voice took on a cooing, wheedling tone. "Now, precious, unlock the door. Papa didn't mean to hurt his darling. Papa only wants to help."

Utter silence.

"Kitty—I—all right, sweetheart, marry whomever you will. You know Papa only wants your happiness."

Kitty's voice rang out, clear and cool. "Will you take him into the bank?"

"Sweetheart, he doesn't want to be a banker." He doesn't want the work, the scoundrel, only the fruits.

"Will you back him, whatever he decides to do?"

"I—of course, dearest. Anything he wants. Now open . . ."

But the door was already wide, and she was in his arms, his good little girl back again, all sunny smiles and kisses for her father. He held her close and thought, Time. All I need is time.

The engagement had to be announced at once, Kitty insisted on that, and the wedding was set for June 2. Taylor balked—June 2 was less than four months away—but Kitty's eyes began to frost, and he hastily conceded. And now he was here in this damnable ballroom, smiling at people he loathed, talking pleasantly with his despicable future son-in-law, his words blithe and affectionate, his thoughts murderous. It was not that he wanted to keep Kitty unmarried. His pretty darling could not be an old maid. He had planned to select as her husband a man seen by the world as desirable, yet one who was easily controlled; there must never be any doubt as to who came first with Kitty. But instead, she had chosen for herself, and the man she wanted had a look in his eyes and a set to his mouth that said he would not be second best or take kindly to direction by his father-in-law. That look said he might do anything once he had the girl, even—though this was beyond imagining—take her away. Over Kitty's head Ethan's bland blue eyes met his, and he parted his lips to show his teeth.

Seeing that smile, Ethan thought, Jesus, I wouldn't want to meet you in a dark alley.

And the two of them went on talking, laughing, bantering with guests throughout the long evening.

Gerald's horse was tethered by the front gate when the family arrived home. Delphine bounced out of the carriage first, invigorated as always after a social evening that included many good things to eat, and she was once again going over Charlotte Winfield's menu in loving detail as she climbed the porch steps. Whenever she paused for breath, Sophy agreed that the food had been delicious. Logan followed silently behind.

Marin came up the path with her hand under James's arm, her step slowed to his, her heart beginning to bump queerly. What was Gerald doing at the house this late on a Friday night when he ought to be out carousing? He had news, that was what, and she had had quite enough unexpected information for one evening. The thought of what his news might be made her mouth go dry with apprehension.

He was waiting for them in the parlor.

James sank heavily into his accustomed chair beside the fire that was always kept going on chill winter nights and groaned as he stretched out cold feet to the comforting warmth. "Gerald, sit down. Take a load off."

Marin closed the door, searching Gerald's dark face for a hint of what was going on behind it. He was smiling beneath his little mustache, and his eyes were blank. Her apprehension increased.

James said, "Bad news, Gerald? Spit it out."

"Good and not so good. I have here the decision of the district court of Little Mountain." He opened the flat black case that so often carried papers that rebuilt or shattered his clients' lives and took out several long, closely written sheets. "This was a complex case, as most of these land claims are. All because of the Spaniards and their half-baked methods of doing business. However, John Baldwin never bungled a job in his life, and that's the good news I have for you. Every inch of land you bought from John—the land the house itself stands on and one hundred and seventy-two acres running southwest to the present La Gracia boundary—is confirmed. You now hold clear title."

After a pause James asked, "And the rest?"

"Unfortunately, Nicolas didn't have John's respect for legalities. Because Fontana's title has been denied and since the remainder of Little Mountain was Fontana land purchased from Nicolas . . ." He lifted one shoulder in a shrug more eloquent than the dry words on the papers he handed over.

James's eyes ran down each page. He handed them back. "Is there anything to be done?"

"We can appeal to the Supreme Court in Washington."

"Should we?"

"You would have to hire a lawyer there to represent you. It would be a long wrangle, and the costs would mount. Frankly, as I told Vail with regard to Fontana's claim, I consider it money down a rat hole but I could be wrong. Think it over carefully, James. Consult with another attorney before making up your mind. I don't want you to go along with what I say and regret it later."

They all sat silent, and Marin wondered sourly where Stuart's prodigious political influence was now that they needed it. All bluster and puffery just as she had suspected. The land would not be wrested from them tomorrow or the next day, but squatters would gnaw at its edges, land developers would pounce on desirable acreage and build stores and houses, dusty streets would appear where once thousands of head of cattle had grazed, and they, the rightful owners, would be forced to stand by helplessly and watch it happen.

"It just isn't fair," she ground out bitterly, anger at the injustice of it beginning to rise now that the first shock had passed. "Papa paid hard cash for that land, he paid it in good faith. It's not his fault if Nicolas was careless. Little Mountain is ours, and we'll fight for it!"

"No," said James, "we won't."

She turned on him, indignation rising, and just in time remembered to whom she was speaking.

"But, Papa . . ."

He looked at her from under beetle brows that had gone completely white in the last year. "I know, daughter. You always want to fight. But there comes a time when fighting is a fool's game; there comes a time to write it off and go on. The ranch . . . it's gone, and I don't need to consult another lawyer to see it. In my heart I've known it for months." He struggled out of his chair and shook Gerald's hand. "Thank you, sir. I know you did your damnedest."

He walked from the room, his step more halting than usual, his cane thumping slowly up the stairs. Out of the thousands of green and gold acres lazing under the sun was left less than two hundred, the puny remainder of James's dream. Marin thought of all that had been lost in the pursuit of that dream and would have wept if Gerald's sympathetic eyes had not been on her. For so long her energy and hope had been focused on the company and the store; until this moment she had not known how much she relied, far in the back of her mind, on the fact of Little Mountain, the everlasting bulwark on which the family could fall back if Gentry and Callendar failed. The debt to Malcolm was paid at last, and substantial reserves were safely deposited in the bank; yet she felt suddenly exposed, like a high-wire walker teetering far above the ground with the reassuring safety net removed.

The next day the mail steamer arrived with news from the East. The eastern branch of Hayes, Harbison & Co., the largest bank in town, had closed its doors. It was news so staggering that Marin did not take in its meaning until Harry explained it to her. There would be a run on the local branch, for the depositors with money at risk would surely panic. It was confidence, belief in the strength and soundness of financial institutions that kept things going. If everyone rushed to withdraw, it would be the end, for no bank, however strong, could pay off every creditor at the same time.

Bankruptcy was common in San Francisco, and Marin had lived with the fear of failure from the moment Gentry and Callendar was formed and the first usurious loan from Malcolm taken. Many times she had danced at parties with prosperous men who a few days later got word of a lost ship, went home, and blew their brains out. Suicide was the dark undercurrent in this exuberant, good-time city, and not the least of the reasons was sudden economic ruin. But up until now the ruin had been sporadic, individual, and you never truly believed it would happen to you. Even the great fires had been surmounted with aplomb by most people. But a general economic collapse—it would be the end for most of the businesses in town, for Gentry and Callendar, the Golden Cathay, and all her hopes.

The run on the powerful Hayes & Harbison bank began that day. The bank stayed open for business through the week, meeting each demand for cash day after hectic day, and then closed its doors abruptly on Thursday morning. But even in the face of such a shock there was cautious optimism; the solid, well-buttressed express and banking firm, T. Davidson & Company, Gentry and Callendar's bank, still faced into the wind with banners flying, and as long as it stood, survival of the town's other, smaller banks was possible. Harry was a bank officer, and Vail was a stock-holder, and Marin took comfort in that. They would not let Davidson's Bank go down.

On Thursday afternoon the run on Davidson's began, and in the small hours of Friday morning Gerald Crown was appointed to accept receivership. He immediately ordered all of Davidson's remaining gold removed to Winfield's Bank before an armed assault could be launched on the building by determined creditors. James went downtown to see for himself what had happened and came home with news that sent hopes rising. The smaller banks in town were not wiped out after all, and Davidson's intended to distribute their remaining gold to every depositor on a propor-tional basis. That meant Gentry and Callendar would get some-thing back, and maybe some other small bank still in business would make them a loan. There might be a future after all.

But James had more to tell, and what he said was staggering. In the presence of Tyler Winfield and the two major stockholders, Gerald had compared the quantity of gold brought from David-son's against the totals in the ledgers that Harry Callendar had certified and William Purcell, the bank manager, had counter-signed. He discovered it was not all there.

"Not there?" Marin repeated, at first uncomprehending. "But how could it not be there if they took it all . . . oh, Papa!"

"Just so," said James. "Nobody knows how it happened, but there sure is going to be hell to pay."

His prediction came true immediately. Early in the morning when the news broke that Davidson's had closed, a snarling crowd rapidly whipped itself into hysteria and assaulted the bank despite announcements by William and Harry that not a grain of dust remained in the vault. Hours later, when the last wounded creditor limped home, heads had been cracked, bones broken, the front window was gone, and desks, tables, chairs, even the railing around the counter had been tossed into a bonfire in the street. William and Harry had barely escaped out the back door with whole skins.

By evening a subtler, more menacing reaction was surfacing as the news of the gold shortage spread. Banks had closed before and paid their customers off pro rata; customers had rampaged and then finally accepted their losses with sour resignation. But gold known to have been on hand only the previous day was missing, and that was intolerable. The questions raged—where was it, and who was responsible?

Rumors flew. One story had it that the missing gold had never been there at all, that the bank had lied about its assets; another that the largest stockholders had somehow carried it away and were shipping it to their banks in New York; another that William Purcell had lost it all at roulette one night last week in the El Dorado's gambling hall; three witnesses swore they saw this with their own eyes. But none of these tales was widely credited. Public opinion, intangible but powerful as armies, came quickly to a generally accepted belief: one man was responsible, and one man only—the man who had certified the accuracy of the count, Harry Callendar. Some people thought he had squandered the money already, for Harry was known to be a high-stakes gambler, but most were convinced he still had it somewhere, the most popular theory being that he had shipped it to Hawaii, where he meant to run off.

The bank's official—and reasonable—explanation was that in the confusion and clamor of the last wild day's business, payouts had been made that were not recorded. Also, a large quantity of coin and dust listed as being on hand had, in fact, been sent during that hectic day to other banks not under siege and had been inadvertently paid out by those banks. The money was gone—it was unfortunate, but there was nothing to be done about it.

That was the explanation, and nobody believed it. The verdict was in, and in the space of a few days Harry could not enter a restaurant or bar without noticing a meaningful hush descending as old friends turned away. He could not walk down the street without ladies crossing to the other side at his approach, whispering among themselves and pretending they did not see him. His close friends were staunch and indignant, but he rapidly discovered how few of these there were.

In an effort to cheer him Vail reported a sharp exchange between Marin and Harriet Venable, whose husband had often sought help and advice from Harry. Mrs. Venable claimed to have known all along that Mr. Callendar was not to be trusted because his eyes were set too close together; men with close-set eyes were invariably false-hearted. Marin, already in a fury for Harry's sake, retorted coldly that Mr. Callendar was a man of impeccable honor, that only the ignorant believed appearance indicated character, and, furthermore, that Mrs. Venable was a simpleminded, slandering harpy. Mrs. Venable swooned with insult and had to be assisted home by two women friends.

Harry smiled at the story. "Marin can strike deeper with her tongue than most people can with a knife. Bless her, if I were an ax murderer, she'd be at the jail with a lawyer and a hacksaw. And so would you."

Vail poured another drink for each of them. He wasn't in the mood for drinking, and neither was Harry, but it gave them an excuse to sit in a saloon and be seen together, while ignoring the undercurrent of gossip that buzzed around them. "Don't let it wound you to the heart, Harry. It will pass."

Moodily Harry swirled the liquor in his glass but did not drink. "Old friends pass me by without speaking, men I have dealt with for years. What can I do to prove innocence? It's a strange, inexplicable thing—the more I deny it, even to myself, the guiltier I feel. Sometimes I begin to wonder, if I did do it. Sometimes I think I'm going mad."

"I know the feeling—all the things we never were punished for but should have been. Maybe it's our sense of original sin, maybe you and I are really very moral men. Ignore gossip, Harry, as much as you can. Work, drink, find a woman, do anything but brood. Surely you're not surprised at the inconstancy of people this far along in life. I can count my real friends on one hand with room to spare."

"Ah, you are right. Self-pity is nonsense. I shall take your advice and give it up. Gerald believes prosecution is possible but not likely. I must take comfort in that. Find a woman, you say." Harry's eyes began to sparkle in the old way. "Up to now I've had no interest, but—would you introduce me to Madame Colette? I hear her young ladies are top drawer, and she's very choosy about clientele. My, my," he added in amazement at what he had just said, "I've never done anything like that in my life."

The firm of Gentry and Callendar did not immediately collapse, as Marin had foreseen in her worst nightmares, but stumbled on, surviving for the present on a lucky shipload of flour and tobacco that arrived during a week when other such shipments were delayed and demand was high. The Golden Cathay, however, was doing poorly. Businesses of all kinds were going down in the confusion that followed the bank closings, and demand for rare objets d'art had dropped close to zero.

Harry appeared moderately cheerful. No one knew what he did after hours, for his friends rarely saw him in the evenings, but during the workday he was bustling and busy, fussing over the unloading of the precious flour and tobacco like a hen with one chick, forcing himself to approach men who had questioned his probity and ask them to buy.

The problem was, he told James, that he never knew who would put on a cloak of courtesy and who would be cold. The crude insults had almost ceased; it was the subtler slights that mortified. James, in a burst of compassionate energy, volunteered to take on the selling job and did so well that he jokingly warned Harry he might take away his job.

At home all appeared serene, although Logan's thin face took on a gaunt look as June and Ethan's wedding approached, and she seldom spoke unless asked a direct question. At such times she appeared to pull her mind back from some distant place, focusing with effort on the words addressed to her.

In the days immediately following his engagement Ethan was ebullient, bounding down the stairs, whistling in the hallways, talking merrily and endlessly at dinnertime about his upcoming nuptials. Marin sometimes had to fight down a strong desire to stuff his mouth with his own superfine, embroidered linen handkerchief. The anxiety and upheaval on all sides seemed barely to attract his notice once he made certain that his Kitty's father was still in good financial health. He's never once offered to help in the business, Marin thought darkly, not that she would allow it if he did. She had been right to talk Papa out of giving him a partnership. He was so busy roistering with friends and being fitted for his wedding clothes that he found it necessary to move to a downtown hotel to be nearer the tailor and the saloons and then, to her fury, blandly sent the bills to her.

But as the limpid days of May slipped by, his lighthearted mood underwent a slow but perceptible change. The wedding was only three weeks away, then only two. He became quiet, preoccupied; he rarely smiled and then, without humor.

Wedding nerves, dear brother, Marin thought, and it serves you right. You'll never get away from Kitty now. She'd have your hide.

And she shrugged off Ethan's problems as she shrugged off Logan's. Ethan had made his own bed, and so, in a way, had

Logan. If Logan had any sense, she would take Dan, who was a decent, attractive man, instead of moping her life away over a charming scamp who could never make her happy even if he wanted to.

Well, it was not her problem, thank the Lord. She had only to worry over cargoes and inventories and keeping the books again herself now that she had had to let one of the clerks go.

All these small concerns kept her mind from the larger problem looming just ahead; in midyear invoices were coming due that had to be paid if Gentry and Callendar was not to go the way of nine out of ten other firms this calamitous spring. The total amount due was only a little over eight thousand dollars; much more than that would come to them when Davidson's assets were finally paid out. But the matter was mired in litigation, and years could pass before it was finally settled. Even so her mind was light. She had the constant assurance of Vail's love. Papa was working almost every day, and Harry had risen out of despair. So much had been survived; surely they were meant to continue. For the present she was still a high-wire walker, but she had her balance. She had only to keep on walking.

The incident that tipped the balance was a small thing, and it came about through a series of minor events. James had a head cold, and Marin, always protective, insisted he stay home in bed. She would see the gentleman who wanted to sell them a fire insurance policy on the warehouse. Only recently Eastern firms had become willing to insure the tinderbox of San Francisco, and agents were selling hard, trading on the memories of old conflagrations. Today's meeting with the insurance salesman was only a courtesy. They couldn't buy the insurance, comforting as it would be; they couldn't afford the premiums.

She had been at her desk for an hour when Harry hurried in with the news that the Golden Cathay's one remaining salesclerk had been shot last night in a most disreputable location and, while not in serious condition, would not be in to work today.

She could not keep the sparkle from her eyes. "Does the disreputable location refer to his person or the part of town he was in?"

"Both, I suspect." Harry chuckled, and she blessed the sound. He had never quite regained his old buoyancy, and it was good to hear him laugh.

"Well," she said, "if we want the store to open, I'll have to do it, although I'm sure it's to no purpose. We haven't had a single sale in two weeks. *Two weeks*, Harry."

"That's because you haven't been there, my dear." He helped her on with her modish little jacket. "You could sell sand to an Arab."

She started down the stairs, smiling at the compliment, turned, and ran back up just as Harry was preparing to leave.

"That insurance man is coming this morning, and I promised Papa I'd see him. Wait for him, Harry."

Harry sat down to wait, his mind in neutral. He no longer thought consciously about the fiasco at Davidson's or the wounds he had endured. It was over and done except for possible prosecution at some time in the unknowable future, and he couldn't live in daily dread of that. It was his wife he was thinking of this morning. He had gone again to Madame Colette's last night. The young lady had been extremely pretty, most accommodating, and able to make him believe for a little while that she really liked him. He missed his wife more bitterly than usual this morning.

The insurance salesman popped in at the exact time of his appointment. Behind his swooping mustache Harry saw that he was very young, with all the brash assurance of one who has as yet met no serious setbacks and confidently expects that he never will. His skin was taut with youth and rosy with good health, his eyes were hard and eager, and Harry thought sadly of the rough edges that would, one way or another, be knocked off this bright young fellow one day.

He smiled. "Come in."

"Good day, Mr. Gentry." The young man pumped Harry's hand. "I have looked forward to this meeting. You have quite a reputation in town, sir. Let me present my card."

"Please sit down, Mr.—ah—Mills."

Mr. Mills spread his coattails and accepted the seat.

Harry sat down in Marin's chair, wondering how fast he could get rid of the man. "Here is my card, sir," he said. "As you see, I an not Mr. Gentry. He is ill today and asked me to offer his apologies."

Mr. Mills took some time reading the card though it said only, "Harry L. Callendar—Gentry, Callendar & Co." Finally he looked up. "Please convey my hopes for Mr. Gentry's speedy recovery. I'll return when he is able to see me."

Harry waved a negligent hand. "I'm his partner. I'll be glad to hear your proposal."

If Mr. Mills had been a more experienced man or a kinder one, he might have kept his thoughts out of his face. As it was, he said,

"I'm sorry, Mr. Callendar. Had I known, I wouldn't have come."

"I don't understand you."

"Well, you see, I knew of Mr. James Gentry, I knew Gentry and Callendar, but I didn't put it together. That is, I didn't realize that you were *the* Callendar. Harry L. Callendar."

"Yes," Harry said, "that's who I am."

Mr. Mills rose, and Harry stood, too.

"I could not write a policy for a firm in which you are a partner, sir. I could not recommend you as a good risk to my company. We find that, distressing as it is to say so, arson is a frequent cause of industrial fires. It is a great temptation to those who want quick money, and a serious drain on the insurer."

"Arson," Harry said quietly. "It is an ugly word."

"Yes, indeed," agreed Mr. Mills in sudden retreat. This little man in the long frock coat was not so comical-looking as he'd thought at first glance; his round, pink face was unreadable, his eyes had the odd look that sometimes preceded a challenge. These crazy Californians were always fighting duels over some fancied insult, and they were good with guns. Mr. Mills wished himself back in civilized, wholesome New York.

But no challenge came. Harry said, "I quite understand your position. Good day, Mr. Mills."

"Well, I . . . that is, it's company policy, you see, nothing personal . . ."

"Nothing personal. No, of course not. Good day."

After the man had gone, Harry sat for a while staring at the toe of his boot. Then he turned to the desk, looked over the papers Marin had left there, set them aside and began to write.

At noon the company's one remaining clerk came in from his cubbyhole. He was a pleasant young man and a good clerk, and he liked Mr. Callendar. Personally, he believed the gossip of this spring to be a pack of scurrilous lies and had often wished to tell Mr. Callendar so. He considered doing it now, but as in the past, his nerve failed. Mr. Callendar was a kind man, but he kept his thoughts to himself and looked particularly unapproachable today. So the clerk put his warm impulse aside and said only, "I'm going to lunch now, sir. Is there anything I can do for you this afternoon?"

"Ah—let me see. Yes, Edward, you can check through this stack of invoices for Mrs. Severance. She will be at the store all day."

"Yes, sir. Good day, sir."

Harry nodded, locked the remaining papers in the safe, took

down his hat from the coatrack and went out into the street. At the corner several hansom cabs, shining with silver trim and polished leather, waited for fares. Harry used them frequently, since he kept no carriage, but this day he decided to walk.

He headed briskly down Montgomery Street, swinging his silver-topped cane, his tall hat at a jaunty angle. How the town had changed since the day he had arrived at a flea-bitten little tent village on the sand hills back in '48—seven years. Most towns would have taken fifty or even a hundred to grow this fast. Substantial buildings, gaslights on the corners, omnibuses, opera, and yet—with all the amenities, beneath its glitter it was still raw and crude, just a jump ahead of the wilderness. He longed for another place, a slower, gentler world, he longed to stop running. His mind traveled back to the little town in New Hampshire where he had grown to manhood, the quiet town he and his wife had left and intended to return to one day after they had made their fortune. His thoughts often turned back to home these days. He stepped out into Clay Street, halted for a beer wagon rumbling by, then moved on more rapidly.

Across the street Michael Morgan, stepping out of his hardware store, saw Harry, raised his hand, and called out. His business was doing better than most, at least his doors were still open, but he was hanging on by his fingernails. He wanted to get Harry's advice and do it in public, too, just to show people where he stood. He called again, but the beer wagon rolled past and Harry did not hear. He moved on down Clay, his natty silk hat gleaming, the silver head of his cane sparking in the light.

He was puffing as he trudged up the hill to his gate. The house was small, nothing like the one he and Mrs. Harry lost in the great fire of '51. They had planned to build a grander house this year. Strange, he thought, looking at the house he had lived in with her, all the years of known probity, the opportunities to cheat safely not taken, the easy lies not told, and now one mischance, the suspicion of wrongdoing, and it was all wiped out, worth nothing. Even had he done the deed, would it be right to balance a single transgression against an entire lifetime of integrity and declare him worthless? Did one act cancel out the rest? In all justice, he thought not. By God's law, he was certain not. By human judgment— savage, capricious, arrogant in its blindness—the answer was yes.

It was the way of this world. It gave no quarter; he should never have expected that it would. He walked slowly through the little house where he had lived with his warm and loving companion. Despair was his only companion now. He went into the bedroom, opened a drawer in the table by the window, took out a bottle, and opened it.

It was a clear, colorless liquid with a smell of peach blossoms and spring. "Oh, God, take me home," he said softly, and drank it all.

Chapter 32

It was a day of shining clarity. Below the little cemetery the town sprawled, clean and orderly at this distance. Beyond it the bay was a mirror reflecting the burnished sky. A cool, salty wind traveled in off the water, brushing Marin's face, fluttering her skirt. She looked out toward the sea. It seemed one could live forever on a day like this.

The other mourners had walked back down the grassy hill, and some carriages were already rolling off toward town. Everyone was tactfully leaving her alone at the grave, believing her the most deeply affected, allowing her the opportunity to weep privately if she wished, but tears were far from her. She had learned about surpassing emotion today. Hate was not fiery, as she had thought; hate was cold and hard, a solid lump in her chest. Near her feet was the mound of newly turned earth and the heaped-up flowers that would soon be as dead as Harry. What should be inscribed on his stone? "Here lies Harry Callendar, killed by public opinion." Or how about "Where the carcass is, there will the vultures be gathered."

Surprising, the size of the crowd. Some of Harry's most virulent detractors were here today, easing disturbed consciences. Yet already the whispers were spreading . . . She had known suicide would be taken as proof of his guilt and had wasted no time destroying the letter he left in the safe; no eyes but hers had seen it. She had begged Charles to put heart failure on the death certificate instead of prussic acid poisoning, but he said he could not falsify a legal document. Legal documents. What did it matter except to those who loved Harry?

Below on the narrow road Logan was standing with Vail and Celia, listening to something Vail was saying, leaning hard on his arm. She looked dreadful today, wan and red-eyed. She had cried more for Harry than she had for her own mother, but lately she was quick to tears, weeping over a lost comb or a torn petticoat.

A fine matched team of horses pranced past, drawing Mr. and Mrs. Tyler Winfield's smart carriage down the hill. Ethan was riding back to town with them, his bright head a shining cap of gold next to Kitty's ruffled parasol. The horses' hoofs kicked up a fine spray of sand as they rounded a curve and rode out of sight.

Everyone but the family had gone. Marin stepped past the low white picket fence that enclosed the graves and walked down to the waiting carriage.

It was almost nine o'clock, well past suppertime, but she was not hungry. Over James's objections she had insisted on being dropped off at the office directly after the funeral and had been there all afternoon going over the books, striking a balance, and coming each time to the same conclusion. The scratch-scratching of pen on paper in the next room was so familiar a sound that it faded from her consciousness and she forgot that Edward Moore, the young clerk, was still there, conscientiously working late to make up for the time he had taken off to attend Harry Callendar's funeral.

The sound of his hesitant footsteps on the bare wood floor broke into Marin's gloomy thoughts, and she straightened her skirt and looked up.

"Yes, Edward?"

"Mrs. Severance . . ." He hesitated, searching for words. "Ma'am, I want to say how sorry I am about Mr. Callendar. There was not a scrap of truth in those stories, I know it. My regret is that I never said so to him. If I had, it might have made some little difference."

Her face changed subtly, as if the lamp had dimmed.

"We can't ever know what made the difference, can we? Some one thing or all of it, piled up. We all have regrets—but I believe he knew we loved him."

"Yes, ma'am. Uh—it is very late. Might I offer to escort you home? The streets are dangerous."

"How kind you are, Edward. Thank you, but Jeremy will be here shortly. You go on home."

"I'd best wait until he arrives."

"No, no, go along."

"Well—good-night, ma'am."

After he left, the room was very quiet. It was a plain room. How many hours she had spent here, working over the books, figuring and refiguring how to meet some impossible debt. Harry had been here then with his astute brain, his courage, his buoyant optimism. Since the beginning of their joint enterprise there had been within her the feeling, never expressed, that she and Papa carried the heavier load, for they were always the ones who came up with the money. Now she realized how great Harry's contribution had been. She felt very alone tonight.

The shaded lamp, the outspread papers on the desk, the blue light of the gas street lamp falling through the undraped window, the chill of the night, her sense of loneliness, brought back another grim evening when she had sat here past the supper hour, trying to find a way to pay off the second loan from Malcolm. That was the night Vail told her he loved her. He had talked to Stuart the next day, and before he was through the loan had somehow been extended for a year and Stuart was building her a new house. But Vail would not be coming here tonight. Immediately after the funeral he had gone across the bay to Fontana to straighten out the Cermeno clan's latest dilemma. And this time money could not be extracted from Stuart. He had banked with Hayes and Harbison, the first to fall. Malcolm—God alone knew what Malcolm might have squirreled away. His bank had not failed, and he rode his acres across the bay in lordly aloofness. The title to Longridge had been confirmed at the end of last year, and all spring he had been quietly buying up city real estate at depressed prices. Malcolm wouldn't lend a penny now.

There were sounds on the stairs. Vail, she thought, her spirits lifting. He must have come back early. How good it would be to see him on this cold, melancholy night. But even as she raised her head, she knew it wasn't his quick, light step. It wasn't Jeremy, either; he invariably bounded up. This was a cautious noise, little more than a faint brush of shoe leather on wood, so slight as to make her wonder if there were really anyone there at all.

She was on her feet and springing across the room to slam and bolt the door. Below, the outline of a man on the shadowy stairs . . . She retreated, her pulses pounding. The man reached the landing and removed his hat.

"Mr. Winfield! I declare, you scared me witless." Her hand was at her throat, her face was white and frightened.

"Dear Mrs. Severance, my profound apologies. I was passing by on my nightly constitutional, and I chanced to notice your light."

She backed into the office, her heart racing with subsiding alarm, and he followed, squinting as his eyes adjusted to the lamplight. He laid his hat on the table and a thin film of moisture on the brim glimmered in the light. The night air rolling in off the sea was damp.

"It is as I feared," he remarked after a quick glance around. "You are alone. Mrs. Severance, I must speak sternly. Promise me you will have your window curtained. Sitting here, you are quite visible from the street below. More important, never stay here without male protection even during the day. It is most foolhardy."

His fine features eased into a smile that took the sting of admonition from his words, and she smiled back uncertainly and offered him a chair. She was never quite comfortable with this man even though he unfailingly treated her with the most gracious courtesy.

He had been an important man in town for several years, and now that his small private bank was one of the few to survive the crash, he was being given credit for immense sagacity; men came to him every day begging advice on a variety of problems having nothing to do with finance. He was assuredly an aristocrat—it showed in his straight, elegant nose and long, thin hands and feet, as well as his cultured Virginia accent. Mama used to say you could always tell the highborn from the common by the width of their feet.

But narrow feet notwithstanding, he puzzled her. She was used to hearty, virile men who filled rooms with their presence, men who were direct and uncompromisingly masculine and left you in no doubt as to where they stood. Tyler Winfield had a quality that was almost feline in its obliqueness. That was it—he reminded her of a sinuous, stalking, enigmatic cat. How silly. He was only a man, and there never was a man born who couldn't be figured out with a little time and patience.

Meekly she said, "I hadn't realized about the window. I shall have draperies made right away. Would you care for a cup of hot coffee, sir, to take off the chill? I can boil up a pot directly."

Tyler was cold. The moist air had seeped through to his bones during the miserable hour he had spent outside in the alley, waiting until Marin was alone. With a graceful wave of the hand he said, "I find these sea breezes invigorating, but if you plan to have coffee, I would be delighted to join you."

She bustled about, pouring water from the pitcher to the pot, adding coffee, building up the fire. He looked around the unadorned room, so ugly and bare compared with his own plush office, and discussed the pleasant weather, the arrival once again of the clipper *Flying Cloud,* the return of Mr. Edwin Booth after his tour of Australia and his thrilling appearance as the Duke de Chartres opposite Mrs. Caroline Sinclair. "Ah, thank you." He took the cup and saucer from her hand and sipped daintily. "Delicious, ma'am. A Colombian brew?"

"A mixture of my own devising, sir. I find blending improves the flavor."

"An excellent practice, one I follow with teas. I see you are an innovative, imaginative young lady."

Marin ducked her head modestly and took a swallow of the hot, strong coffee, her mind working fast. It was plain now that this man's appearance in her office late at night when she was alone was no accident, but what the devil did he want?

He placed his cup on the table. "I cannot tell you how pleased Mrs. Winfield and I are with our daughter's choice of a husband. Your brother is an admirable young man, as I'm sure *you* are well aware." He chuckled, and she smiled, too. "I see before them a long and happy union filled with the honest toil and simple pleasures that make up a dedicated Christian life." He gazed into space as though watching Kitty and Ethan strolling hand in hand down life's sunny trail, and she tried to imagine Kitty engaged in any form of toil or either of them satisfied with simple pleasures. "There is only one slight concern . . ." Tyler's lightness of tone indicated how trivial it was. "Ethan and I do not fully agree on his plans to support my daughter. Not his ability, his method."

Marin set her empty cup on the table beside his. "Method? I don't understand."

"My choice of words is poor. He and I have had a number of discussions, none of them entirely fruitful, as to his occupation after his marriage. He does not wish to join me in the bank, and I confess to the belief that his talents lie in other directions."

"Oh? What directions, Mr. Winfield?"

He chuckled again. "Mrs. Severance . . . my dear, would you give an old man the privilege of calling you Marin? You are as young—almost—as my own daughter, indeed I have come to think of you as another daughter."

"Please do, sir," she answered demurely, and thought, You old goat, you haven't spoken an honest word since you walked in that door.

"Well, then—Marin—I believe Ethan's wide experience of the world, his special abilities, would make him an invaluable asset to the firm of Gentry and Callendar . . . by the by, do you intend to retain the name?"

"We do."

"I should think Gentry and Company . . . well, no matter. What do you think of my idea?"

Warily she replied, "I'm not exactly certain what it is. Do you mean make Ethan a partner? If so, you should talk to my father. I only watch over the little, run-of-the-mill matters. All the big decisions are his."

"Modesty becomes you, my dear, but it is no secret that while James is, of course, the head of the firm, you are a young lady of astonishing acumen. It's well known that anyone dealing with James Gentry had better have Marin Severance on his side!" She poured them both more coffee, and he went on, "But we are speaking of hypotheticals, aren't we—as things stand."

His tone was smooth and kindly. Her muscles tensed. "I don't take your meaning."

"By July first of this year you must meet debts amounting to—let me see—eight thousand and fifty-three dollars, give or take a few cents. $3,274.82 to Jarvis & Company, New York. $1,812.35 to José Delgado, Valparaiso. $2,008.00 to Phillips, James, Limited, London. $958.80 to the California Steam Navigation Company, San Francisco."

Her mind floundered. He knew to the penny, even the creditors' names . . . What was he after? A steal of their pitifully small inventory at rock-bottom prices?"

"Not a great deal of money," she said. It had taken years of practice to learn how to show nothing in her voice or face.

"It is if you don't have it, and you do not."

She looked directly into his expectant eyes and said nothing. It had been her most difficult lesson, one still imperfectly learned, this keeping her mouth shut when every nerve strained to speak. Prolonged silence was a clever weapon; it embarrassed, it pressed one's opponent to fill the void, to say something. If you buckled, you invariably told too much and handed your adversary the advantage. She waited in apparent tranquillity as the silence lengthened.

Tyler cleared his throat. "I am prepared to make you an offer." Marin's wide, candid eyes never wavered. "Because we are to be relatives, I will advance the money to meet your debts."

"At what percent?"

"You misunderstand. I do not offer a loan but an investment in a firm that has good growth potential, one my new son-in-law will contribute to greatly."

The man wanted to buy a job for his daughter's husband. It was a high price, taking Ethan into the firm, but not impossible to meet. It would mean they could stay afloat a while longer, and perhaps later on Winfield's Bank would lend them cash to expand. Even if Ethan was a partner, she could keep the whip hand over him, for he was basically lazy and no more interested in merchandising than in banking.

She said, "You want a partnership for Ethan."

"In a manner of speaking. We might call it a junior partnership. In reality, I would be the partner, the silent partner—I do not wish my name painted on the door. Ethan would be quite free to develop in any direction he pleased." Put very well, Tyler thought. A masterful plan, one that had come to him only in recent days after a detailed investigation of Gentry and Callendar's financial condition, which had involved much quiet work, subtle pressure, one illegal entry, and a little judicious blackmail. Ethan Gentry wanted into his family's firm in the worst way and resented his sister's ascendancy, so—lead the boy along, hand him his heart's desire. In only a little time he would be bound hand and foot and would not dare breathe without applying to Tyler first. Then let him try to take Kitty away, and he would find himself hammered onto the cross.

Marin studied her hands, linked loosely in her lap, to all outward appearances a young woman calmly considering a friendly business proposition. Inwardly a welter of ideas tumbled through her mind so swiftly that she could examine none. Salvation was offered—at a price: Ethan would be on his father-in-law's hook forever. But if ever a man had brought his fate on himself . . . Tyler Winfield, a partner . . . but without him, no company at all . . . this was a last chance . . . grab it, then . . .

She drew a deep, steadying breath. What was it Vail had warned her against? He said she had a bad habit of stating the price she really wanted at the beginning of a bargaining session and trying to hold to it while her opponent battered her down. That was not good negotiation, she must remember that; people expected you to ask for more than you hoped to get. But you must know what your bottom price was. And oh, God, what was that? She must not ask too little. How much was a partnership worth? She leaped through some rapid mental arithmetic, snatched at a number, sent up a silent prayer, and said, "It's an interesting suggestion, worth discussing, though of course my father must make the final decision. What is your offer?"

"I have made it. I will relieve you of the previously mentioned debts."

"Yes, but what price did you have in mind for the partnership?"

"That is it."

She clamped her tongue until the hot anger subsided. "Now, Mr. Winfield, let us be serious. I would not even mention such a proposition to Papa. We grossed over two hundred thousand dollars last year."

"You also lost every cent in the criminal mishandling of Davidson's funds and will be forced to declare bankruptcy in less than a month if your current invoices are not met. I offer you a chance to stay in business."

Her nails cut into her palms, and she thought grimly, I must not lose my temper. He doesn't for a minute expect me to accept.

Her light laughter chimed in the quiet room. "You offer Ethan a mighty poor future if that's the way you see us. We'll get our money from Davidson's soon, and meanwhile we will stay in business. I think you fail to understand us, Mr. Winfield. Gentry and Callendar is a family concern, built through our own hard labor. Harry Callendar was a close, dear friend. We would not be willing to take just anyone in his place, even if our circumstances were as dire as you imagine." Throughout this little speech her voice remained level. She was even able to smile in gentle reproof.

Having probed and discovered the strength of the enemy, Tyler fell back to a prepared position. "Do not believe I underestimate your accomplishments, Marin. Why, my dear, I stand in awe of your success, and I hope to see you continue. My bank is a trust, and prudence must always guide my handling of depositors' funds—have we not recently suffered from the mismanagement of the imprudent?—but I think I could offer . . ." he paused, "fifteen thousand in addition to the payment of all debts. How is that for an offer?"

"Sixty-five thousand, Mr. Winfield. I could not consider less."

"My dear!" He got up, paced to the window, and looked down into the silent street. Even the back of his head conveyed shock and reproach. Marin stared at his back, trying to read in its still lines the measure of the man. Something was eating at him, something had driven him here tonight, and it wasn't just helping Ethan get a job. He could have done that in other ways. Oh, how ticklish it was to deal with a man whose weaknesses you didn't know. All she could do was press on cautiously, like Sophy in a strange room, and hope to avoid falling over the furniture. Her palms were damp, and the nervous quiver in her stomach was becoming more pronounced. It took conscious effort to keep her face blank.

Tyler looked back at her and sighed. "Because it is Ethan, because it is family, I will personally add five thousand dollars. Twenty thousand dollars for a half partnership in a bankrupt firm—more than fair, don't you agree?"

She answered clearly, sweetly, "I would like to work with my brother"—that was a lie—"and it would please Papa. Sixty thousand."

His thin features hardened and became still. "You are talking impossible numbers. Sixty thousand in these times—"

"Very well." She shrugged and started to rise.

"Wait! Thirty thousand dollars. Let us say no more."

"Let us say good-night," she replied flatly and began to clear the papers from her desk. Methodically, she locked each drawer, pulled down the top and locked it, too, as she did every night. Outside was the clop of horses' hoofs, the distinctive squeak of her own carriage rolling down the bumpy street. Jeremy's arrival would break this duel . . . she had to close, and close fast, with no idea of the man's real limit. Beneath his suavity he had a fierce temper, she had seen it flicker in his eyes.

Jeremy was coming rapidly up the stairs. She reached for her cloak hanging on the coatrack next to the hook where Harry's hat had always perched. Oh, how she missed Harry tonight! She slipped the cloak around her shoulders and fastened the clasp.

"Thirty thousand dollars, Marin," Tyler said softly. "You make a great mistake to refuse."

Perhaps so, perhaps so. She put on her bonnet. "Good evening, Jeremy. Mr. Winfield is just leaving."

"Evenin', Miss Marin. Evenin', suh."

"Good evening, Jeremy. Please wait outside for a moment and close the door. Miss Marin and I have almost completed our business."

Jeremy's eyes slid to Marin's. They looked at each other, and he eased out the door but did not quite shut it.

Tyler came closer, into the circle of lamplight. "As one older and possibly a trifle wiser, I advise you to consider my offer carefully. Discuss it with your father. All hinges on how much you wish to save your business."

"No, Mr. Winfield, all hinges on how much you wish Ethan to work here."

He seemed to grow taller and wider; color rose in his face and darkened until she wondered if he was going to seize her by the throat or topple over in apoplectic rage. Slowly the purple flush receded, leaving white patches under his eyes. Through his teeth he said, "Forty thousand dollars."

"And the nine thousand in debts."

"Eight thousand fifty-three—yes, that too."

Now she knew how sharp was the goad that drove him. With a little more push she might have extracted forty-five thousand or even fifty. "It's a bargain," she said. He bent over her hand, and as he raised his head, she felt a wave of thankfulness that she hadn't tried for more.

In a cordial fashion he said, "I am certain this commences a long and happy relationship," and in his eyes was the ugliest look she had ever seen.

It was very late when Jeremy turned the carriage into the drive and pulled up next to the side porch. Marin climbed down, and he clucked to the horses and rolled on to the stable. The big house was silent and dark except for a single lamp left burning near the door.

On the porch step she stopped and looked up. This brick house was a solid shelter. She could rest easy now, knowing she would not lose it. Inside all were sleeping: Papa freed for a few hours from memories of Rose and grief for Harry; Sophy no more blind than any other dreamer; Delphine fed and contented; Logan unhappy in her spinster's bed but shielded from a world that was too much for her; Carey and Belinda deep in untroubled sleep, too young to recognize the precariousness of life. All were secure now, or would be as soon as she got the company back on its feet. Later there would be time to figure how to rid herself of Tyler Winfield. She unlocked the door and went in.

On an evening late in May, Marin sat at the small desk in her bedroom, making up a list of last-minute things to do. Ethan's wedding was Saturday, and she had had to squeeze time from the constant pressure of business to be fitted for a new dress and to deal with a series of small domestic crises. Logan, who usually oversaw the running of the house, had been visiting Celia at Fontana all week, and until she had gone, Marin had not realized quite how much work she did or how necessary she was to everyone's comfort and convenience.

She wrote quickly, her pen making a light rasping sound in the quiet room. Everything had to be done in such a hurry; there were not enough hours in the day for the tasks that had descended on her now that Harry was gone. With new capital available she bore the responsibility that had always been his—deciding, alone and with advice from no one, what merchandise would sell two or three months from now when the ships came in. All the past week she had been ordering goods, fingers crossed, heart in mouth, praying each decision was the right one. All her energy of mind and heart was engaged in laying down bets on the future. She had none to spare for what was going on in the minds and hearts of those around her.

On Friday last she had offered Ethan his job, and although he accepted with expressions of pleasure, it had come as a surprise and a puzzlement how little time he had spent in the office since then. She had expected to find him constantly underfoot, a nuisance, until he became bored with business. Without a blink he had swallowed her story about a new credit line from the bank—she did not mention which bank—and glanced through the tall stack of ledgers she set before him, flipping the pages so quickly that she knew he was taking in nothing.

Halfway into the third ledger he looked up. "This is fascinating, sis, I am spellbound." The ends of his mouth turned down in smiling self-derision, and he shoved the cumbersome book away. "Just tell me about it in language even I can understand."

"That wouldn't be right, Ethan. Papa always says before you go into any business, look over the books yourself, don't rely on what someone else says."

He tilted his chair back and put his fine shoes on top of a partially opened desk drawer. "Oh, I trust you. Come on, make it easy for me."

You are making it easy for me, she thought with a stab of guilt. Sitting there smiling the familiar, jaunty smile that had always been able to win him anything, so handsome, so debonair, so dumb! Anyone with an ounce of sense would look at those books and see that the company had been on the ragged edge of bankruptcy at the beginning of the month; anyone who had been awake and paying attention during the past months of general collapse and ruin would wonder why any bank still in business would open a line of credit for such a shaky firm; anyone who could put facts into logical progression would ask which bank was performing this charitable act and would know the answer before he asked. Instead, just as she had expected, Ethan had looked at that intimidating stack of ledgers and refused to plow through the tedious figures.

But she had tried. Everything was there if he looked, nothing was concealed. If he had asked any of the questions he should have asked, she would have answered honestly. He had decided to go marauding after Kitty, and if he ended up in bondage to his father-in-law, he could blame no one but himself.

She said, "Truly, Ethan, you ought to study those books."

He gave a sigh of mock weariness, swiveling idly back and forth, put his hands behind his head, and yawned; he had been out very late the night before. With a dart of sudden anger at the memory of how late she had worked last night over those damnable books, she thought, So be it! and put on her bonnet. "I'm going over to the warehouse." She gazed consideringly at her reflection in the mirror attached to the inside of the cupboard door and tilted the pretty little hat farther off her face. "Do you want to come?"

He leaped up gladly, leaving behind the dull, humdrum ledgers with their telltale figures that could force him to face reality.

Now, in her bedroom, she set aside the list of things to do tomorrow and began to scribble another list, of minor household problems to present to Logan, thinking that she would stop soon and look in on the children before going to bed.

She was still writing when the clock in the downstairs hallway struck eleven. Shortly afterward there came a light tapping at her door, and a low voice whispered, "Marin, are you awake?"

She hurried to the door and turned the key in the lock. "Ethan, what are you doing here? What about your bachelor party?"

"Oh, that's over."

"Already? I expected you boys would be carousing till dawn."

"No. Can I come in?" He looked very subdued.

She opened the door wider. He moved past her with the fluid grace that was his alone and looked around at the charm of her bedroom.

"Very nice." He lounged over to the fireplace and stood gazing down into the embers dying in the grate, his blond head lowered, the orange light producing dancing shadows that hid the expression on his face. He glanced at her sideways, an odd, shy movement, and in that one quick glimpse she imagined she saw again the man who had come back from the dead last winter, a sick man with a wasted face and haunted eyes.

She closed the door and, worried, whispered, "What is it, Ethan?"

He shifted restlessly, shook his head, then suddenly slammed his fist into his palm. "This—this marriage . . . Marin, I can't go through with it."

She sucked in her breath. He had reasoned it out after all; he saw the trap Tyler had laid. "If it's that you don't want to work for the firm . . ." she began.

"What's the firm got to do with it? Of course I want to work for the firm. I belong there, and you had no right to keep me out this long. But I'm sure as hell not going to marry Kitty."

"Ethan, are you drunk?"

"I haven't had a drink in days, dear sister, and I've never thought so clearly in my life. How can I marry one woman when I love another? All week I've been trying to get up the nerve to talk to Logan. I came here the other day to see her, but she'd taken off to Fontana with that damn ice queen Celia. I should have gone after her, just picked her up, and . . . and . . ." He sat down on the sofa and ran his hands over his face distractedly. "It was always her, I guess, don't ask me why. There never was a girl more different from what I thought I wanted, her with her proper ways and her needlepoint and her books. But when I had the fever up in the Sierras, it was her I saw in my dreams, always her—scolding me for being such a fool and then smiling that loving smile. Sometimes I heard her singing, too. And when I got knifed that time in Sydney and I thought I was going to die, it was her I wanted to see once more, not Mother or Pa. You see, she knows me through to the marrow, and she loves me anyway, in spite of what I am and what I've done. I almost killed Pa. I let everybody down, Mother and Sophy and you. But for you the family would have gone under, do you think I don't know that?"

"Now, honey . . ."

"No!" He jumped up and began to pace. "Don't try to soothe me, and don't pity me. I don't want pity, all I want is Logan. Without her I'm a harebrained son of a bitch, but with her . . . oh, Marin, with her I could do such things!" His eyes came back to her, alight with hope. "She believes in me, she thinks I'm grand. When I'm with her, I believe it, too."

"Kitty thinks you're grand. She adores you."

"Kitty is a man-hungry baggage who can't wait to jump into bed and have at me."

"Ethan!"

"It's true," he said brutally. "I know a slut when I see one. I should, having had enough of them."

Marin stared at the floor, shocked speechless.

"So," Ethan dug in his inside coat pocket, pulled out an envelope, and handed it to her, "do one thing for me, sis. Give this to Logan tomorrow. She is coming home tomorrow?"

"Yes, tomorrow." Marin stared at the envelope. On it in black ink was written "Miss Logan Severance" in Ethan's sloping hand. "What is this, Ethan?"

"Only my life." He jabbed a finger at it. "I told her how I feel, I told her that I love her. If she—if she wants, I'll marry her anytime, anyway she wants it. If she wants it."

Marry Logan? the idea was stunning. Slowly she said, "You should give her this yourself, you should tell her yourself. Don't do it like this."

"She won't listen to me. You know how she can be—so goddamn stubborn, like all the Severances. No, you give it to her. Tell her . . . tell her I'll be at the Union Hotel."

Marin flung the envelope away, and it landed on the floor near his feet. "That's you all over, dumping the dirty work on someone else. You could make her listen, if you tried. God, Ethan, this is no way to treat a woman. You came home after all those years when she thought you were dead, you played with her, teased her, led her on. Then you dropped her and ran off chasing Kitty Winfield. Of course she won't listen to you. What woman would after the way you've behaved?"

"She will when she reads this." He picked up the letter and laid it on the sofa. "Give it to her as soon as she comes home."

"Suppose she turns you down, which she will do if she has any sense. What then?"

The light died out of his eyes. "I don't know. Marry my bundle of fire, I guess." He lifted his head, and back came the old, confident look. "She won't turn me down when she knows how much I need her. When she reads that letter, she won't turn me down." He bent and brushed her forehead with his lips. "Thanks, sis."

For a long time after he had gone she sat looking at the envelope lying on the sofa beside her, thinking back to the time she and Ethan had been children together. He had been a wonderful older brother, handsome, daring, full of fun, and she had loved him so. She still did, but she did not trust him an inch. Ethan had never grown up, only grown older.

She stared into the fire, thinking of those two together. Logan did not even suspect the kind of life Ethan led and would continue to lead, she did not know of his need for a constant variety of women, his desire for easy wealth, his unwillingness to work.

Faithful herself, she did not see that he was unfaithful to everyone, unable ever to keep his promises. She needed and deserved a good, loving man, but if Ethan was an eloquent on paper as he had been tonight, if Logan heard in his written words the throb of emotion that had been in his voice, she would accept him. For the moment he wanted her, or thought he did, but the time would come when he would go on to someone else, as he always did, and she would be destroyed.

Logan must never see the letter, it must be burned, Marin thought, and trembled. Did she have the courage to take such a risk? If Ethan found out, he would not forgive, but if he had the backbone to ask Logan about it, he would face her directly in the first place. A resolute man would never choose this roundabout, almost gingerly way of asking a woman to put her life in his hands.

Marin came to a decision as she did in business, quickly, setting all doubt aside. She would not burn the letter; she would keep it for the time being. Someday, when Logan was happily married to someone else, Marin would take the letter out and show it to her, and they would speculate together on the life Logan might have had if she had married Ethan.

Chapter 33

Tyler Winfield kept his promises. On the day his daughter was married forty thousand dollars was deposited to the account of Gentry and Callendar, all outstanding debts were paid, and the company was as tightly wedded to Winfield's Bank as Ethan was to Kitty.

The attitude of the business community toward Marin Severance underwent a subtle change during the months of struggle and collapse. In the past she had been recognized as sharp-witted, too sharp-witted for a woman, but it was believed that most of her bright ideas came either from her father, as she sweetly maintained, or more likely, from Harry Callendar. But now Harry was dead, and after watching Marin operate in the months following his death, no one could pretend any longer that James Gentry or any other man was the decisive factor in her success. It had to be acknowledged—behind the pretty face, the gentle manner, the soft accent was a soul of steel and a brain that never rested. Where in earlier days she had been referred to behind her back as "the girl" and businessmen dealt with Harry if they could, she was now sometimes called "that damned redhead" or "the Severance woman," but never "the girl." She was not well-liked but she was looked upon with wary respect. Marin recognized the change in attitude and savored it, for like all people with a taste for power she preferred deference to approval.

Logan seemed to have recovered from her shock over Ethan's marriage and was once more her placid, hardworking self. Delphine fussed over her and imagined that she had lost weight and looked peaked, but Logan had always been thin. She had recently stayed at La Gracia for two weeks and when she came home described to Marin the latest calamity to strike the Cermeno family. "Those people are in a terrible state, Marin. I fear for them, truly I do. What will become of them?"

In the parlor fireplace a log burned through and fell with a soft rustle. Marin got up to poke the pieces back onto the grate. "It appears to me that Vail will have to take care of them. Celia intends him to."

Logan stared at her long, thin hands. "It was dreadful the other day when those men came to take over the house. Corona and Soledad and Teodora simply collapsed on each other and cried, and Beatriz was no help. She stood like a ghost, not paying the least attention to the girls, looking at the house as if it were a person dying, and Aunt Isabel was sobbing and saying her beads over and over until I thought I would scream. We hadn't seen Armando all morning, and suddenly he came galloping up from the stables, firing his gun in the air and yelling at the top of his lungs. He jumped the horse over the porch railing and rode all through the house, upstairs and down, shooting out the windows and destroying everything he could lay hands on, all the time shouting in Spanish—curses, I suppose—and then he came roaring out and tried to set fire to the wooden part of the house. He wanted to burn the whole place down before they took it and was so frustrated because there's not much you can do to adobe. Well, finally Vail got hold of the horse's reins, and then Armando slid out of the saddle, laid his head on Vail's shoulder, and cried.

"When we finally got the family over to La Gracia, Vail took his guns away from him and locked him in Mr. Baldwin's study with a bottle of whiskey while Celia gave the girls laudanum and put them to bed. She's very angry with Vail. Terribly polite but distant. You know how she can be."

Marin selected a chocolate from the box Delphine had left on the lamp table, feeling little sympathy for Celia.

"When you think how almost all of Little Mountain is gone and how many of the oldest ranches are being lost altogether—she ought to give thanks she's only losing a little part of La Gracia. But she wants it all and Fontana, too."

"That's true, although I hate to think . . . oh, she's upset just now, but it will pass. After all, she has Vail, who should be enough for any woman, and Alida, too. Such a beauty, that child."

Marin's eyes flashed up. "Is she? I haven't seen her in so long."

Logan tactfully retreated. "She resembles her mother—the same black hair and blue eyes, but truth to tell she can't compare with my darling, sassy Belinda."

Mollified, Marin said generously, "Of course any child of Celia's would be pretty," and opened her book. She knew well the terror of impending poverty and dispossession but the Cermenos carried on over the good old days and their lost kingdom and how things ought to be while making no move to help themselves. Why didn't Armando go to work instead of hurling himself onto Vail and crying about injustice? Why didn't Beatriz and her sisters take in sewing or whatever else would produce a little cash? Great-grandpapa must have been an enterprising gentleman, or he never would have acquired all that land, but the stamina was bred out of this generation. She had no kind feelings for the chickenhearted.

August was unseasonably hot, and people grown accustomed to fogs and cool sea breezes sweltered and complained as the temperature rose. At month's end, when they had been married a little more than a year, Kitty and Ethan Gentry announced the birth of a son named Tyler George after his illustrious grandfather.

Kitty's family thought the boy a marvel. Ethan's family privately bemoaned the fact that the child did not take after his handsome father. Publicly they congratulated the new parents and prepared for the christening and the party to follow.

Sophy had mixed feelings. She knew this birth had reopened old wounds for Logan, but a new baby was always wonderful, and she wanted to get her only brother's child a special christening gift even if the mother *was* Kitty Winfield. Logan had promised to go with her, but on the day was felled by a headache so violent that Delphine sent for Charles.

He came down after spending a long time with Logan in her

room and saw Sophy waiting at the bottom of the stairs, her face upturned. She was smiling directly at him.

If I didn't know, I'd swear she could see, he thought, and before he could speak, she asked, "How is she, Charles? Should I go sit with her?"

"No need for that. Sleep is the best medicine for these minor indispositions."

She came closer. "Why such a scowl, Charles? What's the matter?"

His taut brows relaxed, and he began to smile. Her presence always made him smile. "How can you know what I look like?"

"Because you scowl in your voice, that's how. Truly, Charles, is she very ill?"

"Not at all. She will be quite herself in a day or so, though she will miss the christening tomorrow. You go shopping, Sophy, and take Miss Delphine with you. I would accompany you, but I have a lady in labor out on Mason Street and a gentleman down with malaria, and I must see them both before the noon hour."

"Oh, I don't need Delphine. Jemmy and I do very well by ourselves. Good fortune with your poor lady and gentleman. They have the best doctor in town." She stood on tiptoe, pecked at his cheek, and went off to find Jeremy.

Charles watched her walk briskly down the hall, treasuring the sight of her and the quick brush of her lips. It wasn't proper at all, but she did it whenever she thought they were unobserved, and so far he hadn't had the backbone to stop her. He must stop her the very next time she did it. Or the time after that.

In a town used to incongruous sights, Sophy and Jeremy still drew attention. Eyes turned and watched as the pretty blond walked from store to store holding the arm of the tall, lanky black man with the glowering expression and the low-slung Colt pistol. Few passersby realized that she was blind—her step was so quick and confident—but no man would have considered accosting her, not with Jeremy at her side.

She bought a fine blue wool wrapping shawl for the new baby and then proceeded to Mrs. Fletcher's shop to buy a pair of white gloves to wear to the christening. Her chat with Mrs. Fletcher brought back other memories. On leaving the shop she almost told Jeremy to take her to Mlle. Petra's millinery shop, then decided against it. For reasons she could only guess at, Marin had an antipathy for Petra that time had not diminished, and she was always under so much strain at work. No sense adding to it by bringing home one of Petra's bonnets.

Instead she said, "Take me to Mr. Vail's office, Jemmy."

"Yes'm. I'll get the ca'riage."

"Oh, it's only a block over and two down and such a lovely day. Let's walk."

At the corner of Kearney and Jackson they stepped into the street, and a hoarse voice bellowed, "There's the black bastard! Grab him quick—don't let him get away!"

A tremor passed from Jeremy to Sophy. He stopped short, and with a shattering flash of intuition she understood, jerked her arm from his grasp, and cried out, "Run, Jemmy, run!"

He was shaking life a man with the ague, but he did not move. She threw out blind hands, pushed him, and screamed, "For God's sake, leave me, Jemmy. Run!"

And then they had him. Around Sophy there were the noises of scuffling feet. She heard the hoarse voice growl, "Got you this time, you black ape. Get a good hold on him, boys, he's slippery!" and she cried, "Wait! Please, there's some mistake. I am Miss Gentry, and this is my employee, Mr. O'Connell."

There was loud laughter. Someone said, "No mistake, miss," and Sophy was jostled aside.

The voices and the feet retreated, leaving her in the dust of the street, in a dark world of unintelligible, terrifying sounds and movement.

She reached out. "Oh, please—will someone help me, please?"

A wagon rumbled heavily past, whipping her skirt, and the driver called, "This here's a roadway, lady. Get out of the street."

She was dizzy with shock and fright; her heart was racing toward exhaustion. She drew in a long, slow breath, and momentary calm came over her. She turned up her face, and the afternoon sun's warmth led her west. Cautiously she moved forward, placing each foot precisely, praying that no wagon would roar around the corner. Her shoe touched the plank of the sidewalk, she stumbled and felt the cloth of a man's coat under her hand. A man's warning voice said, "Watch it, honey. Keep your pretty fingers out of my pockets."

She snatched back her hand. "I'm sorry, sir. Could you tell me—am I near the Washington Building?"

"Right in front of your . . ." The man peered into her face and in a different voice said, "I beg your pardon, miss. You got someone in there? Here, take my hand."

"I can find my way if you'll be so kind as to start me up the stairs. Yes, I'm sure. Thank you."

Slowly she climbed, her hand clinging to the banister, the horror of that moment in the street rolling back over her. Up this last flight, turn right, down the hall twenty paces to Vail. Vail would fix things, Vail would do something . . .

By the time she reached his door, control was almost gone. She fumbled for the doorknob, flung open the door, and called, "Vail, are you here? Vail, I need you."

His step was clear and familiar as he came out of his private office. She hurtled into his arms sobbing, "They've taken him, Vail, they've taken Jemmy, and he didn't even try to run!"

Chapter 34

On the night before the court hearing Marin, Sophy, Vail, and Stuart sat in Gerald's office listening to him explain Jeremy's predicament in bald, concise words.

"This Mr. Beaumont claims he had a slave named Jeremy who would now be about thirty years old, that this slave was six feet tall, thin but well muscled, dark-complected, with two long scars across his right side over the ribs. We must grant that Jeremy fits the description. Mr. Beaumont claims he brought this slave and two others to California to mine gold for him in the fall of 1850 and that Jeremy, being of an obstinate and undutiful nature, ran away as he had twice before and made good his escape by hiding in the mountains."

"Beaumont is a cracker and a liar," Marin snapped.

Gerald frowned her down. "He is indeed a Georgian, but I advise restraint in name-calling, above all in the courtroom. It always pays to be courteous, particularly to people you despise." He looked around to see if the others had untoward remarks to make. No one spoke. "Now the problem is this. Mr. Beaumont claims Jeremy is his property and presents a reasonable story to back it up . . ."

Marin twisted in her seat and exploded, "Reasonable story! He's a liar. Jeremy was free when we met him. He works for me as a paid employee, and he's nobody's property."

"What proof do you have of that?"

"I just know . . . that is, Jeremy told me."

"He tells me he had no papers of manumission."

"Of course he hasn't. He's the son of a free man. His family has been free since the year one. Just wait till he testifies—he'll convince the judge."

"He can't testify, Marin. I can't put him on the stand."

"But why not?" Sophy burst out, tears coming to her eyes. She had been in tears most of the time since Jeremy was taken, blaming herself for his misfortune even though everyone told her how illogical that was.

"He is a Negro," Gerald explained quietly. "When whites are also parties, Negroes cannot testify in court any more than Mexicans can."

"Not even in his own behalf?"

"Not even then."

"But that's so unfair!" cried Marin.

"Certainly it's unfair. It is the law, and the law in this great democracy is whatever men in power decide it shall be, no matter what high-flown rhetoric you may have heard in Fourth of July speeches."

"But this is a free state . . ."

"I am weary of these interruptions. Sit down, Marin, and listen to me as attentively as if you were paying for my services. Jeremy cannot take the stand in his own behalf, but his friends can because they are white, and since they are also affluent and have standing in the city, they may be able to influence the outcome. I emphasize *may*. Don't start counting your chickens because so far in every case of this nature the runaway has been returned to the owner. I want you all in court tomorrow looking like the pillars of the community that you are. You especially, Stuart. A state legislator and a prospective congressman will make a tremendous impact. You, Marin, and you, Sophy, will be the most crucial witnesses." The two girls sat straighter. "Listen very closely once more to my explanation of Jeremy's problem, and then search your memories for the circumstances of your first meeting with him. I do not presume to tell you what those circumstances were, for only you can know, but remember—everything depends on what you say and exactly how you say it." Gerald paused to allow the words he had just spoken to sink in. "Now this is the crux of the matter: Mr. Beaumont states that his slave, Jeremy, ran away in the fall of 1850 and hid out in the mountains. Obviously persons such as yourselves, coming across the slave at about that time, would have no way of knowing his legal condition. Regardless of what you believed his status to be, the court unquestionably would return him to his rightful owner. However, anyone who knew your employee, Mr. Jeremy O'Connell, at some substantial time before that date and knew him to be a free man—well, as you can see, such testimony sworn under oath, on pain of perjury, would be invaluable. Together with the support of prominent friends it would quite probably establish Mr. O'Connell's free status and send Mr. Beaumont looking elsewhere for his lost property. Is everyone quite clear as to the situation?" He paused again to allow them to think about it. "Are there any questions?"

No, no, they all murmured. The ladies put on their cloaks, worried, thoughtful, and departed with Stuart their escort. Stuart looked neither thoughtful nor anxious. He had wanted no part of this business and considered Marin a fool to put herself in the forefront of a cause that was not popular. Jeremy was arrogant and swaggering, and the best people in town, most of them Chiv Democrats, considered him uppity. Stuart did not approve of slavery, but one did not like swagger in one's servants, whether they were slave or free. However, it pleased him that Gerald said his appearance on Jeremy's side was especially important because of his stature in the community. He, not Vail, was needed in this matter, and he had decided to willingly spend a little of his influence on an inferior. He only hoped Marin was grateful.

He bowed and smiled at Gerald as he went out.

Gerald and Vail were left alone in a room that suddenly seemed very quiet. Gerald pulled a bottle of French brandy from the lower drawer of his desk, poured a tot for each of them, and joined Vail beside the fire.

Vail asked, "What do you know about Judge Chaffee?"

"Not much, except that he's from Tennesse and a friend of Senator Gwinn's, which isn't good. Tennessee is a border state, so it's a toss-up as to his position on slavery, but we all know how Gwinn stands."

"Does he owe his job to Gwinn?"

"Uh-huh."

The two men sipped brandy in silence.

Gerald said, "Chaffee hasn't been in town long enough to get into trouble. No telling what mess he left behind in Tennessee, but I haven't enough time to pursue that. He's married, doesn't drink much, doesn't gamble, doesn't frequent the brothels, no one's been able to bribe him yet, he attends the Presbyterian church every Sunday—hell's bells, the man's a saint."

Vail's eyes gleamed. "I lived with a saint during my formative years, so I know the breed well. Chaffee sounds unreachable in the usual way. The thing is—" he swallowed the last of his brandy and set the glass on the floor, "the thing is, most saints are enormously proud of their virtue. A fine lawyer like you can surely turn that to advantage if you go about it properly."

"I take your point. Yes, he is a good man. We ought to be able to do something with that."

As Delbert Chaffee entered his courtroom, gratification welled within him. It was a fine beginning to each day, and he looked forward to it, this moment when he stepped from his chambers, when the bailiff called, "All rise," and people got respectfully to their feet with much scraping of chairs and nervous coughs. He never looked at them but moved with magisterial tread to the dais, aware of their anxiety, their tension, their fear. And well might they fear, for no one appeared in this room unless he was embroiled, one way or another, in a great dilemma.

Each day when he covered his plain business suit with the black robes of office, Judge Chaffee felt his meager height increase, felt himself expand, become a being apart and above ordinary men. Bill Gwinn had been right about him. He did have judicial temperament. He knew right from wrong and had no doubts about the difference. His reputation for probity, rare among San Francisco jurists, he guarded as a good woman guards her chastity. Not by the smallest misstep would he jeopardize his position on the bench. Although not an introspective man, he could admit (to himself only) that a tiny part of him enjoyed the prestige, the good pay, and the power, and he was proud of his self-honesty.

He did not dream that buried far beneath his forgivable human weakness lay impulses he hated and could barely control, desires that he suppressed in himself and condemned in others. Never did he shrink from listening to the details of a sordid case or from handing down a harsh sentence; the details were fascinating and the sentence necessary. Often, just to test himself, after studying a case but before the trial began, he would write down in a small notebook the way he thought the trial would go. It never ceased to amaze him, the regularity with which his original assessment and the final verdict turned out to be the same.

However, today's case was different. No vicious murderer or robber or common thug stood before him, but a runaway slave claimed by a friend of Bill Gwinn's. The law in these matters was comfortingly clear—runaways must be returned to their owners—

and ordinarily he would have made a quick decision and gone on to the next case. The trouble was, this particular slave had friends too, white people of importance. The judge had made no entry in his little notebook today.

Was the ebony-faced, stolid defendant sitting alone and gazing down at his handcuffs a runaway, or a free man, as his supporters maintained? Judge Chaffee stole a glance at the supporters. The whole overwhelming family, Severances and Gentrys, were present today, along with members of the public drawn to an unimportant hearing by the prominence of the witnesses. James Gentry, silver-haired and gaunt, with lively eyes and the thin, nervous hands of the invalid, fidgeted with his cane and then turned to murmur something to the giant of a man beside him. The judge's eyes moved on.

At first glance Vail Severance looked like the man who ought to be in the dock today, for all his fine clothes and cool self-assurance. He was a pleasant-spoken man, serious, notably abstemious, with no scandal attached to his name in this town of scandalmongers, yet there was something in the taut, hard-boned face, in the singular intensity of the gray eyes that the judge, who prided himself on his ability to read character in men's faces, had seen in the reprobates who regularly appeared before him, a reckless intransigence that inevitably led to evil deeds.

In the next row sat Ethan Gentry, related by marriage to Banker Winfield. Beside him was a dainty blond girl Judge Chaffee did not know, but who was certainly a comely little thing. Mrs. Marin Severance he had met once, briefly, at her brother's wedding. He had heard nothing against her except that she was too forthcoming for a woman, but as with Vail Severance, he saw an ungovernable quality in her face that he could not like. He would wager she led her husband a merry chase.

It was her husband who interested him most. Stuart Severance had been a power in the legistlature for years and was already running for one of California's two congressional seats, although the election was months away; he had switched allegiance and was no longer a Whig but a member of the new antislavery Republican party. A man fast on his feet; a man the judge could admire. Senator Gwinn was a powerful man and a benefactor, but Mr. Severance had power, too, and might soon have more. Besides, Gwinn was in Washington, thousands of miles away, and Stuart Severance was sitting right here looking at him. The best way to handle this imbroglio was cautiously, with a clear and unimpeach-able record, allowing everyone to have his say. The two lawyers in the case, Gerald Crown and Otis Marley, were contentious fellows who liked the sound of their own voices. Well, he would feel his way carefully, and let the evidence fall where it would. He brought down his gavel.

Mr. Beaumont, guided by his lawyer, presented his evidence with a thick Georgia accent and a straightforward manner. He had bought the slave, Jeremy, for fifteen hundred dollars in Savannah in February of 1850 with the intent of bringing him west with two other slaves to dig for gold in California. (The bill of sale was accepted into evidence.) From the beginning Jeremy had made trouble, but foolishly Mr. Beaumont had considered only the man's youth and strength and ignored the rolling of his eyes, which you could not overlook in selecting a slave any more than you could in a horse—they could both turn mean. Even so, Jeremy was his property, and Mr. Beaumont wanted him back.

Gerald opened with a genial, low-key statement that granted Mr. Beaumont's right to his property if such Mr. O'Connell had happened to be. All right-thinking men would agree to that. However, Mr. O'Connell was not Mr. Beaumont's slave, Jeremy, but the unfortunate victim of mistaken identity. He was a free man, and Gerald would now undertake to prove that such was the case.

First he called Stuart to the stand to testify to Jeremy's sterling character and impeccable record of service with the Severance family, and to state his firm belief that Mr. O'Connell was, indeed, a free man. Mr. Marley chose not to cross-examine. The next witness called was Sophy.

"I had traveled to Dead Man Bar with a childhood friend," Sophy related softly, her head tilted down. Sunlight gleamed on the curls beneath her bonnet and turned them to gold. "And—and I suddenly became ill."

"Speak up, child," the judge ordered with an indulgent smile. "The reporter must take down your every word."

"Yes, sir. I became ill, dreadfully ill. My—my friend ran away when he found out what was wrong with me. I had cholera."

There was a sharp intake of breath from the court officials and the spectators. All knew what cholera meant, knew that a survivor had been to hell and come back.

Sophy's voice went on, quiet but clear in the listening room. "I was alone in a bare cabin without water, without medicine, unable to help myself. I was shivering with cold and so thirsty. I was dying. Then I heard a voice calling to me, calling me back. The voice wouldn't let me go. I opened my eyes and saw Jemmy—Mr.

O'Connell—leaning over me, saying, 'Poor missy, I'll take care of you, missy.' He did care for me, Your Honor. My own mother couldn't have been more tender or more kind. He bathed my face, he held me when I vomited and then fed me the water I needed to live. He comforted and reassured me, he never left my side until my sister and brother-in-law arrived. He was truly a Good Samaritan."

The courtroom was utterly still.

Quietly Gerald said, "Thank you, Miss Gentry. Your witness, Mr. Marley."

Marley hesitated. He had decided as soon as he saw this witness that he would not touch her with a ten-foot pole. She was pretty and gentle, a little frightened and altogether captivating. He hated captivating witnesses unless they were his own. But there was a way to undo any harm she might have done without roughing her up and damaging his own case. He rose and came toward her slowly, maintaining an unthreatening stance.

"Miss Gentry," he intoned with a friendly smile, "never have I heard so poignant, so heartwarming a story. I speak for all here when I say I am moved by your sufferings and honor your courage. While at death's door you were aided by Jeremy, and it is most understandable that you wish to repay his kindness."

"Repay? I can never repay him. He is the finest of men."

Good, good, thought Marley. A little more, and we shall have you agreeing that you would lie for him. But then a tear appeared at the corner of Sophy's eye, and he asked hastily, "Miss Gentry, when did you first meet Jeremy?"

"Why, at that very time, when I was so ill. He didn't know me at all, yet he did what few others would." She turned to the judge, her blind eyes wet and wide. "Sir, my friend of many years, a white man, abandoned me for fear of his life. Mr. O'Connell, who owed me nothing, stayed with me, cared for me through a hideous, repulsive sickness, risked his own life because of the compassion in his great, good heart. A black man, Your Honor. A black, free man."

As Gerald led Sophy back to her seat, there was much clearing of throats and surreptitious digging for handkerchiefs. Judge Chaffee, deeply moved, made a pretense of jotting down notes until his emotions were under control.

"Gentlemen." He beckoned the lawyers forward, and the three men quietly conferred. "Off the record, Gerald," said the judge, "Stuart Severance's word is impressive, and Miss Gentry's testimony is heartrending. I declare myself to be most touched.

But you know that the Negro's pluck and good heart, which I do not deny, are not at issue here. The question remains, is he Mr. Beaumont's property? We have Mr. Beaumont's word that he is, and your witnesses, affecting as they are, do not contradict his claim with facts. I do not see where you are going."

"Bear with me, Your Honor. I would like the court to hear from Mr. James Gentry, Mr. Vail Severance, Dr. Charles Towle, Miss Logan Severance, Mrs. Delphine Whitmore . . ."

"Your Honor!" muttered Otis Marley in sotto voce indignation. "At this rate my learned friend will bring the entire population of the city before this court to no purpose but to prolong these proceedings."

Judge Chaffee peered sternly down his long nose at Gerald. "As you well know, counselor, I do not permit dilatory tactics in my courtroom. If we are to hear only more tributes to the Negro's moral character and unsubstantiated opinions as to his legal status, I must ask you to call a halt now. Do you understand me?"

Gerald looked crestfallen. "Yes, Your Honor, I shall try to make do. Allow me to call only one or two more witnesses, and I guarantee to conclude before the noon hour." The judge eyed him with skepticism, and Gerald earnestly added, "It is a man's freedom we are determining, your honor, not a matter of dollars and cents."

"It's dollars and cents to my man," remarked Marley.

"We cannot put a price on freedom, Otis," the judge said reprovingly, and liking the sound of it, went even further. "Freedom is dearer than rubies. Reflect on that, gentlemen. I'll allow you one more witness, two if you must, Gerald. No more."

"Yes, Your Honor. Thank you."

Marley went back to his seat and talked quietly with his client while Vail Severance was being sworn.

Gerald stood reading over his notes, allowing time for the spectators—and the judge—to fully take in this witness's forceful presence and to recall his social position, his wealthy wife, his many connections with the rich and powerful. "Ah, Mr. Severance." Gerald walked slowly to the witness stand. "Are you, sir, the brother-in-law Miss Gentry mentioned as coming to her rescue?"

"I am."

"She has testified that at that time she was suffering with cholera—a formidable disease, as we all know to our sorrow. There are few present in this courtroom who have not lost a friend or loved one to its savagery." A murmur and a sigh in the crowded room. "Mr. Severance, please describe for the court the condition in which you found Miss Gentry in that lonely, faraway mountain cabin."

"She was still in the collapse stage of cholera, desperately ill, with frequent vomiting and violent purging. Her limbs were cramped, the skin was cold, blue, and bathed in sweat. Her fingers had the typical wrinkled, shrunken appearance, her tongue was cold, her pulse weak, her thirst intense. Cholera victims, even strong men, commonly die in this critical stage. That she survived it is as much a tribute to Mr. O'Connell's nursing care as to her own reserves of strength. Shortly after we arrived, her fever rose, her heart rate quickened, and the delirium increased. But though the night was difficult, she held on. Eventually she recovered and came back to the blooming health you see her in today."

"Thank you, Mr. Severance," said Gerald softly. His eye cut toward the opposition. "Your witness, Mr. Marley."

Marley advanced with an expression of smug content. He was about to nail this witness and nail him hard.

"Mr. Severance," he began smoothly, "you have testified most knowledgeably as to Miss Gentry's condition and set forth the opinion that without this slave's ministrations—he gestured negligently toward Jeremy—"the appealing young lady would have died. Yet it would, in fact, take a physician to make such a judgment. Are you, perhaps, a physician?" He let the question fall almost casually and smiled.

There was the slightest of hesitations, and then Vail said, "Yes, I am."

A ripple of sound passed through the room, and Judge Chaffee cracked his gavel sharply.

"Indeed," remarked Marley, so nettled that for a second time he forgot the stricture of his mentor when he was reading law and asked a question that he did not already know the answer to. "And what kind of physician are you, sir? A hydropath or homeopath? An electic or botanist or possibly a phrenologist?" Marley allowed himself a scornful chuckle, and his voice rose dramatically. "A variety of quacks infest our fair city, Mr. Severance. Which kind are you? From what medical school did you graduate?"

His face sober and his eyes amused, Vail answered, "Harvard Medical School."

Judge Chaffee brought down his gavel several times, glared ferociously at the suddenly noisy crowd, and then turned interestedly to watch Marley try to climb out of the hole he had just dug for himself.

Marley cleared his throat and shot a bitter glance at Gerald, who bowed slightly in his chair, his teeth showing under his clipped mustache.

"Harvard," Marley rumbled, pulling himself together. "Most impressive, sir. Yet you do not use the title of doctor. Why is that?"

"I see no need, since I am no longer in general practice," Vail answered in a flat tone that dared Marley to probe further.

"Ah, yes. And though Miss Gentry was on the point of death when you arrived and according to your own testimony the cholera then progressed in severity, it is your opinion, your *professional* opinion, that it was the slave Jeremy who saved her. I submit to this court that it was, rather, the fortunate presence of a learned and highly trained physician that pulled her through. Isn't that the truth, Mr. Severance?"

"No. But for Jeremy O'Connell I could have done nothing. She would have been dead before I got there. It was he who used hot applications to keep up her body temperature, he who gave her water to assuage her thirst and prevent dehydration. It was his intelligence, skill, and selfless courage that saved her when most people would have passed by on the other side. He is, as Miss Gentry said, truly a Good Samaritan."

When Marley again took his seat beside his client, he knew he had been sniggled with bait that should not have fooled a fledgling, switched off the track and done in. Though there was no one to blame but himself, he resolved to pay Gerald back in kind one day. With a cool smile he cut off Beaumont's furious whispers. "Do not concern yourself, sir, we are in fine shape. All of that was sound and fury, signifying nothing. Indeed Miss Gentry, in her zeal, aided our cause by stating that she first met him at the time of her illness. She was a stranger, yet he helped her. That means she could not have known his status before that date, and neither do any of the others." He glowered at Gerald. "Let the bastard try to repair that."

Gerald called Marin Severance to the stand.

Marin stepped past Logan and Delphine and walked forward with her midsection quivering and her heart beating double time. Before the hearing began, Gerald had said he might or might not call on her, depending on how things were going, and she had earnestly prayed that he would not. It was exciting to read about trials or watch others sitting in that chair just below the judge, with every eye on them and every word and fleeting expression weighed and measured, but how terrible to be on the spot yourself and know that the outcome might depend on your wit and presence of mind. Jeremy sat alone, his handcuffed hands hanging between his knees, his dark face blank and stupid. But she knew him so well; she could see the wildness and the fear in his eyes. Oh, why had they handcuffed him? Even if he bolted the courtroom before the bailiff shot him, where could he run? The burden of his freedom was on her shoulders.

The clerk held out the Bible. With her gloved hand on it she swore before God and all present to tell the truth and only the truth. She glanced up at Judge Chaffee, her wide, awed eyes framed by her prettiest bonnet. How could she possibly do as Gerald had advised and imagine the judge in his underdrawers when he looked like he'd been born with black robes and a full head of white hair? With a graceful flutter of skirts she took her seat.

Gerald was standing before her, smiling his impudent, mocking, comforting smile. The knot in her stomach eased.

"Mrs. Severance," he began, "Jeremy O'Connell is your employee?"

"Yes," she answered with a slight quaver. She swallowed and cleared her throat. "Yes, my husband and I have employed him as our carriageman and houseman for over five years. He has been a loyal, hardworking, exemplary servant."

"Exactly when and under what circumstances did his service with you begin?"

"In October 1850 in Dead Man Bar. Mr. Severance and I had found my sister horribly ill and being cared for by Mr. O'Connell. I offered him employment, he accepted and has been with us ever since."

Gerald gazed at the floor, seeming for the first time unsure as to what question to ask next. Then, as though starting up a social conversation, he remarked, "I suppose, like all of us Californians"—his smile included the entire room—"you have come here from somewhere else, Mrs. Severance. What is your home state?"

"Maryland. My father owned a horse farm near Baltimore."

"Ah, you are a Southerner then, ma'am. And did your father own slaves?"

"Yes. At the time we left to come out west, our people numbered twenty-six."

"Men, women, and children?"

"No, that's only the adults. We had nine children born at the farm."

"Altogether, then, your family owned thirty-five slaves, a substantial number . . ."

Otis Marley was on his feet. "Your Honor, Mrs. Severance's background is interesting but hardly relevant to this case. Learned counsel is on a fishing expedition, searching for a way to complicate a very simple matter."

Judge Chaffee tilted back his head and scowled at Gerald. "I warned you before, Mr. Crown, I do not take kindly to a deliberate muddying of the waters. Let me see your destination or cease this line of questioning."

"Yes, your Honor, I apologize," Gerald murmured humbly. "I have only one or two more questions, Mrs. Severance, and then you may step down. Now, we have established that yours was a slave-owning family."

"But we were very close to our people. They were treated well, and my father never separated families. When we left Maryland, he refused to take the highest bid for our best horse trainer because the buyer didn't want the man's wife and two children. Papa said that if he couldn't keep a family together, he wouldn't sell, and he ended up accepting a lower bid at quite a loss."

"But he did sell his slaves? He did not manumit them?"

"Well, no. He had to get his capital out."

"Of course. So, ma'am, you are a Southerner from a salve-owning family. You are not, by any chance, an abolitionist?" Gerald's eyes twinkled.

"My stars, no! That is all a great lot of nonsense that the Northerners have invented just to stir up trouble."

"And if you came across a runaway slave, you would feel duty bound to hand him over to his owner?"

"Indeed, yes. Anything else would be . . . well . . . like stealing."

Absently Gerald fingered his immaculate shirt cuff. Then he looked sharply at Marin, all humor gone, his narrow face intent. "When you came across Mr. O'Connell in a lonely cabin in the mountains, a place where no other Negroes worked, an excellent place to hide out if one was hunted, why did you not suspect he was a runaway? Why did you accept his story that he was a free man?"

Marin looked up. The spectators, the judge, and even Gerald were a blur, but she saw Jeremy's eyes plainly. Her palms were damp, but inside she felt a great calm. She said, "Because I knew him before I left Maryland. I knew him to be a free man."

Beaumont was on his feet, bellowing, "He's my nigger, by

God!" and it seemed that only his lawyer's restraining hand kept him from leaping over the table and strangling Marin. The general noise in the room drowned out the judge's gavel at first, but his steady pounding and fierce glare had its effect, and gradually the tumult lessened until his voice could be heard.

"Another such unmannerly uproar, and this court will be closed to the public. You, sir," he said icily to Beaumont, "will sit down and contain yourself or be subject to the penalties of contempt."

Slowly Beaumont sat, puffing and blowing, his face purple with fury. Judge Chaffee leaned down toward Marin.

"You state that you knew Jeremy O'Connell in the East, ma'am, and that he was free at that time?"

"Yes, Your Honor." Marin gazed up at the judge with candid eyes. "I first knew him in Virginia at my Aunt Vetta's. He worked for my aunt, and he was a free man, born free because his daddy and mama were free. That's an unusual situation in Virginia, sir, and everyone in town knew about it. He was very well liked."

The judge looked from Gerald to Marin and back to Gerald again. "Continue examining the witness, Mr. Crown."

"Thank you, Your Honor. Mrs. Severance, please elaborate on your first meeting with Mr. O'Connell."

Marin turned slightly, speaking at much to the judge as to Gerald. "My father, James Gentry, was Virginia-born, and being an adventurous gentleman, he traveled a great deal in his youth. But his sisters, Vetta and Jessie, they stayed home and never did marry, so when Grandpa and Grandma Gentry passed on, my aunts inherited the home place in Montrose, Virginia, which was only right, Papa said, and they live there till this day. We often received letters from them, but I had never met them. Then, in the year 1844, while Papa was traveling west to see if our family should move out here, my mother decided I ought to know my relatives." Marin lifted her eyes to the judge. "In case we did move way out here and I never got to know them, you see."

Judge Chaffee, for no very clear reason, felt obliged to agree, "Yes, I see," and then was vastly irritated with himself.

Leaning on her arm, Marin continued confidentially, "So I took the train down to Virginia and stayed the summer at my aunts' farm. Mr. O'Connell lived with his wife, Seline, in a little house right near the big house. He was their gardener and handyman—he can fix anything, your honor. Aunt Vetta often said she didn't know what she would do without him. Seline was their cook, and a seamstress, too. While I was there, she made me a blue dress rather close to the color I'm wearing today, and when

I got home, my mother said she'd never seen such tiny stitches."

Judge Chaffee turned his face away and gazed out the window.

Gerald asked, "Then, Mrs. Severance, you declare unequivocally that you knew Jeremy O'Connell in 1844 in Virginia, that he was at that time known to have been born a free man and so could not possibly be Mr. Beaumont's slave, Jeremy."

"Indeed I do."

"Your witness, Mr. Marley."

Marley got to his feet, his mind sorting through a number of possibilities. That innocent-eyed young woman on the stand wouldn't know the truth if it walked up and slapped her in the face, she was perjuring herself with every breath, but it would cost him more than his client's case to come right out and call the wife of Stuart Severance a liar. He had to tangle her in her own deceptions, lead her into such contradictions that her story fell apart of its own deceit. She was frightened—her voice had trembled as she took the oath. That was his advantage. He would pit his trained mind against her amateurish inventions and let her impeach herself.

In a voice as sweet and smooth as warm honey he began, "Ma'am, your mention of Virginia brings back happy memories of my own youth, when I also visited in that beautiful state." He paused to ruminate on the many attributes of Virginia. Then, with a gentle smile, "And you are such a charming and very young lady. 1844 . . . twelve years ago. You must have been exceedingly young, a tiny child. So young, in fact, that perhaps your memory is a trifle faulty."

Marin ignored the appeal to feminine vanity. "I was twelve, sir, Old enough that my mother allowed me to travel by train all the way to Virginia with only my maid in attendance. It was a great event for me, my very first trip alone, and I remember every moment as clear as if it were yesterday."

Marley knew that if he turned to look, Gerald would be smiling, the whole damned phalanx of Gentrys and Severances would be smiling, and the knowledge goaded him. "I see," he said in a tone slightly less warm. "And you say—you *say* that the O'Connell you knew had a wife named, most poetically, Seline. Where is that wife now? Did this noble, upstanding fellow abandon her? Where is she, madam?"

Marin sighed and closed her eyes against painful memory. "That is the sad part. Seline took the cholera and passed on, although Mr. O'Connell gave her the most dedicated care. That's where he learned what to do for cholera and why he worked so hard to save my sister. He said he didn't want to see another fine woman die of that dreadful disease. It was a great tragedy for him, losing Seline like that. She was so pretty and there never was another couple, black or white, more devoted, even though they had no children. That's the reason he came to California—to forget the past and strive to make a new life, which he has done so successfully."

All the spectators were busy picturing the happy home, the loving couple sundered by death, the heartbroken widower courageously coming West to start life anew, as they themselves had done.

With sarcasm he did not attempt to hide Marley inquired bitingly, "Madam, are you asking this court to believe that, contrary to all reasonable expectations, a Negro whom you *just happened* to know in Virginia as a free man and a servant of your aunts *just happened* to come across Miss Sophy Gentry quite by accident at the moment she most needed help in a mining camp in the high Sierras, and he then cared for her, not knowing she was your sister? I repeat, madam, are you asking the court to believe such an outlandish, trumped-up, shameless, humbugging string of fabrications?"

Sober, unwavering, Marin replied, "Sir, it is a fact that has led me to reflect often on the hand of Providence in our affairs. How else to account for such an amazing and beneficent coincidence?"

There was a respectful hush in the courtroom, for the last words were very like a prayer.

Into the silence the judge asked, "Are you through, Mr. Marley? Then you may step down, ma'am. Have you more witnesses to call, Mr. Crown?"

"No, Your Honor."

"Gentlemen, see me in chambers. Court is adjourned."

In his small office in the rear of the building Judge Chaffee sat behind his desk and contemplated the hairs on the back of his hand while the two lawyers waited deferentially. There was only one issue: was that bright-haired, sweet-faced girl the most accomplished liar in Christendom, or had she told the plain, unvarnished truth? At the beginning of her testimony he had been inclined to disbelieve her, but her eyes, her enormous, honest eyes there at the end, the heartfelt conviction in her soft voice when she spoke of Providence . . .

Otis Marley was a known terror in the courtroom, the judge had seen him demolish many a strong man, yet Mrs. Severance had not once faltered under the barrage of the lawyer's scorn. As she told it, her unlikely tale seemed utterly plausible. That was the problem. She was so calm, her story was so neat, every detail was perfectly recalled, but it had been Judge Chaffee's experience that an honest person under the pressure of cross-examination, faced with the threats and unknown pitfalls of the courtroom, was usually ill at ease. The voice fluttered, the eyes darted, the hands twisted with a life of their own. Often the testimony ended in a shambles. It did not always happen, but it happened often enough to give the judge pause.

Judge Chaffee looked at the waiting men. "Well, gentlemen, it comes down to a question of credibility."

Otis Marley cleared his throat. "If I may, Your Honor, my client is a man of known probity. It is a sad misfortune that his good friend, Senator William Gwinn, is not here to testify to his character, but is in Washington overseeing the affairs of our federal government."

Marley had a wart on the right side of his nose that wiggled when he talked, and it looked particularly unattractive to Judge Chaffee this morning. The judge had never admitted to anyone, even himself, how desperately he craved an appointment to the federal bench, and Marley's delicate reminder of Gwinn's power in that direction stirred unpleasant sensations. His need to see himself as a man of shining integrity outweighed even a federal judgeship. "Indeed," he remarked coldly, pushing away the image of himself presiding in the district court, and retreated into silence.

Moments passed, and the judge was about to announce that he would take the matter under submission when Gerald spoke.

"Your Honor, in considering the merits of Mr. O'Connell's claim of freedom, I would beg you to keep in mind the remarkable nature of the man. His legal status, not his character, is at issue, and in that regard we are faced with directly conflicting testimony. In such an impasse the trier of fact must look to sources of the heart as well as the mind to resolve the question.

"Your Honor," Gerald rolled onward with heightened fervor, "this is without doubt the most difficult case ever to come before a San Francisco court. Before trial began, I was asked what manner of man was sitting on it, and I was able to reply, 'A jurist virtuous, compassionate, and wise, who will see past the superficial to the heart of the matter.' Your Honor, Mr. Beaumont is not wicked, he is merely mistaken. We have Mrs. Severance's prior knowledge of Mr. O'Connell's free status. We know of his exemplary character." His resonant voice dropped so low that the judge had to strain to hear. "Sir, to stand against the wind, to refuse the easy path takes great strength of purpose and humbleness of heart, but before that God to whom we all pray I have faith that Your Honor harbors both qualities in abundance. Jeremy O'Connell's fate is in your wise hands."

"Oh, Jesus," said Otis Marley.

Judge Chaffee's silver brows drew together. He never used profanity and did not like to hear it from others. As Gerald had rightly pointed out it was a difficult case, but now he saw a way through it. Many a judge's reputation had been made by the flair and originality of thought in his decisions; the way he would write it, solid as oak, no higher court would lay a hand on it. Several felicitous phrases had already occurred to him. He felt good, he felt warm, it would be something to tell his wife about tonight. A jurist virtuous, compassionate, and wise . . .

He said, "Thank you, gentlemen. Case is submitted. My decision will be handed down within the week."

Chapter 35

Autumn arrived with only the scorching rhetoric of a presidential election to heat up the cool, clear days. The new Republican party had nominated the former California senator, John C. Frémont, whom the South loathed. The Democratic candidate was elderly, pussyfooting James Buchanan, a Northerner not unreasonably opposed to slavery. Buchanan won the job he had wanted for so long, but his victory was painfully narrow, clear evidence of the nation's bitter division to anyone who cared to look. No national notice was taken of the fact that in the same election California chose a new congressman, Stuart Severance of San Francisco.

After a celebration party notable for its good-fellowship and the quality and quantity of liquor served, Stuart left for Washington on the steamer *Golden Age*, taking with him his father's admiration and a certainty that he was meant to do great things. The loss of most of Little Mountain's land had put him out of the cattle business, but election to high office opened up new and exhilarating prospects. As Glenna had said at their last secret meeting, there were now no heights to which he could not climb.

For Marin life was not as good. She could not have what she wanted most; it was difficult even to see Vail alone now that Celia was living in town. At times she wondered how she would survive if she did not have her children to love and to worry over. Carey was easy to live with, but in her beautiful little girl she sometimes saw herself—agile of mind, quick of temper, and with a will of tempered steel. Belinda, for her own sake, had to be curbed, and it took much of Marin's energy and determination to do it. Gentry and Callendar took the rest. As she had expected, Ethan accepted his share of the profits and left the running of the business to her. Tyler Winfield was an irritant, but he was, at present, absorbed in his grandchildren, for Kitty had presented Ethan with another child, a girl named Dorothea and called Dottie.

Stuart wrote home with moderate frequency, but he did not step off the boat onto the San Francisco wharf until a few weeks before the election he hoped would return him to Congress for another two years. Marin stood at his side while he gave a statement to the press, and attended every speech he made. His voice was resonant and reached the back row of the largest auditoriums, he was good at the florid oratory everyone expected, and he was tall enough to be easily picked out in a crowd. He won handily.

Late on election night he made a long and rousing victory speech on the front porch of the house to a torch-lit crowd of well-wishers. In the backyard Sophy sat on a bench in the summerhouse Marin had built the year before and tucked the last leaves into the wreath she had plaited from strands of ivy. She put it on her head.

"There. How do I look?"

"Like a wood nymph," said Charles. She had dragged him back to the summerhouse, complaining that Stuart's speeches gave her a headache. They had been there for almost half an hour, and he had not yet thought of a way to get her back to the party in progress at the front of the house.

"Quit pacing and sit beside me, Charles. I have something to tell you." He sat, suddenly nervous for no reason he could think of. "What would you say if I told you I was going to marry Tom Anderson?"

It was odd, how one could go hot and cold at the same time. He said, "I wish you every happiness. You deserve it."

"Do you think I can be happy with Tom?"

"He is a fine man."

"A fine man whom I don't love."

"But you said . . ."

"I gave him his walking papers today. He won't be coming around here anymore."

Charles, who was not a slow thinker, felt simultaneous relief and befuddlement. After a silence he remarked dryly, "You've already sent George Winfield away. Now Tom. You are prodigal with your suitors, my dear."

"I don't save what has no value." She bent forward to rearrange her skirt. The wreath slid rakishly over one eyebrow and fell to the ground. "Charles, when I went blind, you told me the truth . . . that there was no hope of a cure. When I acted like a hysterical child, you told me that, too. It couldn't have been easy either time. Will you be honest with me now?"

"I'll try," he replied slowly, wondering what he was committing himself to.

"Tell me—what is the night like? Can we see the town from here?"

"Yes, it's a spectacular view. There is no fog, and the lights twinkle like fireflies. Hundreds of ships are anchored in the harbor, and their riding lights wink as they rock. Far across the bay there are pinpoints of lights. Oakland, I suppose. I doubt we can see Benicia from here."

"Is there a moon? Are there stars tonight?"

"Thousands of stars, a path of stars through the sky. The moon is full and white."

She turned her face to his, and the pale light gave her skin and hair a silvery sheen. "What do I look like now? Have my eyes gone all small and strange? Am I still a little pretty?"

"Your eyes are as lovely as ever. And just as expressive . . . You are no longer pretty, Sophy. You are beautiful."

She chuckled at that. "How vain I am. Even if you're lying, it's a kind lie."

"I'm not lying."

"Then don't lie to me now. I've done everything you asked of me, taken up my life as if nothing had happened, gone to parties, danced with men who bored me, even let one or two of them kiss me—what do you think of that? I have taken your prescription faithfully all this long, long time, and just as you promised, I found the man I can truly love. He is still you, Charles." Her hands went out to him in appeal. "I love you, and only you, most dearly. I can live with the blindness, I can live with anything if I am your wife. Tell me if you care for me just a little. Tell me the truth."

Old memories returned. Her child's face uplifted and laughing in that moment years ago when he first saw her through a dirty windowpane. Her face, terrified and disbelieving when he told her she would never see again. Her face, in sickness and in radiant health, happy, sad, angry, loving . . . He fought down the rising desire and said nothing.

She whispered, "I know you love me, I feel love surrounding me whenever I'm with you, but you will not speak. Take a good look at me. I'm no longer a little girl waiting for her first beau, I am twenty-three years old, an age when girls are either married or on the shelf. But I'm not meant to be an old maid, I need a home and babies and my own man. Do you want me to end like Logan, beaten and old before my time, living without the man I love? I can't be like her, I'll fight for what I want! Oh, Charles, you do love me, don't you?"

Professional composure came to his aid.

"You know I care greatly for you and for your well-being."

Her hands fell to her lap. With a shamed laugh she said, "I guess I've put my foot in it again. All this time I thought if I did what you asked, if I showed you that it wasn't just a schoolgirl crush . . . But I was wrong. You were trying to tell me in a kind way that you really don't love me. No wonder you don't come to the house much anymore—you never know when I'm going to throw myself at you. Well, you can come anytime you like from now on, for I'll never do it again."

The hurt in her voice, the humiliation in her flaming face burned through him as even her declaration of love had not. Every reason he had given himself for never speaking went down before the strength of his need. "Oh, darling, don't!" he said in a muffled voice, and the soft little body he had cared for with such detachment was in his arms, where he wanted it, his face was buried in the sweet-smelling curve of her neck. "Of course I love you, how could I help it? I've loved you for years, since long before you knew I existed. Oh, my Sophy, I used to watch you walk down the street with your pretty skirts swaying, I saw you in shops and restaurants . . . I used to follow you sometimes, isn't that a disgraceful admission? I'd find out where you were going to be and then be there, too, just to look at you from a safe distance . . . Sophy, stop crying."

"I'm crying because I'm happy . . . and mad. If you cared so much, why didn't you ask someone to introduce you? In all the years you've been my friend why haven't you spoken up?"

He took her arms from around his neck, pulled out a handkerchief and dried her face. She smiled, her face radiant, and tried to embrace him again. He took her hands firmly and held them. "Darling, I want you to listen to me calmly and sensibly."

"I don't feel sensible, not when you call me darling."

"Well, one of us has to be. I do have reasons for acting as I have, odd though I must seem to you." He drew a quick breath. "Sophy, I am not like the other men you know, big, hearty, handsome men who can aspire to a girl like you. I have been an invalid a good part of my life. I have chronic bronchitis and asthma that could grow serious someday. Twice I nearly died of pneumonia. You know that I am a cripple, but you don't realize how badly twisted I am. My left leg is wasted, and my foot turns outward so that I walk more like a duck than a man. As for the rest of my appearance—if you could see me, if you looked once on my face, you could not imagine yourself in love with me. I am—I am not just a plain man, Sophy. I am ugly."

"I did look on your face, more than once," she answered tenderly. "Don't you recall leaning over my bed and talking to me when I was so sick? I wasn't blind then, I saw you—a pale young man with the kindest eyes in the world and a smile so sweet that I thought you were the angel of light."

"You were desperately ill then, delirious most of the time. Don't rely on your memory of me then, for nothing was really as it seemed to you."

"So you would have me believe you are grotesque and deformed? Very well, I'll take another look." Smiling, she reached up, and her fingers fluttered over his face. "A high forehead. Silky hair—I remember it was fair, like mine. Deep-set eyes. A thin, straight nose. Rather full lips with a definite curve to them—are you a voluptuary, Charles? A long, firm, *stubborn* chin. Splendid side-whiskers. Ears that fit neatly close to your head. Nothing bizarre so far. You have a good height but are, I confess, a trifle skinny. I'll fatten you up after we're married."

"Sophy, please." He pulled away from her light touch. "I'm a sickly cripple, a homely man who could never compete with men like Tom and George if you could see."

"Do you mean, I'm so shallow that if I saw a more handsome face, I would promptly fall in love with it and never treasure your qualities of mind and heart? I believe I have just been monstrously insulted."

"You know I didn't mean that. In the early days, before your illness, I didn't declare my feelings because I was very busy building my practice."

"You were afraid I'd turn you down, that's what. Men are supposed to be the logical sex, but look at you. You walk into rooms filled with contagious disease and don't turn a hair, you like nothing better than to try your luck with the ponies—oh, I know about your trips out to the racetrack. You gamble your money and even your life, but you wouldn't gamble your pride. You wouldn't tell the girl you love that you love her."

He reddened to his ears, and although she could not see his sheepish face, he turned away and looked down at the bay. "I am a fool, I admit it. I'm also cranky and unsociable. It isn't in me to be warm and outgoing like you."

"Do you want a list of my defects? I assure you I have thousands, which you will discover in due time."

As if she had not spoken he went on, "And though my health has been good the last few years, I can't guarantee the future. I could get sick and be unable to support you."

"My darling, I can't guarantee tomorrow morning, no one can. All I ask is that whatever comes, good or bad, we share it. Isn't that what marriage means? I can't imagine a future that doesn't include you. If you feel the same, then what is to prevent us?"

They sat for a while holding hands, closer to each other than either had ever been to any other human being. Then soberly, Charles said, "There is more to tell you, Sophy. You don't know everything about me."

"You haven't a wife and nine children hidden somewhere?"

"No. But when you hear what I have to say, you may consider it almost as great an impediment."

Her face went bleak. "Don't offer me any secrets or I'll have to confess things I would rather forget."

"You need never tell me anything, ever!" Charles said quickly. "But you must hear about me, and then—well, we shall see."

On the day Sophy's engagement to Dr. Charles Towle was announced, Marin received two callers. It was Saturday afternoon, and the house was quiet. Vail had taken the children to a puppet show at the American Theater, and Sophy, too energized by happiness to stay home for an afternoon of rest, had decided to go along. They were late returning, and Marin had put the time to good use, changing her dress twice, letting down her hair and redoing it, taking extra care over her appearance as she always did when she knew Vail would be around. She wore her hair much more simply than was the fashion, looping it back over her ears so that only the tips with their tiny gold studs showed. No plastered down curls hid her high forehead, no fussy ringlets detracted from the gracious curves of her cheekbones and throat. The heavy chignon on her neck shone deep, dark red, only hinting at the richness that would be revealed if she allowed it to fall free. Vail had once remarked that frizzled curls and false braids made women look like feather dusters. She had promptly adopted this classic style and never varied from it.

Just now, however, she felt like making some drastic change, like taking the scissors and cutting bangs, or something equally dramatic. She frowned into the mirror, wholly displeased with her appearance. She had felt dissatisfied and angry with the world all week, ever since Sophy told the family her amazing news. How had the girl managed such a romance with no one aware of it? And who would have thought it would be Charles? Never once had either of them shown more than the affection natural between good friends, so far as she could tell. It was hard to believe that her baby sister was going to get the lover she wanted, to have and to hold for the rest of her days, while she, Marin, had to be content with a hungry, empty life, always looking on from the outside, always denied what she most desired . . .

Tears burned in her eyes. What a bad person she was to envy Sophy, the sister she dearly loved, who had borne so much so bravely and was entitled to the best. Charles was the finest of men, and he loved Sophy completely. It showed in his every look and gesture. He would be the most devoted husband God ever made. She turned away from her mirror, sat down on the bed, and wiped her eyes. The rush of anguish was receding, leaving only the familiar dull ache in her chest, the ache she had learned to keep at bay most of the time. When Luz knocked at her door, she was able to answer with a steady voice.

Luz's head appeared around the door. "Mrs. Winfield an' Mrs. Parrish to see you . . . Are you all right, Miss Marin?"

"Quite all right, thank you. Seat the ladies in the parlor and tell them I'll be down shortly."

In a few moments Marin came downstairs. Charlotte Winfield was an affliction that the family had to bear, thanks to Ethan, but why was the woman calling so late in the day, and on a Saturday, of all things? Margaret Parrish was a kindly soul, wholeheartedly involved in good works, and that must be the point of the visit. Probably she was going to ask for another contribution to one of her charities.

"Mrs. Winfield, what a pleasure. Mrs. Parrish, how kind of you to call." Marin took a seat on the sofa and resolved not to ring for tea. She must be rid of them before Vail returned, or else it would be awkward to invite him to stay for dinner.

"Forgive us for this late call," Mrs. Winfield began, "but we have struggled with our consciences all day and have decided what we must do."

Marin's smile of welcome remained fixed. The picture of Charlotte Winfield struggling with her feeble conscience tempted her to laugh, yet somewhere an alarm bell rang. Mrs. Parrish's conscience was far more developed, and she looked very serious.

"I was, to say the least, thunderstruck when I read of Sophy's engagement in this morning's paper," Charlotte continued.

"We were all surprised," murmured Marin. What could this woman have on her petty mind?

Mrs. Parrish leaned forward. She was a plump woman, and her stays creaked. "My dear, we bear unfortunate news, facts of which you and your father and Sophy herself must be unaware."

"Something about Charles, I take it," said Marin, her voice as sharp as the sinking unease in her stomach. What could Charles be involved in that would preclude his marrying? That was what these women were hinting at. Surely Sophy had had enough pain in her short life, surely God wouldn't take this good thing away from her, too. The violent envy she had felt only moments before was swept aside by utter protectiveness.

Charlotte drew herself up very straight. "Marin, I regret to tell you that Dr. Towle is—" She hesitated. Then, in the low voice she used when forced to refer to matters of elimination or ladies' diseases, she said, "He is a person of Hebrew descent."

After a moment of total surprise Marin laughed. "Oh, dear life, where did you ever hear such a story? He is English, Mrs. Winfield. His parents came to Boston from England years before he was born, and his family had lived in London since time began."

"Is that the story he gave you? Perhaps it is true as far as it goes, but they were Jewish, and at some time in the past his ancestors came from—" she exchanged a glance with Mrs. Parrish, "Palestine, as Margaret can vouch for of her own certain knowledge."

"Yes," Mrs. Parrish agreed, reluctant but firm. "My cousins, the Ballards, knew the family in Boston. The Towles were Jews and made no secret of it."

Marin was on her feet, her cheeks very pink. She must not lose her temper; bad things always happened when she did. But it was Sophy's whole future these women were hacking apart. For if it was true . . . she knew that Jews were unacceptable in the best society, except for a few very rich individuals.

"I do not believe it. Your cousins are mistaken. Dr. Towle has no connection with the Jewish community in this town, and he has several times attended church with us." Once, she thought, the time Logan sang the solo with the choir at Christmas. And he was present at the small ceremony at Fontana when the priest baptized Alida.

"Dr. Towle fancies himself a freethinker, but his antecedents are as I have described," Mrs. Parrish replied with gentle certainty. "Have you never wondered why he was forced to leave his homeland to take his degree in medicine at the University of Vienna when the great university, Harvard, was right in his own backyard? It was because he is Jewish and Harvard would not have him. As you must know, I do not lend myself to idle gossip, and I do not enjoy carrying news that will bring grief to Sophy. She bears the cross of her blindness with fortitude that is a lesson to us all. Indeed one wonders—but the ways of the Lord are mysterious. You are her closest female relative, dear. You must do a mother's task and guide her wisely in this most difficult circumstance. If necessary, point out her duty to her religion and the onus that would fall on her family and her unborn children, though I do not doubt that once she hears the truth, she will know what to do. A simple announcement in the newspaper stating that the engagement is ended—it can be handled with dignity."

"Yes, dignity, that's the important thing," Charlotte put in, wringing her gloved hands. "Think what it would do to our family, to our bloodlines. We go back to the Pilgrim Fathers. I am a Claibourne, you know, and the Winfields are also FFV. Why, her children would be half Jewish—cousins to little Tyler and Dottie."

Marin's mind leaped from thought to half-formed thought: Charles struggling for Rose's life, saying, "I never give up until I must . . . I am not God"; Charles nursing Sophy as tenderly as a mother and then ruthlessly bullying her into living again. It was such a man that Charlotte Winfield feared would contaminate her precious First Family of Virginia. Dislike of the malicious woman, despair at the news she brought, rage at this latest blow to Sophy all combined to overwhelm caution.

"How dare you," she said, soft, distinct, and deadly, and Charlotte's mouth fell open. "How dare you come here prattling about bloodlines and the FFV." Her voice rose, and on the hearth Angus lifted his noble head to look at her with clear, gentle eyes. She pointed a shaking finger at the collie. "Do you see that dog? He has finer bloodlines than you and far more generosity, integrity, and loving-kindness. Get out of my house, both of you. Get out before I have Jeremy escort you out."

The two ladies sat dumbfounded by the unexpected onslaught. Then, red-faced, lips clamped, they rose and marched from the room. Marin watched them go, shaken by the depth of her rage at them and pain for Sophy. Those odious women would never forgive her, and subtle, dangerous enemies they would be. But she regretted nothing. This once she had not equivocated or maneuvered or finessed, this once she had taken an honest stand, had met the foe head-on regardless of consequences, and it was exhilarating.

Outside came the creak of a carriage. Vail, returning with Sophy and the children. She flew to the front door as the ladies descended the steps, their backs rigid with indignation and insult. Vail lifted his hat, and they nodded coldly. "Good afternoon, Mr. Severance, good afternoon, Sophy." They continued on and climbed into Charlotte Winfield's barouche.

Sophy came up the steps with Carey and Belinda, and Vail followed, carrying Alida, his eyes filled with laughter.

"Who are they mad at?"

"Me, I guess," said Marin. "We had a little dispute over genealogy."

Sophy giggled. "Who won?"

"I'm not sure." Marin kissed the top of Carey's head and hugged Belinda, who had grown so rapidly this last year. "Hello, honey," she said to Alida. "Sophy, why don't you take the children out to the kitchen? Mrs. Victoria has hot chocolate and muffins for them."

She watched them go, Sophy's blond curls only a little higher than Carey's dark head. To Vail she said urgently, "Come in here. I have to talk to you," and dragged him into the parlor.

With the door shut tight she ran to the window and pulled back the draperies in time to see the Winfield barouche disappear down the street. "The old biddies. Charlotte Winfield doesn't surprise me—she's mean and she's vicious—but Mrs. Parrish! How could such a good, Christian woman be so cruel?"

"God deliver me from good Christian women, especially the kind that make a great point of it. They're the ones who smile so lovingly as they stick the shiv in your ribs. For your own good, of course. What have those two humanitarians done to you?"

"They told me—oh, Vail, did you know Charles is—is Jewish?" She whispered the last word with utter desolation.

"Yes, I knew his family well, or his father at least. Old Mr.

Towle was quite a fellow. A lawyer, a scholar, an independent thinker like Charles, who went his own way without worrying too much about what his neighbors thought. For a while he considered converting to Christianity but decided he couldn't tie himself to one creed. When he died, he was investigating Buddhism. He liked to race horses and jump them, too. That's how he died—fell off his horse in a steeplechase and broke his neck. Charles's mother was a charming, frail woman, a little vague. Your mother reminded me of her in some ways. His sister, Lydia, died at fourteen, and Mrs. Towle never got over it—she spent most of her time lying down. I think it was his sister's death that turned Charles toward medicine and made death his enemy. He knows he can't beat it in the long run, but he keeps trying."

His talk about the Towle family went past her, scarcely registering. "You knew all the time. How could you let it reach this point without telling us? What is Sophy to do?"

"Marry the man if she loves him. Don't worry about his agreeing to the parson. He won't object to a little thing like the ceremony, no matter what he may privately think."

"That's the least of the problem, and you know it."

He sat down in James's chair by the fireplace, and Angus got up, slowly padded to him, and insinuated his silky head to be patted. "No, I can't say that I do. What is the big part of the problem?"

"You know perfectly well what I mean. People will never say anything directly, not to her, but there'll be the little snubs and silent insults. Her children will never be truly accepted, not in the best homes, and neither will she, no matter what her family is or what we do to help her. Saints in heaven, we can't let her marry him."

"I don't see how you can stop her."

"She won't want to, once she knows."

"Do you really think he hasn't told her? Of course she knows. Obviously it doesn't make any difference."

"But it has to. Charles is such a good man, so decent and honorable. He just doesn't realize what this would do to her."

He looked at her, his fingers idly rubbing the dog's ear. "Charles is so decent, so honorable, such a good man, but not good enough for your sister?"

It was not easy to face the censure in his eyes, for she treasured his good opinion, but at the moment Sophy came first. "You know what I mean. I've got to tell her."

"Go to it then, and good luck to you."

In the kitchen the children greeted her happily, with circles of chocolate and crumbs around their mouths. She smiled and said under her breath, "Sophy, would you step outside for a minute?"

On the back porch she said, "Let's walk down to the summer-house."

"What is it? Is something wrong?"

"I guess so, honey." They came to the latticework structure, a pretty place with ivy climbing over it and already looking as if it had been there for years. "Here, sit beside me. Sophy, I want you to try your best not to get too upset. Try to take the long view. I was told something today, and much as I hate to, I have to tell you right now, for we can't afford to wait. Sophy . . . honey . . . I have learned on good authority that Charles—" oh, this was horrible. How could she put it gracefully? Mrs. Parrish's genteel words came back. "Charles is a person of Hebrew descent."

To her unbelieving ears came the sound of Sophy's chuckle. "Oh, Marin, what a mouthful. You mean he's a Jew."

Marin gave her a hard stare. She had expected shock, tears, and protestations, but never laughter. "You mean, you know?"

"Certainly I know. He told me right here"—Sophy's voice softened, "the night he asked me to marry him. Can you imagine, he thought it might make a difference."

Marin looked into her sister's wide, unseeing eyes and felt tears in her own. How far Sophy had come from the petulant child she had been, how many tragedies had descended on her. More unhappiness was the last thing she needed, but how could it be avoided when this thing she wanted so much simply could not be? She was blind in more than her eyes and had to be told the blunt truth even if she hated the person who told her.

"Darling, listen to me. Charles was right, it does make a difference. It shouldn't, but it does and it always will. He is the best of men, and when he thinks about it, he won't want you to bear the same burden he does. You have a choice he doesn't have. If you marry him, people will turn away from you and your children and your grandchildren. You know it, if you're honest with yourself."

She waited for the indignation and the arguments, but none came. Sophy put out her hand and found Marin's face.

"Sister, Charles said it all. He told me what has happened to his people over and over, terrible things that I'd never even heard of. He's been hurt many times; maybe I will be, too, but I have to be with him. Should we live without each other, should our children never be born because of ignorant people who aren't fit to polish his boots? I'm going to marry him on the first Saturday of next month, just as the newspaper said, and whatever comes . . . well, we'll face it together."

She rose and walked slowly up the path, feeling her way with her cane, and Marin watched her go, recognizing defeat when she saw it. Vail was right. She could argue and order till doomsday, and Sophy would never budge. There were to be no tears, no quarrels, no fireworks, but she would marry Charles when she said she would, and anyone who loved her would be welcome to attend the wedding.

Chapter 36

 Southerners—the Chivalry, as they liked to call themselves—were a minority in San Francisco, but a vocal, rich, socially prominent minority, always quick to redress a slight, never hesitating to make their opinions known. Ethan Gentry was in the forefront of this element of society, one of the young bloods around town. Handsome, free-spending, dressed in the latest exaggerations of fashion, he was generally regarded as the *ne plus ultra* of a young Southern gentleman— virile, a hard drinker, a fine horseman, a good shot, passionately defensive of his honor, and pugnacious to a fault. Kitty thought it a great credit to her that her dashing husband had gotten himself involved in two duels before the summer was well launched. James professed himself annoyed and was secretly more pleased with his son than he had been in many years. Marin, unlike most Southern gentlewomen, thought dueling an absurdity and told Ethan he was a quarrelsome idiot who was lucky he had only wounded, not killed, his opponents, and even more lucky that he hadn't gotten killed himself.

Ethan shrugged off her scoldings and went his aggressive way with a chip on his shoulder so big the whole world could see it. He was bored, he was lonely, he despised his pretty, lustful wife, and the young men he ran with were all hotheaded Chivs filled with Southern rhetoric and looking for a fight. Soon he was caught up in the rising wave of political excitement and expounding theories of states' rights and the social benefits of slavery as if he were a plantation owner with a hundred slaves and a vested interest in the status quo.

It was luck, not wisdom, that kept him out of duels through the rest of the summer, but on a pleasant day in mid-September he was one of many witnesses of a duel between two of the most prominent men in California. State Supreme Court Justice David Terry, a proslavery Kentuckian and an experienced duelist, shot to death David Broderick, a Democratic senator himself, but an antislavery, Northern workingman's Democrat. By the time of the funeral, rage between the pro- and antislavery people was ready to explode into more violence.

On the night of the funeral Ethan swaggered into the Red Garter saloon with three of his friends, more than slightly drunk. He had been closeted with a bottle all afternoon and was blustery and combative, a stage that would be followed by bathetic sentimentality and tears just before he passed out. He placed his varnished boot on the brass rail, leaned on the bar, and demanded a bottle of the barkeep's best whiskey. With his friends to help, the contents of the bottle diminished steadily, and as the last round was poured, he noticed Vail at the opposite end of the bar talking to the manager of Davidson's Bank, William Purcell. He raised his glass airily in their direction and boomed, "A toast, gen'lemen. A toast to tha' defender of Southern womanhood and the democracy, tha' flow'r of Kentucky, David S. Terry!"

His friends drank, but not Ethan. He moved down the bar, full glass still in his hand, until he was only a foot or so from Purcell. He leaned close and inquired, "You do not drink, sir?"

Purcell not only was a pudgy banker who was known as a "feeler" by every pretty woman in town, he was a staunch abolitionist, a grief-stricken friend of David Broderick, and the author of a letter printed in the *Alta California* that morning denouncing the killing as a political assassination and recommending that his murderer, Judge Terry, be tried and then hung by the neck until dead. Purcell was also an excellent shot. He gazed coolly at the bleary-eyed, red-faced young man, said, "I do not drink that toast, sir," and turned his back.

Ethan stared at the wide back, wavering slightly. Beyond Purcell's shoulder he could see the warning in Vail's eyes. His lip curled, and his hand came down on the heavy shoulder; he tried to spin Purcell around and spilled his whiskey down his own trousers.

Purcell half turned and rumbled, "Remove your hand, sir."

Ethan was looking down, puzzled, at his dripping pants. "You threw whiskey on me. Why'd you throw whiskey on me?"

"You spilled it on yourself, you drunken fool. Go home to your unfortunate wife before you have to be carried there."

An interested crowd was beginning to form. Judge Terry had been arrested and released on a modest ten thousand dollars bail, but the prevailing sentiment in town was one of moral outrage, and most Southern sympathizers were lying low. Even Ethan, hotheaded as he was, would have kept a prudent tongue had he been sober.

But he was not sober. He looked at Vail, who had moved forward until he was almost in front of Purcell. "That man 'sulted my wife," he told Vail plaintively. The color in his face deepened. "You 'sulted my wife, sir!" he roared. "Per'aps Yankees don' know gen'lemen don' mention ladies in a saloon. You are a rare scoun—" Something brushed against his jutting jaw, and the room went dark. He sagged into Vail's arms.

"Sorry, Bill. The boy was just too deep in his cups. He'll send his apologies in the morning. See to my horse, will you? I'll take him home in a cab." Vail heaved Ethan over his shoulder and pushed quickly through the crowd. On the street he hailed one of the hansom cabs that always waited near the better hotels and saloons, shoved Ethan's limp body onto the seat, and climbed in after him.

The cab rocked past Portsmouth Square and rounded into Kearney Street. Ethan slid sideways, twitched, groaned, and opened one eye. The other eye appeared to be stuck shut. "Bastard," he mumbled. "Y'broke my jaw."

"I hope so," Vail replied with brutal unconcern. "You need your mouth taped. I made your apologies for you."

" 'pologies!" Ethan tried to sit up and look indignant, but his head was spinning and the lights of street lamps flickered and danced in a crazy, dizzying pattern. He gave up the struggle and slumped down, muttering, " 'pologies, by God."

Vail grinned. "But you'd better write a masterful letter of apology tomorrow, or you may yet find yourself on the field of honor. Purcell has killed two men in the last year for less reason than you gave him tonight."

"I'm the bes' shot in town. I can kill the sombitch anytime." Ethan closed his eye and went back to sleep.

It was ten past eleven when Kitty heard the French door chimes tinkle. She called to the Chinese houseboy, "I'll get it, Ling," and went to the door thinking that Ethan had forgotten his key again, pleased that he was home early.

There stood her husband, suffused in whiskey-stink, his face flushed, his blond hair flopping into bloodshot eyes, one arm draped around Vail's neck. The beautiful new beaver hat she had given him was gone. Her face hardened. "In there," she said briefly, and pointed to the bedroom.

Ethan said, "I c'n walk," let go of Vail's shoulder, and fell forward on his face. "Sombitch," he muttered to himself. Unsteadily he climbed onto hands and knees and wobbled back and forth. Then his head sank slowly down to the floor, and there he stayed.

Kitty uttered a word ladies did not use. Vail hauled Ethan onto his feet, carried him into a bedroom, and rolled him onto the fancy satin coverlet. He loosened the polka-dot silk cravat and unbuttoned the ruffled shirt and then went out, leaving husband and wife together. Kitty stood looking down at the red-faced, snoring, disgusting creature defiling her bed. He would be out cold all night and revoltingly sick in the morning. She repeated the same improper word and walked out of the room.

In her parlor Vail waited, hat in hand, ready to say good-night.

Large, she thought. Exceedingly big, muscular men made her feel smaller, more womanly, made her feel they could overpower her so easily. Why had she chosen a slender fellow like Ethan when big men were so exciting?

"Thank you, Vail," she murmured in her sweet, husky voice. "I'm so embarrassed I could die."

He turned. A harsh face, not at all like his refined-looking brother. Big, bold nose, deep lines around his mouth, oddly beautiful gray eyes with something in them . . . She could have had him back in the old days before he married Celia, she could have had him if Mama had handled things right.

He said, "No need for embarrassment. Ethan has put me away in like condition. We men are such a great lot of trouble I fail to see why you ladies put up with us so charitably."

And what a charming smile! Kitty breathed deeply. "I expect you all are worth it in the long run." She moved toward him. "Vail, you mustn't leave right away. I had a midnight supper planned for Ethan, and now he—please do join me."

"I've eaten, ma'am."

"Well, a cup of coffee then, and a taste of my pecan pie. I insist."

In the small dining room a table was set for two beside a low fire. Candle flames wavered, reflected in the shining crystal and silver. Kitty had him by the arm. "Come along now. You sit there, and I shall take your hat and coat." She rang a silver bell, and almost instantly the houseboy came in on silent feet. "Coffee, Ling, and bring the pie now, if you please."

She turned then to Vail, her lashes fluttering. "I visited with Sophy today. We've become dear friends now that she is a matron, too. It's so remarkable, the way she keeps house and even cooks sometimes, and she's just the happiest little thing in her marriage. The family must be pleased that it's worked out so well."

"Remarkable is the word for Sophy. Yes, we're very pleased. She married a fine man." Vail dug in his pocket for a cigar. "May I?"

"Oh, please do! I love the scent of a good cigar. If only Ethan would give up those vile cigarillos. Papa smokes cigars, so the smell always makes me think of home."

He struck a match inelegantly on his boot sole and drew deeply until a cloud of blue smoke circled his head. He said, "I didn't know you and Sophy were so close."

"We have become so in recent months. I grieved with her after her sad illness." A refined, roundabout allusion to Sophy's miscarriage three months ago. "But she bounced back to her usual cheerful self in no time."

"Sophy has a gift for bouncing back."

"So brave," Kitty murmured. A touch of complacency entered her smile. At one time in the long ago, Sophy had been a rival in the quest for beaux and popularity, and even after blindness overtook her, Kitty had felt sour envy at the way attractive men hung around her and vied to take care of her. But ever since Charlotte Winfield and Marin had had their cataclysmic falling out, Kitty, in sheer perversity, had endeavored to make Sophy her special friend. So far, to her mother's intense aggravation, Sophy and her odd, quiet doctor had twice been present at the Ethan Gentrys' small, intimate dinner parties. Carefully she brought the touchy subject a little way into the light. "Dr. Towle is a dear, dear man, as you say. I hear there are those who no longer have him attend them out of misguided loyalty to Mama. One should not criticize one's parent, but Mama was wrong, which I'm sure she realizes and is just too stubborn to admit. Personally, had I agreed with her, as I certainly do not, I would still have him as my doctor. Good gracious, the children are always ailing, and where would I turn without his guidance? He is just so *smart*—all those people are terribly clever, aren't they? I don't know what they do with their dullards. They must not have any."

"They have them, just like any other people."

"No doubt," she agreed quickly, aware that she had somehow

struck a wrong note and relieved that Ling was finally bearing in
the coffee tray. It was never good manners to call attention to the
quality of one's possessions, but she hoped Vail noticed that her
china was Limoges. She made a gracious ceremony out of pouring
the coffee, and as she handed him the fine china cup, her hand
touched his lingeringly. "You must be lonely in that big house
now that Celia has gone back to La Gracia."

"I am desolate, but I try to keep busy."

I'll bet you do, she thought. Vail Severance's comings and
goings were matters of fascination to her, but even when drunk
Ethan was annoyingly closemouthed about his family's affairs.
However, Bridie, her mother's maid, was an invaluable source of
gossip and rumor, and Bridie said there had been a donnybrook
when Celia Severance decided to go home for an indefinite stay,
not because her husband wanted her to stay, but because he made
her leave their daughter, Alida, behind. "Mrs. Moon heard it with
her own ears," Bridie had related with large eyes. "Miss Celia said
she would come and go as she pleased, and Mr. Vail said that was
fine, she could go and stay for all of him, but Miss Alida was to live
on this side of the bay. Well, Miss Celia was mad as a wet hen,
though she never raised her voice—Mrs. Moon says she *never* raises
her voice—and she said that it was his fault she lost some of her land
and that he couldn't force her to abandon her child. She's gone back
to La Gracia though, and Miss Alida's still here. Mr. Vail usually has
his own way when he gets his back up."

Kitty stirred more sugar into her coffee. She liked it thick and
syrupy. "At least you have Alida to console you. She is such a
darling."

Vail's eyes lit with genuine feeling. "Yes, I must agree, she is.
But she will go to La Gracia soon and stay for the next few
months. Celia makes the point that the climate is warmer and more
healthful on the other side of the bay in winter, and she's right.
Also, the ranch is Alida's inheritance, and she should learn to love
it. Celia's right about that, too."

"So you will be alone all winter." The ruffle of lace at Kitty's
bosom rose and fell quickly, a delicate shimmer in the candle
light. Her skin was pink with the tide of warmth that had started
to rise when she touched him. She took a silver knife, cut into the
spicy, sugary pie, and lifted a piece onto a plate. "I know what it
is to be alone, even in a crowd of friends. Do you ever feel that
way? My husband—sometimes he could just as well be off on
some old ranch for all the company he is to me. For instance"—
her voice lowered, "he will sleep like the dead all night and never

stir, not if the house burns down around him." She put the plate of pie into his hand, and this time her soft fingers slid up to his wrist and rested there. God, the energy in the man! She was shaking. The sticky wetness, the never satisfied throbbing increased. "Do have all you want," she whispered. "There's plenty, and we have a long night."

Vail set the pie on the table and gazed at her with a faint smile. "It looks delicious, but I must decline. In the past I've found pecan pie to be most tasty but so sweet and overrich that I've come to regret it later." He crushed out his cigar in the silver ashtray, shoved back the chair, and rose.

She got to her feet, too, her eyes like her father's, shiny and unblinking.

He picked up his hat and coat. "Good-night, ma'am. Thank you for a most entertaining evening."

She stood in the middle of the room, fists clenched, hearing the front door click, hearing his footsteps fading into the night. Then with a howl of frustration and fury she threw herself onto the sofa and pounded her fist into the pillow again and again.

By year's end the political fires were burning hotter than ever. Marin was aware that another acrimonious presidential election was coming in 1860 and that there was increasingly serious talk of war, but it did not worry her. Her concern, as always, was, Is it good or bad for the Gentrys? And as her reading of history told her that wars were usually good for business unless you were too closely involved, she could not see that the possibility of war back East was something to lose sleep over. She had listened to endless rhetoric from Stuart when he was home and was glad to receive it now only in his infrequent letters. Reading them, she could quickly skim the political part and get on to the social doings and gossip of the capital city. The newspapers she ignored.

But Logan subscribed to all the city's newspapers and devoured her *Atlantic Monthly* and *Harper's* magazines. She read every detail of the trial of the wild-eyed John Brown, the fanatic who had stormed the army's arsenal at Harper's Ferry in October, and when the stunning news came that he had been convicted of treason and hanged, she wept tears of angry grief and insisted to Vail that the great man was a martyr and a saint in the cause of freedom.

Vail shocked her by replying coolly, "A few more saints like that, and we'll be dragged into a holy war that nobody wants but the saints."

"The newspaper quotes Mr. Emerson as saying that John Brown makes the gallows glorious like the cross!"

"Ringing words, but if war comes, you may be sure Mr. Emerson won't be one of the boys in the front line."

James, in his chair by the fire, began to rumble about states' rights and crazed abolitionists, and Marin interposed quickly, "Why do you two carry on like that when you know war is out of the question? Stuart says so." She looked hopefully for signs of a smile on Logan's cross face but saw no response. "Stuart also says there's a rumor around Washington that the Prince of Wales may come to visit this year. Imagine, real royalty right in our own country."

Logan ignored the chance to peacefully change the subject, took up her sewing, and went to sit in a corner of the parlor, stabbing her needle so violently into the cloth that she might have been impaling a slave owner with every thrust.

Vail moved nearer the fire and began to agree with James about the unlikelihood of war despite the best efforts of iniquitous rabblerousers, ideas Marin knew he only partly believed. Why hadn't he shown as much tact with his sister? Usually he was so gentle with Logan, but lately he'd been restless and touchy and likely to fly off the handle at the least provocation. Much as she loved him, she could not always see into his mind; sometimes she had the odd, uncomfortable feeling that there were areas of his life she knew nothing about.

On the sofa Ethan watched quietly. It wasn't often that he bothered to observe the reactions of other people, for he was usually immersed in himself and more than half drunk, or listening to Kitty's chatter, or both. Tonight, though, he was stone-cold sober, and Kitty hadn't come to dinner with him. She had announced the arrival of a severe headache as soon as she learned that Vail would be there, too. Recently she had developed a violent dislike of Vail and never went anyplace he was likely to be. When inadvertently they did meet, she was cold, distant, and almost rude, although Vail appeared not to notice. Ethan would have liked to know what had passed between them on the evening Vail brought him home three sheets to the wind, but Vail professed not to understand what he was talking about.

Whatever the reason, it meant he was blessedly without her company tonight. He uncrossed his slim, elegantly clad legs and went to Logan, sitting alone, sewing furiously.

"Don't let Vail bother you, little abolitionist. He's on the prod these days. He'd have to be to argue with you."

"I know it. He is really very good to me and I ought not to get so aggravated." She glanced up with the beginnings of a smile. "You and I are the ones who should be quarreling, Southron that you are, yet we never do."

"Ah, that's a nice smile. Let me see a little more of it. As I suspected, a dimple just north of the lefthand corner of your mouth."

"Shame on you, you prevaricator. I haven't a dimple to my name."

"Well, I saw one just then." He settled on the floor at her feet. "It's good to talk to you alone. Do you know how long it's been?"

She placed her needle with close attention and drew it through the cloth. "Yes, I know."

"I miss our talks. I miss you."

"You have so much to keep you busy. Your—your family and the business . . ."

Ethan uttered a short, sharp laugh. "I have nothing to do with the business. Marin won't let me do anything that matters. You know how she is, wants her fingers in every pie, and Pa backs her up. I wish—Logan, could I come to see you once in while, just to talk? I know you think I'm a waster and a loafer, and I don't blame you for not caring to have me around, but it would mean so much."

She raised her head. New lines had appeared around her eyes and mouth in the last year, but just now her blue-gray eyes were bright. She studied his features thoughtfully. "I don't think you are a waster and a loafer. I never did. This is your family's home, and you are always welcome here."

"That isn't what I mean. May I come to visit you, spend time with you? Will you receive me if I come? Logan, I've got to have a real friend in my life, someone I don't have to explain things to, someone who knows me to the bone. I'll go crazy if I don't."

"Of course I'll receive you and be your friend. I always have been."

She lowered her eyes to her needlework again, the icy lump that had been in her chest since the night Ethan announced his engagement beginning to thaw just a little. He said he needed her. She could not be his wife, share his life, bear his children, she knew now that it had never been possible. But she could be his friend. She could listen to his woes and help him in ways that Kitty apparently could not. A platonic, affectionate relationship was not what she had dreamed of, but it was far better than nothing.

Chapter 37

✦ The grove of stately sycamores echoed with band music and the sounds of many people talking, laughing, calling to friends, and singing along with the band, which had finished "Camptown Races" and was launching into the opening bars of "Yankee Doodle." There were catcalls from some rambunctious Chiv Democrats, but they were drowned out by the horns and drums. Bright red, white, and blue bunting had been strung between the trees, and in different parts of the grove speakers of various political persuasions held forth, expounding their parties' opinions and warming up the crowd for the important speeches that would be delivered after the meal, which was now cooking over a slow fire. Great joints of beef, venison, lamb, and pork had been spitted on long iron rods and laid across a fire-filled trench. The mouth-watering smells drifted through the tall trees and whetted appetites of people only half hearing the speeches.

They had been arriving since midmorning, a steady procession of carriages, buggies, fine landaus, and buckboard wagons carrying young girls and their beaux, husbands and wives, politicians down from Sacramento City for the day, ranchers from the Contra Costa, the cream of San Francisco society, and as many ordinary citizens as could find a means of travel. The ladies carried ruffled parasols or wore wide-brimmed, beribboned straw hats to protect delicate skin from a sun still warm in November, and the bright colors and pretty pastels of their spreading hoopskirts dotted the woods like great bell-shaped flowers springing up from the matted grass.

The grove was near San Jose, a favorite picnic spot, and today's barbecue and speech making was the last great political meeting before the election tomorrow, an election that could set the land to reeling more violently than the earthquake that had opened the earth, diverted streams, and knocked people down in the street last month.

There were four presidential candidates before the voters, but the real battle was between the great orator and Democrat, Stephen Douglas, and the Republican, Abraham Lincoln of

Illinois, a man not well known outside the Middle West. As the campaign had progressed, Californians, sitting on the far western side of the continent, isolated by deserts and mountains, arrogant with riches, influenced more than they knew by the foreigners in their midst, debated whether the Union was paramount or whether, if secession came, they would side with the South, remain above the battle, or even become a separate republic. Then, as summer moved into fall, Union sentiment began to build. With threats of secession if Lincoln was elected coming out of the South, fidelity to the federal government grew and the Chivalry of San Francisco became quieter as they realized they were in the minority.

Through it all Marin watched and listened and said nothing, but she gave up trying to ignore the uproar and took to reading the newspapers as closely as Logan did. News was coming in swiftly now that the pony express, established last April, was making the trip from St. Joe, Missouri, to Sacramento City in eight days. Much too swiftly, Marin thought with unease, remembering the comfortable time when a month, or two or three, could go by with no disturbing news of the outside world. They were all crazy back East, and she wished they would fight their war, if war there must be, without sending word to California. No longer could she pretend to herself that there was no chance of a conflict. She could only thank God that her own son was still a child, that the men she cared most about were too sensible to get involved, that it was all taking place so far away

She walked through the shady grove chatting with friends, flirting a little—Stuart was off somewhere holding forth to a group of his admirers and wouldn't notice—keeping an eye on the children and listening with both ears to the speeches going on around her.

Mr. Lincoln's attributes she knew by heart. Stuart, a former Whig, had recognized an up-and-coming party when he saw it and had agilely leaped onto the Republican bandwagon some time back. He was now heart and soul for Lincoln, although he didn't know much about the man, and tried out his speeches on her. "An honest man is the noblest work of God," he would intone, "and Abe Lincoln is as honest as the day is long. He is a great man, a man of the people, a man for our time! Do we want the insidious institution of slavery spreading throughout our fair country, or do we want free white laborers who work the land with their own hands, feed their families, care for their own? Does Abe Lincoln spend his days lazing on a veranda with a mint julep in his hand watching his Negroes work? No, gentlemen, he was born in a log cabin, he split rails when he was a lad no bigger than my son over there." Here Stuart would gesture toward twelve-year-old Carey, who was kept nearby for the purpose, and then he would fling out his hands in wide appeal. "Abe Lincoln's hands are callused and worn from hard labor. He knows what it is to work up an honest sweat, to need a job and not have it, to be a farmer with no money to buy land. A vote for the Railsplitter is a vote *against* the extension of slavery, the honest white man's most dangerous enemy!" At this point Stuart's voice would drop, and with somber passion he would begin his peroration. "The South shouts that it will leave the Union if Abe Lincoln is the next president. Well, sirs, that is an empty threat. Call their bluff, vote against slavery, vote Republican, and see our great nation grow ever greater in prosperity, peace, and freedom!"

Stuart always got many huzzahs with this speech and was considered one of the party's most effective spokesmen. None of his hearers, except Marin, seemed to find this big, handsome, elegantly dressed man's references to honest sweat and callused hands in the least amusing. Stuart's hands were soft and well manicured since he had given up ranching, and it had been several years since he had worked up a sweat. The same was probably true of Mr. Lincoln. She had heard he was a corporation lawyer, which meant it had been many a long day since he had split any rails.

She walked down a slight incline at the north end of the grove and there found what she had been looking for. Stuart was standing on a small platform decorated with bunting, making the speech she had heard so often to a good-size audience. Beyond the crowd, leaning against a tree and watching with a smile, was Vail.

She came up to him. "Are you impressed? I hope you're going to vote right."

"I'm going to move to Hawaii and watch the crack-up from a safe distance."

She closed her parasol and stepped into the shade of the tree. "You think Stuart's wrong? You think they really might secede? They're always blustering, but—"

"I don't think it's all bluster this time. They're fighting for their lives, and nobody up north seems to see it. The South is hooked on cotton the way a drunk is on liquor, the whole economy depends on it, and they can't grow cotton without slaves."

"I understand how they feel. People can't be expected to throw away their livelihood. But it's a matter of dollars and cents, so surely something can be worked out without a war if everybody just tries."

"Ah, Marin, it's more than money. You're a Southerner. You ought to see that."

She looked at him blankly.

"Think back to Jeremy's trial. Why did you go out on a limb for him?"

She reddened, recalling her monumental lie under oath on that frightening day. "Because . . . because I had to, somebody had to, or that man would have taken him back to Georgia. And people were hateful about it afterward, as if it makes any difference to them."

"But it does make a difference. Jeremy is considered a 'smart nigger,' and people don't like that. The idea scares them."

"Of course he's smart. That's why I want him around. He's smart and ambitious, and he makes money on the side—I know that, and good for him if he can. But he wouldn't hurt a fly. How could anyone be scared of him?"

Vail looked up at Stuart, who was well launched on his speech and gesturing expansively.

"Listen to what your husband is saying. He speaks for Mr. Lincoln and what does he say? Keep the Negroes out of western land and protect the white man from slave competition. Not a word about the moral iniquity of slavery. If you took a vote today, everybody here except the Chiv Democrats would say the slave system is an evil that ought to be ended, but nobody wants to face up to what would happen then. The truth is, Northerners and Southerners aren't much different. Nobody wants free Negroes around, not the most rabid abolitionists, not Honest Abe himself. Northerners fear blacks on the loose as much as Southerners do."

It was true. For all his antislavery talk Stuart never had been comfortable with Jeremy, never had understood him, had feared giving him a gun even though it was for the protection of her and the children. She watched him making his point about the child Abraham splitting rails, and smiling fondly at his son, stationed strategically on a nearby tree stump high enough that everyone could see him. The crowd turned to look approvingly at Carey and then back to the platform as Stuart roared on.

Flushed, his hair flopping untidily into his eyes, he bellowed, "The Union must and shall be preserved!" and the crowd broke into loud applause and shouts of approval. Smiling, bowing, he climbed down, mopping his face and accepting congratulations.

Beneath the tree Marin said, "Well, I can't see it's as hopeless as you say. Southerners are reasonable people, it's only a few fanatics that talk so wild. Oh, Lord, there's Ethan. I hope he and Stuart don't tangle today. Lately every time they meet, they sniff and growl at each other like two strange dogs."

Vail laughed. "Ethan's got Carey to keep him out of mischief."

Carey had abandoned his post as soon as his father had no further use for him and was swinging along beside Ethan, stretching his long, thin legs to match Ethan's stride. Marin smiled at the sight of him. Sometimes it did seem that Carey was the adult and Ethan the boy. Carey liked his uncle with the romantic past who had so astonishingly come back from the dead, but he viewed him with clear-eyed skepticism and took little that he said seriously.

Ethan strolled up looking dissolute and handsome in tight plaid trousers and a fine tweed coat.

"Little sister, you look sweet as a peach." In high good humor he kissed her cheek and grinned at Vail. "Ain't you proud of your brother? Hey, Stuart, that speech was a humdinger. By God, you won me for Lincoln today."

Stuart, standing a few feet away with a group of enthusiastic gentlemen, gave him a sour glance and went on talking.

"Ethan, do shut up," Marin said with an anxious eye on her husband. "I want to have a nice day and not worry about you two shooting each other's heads off."

"We're not going to fight, honey. I like to listen to the damn fool mouth off. Who do you think will win, Vail?"

"With the Democrats split up and clawing each other like alley cats, it has to be Lincoln, you know that."

"Sure I do, and I'm all for it. I may even vote for him myself. Because you know what will happen the day after he's elected? We're going to say good-bye, and about time, too. We should have done it years ago. To hell with the North. We're going to have a by-God empire, Vail. We're going to take Mexico and maybe Central America, too. The tropical climate is just right for slaves. We'll trade with Europe and the Orient, we'll be the greatest, richest civilization the world has ever seen, and you know what that'll mean? Leisure time and ease, so a gentleman can think and read and write, like in ancient Greece. Statesmen and poets . . . I always had a bent for poetry . . . and philosophers to figure out things and set the rest of the world straight. What do you think of that, Marin?"

"I think you've been at the opium. Honestly, Ethan, you

shouldn't go around talking like that where people might hear you. They don't know you like we do."

Ethan's grin vanished, and his eyes changed, became remote. "You think it's a pipe dream? You're wrong, sis. It will happen. It will be made to happen." Then the smile was back. He sauntered off and was almost instantly surrounded by a group of men, his cronies, all young, elegantly dressed dandies, and every one of them a Southerner.

Beyond Ethan, near the creek bank, Marin saw Belinda astride a high branch of a cottonwood tree, her pantalette-clad legs dangling in full view of people passing below.

"Carey, go get your sister down from that tree and tell her if she climbs up there again, she'll be sent home without any barbecue." Carey loped off, and her gaze went worriedly to Ethan's retreating figure. "What in Heaven was he raving about, Vail?"

"You read the papers. Haven't you heard of the Great Southern Confederacy stretching all the way from the Mason-Dixon line to beyond the gulf? Every white man will be pondering deep thoughts and composing music on his piano while his slaves chop cotton. It's going to bring mankind a new age of enlightenment and make everybody rich."

"You can't be serious."

"They are. They're deadly serious."

"But it's the wildest gibberish. Most Southerners aren't crazy like Ethan. Such a thing is out of all reason. Ordinary folks know that."

"I wouldn't bet on it. Ordinary folks, if they're angry and scared enough, believe what they want to believe."

Her eyes returned to Ethan. He had stopped to speak to Logan and was looking down into her face with the gentle, faintly teasing smile he always had for her. But Marin remembered how he had looked when he'd said, "We're going to have a by-God empire," and she shivered. That same, breakneck, headlong expression had been on his face so many years ago when he announced that he was going after gold.

Under the cottonwood tree Carey looked up at Belinda and ordered, "All right, come on down. Mother saw you."

Belinda stared back obdurately. Her skirt and petticoats were hiked up to allow ease in climbing, and her underdrawers showed plainly from below. At ten she was a dainty blond child with eyes as luminously blue and full of devilment as her Aunt Sophy's once

had been, and a mind as tough and resilient as her mother's.
"No!" she answered shortly, and inched farther out on the branch.
It sagged, and she cried out, "I'm stuck, Carey. I can't move."

Below Alida gasped and craned her neck to see better. She was
only eight, quiet, credulous, a little timid, a tail to the comet of
Belinda and Carey, with her mother's beauty already showing in
her little face and a wide-eyed gullibility that gave the family
much amusement. Belinda took regular, shameless advantage of
her by spinning wild tales out of a fertile imagination, tales she
half believed herself. Once Alida came puffing into the house to
announce to Marin and Logan that there was a dreadful shipwreck
down in the harbor at Monterey and sailors were drowning and
silks from China had spilled and were floating on the water,
spreading out so that the whole bay was turned white and emerald
and red. Marin said, "Now, Alida, you know that isn't so. We
can't see all the way down to Monterey." Alida had responded
eagerly, "No, ma'am, we can't, but Belinda can," and wondered
why her aunts dissolved in helpless laughter.

For both little girls Carey was a hero without peer. Belinda
adored him but hid it well. Alida was openly worshipful. Both
girls would have died for him.

He was now assessing Belinda's situation on the swaying
branch almost thirty feet above. As often happened, her daring
had exceeded her understanding of the problems involved, and she
was now trying to figure out how to save herself without losing
face.

With resignation he said, "Stand back, Alida," found a knot on
the tree trunk that was a good foothold, and quickly scrambled up.
In moments he had her safe on the ground, and when Alida
hugged her in vast relief, she was able to say, "Don't be such a
silly, I'm perfectly fine," but she said it in a good-natured way
and, without looking directly at her brother, added, "Why don't
we go down to the creek and catch Alida some polliwogs?"

"You can catch frogs maybe, but there won't be polliwogs till
spring."

"All right, frogs, then. You'd like some darling little frogs,
wouldn't you, Alida? Come on, Carey, let's hurry."

Adults smiled at the three children marching down to the creek
bank. Exceptionally well-favored young persons, all of them, the
little girls so pretty in their pastel flounces and ribbons, and the
boy so manly and grave, shepherding the girls. Everyone knew
Carey, and even people who found most children nuisances liked

him. For Carey was one of those fortunate beings born with the gift of charming others without compromising his own integrity.

His good looks helped. At twelve he was big for his age. He had the Severance height and was beginning to develop the masterful Severance nose, or "the Nose," as Logan ruefully referred to her own version of it. It was possible to see now in his boy's face the man he was going to become. His skin was olive, his eyes as black and brilliant as Marin's, his hair almost black with russet lights and a tendency to curl across his high forehead and behind his ears.

Marin knew him in much the same way James had known her when she was a child, for she observed him clearly and was pleased with everything she saw. He was mature for his age, quick of mind and kind of heart. It was a source of immense pride to her that Carey was well liked by so many people who ordinarily would have no time for so young a boy. "Smart as a whip, that boy," and "Fine, upstanding young man," people said, and Marin glowed.

He observed the world with a realistic but friendly eye, for the world had always been benevolent toward him. That there was no real affection between his mother and father he knew instinctively, but then, there was no such feeling between Vail and Aunt Celia, or between Uncle Ethan and Aunt Kitty, either. Never having seen a marriage that included true intimacy, he thought indifference was the normal married state. A man and a lady married and stayed together all of their lives but did not necessarily love each other. True, Sophy and Charles were very close and loving, but Sophy, being blind, needed special care, and besides, as Mother had once pointed out somewhat sarcastically in Carey's hearing, "The honeymoon is scarcely over with those two." He supposed that when the honeymoon was over—whenever that was—they would also become distant and aloof and sometimes speak sharply or with double meanings to each other, as Mother and Father did; he supposed his parents' honeymoon must have been over long before he could remember. It was sad, but it was the way things were.

His major problem and chief ambition in life was to please his father, an achievement he had decided was nearly impossible although he wasn't giving up. The trouble was, just when he had pleased Father about one thing, something else cropped up where he had not. Last week's accomplishment meant nothing if he failed today. But on this sunny morning Father was in such a fine mood that he had refused to cross verbal swords with Ethan and had even spoken pleasantly to Vail, an event that occurred rarely.

Why there was such enmity between Father and Vail, simmering always just beneath taut good manners, was a puzzlement. Once Mother, in answer to Carey's questions, had shrugged and said merely that those two had never gotten along even as boys, a reply that only intensified the mystery. For they were both good men. Father was Father, and Carey loved him accordingly. Vail was Vail, so big, so powerful, the best horseman, the best shot, the best storyteller, the most fun to be with, unfailingly kind to him and to Belinda. Like Ethan and Michael and many other young men before him, Carey hoped to be just like Vail when he got older.

Vail knew so much about so many things, like what to do about an ailing horse or dog, how to take unhurried aim with a gun and squarely hit a standing or moving target, how to teach a recalcitrant horse who was master without mistreating the animal or breaking its spirit, how to play poker and bluff if you drew a poor hand. And he shared all this magnificent knowledge with Carey, even teaching him things Mother didn't approve of, like the handling of pistols and rifles.

Vail was also very good to talk to about feelings and fears and dark, secret thoughts that he couldn't discuss with Mother, anxieties that preyed on his mind and kept him awake nights. One such problem had plagued him many years ago, when he was a very little boy, and it had lasted for some time; it had been an occurrence he did not understand and could not control but was a source of hideous embarrassment. The problem was that at almost any time, whether he was racing with Angus or eating dinner or sitting in the parlor listening to the grown-ups talk, his male organ would suddenly, of its own volition, stiffen and pop straight up, pooching out the front of his trousers and making him pray to die. He would scoot back in his chair and lean forward, hoping no one would notice and causing Mother to ask if his stomach hurt. Nothing he could do would make it conduct itself properly. He could order it down with his mind, but the rebellious thing would not behave. Belinda was the only one who knew about it, and she was no help at all, saying that he was making a great fuss about nothing. He had no other playmates, no boys his own age to compare notes with.

Eventually he told his troubles to Grandpa, and James leaned back in his chair, laughed until tears came to his eyes, and then patted his head and said he was a fine, lusty lad. Humiliated, Carey kept quiet about it for months, and then one day when Father was in an especially good mood, he had brought up the subject with him. But Father had been profoundly shocked and ordered him to stop doing it immediately, even though he had already explained that he'd tried to and couldn't.

"Nice little boys do not do such things," Father had announced thunderously, and that was the end of that.

So, he had been laughed at and castigated, and he wanted no more of either, but the problem continued to plague him. Finally, fearing for his soul's salvation, he had told the truth about himself to Vail and then waited to be scourged. But Vail neither laughed nor frowned. He said matter-of-factly, "That's normal, Carey. It happens to all little boys at about your age."

"It does?" Carey was flattened with relief. "Even good boys?"

"All boys."

"Even Father?"

"Even Father."

"But why did he say I was bad if it happened to him, too?"

"I suspect he's forgotten. He was a little boy a long time ago."

Carey thought this over. "Yes, but so were you, and you haven't forgotten."

"No, I haven't forgotten. Don't worry, Carey. It's just the way God made us. It will get better as you grow older."

"That's a load off my mind." Carey heaved a tremendous sigh at the prospect of ultimate deliverance. "To think I won't have any trouble with it when I'm grown."

A flicker passed through Vail's eyes, and for a terrible moment Carey thought he was going to burst out laughing like Grandpa, but he answered with perfect seriousness. "I can't promise you no trouble at all, but at least you'll have a fighting chance."

After this discussion they had sat for a time in companionable ease, Vail smoking a long cigar on the porch swing, his eyes on the boy he loved so much. Perhaps it was only pride that made him want to claim Carey for his own. What man wouldn't be proud of such a son? And it was part of his punishment that it could never be said, for Carey's own sake. He knew, had known for a long time, that Marin intended never to admit it, not to him or to Carey, and how could he say she was wrong?

Carey, straddling the porch railing, was feeling much better about his unruly body. He liked it that Vail talked the same way to him as to adults, as though Carey had a brain in his head and could discuss matters sensibly. After a while he said, "Belinda thinks it's better to be a girl. She says boys do stupid things and have lots more problems."

"Belinda has a very high opinion of herself, which isn't necessarily bad. It may smooth her path."

"Do you think boys do stupid things?"

"They sure do, but so do girls. Everyone has troubles in this life, Carey, men and ladies, too. Being human is a hard row to hoe. I haven't quite figured it out myself."

Encouraged by the quiet confidentiality of Vail's mood, Carey ventured a subject he'd long wanted to bring up. "You're not an ath—a—one of those people that doesn't believe in God, are you? I mean, you said God made us, so you must believe in Him."

"Atheist, Carey. Did I say that? Well, something made us, so I suppose it might be God."

"You really ought to tell Grandfather Severance so you can be friends again." It bothered Carey very much that there was hard feeling between Vail and his awesome grandfather.

Vail's eyes came quickly to his with the cool, hard gaze that could be so disconcerting. "Where'd you get that idea?"

Carey looked away, wishing he had left the delicate subject alone. "I asked Mother why Grandfather is always mad at you, and she said it's because you're an ath—atheist."

"It's not exactly the reason, although your grandfather's ideas and mine do differ on that subject. We don't agree about a lot of things. We don't like each other very much."

"You don't love your father?"

Vail looked consideringly at the tip of his cigar. "No," he said, "I don't."

It was a staggering concept, one Carey could scarcely take in. How could one not love one's parents? It was a given, like the sun's coming up in the morning. But Grandfather Severance seemed not to love Vail, which wasn't possible, either, for parents had to love their children, didn't they?

However, there was no doubt about it; Grandfather did not love his own son, his older son, and today at the picnic he was making it clear to everyone, warmly and proudly introducing his younger son, the congressman, to business friends come all the way from San Diego, and ignoring Vail as if he did not exist. Carey looked back from the creek bank. They were staying at opposite ends of the grove, Grandfather and Aunt Glenna with Father down near the barbecue pit, and Vail walking along the meadow's edge with Mother. Mother said something, and Vail threw back his head and laughed, Carey wondered how it was possible to be so carefree when your father didn't love you.

Belinda and Alida were begging him to find some frogs, so he pulled off his shoes and stockings, rolled up his trouser legs, and waded into the water. When he brought back two green, dripping, wriggling frogs, the little girls screamed most satisfactorily and ran away.

From her place on the long bench next to Celia, Kitty flirted over her fan and blushed and accepted her share of compliments from the gentlemen surrounding them and at the same time kept an eye on other activities at the picnic. Ethan was behaving himself, she made sure of that. He hadn't so much as looked at another woman all day, confining himself to a long chat with Logan Severance, who didn't matter, and spending the rest of the time with his male friends.

Her eyes traveled back to the one person they had rested on most of the day. Vail was with Marin in the meadow, and they were picking late fall wildflowers. Kitty had seen them under the tree while Stuart, all unaware, was making his fiery speech. She'd seen the long, long talk, the intensity in their faces, the utter absorption in each other, the careful space between them. Often in the past she had wondered if there were more going on there than anyone guessed. It would be unspeakably dangerous, considering Stuart's temperament, if he ever caught on, but beneath Vail's smooth good manners he was a risk taker, she had seen it in his eyes, and Marin—who knew what an arrogant woman like her might do?

Now they were strolling back through the tall grass, Marin carrying the flowers, her pale yellow skirt spreading out like a great blossom and fluttering in the light breeze. Vail's dark head was bent as he listened to something she said. The silk fringe on her parasol danced and shimmered in the sunlight as she tilted it back to look up at him. She wore no wide-brimmed hat, relying instead on the parasol to protect her skin, and that was no accident. She wanted to show off her red hair. Look at her now, slipping her arm through his so casually, as if she had the right to touch him any time she wanted. Kitty's heart contracted with malignant jealousy. What a fool Celia was, sitting there so confident in her beauty and her admirers, blind to what was going on right under her nose. She, Kitty, would know instantly if her husband even thought of another woman. And Marin, the predatory bitch. Self-satisfaction was written all over her smug face. If only she knew what lots of people knew, she wouldn't give herself such airs.

I could tell you news that would bring you down to earth in a hurry, Kitty thought in spiteful fury. Through the servants' network, which spread gossip faster than the telegraph, she had discovered what she had been unable to pry out of Ethan even when he was in his cups. Vail Severance did have a woman on the side. Her mother's maid, Bridie, had said, "I was early at Mademoiselle Petra's house, seven o'clock in the morning it was, because your dear mama wanted her new bonnet to wear that day, and there, big as life and twice as handsome, was that darling Mr. Severance—Mr. Vail, that is—kissing Mademoiselle Petra good-bye as he was leaving, and her so pretty and indecent in a wrapper you could see through. Well, far be it from me to jump to conclusions, but gentlemen don't leave unmarried ladies' houses at the crack o' dawn unless they've been there all night, do they now, ma'am? And my friend Mary Clare, who works for Mrs. Parrish, heard that it's no new thing, either. They say Mr. Vail used to have Mademoiselle Petra at his house and then they stopped seeing each other when he married Miss Celia. But it's back on the fire now." Bridie's blue eyes had been bright and her cheeks pink with the pleasure of such a delicious tidbit of scandal, and, oh, the pain and mortification that would be in Marin's face if she knew. And someday, Kitty thought viciously, I may just tell you.

The dinner bell began to clang, calling all to the long tables spread with glistening white clothes and loaded with salads and steaming hot meats, tall, thickly frosted cakes and rich pies.

As the sun dipped in the west, speakers stood up once more to predict the immediate demise of civilization unless their own candidate was elected. Stuart repeated his speech word for word for the delectation of the entire crowd this time, and again received hearty applause along with shouts of "The Union forever!" and "Hurrah for Honest Abe!" There was some muttering among the gamecocks of the Chiv Democrats, but everyone was too full of food to get really angry, and the afternoon ended with no insults passed that could not be ignored.

In the coolness of evening carriages streamed out of the grove, and as they rocked and jounced their way home, almost everyone felt that it had been a marvelously satisfactory day.

The next morning men went out to vote and ten days later the election results from the East arrived by pony in Sacramento and were telegraphed to San Francisco, and Californians knew that their state had given its votes to the next president, Abraham Lincoln.

Chapter 38

✦ "I'll take these deposits to the bank, Mrs. Severance, and stop for lunch, if that's all right."

Marin looked up with an automatic smile. "Fine, Edward. Take your time." Her mind went back to this morning's unpleasant conference with Tyler Winfield. Only by proving to him, chapter and verse, that it would be profitable to buy the *General Randolph*'s load of flour as well as its tobacco and whiskey had she prevented him from countermanding her orders at the dock. For a silent partner he had become very active, and her tilts with him were increasingly disagreeable. Just because he'd bought Ethan a job by paying off the company's debts, just because he'd made another paltry loan when she was short of cash, that needn't give him the idea that he owned the company. Soon, very soon, she must straighten him out. But in the back of her mind there was always the secret worry over the papers she had signed when she and Tyler first entered what he liked to call their partnership. He was no partner of hers, but though the words in those papers had seemed innocuous, it was the first time she had ever signed anything that Gerald had not looked over first, and sometimes she wondered if there might have been more there than she'd seen. She hadn't wanted advice from Gerald; she had closed her eyes and jumped, hoping that somehow it would all work out. One of these days she would manage to dump Tyler in spite of his slippery, double-dealing ways.

Outside her window the day was soft with spring, the bay glittered, the streets stirred with life. Oh, she wanted out of this stuffy, cramped office for just a little while, wanted to stride briskly along the waterfront listening to the slap of water against the sides of gently rocking boats, sniffing the tangy air, letting the stiff breeze lift her hair and sting her cheeks and clean the cobwebs out of her mind. There was excitement to be found outside this office; as a matter of fact there was noticeably more excitement than usual today.

She raised the window and leaned out to see people running and hear a man's high-pitched, demented shout, "It's war, lads, it's war!"

In the next instant she was running, too, down the stairs and out into the suddenly boisterous streets, without cloak or bonnet, fear sweeping her, hurrying, hurrying to the building where the *Bulletin* produced each day's newspaper. The dispatches were up, the words printed out hastily in chalk—short, peremptory head-lines on long blackboards—and they said that shots had been fired at Fort Sumter, people were dead in a riot in Baltimore, and Congress was meeting in war session.

In a fever of panic she turned away. It had come, it had come. Instinct ordered her to run straight to her strong brick house, gather all her loved ones into it, close the draperies and bolt the doors, and huddle close until the storm had passed. But how could she bolt the doors against war? Why had she thought that being far away would save them? Thirty thousand troops from New York. Free states arming. Good God, California was one of those free states! How many troops would be taken from here? Why, oh, why had it ever seemed like a good idea to join the Union? Bloody riot in Baltimore—riot in the quiet, gracious streets of home. Baltimore, so close to Washington, where Stuart was. He would be in that session of Congress.

She was moving at a fast trot, caught up in her own inner turmoil, blind to the commotion around her. A man bumped into her, pushed her aside, and rushed on, laughing and hallooing, not bothering to apologize. She stayed where she was, for the first time really seeing the faces around her. Many were jubilant, and she knew they could be on either side. The more fanatic abolitionists and ardent Unionists were as hot for war as the excitable, militaristic Southerners. Crazy, all of them. But some faces were sober, some men stood talking quietly. A well-dressed woman passed, her handkerchief pressed against streaming eyes.

Marin walked on, turning over in her mind the ways in which war might hurt her personally. Not one man she cared about was a member of the state militia and subject to call; not one had military experience. She began to breathe a little easier. Even Ethan, so rabidly belligerent, had never talked of going to fight himself. Lately he had been talking up the old dream of South-erners in California—to take the state out of the Union and form a Pacific Republic.

Rumor said that there were thirty thousand secessionists in California ready to fight if the state government tried to enforce federal laws. Rumor also said that federal arms had been illegally removed from arsenals in the East and were now secretly stored in California, waiting for the Rebel uprising. The rumors were wild, especially the part about secret caches of armaments in the state, but the idea of a republic was appealing, particularly to a man like Ethan. She could see him as he had looked last week standing in the doorway of the El Dorado Saloon, his favorite hangout, hatless, his hair tousled, his face flushed, raving to his Hotspur friends. He was probably wrong about the practicality of a separate republic, but a sensible neutrality was possible, and surely everyone would soon see it.

But Marin was mistaken. Inclinations toward neutrality dissolved in the heat of passion over Fort Sumter. The Stars and Stripes flew everywhere. Republican clubs, campaigners for Lincoln during the election, met to change themselves into a Union club with the banker and former army officer William Sherman chairing the meeting and lending it the desired military tone. One staunch Southerner defiantly raised the Palmetto flag of South Carolina and was kicked out of the meeting with the flag tied around his neck.

The rumors about secret military stores in California turned out to be true. John B. Floyd, the disloyal secretary of war, had quietly transferred fifty thousand guns out west to be furtively cached around the state. More than half were returned as soon as they were discovered; the remainder were turned over to the army at the Presidio and the forts on Alcatraz Island. Several high army officers with Southern sympathies resigned and headed South, and the defections shocked loyal young men into volunteering at once. Some few went east immediately.

Harlan Gentry was one of these. He passed through town on his way to New York and, accompanied by Dan, came to call at the house to say farewell to his relatives. Harlan was a lanky young man with a luxuriant mustache and full beard, leaner and taller than his brother and with far more mischief in his eyes.

He's the first of our own to go, thought Marin, heartsick. Look at him, eyes sparkling and full of devilment. You'd think he were going to a party.

She glanced at James, wondering how he would take a Gentry's coming down on the side of the Union. He had never hidden his loathing for abolitionists or his love for the state of his birth, Virginia.

He was gazing at the floor, rubbing a finger over his lower lip, staring into a past the others could not see. "My grandfather, Thomas Gentry, was in the Virginia line for three years while my grandmother, Catherine, brought in the crops and raised his sons. He marched and starved and fought in many a bloody action. He was at the battle of Guilford Courthouse and at Yorktown when Cornwallis surrendered." He looked up at Harlan. "Did you know your great-grandfather was at Yorktown? I must have heard him tell about it a hundred times. He was proud of what he'd done in that war. He believed—they all believed they were building something better than had ever been seen in this world before. Now people say the country is washed up, that if a state can't leave peacefully when it wants to, there's no democracy and no freedom. Well, I don't know. I wouldn't fight to free one slave, although I don't own any and don't intend to. But the Union— that's the thing. There's too much of my family's heart's blood tied up in this country to let it go because the South has decided to pull its marbles out of the game." He leaned forward and tapped Harlan's hand. "Listen to me, boy. War is no jolly picnic. Take care of your rifle, keep it oiled, keep it dry. Keep your feet dry, too. Carry an extra pair of socks. A Southron is a hell of a shot and loves a fight, so you keep your head down and don't be a hero. What does your pa think about your going?"

"Well, sir, Pa and I don't get on, and I've been gone from home a while. But I stopped by to see him on my way down here. He's for the South, but he wished me well all the same. He's married again, did you know?"

James sat back, startled. "Dan never told us."

"It happened just at the end of the year. A nice enough woman. I guess."

Cole married, and I didn't know, James thought sadly. He could be dead and I wouldn't know. What a far road we've traveled. He said, "Stay for dinner, son, stay here tonight. The whole lot of us will give you a good send-off in the morning."

Not too many men were as yet prepared to take Harlan's path. Most of the early volunteers expected to stay in California to hold the great harbor and the state for the North. But the patriotism of newspaper editors was at white heat, and Confederate sympathies became anathema. Anyone harboring such feelings stopped talking in public, but in the homes of certain wealthy families on Rincon Hill or in South Park, where the Southern aristocracy had built fine houses, or in boardinghouse rooms or unpretentious dwellings in less affluent parts of town, pictures of Jeff Davis were hung above the Stars and Bars, "Dixie" was softly sung, and later, as Southern battle triumphs began to mount, quietly exultant parties were held.

Tyler Winfield, prudent as always, hedged his bets by making a large and very public contribution to the U.S. Sanitary Commission, an organization formed to provide medicines, clothing, and personal articles for the boys in blue, while his son, George, traveled South to take up a commission under General Beauregard, the man who had pounded Fort Sumter into submission.

Stuart wrote that the Federal City was in mortal danger from a host of Confederate troops infesting Manassas Junction, only thirty miles away. It was his opinion that Union forces must move into Virginia without delay, occupy Richmond, and end the war before things got out of hand. He was pressuring friends in the War Department to get him a commission quickly, before the rebels surrendered, for a war record would be essential to anyone hoping to run for higher office in the future.

As Marin had expected, business boomed. War, as always, was making money for those who didn't have to fight it. Rates of exchange on gold had shot up owing to the ever-present specter of piracy on the high seas. One shipment of California gold captured by the Confederacy could mean as much to the South as ten battles won. But if the war ended as soon as Stuart predicted, costs would be back to normal by Christmas.

Then came news of the battle of Bull Run, the little stream near Manassas Junction that Stuart had mentioned. After three days of fighting, Federal troops had stumbled back to Washington—routed, panicked, beaten. Colonel William T. Sherman, the former San Francisco banker, was mentioned in dispatches. Among the Confederate dead, killed when a cannon exploded in his face, was Lieutenant George Claibourne Winfield, C.S.A.

Just before Christmas, Stuart wrote gleefully that he had obtained a colonelcy under the command of General McClellan, but that Marin was not to worry. He was on detached duty in Washington and was in no danger. No major battles had been fought anyway—a good thing, as the army was made up mostly of raw recruits. His only worry was that President Lincoln, a crude man with an odd sense of humor, would push the general into making a move before the army was ready. He enclosed a daguerreotype of himself in a well-tailored uniform with gold-fringed epaulets and a sword at his side. He had grown a mustache, which drooped down around his lips, his eyes gazed steadily into the camera, and everyone who saw the picture commented that with only a few more men of such resolution the war would soon be over.

There was little fighting during the remainder of the year as the two armies struggled to organize. The first good news came in February, when Ulysses Grant, an untidy West Pointer, a former captain in the Mexican War with a history of failure at every civilian job he tried, took the forts of Henry and Donelson, which controlled the Tennessee and Cumberland rivers, a feat that came close to wresting Tennessee from the South. People said happily that this showed what Yankee farm boys could do under a good general. On the heels of this achievement Manassas was occupied by the Federals, and the town went wild. Manassas was the gateway to the Shenandoah Valley, the pathway to Richmond, the scene of the miserable humiliation at Bull Run. Now all was redeemed, the war could not last long now! Guns were fired, firecrackers set off, bands played "The Star-Spangled Banner," and people crowded around the newspapers' blackboards for further details. A direct telegraph line was in now, and news streaked from east to west with miraculous speed. Soon word would be tapped out across the thousands of miles of wire that the war was over.

Then, only a month later, a year to the day after the surrender of Fort Sumter, dispatches flashed in telling of the struggle near Shiloh church. Grant's army, caught unprepared, had been fallen on by Beauregard and Albert Sidney Johnston, once commander at San Francisco and one of the Confederacy's finest generals. After two days of savage fighting both armies were exhausted; the Confederates had retreated, leaving the Northern army in control and General Johnston dead. The news was received as a great victory. People cheered and paraded and sang, cannon boomed, and many patriotic speeches were made. Only a few worriedly noted the bloodiness of the battle. The Union force had lost over a quarter of its troops. It was victory, but at what cost?

During all the celebrations Ethan remained calm, even cheerful, and Marin watched him with puzzled eyes. He rarely mentioned states' rights or King Cotton, but that was natural; no Southerner talked much in San Francisco these days. He was sober most of the time, too, and that was not natural.

Chapter 39

Pike Street was not a street at all, but a dark alley in the heart of San Francisco's Chinatown, where the Chinese lived their own lives in their own way. White cutthroats hid out in Chinatown, as did some very sophisticated elements of the underworld, but noncriminal Caucasians did not venture in except to sample the exotic wares of the exotic ladies available there. Along the alley and around the corner on Clay Street, plush parlor houses, where an all-night stay with an exquisite young lady could cost six hundred dollars or more, sat alongside the worst of the cribs inhabited by Chinese peasant slave girls, many of them only children, imported by wealthy Chinese entrepreneurs.

The cribs were relatively cheap and patronized by men who couldn't afford better. Respectable gentlemen who came regularly to Chinatown for their thrills went only to the best houses. They came cautiously and usually with a friend. Vail had come alone, in canvas work pants and an old jacket with no gold watch chain or cuff links, but a gun on each hip and a small dagger in his right boot. The sensation of impending danger reminded him of the early days when he had slept at all times with a loaded gun at his side.

He had come to Chinatown on business. Frank Maguire, the owner of the Restaurant Rondeau, had finally made an offer for the land Vail held on either side of the restaurant, but Frank was recovering from a gunshot wound at the Joyful Joss House, a high-priced brothel he owned in partnership with his Chinese mistress. The only way to get the money was to meet Frank there. Vail damned Maguire for his tastes and kept his hands near his guns.

When he left Frank after their meeting, it was long past sunset and he was carrying five thousand dollars earnest money, too much for this part of town at night. Pike Street was completely dark except for an occasional door lit by a small red lamp. Most of the doors and niches lay in shadows so that no one could see who came and went. Far down the alley, at the corner of Pike and Clay, a saloon was going full blast, and light from its open front fell on the narrow dirt street and briefly illumined men hurrying furtively past. Two men stepped out of the saloon and stopped before it, heads together; the dark, wide-shouldered, shabbily dressed man listened with intent eyes. His taller, golden-haired companion talked rapidly, then glanced around, suddenly aware of the light. He said a few more words, put his tall hat on his head, and walked off down Clay Street, swinging his malacca cane. His down-at-the-heels friend stared after him, balled hands shoved deep in his pockets, tense excitement in the pose of his hunched body.

A heavy hand fell on his shoulder. "Hello, Wes. Fancy running into you after all these years. How's the world treating you?" John Wesley Morgan found himself being walked back into the saloon despite a mighty desire to be off and running down the alley.

"Vail?" He sounded as though he could not believe his eyes or his ill luck. "Uh, grand to see you. Look, I got to be going . . ."

"Oh, let me buy you a drink, Wes. I insist." With a friendly, firm hand Vail shoved him across the smoky, crowded room. At the bar he tossed a gold coin to the bartender and got two bottles in return. He then propelled Wes to a table in the back corner, sat him down in a chair, and sprawled opposite, grinning genially.

Wes considered the obstacles between himself and the door and decided he couldn't make it. Jesus, what a break. The Severances were always bad news.

Vail opened a bottle and passed it across. Wes accepted it gingerly, took a deep breath and then a long, long swallow. He shuddered, wiped his mouth, said hoarsely, "Damn, that's good stuff. Wes, I got to be . . ."

"Nothing but the best for an old friend. Sit down, Wes."

Wes sat down. "Look, Vail, I got nothing against you, and I hope you got nothing against me. That old business with Stuart . . ."

"Oh, Stuart. Did you tangle with him? Well, I'm not on the best terms with him myself. He's a big man back in Washington now, a colonel in the army. Have another drink."

"That a fact?" Wes drank, slightly more at ease. Washington was a long ways away, and Vail looked relaxed and friendly. He'd always been a right kind of man, decenter than his brother, that toad. Wes tilted the bottle again. His face behind the ragged beard was thin, his skin an unhealthy yellow, but he had developed heavy shoulder muscles, and his eyes were still brown and prominent, like Glenna's, and still impatient. His trousers were threadbare, his flannel shirt frayed, his leather jacket sweat-stained and stiff with dirt. The soles of his boots had worn thin, and the heel of one was pulling loose. He was no longer the lanky boy who had loved Marin Gentry's red hair and slender body, or the dashing young man who had stolen Sophy Gentry's heart and virginity. He was thirty-two years old and looked forty, he lived in a rat-infested back room in the heart of Chinatown, and until Ethan had bought him a meal an hour ago, he had been starving and planning to rob some passerby soon if Ethan didn't come through.

Ethan had come through, however, and he was replete, with only a touch of the indigestion that plagued him. He took out a new cigar, one of a half-dozen given him by Ethan, sniffed it, rolled it delicately between thumb and forefinger, struck a match. With satisfaction he drew the aromatic smoke down into his lungs and leaned back, enveloped by a sense of well-being. "So what're you doing down here with the chinks and bully-boys, Vail? Come to see how the other half lives?"

"Something like that. I hear the ladies are a trifle different."

Wes laughed loudly. "They're different, all right. You've come to the right place if you're looking for the unusual." His voice lowered to confidentiality under the babble of noise. "These China girls are the hottest stuff it's ever been my pleasure to climb aboard. Better'n the Frenchies and señoritas by far. They got the damnedest imaginations. Here, have a drink. I been hogging the bottle."

"Thanks, no. Liquor and I don't always mix. Sometimes it causes me problems, so I don't drink when . . . that is . . ."

Vail looked embarrassed, and Wes said, "Oh." After a pause, "Yessir, as I say, you've come to the right place. The girls down here know things white girls never even heard of. They use these . . . they've got a name for 'em, but I don't speak the lingo . . . these here gadgets that'll get you started and keep you going, world without end, amen!" He launched into shrill laughter that ended in a hiccup. The first bottle was empty. Vail opened the second and shoved it over.

"Any recommendations?"

The laughter drained out of Wes's face, and he leaned forward until his breath, foul from whiskey and decaying teeth, reached Vail. Very seriously he said, "Stay away from the cribs, the real low-class ones anyway, because the girls're likely diseased. They ain't allowed to turn down any man no matter if he's all over sores and sick as a cat, so it's not worth fooling with 'em. I had the pox a while back myself, but an old witch-woman dosed me, and I'm fine now. Too bad about those cribs. They got dollies maybe ten, eleven years old. Now that's different."

He giggled drunkenly, and Vail's eyes flickered over him, noting the miotic pupils, the jaundiced, scaly skin, the hoarse voice and stertorous breathing.

Wes took hold of himself. "If you got the money—sure, you got the money. Go to Ah Choy's or the Joyful Joss House. Now that's class, I hear. Never been there myself, though I will real soon. Look out, ladies, Wes Morgan's a-comin'!" He whooped with laughter at his own humor and ended in a violent paroxysm of coughing.

When the spasm had passed and he had wiped the tears from his eyes, Vail said quietly, "How would you like one of Ah Choy's women right now?"

They looked at each other.

"Those gals cost six, seven hundred dollars."

"I know."

Wes drew back, unease moving in his face. "What do I have to do?"

"Nothing much. Just tell me what you and Ethan were talking about tonight."

He was up and battling in the direction of the door, but Vail had him by the collar, choking, choking . . . He was slammed down in his chair, and Vail found the knife hidden under his belt.

"Any guns? I said, *any guns*?"

Wes shook his head, his pupils pinpoints in the shadowed corner.

Vail patted over his body, found the ammunition in his pocket, and pulled out the Colt pistol from the holster under his arm. Wes drew as close to the wall as he could get and watched Vail sit down and examine the gun.

"A nice piece for a ragpicker who can't afford a meal, let alone a girl. Did Ethan give it to you?"

"Go to hell."

"What is Ethan hatching, Wes? Tell me, and you can go on your way with a thousand dollars in your pocket and no one the wiser."

Wes leaned across the table, lips drawn back over his teeth, his face white with the rage that suddenly consumed him. "Piss on your thousand dollars. I hate your goddamn guts. Shove your putrid money up your arse, I don' need it, 'cause I struck the richest vein in California, yessir, El Dorado, by God. Af'er t'night I'm gonna be richer'n you bastards . . . Gold'll spill outta my pockets, an' will I stoop to pick it up? No, I won't. You'll be sayin', 'Yes, indeedy, Mr. Morgan,' an' 'Just as you say, Mr. Morgan.'" Color was returning slowly to his face, pleasure replacing anger at the rapturous thought of himself, guns blazing, chasing the despicable Severance brothers out of town.

"Where are you going to strike that rich vein, Wes?"

"Wouldn't you like to know," Wes chortled. "M'lips are sealed . . . promised my frien' Ethan. Good man, Ethan, fine frien'." His eyes struggled to focus on the tense, alert man opposite, and the second bottle of whiskey, still almost full, wavered into view. Tears welled and trickled down his mottled cheeks. "Poor li'l bottle, don' nobody love you? Don' nobody love Wes either. Poor Wes." He lifted the bottle and missed his mouth; slowly his head sank down to the tabletop. The bottle rolled off and landed beside his boot, whiskey pooling on the rough wood floor.

Vail hauled him up, dragged him through the crowd and out into the night. Not one man in the room lifted his eyes from his drink or his cards to take note.

Michael Morgan peered through the crack in the door, his gun ready, the light of the lamp throwing odd shadows upward onto his broad, well-fed face. It was a face grown cautious with the years—he was a shopkeeper now and had property to husband and nurture—but suspicion departed when he saw Vail. He recognized the body slung over the big man's shoulder, set the lamp down quickly, and unchained the door.

"Come in, come in. What happened? Is he dead?"

"Not yet. Where can I put him?"

"In the back room. There's a cot."

Michael hurried ahead, holding the lamp high, drawing back the curtain that hid his little office from the front of the store.

Vail brushed past and lowered Wes onto the narrow canvas cot. "Get some water, a bucketful. Hurry!"

The sharp command moved Michael out of the room. In a moment he was back with two pitchers. "I was just going to wash and make some coffee . . ."

Vail took both pitchers and dumped the contents into Wes's flushed face just as he was inhaling in a loud, rattling snore. He choked and rose up, gasping like a fish in a net. "Jesus God!" He strangled again, wiped his dripping face and looked around, wild-eyed. At the sight of Michael some of the panic faded. He wiped his face again, snorted, and sank back down. Before his head hit the cot, Vail had him up and swaying on his feet. "Get that coffee started, Michael, and come right back. I need you."

Michael, thoroughly galvanized now, ran out, fumbled at his little stove, and hurried back to help walk Wes around the room.

"Lemme alone," Wes mumbled. "Lemme sleep."

"Can't we just let him sleep it off?" Michael asked. "He's soused to the gills."

Vail gave Wes an upward tug that snapped his head back, at the same time booting him in the rear. "I was in Chinatown tonight. Ethan and Wes were in a saloon down there with their heads together having a long, confidential talk."

"Ethan?" Michael hitched Wes higher. "Come on, old bud, walk!" He looked across his brother's sagging shoulders. "What business could Wes have with the likes of Ethan?"

"That's what I spent a bottle of good whiskey trying to find out. He says he's struck a rich vein and after tonight he's going to be swimming in gold, but he can't tell why because he promised his good friend Ethan. Stand up, you bastard." Wes had sunk toward the floor and hung there, a deadweight. The two men pulled him up and dragged him across the room again.

Michael groaned, "Please, God, not another robbery. He wiggled out of the last one by the skin of his teeth. But I can't picture Ethan getting himself into a snare like that."

"Can you picture Ethan trudging off to the mountains again with a pick and a shovel? I offered Wes a thousand dollars hard cash for information tonight, and he told me what I could do with it."

Michael stared. "He'd sell me for a thousand, no questions asked. What do you think their target is, Vail? A bank?"

"I think it's nothing small-time. I think it's the whole damn state."

Michael's mouth opened. He let go of his brother, and Wes swung around, clutched Vail in a drunken embrace, and slowly opened his eyes. "Ho, there, ol' frien'." He rested chummily against Vail's shoulder and introduced him to Michael. "This here's Vail, my good ol' frien'." Another thought struck, and he frowned darkly. "Not his brother, though. His brother's *merde*. Yer brother's shit, ain't he, Vail?"

"He sure is. Michael, get the coffee."

"See?" Wes bellowed as Vail shoved him down on the cot and held him there, "Vail thinks he's shit, too. Vail's m'frien'."

Michael bustled back with the coffeepot and a mug. "Here you go, buddy, swallow a little. That's it, drink up. Good boy. Now bottom's up. Good job, Wes."

Wes smiled happily at the praise, and Michael slopped more coffee into the mug. "Let's see how fast you can get it down. Atta boy!" He filled the mug again, held it to Wes's lips, and Wes, suddenly petulant, batted it away. The mug flew against the wall, shattering, and brown coffee spread a dark stain on the white paint and trickled to the floor.

"Had enough pukin' coffee," he muttered, and then, alarmed, "Gonna puke!" Michael rushed for a chamber pot and held it under his retching brother's face.

When the spasm had passed, Wes rubbed the back of his hand across his mouth, sighed, and murmured piteously, "Wanna sleep."

"Later," said Vail. "Right now we're going to talk. Where are you meeting Ethan tonight?"

Wes grinned triumphantly. "You ain't so smart. I ain't gonna meet him tonight."

"Tomorrow then."

"Go to hell."

"Come on, Wes, I'm your friend. Michael's your friend. You can tell us."

"Tell nobody. Ethan said, 'If you wanna be rich as Solomon, tell nobody.'" Wes's eyes began to droop again.

Vail took him by the shoulders and shook him so violently that his head snapped, and his struggle for breath ended in an eruption of coughing. "Now do I have your attention? Then listen closely. The witch-woman's dosing didn't cure you of pox, Wes. You've got it now, and you're dying."

Wes's eyes flew open. His face turned dark red. "You're a liar!" He tried to lunge from his chair, reaching upward for Vail's throat, but his hands were weak and trembled, his traitor body would not obey.

Vail knelt beside him, his voice rough and brutal. "You have trouble walking, don't you, especially in the dark. You spread your feet apart to keep your balance. You have stabbing pains in your legs, lightning pains that hurt like hell. You can't eat like you used to, and when you do, you end up vomiting, sometimes for hours."

"That was bad liquor made me spew. You bought me bad liquor."

"You don't see so well, either. Sometimes you can't stop coughing, sometimes it hurts just to breathe, and when you crap or piss, it hurts so bad, you put it off as long as you can. Got any sores on your feet that won't heal? How are you with women? Have you been able to make it lately?

Wes stared into Vail's face, his lips working to form words that would not come. In the room there was only the sound of a clock ticking. Outside in the street a horse clopped slowly by.

Quietly, almost gently, Vail said, "You are in the late stage of syphilis, Wes. *Lues venerea, Morbus Gallicus* . . . pox. I'm a doctor, and I know."

Wes still stared, shocked into cold sobriety by the hideous phrases, hypnotized like a snake before a snake charmer, more convinced by the formal Latin words than by the exact description of all he had suffered lately.

"What—what do I do?" he whispered hoarsely, and then clutched at Vail in wild supplication. "Oh, God, I don't want to die! Oh, God, Vail, save me. Michael . . ." Desperately he looked up into his brother's stunned face. "Michael, make him save me."

"I will save you, Wes, I'll give you medicine," Vail said softly, "but only if you tell me the truth, and tell me now. What is Ethan planning?"

"I'll tell—I'll tell you everything, only save me."

"I will save you, Wes. Start talking, and don't leave anything out."

Wes swallowed. "Well—it's a kind of club, see? Knights of the Golden Circle, that's us. A lot of grand fellers in it. We're sworn to eternal silence, and we stand for things like states' rights, and all that. We don't mean to see California crushed by the despot's heel. That's what Ethan says. There's this one feller, Mr. Pettingill, who's an officer in the Confederate navy with a letter signed by Jeff Davis himself, a special kind of letter that says he has the right to fit out a ship and capture the enemy's ships and treasure. And that's what we mean to do." His eyes began to glow as excitement rose and wiped out for the moment the dread those awful foreign words had brought.

"The *Columbia* is sailing tomorrow afternoon," Vail remarked casually. The *Columbia* was one of the mail steamers sailing regularly from San Francisco, laden with gold destined for New York. A single shipment commonly amounted to upwards of two million dollars. New York bankers were saying that the massive, steady influx of Western gold was keeping the economy growing and the federal government solvent, and, in fact, was paying for the war. But the Confederacy was strapped for cash. California's gold would buy the South bountiful military supplies and armaments from European suppliers who demanded cash on the barrelhead.

"Yeah," breathed Wes reverently, "the *Columbia*. Do you know how much gold there is on just one of those steamers? Two, three million each sailing. Plenty for the Confederacy and a lot left over for us boys who take the risks. Plenty for you fellers, too. Say, why don't you join up and be Knights along with us? Ethan's always saying we need more men and, hell, I'd go bond for you."

"Would you?" Vail pulled up a chair and sat down beside Wes. "That'd be something, being a Knight, wouldn't it, Michael? Michael? Don't just stand there, man, get Wes and me some coffee."

Michael still stood frozen, seeing his endlessly troublesome brother in a new and harrowing light. The boy was mad with impossible dreams of glory, the boy was sick unto death. He said, "Uh, yes, coffee," and hurriedly poured two mugs, handing Wes his without looking directly at him.

"Sit down, Michael, relax. That's some offer Wes has made." Vail sipped at the bitter, overboiled brew and mused, "A Knight. Well, I, for one, would have to know more about it. If Mr. Pettingill is going to use his letters of marque against U.S. shipping, he's got to get a ship for himself first."

"He bought one right after he got here," Wes cried eagerly, "a fast honey of a schooner, the *Mary Mulhane*. Maybe you've seen her down by Lombard dock."

Vail's brows rose in amazement. "Right out in the open where everyone can see?"

A crafty expression entered Wes's bloodshot eyes. "Looks funny, doesn't it? I thought so, too, at first, but here's the way it works. We do everything aboveboard because we got nothing to hide, right? We're just merchants carrying guns and ammunition down to Mexico. The Mexicans are having a hell of a time fighting off the Frenchies down there, and they need help, right? It isn't legal to sell military supplies here, but you know how it is—we offer good money to local businessmen, they wink their eye at the law and pretend they're selling us food and machinery. After all, it's for a good cause—except here's what we really do. We sail out of port, innocent as can be, just honest merchants turning a buck, and we lie doggo till the *Columbia* comes along. We take her, put our guns aboard her, and use her to take the next steamer. After two or three like that we run up to Vancouver Island, send part of the gold south, and divide up the rest. Millions and millions!" He chortled. "And that's just the beginning. We've got our men in every town in California—there's a lot of us Confederates out here, you know—and when we're ready, we'll cut the telegraph wires, grab the arsenal at Benicia, take Alcatraz and Fort Point, and then . . . what's the trouble, Michael?"

"No matter, no matter. What then, Wes?"

"Then, gentlemen, we make California one of the Confederate States of America. How do you like them apples! Ain't that one hell of a plan?"

Vail rubbed his chin. "It's a hell of a plan, all right. How many guns on the *Mary Mulhane*?"

"Four twelve-pounders that I know of. There's a lot of boxes down in the hold marked 'Flour' and 'Machine Parts,' but my guess is it's rifles and powder. I'm not one of the high-ups, and they don't tell me everything."

"How many men will be aboard?"

"Twenty of us Knights—if you and Michael come, that'll be twenty-two. And a half-dozen sailors to run the ship."

"When do you leave?"

"On the morning tide. Hey, I got to meet Ethan by two o'clock." Wes fumbled in his pockets with stiff, clumsy fingers, searching for the gold watch he had long ago hocked. "What time is it getting to be?"

"The evening's young," Vail murmured soothingly. "You have a lot of time." He pushed Wes's shoulder gently; Wes rolled backward and lay prone on the cot, blinking his eyes. "You're tired, Wes, and you've had too much to drink. Sleep for a while, and we'll wake you when it's time to go."

"Good idea—think I'll do that." Wes yawned, and his eyes closed. Then, "Vail? When you gonna give me that medicine?"

"Tomorrow, when all the booze is out of your system."

"An' it'll cure me, sure?"

"It will cure you. Go to sleep now."

In moments Wes lapsed into a rasping snore.

Vail stood looking down at him. "Got a blanket, Michael? He'll be cold in a little while."

"Sure, I've got one somewhere." Michael hunted through his cupboards, glad of something to do, found an old blanket, and laid it over his sleeping brother. "I'll never forget what you've done for him tonight."

Vail shrugged. "Rolling home drunks is my specialty. Besides, I got him drunk."

"No, I mean about—the pox. Thank God you could recognize it and you know what to do. I'm forever in your debt."

Vail looked up with an odd smile. "Are you? Enough to come with me to Lombard dock tonight?"

"For God's sake, why? Stay away from there, Vail. The navy will be on those dumb bastards before they're through the Golden Gate. Let 'em hang."

"I can't. One of those dumb bastards is Ethan."

Michael thought that over. "For Marin's sake?"

"Partly. For someone else, too."

Kitty? Michael wondered. Not likely. Vail's good manners barely hid his contempt for her. Was there another woman in Ethan's life, someone beside high-class tarts? Unwillingly, under the pressure of obligation, he said, "You can count on me. What do you have in mind?"

"First locate Usual McIntyre. He's taken up residence with Mrs. Tierney and lives behind her shop. He'll be either there or playing poker at the Union Hotel. You won't find him in a saloon—he had to take the pledge before she'd let him move in with her. Tell him to come here and keep an eye on Wes while we're gone." Vail bent over the snoring Wes, listened to his heart, lifted an eyelid. "He may sleep through the night, or he may come out of this suddenly, roaring like a lion and ready to take on the world. We can't afford to have him loose on the town tonight. Tell Usual to keep him here if he has to chain him to the wall. I have a small business matter to attend to, but I'll meet you back here in an hour."

"All right. Ah—no doubt it's occurred to you that there's twenty-six of them and two of us. Just how do you propose to stop them?"

"That's what I have to figure out."

Fog thick as drifting eiderdown hid their movements. In the shadow of the warehouse they crossed the wharf carrying a dinghy. They lowered the dinghy, let themselves off the edge of the wharf, and silently dropped the few feet to the rocks below. To the north of town, in midchannel, rose the rocky outcropping of Alcatraz Island, confronting the entrance to the bay, its lighthouse struggling to beam a path through the dark and the fog, its recently reinforced gun emplacements ready to do battle with any intruder. Much farther to the north, in San Pablo Bay, lay Mare Island Navy Yard, where the few vessels the government had seen fit to allot to the west coast were based. Due west, close by Lombard dock, were the red cliffs of the Golden Gate and Fort Point, the

Presidio's jutting promontory guarding the Gate with the heaviest guns in the harbor. On the north side of the Gate lay Point Bonita, its lighthouse defeated tonight here at the entrance to the bay where the fog was always the worst. Its lonely cannon fired a fog signal every half hour for shipping in the channel. Off Point Bonita the simmering, deadly Bonita riptide was beginning to form. Any ship leaving port on this night, in this fog, would need a master pilot at the helm as well as enormous luck.

But the tide was ebbing westward fast, and the schooner *Mary Mulhane*, half hidden by the swirling mist even at this close range, was preparing to leave. She was a rakish lady, her long, sleek, black hull shouting speed, her masts slanting aft, her sails ghostlike clouds in the fog. Cries issued from the deck, men scrambled in the rigging, pinpoints of light gleamed and disappeared as the fog moved with each faint stir of the quiet air.

"They're all aboard," whispered Michael. "We're too late."

"Not if we use the dinghy."

"It's a damn fool plan, and you'll get yourself killed if you try it. Let them go."

Vail pulled the rope off the dinghy, coiled it at his belt with the grappling hook, and fastened his knife in its sheath, every movement of his big frame smooth and economical. There was a controlled vitality to his face that Michael had not seen in years, and he was smiling—smiling, by God—as if this lunatic adventure was a dinner dance at the St. Francis Hotel.

In disgust he said, "I believe you're enjoying this. Ethan be damned, I think you're doing it just for the monumental, pie-eyed hell of it."

Vail laughed with barely contained excitement and Michael, wanting to take off for home and unable in honor to do so, thought with sour accuracy that the man was like a big, restive racehorse kept too long at a quiet trot. He had the bit in his teeth, there was no force on earth that could stop him, and he, Michael, was going to be dragged along willy-nilly in a flat-out, neck-or-nothing race.

With mock sympathy Vail said, "I can see how you're yearning to go on board, but I reserve that pleasure for myself." The sardonic tone said that he knew exactly how unhappy Michael was and thought it was funny.

Michael set his teeth. "Come on, let's get the damned boat in the water."

The dinghy was a lightweight rowboat they had furtively removed only a half hour ago from a fishing vessel tied up at the next dock.

"This is stealing, you know," Michael grumbled.

"We'll return it when we're finished."

"Finished is what we'll likely be, and then we can't return it."

"Leave some money if your conscience hurts."

"It doesn't hurt that much," Michael replied, and grinned as he heard Vail laugh in the dark.

They carried the dinghy down to the water and climbed in. The water was black as the sky. Only the great sails on the slanting masts gleamed mistily through the obscuring dark, only the occasional moving flame of a lantern on the deck above them shot a slender beam through the fog, a yellow shaft of light with particles of moist air swimming in it. Fog muted sounds. The splash of the dinghy's oars was faint, the shouts of the men on deck and in the rigging as distant as a dream. They rowed close to the slim, dark hull at a point farthest from the working sailors.

Vail stood up, rocking with the gentle movements of the dinghy. He hurled the grappling hook upward, and it landed on deck with what seemed an explosive noise, slid back, and caught on the gunwale. No shouts above, no running feet. "Here goes nothing." He swung up the rope and disappeared into the night and the fog.

He was behind the cabin. Forward he could see Ethan, a knit cap pulled low over his ears, his hands jammed in the pockets of his heavy jacket, his face taut with elation, watching the sailors swing like agile monkeys up the shrouds. He was with Rufus Pettingill, a drab, rabbity little man whom Vail had met once, a man with the dry, cautious look of a banker and a habit of repeating himself, the last man in the world to be a spy, a pirate, a fomenter of rebellion.

On deck, working along with the sailors, were Ephraim Parrish, the son of Hugh and Margaret Parrish, Cade, the Venables' oldest boy, and several other young Chiv Democrats. More surprising was the sight of Tony Purcell, the son of the passionate Unionist William Purcell, calling to one of the sailors above and then excitedly scrambling up after him. There were others Vail did not recognize, but they were boys, all of them, boys aflame with the thrill of adventure and danger, even Ethan, who would always be a boy. The only adults among them were the six professional sailors, hired for a job, and Rufus Pettingill, calm, cool-eyed, and plainly in command.

Pettingill walked back toward the cabin, and Vail crouched, knife in hand, his gun a comforting weight against his hip. Pettingill went down the companionway to the cabins below.

Ethan was moving after him. He stopped, glanced up again at the sweating sailors above him, and in that brief instant Vail climbed down the companion ladder. Light showed under the door at the end of the passageway. He tried the door of the first cabin. It moved under his hand, and he stepped inside as Ethan scrambled down the ladder.

Ethan turned toward the captain's cabin, humming under his breath. In the next moment a heavy hand clamped his nose and mouth, the edge of a blade, razor-sharp, pinked the skin of his throat, and he was dragged backward into the dark. Beside his ear a whisper said, "Do you want to breathe?"

He nodded frantically. The hand released his nose but still clamped his mouth. He drew in a sharp breath in fear and astonishment, and the knife cut his skin slightly. He froze.

"Cross your wrists behind you. Quick!" The knife left his throat, and cold metal locked his hands together. The knife returned. "I'm going to take away my hand. Make a sound, and I'll cut your throat. Do you understand?" He nodded and the hand withdrew, but the knife did not move. He swallowed convulsively and waited.

"Does Pettingill expect you in his cabin?"

He shook his head.

"Good. You're coming off the ship with me, under your own power or not. Which way do you want it? Answer very quietly."

"Jesus, Vail . . ."

"Which way?"

"I'm not going!" Ethan whispered furiously. "How did you find out?"

"You left a trail a mile wide. The minute you pull away from the dock, the navy will jump on you."

"The navy don't have a suspicion . . ."

"Do you really think they're all fools? If it's obvious to me, others must know, too. They'll take you and hang you for treason."

"Butt out of my business! If I hang, I hang. What do you care?"

"I don't, but others do. Are you coming peaceably, or do I have to assist you?"

Ethan was silent, thinking of his own sister and of Vail's sister. "You took a hell of a risk, coming here. This isn't any small-time enterprise, and I've given my word. Would you mind taking that knife away? It makes me nervous."

"Since your word means so much, do I have it that you'll keep quiet?"

"Yeah, you have it."

The knife moved away, and Ethan took a long breath and let it out slowly. He looked through the porthole. There was only blinding fog; the town was blotted out as completely as if it did not exist.

"Not even a last look. I'm sorry to leave, but I'll be back one day. I thank you, Vail, truly, for I know you meant well, but I'm committed with all my soul, and I can't turn back. It's a matter of honor."

Behind him Vail sighed. "I was afraid you'd say that. Well, I've done my best . . ." There was a pungent odor as a cloth came down over Ethan's face. He choked once and went limp.

In the dinghy Michael, working constantly with the oars to remain in position, looked up to see a large object being lowered at the end of a rope. He reached up, almost lost an oar, swore, and snatched again at the swinging body. He guided it, trussed hand and foot, into the dinghy and cut the rope free, then Vail came down.

"Let's get out of here."

They rowed back under the wharf, tied up the boat, and staggered over the uneven rocky ledge with Ethan a burden between them. Inside the warehouse that fronted on the water, they dumped him and sat down, breathing heavily.

"We could be charged with breaking and entering if we're caught here," Michael said gloomily. "You might offer me one of those."

"Here, take two." Vail struck a match and drew until the tip of his own cigar glowed brightly. "You ought to get married, Michael, before you turn into a fussy old maid. I don't recall your worrying about illegalities in the old days."

"I didn't have so much to lose in the old days. How would it look for a respectable hardware dealer like me to be caught stealing a dinghy and busting into somebody's warehouse?"

"Terrible. The respectable people—all dear friends of yours—would probably string you up."

Michael grunted and glanced at Ethan. "He looks like a turkey ready for the oven. What did you hit him with?"

"Just a little chloroform. I got it from Charles."

"Charles, huh. What story did you tell him?"

"The truth. He wanted to come, too. He's not so dainty as you."

Ethan groaned and rolled over onto his back. He groaned again, turned his head slowly, and then began to struggle to a sitting position. "Where's my ship? I've got to get back on my ship. Oh, God, I feel sick."

"Lie down. It will pass."

Ethan looked toward the shadowy men. "Vail, you blackguard, you filthy Judas . . ."

Michael chuckled. "Tell him, Ethan."

"Michael? You there? Set me loose quick, man!"

"Can't. Too much trouble getting you here."

"God, oh God . . ." Ethan lay back weakly, near tears.

Vail went to the window and through the dirty pane saw the *Mary Mulhane* moving away from the pier. "They're pulling out. Either they haven't missed you or they've decided to go without you."

"Help me up," Ethan begged. "I've got to see."

Michael hauled him onto bound feet and held on to him as he hobbled across the floor. At the window he leaned forward to steady himself, his head resting against the glass. "There she goes—without me." Tears ran down his cheeks, and he looked at Vail with honest hate. "You swine. You don't even know what you've done."

"Oh, but I do. Get the buggy, Michael. We'll move him over to the Gentry and Callendar warehouse, and you'll feel better. Ethan being one of the owners, we'll have a perfect right to be there."

At 3:32 A.M. the *Mary Mulhane* pulled away from Lombard dock. At 3:46, in midchannel, the sloop of war *Liberty*, guns primed, cut across her bow and ordered her to stop. She was brought ignominiously back to the wharf with the crew and the Knights of the Golden Circle in irons.

At midmorning, as church bells called the faithful to services, Vail climbed the stairs to the second story of Gentry and Callendar's warehouse, where Michael was guarding Ethan. He brought a pot of hot coffee and the latest news. Since dawn he had been drifting through the gambling houses and saloons, which never lacked customers at any hour, listening to the gossip around him and chatting with friends, including two young naval lieutenants. Although the matter was still officially secret, word had blazed across town as soon as the *Mary Mulhane* had been brought back to the dock that a dastardly conspiracy, known to the authorities for weeks, had been nipped in the bud by the navy and the traitors were safely in jail awaiting trial. Everyone was astounded at the involvement of colorless, conventional Rufus Pettingill and the scions of some of the best families in town in a treasonous, piratical plot.

"They'll be tried for treason, right down to the cabin boy," Vail said. "The navy found arms, uniforms, and papers when they searched the ship. Ethan, were membership lists made? Did you sign anything?"

Ethan, still sick from the chloroform, raised miserable eyes. "An oath of loyalty and silence. We all signed." He stared moodily into his coffee as though he saw the future in its dark depths. "That gold—it could have made the difference. It would have made the difference."

"You have to get out of town, now, before they find you. There's a Mexican fishing boat leaving for Mazatlán tonight. We'll smuggle you on board as soon as it's dark. The captain is an old friend of mine. If you're so hot to fight for the South, you ought to be able to make your way from there."

Hope flared in Ethan's drawn face. "I could get down to Panama and take the railroad across. I could tie in with some blockade runner, get into port and join up with the army."

"Lucky you. Your passage as far as Mazatlán is free. Five hundred dollars will have to see you the rest of the way. It's all I'll spare to finance this insanity."

Ethan gripped his arm, a half-smile beginning to form. "You are a bastard. Get the money from Marin."

"I will. I'll have her take it out of your salary."

Ethan gulped down his coffee. "Tell me the truth, Vail. How did you find out?"

"I had business in Chinatown last night and ran into Wes. He got a tad drunk."

"Wes. When he didn't show, I figured either he was drunk in some brothel or he'd chickened out. I was a fool to bring him in on the deal."

"It was dumb luck that you did. Otherwise you'd be sitting in jail with your friends right now, looking at a noose."

Fog swirled in again as night fell, but it was less dense than on the previous night. The *Columbia* had sailed triumphantly out through the Gate in midafternoon, bearing her mighty load of gold eastward, another strengthening infusion for the Union. A cheering crowd had packed the wharf as the steamer chugged into the open sea, but now the waterfront was quiet. The night was black and cold, and people had gone home or retreated to restaurants and saloons for food, for safety, for the warming glow of heated stoves, whiskey, and human companionship. Word had gone out that the names of Ethan Gentry and John Wesley Morgan had turned up in papers discovered on the *Mary Mulhane* and that they were wanted for questioning, but with the conspiracy shattered and the ringleader, Pettingill, in custody, the search was not intense. During the day a squad of soldiers from the Presidio had gone aboard ships riding at anchor, asked questions, and found nothing out of order.

So it happened that when a Sonoran in a broad sombrero and tattered serape shuffled aboard the fishing smack *Gaviota* shortly before she sailed, no one took notice except the captain, the first mate, and the Sonoran's two friends.

At the gangplank Ethan paused. "Mike, I'm beholden. See you after the war."

Michael shook the hand held out to him and said, "Go with God."

"Vail . . . well . . . explain to Kitty why I couldn't see her before I left. I'll get word to her somehow about where I am. Tell her to kiss the children for me. Give my love to Pa and Sophy and Marin." He hoisted onto his back the bundle containing the clothes that had been brought him and stepped onto the ramp. He stopped. "Vail, tell Logan for me—ah, what the hell. Tell her good-bye." He trudged up the gangplank without looking back.

Vail and Michael leaned against the wooden railing beside the wharf, smoking and watching until the *Gaviota* moved out on the ebbing tide. No navy man-of-war signaled her to stop, no other ships took notice of the scrubby little fishing vessel slipping out, southward bound, vanishing silently into the mist.

Michael shrugged his coat close against the damp night air.

"I'll be going. I promised Wes I'd come home early. He was feeling a lot better when I checked in with him today. Said the medicine you gave him this morning tasted so bad that it had to cure him. Now I've got to work out how to keep him hid till he's well and then get him out of town, too."

Vail dropped his cigar butt and ground it under his heel.

"About the syphilis . . . I lied to Wes."

"Lied? Why you son of a gun!" Michael's laugh boomed out. "He'll be so relieved, he won't be sore at you."

"He's in the late stage of syphilis. I lied when I said I could cure him. I can't."

After a silence Michael's voice came oddly, thinly in the dark. "You serious?"

"Yes."

"Are you sure?"

"Charles is coming over to take a look at him, but, yes, I'm sure. Say anything you want to me, I won't blame you. I had to pry information out of him somehow, and I wanted you feeling grateful. I couldn't get Ethan out of this by myself."

Water slapped against the pilings as a boat moved slowly past. Michael said, "Maybe you sized me up right. Maybe I wouldn't have helped you, but for Wes. I didn't want any part of this." He started to walk, talking out his agitation, and Vail kept pace with him. "You never liked him—oh, it's true, and I don't blame you. He's pulled a lot of stunts. But maybe I didn't put out for him as much as a brother should. He never had the knack of making people like him, even his own pa. Pa always said he'd come to a bad end. I keep thinking of him when he was young. Such a little kid for his age that we thought he was going to be a runt, always scared of the other boys, always in trouble over something. Pa'd whip him with a strap or clout him with his fists. Pa was a strong man, and Wes would be black and blue. Pa said he was beating the sin out of him, but I always thought that punishment never makes a man good, it only makes him mean."

"I always thought that, too," Vail said.

They came to the place where their horses were tied. They mounted and rode into town together.

Chapter 40

"I won't drink it, you can't make me!" Kitty screamed, and buried her face in her pillow. "He'll be killed, I know it," came her muffled voice, "and I'll be a widow. Oh, how could he do this to me!"

Logan took the glass of sedative from Charles. "Leave it here, and she'll drink it in a little while."

Kitty raised her swollen face. "I will not!" She pulled the covers over her head and lay still.

Logan shrugged. She went with Charles to the door.

"Call me if she grows worse," he said, very low.

"She won't. I'll get it down her soon. Thank you for coming so quickly."

Charles closed the door, and Logan tiptoed back to the bed. "Kitty, do you want to see your parents? They're downstairs."

"No!" cried Kitty, pushing back the blanket. "Mama will say I told you so, and she *wanted* me to marry Ethan. Papa—I don't want to see him, either."

Logan helped her to sit up, and she lay on the piled-up pillows, exhausted by the long Sunday's vigil when the news of the *Mary Mulhane* first came and the two hours of hysterics after she was told that Ethan had left for points south. "Oh, Logan, how could he do this to me?" she whimpered, wiping her wet face with the edge of the sheet.

"You are a Southerner, my dear, and he's gone to fight for the South. Isn't that some comfort?"

"My brother's dead—a sacrifice on the altar of liberty, Mama says. *I* say a fool. And now Ethan. Oh, I can't bear it."

Logan picked up the glass from the bedside table. "Drink it, please, Kitty. For my sake. Dr. Charles says sleep will do you a world of good."

"I don't want to sleep!"

"Drink it. Then I can honestly tell your mama and papa you are resting, and they will leave." She held the glass to Kitty's lips. Reluctantly Kitty swallowed. She lay back on the pillow and murmured tragically, "I shall be a widow and alone."

"Even in such a dreadful pass, and it is by no means certain, you would have your children."

"Oh, them. Children are all very well, but what do you do without a man?"

I would trade my soul for his children, Logan thought, and you say, Oh, them.

She tucked the covers around Kitty, her face placid, her heart burning with the news of Ethan's going and the other news Vail had told her this evening.

Kitty yawned. "You are a good-hearted girl, Logan. Men just don't look further than a pretty face . . ." She yawned again. "They are such fools . . ."

Logan watched the swollen, long-lashed eyes close and the sulky mouth relax. When Kitty was breathing deeply and regularly, she turned down the lamp and left the room.

Mr. and Mrs. Winfield were waiting in the parlor. Charlotte's nose was pinched as if she smelled something bad, for Marin was in the next room and it pained her to be within miles of that dreadful young woman who had said such monstrous, rude, wicked things to her and then compared her unfavorably with her dog. Tyler paced, ignoring his unhappy wife and casting many worried glances upward to where his daughter lay in torment.

"Ah, Miss Logan." He whipped across the floor as Logan entered. She felt as though pounced upon by a thin, groomed tomcat. "Is Kitty . . ."

"She is asleep, Mr. Winfield. Now you must not be too distressed. Dr. Towle has given her a sleeping draught, and she will be much improved in the morning."

"Umph," remarked Charlotte. She hated Kitty for continuing to have that peculiar man as her doctor, hated having to face him when he undoubtedly knew what she had said about him. Not that he ever showed her less than the utmost courtesy, which proved he would do anything to make her uncomfortable.

Logan was helping Tyler on with his greatcoat and handing him his hat. "Do go home now and rest, ma'am," she said with her hand under Charlotte's elbow. "You have been too much afflicted lately and must save your strength."

Tears came to Charlotte's eyes at the understanding in Logan's voice. She dabbed at her face as she and Tyler found themselves being ushered out the front door.

Logan went to the dining room. "They're gone," she announced triumphantly.

Marin looked up. She had been sitting for an hour at Kitty's large and very expensive cherrywood dining table, drinking coffee she didn't want and prodding Vail with questions he couldn't or wouldn't answer. "I thought they'd camp here for days. How did you get rid of them?"

"Tact and diplomacy, I'll wager," said Vail. "Logan should be in the State Department."

Logan smiled wearily and sat down with them. "Kitty is asleep, thank heaven, and the children, too. I told them Daddy had gone off to be a soldier for the South, and little Ty asked if he would bring back Mr. Lincoln's head. Of course he hadn't the least idea what he'd said, but where do they hear such things?"

"Where do you suppose?" Marin replied tartly "Underneath Tyler Winfield's nasty face lies a heart of pure bile." She frowned at Vail. "I don't see why I shouldn't know exactly what happened. He is my brother. Why was he the only one of those idiots that got away? How could he ship south when the navy is watching everything that moves?"

"If you don't know, you can't answer questions."

She looked at him in some alarm. "You think they'll question us? Oh, I wouldn't like that at all."

"Maybe. If they do, tell them the truth. Your husband is a Union officer, and being completely loyal, you disapprove of your brother's activities. They'll go away charmed." He rose and looked into Logan's desolate eyes. "Get some rest, honey. Kitty may start in again in the morning. Marin, walk with me to the gate. I have something to tell you."

Outside, fog wrapped the town in a tight, gray shroud. Marin drew her shawl close, cold in more than body. When the news came, a bleakness had descended on her soul. She had been utterly right about Ethan; he had learned nothing and could be faithful to no one. Now he had abandoned his wife, run out on his responsibilities just as she had feared he would, and was gone on another wild goose chase, leaving those who loved him to grieve and wait. What a fool she had been to think that the war could not touch them.

"Marin." They were at the gate. Vail's horse, a big, muscular animal, whickered and stamped, and he put a hand on its bridle. "Marin, this isn't a good time to tell you, but if I don't, you'll hear it elsewhere. I've joined the army, the Union army, that is. I'll be leaving at the end of the week."

She stared at him, hearing the words but not quite taking them in. The night was very cold, and somewhere, in one of the houses down the street, a child was crying.

New Year's Day, 1863, was a somber time for the North. Burdening every heart was the bloody horror of Fredericksburg, only three weeks before, when Federal troops made a frontal assault against Lee's army entrenched on the thickly wooded heights south of the little Virginia town. Confederate rifle and artillery fire slashed through the oncoming Federals like a great scythe. Before the bloody day ended, the blue lines were ordered into six crossings of that deadly open area, into a hail of minié balls, and their torn, bleeding bodies lay piled on the field, thousands of young men squandered by the incompetence of stubborn, blundering General Burnside. The battered Army of the Potomac had then pulled back to think the matter over and prepare to fight again.

News of Fredericksburg brought terror to the two houses on Rincon Hill, for Vail was an infantry captain in Burnside's army. But no dreaded telegram came, and when Celia brought a letter from Vail saying that he was well, she and Logan and Marin wept together in relief and thanksgiving.

One morning in early spring a letter arrived from Ethan. It had come by circuitous routes, and it told them he was riding with Nathan Bedford Forrest, the great rebel cavalry general, and was having the time of his life. He had, he wrote, found himself at last. Hard riding, fast shooting, daring, slashing raids against the enemy, the comradeship of other good fellows—this was the only way to spend one's allotted time on earth.

The letter sent Marin and Logan searching through old newspapers, reading reports from the East, trying to discover the area of General Forrest's operations. Between them was the unspoken fear that someday Vail and Ethan would find themselves opposing each other, that somehow it would be the bullet of one that found the heart of the other and make death more hideous because it came from a friend. But Forrest appeared to be active in Tennessee, far from Virginia and the Army of the Potomac. Unreasonably, both women felt better. The brother of each was still alive, at least when the last letters were written. One could hope for no more comfort than that.

Then, in May, came Chancellorsville, a savage battle only a little distance west of Fredericksburg. It ended in another staggering defeat for the North. Once again the women waited, not knowing if their men had been on the line. Stuart commanded a brigade under General Hooker, and Vail, now wearing the two oak leaves of a major, was in General Howard's XI Corps. The days passed. There were no letters, but no telegrams from the War Department arrived, either.

In early summer malaria broke out in town, as it did periodically, and Delphine and Celia came down with it. Barely had Charles pronounced them recovered when rumors began to fly that the Army of Virginia had crossed the Rappahannock and moved audaciously into Pennsylvania. "Lee Invades North," the headlines screamed, and Marin, sitting in the side garden at Vail's house, read the latest dispatches aloud while Celia knitted.

Celia was living in town now, for as the war intensified, she wanted to be nearer to the sources of news. She was frowning over the blanket she was knitting for the Sanitary Commission, tired from lack of sleep. Consuela, her maid, was ill again with another bout of lung inflammation, and Celia had been up with her most of the night. She looked up from the brown wool in her fingers. "What do they say about this new general?"

"Oh, the usual. 'Major General George Gordon Meade is known to be a valiant, stern, hardworking soldier who demands the best from his men. The army is in capable hands.' They're not quite as thrilled over him as they were over Burnside, are they? Maybe it's a good sign."

In the days that followed, Marin walked the three blocks from her own house each morning with the latest newspapers, and she and Celia pored over them together, trying to piece together from rumors and partial reports what was happening far to the east in the rolling Pennsylvania farmland near a tiny crossroads town nobody had ever heard of.

"It's called Gettysburg," said Marin. "They say it's only a stone's throw from Philadelphia. How is it possible Lee got so far north without our army stopping him? I swear, he's a devil, that man."

Celia began to knit, her white, slim fingers flying, and Marin decided that she would bring her own knitting next time, just to keep her hands occupied and prevent them from wringing in anguish. Uppermost in her mind was the newspaper headline "Union Losses Are Reported to Be Heavy!"

The next day, singing over the wires, came word. A major battle had been fought in the Pennsylvania fields under a hot July sun. Lee, the invincible, Lee, the master, had hurled his best divisions against Cemetery Ridge and had been beaten back with great slaughter.

It was a smashing victory for the North even if Meade did fail to follow up his advantage and prevent Lee and his surviving soldiers from slipping back into Virginia. To underscore it, reports swept in that on the Mississippi, Vicksburg had fallen to General Grant after a campaign as daring as any Lee had conducted and the great river was now open to the sea. In San Francisco people wept and cheered and gathered in Union Square to sing the new words written by Julia Ward Howe to the tune of "John Brown's Body," words that lifted the heart and exalted the soul. As they roared out "Glory, glory, hallelujah!" everyone knew that at last, at last, the war was nearly over.

Not many of the celebrants in the city had loved ones in those far-off battles, so almost everyone could thrill to the victory without truly counting the cost. It was easy to sing songs and shout "Death to the rebels!" and argue military strategy when it was other men's sons who were doing the fighting and the dying.

A letter came from Stuart, a brief one saying that he had come through Gettysburg without a scratch and was with Meade in Washington. After several weeks another letter arrived, long delayed in the mail. It was written in a feminine hand, but it was from Vail. He was in a military hospital in Washington, and a kind lady was writing this for him, as his right arm was temporarily disabled. It was a minor wound sustained on the first day of battle on Cemetery Ridge, and he expected to return to duty soon.

"A minor wound," repeated Celia, who had been reading the letter aloud. Marin's eyes met hers, and then they both looked quickly away. He would say a minor wound no matter what it was. And there were so many stories about wounds that really were minor until infection or gangrene set in, and then pneumonia . . . there were so many stories.

One afternoon Dan walked up to the house with a telegram in his hand that said Harlan was dead. He had died of dysentery in an army hospital in Baltimore.

"Strange, isn't it," Dan said in a faraway, musing voice. "After surviving Chancellorsville and Gettysburg, he died of disease at home." He was very calm, sitting in the parlor talking about it. Just before he left, he told them what had been evident since the moment he arrived. He could no longer stay out of it. He had been considering for a long time, and now he had to go.

Marin watched him walk down the path to the gate, wondering at herself. These past months had wrought a change in her; she saw it, despised it, and could not help it. No longer did it seem mad folly to go to war but the right thing, the only thing to do. More than once she had caught herself looking at Michael in his prosperous hardware store with something close to contempt, and Gerald's witty cynicism no longer amused her. This was what war did to you; it took your mind and twisted it until endless suffering and monstrous death seemed acceptable, even admirable. And in what cause? Abstract ideas like "union" and "emancipation." Slavery would have ended eventually without this war. People would go on living whether the Union held together or not. For, in truth, what was life but the survival of individuals, their families, their homes, their personal, private lives? As long as you were alive, regardless of governments, you could still see the sun rise and set, still watch your children grow, and sing songs and laugh with friends. There was cool water on a hot day, the smell of bacon frying, restful sleep in a soft bed, the snug comfort of a fire on a winter's night when the wind howled outside. Most of all, the happiness of simply being with those you loved.

The many, many dead of this war had given up these things forever while stay-at-homes safely declared that it was all necessary and worthwhile. But few causes, in the long view of things, were worth such sacrifice. There was no glory in dying, only ugliness and pain, only lonely women and fatherless children and empty chairs on both sides. This was a vile, stupid, cruel war, as were all wars, and she must never forget it. And yet—fool that she was—she was proud of Dan.

Chapter 41

"There's my sweetheart," Sophy crooned, lifting little Jefferson out of the bathwater. "Now Mama will get you dry and warm, and you will have your nap."

Marin sat on the sofa, observing Charles's handsome baby son and recalling Charlotte Winfield's fears for the purity of Sophy's children. A sense of quiet contentment stole over her. The world was in shambles, everything was out of joint, sometimes it seemed that the ache in her heart would never ease, but in this snug house there was a peace that held loneliness at bay and made war and death seem only a dark delusion.

Sophy had been so well since the baby came and so happy in her marriage. As often as she saw it, Marin was always amazed by the way her sister's expert hands moved surely over Jefferson, drying him, pulling his dress over his head, tying on his booties. Every towel and article of clothing had its place and was always returned to the same spot after washing. It was an ironbound law in her house that nothing was ever moved without her knowledge, so that she could walk through the rooms with confidence and take care of her baby herself. Charles had hired a Chinese cook and a young Irish girl as a maid, and with their help Sophy ran the household during the days when he was in his office and the nights he was out on calls.

She laid the sleepy baby in his crib, drew a light blanket over him, and placed her hand comfortingly on his back as he yawned and drifted into sleep. "I believe Charles will go soon," she said.

"You can't be serious."

"Yes. I think he's going to go."

"But he's a healer. He couldn't kill, not in a million years."

"That's just it. He reads everything he can get his hands on about the military hospitals and says they are a horror, the ones in the cities almost as bad as the field hospitals. Charles says more men are dying of sickness than from enemy action, many of them because of poor care. The army is desperate for doctors, medical supplies don't get to where they're needed, it is all so badly organized . . ."

"But that's what the Sanitary Commission is for, seeing to it that the hospitals have what they need."

"I know." Sophy walked the short distance to the sofa, felt for the seat, and sat down beside Marin. "They do their best, I suppose. Charles had a letter about it from Vail."

"He did? He never mentioned it."

"Well, it was full of medical things that they love to talk about. You know how they are. He said the hospital he was in was frightful. Dirt everywhere. Even the bandages were filthy. Ignorant nurses, though some of the volunteers try very hard, no idea in the world of basic sanitation, sloppy surgeons whose answer to everything is 'Cut it off.' They wanted to amputate his arm, did you know that? He fought them off. Kept a gun under his pillow and threatened to shoot the first man who came near him with a knife. He finally got some friends to carry him out of the place."

"A minor wound, he said."

"He only meant to keep us from worrying. He's back with his regiment now, so we know he's all right."

"If they had to carry him out of the hospital, he must have been terribly sick."

"I thought that, too. But Vail is so strong. He pulled through in spite of everything."

So strong, yes, but only flesh and blood. No man, however powerful, was proof against bayonets and bullets and ripping, tearing shells. And what of Charles with his twisted leg and vulnerable lungs? Sophy's love and good cooking had improved his health. He had gained twenty pounds since his marriage. But how could he survive the rigors of exhausting work in drafty tents along with bad food, cold, rain, mud, and rampant disease?

"Oh, Sophy, you must not let Charles go."

"How can I stop him?"

"Well . . . put your foot down. Tell him you can't manage without him because of your blindness. Fall down or something, that ought to worry him. Remind him of his responsibilities. He's a father now, not a flighty bachelor. Get in a fix if you have to."

Sophy grinned. "Oh, honey, you are a caution. I promised myself when we got married that I was never going to let the blindness get in his way. As for getting pregnant, I hardly think I have the time. He's out at the Presidio this morning talking to the commandant. He tried to enlist a year and a half ago and they turned him down because of his leg, but this time it looks as if Washington is going to say yes."

"You," said Marin, "are the sappiest woman I've ever come

across. I could certainly find a way to keep him home. What will we all do for a doctor?"

"Tom Anderson is a good man."

"Twaddle. If Tom Anderson were in the army, he'd be hacking off arms and legs with the best of them. And, come to think of it, why isn't he in the army?"

"He's not a young man, Marin, for all he tries to look like one."

"Tom Anderson. I haven't seen him to speak to in years. He hasn't been to the house once since you married Charles. How could you take the baby to him? And what if you need care?"

"I'll go to Dr. Bauer. He's old, and he doesn't like to make night calls, but he did a good job delivering Jeff."

Marin gazed at her gloomily. "So it's settled. He really is going."

"I expect so. I've been wondering—when he leaves, would it be all right if I moved back with you, just till the men come home?" Sophy's head was bent, her fingers moved in the folds of her dress with a distress she kept carefully out of her voice.

Marin's ill humor evaporated. Poor baby, she's scared to death for him and trying so hard to hide it. I could choke Charles!

She said: "Darling, we'll love having you. Logan can spoil the baby rotten." She thought: Till the men come home. Dear God, how long will that be?

So it was that Sophy came back to the house on Rincon Hill. With a new baby to fuss over, Logan was happier than she had been in years. Even Delphine dragged her enormous weight around the house more cheerfully, for Sophy spent time with her, patiently listened to her interminable stories of the great old days when she was a belle and every young man was in love with her, and endured her childlike pouts and frequent lapses of memory with more kindness than the other members of the family.

Marin, isolated in her anxiety and loneliness, prohibited forever from speaking of their true source, smilingly accepted everyone's reassurances that Stuart was in little danger since generals were seldom in the thick of the fight, and lived with gnawing inner fear.

Oddly, she got most of her comfort from time spent with Celia. From her she heard the latest news of Vail; with her she could talk of him anytime she wished, for Celia, always completely self-absorbed, thought it natural that others should be as interested in her husband's fate as she herself was. Marin took to leaving the office early, and they whiled away afternoons together, gossiped about mutual friends, and it was almost as though the old days of girlhood friendship had come back.

One afternoon Celia had an especially good piece of gossip.

"Anna von Helsdorf has left town, did you hear?"

"Anna? I haven't seen her in months. For how long?"

"Forever, I think. Did you know that she . . ." Celia paused, ". . . was not quite the thing?"

"I've suspected, but how she fooled me at first. I thought she really was a baroness."

"Not quite. They say Harriet Venable caught Anna with her husband in . . . well, in a state of undress at the Union Hotel. It's been kept very quiet, but she's had to leave town. When I think of Harriet, so busy looking out for everybody else's morals . . ." Celia laughed, and Marin smiled, too, glad at Celia's merriment. It had been only two months since Consuela, her quiet, gentle maid, had died so unexpectedly of lung inflammation. Celia herself had cared for Consuela at the end. She had cried more tears than she had over Nicolas and had been low in her mind ever since. Recently her malaria had recurred, as it commonly did, and because she ran a fever for three or four hours every day, Tom Anderson had ordered her to stay in the house or sit only in this most protected corner of the garden. The dappled shade fell gently on her face and she looked especially lovely today, the pink of her cheeks causing Mrs. Moon to exclaim at breakfast that she looked just like a dew-kissed rosebud.

Later, after Tom had made his thrice-weekly examination, he was not as pleased as the housekeeper.

As he put on his coat in the entry hall, he said with a frown, "Miss Marin, we have made our diagnosis. It has been a mysterious case, most difficult, but at last we are satisfied." Tom always referred to himself in the plural when he spoke in his professional capacity.

Marin, who was preparing to leave for the office, put down her bonnet. "But I thought it was the malaria again."

"At the beginning we assumed that as well. But there were no chills, no stupor or vomiting, no copious perspiration. We dismissed malaria on the second day of the fever. Next we considered scarlet fever, but the typical rash was missing. She had measles as a child, so that was eliminated. Typhus . . ."

"Oh, dear," said Marin, going pale.

". . . Typhus would have shown a rash by the fifth day."

"Then what is it, Tom?" Pompous man. Why didn't he get to the point?

"We have debated, for there was catarrhal pneumonia to consider. But now four weeks have passed, and our diagnosis is secure. Even though there has been as yet no hemoptysis or cough, we heard rales in the chest today, and we are certain that Miss Celia is suffering from acute phthisis—or, as the layman calls it, galloping consumption."

Marin went cold. "How could it be? Celia's always been so well except for the malaria, and she's always lived such a healthy life out there in the country."

"Exactly so. We believe her to have been debilitated by the malarial fever. Also, mental strain drains the powers of the constitution, and she is, of course, deeply anxious all the time her husband is in danger."

"Will she get well soon?"

His lips pursed, "Acute phthisis, as opposed to chronic phthisis, runs a swift course. Under adverse conditions the prognosis may be grave, but in Miss Celia's case we expect that after a few weeks of good care the moist chest sounds will disappear, the temperature will drop, and her strength will return. Recovery always depends on a strong constitution and the availability of modern medical care. She has both. Now we must work together, Miss Marin. Keep her mind off the war, keep the newspapers and the accounts of battle away from her. We will build her up with good, fresh milk and eggs and draughts of porter every day and regular doses of cod-liver oil. Be of good cheer!"

He clapped on his hat and strode out the door. From the window she watched him leap on his horse and canter off and thought, Oh, Charles, if only you hadn't joined the army.

Tom would have been hurt and offended if he had known how little faith Marin had in him. As it turned out, he did a better job than she expected, for in the seventh week of Celia's illness her fever returned to normal, as he had predicted, and while a slight hacking cough sometimes plagued her, no blood appeared.

On a bright November morning lounge chairs were moved into the garden, and Marin and Celia settled themselves in the warm sun to wait for Tom's visit; recently he had taken to stopping by every day, more for a social than a professional visit, they believed. In these last weeks Marin had been spending more time with Celia than she did at the office, knitting, chatting about inconsequential matters, steering the conversation onto pleasant subjects. Since Chickamauga the war in Tennessee had been quiescent, and in the East the Army of the Potomac had settled into winter quarters, content for the present to rest and glare across the river at the weary, defiant Army of Northern Virginia, so there were no disturbing news bulletins to worry over.

A letter had arrived that morning from Vail, a cheerful, superficial letter that revealed nothing of his thoughts or inmost feelings. His letters never answered the questions uppermost in Marin's mind. Was he well in spirit? Did his wounded arm ache in the night? Was he exhilarated by battle, or had he grown to hate it? Was he sometimes, ever, afraid? Papa said a soldier was always afraid before battle, before blood lust and the driving desire to survive took over, and after battle, when he remembered what he had done and what could have happened to him. It hurt her to think of him afraid in the night and no one there to comfort him.

Celia, never introspective herself and not liking it in others, seemed unaware that anything was missing in his letter. She read it twice, smiled, and laid it aside, perfectly content. Marin picked up the half-finished blanket for the Sanitary Commission that had now become a joint effort and knitted a few rows. Celia got up and wandered through her garden, examining the fine winter roses and choosing a velvety bud to fasten to the corsage of her dress. Some of the lush curve was gone from her cheeks and bosom, Marin noted, and she still tired easily and her appetite was poor. But her eyes were bright and her color excellent; she would come back to full health quickly now that the fever had left.

Mrs. Moon came out of the house bearing a mug of porter, the dark malt beer Celia detested.

"Come, dear, here's your midmorning treat."

Celia wrinkled her nose. "I'd rather have chocolate. I'm sure it's just as good for me."

"Porter now, chocolate later, there's a good girl. We must follow doctor's orders." Mrs. Moon gazed fondly at her charge. Celia was a kindly mistress and left the running of the house completely in her hands.

Celia sat down and obediently took a swallow, but as soon as Mrs. Moon was out of sight, she set the mug on the grass. "I shall smell like a brewery and become a toper if I keep this up."

She picked up the new kitten Logan had brought her, lay back in her chair, and watched Marin unravel a skein of yarn. From far down the street come the sound of hoofs on the dirt road. It was Tom coming for his regular visit. Marin raised her hand to wave, but he drew rein and stopped at a neighbor's house to talk, and she put the ball of yarn in her lap and took up her needles.

Celia said, "Shall I tell you a secret?"

Marin looked up. "If you like."

"I've often wanted to tell you. You won't believe this, but for most of the time after Vail and I were married I doubted that he really cared for me as he should. I even imagined—now don't get mad, and don't laugh—I imagined he was in love with you."

Marin's hands lowered slowly to her lap; her eyes were locked on Celia's face.

Celia said, "I knew you'd be shocked. It was such a silly idea, but he was different from the old days before I married Nicolas. Somehow I thought he didn't really love me anymore, that he wished he hadn't married me. And he was always so fond of you."

"What rubbish, Celia."

"I know." Celia looked abashed. "The night Alida was born, it was so bad, I thought I would die. I planned to forgive him and be marvelously generous and good." A dimple crept into her cheek. "It would have been wonderfully dramatic."

Marin grinned, too, and resumed knitting. "Why tell me now, for Heaven's sake?"

Idly Celia stroked the kitten, who stretched and began to purr. "I don't know, except that I think of him so much lately. I even dream of him sometimes. Our marriage hasn't been all it should be—there's not another soul I would admit that to—and it's been mostly my fault. Not entirely," she added after a moment's thought. "Vail can be very difficult. But some of it was my fault. When Fontana was lost, I blamed him most unfairly. I wish I'd said I was sorry before he left. Every time news comes of another battle . . ." In her agitation she squeezed the kitten, and he squawked resentfully and leaped from her lap.

"Why don't you write and tell him?" asked Marin, disturbed.

"Because I'm not good at writing how I feel. If I could talk to him, I'd tell him that things will be different after the war. I just . . ." She lay back and put her hands to her temples. "Give me the porter please."

Marin leaped to her feet in alarm, for Celia had gone ghost white. In an instant she was across the short space between them and had the mug at Celia's lips. "Here, darling, take a swallow. Mrs. Moon, help me!"

Celia tried to drink, choked, and slumped back, coughing. Her eyes were wide, the pupils dilated. There was a faint blue tinge to her lips.

"Oh, my God," Marin whispered in cold terror, and she raced for the house. As Mrs. Moon appeared in the doorway, she shouted, "Send for Dr. Anderson, he's just down the street! And get the priest—quick."

She ran back to the garden. Celia had half fallen off the chair, and a desperate gagging sound ripped her thin chest. Marin's arms were around her, lifting her, and the feel of the light, sharp bones made her heart sink. Rapidly she unbuttoned Celia's bodice and loosened her stays. "There now, is that better? Tom is coming, Celia."

". . . priest . . ."

"Yes, yes, the priest is coming, too. Hold on, darling!"

Celia gasped and drew in a shuddering breath, and as air entered her lungs, her rigid body relaxed. A smile trembled on her lips. "It's passing. Oh, what a spasm . . . the worst I've ever had."

Marin shifted her arm so that Celia's head could rest against it and smoothed her dark hair, feeling sweat on the ivory brow. "Don't try to move, let me hold you till Tom gets here." She laughed shakily. "What a scare you gave me."

Celia laughed, too, and the laugh turned into violent coughing. She bolted upright, straining for air, and then fell back into Marin's arms, wild fear in her eyes. She whispered, "Please . . . I don't want to die . . ." Then, "Say an ave for me . . ."

When Tom ran into the garden, he found Marin on the grass with Celia's head against her breast, her cheek resting on the black, tumbled hair. Without words he took Celia from her and placed his ear against the bare chest where the bodice had been pulled open. After a long time he raised his head and gently laid Celia on the ground. "She went downhill so fast in the last two weeks." Grief and anger were plain in his face. "I couldn't save her . . . couldn't save her."

Marin sat where she was, seeing everything with great clarity. Mrs. Moon, horror-stricken, her hands over her mouth. Father Moreno, kneeling, praying, making motions with his hands. The sun, very bright, the roses brilliant in the light, the kitten stalking a fluttering blade of grass. In a treetop a bird sang merrily.

And Celia lay still, eyes half open, pale lips parted, the pretty dress a sweep of blue on the grass, the thin, perfect face marble white and empty. Lonely, frightened, Marin whispered, "I didn't know how to say an ave."

My dear Vail:

Forgive me. This letter brings you the saddest news. I must tell you that last Tuesday Celia passed away after an illness of two months. We had thought she was recovering, but it was not to be. Tom is writing you the details, but because I was with her at the last, he has asked me to write, too.

As you know, she had malaria in the spring but seemed well over it. She was always so strong. Tom says she was run down because of the malaria and that is why she developed galloping consumption. She believed she was getting well (as did I) and on the morning of her death spoke most lovingly of you. She regretted holding you at fault (unfairly, she said) for the loss of Fontana and was looking forward to your life together after the war. Then without warning she became very ill. I called Tom and sent for her priest, but I think she was gone before they arrived. However, Father Moreno assures us that he was in time and that she received absolution. Since we did not know the forms, we followed his advice and have done all that is required. She is buried at La Gracia beside her father, which we believe she would want. Although Beatriz very much wants Alida to live at La Gracia, she is presently with us. She grieves for her mother but has been very brave. She is such a quiet child that one never knows her deepest thoughts, but I believe she is not too unhappy with us. The children devote themselves to her and keep her busy every day to hold off sadness. She has your picture beside her bed and speaks of you often and with great pride. If you wish it, we will send her at once to La Gracia, but if it meets with your approval, she has a home with us for as long as need be. She will continue to receive instruction in her religion, and we will care for her as you would care for Belinda and Carey in like circumstance. We think of you daily. You are always in our prayers. Alida sends her love to you, as do we all.

                                                              Marin

She read it over once more. Was it too short? Too blunt? Had she said too little or too much? Should she have led up to the terrible fact more gently? Nothing could change the truth, no matter how long she took to say it. In any case, it was the best she could do.

Outside her bedroom window the lights of town glittered diamondlike in the dark, but the sight held no pleasure for her. It had been a disagreeable day, the funeral this morning as harrowing as she had expected, and to make matters worse Beatriz had been at her most unbearable, alternating between cold anger when she found out that Alida was going back to town and fits of hysteria at the graveside.

The fact of Celia's death was still hard for her to grasp.

Astonishing to discover how much she missed Celia. How could Celia be dead—so beautiful, so young, only two years older than she? Yet if Marin looked in her own mirror, she would see not a girl but a woman of thirty-one whom life had passed by. Looking back, she could recall with aching sadness the innocent, ignorant, desiring girl she had been, envious of Celia's looks, popularity, and wealth, craving the best things life could offer and confident of getting them—beauty, possessions, a great love that would end her loneliness. Well, she had possessions, and little they meant once she got them; she had turned out pretty enough, and much good it had done her; the love that passed understanding—that was impossible, too. Life was only a series of losses with nothing to look forward to but endless war and the men gone away forever.

The house was very quiet. In an effort to distract Alida, Sophy had asked her to help with the baby's bath, a privilege the little girl loved. Carey was playing checkers with James downstairs, and Belinda, profoundly upset by her first true awareness of death, had gone to bed early. Logan was in her own room, attempting a letter of condolence to her brother, but her heart was elsewhere. Over the wires this morning had come news of a great battle at Chattanooga. The hardened veterans of Sherman and Thomas had beaten the Confederates badly, and now they were on the Tennessee border, in position to drive on into Georgia, the heartland of the Confederacy. Logan had read the news in terror, for Ethan was with General Forrest somewhere in Tennessee. If he were to fall in battle, they might never know of it for certain— Confederate casualties were not reported to Northern families. Vail and Stuart and Dan were with the Army of the Potomac on the north bank of the Rapidan. God alone knew when that mighty army would attack the Rebels, but attack it would, again and again, until Lee and his slippery, gallant soldiers were finally broken.

What a coil it all was. Wearily Marin leaned her head in her hands and closed her eyes. She could still feel Celia's thin body in her arms, see the life slipping out of her face even as she begged to live; she could see the faces of all the beloved dead and those who might die at any time. Oh, for tears to ease the heart, scalding tears of sorrow in the face of death, of fear for those who were in danger and so far away. But she could not cry. Late into the night she sat by her window, staring at the lights below and looking bleakly at a future that was all ruin and despair.

• • •

By the beginning of 1864 there was soaring optimism in the
North. Everywhere the rebel armies were in retreat, still dangerous and capable of lashing out, but slowly wearing down.
Southern men had been fighting and dying for three years, and
there were fewer and fewer reserves for Southern generals to draw
on. The Army of Northern Virginia, now weakened and tired, was
the sole obstacle before Richmond. Sweet victory could not be far
away.

In San Francisco the war was a drama played on a distant stage.
Only those families with relatives in the fighting suspected that
Lee's veterans were not beaten yet or that the rebels might not give
up Georgia easily.

With every ship that docked, more young, healthy men appeared in the city, many of them draft evaders who had chosen to go
west and hunt gold rather than escape to Canada as others were
doing. No one looked down on them. The stupidities and inequities
of the draft were well known; if a man with money could avoid
service by a payment to the government or by hiring another to take
his place, what was immoral about skedaddling if you didn't happen
to have the cash? Besides, other young men, eager to be in the fight
when final victory came, were joining up at an increased rate. The
Union was in no danger of running out of sturdy, high-hearted
soldiers.

That was Glenna's opinion, expressed during one of her
periodic visits to town. "So many fine young men are volunteering, they say, and all of them so strong and brave, like John
Wesley . . ." Her voice broke.

Luz bore in the tea tray, and Marin signaled her to put it down
and leave quickly. Glenna had broken down twice since arriving
this afternoon. Wes's death last week was quite unexpected, she
said. He had been caught in a sudden rainstorm and suffered a
chill on the lungs, which turned into pneumonia. "He was
gone"—she snapped her fingers—"just like that."

Marin made a sympathetic noise and poured the tea. She hadn't
even known Wes was in town, and now it turned out he had been
living in Michael's back room for some time. Glenna's grief seemed
real, although several years ago she had turned her younger brother
away from Longridge when he came to her broke and in trouble. She
had grown closer to Michael, too, during the past few years. Never
the month went by that she did not come across the bay to visit him,

usually without her husband. Mr. Severance, she said, was very busy raising beef for the army and could not be spared from the ranch.

Mr. Severance is busy making an outrageous amount of money on army contracts arranged by friends in Washington, Marin thought. She said politely, "I hope Carey is no trouble to you. His visit has stretched out so. You really must send him home, Glenna."

Glenna was in the process of lifting a forkful of cake to her mouth. The fork paused in midair. "But we haven't seen Carey since before Christmas. In fact Mr. Severance gave me strict orders to bring him home with me . . . whatever is the matter, dear?"

Marin set down her tea, and the cup made a light rattling sound against the saucer.

"He's been with you for almost two months. Mateo stopped by just before New Year's with a message that—that his grandfather wanted him to stay . . ." Mateo, who had grown up to be so handsome and brawny, explaining in his boyishly charming way how much help Carey was on the ranch, explaining . . . Her hand went up as though warding off a physical blow, warding off the truth that leaped into her mind even as she tried to deny it.

From a great distance she heard Glenna say, "Mateo? Dear me, *that* young man went off to join the army right after the first of the year and left us in a frightful pickle. We haven't seen hide nor hair of Carey."

But Marin was out of the room and running up the stairs, running blindly to her father as she had not done since she was a child. In the next hideous hours her family tried to console her, and she tried to believe that her boy might be visiting friends, might be adventuring in the gold fields, might have taken ship to China, anything but that he had gone to the war. In cold panic she recalled Carey's face as one by one the men he most admired went off to fight; she recalled the shine of his black eyes as he took in the dazzling uniforms, the gilt, and the sabers, and the excitement in his voice as he read and reread letters written after battles. He had pored over the newspapers, followed the armies on the map, argued military strategy with James . . .

"He's only a baby," she wept, "only fifteen! Papa, they don't take them at fifteen, do they?"

"Of course not, chicken. They'll pack him straight home with a flea in his ear," James answered comfortingly, and they both thought of Carey, broad-shouldered, already over six feet tall and growing fast, with a dark beard plentiful enough that he had to shave every other day and an easy, adult manner that could fool anyone who wanted to be fooled, such as a recruiting sergeant with a quota to fill.

Inquiries to friends were answered quickly. Carey had not been seen around town in weeks. Belinda and Alida were interrogated. Both girls had believed him to be at Longridge, and to Marin's disgust they were tremendously impressed and excited that he might have gone to the war. Telegrams were dispatched to Stuart, care of the War Department, and to the Pinkerton Detective Agency in Chicago. Allan Pinkerton himself replied, promising that his New York branch would have a detective meet every ship that docked in New York, and in Boston as well. An agonizing time passed before word reached Stuart and he was able to reply, his exasperation with his son resounding in the telegram's clipped words.

"But why can't he do something?" Marin wailed after she had read the message and flung it aside. "Couldn't he tell the other officers to be on the lookout? What's the use of being a general if he can't do something?"

The days dragged past, every ring of the chimes sending Marin flying to the door before the maids could get there, hoping for word that Mr. Pinkerton had Carey in his custody or that Stuart had located him and was sending him home. But no such word came. Most of the time she crept around the house or huddled near the fire like a wounded animal, not crying but simply staring, hour after hour, and seldom speaking.

Delphine had to be told, for she doted on Carey. It was Sophy who took on the task.

"He is gone, Aunt Delphine. No note or message of any kind, but we have reason to believe he has gone east to join the army."

Sophy waited, wondering if Delphine, whose mind wandered now, had understood the import of her words.

Delphine nodded, her eyes narrowing shrewdly. "Yes," she muttered, "yes. They're killing all the boys. God means to leave us women alone, all alone forever. God hates women." She resumed rocking in the chair she could barely fit into, staring at the wall and humming tunelessly.

Sophy went out of the room and felt her way down the long flight of stairs. Door chimes echoed through the house, and Logan's light step sounded on the marble of the entry hall. As Sophy reached the bottom of the stairs, she heard Logan running and her sibilant whisper, "A letter from Carey. Oh, sweet Lord."

When Marin ripped the letter open, she read it through silently. Then, realizing that others were waiting, she read it again, aloud.

Sunday evening
February 7
Dear Mother,
By now you will know I am gone and maybe have guessed where, but I must write to put your mind at ease. I am fine. Mateo and I have joined the army, and he is looking out for me. (Ha, ha!) You would be proud if you could see me in my uniform, as I look the picture of a good soldier. We are in with a grand bunch of fellows and have been given an important job. We are to be replacements in a regiment that is short of men. You will understand why I can't tell you more than that. Maybe one day I will run into Father or Vail or Charles, and won't they be surprised to see me. Tell Grandpa I remember his advice to Harlan about carrying an extra pair of dry socks and keeping my head down. Give Belinda and Alida a kiss for me, and wish Belinda happy birthday. There is a present for her in the bottom drawer of my dresser. Well, that is all for now. Don't worry if you don't hear from me for a while, as I expect to be very busy.

Love to everyone from
Your son,
Carey Severance

Not a hint as to where he was, where he was going, or even what kind of outfit he was in. Like Ethan, he might be in the cavalry, for both he and Mateo could ride like the wind. But more likely he was an ordinary soldier in the infantry, as were most of the young men who offered themselves up to the military. More healthy young bodies for generals like Stuart to hurl into brainless assaults, never mind that at home their mothers were suffering as if their bodies were being torn apart. Damn war and damn the men who made war, damn governments and flags and Causes and martial music and patriotic slogans that seduced naive, idealistic children into believing that they owed their lives to their country. Replacements. That meant he was being sent to a regiment that had suffered heavy losses. The letter had been mailed in New York, but he would be long gone by now. Much help the vaunted Pinkertons had been. But there must be lists, surely the army would have lists of its soldiers. Somewhere there were names written down with army corps, brigade, regiment, battalion, and company written after, and a mother with the necessary determination could locate one very young, foolish boy and bring him home.

She raised her head. "I am going to Washington. I'll take Jeremy and leave on the next eastbound ship."

As if she had been expecting some such statement, Logan nodded. "I think you should. I'll go with you."

BOOK FIVE

Chapter 42

Marin and Jeremy left the columned brick building that housed the War Department and picked their way across the mud of Seventeenth Street to Pennsylvania Avenue. Rain had fallen in hard bursts during the night and intermittently this morning, and the wide street, its cobbled surface crumbled by constant heavy traffic, was churned into a quagmire.

"Reminds me of a hog-wallow," she said, looking in disgust at the red clay mud on the hem of her skirt.

"Yes'm," Jeremy agreed. "Sounds a lot like one, too."

Near the iron fence that ran in front of the White House, two pigs rolled and grunted ecstactically in the ooze.

The barnyard capital of the world, Marin thought, not relishing the prospect of struggling across to the north side of the avenue, where there was at least a brick path to walk on. You were as likely to see a gaggle of geese parading up the broad street, or chickens or goats for that matter, as prominent politicians and the heads of government. She'd just about as soon deal with a goose, too, as that idiot clerk who had kept her out of Mr. Stanton's office for the third day in a row. She was furious at the treatment she had received since arriving in this chaotic town, furious that she had gotten nowhere with the army despite her name and that Stuart had not yet spared the time to come up from Virginia to see her. She knew what they thought, those men back in that government building—they thought she was just a foolish woman, blind to the important issues of the day, fluttering and wringing her hands over a grown son. They could not grasp the fact that her son was not grown at all and must be released from the army immediately. They asked, so politely, for his regiment, his brigade, and lifted eyebrows when she could not tell them. They were not impressed by his extreme youth, but informed her that the army contained many men of fifteen and even younger, some of whom had distinguished themselves on the field of battle. It was a hard stone wall she had run into, and unless she got help from higher authority, that wall was going to defeat her.

She felt defeated now and tired, and the tiredness made her peevish. She glared at Jeremy. "Well, don't just stand there. We'll never find a hack this late in the day and I will not be thrown around on one of those benighted omnibuses, so you'll have to walk."

Jeremy ducked his head. Meekness was the better part of valor when she was in this mood. He both pitied and admired her, each day determinedly assaulting the mare's nest of government, her bright head gallantly high, each day being turned away no closer to her goal. They started down the street together.

To Marin, expecting the glamour and sophistication of a great capital, the city was deeply disappointing. Its conception had been grand enough, but only a few impressive buildings had actually been constructed, and there were vast distances between them. Much of the rest of the town was jerry-built and shabby. Bordellos and saloons did a booming business, and although gambling was illegal, gentlemen could always find a quiet game. It was a malodorous city as well, for a sensible sanitation system did not exist; stinks from polluted Tiber Creek down on the south side of the White House drifted across town whenever the breeze turned in the wrong direction. As soon as the sun set, toughs, many of them Confederate sympathizers, prowled the poorly lit streets, and robbery and murder were commonplace. Ladies dared not venture out at night, and rarely did a gentleman leave his well-lighted, convivial hotel lobby after dark without a gun in his pocket and one or two friends for company. In a shocking, completely unexpected way Washington had turned out to be not a cultured eastern metropolis but a dangerous, disorderly, scrabbling boomtown. It was almost as if San Francisco, that frankly raw frontier town, had been physically situated in the middle of a war with responsibility for the conduct of that war lowered suddenly upon it, a maddening, impossible task.

Yet Washington was conducting the war, incompetently but with increasing energy and determination. Above the newly expanded Capitol building the Old Flag flew, glorying in its thirty-five stars representing every state in the Union, North and South, and by so doing proclaiming the unalterable conviction that the Union would, in the end, endure. And all during these last years of panic and stupidity and defeat and stubborn fortitude, work on the marble house of Congress had continued, another demonstration of faith.

But for all its dedication to the Northern Cause, Washington had been a city peculiarly Southern in atmosphere, culture, and habits. Many of its permanent residents were members of uppercrust Southern families, and until barely two years ago slaveholding had been legal, but the languid tempo of life had been replaced by a steady, driving excitement. For three years the city had lived in fear of invasion from the south. It had never happened, but invaders of another sort had taken over. The entire city was an army camp, and the streets were blue with uniformed men. Prostitutes, always substantial in number when Congress was in session, had swarmed into town following the troops, and the unashamed public consorting of soldiers with painted strumpets was a local scandal. Other conspicuous newcomers were the ambitious men come from all over the country to do business with the government. These men had grown rich supplying the military with uniforms made of inferior cloth, boots with cardboard soles, defective shells, harness that broke when mules strained to pull heavy guns and wagons through deep mud. Countless Union soldiers had died as a direct result of such cheating, and the wealthy contractors swanked down Pennsylvania Avenue in splendid carriages and were welcome guests in the best homes, including the President's House.

That great mansion was the heart of Washington. In the midst of mud and turmoil it sat behind its ornamental iron fence and straggling lawn like a Greek temple dropped into a rather seedy neighborhood. Marin looked up at the classic white pillars of the North Portico, awed and a little intimidated. There resided the higher authority she needed. Men who wanted something from Mr. Lincoln filled the halls every day, pressing for favors. Suppose she got in to see Mrs. Lincoln? Gossip said the

President's wife was in a perpetual panic that her oldest son, Robert, might go off to the army. She would understand.

The main gate leading to the north entrance lay just ahead. Marin walked through it onto the grounds of the White House, and Jeremy, who had been watching her face, said, "It ain't a good idea, Miss Marin. You ain't gonna get no fu'ther in that place than you did over to the War Department."

"I have no intention of going in," she retorted. Jeremy was one of the few people who could sometimes guess her thoughts. "I prefer this path to getting splashed out there on the street every time a wagon rolls by. We'll cut down by the State Department and be almost home."

Home, for the present, was Willard's, the best hotel in town, she had been told. Now that she had lived there for two weeks, its desirability remained a mystery to her. The parlors and barroom were choked with cigar-smoking politicians, diplomats, army officers, contractors, and other men on the make, eating and drinking too much, waving their hands a great deal, aiming brown juicy streams at the big brass spittoons, and missing as often as they hit. A constant rumble of footfalls and voices sounded in the corridors, and for Marin and Logan, used to the privacy of a large house, life in a cramped hotel room was close to intolerable. They had gone to the Willard when they arrived in Washington with the intent of immediately finding a small house to rent for the rest of their stay. Each day when Marin left to assail the halls of government, Logan went out to hunt for a decent place to live. Her search had brought her in contact with several ladies of high position in Washington society, and she had become friends with two of them, pretty, gentle Lily Pell and her young sister, Clara Pell, of Virginia. These ladies made no secret of their secessionist sympathies, but remained friendly with many high-ranking Union officials and often entertained Union army officers. It was at their house on E Street that Logan was visiting this afternoon.

As Marin and Jeremy entered the smoky, crowded lobby, the chief desk clerk saw her and hurried from behind the counter, smiling broadly. "Mrs. General Severance, I have excellent news for you."

They've found Carey, she thought, and her heart seemed to leap and stop in her chest.

The clerk rushed up to her. "General Severance has just arrived from the field and is waiting for you in your room. I was sure you would want to know immediately."

Color flooded back into her face, and she almost laughed with elation. Stuart had come. Now the War Department would have to help her.

He was waiting by the window in a crisp, unsullied uniform, his golden sash adorned with swinging gilt tassels, his dress saber at his side, his shoulders bearing gilt epaulets with the single star he had coveted and fought for and finally won. His new beard was full but neatly trimmed in the style affected by so many high-ranking officers. He looked harder, older: there were lines around his eyes, and the hint of a paunch that had been present when he left San Francisco four years ago was completely gone.

He swept off his hat, descended on her with customary vigor and pecked at her cheek. She looked tired and not as pretty as he remembered. Her hair was as vivid as ever, but its brightness made her face seem pale. Then she smiled, and it was like a blow to the heart. By God, she was a striking woman. She would do him proud in this city of surface friendships where people were judged, and judged brutally, by the appearance they managed to present. That is, she would do him proud if she could be made to behave.

She said, "You look so well. Come, sit down and tell me how you've been."

Good thing he'd cleaned up first and worn his dress uniform. He suspected there was admiration in her eyes. He settled into the large, overstuffed chair, the only comfortable seat in the room. "No, you tell me. How is everyone at home? Is Belinda a grown-up young lady? Does she still remember me?"

"Of course she does. She's so proud of you that she has to be reminded not to brag. She's as tall as I am and very pretty. We are going to have young men lined up outside our door in a year or two. Papa is well and sends his regards. Sophy and the baby are with us now that Charles has gone. He shouldn't have, but no one would stop him."

"He did the right thing. No self-respecting man could have done otherwise, and the need is desperate. I'm sure lives have been spared because Charles was there."

There was more warmth in his voice than she had ever heard when he spoke of Charles. How odd if the war had made a human being out of Stuart. There was a tap at the door; Jeremy came in bearing coffee. He greeted Stuart with just the right note of respectful admiration and retired speedily.

Marin made a little ceremony out of pouring the coffee and handed Stuart his cup. "I haven't seen your father in many a long age, but Glenna says he is fit as ever and working the ranch like a demon."

"I can imagine. And how is Glenna?" It was the question he ached to ask and dared not until she brought it up. Glenna's most recent letter lay tucked in his inside pocket waiting to be read again and again, yet he needed to speak her name, to savor it freely on his tongue. Who would have believed when he set sail the last time that four years—and God only knew how many more—would pass before he looked on her face again. Without Michael as intermediary neither of them could have survived, for without him the letters that flew between them could never have been received and sent.

"Glenna is as always. Perhaps a touch plumper. The last time I saw her she was grieving—oh, you won't know. John Wesley passed away in March, caught pneumonia and died—'just like that' Glenna said. She seemed quite to pieces, but I suspect it was a pose. He was always an embarrassment, and she never cared two cents about him when he was alive."

"You do her grave injustice," Stuart replied as soon as he could speak without spluttering. When he thought of the sorrowful letter that had told him of Wes's death, when he thought how the dear girl had suffered . . . "Glenna is reticent, as a lady should be, but she feels more deeply than others realize. I'm sorry to hear Wes is gone."

"My, you have grown forgiving in your old age. You used to think shooting was too good for him, and you called Glenna a conniving social climber when she married your father."

"I never said such a thing. She's been an excellent wife to Father, and I feel nothing but the deepest respect for her. As for Wes, he was a wild boy, but people change. As I have always said, 'Judge not, lest ye be judged.'"

"If you always said that, it's news to me. The war has changed you, Stuart."

"War changes everyone," he answered stiffly. "I was saddened to hear of Celia's passing. Unbelievable, how swiftly it happened. It put me in fear for you."

She shrugged. "I'm very well. Do you ever see Vail? His letter was so composed, but we wondered how he really is taking it."

"Bearing up, I should say."

She looked at him sharply. There was an edge to his voice, but he was taking a long swallow of coffee and she could not see into his eyes.

"That is," he went on, drying his lips with the tiny napkin,

"I've run into him only once, when he first enlisted, but I should guess he'll recover quickly, considering the state of their marriage."

"Whatever do you mean?"

"I had the impression things were lukewarm between them, didn't you? She was always a cool one, and he married her for her money."

"How can you say such a thing? He's never touched her money, you know it as well as I do."

"You think not? Well, perhaps." He set down his cup. "Marin, certain stories have come to my ears that upset me greatly. A brother officer has got word to me that you are in constant attendance at the War Office, plaguing them about Carey and even trying to get an audience with Mr. Stanton. I'm delighted to see you, though you should never have made the trip and Logan shouldn't have encouraged you, but this throwing about of my name in high places has got to stop."

No more polite sparring; they were down to serious combat. Marin smiled coolly. "Well, you've finally mentioned his name. I was beginning to think we'd discuss every friend and acquaintance first before getting around to Carey."

He leaped to his feet and began to pace. "Do you think I'm not concerned? Do you really believe I'm so coldhearted? I didn't want the boy to do this any more than you, but he's exactly like you, bullheaded and unmanageable. Always has been. I never could control him any more than I can control the weather. He's chosen his bed and he can lie in it."

"He's only a boy!"

Stuart stopped pacing and looked at her irritably. "A good many are only boys. It's a terrible war."

"But surely—"

"Dammit, what do you want me to do? Stop the whole goddam war, line up the troops and go looking for one runaway? It can't be done. I swear to God, Marin, if it was Mr. Lincoln's son, it couldn't be done. Carey has taken on a man's responsibility whether we like it or not, and there are worse things a boy might do. I do not doubt he'll acquit himself well."

She looked into his flushed, handsome face and thought in bitter realization, you aren't really sorry. You think it's fine and admirable that he's gone to fight. In your heart you don't fear for him, you only hope he'll distinguish himself and be a credit to you, even if he gets killed doing it. You talk about how dreadful the war is and how you're only fighting for noble ideals, but the truth is you love it, all you men. Vail and Ethan and Dan and even Charles—they couldn't stay out because it's such a grand adventure, too good to miss. And Carey had to follow, the poor foolish baby, so eager and honorable and anxious to do the right thing. There wouldn't be wars if there weren't fools like you all to fight them.

Oh, it was no use. Stuart wouldn't help her, no one would. She was alone in this, the only one in all the world who saw the issue clearly. Somewhere, in the midst of brutal war her child marched and ate and slept and was the target of some other boy's gun; her child, born at such risk, who had taken possession of her heart when he was so very tiny. Well, she would not give up because she could not. For the present this hateful town was the closest she could get to Carey, so here she would stay. She would not stop trying to see important people, no matter what Stuart said or did. She would go on and on until one day the miracle occurred that would lead her to him and let her bring him home.

It had rained without ceasing for more than a week, and the roads were a morass of thick, oozing mud churned by the hoofs of mules and horses and the heavy wheels of wagons and artillery caissons. The men slouched along bearing heavy packs, water dripping off forage caps, the lucky ones bundled in overcoats. The coats cost nine dollars, and since the ordinary soldier was allowed only forty-two dollars a year, some had elected to draw an extra blanket instead. During the frosty nights in Tennessee last fall the choice had seemed wise, but now as they struggled through cold rain, swaddled awkwardly in blankets, many yearned for the warm, comfortable coats.

In early May the Union armies in the West, General William Sherman's army now, had stripped itself of excess baggage, moved out of Chattanooga and crossed the border into Georgia, a lean, hungry animal sweeping down on its prey. The only obstacle between Sherman and the rich heartland of the Confederacy was cool, steadfast Joe Johnston and his hardy veterans dug in at the little town of Dalton in northwestern Georgia. Sherman, always daring, always flexible, sized up the solid Confederate lines and instead of ordering an assault sent his right flank wheeling behind them toward the railroad line at Resaca. Johnston, with the Federals threatening his rear, was forced to drop back and dig in again before Resaca.

All during the wet, miserable days of May the two armies

skirmished and suffered small but steady losses. Sherman's army lived on short rations. High-ranking officers, their tents and other comforts left behind in Chattanooga, ate skimpy meals and camped in the rain like lowly privates. The two armies were never out of contact, but when night fell, soldiers on both sides searched for cover from the dampness and warmed themselves by campfires when they could.

An experienced man like Sam Pryor had an advantage over the greenhorns. Before the last light died, he had spotted an indentation in the rock near the base of a stony ridge and already had a fire going and his coat nearly dry. The wet wood sizzled and smoked, but it produced warmth and it was going to cook the chicken he had freed from a farm at midday. He had been in the army two and a half years and at Chickamauga had acquired a scar that cut down into his ragged beard and gave him a fierce, wolfish look. He was, in reality, a thoughtful, studious man, a twenty-nine-year-old schoolteacher from a little Illinois town, but battle had toughened him. He was reliable in a fight and so was respected by his comrades, but he had no close friends and preferred to do his foraging and housekeeping alone.

So it was out of character when, after watching for over half an hour while the tall, lanky boy struggled in the rain with various fire-making strategies, he called out, "Hey, O'Connell, come here."

Carey looked up and saw the fire and the man. He climbed over rocks and fallen tree limbs to the foot of the escarpment.

"Yes, sir?"

"Don't call me sir. I'm not an officer. Come on up."

Carey found a foothold and scrambled up to the ledge. "Say, this is snug." The cave was so low that he had to stoop, but it had space enough for several men to spread out their blankets and was wonderfully dry.

"Snug as a bug," Pryor agreed cheerfully. "Like to join me?"

"Yes, Sam, I sure would. But my friend will be along. Is there room for both of us?"

"Can you contribute to the pot?"

"I've got a poke of cornmeal, and Mateo found some sausage in a smokehouse this morning."

"A fair trade for some bites of chicken. Sit yourself down."

"Thank you." Carey sat down, and an ecstatic shudder passed through him as the heat of the fire struck his chilled body. He laughed in embarrassment. "Didn't know how cold I was."

"The pleasures of a Georgia spring." Sam's eyes were on

Carey's bulging pack. Remembering his manners, Carey dug out the all-purpose pan and the package of cornmeal, poured water from his canteen, and mixed a batch of dough. He had developed a nodding acquaintance with Sam Pryor in the last few days and knew the man was a loner. The other men said he wrote poems home to his wife, but how could they know that when Sam never talked about himself? For some reason he craved company tonight, which was a lucky break, for a stiff wind had risen and was blowing the rain in gusts.

In the gloom a soldier came loping from the direction of the colonel's camp.

Carey stood up. "Mateo! Up here."

Mateo spotted him and came clambering up, little rocks kicking loose under his boots and rattling away in the dark.

"Our lodging for the night," Carey said, "courtesy of Mr. Pryor."

Mateo looked admiringly around the cave. "Ho, there, Pryor. To what do we owe this honor?"

"Ho, yourself, Vasquez. Where're the sausages?"

"That's the reason, huh?" Mateo pulled a string of fat sausages from inside his coat. "What I went through to get these beauties. Just when I am finding all sorts of good things in that smokehouse, this girl comes chasing me with a broom."

Sam took the meat and dropped it into his pan. "Did you give her a kiss?"

Mateo hunkered down by the fire, sighing with pleasure. "Gave her a kiss an' a swat on the fanny, an' she begged me to take the cow, too. Jesus, Mary, an' Joseph—chicken. Hey, what a banquet we're gonna have."

After eating, they did their housekeeping chores with the tidiness of experienced soldiers, added wood to the fire, and settled down in comfortable repletion to smoke.

"Full stomach, warm feet," Carey said happily. "What a grand war."

Sam tossed his stub into the rainy night and lit a second cheroot. "How long have you been in the army, son?"

"We joined up in March."

"Why?"

"Pardon?"

"Why did you join up?"

Carey looked down at his scuffed boot. "Well—for the same reason as you, I guess, and all the men. To fight for the right."

"To preserve the Union and free the slaves?"

"Yes, sure. And to be in on the finish. It will be over soon, and we've missed the best part already."

Sam's beard parted in a grin. " 'deed you have. Vasquez, is that why you joined? To fight for the right?"

"Oh, I came along just for the hell of it"—Mateo darted a sparkling look at Carey—"an' to take care of the kid here." Carey gave him a shove, and he toppled over, laughing. "That's right, sonny, pick on me. You'll be sorry someday when I save your life. Hey! Why don't you write a letter to your mama tonight? I keep telling you, and you don' do it."

"I wrote a letter."

"A long time ago. Poor little Mama—crying her eyes out, I bet." Mateo yawned. "You fellas can stay up all night, but me, I got the colonel's horse to get ready before dawn. The colonel couldn't fight the war without me." He rolled up in his blanket, feet to the fire, and pulled his cap down over his eyes. After a moment he gave a long, rolling belch. "Bes' chicken I ever ate."

Sam and Carey smoked for a while, listening to the rain, letting the heat of the fire beat against their boot soles. Carey had no real taste for cigars but had learned to smoke them without getting sick. It was necessary because everyone did it.

Sam said, "Your family all hot for the war, are they?"

"My father and my uncles are in it. One of my uncles is on the other side, though I don't see how he can be."

"I expect he's fighting for the right."

Carey looked up quizzically, but Sam was merely smoking and staring into the fire. "My mother wasn't for it. You know how mothers are."

"Women don't understand."

"She needn't have worried. We haven't had a good fight yet. I'd hate for the war to be over before we have a good fight."

"How old are you, son?"

"Eighteen. Why?"

"Just wondered. Your father in this army?"

"He's over in Virginia with the Army of the Potomac. He's been in since the beginning. He was at Fredericksburg and Chancellorsville and Gettysburg. My uncle was wounded at Gettysburg."

"A lot of battles. Ever talk to them about it?"

"I haven't had the chance. I haven't seen either of them since they left home."

"Too bad. Well, if it's a big fight you want, I think you're going to get it in a day or two."

Carey's stomach lurched, and he felt a sudden great excitement. "You think so? About time. We could have beat the pants off the Rebs weeks ago if the general had let us. Instead it's been nothing but a lot of puny skirmishes."

"Ever been in one of those skirmishes?"

"I haven't even fired my rifle. Up to three days ago we were stuck in the rear guard. We wouldn't be up here now except the colonel found out how good Mateo is with horses."

"Well, sir, until you've been in one of those puny skirmishes, don't throw off on 'em. One Reb with a gun is just as serious a matter as a whole battalion if you happen to be the fellow he's looking at down his sight."

"I know I'm green, but I'll learn fast. It seems to me we ought to attack. We outnumber the enemy, and we're better."

"Sherman knows what he's doing, don't ever doubt it. He's the best general we've got, better than Grant, better than Robert E. if the truth be known, and do you know why? Because he understands what war is about. No play-party and no grand adventure, but a mean, dirty business to be gotten through any way you can. Old Joe Johnston is one hell of a smart general, and if we had attacked every time he dug in this last month, a good many of us would be dead by now and the Rebs would still hold the railroad. Sherman doesn't waste men if he can help it. He's been outflanking Johnston, forcing him back, but soon now—" With his finger Sam drew marks in the dirt. "There's Atlanta. There's the railroad coming up through Marietta. Here we are, and here's the creek line right ahead of us with Johnston entrenched on the other side. Now we have to get hold of Marietta, and the area right around here is not bad terrain. I smell a battle coming that we're all going to be in on."

After they had rolled up in their blankets and closed their eyes for sleep, Carey lay thinking. Mateo was right. He should have written Mother and let her know where he was. No one but Mateo knew his real name. If in the big battle that Sam said was coming he were killed—he swallowed—if he were killed and Mateo were to die, too, Mother would never know, no one would ever know . . . He hoped he would not be found wanting, he hoped Father would be proud if he knew. That was the bad part. If he did fight well and became a hero, Father would never know.

They were running. Blood roared in his ears. He could not hear the sergeant but only saw his open mouth. He threw himself on the ground, smelled the earth and the grass, heard a loud burst close over his head. He could hear everything now, the thudding of his own heart, the hard breathing of the man next to him, a gurgling groan only a few feet away, the wild, trumpeting shriek of frightened horses, the blood-chilling "Eee-ayyy" of the enemy. He had to get up, had to go ahead, but he could not move.

"Come on!"

It was Mateo.

Get up, stumble on, follow Mateo. They're ahead there in the bushes, in the trees, faceless terrors with sharp flashes of fire that never missed. Something cracked near his ear. He ran on. Men in blue lay sprawled in the field as if sleeping. Some moaned, some didn't move. Another fusillade. The man running beside him went down, and fear and hate swamped him. He ran, face contorted, eyes bulging, lips drawn back. He fired, reloaded, fired again. In a dizzy flash he saw Mateo's face, a twisted, snarling mask. He went ahead, saw a soldier in butternut rise up. He fired, and blood spurted from the man's chest as he fell. The devils were pulling back, scrambling to the rear as the blue lines overran their breastworks. There was a cheer from the boys on the left, and far away the sound of continued firing.

He was walking back, picking his way across the field. The blue bodies looked awkward now, doubled over, or with their arms and legs flung out like discarded dolls. He looked into each face. They were terrible faces, but they didn't bother him, nothing bothered him. Some of the bodies moved or twitched jerkily. An antiphony of groans rose from the battlefield, and the sound hung low, like the powder smoke and the morning mist. Men were stumbling back, some trying to hold together gaping holes in their bodies, some helping others. Bodies of men and horses were strewn everywhere. One soldier lay with a knee drawn up as if about to leap to his feet, but his neck ended in a bloody stump; the head was not there. In the long ditch they had had to cross this morning lay the bodies of young men who only an hour before had breathed and sweated and trembled and hidden behind bushes to relieve liquid bowels and then gone out to charge the enemy. Now they were heaped like discarded garbage. Carey tripped over a soldier whose mouth was open in a yell and mumbled "Pardon me" even as he realized the man was dead.

But not everyone was dead. He climbed out of the ditch and saw a soldier with a bloody arm struggle to his feet. A few yards onward he found Mateo looking up, glad to see him. He got down on his knees, groaning like an old man, slipped his arm under Mateo's shoulders, and lifted him. The back of his head was gone.

•   •   •

New Hope Church lay behind them and the cliffs of Kennesaw Mountain, where a valiant assault was repulsed with three thousand Union troops dead and little loss to the enemy. But the drenching rain was ending, the roads were becoming passable, and although the supply lines stretched thinner with every day's march, trains were chugging through from Nashville over rails rebuilt by the U.S. Army Engineers as soon as the Rebels tore them up. Onward the blue army came, pressing south toward Atlanta, where the arteries of the Confederacy, the railroads, met and crossed and pumped out men and supplies. As the first Federal detachments forded the Chattahoochee, platoons were sent out to watch for the enemy; the army was at its most vulnerable during a river crossing, and Rebel cavalry could do great mischief if allowed to sneak up unobserved.

Carey sent his companion down the trail to the left and moved quietly under the trees. Sunlight slanting through the leaves warmed his face, and birds sang far above his head. Sam Pryor would likely choose the ditch behind the bramble of wild blackberry as a good spot to sleep tonight—but Sam was rotting at the base of Kennesaw Mountain. A crackle and a light brushing sound, and he swung around, his eyes squinting down his rifle barrel, his finger tightening on the trigger.

A horseman moved cautiously down the slope, half hidden by low-hanging branches. His butternut uniform was patched, his blond hair long and streaked with gray, his face gaunt, with a look of unspeakable weariness. He sensed a presence; in one motion his hand flew to his holster and he turned to look down, unbelieving, into the tense face of the young soldier with the raised rifle. They stared at each other. Then the rider slammed in his spurs, and the horse bolted up the slope and vanished behind the sheltering trees.

Into the clearing ran the other soldier, back from his reconnoiter. He lifted his rifle and fired fruitlessly into the woods.

"God almighty, corporal, that Reb sure can ride!"

"Yes," said Carey, "he sure can."

Chapter 43

At the beginning of the war, the hospital Marin worked in had been an Episcopal church. Now the narthex served as the admission office, the pews had been removed, the altarpiece and organ covered, the altar cloths and prayer stools stored; wounded men lay row on row, their pain no easier to bear in this house of God than if they had been dumped in one of the whitewashed huts near the depot. Washington knew the real price of war as no other Northern community could, for after each desperate battle across the border in Virginia the casualties poured in. Every train rolling into the depot, every riverboat plowing up the river arrived loaded with diseased and wounded men, many of them near death, who must somehow be housed and fed and cared for. After three years of bloody war the town had become one vast infirmary. Government buildings, sprawling warehouses, canvas tents, broken-down hotels, churches, and the confiscated homes of Confederate sympathizers gone South all sheltered hurt and dying men. Ambulances rumbled constantly through the streets, and intinerant carpenters who normally lived hand to mouth found steady employment slapping together coffins for undertakers who held government contracts and grew richer as the battle toll mounted. At times the carpenters could not keep up with demand, and Marin and other nursing volunteers experienced the horror of having to step around dead bodies, piled up and waiting for decent interment, as they entered the hospital.

During their first weeks in Washington neither Marin nor Logan even thought of volunteering for hospital work. Marin spent all her time and energy in vainly assaulting government offices and demanding to see the person in charge. Logan developed a busy social life in a surprisingly short time for one so shy. With the help of her new friends, Lily and Clara Pell, she accomplished the impossible in the crammed-to-bursting town and located a small but acceptable furnished house near the Pell residence on E Street. The Pell sisters were helpful in other ways, too; they contributed inexpensive bric-a-brac to dress up the place and make it homier and were the first visitors to call. Stuart disliked the association intensely and wrote a stiff letter to Logan listing all the drawbacks to a friendship with known Southern sympathizers and ordering her to break it off immediately.

Logan read the letter aloud, her jaw hardening. "Of all the gall! Who does he think he is, telling me what I shall do and not do? Oh, I could just . . ." She crumpled the letter and threw it to the floor. "Stuart's been a general too long."

Marin grinned, yet this once she understood Stuart's side of the matter and privately agreed with him. While some Southerners had demonstrated their loyalty to the Union in costly ways, many others were suspected of the worst kind of treachery. As the tides of battle shifted, conspirators were seen under every bush, and Marin knew that her own position was none too secure. Luckily her native state of Maryland had not seceded, but every time she opened her mouth, out came that damning accent. She kept Lily and Clara Pell at arm's length, although they were two of the silliest women she had ever met, foolish, flirtatious Southern belles who could not be accused of having a sensible idea in their heads, let alone a treasonous one.

One evening as twilight was deepening she came home from the hospital to find a letter from Michael waiting for her on the hallway table. Logan had not yet returned from the Misses Pell's afternoon tea, and the house was silent. She went into the small parlor and lit a lamp. What a dreary room, dark and shabbily furnished; what a dreary life, filled with pain and death and all to no point. She sat down and looked at the letter. Her last act before taking the steamer East had been to talk Michael into coming to work for Gentry and Callendar—"for just three or four months, Michael, that's all I ask. I'll make the fur fly once I'm back there, but I can't do it from so far away."

Michael had had doubts. "I know hardware, Marin, but all of this . . ." They had been standing on the first floor of the warehouse, and sacks of coffee off a ship just in from Valparaiso were being trundled through the wide door. "And as for the Golden Cathay . . ."

In her impatience to tidy her affairs and be off she swept aside his doubts along with her own. "Fiddlesticks. You're a business-man and a mighty successful one. I notice Morgan's Hardware stayed afloat back in fifty-five when nine out of ten merchants were going under. You can run the hardware store with your left hand, you know you can . . . and in addition to the salary you get here I'll—I'll give you a piece of the profits, how's that for fair?" The offer had been a wrench—no one but the Gentrys and Harry Callendar had ever shared in the profits—but Michael's obdurate look told her he must be tempted by more than a salary.

So he had accepted, and now she read the details of his day-to-day difficulties and dropped the letter into her lap. He wanted advice, but how could she give it at this distance? The company, Tyler, even Papa and Belinda and Sophy seemed so far away, and Michael's worries part of a life she could barely remember. Why had it mattered so much whether Gentry and Callendar succeeded or failed? Why had money seemed so important and a grand house so necessary? Here, close to the war, all that mattered was that the name Severance did not appear on the ever-lengthening casualty lists, all that mattered was that she find Carey soon. And after she went to work at St. Francis Hospital, all that mattered was that she keep her breakfast down while changing the dressings on infected stumps and hopeless belly wounds and stay on her feet until it was time to go home.

It was Ellen Stanton, the wife of the secretary of war, who first suggested that she volunteer. "You might 'adopt' one or two soldiers, my dear, as I have done. Bring them little gifts and write letters home for them. I believe it would ease your mind."

Ellen Stanton was pretty and self-assured, and much younger than her explosive husband. She had been very much the social leader in the early days of the war. Marin was a little afraid of her because of her nearness to power and her lack of warmth, but she had maneuvered an introduction and deliberately cultivated the woman with the idea of talking to Mr. Stanton in his home, away from the hurly-burly of the War Office.

Opportunity arrived more swiftly than she could have hoped. She looked at the squat man with the choleric, perspiring face who sat beside her in his lavishly furnished parlor, and her courage almost failed. A stern man, unswerving in his devotion to the Union, proud of his incorruptibility in this most corrupt of cities, the predominant man in Washington after the President, he was every bit as unattractive as everyone said. Yet power seemed to emanate from him. His short legs barely reached the floor, but his eyes, behind steel-rimmed glasses, seemed to see into every corner of her mind.

When she haltingly explained the favor she wanted, he directed those pitiless, all-seeing eyes at her and said, "Have you discussed the matter with your husband, madam?"

"Yes, sir."

"And what was his advice?"

"He feels that—that our son has chosen his path and that it would be impossible to find him in any case, but sir . . ."

"Just so. Just so. Madam, you will pardon me, but you should listen to your husband and be guided by his greater wisdom. Your son has chosen honor and duty. Take pride in the fact and cease moping. Go out and do something for our brave fighting men, ask Mrs. Stanton. She will find something constructive for you to do. Our country asks our all, madam, and we must give it." He hopped up, bowed, and moved on to his other guests with the ungainly walk that was the result of a stiff knee.

Mrs. Stanton watched him go and then came across the room. "Not good news, my dear?"

"No, ma'am. Secretary Stanton agrees with my husband." Give our all to our country, the little troll. What was he giving? "He cannot take time from the war effort, ma'am, to find one boy." Oh, the bitterness had shown then. Stuart would have apoplexy if he knew.

Mrs. Stanton sighed. "It is as I feared. Now you must come with me to the hospital tomorrow, I won't take no for an answer. It will do you a world of good."

So Marin had gone. Timorously, with a trembling in the pit of her stomach, she stopped by the bed of a young soldier who smiled when he saw her but did not speak. She sat beside his bed and talked of the world outside, wondering what his wound was, and his eyes lit as she told him about California. When she rose to go, she left a jar of jelly tied with red ribbon and a packet of needles and thread and promised to return the next day. But a week passed before she went again, and when she arrived, another man was in his bed. When she inquired, the nurse explained, "That young feller—oh, he had a bullet in the lung. Lung cases don't last long."

"No, of course not." Marin turned and walked outside, feeling the spring breeze on her skin, drawing air deeply into her own lungs, and thinking she would never go back into that pesthouse again, no matter what Mrs. Stanton said. But the next day she did return, and the day after, and soon she was in the wards four long days a week, sometimes staying into the late night hours. At first she only brought gifts and chatted with the less seriously wounded, but then in early May came the purgatory of the Wilderness and the wounded poured in, an avalanche of terribly burned and injured men, and she learned to give baths and dress the wounds of naked, hairy men who wept and swore and sometimes screamed with pain.

The newspapers shouted that although the losses in Virginia were great, the Union at last had a general who would fight, and in rolling phrases lauded Grant for his unyielding courage and stubborn perseverance.

Marin read dispatches describing the bitterness of the fighting and then the glowing editorials and threw the paper down. How could any sensible person speak of Grant's courage when all the man had done was bravely order other men to go out and die? "And die and die. He says he'll fight to victory no matter how long it takes, but who's doing the dying? Not General Grant, the cold-eyed scoundrel."

Logan was taken aback. It had never occurred to her to question the judgment of those in authority or to wonder if wiser men might have found a solution other than battle to settle the nation's dispute, but the mention of the wounded stirred buried guilt. Remorsefully she said, "You've been so brave, going into that hospital and facing up to all the dreadful sights. I feel like a slacker. If I hadn't promised Lily to come to her musicale this evening, I'd go with you. I will go tomorrow and every day after that. I'm ashamed I didn't do it sooner. I—I guess I haven't been able to get up the nerve."

Marin warmed to the praise. "Oh, it's not so hard. You just turn a blind eye to the worst of it and try not to think."

But when she arrived at the hospital, she almost turned around and left. Moans and putrid odors assaulted her before she was up the steps, and inside was pandemonium. New steamerloads of wounded had arrived at the wharf early that morning, and every hospital in town was overwhelmed. She walked between the beds in a daze. So many burn cases, and no way to ease their pain but morphia and more morphia until they died; never after any other battle had she seen such savage burn cases. And the amputees. God, there were so many. Before long the surgeons would be trying to cure dysentery with the knife.

Throughout the long afternoon of May 9, while rumors flew that Grant was pressing battle and blood was flowing again in the woods and fields of Virginia, Marin worked, dousing burns and wounds with cold water, bandaging, comforting, giving spoonfuls of laudanum; to her every lanky young boy with part of his face shot away or an arm or leg missing was Carey, every horribly burned officer was Vail. Once, when she lifted an arm and it detached from the body and hung limp in her hand, she came close to hysteria, but after a deep inhalation of smelling salts held to her nose by an orderly and a few minutes spent sitting on the front steps in the warm May sunshine, she marched back inside and went to work again.

Dusk fell, and outside the torches were lit and flared upward into the darkness, the ambulances still came, and the dead carts still rumbled away. Inside the groans dwindled as laudanum and morphia brought temporary deliverance. Marin had forgotten supper, but she gulped a cup of coffee in the narthex before going back into the ward to help with the new arrivals. The nurses moved quietly, burdened with the suffering around them and their own lack of training. Most of the doctors had gone home— amputations would resume in the morning—and no more heart-breaking shrieks issued from the operating room. A man in a drugged stupor half-woke and cried out for his mother. It had astonished Marin to find that grown men in extreme pain often begged for their mothers like hurt, puzzled children. Every one of them was Carey crying out for her.

A groan, a whisper. Her name. She whirled toward the bed from where that miserable whisper had come, hopeful and afraid.

"Vail . . . is it Vail?" She lifted her lamp, and light fell on the man in the bed. "Dan! Oh, Danny, my dear, whatever has happened to you?" She went down on her knees, her hands cupping his face.

". . . saw your hair in the lamplight . . . couldn't be you, but it was . . ."

"Yes, yes, it's me . . . oh, Dan . . ." She smoothed back his hair and kissed his forehead gently. Her cousin's eyes were dark with suffering, the flesh around them bruised. His square, blunt-featured face was gray-tinged. "Are you in pain, Dan? Have they given you anything?"

"A while—a while back, something . . . It dulled down a bit, but now it's back. Some mean old devil is burning the soles of my feet."

"Let me look." She drew back the covers. "I'll get you something that will help."

Get to your feet, walk to the dispensary, take the bottle and the spoon. Walk back, pour the medicine, get it into his mouth. Don't look at the blanket, so flat below his hips, where there are no legs. Don't think, don't let it get inside your mind, or you'll begin to scream and never stop.

He swallowed the laudanum, and a frail ghost of his old merry smile curved his lips. "So good to see you . . . I'm halfway well already. How do you come to be here, honey-girl?"

Her hand stroked his cheek lightly. "Carey ran off and joined the army the first of the year, following the bad example of you other fellows. I've tried to find him, but so far no luck."

"Mama wants her baby back, huh? I don't blame you . . . the war's no fit place for a kid . . . no fit place for anybody . . ." A spasm gripped him, and his face twisted in pain. When it passed, she said, "I've taken a house here in Washington. As soon as you're better, we'll move you there, and Logan and I can take care of you."

His eyes opened, wide and lit with hope. "Logan . . . she's here, too?"

"She came east with me. Oh, I'm such a fool! I should have sent for her right away." A man was moving slowly between the beds—Sergeant Evans, the kind convalescent soldier who had given her the smelling salts earlier in the day. She hopped up, and her low voice came to Dan in snatches. ". . . Miss Pell's house on E Street . . . Captain Dan Gentry . . . Miss Severance is to come immediately . . ."

She went back to Dan, pulled up a stool, and settled herself beside him. "She'll be here very soon. You must sleep now."

Laudanum was easing the lines of pain in his face. He said, "I don't want to sleep—want to visit with you. It's so good to see you, Marin. Is home still there? Is it still the same?"

"Wild and woolly as always. Dan, have you ever run into Vail? Do you know how he is?"

He smiled. "I was transferred into his battalion in the reorganization just before this campaign started. He's my commanding officer now, luckily for me."

Her heart began to beat in queer leaps. It was as she had feared. Vail had been in this hideous battle, too. "What happened to him, Dan? Where is he now?"

"Beats me, honey. I last saw him when he loaded me into the ambulance. But for him I'd be making bones somewhere in the Wilderness instead of lying here in luxury talking to you. He's a fine officer, Marin, a fine man. I wish I'd known him better before the war. He'll never make colonel though."

"Why not, if he's good?"

Dan chuckled low in his throat. "He has a talent for antagonizing higher command. Thumbs his nose at authority and makes sure they know about it. You can't do that and get ahead in the army. They'll promote fifty incompetent toadies before one good man who rocks the boat. Our colonel, for instance. Every man in the regiment hates him. He's not so much mean as dumb, and dumb is the worst an officer can be, because he's the kind that gets men killed. When Colonel Mercer gives an order, Vail says 'Yes, sir,' and then does as he pleases." Dan smiled in fond reminiscence. "The colonel is a stickler on rank and privilege. No matter where we are, in camp or on a forced march with Johnny Reb having at us, the colonel has his own supply wagon with him, and when mealtime comes, his orderly sets out a table with a tablecloth, china, and silver, and serves him, and the fool orders his officers to eat with him. Mind you, the men are sitting in the mud scrabbling for hardtack and beans. Well, Vail wouldn't do it. He took his food and sat with the men, which gave me and a couple of other officers the courage to do the same. He'll never get a recommendation from Colonel Mercer, but a lot of us owe our lives to him."

A warm rush of pleasure passed through Marin, as if she herself had been complimented. "How so?" she inquired almost shyly.

"Colonel Mercer insisted that patrols be sent out every night, with the Rebs only a few yards away looking down our throats and firing at everything that moved. We knew exactly where they were. It would have meant men dead for no good reason every time a patrol went out, so Vail says, 'Yes, sir, Colonel Mercer, sir,' and has the fellows take a couple of steps out to a tree and come back. Later on he reports that the patrol is back safe and the Rebs are thirty yards or whatever over that way. Colonel Mercer got to wondering out loud why we never lost any men, but the reports were always right so what could he do? When the bad time came—" Memory entered Dan's eyes. He looked away. "It's not fit for a lady's ears, but—it was a rough go, Marin. We were sent straight in, straight in . . . I don't know why any of us are alive. My boys got lost in the smoke and stumbled into a bog, and the enemy fire was coming right down on us. The Rebs have a way of screeching that chills your blood, and here came a bunch of men hollering like banshees, and I thought it was more Rebs and it was my end. But it was our fellows, with Vail out in front as if bullets couldn't hurt him, roaring like a maniac. His horse was shot down under him, and he just scrambled up and kept coming. I never was so glad to see anybody in my life. His fellows poured fire into the Rebs and chased them off and then dragged us out of the bog. The enemy was on the run, firing back at us, and we took off after them. That's when I got hit. It was Vail who hauled me back and found an ambulance. He gave the driver a lot of orders about how to take care of me, and we went bouncing down the road back to Culpepper. I was out most of the time, thank God—those ambulances see to it that you feel every bump. The last I saw of Vail he'd found another horse and was flying back down the road, back into the fight . . . God help him . . ." Dan's burst of energy was gone. His pupils had narrowed to pinpoints as the drug took effect.

Marin whispered, "Sleep, Dan. You've talked enough."

"No sleep . . . want to see Logan . . ."

Her hand passed across his eyelids, closing them. "Let the medicine help you. Sleep, and I'll wake you the moment she comes."

"Promise . . ."

"I promise," she said.

Since St. Francis Church had become a hospital the bell in the steeple had not been rung, but from somewhere in the city another bell was marking the slow passage of the night. Midnight and then one o'clock. Logan did not come. Two-thirty. Marin shifted on her seat, put her hands to her tired back. Dan still slept, his breathing quick and shallow.

At a little before three he waked. ". . . thirsty . . ." She spooned water into his mouth and wiped his face with a cool, damp cloth. "Ah, that's good." And after a moment, "Logan?"

"She'll be here soon, Dan. Go back to sleep." Why doesn't she come? Why doesn't she come? Marin chanted silently. I should have gone after her myself.

Toward dawn he woke again and whispered, "Hold my hand."

She took his square, strong hand in hers and held it tight, remembering the party where he had danced all evening with Logan, whirling her around and around the room until her cheeks turned pink and her eyes glowed, remembering another night much farther in the past, John Baldwin's birthday party at Fontana when Dan and Harlan had challenged the other boys, and Dan had leaped higher than anybody on his long, sturdy legs. Now Harlan was in his grave these many, many months, and Dan had only half a body.

He stirred and sighed and muttered; his hand still clung to hers. As morning bells rang distantly from the steeples of other churches, he opened his eyes and said distinctly, "Keep going, boys. It can't be much farther now."

The sky was fully light when Sergeant Evans limped into the church and found Marin sitting on the stool, still holding Dan's hand.

He bent down, took the hand from hers, and closed the staring eyes.

She got up and walked down the aisle, out into the bright May morning. The sergeant followed, his left leg swinging awkwardly. He said, "Go home now, ma'am. Eat and get some rest."

Marin shook her head. She felt that she could become an assassin this day, kill Grant and Lee and Lincoln and Jeff Davis and all the vainglorious, hypocritical old men who believed that political theories were worth dying for as long as it was someone else doing the dying. "No," she answered, low and bitter, "I'm not leaving here until they give me his body. He's not going to be hauled out to the cemetery in a pine box and dumped in the ground like so much rubbish. He's going to have a fine rosewood coffin and a headstone and a minister to say prayers, much good it will do him. May God damn them all."

"Yes, ma'am. I looked everywhere for Miss Severance, but never did find her. No one was home at the Misses Pell's house nor at your house, either. I talked to some of the neighbors, and nobody knew where she was. They said your Negro servant had gone out looking for her. I left messages everywhere I stopped."

"It doesn't matter now. It's too late, too late for all of us." She looked into the man's compassionate eyes. "But it was good of you to try. I thank you."

"Not at all. Ma'am, if you'll go on home, I swear before God he'll be taken care of right."

As Marin walked up the front path, old Mrs. Hall, her curious eyes bright as a bird's, hailed her over the fence. "Mrs. Severance, did that soldier boy ever find your sister? My gracious, she's been out all night. How is the poor wounded captain? Better, I trust?"

"He's dead," Marin said, and shut the door on her neighbor's cries of dismay.

Slowly she climbed the stairs to her room, weary in body, sick at heart. The little house was quiet in the hush of midmorning. She stretched out on the bed, prepared to cry her eyes out, and instead dropped immediately into sleep. Downstairs the front door opened and closed, but in her sleep no outside sound reached her. After a time she turned on her side and then jerked and groaned and clenched her fists. She cried out loudly and sat up, her eyes wide open. Half drugged with sleep, shaking with shock, she leaped from the bed and ran out into the hallway. Near the stairs she stumbled and went down in a heap at the edge of the top step, trembling and sobbing.

From inside her room Logan heard and came running.

"Darling, what is it?" The peculiar gulping, wrenching sound that came from deep inside Marin was frightful. Logan tried to lift her, failed, and bent down to see her face. "Marin, please . . ."

Tears streamed down Marin's face. She held out her hand in supplication, and words tumbled from her shaking lips. "It was a dream, oh, Logan, a horrible, horrible dream. We were in a house in the middle of a battle, and the house was all windows so we could see everything. Shells were exploding all around, and the earth was going up in great, awful puffs. You were there, and Mama and Papa and Sophy, and I was trying to get you all away from the glass. Belinda was like she is now, and she kept trying to run outside so she could see better, but Carey was a tiny baby. I had him in my arms and was dragging Belinda back inside. Then all of a sudden Carey was grown-up. He was one of the soldiers running across the battlefield, and I could see his face as though I were right next to him. His eyes were standing out and full of hate, and he was screaming, 'Kill! Kill!' Then he wasn't Carey anymore, he was Vail, and he was hollering and running and shooting. And it was so thrilling, and I thought, Now I understand why they do it, and then he was running right into the enemy, and they were raising their guns to fire . . . Oh, Logan, I know we'll never see them again. I know they're both dead!"

The words, spoken with such desperate certainty, shook Logan to the core, but as always in an emergency her native good sense took over.

"Nonsense, dear. You can't know that, and there's no reason to believe it. It was only a dream, a dreadful dream, and no wonder with all you've been through. Let me wipe your eyes, poor thing. Now blow your nose. It was only a dream." She went on talking softly, reassuringly, until Marin sat quiet on the top step, sniffing and blinking. She looked at Logan and saw that her eyes, too, were swollen from hard crying.

"So you've heard. He wanted to see you, he asked for you over and over."

A wave of pain and shame passed over Logan's face. "Don't, please. I just found out when I got home. Mrs. Hall caught me at the front door. I believe she took pleasure in passing on bad news."

Marin blew her nose again and stuffed the handkerchief in her pocket. "Where on earth have you been? Sergeant Evans looked everywhere."

Logan's head was down. "He didn't look in the jail."

"Jail?" Marin gazed at her, uncomprehending.

"They came for Lily and Clara last night and locked them up, and they questioned me for hours. Oh, Marin, they think I'm a Confederate spy."

Dumbstruck, Marin's mouth opened and closed. "Logan Severance, are you stark, raving crazy?"

"They do," Logan insisted miserably. "They suspect me even though they finally let me go. They said that the Pells have been watched since the beginning of the war. I think they weren't arrested sooner because they've got so many friends high up in the government. That's how they got their information."

"Don't tell me you think those two are really spies. They're the silliest women in Washington."

"No, they're not. Marin, I didn't come east with you just out of love for Carey. I came because . . . because I hoped that once I got here, I could somehow find out where Ethan is, maybe even get to see him. When I met Lily Pell—well, you know how she's always talking about her connections. Jefferson Davis really is her second cousin, and she knows lots of important Southerners. I did wonder why girls so hot for secession would entertain so many Republicans. They have that way about them—it seems to be a gift Southern women have—of listening so sympathetically, and there was a great deal of talk in that house, things that never should have been said, by government officials and army officers, too. The gentlemen who questioned me said they believe several battles have been lost because of information the Pell sisters supplied."

Marin swallowed, completely stunned. "But how—my goodness, even if they are disloyal, how could they get information south, how could . . ."

"Washington is a sieve, you know that. It's easy to get out of town, and the enemy is just a whoop and holler down the road. And half the town is secesh—anybody could be a messenger, but not just anybody could get information. Oh, Marin, I doubted those girls, I knew they weren't as empty-headed as they seemed, that was the very reason I cultivated them. I thought maybe—I hoped they could put me in touch with Ethan, and if they could, I didn't care if they were sending information to Robert E. Lee himself. There, that's the truth."

Marin watched Logan knead the brown taffeta of her skirt with nervous fingers, seeing her sister-in-law in a new and stupefying light. Logan the timid, Logan the arch-abolitionist taking up boldly with spies and traitors, risking her reputation and the Cause she believed in, all for the love of a man. A married man. Stuart had been absolutely right when he ordered her to break off with the Pells.

Cautiously she inquired, "What exactly did you tell those men who questioned you?"

"I told them I am a loyal citizen, Massachuetts born and completely opposed to slavery, that my two brothers are high-ranking officers fighting for the North, as well as my nephew and my dear friend Captain Daniel Gentry—" Logan's eyes filled, and she turned away.

"Did you mention your other dear friend, fighting for the South?"

"Stars above, no!"

"Thank the Lord for that. What else did you say?"

"Nothing much, except that I was a stranger in town and lonely and the Pell sisters had entertained me in their home, as they had many other loyal citizens. And that I was completely innocent of wrongdoing."

A cagey statement. Logan hadn't lost her head. Marin asked, "So how was it left?"

"They said I was free to go home but not to leave town. They suspect me, and I can't blame them. I can't blame anyone but my own stupid self. I sneaked out of there feeling so guilty, as if I really had helped the enemy, and then when I got here and heard about Dan . . . oh, I'll never forgive myself."

The two girls sat on the steps, Logan with her head in her hands, Marin considering the ways in which this news might effect her. Living with Logan, she would be tarred with the same brush even if she was Stuart's wife. Lord, what if they knew her real opinion of the war?

From this moment on she must guard her tongue, her actions, even the expression on her face. She would work longer hours at the hospital and polish up her friendship with Ellen Stanton. Otherwise even if she located Carey, the authorities wouldn't let her leave town; even if she proved that he was underage, they would believe she was only trying to weaken the army and refuse to listen.

Chapter 44

Peachtree Creek was behind them, a sudden, bitter battle where the Confederates lost twice as many men as the Federals. The rooftops of Atlanta were in view now. The city and its railroad were the prize, and their loss would be the beginning of the end for the South.

For Carey each day was another mindless battle, each night a different kind of nightmare, for no one knew when that madman General John B. Hood might launch another of his lunatic assaults and his shrieking troops would descend like wild beasts. No one slept well, each man kept his dearest possession, his rifle, loaded and close at hand. Foraging parties brought in victuals every day, for supplies coming in over the long rail line from Tennessee were undependable, and in any case guns and ammunition took precedence over food. It was an army living off the land.

Carey's usual practice was to forage for himself. Although he ate and slept and fought in close proximity with other men, he was regarded as a loner, a good enough fellow but quiet, one who never engaged in horseplay when the fighting slackened or talked of home and what he was going to do after the war or, indeed, revealed anything of himself.

One hot August morning while the cannon thundered outside Atlanta and shells screamed overhead, a foraging party left camp for Woodford Plantation, more than a mile away, where those in the know said there were fat hogs and chickens feeding happily, a smokehouse filled to bursting, and other kinds of wonderful food untouched as yet by the Union army. On impulse, thinking of fresh pork and sweet potatoes for dinner, Carey joined the party. He had grown an inch and a half in the eight months he had been gone from home, and for some reason that he could not understand, he was always savagely hungry.

Toward noon rumors began to circulate through camp that a detachment of Wheeler's cavalry was hovering on the Union flanks, no threat to the main body of troops but a danger to stragglers. Carey was in the henhouses at Woodford Plantation, helping himself to some eggs, when a voice said, "Hold it right there, mister, or I'll blow your head off."

He turned, the eggs in his hands, his gun strapped to his shoulder. A girl who he guessed to be about Belinda's age held a rifle on him, steady as a rock. She looked a lot like Belinda, too, with her long, blond curls, her small, turned-up, lightly freckled nose, and the belligerent fire in her eyes.

"Good day, miss," he remarked genially, gazing down at her from his great height. "A dandy plantation you have here. Makes me think of home. We have a fine lot of layers on my farm, too, and more cattle than you've ever seen."

"That so? Why didn't you stay there then? Keep those hands up, you thief."

"Yes, ma'am. But, beg pardon, I'm not a thief. I only meant to borrow the eggs. I was going to pay for them as soon as I found the owner. See, I've got the money right . . ."

The rifle jammed in his lean stomach. "You make a move like that again and you'll never eat another egg. Now put them back where you got them and get out of here."

"Yes, ma'am." Smiling, Carey set the eggs down. His fingers rested on the straw for a moment, and then the rifle was out of her hands and in his own.

She leaped forward, screaming, "Give me that, you rotten coward, give it to me!"

He held her off with one arm. "Afraid I can't, ma'am. You run along now before I paddle you, and stop that screeching or I'll go home with a mighty poor opinion of Southern womanhood."

"I'll kill you, you dirty Yankee!" she yelled as he pushed her in front of him out of the henhouse. As they reached the door, he gave her a little shove and stepped out, laughing, the rifle he had just commandeered loose in his hand. He walked into a gun. Behind it was no young girl but a man in ragged butternut, a man with a scraggled, clawed beard and the coldest eyes he had ever seen.

"Drop it slowly, soldier." Carey dropped the rifle. "Now yourn." He allowed his own rifle to slide down to the ground. "That's fine. Now turn around and march."

There was sporadic firing some distance away, and a man from Carey's company lay dead near an unkempt hedge. The others had disappeared. Rebel cavalrymen were rounding up the scattered hogs—no dashing cavaliers these, but beggarly, disreputable-looking men with hard, haggard faces and horses that were thin and ill used. Carey cursed himself for a fool. He'd been so busy playing with the girl in the henhouse that he'd missed what was going on outside. And the others had taken off without him. This was no way to live through a war.

The man with the gun growled, "Give me your pocketbook, damn you," shoved his rifle in Carey's ribs, and clicked back the hammer. Carey dug out his purse and handed it over.

"Git his watch," yelled a soldier with a wriggling sow in his arms. "Them rich Yankees allus has gold watches."

"Hand it over," said the man with the rifle. "The ring, too. Now turn out yer pockets." The rifle barrel trembled as he spoke. Carey noticed the saddled horse only four feet away and the clear path back to camp, barred only by a hedge lower than ones he had jumped when he was ten years old. He also noticed the alert eyes of his captor, the trembling of the rifle, and the heavy armaments of the other men.

I could grab that gun, fight my way out, and come back to camp a hero. I could be dead, more likely. Well, now's my chance to sacrifice all for the dear Old Flag and I don't think I'll take it.

He emptied his pockets.

"Now git a move on, soldier." The man gave him another sharp jab in the ribs, and he started down the long, curving drive past the porch of the plantation house, where whites and Negroes stood watching. Behind him he could hear the girl shout angrily, "Put that sow down, you thief, give me back those piglets!" And then a wail, "You all are no better than the Yankees."

It was a long run, trotting beside the riding cavalrymen, and Carey was winded as he stumbled into the enemy camp and got his first close look at the men he had been fighting all these months. They looked unutterably tired and as though they hadn't eaten well in many weeks. Their uniforms were worn, and rags covered the feet of some, but the greatest difference between them and the Union troops was in their faces, especially their eyes. Union soldiers, even the most hard-bitten, could still sometimes have a merry look; these men rarely smiled, and most wore stony, incurious expressions as they glanced at him and then went on about their business. Apprehension passed through him like a chill. If this was a brothers' war, it was between brothers who detested each other.

He was turned over to a major called Furgeson, who marched him to a tent where a guard stood at ease.

"This is General Patterson you're going to see, son," said the major. "Look smart now." They stepped inside.

The man behind the table wore a gray uniform, the first actual gray that Carey had seen today. The Confederate army appeared to be mostly a ragtag group dressed in varying shades of yellow-brown with additional garments consisting of whatever they could scavenge. The general looked up.

"This is the prisoner, sir," said the major.

General Patterson fixed him with a cold eye. "What is your name and rank?"

"Corporal Carey O'Connell, sir."

"Your regiment?" The general waited, watching him, and after a moment said, "We know Howard is on our right and Slocum has the Twentieth Corps. I want you to state as well as you can the number of men and heavy guns in Sherman's army."

Carey fidgeted and lowered his head. This general had the vengeful look of an ill-natured, angry man, uncomfortably reminiscent of Grandfather Severance. He cleared his throat. "About two hundred thousand men, sir, and four hundred and eighty guns or thereabouts. To the best of my knowledge, general."

General Patterson leaned back in his chair and said in an even voice, "You are a lying son of a bitch," and Carey had the sickening conviction that the man was going to order him shot. But instead the general said tiredly, "Take him away, Major. Get the bastard out of my sight."

Outside, the camp was stirring, preparing for an assault on the Union lines little more than a mile away. Carey was being sent to the rear, where a dozen other prisoners were being held.

An hour later Major Furgeson rode up and called, "Move out! On the double-quick!" and across the fields the Rebel assault force came running, pursued by Union troops. There was heavy firing, several Confederates went down, and the little group of prisoners trotted out, following the major's horse, bullets slapping into the dirt around them and singing over their heads. Five miles down the road they came to a wagon train and a group of about forty prisoners who had been taken during the previous day's skirmish. They marched onward down dusty roads and across open fields, heading always in a southeasterly direction until, near midnight, they halted for the night.

Supper for the prisoners was weevilly hardtack, beans, and parched corn "coffee," but it was the same fare their captors ate. Carey looked at the food, turned away, and sat down on the ground a little distance from the others. There was a great lump blocking his throat so that he could not swallow. He had not bargained for this. Death in battle—yes, perhaps. But not prison.

He had heard about Confederate prisons. Hellholes where men died rapidly of starvation and disease and brutal treatment. Or if they did come out, they were not whole men. He did not want to die of starvation, he did not want to die at all. He would never see home again, and it would kill Mother. Father would never know he had been brave. Belinda would not jump up and down with excitement when he came home a hero. None of the great things he had planned for his life would ever happen. To his horror he felt tears forming, and the lump in his throat grow larger. He swallowed painfully and got control of himself, but when another prisoner brought a plate of food and urged him to eat, he shook his head and did not speak.

They were up before the sun and were ordered into columns, seven men side by side, forming a long, snaking line. There was some skirmishing, a few disagreements that led to fist fights that were quickly stopped by the guards, but the roads were very sandy and the marching difficult, and most of the prisoners walked in silence under the broiling August sun.

Late that night they halted for rest, and Carey sat by himself, aching, exhausted, sick at heart. Not once during the long day had there been the slimmest chance for escape, and they were marching deeper and deeper into Georgia, toward what, only God knew.

As Carey and the other prisoners were marched down the main street to the Augusta depot, a crowd formed, clamorous, fearful, expectant, straining to get a good look at the dreaded enemy. Hate was in the faces, in the shouts and threats and mockery, hate born of overwhelming fear. The Yankees were at Atlanta, little more than a hundred miles to the northeast, and coming on relentlessly; there were rumors of women ravished, homes burned, the old and sick driven out into the night to die. Oh, there was no end to the atrocities those blue-coated fiends were guilty of, and the bravest and best men who ever stood up to defend their homeland could not stop them.

A half-loaf of bread was passed to each prisoner, the first food they had had in two days. At the sight of the dirty Yankees ravenously devouring good bread when they themselves were on short rations, the crowd began to murmur and press against the cordon of guards. One old lady pushed her way through the throng and said loudly, "My land, are those Yanks? They look just like our men."

"Well, they're not like ours," the younger woman next to her spat out. "They're devils, and they ought to be shot instead of fed. You all ought to be shot!" she cried, and there were cries of "Hang 'em! Kill 'em!"

A man better dressed than most in the crowd, wearing a tall hat on his gray head and a gold watch fob dangling on his vest, strode back and forth in front of the prisoners. The mayor of the town, someone said. He stopped before a prisoner with lieutenant's bars on his shoulders, dragged the man out of line, and shouted rhetorically to the mob, "Is this the hell-born archfiend that has desecrated our places of worship, destroyed our homes and our sacred way of life?" He slapped the lieutenant's face twice and cried, "See how the coward cringes! Not so brave are you now, sir, without a gun held to the heads of innocent people."

He shoved the man back into line, and the prisoner next to Carey murmured, "By the Almighty, a campaign speech this far ahead of election time. Some things never change," and Carey could have laughed but for the fury licking through his veins.

Then the public humiliation was over, and they were being herded into freight cars no more than half as big as those used up north. Almost a hundred men were jammed in and stood shoulder to shoulder with no room to sit or turn.

Once the train was moving they rocked and jounced, and the man who had laughed at the mayor back in Augusta said quietly to Carey, "I believe we're the last car on this train. You know what that means?"

A riddle, Carey thought dully. What does the last car on the train mean? He'd always been good at riddles, but right now his brain wouldn't work. It was dead, just like the rest of him. "The last car?" he echoed, puzzled.

"It means if we can cut a hole, we can reach through and pull out the coupling pin, and the train will go scampering off without us. We can escape, boy."

"Escape?" The word was familiar but had no meaning.

"Not so loud. M'name's Jim. Stick close by me. I've got a knife in my boot."

They pushed their way to the front of the car, maintaining extra space for themselves by refusing to budge when others pressed against them. A lantern swung overhead, but the shadows were black and protective where the light did not reach. Jim hunkered down and went to work on the old splintered wood, and Carey turned his face to the dark, half asleep on his feet.

• • •

"Wake up, boy. I've broken through," came a low voice.

Carey looked down. The clack of the wheels was louder, and air rushed into the jammed, smelly car, cooling and soothing his hot face and prodding his mind into motion. "What do we do now?"

"You stand and hide me while I reach through."

A good way to lose a hand, Carey thought, but he stood very straight, his lanky body braced, his face unconcerned. There were scraping sounds. "What're you doing down there?" he whispered. "They'll hear you!"

"Making this hole bigger. Can't reach the damn pin. I've got to crawl out there. You keep watch and nudge my leg if the guard looks this way."

Carey glanced around, dragged out of his strange inertia by sudden hope and the cold wind in his face. Most of the men near him looked scarcely conscious; the few who weren't awake kept blank faces turned to the front, fully aware of the exciting prospects of that opening behind their backs.

Jim pushed his head through the hole, hunched his shoulders, and wriggled painfully forward. He pulled one arm free and reached out as the coupling swayed with the train's increasing speed. There was an imperative tug on his trouser leg. "Hell!" he whispered savagely. Another tug. He wriggled back inside and looked up into the barrel of a rifle.

At dawn, ten days after he had been taken prisoner at Woodford Plantation, Carey stumbled into the Confederate prison at Florence, South Carolina. Once a day water and sometimes raw cornmeal had been given to them, but the bread at Augusta had been their last meal. Carey had passed from desperate hunger to uncaring numbness.

A cold rain was falling, and the prison yard was a morass of soaked earth. Carey stumbled over an object that turned out to be a small log. He sat down on it. Anger and indignation were long gone. His chest had been hurting since yesterday, his face was hot with fever, and although the pangs of hunger had ceased, he was slowly starving.

In the morning four prisoners were dead, and that night seven more died. All the next day it rained. He wandered about the prison yard searching in vain for a familiar face. He had not seen Jim since he climbed out of the freight car, and every man around him today was a stranger. The rain diminished to fine spray, but a cold wind had come up that cut to the bone.

Suppertime again; a pint of cornmeal and the announcement that it would be considered full rations. He ate, sitting in the mud beside the body of a man who had died shortly after noon. He lay down in the mud, pleasant unconsciousness stealing over him. Let me sleep and forget all of this he thought; let me die and escape.

A tug at his arm. Someone was lifting him. "Lemme alone," he muttered, pushing feebly at the hands.

"Now you help me, boy. Get up onto your feet and walk, 'cause I'm not so brisk myself."

Carey peered through the gloom. "Jim?"

"Come on—walk, you dumb kid. You're twice my size and half my age. I've got a lean-to built, and there's room for you. Walk, goddamn it."

It was a palace. Sticks braced in the mud and an old scrap of canvas. Carey rolled under and lay there trying to express his thanks. But in a little while he was coughing miserably again, and purple visions were beginning to dance before his eyes. In his last lucid moment he knew that he would not survive this place.

Chapter 45

The Wilderness, Spotsylvania, Cold Harbor. The North read the casualty lists, disbelieving. They wanted victory and expected to pay for it, but they had not dreamed the price would be so high. Sixty thousand casualties in a little more than a month? The army had been a hundred and twenty-two thousand strong at the beginning of the campaign. No country, however strong, could sustain such losses indefinitely. What was in General Grant's mind? People who at the beginning of May had cheered Grant to the rafters now, in the hard afterlight of June, began to use the word *butcher* when they spoke his name.

No sooner had the ink dried on the casualty lists of Cold Harbor than another battle came, three bloody assaults on Lee, snugly entrenched again, this time at Petersburg, and again a failure, with eight thousand more men added to the list of the lost.

Sadly, bitterly, Marin went on working at the hospital for the reason that she could think of nothing else to do. The burning days of August dragged past, the heat made more intolerable by a sticky, oppressive humidity. September came, and with it arrived the news, hard to take in at first, that General William Tecumseh Sherman, that skilled maneuverer, had taken Atlanta and rubbed the Rebel nose in the dust. And he had done it without great loss of life. "Hurrah!" shouted the crowds. "Uncle Billy has done it!" And they gathered in the streets to cheer and sing "The Battle Cry of Freedom," the exultant song from early in the war, a song that hadn't been heard much recently. But after the jubilation they remembered—Grant was still in the lines before Richmond, men were still dying, and the Army of Northern Virginia was still tough, determined, and ready to fight.

One balmy autumn afternoon Marin was told that there was a messenger waiting for her in the narthex. She covered the man she was bathing, dried her hands, and walked to the front door, hiding her nervousness with a pleasant smile. She feared messengers; they always brought bad news.

This messenger was a soldier, a man in the uniform of a captain of infantry. One empty sleeve was pinned to his coat, and a long, white scar ran down his cheek below the patch that covered his empty eye socket.

He bowed. "I bear a message from Mrs. Stanton, madam. She requests that you come to see her immediately."

The drumbeat of her heart increased. "What news, Captain?"

"I couldn't say, madam. Only that she wishes to see you most urgently."

She took off her apron and got her bonnet, her fingers so cold and awkward that she could scarcely tie the strings. One of them was dead, she knew it. The word had just come through, and they were breaking it to her gently, before the name Severance appeared on the casualty lists. That was the fear she lived with through the long days and nights, that the time would come when the name would be there, possibly not just once but three times. She could lose all her men. It had happened to other families. There was no reason that her family should come through intact.

But when she walked fearfully into Ellen Stanton's parlor, she saw that the woman was smiling. Surely she wouldn't smile if the news were bad.

"Marin, my dear, word has just reached me—actually I heard yesterday but decided to wait for confirmation. I believe your son has been located."

The room swayed. Marin begged her pardon and sat down, and

Ellen Stanton hurried to her, all concern and apologies. "Such a shock, I know. Could you take a little sherry?"

Marin shook her head. "Please . . . where is he?"

"In a field hospital near Fredericksburg."

"A hospital . . ."

"Now, now, he has been very ill, but the doctors say he is improving. We captured a Confederate train last week. Ten freight cars filled with our men, prisoners the Rebels were transferring. Perhaps you read of it in the newspaper."

"I did, but I never thought . . . Please convey my profound gratitude to Secretary Stanton."

Mrs. Stanton snapped open her fan and began to fan herself contentedly. "As it happens, Mr. Stanton does not know of this. I have sources of my own. I cannot tell you more except to say we feel very certain this is your little boy. Of course he is not using his own name, but the first name is the same, he is dark, very tall, very young. Most importantly"—the lady's smile grew until her pale, pretty face sparkled, "it appears that he came from California to join the army. We don't have many California boys in our army."

Tears spilled down Marin's cheeks. She could have kissed Ellen Stanton's well-tended hands. "What can I do to thank you? I . . ." Her voice broke.

Ellen Stanton's fan slowed. "I know, I know. My baby, James, died only two years ago." It was the most human thing Marin had ever heard her say.

Promptly at ten o'clock the whistle tooted, the gangplank was pulled up, and the space between the steamer and the dock began to slowly widen. In the crowd left behind on the wharf Logan stood, miserable but waving with a cheery smile whenever she could catch Marin's eye. The authorities had black-heartedly refused to give Logan a pass in spite of her declarations of devout loyalty, her explanations of past conduct, her invocation of Stuart's name, and Marin's appeal to Mrs. Stanton. Logan Severance was under suspicion and could not leave the environs of Washington, let alone cross over into Virginia, where contact with the enemy was not only possible but likely. It was insulting, humiliating, and she would never live it down. And she suspected that Marin didn't at all mind going without her.

"You'll be alone," she had mourned, "in that strange town, all topsy-turvy and full of soldiers, I'm sure. Where will you stay?

Why not wait till they bring Carey here?" But it had been like reasoning with the wind. Carey was in Fredericksburg, and Marin was going to him if she had to swim down the Potomac and walk the dusty miles to that Virginia town.

"Jeremy will be with me. As for where to stay, I have that all planned. Papa's sisters live in Montrose, and that isn't five miles away. I can ride over to Fredericksburg in no time and see Carey every day until he's well enough to travel."

"You haven't heard from your aunts in years, and they've been right in the path of the war. They could be dead or moved away or—anything could have happened."

"Oh, they're still there. We'd have heard otherwise," Marin replied serenely, and went on packing.

I'll see Carey every day, she thought, savoring the words, and leaned over the railing and waved vigorously until the wharf and Logan were out of sight. Poor Logan. How she hated to be left behind.

Once they were in midstream, she made her way to the bow, the breeze blowing her skirt, the precious passes for herself and Jeremy resting securely in her reticule. Oh, she felt so powerful with those passes!

She leaned against the railing and looked up at him. "Does it seem good to you, Jeremy, coming back home after such a long time?"

His face creased into a grin. "The South ain't home to me, Miss Marin, not anymore. California's home now. Can't wait to get back."

Her laughter bubbled up. "Before long we'll be going back together. All the Severances and Mr. Jeremy O'Connell." Only two days before she would never have said such a thing, never even dared think it. It was tempting fate to talk with such certainty about the future. The gods had a way of knocking you flat whenever you got too confident. But today she wouldn't genuflect to those frowning gods. Today the sun shone, the river was a smooth, open path, and Carey was in Fredericksburg, safe and getting well. He had been very ill, Mrs. Stanton said, but . . . She pushed the nagging worry away. It was a lovely day, the best of days, and everything was going to be fine.

"Course, there's one thing might make me change my mind about the South," Jeremy went on. "Miss Marin, do you s'pose Miss Vetta and Miss Jessie got any more cooks like that Seline? She shore was the sweetest, purtiest l'li gal. I thinks about her a lot."

"Don't be smart," replied Marin with a grin. "Tell me something. How did you come to pick O'Connell for your name? I've always wondered."

"I reads a book now and then. Mistuh James got a lot of good books in his liberry. I read this book about a man named Daniel O'Connell. He was an Irishman, and they called him the Liberator. That means to make the people free. So I figgered that's a good name, O'Connell." He looked off down the river. "The Liberator," he said to himself.

Marin stood beside him, watching the riverbank rush by, and said nothing more.

They had ridden in the hired wagon for two hours, and the sun had long ago dropped behind distant trees when they saw the lights of Montrose. Marin was for traveling on directly to the army encampment. How could she stop and wait till morning when Carey was only five miles away? But Jeremy held firm, arguing that a sick boy needed his rest and shouldn't be excited in the middle of the night.

"You *say* you'll just look at him, but I knows you. First you'll want to touch him, and then you'll cry and wake him up and get him all wore out. We're gonna stop at your aunties' house tonight, so don't give me no more arguments."

As she walked up the path, the house seemed so small to her—it had loomed so large in memory. It was a spreading, three-story house with many rooms added on as afterthoughts, a vast establishment for two elderly maiden ladies, but in her mind it had been a mansion. The picket fence had many gaps, and the gate sagged on one hinge. The garden, once magnificent, was in ruins. Only a few bedraggled roses raised their heads along the path. Climbing the steps to the porch, she saw that the posts were oddly splintered and the paint around the door was peeling. After a hesitation she banged the knocker. Silence within. She and Jeremy looked at each other.

Jeremy said, "S'pose Miss Logan's right? S'pose they've gone away someplace?"

"Oh, they haven't. They're here, they must be." She banged the knocker again, loudly.

A rustle and then footsteps. The door opened a crack. A frowning black woman held up a lamp and peered out. "Who dere?"

"Mrs. Severance, from California. Please tell Miss Vetta and Miss Jessie I'm here."

The woman disappeared, and there was a whispered conference behind the door. It opened again, this time a trifle wider. A white face, round, worried, querulous, came into view.

"Aunt Jessie, it's Marin. James's daughter from California."

"California," Jessie echoed, as she might have said "the moon." "Marin? Land sakes. Vetta," she caroled, "it's James's little Marin, come from out west to pay us a visit."

They sat up late around the fire, and Marin longed for bed, but courtesy required that she visit as long as her aunts wished and answer every question in detail. The two ladies were not quite alone in the house. They had living with them Cousin Sally, an ancient woman whose actual connection with the Gentrys was difficult to follow (doubtless Rose would have understood instantly). Cousin Sally spoke little and was so bent and shriveled that Marin thought she must be well into her nineties, but her eyes were alert, she had eaten like a field hand at supper, and she followed the conversation with no indication that she was as tired after a long day as Marin was.

The sisters also had Ornelle, the servant who had answered the door. They fondly remarked that Ornelle was their maid, cook, seamstress, and gardener and that she, of all their people, was the only one who had not run off as soon as that Black Republican, Lincoln, had wickedly emancipated them.

Marin smiled and privately decided that Ornelle was not an unmixed blessing. She ruled her elderly mistresses with an iron hand, and they hurried to agree with her lightest pronouncements, so terrified were they that she would leave them, too.

Vetta was seven years older than Jessie, a down-to-earth, horse-faced woman with snow white hair that had once been black and shining. She had far more sense than her sister, but she, too, looked shocked when Marin explained her mission and told them that her son was in the Union army.

"A Yankee in our family?" Vetta cried, aghast, and Jessie, her round eyes saucer-large, exclaimed, "Oh, what would dear Papa say to that?"

"I do not see how you could allow such a thing, Marin," Vetta said with frigid disapproval.

"I didn't allow it, Aunt. He just went. You see, all our men have gone. Dan and Harlan—they're both dead now . . ."

"Oh, mercy!"

". . . and my husband is a brigadier down on the peninsula.

You can see how it would influence Carey with his father in the army. And his uncle is an army officer, too, a major with Grant. All Union soldiers aren't wicked, Aunt Vetta, and Carey admires his father and his uncle very much."

"Colonel Hill has been nice to us, Vetta. You know he has," Jessie agreed, still a little breathless from the shocking revelations. To Marin she explained, "He's the commanding officer over at the army camp."

"Colonel Hill is a gentleman," Vetta admitted. "He could have taken our pigs, and he didn't. He left us the cow and the horse, too. But Marin, you don't know how we have suffered. Back in sixty-two the Yankees poured in here and rode roughshod over us. Horses tearing up our garden, trampling our vegetables that we needed for the winter. Oh, that was a bad, harsh winter after Fredericksburg, let me tell you. They fought right down here near Telegraph Road, and the cannon boomed all day and half the night. We had to hide in the cellar."

"Yes," put in Jessie, "and we had the livestock in the cellar, too, for fear they'd get shot, and it was dreadfully uncomfortable and smelly with the horse and the cow and the pigs and our nanny goat. You don't know what discomfort is until you've tried to sleep with a chicken sitting on your head."

"That was the least of it, Jessie," said Vetta. "We feared for our very lives. Shells were flying in all directions, and we thought each moment was our last. The next day we found bullet holes in the side of the house, and some of our windowpanes were broken. The front veranda faced toward the battle, and the wood is all chewed up where the minié balls struck."

"Think what minié balls do to a man's body," Marin said quietly.

"Yes, we saw the Yankee wounded, for our gallant lads delivered them a spanking blow and drove them off handily. They came hiking back down the road and took over this very house for some of the worst ones. We helped as best we could. They're human even if they are Yankees. We went so far as to give them some of our milk and eggs, though I'm not certain if that was disloyal. I don't know what General Lee is thinking of, letting them hang around in Virginia, disturbing honest folk. I wish he would chase them off for good. All this trouble, it's the Yankees' fault, and you can't expect us to be pleased that a nephew of ours is one of them."

That was the war to the Gentry ladies—the bloody horror of Fredericksburg and the endless slaughter ever since came down to inconvenience and discomfort and broken windowpanes. But that was unfair. They were old and frightened and without a man. Through no fault of theirs they found themselves in the middle of chaos and they didn't know what to do.

Marin said, "Of course you're not pleased. Neither was I, but it's over for Carey now. He'll come home and never fight again."

"Well, I'm glad to hear you say something sensible. What did your Papa say when Carey ran off?"

Marin considered explaining James's views on the rights and duties of the states and his overriding loyalty to the federal Union and decided not to try. Instead she said vaguely, "Oh, Papa takes the bitter with the sweet and always tries to look on the bright side. He's had many hard knocks in this life."

"I should say," cried Jessie, scooting forward on her chair and preparing herself for an enjoyable gloomy discussion. "Rose Landrini was the dearest, prettiest girl I ever saw. When I first met her, I thought, 'That is the prettiest girl I've ever seen,' and James doted on her so. She was too finely made for such a rough life, don't you think that's true? I don't know what was in James's head, dragging her all the way out to California, of all places. I suppose he's suffered greatly, knowing it was all his fault."

After a moment spent pushing down anger, Marin said in a controlled voice, "Papa doesn't look at it that way." What business was it of this babyish old fool how much James had suffered or why? But Marin had to be polite if she was to stay here. She turned the drift of the conversation. "He will never be the same as before the stroke, but he can walk quite some distance now, and his speech is very good. He finds what good he can in life though naturally it can't be the same without Mama." Deliberately, she offered a new tidbit. "Aunt Delphine is not at all well, though."

"Oh?" The eyes of all three old ladies brightened. Misfortune was their meat and drink, and they were never happier than when hashing over the grisly details of a serious illness or death. Funerals were their favorite social events, especially if the manner of death had been notably tragic and the mourners inconsolable.

"Yes, indeed," Marin went on, hiding grim amusement. "Dr. Towle, Sophy's husband, believes Aunt Delphine has suffered some strokes over the last few years. Not great ones like Papa's—several little ones, so slight that we would hardly notice but that have affected her brain."

"Ah," sighed the ladies.

"She has grown enormously fat and sits in her room most of the time, staring at the wall and singing to herself. She's dreadfully forgetful and often doesn't seem to understand what we're saying. Then all of a sudden she'll come out with something so sharp and witty that I wonder if she's been fooling us, but Charles says that's the way it is with strokes, sometimes the brain works, and sometimes it doesn't."

"Fancy . . . Delphine fat," Vetta said in a wondering voice. "I remember her slim as a wand. And smart, too. Delphine always knew what time it was. I can't imagine her touched in the upper story."

"She's not crazy, just a little cracked." Having tossed Delphine to the wolves—better her than Papa—Marin sat back and listened to them gabble. How jealous they must have been as girls to so enjoy Delphine's downfall. She waited a while and then stretched and yawned delicately behind her hand.

Immediately Vetta was on her feet, her duties as hostess recalled. "You must be exhausted, child. How wicked of me not to put you to bed hours ago. You shall have the front bedroom because it's the sunniest in the house. Come along."

The town was a vast army encampment. Public buildings had been commandeered for army use, a little city of tents sat on the outskirts, and wagons and caissons rumbled through on their way south, raising great clouds of dust and digging craters in the roads; as Vetta had said, the army was hard on roads. The Stars and Stripes flew from the flat roof of a battered wooden building that wore the unmistakable, utilitarian look of an army headquarters.

The hospital was an enormous tent on the south side of the parade ground, and outside it Marin hesitated, irresolute now that the moment had arrived. But as Vetta and Jessie had said, Colonel Hill was a gentleman and a perceptive one, for he saw her distress and said kindly, "The doctor tells me he is sleeping, Mrs. Severance. You may stay as long as you wish. It will be quite private."

They had done everything they could to make it easy. A screen had been placed around his bed, and a chair provided for her comfort.

Alone, she looked down at the long body of the boy in the bed. His face was very thin and faintly flushed, his dark hair was tousled, his breathing slow and regular. The chart at the foot of the bed said that his name was Carey Miller, and one glance told her that he was not her Carey. She wanted to snatch him out of that bed, shake him awake, and demand to know why he wasn't her son. She wanted to hurl herself against the canvas wall, knock down that mocking screen, claw and scream at Colonel Hill and the doctors who had stupidly decided that this was her boy and cruelly led her to hope. They had promised, *promised* her! She sat down in the chair, doubled over against the pain in her chest, trying to accept, trying to bring common sense to the fore and bend her will to reality. She had known all along; in some deep part of her she had known. Carey was lost somewhere in the war and was not to be found. Not even Mrs. Stanton had the power to perform that magic for her. The boy opened drowsy eyes, pale blue eyes, not black like Carey's.

"How do, ma'am," he murmured dreamily, still under the influence of morphia. "You an angel come to set me free?"

"Just a lady come to visit you. You won't see any angels for a long time yet." So many of the very sick thought constantly of death, especially if they had been in a bad battle. How she hated him because he wasn't Carey. How young and sick he looked.

She stayed for a long while, holding his hand, smiling and talking and fighting the urge to lay her head on the bed and sob. When she left, Carey Miller was asleep again and the pain in her chest had eased a little. Colonel Hill, grieved by her stricken face, berated himself for a fool, apologized profusely, and promised aid she knew he could not deliver.

She gathered her strength. "Don't think about it for a moment, Colonel. It was not meant to be."

"You are kind to forgive me but I shall not forgive myself. The last thing I meant to do was bring more grief to the wife of a brother officer."

"Do you know Stuart well?"

"Only by reputation," he answered, and immediately wished he had put it another way. Last May, Ben Butler's army had tried to move on Richmond by coming up the James River and had been stopped cold by Beauregard's few troops at Drewry's Bluff. One of the reasons was that Severance had weakheartedly pulled his brigade back with considerable loss of life at the first probing thrusts of the Rebels. Butler was a poor excuse for a general, but Severance's part in the bungling operation was an embarrassment in an army with many bunglers. Colonel Hill would not humiliate the man's lovely wife for anything, not even for four stars on his shoulder.

In an effort to repair any damage done he said heartily, "I am fortunate enough to be acquainted with his brother—a fine officer," and was surprised at the light that came into her face.

"Oh, have you seen Vail recently?"

"Not in some months. I believe him to be with Grant down at Petersburg." There it was again, damn it. Grant wouldn't be stalled in the trenches before Petersburg and men wouldn't have been dying by the thousands all summer if Butler and his generals had played their cards properly.

But she never so much as batted an eye. She thanked him again and walked to her waiting buggy. He watched her servant hand her up, impressed by her dignity in a bitter situation. What a lucky man that blowhard Severance was. Remorseful at the pain he'd caused her, he walked back to his headquarters and tongue-lashed his unfortunate aides all afternoon.

Marin rode home in the aunts' old buggy, silent and unapproachable, and Jeremy had the sense to restrain his condolences, but once back in Montrose she had to tell her aunts the truth and accept their cries of sympathy with as good a grace as she could muster. Why had she promised the Miller boy that she would come back? Hadn't she seen enough heartbreakingly sick boys by now to be tough and unsentimental? But she had promised so she had to go; she knew too well what broken promises could do to the very ill.

That night she wrote Logan that her trip had turned out to be a wild-goose chase but that she was staying a while longer to visit with her aunts. The next morning she went back to the hospital.

Every day after that she appeared faithfully at Carey Miller's bedside. He was a nice young man of almost twenty who had left Indiana three years earlier to go adventuring in California and had come back last year, eager to get into the war before it ended. He was good-looking and intelligent and decent and she didn't care a rap. But she wrote a letter for him to his mother, brought him Ornelle's homemade preserves, and tried not to resent the fact that he was coming swiftly back to health.

One evening two weeks after her arrival she came home from the hospital late, and Ornelle sang out from the kitchen, "Supper on de table, Miss Marin." Then in a lower but distinct voice, "People comes home anytime dey feels like it and espects a hot meal all ready."

In her bedroom Marin washed her hands and face and sat down before the mirror to tidy her hair. But instead she only sat. Nothing much had happened today so why did she feel so blue? The doctor had told her Carey Miller was greatly improved and would be transferred to a hospital in Baltimore in a few days. So it was time to go back to Washington. She had left the hospital, thinking that two weeks of Jessie and Vetta and Cousin Sally were quite enough. As she was crossing the parade ground to Jeremy and the waiting buggy, a horseman, riding hard, pounded across the field and cut directly in front of her. She stepped back out of his path and looked up into the last gleam of the lowering sun. Outlined in the light the man on the horse appeared enormous, an officer with greatcoat flying, digging in his spurs and urging his big horse on. For one dazzled, heart-stopping moment she thought, "Vail," and then she caught a clear look at his face as he raced past her. Not Vail at all but some stranger. It was always a stranger, never him. She had walked on, her head down, and climbed into the buggy without a word.

No, she told Vetta through her bedroom door, she was not a bit hungry and planned to retire early.

"But, dear, Ornelle made a special dessert and her feelings will be hurt if you don't eat it. You know how she is when she gets her feelings hurt."

Marin was tempted to describe what Ornelle could do with her feelings but said, "All right, Aunt Vetta. Tell her I'll be there directly."

At the dining table she ate and listened to her aunts complain about high prices and the lack of luxuries and the upset conditions that made a comfortable social life impossible. Ornelle slapped down little bowls of bread pudding—her special dessert—and Marin shoveled it in without tasting it. Across the table Cousin Sally licked her lips, enjoying every morsel. How wonderful to be very old, so that you needed only food and a fire to warm your bones. How wonderful to be so old that all the painful emotions were gone and you felt nothing.

Cousin Sally looked her over with smiling eyes and said in her reedy voice, "What a bonny thing you are, dearie. I had red hair once upon a time, all shiny and bright like yours; had curls so long, I could sit on 'em. Ah, the boys swarmed around me then." She laughed softly, looking back a long distance. Out on the road horses thundered by; then came the rumble of wagons and the shouts of men. Her old eyes darkened. "Soldiers," she said, and her fingers fidgeted with the folds of lace at her throat. "I do hope there ain't going to be more battles around here. I tell you, Marin, I was that frightened cooped up in the cellar with the boomin' and the whistlin' and ca-thump, ca-thump right outside this very house. I expected to meet my maker any second. And afterward those poor boys bleedin' and dyin' in the parlor—Yankees or not, it near broke my heart. There was one young feller had yellow hair and the bluest eyes. Looked like my own true love, Johnny Owen. Vetta, you remember me tellin' about Johnny." She swallowed, and the crumpled skin of her throat quivered. "He went away to fight the Indians and never did come back. I never knew where he was buried."

In horrified realization Marin looked at Sally and for the first time saw her clearly. Beneath the ancient outer shell the old woman's brain and heart still felt as much as ever they had in youth, still endured pain, feared death, and needed love. What a fool she had been to think that great age brought release. The suffering never ended. You never escaped, not until you died.

Chapter 46

The next day was Sunday, Marin's second Sunday in Montrose, and once again she accompanied her aunts to church, wishing she could plead great age like Cousin Sally and stay home. The church was a small white wooden building with a slender bell tower much like the one she had attended as a child in Maryland, but she had gotten out of the habit of churchgoing in recent years; the hard benches chafed her body, and the minister's platitudes galled her soul. How could anyone live through those years and still believe that there was a loving God who cared for His people? How could anyone believe that underneath were the everlasting arms?

The only enjoyable moments came during the singing. Even if she could not believe the words, the old hymns took her back to childhood when her family had been together in their own pew, Ethan buoyant and full of fun, Sophy frivolous and mischievous and sighted, Papa and Mama young and beautiful and certain to live forever.

That afternoon Marin went early to the hospital and stayed with Carey Miller for over an hour. As she was leaving the tent, a young captain, one of the commanding officer's aides, approached her.

"Colonel Hill's compliments, ma'am. Will you spare a moment to step over to headquarters?"

She walked with him across the parade ground, wondering how to gracefully refuse another dinner invitation. Making conversation with the colonel and his senior officers was not the way she wanted to spend her evenings, and she had run out of acceptable excuses.

Horses galloped past, and she drew back her skirt to avoid the dust. There had been much movement of troops yesterday and today; since early morning men had been marching out of camp, and officers had been thundering in on tired horses and then rushing out again. God only knew what Grant, stuck in the trenches before Petersburg, had on his mind now.

Colonel Hill met her on the headquarters steps with a beaming smile and an almost tangible air of gratification.

"Dear lady," he exclaimed, "yours is quite the loveliest face I've seen in days. It lightens this hard old heart just to look at you."

Marin accompanied him up the steps, thinking wryly that in this utterly masculine army camp the competition was not great. She stepped into his office, formulating a refusal of the invitation that was coming, and an officer standing by the window said, "Hello, Red."

The mask of social courtesy faded from her face, leaving it blank. Then she was across the room and in his arms. Her head was pressed against his chest, her bonnet knocked off and dangling by its ribbons. His lips were on her hair, his eyes were closed. The heavy brass buttons of his coat dug into her cheek, and his arms were crushing her ribs, but she didn't care. She could only cling to him and cry, all the pain and fear of the long years flooding out.

Colonel Hill danced about them, rubbing his hands at the success of his surprise. The dear girl, how brave she had been when the Miller boy turned out not to be hers, how guilty he had felt at being the partial instrument of her disappointment. It was a bastardly war but the rare moments like this made up for a little of it.

Dimly, through torrents of emotion, Marin became aware of Colonel Hill's merry face. She raised her head and fumbled for her handkerchief, and the colonel said, "Take mine, take mine. Oh, what a fine day this is. Were you surprised? Indeed you were, I'll be bound. This is the bravest little lady in the world, Major, as I'm sure you are well aware. Now I have a thousand things to do, and you two must have a lot to catch up on. Just make yourselves at home." He shut the door softly.

Marin wiped her face and blew her nose. "I'm making such a
fool of myself, but, Vail, you can't know . . . My stars, I'm
knocked breathless!"

She wiped her eyes again and then really looked at him. So thin,
was her first thought, lean and taut as a bowstring. His uniform
was dusty and his boots were worn but he looked healthy, and
happier at this moment than she had ever seen him.

She smiled at him sunnily. "When did you get in?"

"About an hour ago. Hill almost leaped out of his skin when I
walked in. When he told me you were here in camp, I wanted to
come right over but he was determined to make me wait until he
got you here."

"He's a kind man," she said, and the tears spilled over again.
"Oh, I'm so silly. Pay me no mind. How long will you be here?"

His eyes traveled over her face. "I have all the time in the
world."

"You don't have to go back? How wonderful! Oh, Vail, come
stay at my aunt's house tonight and eat a real home-cooked meal.
They'll be thrilled to have you."

In actual fact Vetta had sworn that no Yankee would ever step
over her threshold again unless he was behind a drawn gun and
when she first saw Vail her hospitable smile froze and she shot
Marin a poisoned look. Kin by marriage or not, he wore the
infamous blue uniform. But by the time supper was over she had
been charmed into making him an exception and was almost as
pleased to have him in her house as Marin had said she would be.

Supper was a long meal and a delicious one, for Ornelle had
outdone herself. This major Miss Marin had brought home was
one of Mr. Lincoln's men. He had greeted Jeremy like an old
friend and treated her with respect. She fried two of the last
chickens in the henhouse and used some of her canned cherries in
a large, juicy pie. At the end of the meal Vetta brought out the last
bottle of her father's peach brandy for Vail and even the ladies had
a thimbleful.

There was only one bad moment and it came at the beginning
of the meal. As they all bowed their heads Vetta clasped her hands
before her and said, "Dear Heavenly Father, we thank Thee for
Thy bounty here on our table, we thank Thee for our home and our
warm fire and the peace that is presently in our neighborhood. We
ask that the accursed Yankees soon be driven from our homeland
if it is Thy will. We . . ." She hesitated and then went on firmly,
"We thank Thee for the preservation of the young man who sits at
our table this night and pray that he may come through the scourge

of war unharmed even if he is a Yankee. We pray for the souls of our nephews Harlan and Daniel, knowing they are safe in Thy loving arms. In the name of Thy Son we pray."

Jessie echoed, "Amen," but Marin raised her head and looked at Vail. His face was utterly still. She said, "Dan was brought into St. Francis, the hospital in Washington where I work. They had cut off his legs just below the hips . . ."

"The bastards," Vail said in a low but distinct voice, and did not apologize to the ladies.

"I couldn't help him. He barely lived through the night."

Vail stared down at his plate. "God rest him. He was a fine man. I wish I'd gotten to know him better before the war."

The very words Dan had spoken about Vail. Marin looked down, too, and bit her lip. She hadn't wanted to tell him about Dan now, when she was still glowing with the thrill of his presence, when they were both so happy just to be with each other. Why did Vetta have to put in everything but the kitchen sink when she said grace?

The silence lengthened. Ornelle brought in a huge platter of chicken, and Vail passed the yams. They began to eat.

During the rest of the evening Vail managed to avoid further mention of the war by telling some of his old stories about the California gold camps. Watching the responding approval in the faces of the other women, Marin felt her heart swell with warmth toward her relatives. They liked him; they recognized his many admirable qualities. Of course they did, how could anyone fail to? But not knowing him so well, they could not see the weariness behind his smile, the loss of weight, the tense movements of his hands. His face was dark brown from sun and weather, and flesh had dropped away, emphasizing the strong bone structure beneath. His eyes had changed, too; his eyes never smiled at all.

Late in the evening Vetta brought out a dressing grown folded in tissue paper and gave it to Vail. "This was my father's. Peter Gentry, your grandfather, Marin. My mother, Maria Carey, gave it to Papa on their twentieth wedding anniversary, but he never wore it because he was saving it for a special occasion. I reckon this is special enough."

They all said good-night at the foot of the stairs and Marin went up to bed, wishing she could have just a few minutes alone with Vail but content in the knowledge that there were many days ahead for quiet time together.

She undressed and unlaced her corset without help, as she did every night—Ornelle had made it clear that she was not available as a lady's maid. Ornelle didn't build fires, either, and the room was cold, but instead of climbing under the covers and brushing her hair in bed as usual she pulled on her old wool wrapper, sat down at the writing desk, and began a letter to Logan. Vail was out of the war at last, and she needed to share the great news with someone who would care almost as much as she did. She stopped writing and raised her head. There were muffled noises somewhere downstairs. The old house creaked, especially at night, but those were footsteps. Jeremy making his nightly pilgrimage to Ornelle's room, she thought in disgust. Not that she cared, except that he was too good for the domineering wench.

The sounds continued, an endless, restless pacing. She laid down her pen and listened. Jeremy would be back behind the kitchen by now, well established in Ornelle's bed. She went to the window and looked down. An October chill was in the air, and the white full moon lit the ravaged garden. Only ladies slept in the sacrosanct upper rooms. Vetta had put Vail, as she did all her infrequent male guests, in the downstairs bedroom on the other side of the parlor. As Marin watched he came onto the little porch outside his room, stood for a while, his hands shoved deep in his pockets, and then went back inside. The slow, restless pacing began again.

She took up the lamp and went into the hall. It was dark, and every door was shut. From down the hall she could hear Vetta snoring. She moved down the stairs without a sound, crossed the entry hall and the parlor, the lamplight darting like a yellow moth over walls and ceiling, and outside his room she hesitated, wondering what to say when he came to the door. The pacing began again and then stopped. Instead of knocking she turned the knob and went in, holding the lamp high.

He was out on the porch again.

"Vail?" She went to him. "My dear, what is it? You'll wear out the floor with this pacing."

She lifted the lamp higher, trying to see his face, and he said, "Put that thing down." With an irritable gesture he took it from her and turned out the flame. "Go back to bed, Marin. If your aunts caught you here they'd faint."

"I was writing to Logan and I couldn't help but hear you. What's the matter? Can't you sleep?"

He sat down on the porch step. "It's the house. I haven't been under a roof in so long . . . The bed's too soft."

She sat beside him. A breeze whirled leaves down the path, and the battered rose trees bent and nodded. In spite of war and depredation they still bloomed valiantly. From here the garden looked inviting, the filmy moonlight softening the damage, the shadows hiding it. Beside the front gate the huge magnolia, taller than the house when James was a boy, lifted sturdy branches to the sky.

She said, "I've wondered and wondered why you joined up. Was it because Stuart was in?"

"No. I don't know if a woman can understand."

"Try me."

He smiled. "I didn't mean you weren't smart enough. Women have different needs . . . at least, I think they do. More than anything they seem to want security, something they can count on, but, Marin, for a man to be too secure is a kind of death. Sometimes he has to break free, no matter the cost, just to be sure he's still a man. All my life I've struggled toward something, never getting there. Eventually I realized I never would and I started looking around for something to smash. A war's a great place to smash things."

"But you hate it. I can see it in your face."

"Most of us do, once we're in it. I found out what I should have known all along. War isn't excitement or freedom. It's obscene. There is heroism sometimes from the most unexpected people, but most of the time you live in squalor, you wait and wait for someone higher up to decide something and you end up so bored that you hope for a fight to liven things up. You either choke in dust or sink to your boot tops in mud, and you live with fear, knowing you have to go out again and next time you may die. Then you're thrown into battle and you run screaming after the flags. You order men to go forward and die and they do, dropping all around you. The earth shakes, the noise deafens you, the glare from the shelling blinds you, and you can't see where you've been or where you're going. After a while you can't remember what it was like not to be always at the moment of death. You just go on killing over and over like a machine. Do you know what fighting soldiers really look like? Dirty, unshaven, tired, scared, and mean. And determined to live. That's all you're fighting for—not flag and country, but to kill that man coming at you before he kills you. You learn not to make friends. One night just before the Wilderness we were in the woods and it was black as pitch. A man came up to me suddenly in the dark. I went for my gun and he said, 'I'm Lieutenant Barnes, sir. I'm new.' He was a replacement, he had to be inexperienced to come at me out of the dark like that. Well, we talked for a few minutes and though all I'd met was a voice, a shadow in the woods, I thought, 'I'd like to get to know that man.' We moved forward before dawn and as we were forming up I asked where Barnes was. It turned out he was dead, killed by a random shot as he passed through a clearing. I never saw him in the light. War is brutish stupidity, Marin, and anyone who says different is a liar."

Through it all she listened, her hands clasped tight, keeping her feelings out of her face. Soldiers seldom talked honestly to women; they told fables for those too weak to look at the truth.

She said, "Stuart thought Carey was right to enlist, and he wouldn't try to find him. He said a good many of the soldiers are only boys."

"He told the God's truth. Most of the men under my command aren't much older than Carey and so innocent and idealistic at the start. We drill them and order them and strip them of individuality until any will of their own is beaten out. Every time I take them into battle, I think of Carey. To me it's always his body that is squashed or blown apart so that nothing is left but part of a hand or a foot or a lump of bloody slime. I shouldn't talk to you like this."

"I'm not a baby that you have to lie to. I've seen it in the hospital. Not the way you have, but some of it. Oh, I wish it weren't this way, I wish I could make it better for you."

"That's my Marin, always wanting to fix things for her people." He turned, and in the pale light she saw that he was smiling. "When I've been away from you for a while I forget how lovely you are and how young."

"Not so young. I'm almost thirty-three."

"Is that so? Right now you look about twelve." His hand moved down the line of her cheek. "During the waiting before battle I used to hold off fear by trying to remember this face, and it was surprising how hard it was, considering that I know every angle and curve of you." He pulled the pins from the knot on her neck. Her hair uncoiled and fell below her shoulders, and he picked up a strand and ran his fingers over it. "This was hardest part, recalling the exact color. It's richer and redder than I thought." He laid the hair on her shoulder and his voice went on, thoughtful, remembering. "But I could see the shape of your face, this bone, the dimple here in your little chin, the way your mouth turns at the corners. I didn't know your skin was this soft. Your eyes were hard to remember, too. I could see the shape and color, but what was in them . . . I'm never sure of that even when I'm with you."

His low voice caressed her. She did not speak or move. He kissed her forehead and the indentation below her cheekbone; he pulled down her high-necked nightgown and kissed the hollow of her throat. Her body arched to make it easy for him. He whispered, "Oh, my sweetheart," and his mouth moved down onto the yielding flesh of her breast. Sensation shot through her, fierce, fiery, exquisite. She was sharply aware of his body warmth, of the rough feel of his shirt as she unbuttoned it, of the beat of her own heart.

This was what she had wanted all the long years ago when they slept on opposite sides of a campfire in the Sierras, when they quarreled and he married Celia and she wanted to die, when they danced together while Stuart and the whole town watched, when he told her in Gentry and Callendar's little office that he loved her, when she came down the stairs to his room tonight. This was what she had wanted all through the lonely years—to be alive at last to her fingertips, to quiver and glow and give herself completely.

"Ah . . . there . . . that's where you belong."

"The floor is too hard. Let me put you on the bed."

"No! Don't stop. Ah, you feel so good, so good . . . you fill me up . . ."

Tender autumn breeze, intense fragrance of roses, a cool moon fading and the mind gone inward; darkness, all darkness spinning up and up into shattering light.

Quiet breathing, smiles in the dark.

"I didn't know a man could be so sweet to hold . . . darling, what are you doing?"

"Putting you on the bed, my love."

"But it's too soft, you said."

"Not now, not now."

Sometime in the night she awoke, knowing before she was fully conscious that he was not beside her. The lamp on the writing desk was lit, and light fell softly on the wall and on his face. She sat up. There was pen and paper on the desk but he was not writing.

"Vail? Is anything the matter?"

Without turning, he answered, "I'll be finished soon. Go back to sleep, sweetheart."

She lay back contentedly and put her arm over her eyes to block the light. How she loved the sound of the word *sweetheart* when it was on his lips. She drowsed.

When she woke again, the lamp was out but he still was not beside her. She raised up on one elbow. He was sitting on the porch step. She wanted to climb out of bed and go to him, but even after all that had happened tonight, even in the sheltering dark, she was not brave enough to cross the room naked. Where was her nightgown? Her hand, feeling along the floor next to the bed, came upon her wrapper. She struggled into it under the blanket and got out of bed. Quietly she came up behind him and laid her hands on his shoulders. "What's the matter, Vail? Can't you rest?"

He reached for her and pulled her down beside him. "There is something I want you to know. Before I left home, I sold the lot on Mason Street and invested the cash in government bonds. Gerald wrote my will." He ignored her gasp and her quick hand on his arm. "When Celia died, her estate went into a trust for Alida, and my will—"

"Don't talk of wills, I don't want to hear about wills."

"You said you weren't a baby and I believe you, so conduct yourself like a grown-up woman and listen to me. If I die, my house is to be sold and the money goes to Logan. Everything else will be divided equally between Carey and Belinda."

"The children? But they're my responsibility. Anything I can't provide they can get from Stuart."

"That's what I don't want. Belinda can sweet-talk him into anything now, and she'll get better at it as she gets older. I don't want her turning into another Kitty Winfield."

"What about Alida? Her feelings would be so hurt if she were left out."

"Alida is realistic, like her mother. She has La Gracia, bonds, jewelry, cash—everything that was Celia's. She's a very rich young lady. I love her, but to be honest I love Belinda just as much. How could I help it when she's so much like you. I flatter myself that she wouldn't be alive if I hadn't found you that night. It makes her my responsibility."

I wouldn't be alive, either, Marin thought, remembering the night of Belinda's birth, the fearful dark, the pounding rain, the pain that battered her, and then his face in the lamplight, his hands pulling her back to life and wholeness.

"As for Carey," Vail went on, "since he could walk he and Stuart have been at odds. What do you think it will be like if he survives the war and comes home a man? I guarantee you, what he wants won't be what Stuart wants. He'll never knuckle under, and that will drive Stuart wild. If he has a little money of his own, he can

live as he chooses and someday make peace with Stuart, which is
more than I was able to do with my father."

"It's very . . ." She cleared her throat and started over. "It's
very good of you. You have the children figured out better than I
do. I guess Alida would understand if you put it in a letter and told
her just as you've told me. Oh, why are we talking like this? The
war's over for you, so the benighted will won't matter. If the
children need help, you'll be there yourself." She snuggled into
the curve of his arm, pleased not because of the money but
because of his concern for her children. He had said "I love
Belinda . . . How could I help it when she's so much like you?"
It was only one of many beautiful ways he had told her he loved
her tonight. His right arm was around her, the arm that had
sustained such a terrible wound; she shifted so that her weight
would not strain it and kissed the wide, deep scar that ran across
his shoulder and down to his elbow, the reminder of the minié ball
that had almost taken his arm and his life. She reached up and
stroked his hair, delighting in doing it freely, with honest love, not
hiding anything; she touched his cheek lightly and said, "This is
the dearest face in the world."

He looked at her in a considering way. "Is it? Sometimes I
wonder why. I know you love me and yet I've always wondered
how you could after what I did to you."

"You've done nothing but good for me ever since I can
remember."

"Then your memory doesn't go back as far as mine. That night
I came home and found out Celia was married . . . you were
wearing a white dress and a necklace of red stones, and your
beautiful hair hung down your back. Everyone wanted to dance
with you, but you chose me. I got just about the drunkest I've ever
been in my life that night." She turned away so that she didn't
have to look at him; she would have walked out of the room but
for his grip on her arm. "We were by ourselves, dancing around
a little fountain, and you were tipsy on champagne. You looked
like a princess. There was a fire in one of the rooms, so we went
inside. I didn't care about you, I didn't really know you, but I took
you anyway. It was easy. You didn't even understand what was
happening."

"You have me mixed up with some other girl and I don't want
to hear about it. You did go off and drink that night and you left
me on the dance floor with Gerald. I never went with you to any
little room with a fire in it. Ask Gerald if you don't believe me.
He'll tell you the same thing."

"I sure he will if you get to him first, but, Marin, I know."

"Ethan told me you couldn't recall anything about that night, and Papa always said men often don't remember things when they've been drinking." She spoke almost plaintively, as if Ethan and James had let her down.

"Sometimes they don't. More often they do but they'd rather forget. There's a code of sorts among men. You take what you can get if it's freely given, but never a girl who is too drunk to know what she's doing. In the hard light of day I was very ashamed, but instead of coming to you, I took off for San Francisco and kept myself more or less drunk for weeks. When I began to think again it took a while to drum up the courage to face you. Then I heard you'd married Stuart."

In a voice that did not sound like her own she said, "Were you relieved?"

"I can't remember feeling anything to do with you but shame. I was glad you had him, since he seemed to be what you wanted, but it was a hair shirt to me—as it should have been—especially because I knew I'd have to go all my life without Carey ever knowing he is my son."

She turned on him, astonished. "Is that why you've been so nice to me all these years? Because you thought Carey was yours?"

"Have I only been nice? I tried to give you all of myself that I could."

"Oh, you have, you have—but is he the reason? Not because you love me? If it is, you've wasted your time. Carey is Stuart's child."

"He was a month early, Marin, and not because you walked in front of a wild horse."

"Is that what you thought? Oh, God, Vail, I wish you'd said something sooner. That night . . . all right, it's true about that night, and it was my fault, too. I always did want whatever Celia had. But can you blame me for hiding it? Ethan would have challenged you and you'd have killed him . . . oh, it would have been a terrible thing. And I was afraid for a while that I might be—but I wasn't."

"Don't lie to me, not now."

How easy it would be to tell him what he wants to hear, she thought, but I can't do it. Slowly she said, "Oh, darling, don't you think I wish Carey were yours? He's like you in so many ways, rebellious and stubborn and so good. And I know how much you love him. Vail, look at me. He loves and respects you far more than he does Stuart. You've always been the one he's turned to when he's needed a real father. Can't that be enough?"

He looked at her for a long time. "I guess it will have to be."

She breathed again when she saw that he was smiling. He drew her head onto his shoulder, and she asked, "Do you love me anyway?"

"Oh, yes, I'm afraid I do."

Thank God he wasn't angry, and he wasn't cold. What he felt for her did not depend on Carey. After a while she asked the question lovers always asked. "When did you first know you cared?"

"You won't remember the occasion. I hadn't seen you since Celia's party, and I didn't know what you'd do or say. It was suppertime, and I walked into your kitchen at Little Mountain. There was a smell of baking bread that I remembered from my childhood. You had flour on your arms, and the room was so warm and full of steam that your hair had curled in ringlets around your face. I thought you might throw knives at me or order me out of the house, but instead you smiled and said, 'Welcome. Vail,' and I thought, 'That is the bravest, most beautiful girl in the world.' "

With an overflowing heart she murmured, "I remember the occasion very well," and took his hand and kissed it, dizzy with happiness, drugged by the touch of him. She rose onto her knees so that her face was level with his and kissed his eyelids and the high bridge of his nose and the corners of his mouth. "Come, darling," she whispered. "Come back to bed with me."

Much later that night she was still awake. He slept quietly, at peace at last, and she lay looking into the dark, thinking over the mistake she had made tonight. There had been a chance to tell the truth and she had not taken it, but tomorrow she would make it right. She would talk Ornelle into fixing a picnic basket, and she and Vail would walk down to the river—there was a stretch of riverbank where the depradations of battle were not too obvious— and there she would tell him that Carey was his son, their son.

Then for the first time they could talk together as parents did about their child, how fine he was, how handsome and intelligent, how altogether splendid. It would be a wonderful morning, and there would be so many more. Somehow, she thought as she settled into sleep, everything would work out well for them.

• • •

Shortly after dawn she woke. He was gone, but she wasn't surprised; he had said that he had to report into camp very early. Half asleep she nestled under the covers. Soon he would return, and they would eat breakfast together.

Her eyes flew open. What time was it? If she were caught in this room Vetta and Jessie would order her from the house and might even write to Papa. She scrambled out onto the cold floor, threw on her wrapper, and peeked into the hall. Luckily all was silent; the ladies still slept. She crossed the empty parlor and skimmed up the stairs. With her own door safely shut she dressed, humming the hymn sung in church yesterday. Never, not in the full flood of youth, had she felt so young or so joyful, and only a day ago she had believed there was nothing left in life for her.

She went to the window. The sun had risen above the rim of the low eastern hills, and the sky was a great pearl. Birds fluttered and swooped across the fields. A beautiful day, a shimmering Indian summer day, but it could have been spring, for to her everything looked new-washed and blooming.

She thought, Forgive me, Carey. You may be lying dead in some dark wood or on some battlefield, yet this morning I must be happy.

Last night a door had been opened to a part of life she had never suspected was there—love given freely, undreamed of riches poured out with nothing of self held back, the mystery of mysteries made plain at last. By hints and insinuations the world taught that physical love between a man and woman was ugly and dirty, an obligation to be stoically borne; in truth it was a blessing beyond imagining. Or so it had been last last night with Vail. How strange that two people, so fearfully separate, could come together in an intimate connection of body, mind, and spirit and give to each other ravishing strength and tenderness, so that for a little while they were no longer alone. Last night she had been lifted up to a high place of such beauty that she wondered if perhaps a loving God did exist after all and had allowed ordinary mortals to know a little of Him.

She loved her children, father, sister, brother deeply, but only with Vail was there this healing, vitalizing element that bound up the wounds of life and made it possible to go on with hope for the future.

After the war—what would they do after the war? She couldn't go on living in the old way, seeing him at family gatherings, talking politely across a dinner table in full view of everyone; after last night she could never be satisfied with the fleeting touch of his hand as he helped her into a carriage or the brief embrace of a dance. And neither could he. Divorce . . . perhaps, somehow. A way would be found; there had to be a way, for she and Vail were meant for each other as surely as the sun outside her window was rising in the east. In the very nature of things they could not be kept apart.

There was a rap at her door, and she ran to open it.

"Oh. Good morning, Ornelle."

"Mornin', ma'am." Ornelle sidled in, her eyes wandering over the room. "I thought as how you mought need me ter tighten yo' corset, but since you is already dressed . . . an' got de bed made, too." She clicked her tongue. "Ma'am, you oughten ter be doin' housemaid's chores." She pulled a wad of fabric from under her arm, let it unfold, and held it up like a shopkeeper displaying her wares. "I found dis nightgown when I was making de major's bed. I don't s'pose it would happen ter be yourn?"

Having washed it several times, Ornelle knew perfectly well it was hers. Why, oh, why hadn't she checked that room before leaving? Because she wasn't practiced in this sort of thing, that was why. Much credit she'd get if the aunts found out. Well, Ornelle could blackmail her, but she'd be damned if she'd blush for her. Coldly she said, "Yes, it's mine. Thank you, Ornelle. You may go."

If Ornelle was disappointed, she kept it well hidden. At the door she dug in her apron pocket. "Almos' fergot. Ah found dis on de major's writin' desk. It's fer you."

An envelope with her name on it. She had it ripped open before Ornelle closed the door, her hands trembling so violently that the scrawled lines moved before her eyes.

Marin—
Since you believed I could stay, I thought it best not to tell you that I must return to Petersburg today with a replacement battalion. Don't let the will worry you. I fully intend to stay alive and come home.

Good-bye, darling—
Vail

A brief note, quickly written. A good-bye note without a word of love in it except for that last. She flew down the back stairs and out to the barn without hat or shawl, without stopping to hunt for

Jeremy. With clumsy, shaking fingers she hitched up the horse, climbed into the buggy, and slashed the whip over the startled horse's head. He bolted forward, and the buggy lurched out of the barn. As she rocketed past the house, Jeremy ran out the kitchen door, hauling his suspenders up over bare shoulders. He stood in the dirt of the yard watching her urge the horse on, consternation and surprise written on his face.

Troops had been on the move for the last several days, but today was the worst. On every byroad wagons were moving, and the main road was jammed with men whose marching feet stirred up clouds of choking dust. They seemed to be not individual men with fears and hopes and women at home who loved them, but faceless parts of a single powerful animal that snaked south toward the war. They marched from the vast tent city that had housed them in camp and from the boat landing on the Potomac, where replacements from the north landed almost daily.

She drew up at the entrance to the main road, waiting for a chance to cross. A New York regiment went by singing "The Girl I Left Behind Me," but after them there was only the muffled thud of boots on dirt. Heavy cannon rumbled past, wagons rattled and jounced, harness jingled and saddles creaked, and officers on horseback shouted, "Close up!" Marin searched each face with frantic hope, looking for Vail's harsh, beloved face under one of those dark blue hats. She saw a major's gold embroidered leaf on a broad shoulder, and hoped leaped higher, but he was a stranger; they were all hard-eyed strangers, tired men who had been up hours before dawn, preparing to leave, enduring the endless waiting that always plagued an army on the move. Not one officer cared for her plight, not one would hold up his men long enough to let her pass.

From the high seat of the buggy she could see far down the road. The columns were unbroken; they would take all day to pass this point, and she had to get through, she had to locate Vail and say just a few necessary words to him before he went away, this time perhaps forever. She clucked to the horse and turned into the road beside the marching men, hoping to squeeze past them if she drove carefully. But an officer yelled furiously at her and raised his sword, and the horse shied and dragged the buggy into the soft dirt at the side of the road.

Slap the horse, shout at him. Leap down and tug the harness, push at the buggy's wheel. But she could not budge it; it was beyond her strength. A soldier stepped out of line to help her, but his captain ordered him back into the ranks with a stream of profanity, and he slouched off.

The buggy was stuck in the dirt, immovable. But she couldn't stay here, she couldn't let him go without seeing his face one last time! She grabbed the whip from its place beside the seat and lashed her aunts' pampered horse fiercely, something she, who loved horses, had never done in her life. She tugged and urged and lashed him again, standing dangerously near his forelegs, and in shock and pain he leaped forward, almost catching her with his hoofs.

"Hold up!" she cried, clinging to the reins with her last strength. He bucked once, then halted and rolled melancholy eyes at her as if to say that he did not deserve such treatment but would obey her in spite of it.

The buggy wheels were back on the hard-packed road. She climbed up to the seat and snapped the reins, and the horse moved out. Slowly, with great caution she guided him beside the marching column, easing toward the regimental flags ahead. At the crossroads the shouted orders to halt came echoing back, and artillery caissons rolled out from the side road. Now was her chance. She stood up, cracked the whip over the horse's head, and moved in front of the column, past the powerful draft horses pulling the caissons, and bounced across the road.

The camp was a bedlam of ordered frenzy. Troops were lined up, ready to march, holding their position as huge canvas-covered wagons loaded with supplies bore down on them. The wagons swerved and continued their headlong dash, and she was barely able to get out of the way before they rumbled past her. At the main road they rocked to an abrupt stop, forced after all the rush to wait their turn. On the parade ground orders were bawled, the regimental band struck up a jaunty tune, instruments shining in the sun's rays, and the men began to move. Automatons, all of them, she thought, remembering Vail's words last night. Husky, naive farm boys and hopeful young immigrants, drilled and trained to become killing machines when the moment arrived, all of them believing they were fighting for the right. Maybe they were. Only God knew the truth of it.

A young lieutenant shouted at her, "Get that buggy out of the way! You're in the line of march."

She lashed at the horse. The buggy jolted farther to the side, and she cried out, "Please, sir, where can I find Major Severance?"

The young man gave her a once-over glance that she did not like, and then his manner became rushed but respectful. "Sorry, I don't know the man. You'll have to keep to the side, miss. We're moving out today."

He started past her, and she called after him, "Can you tell me where Colonel Hill is?"

"Down by the commissary, the last I saw him." The young man hurried on.

Colonel Hill was pulling on heavy gloves and preparing to mount as she drove up.

"Colonel!" She jumped down from the seat. "Colonel, wait!"

He looked back, the smile he always had for her coming over his face, and swept off his hat in a courtly gesture. "Dear lady, what a pleasure to see you once more before I leave."

"You're going, too?"

"Yes, I've been ordered back to active duty." He grinned happily. "At last. These housekeeping chores are no sort of business for a soldier. How can I serve you, ma'am?"

She was breathless from exertion, shaken by the upheaval around her. "I want—I've got to find Major Severance. I must talk to him before he leaves."

An odd look came into the colonel's eyes. The warmth of the greeting yesterday between this remarkable-looking woman and Vail Severance had not been lost on him, and he was a conventional man. But he liked Vail and heartily detested Stuart Severance, who not only was a bungling general but had been promoted when he himself was passed over. And the war had changed him as it had most men. He was no longer so certain of a good many things.

"Dear ma'am, I wish I could help you. Major Severance left at dawn."

"But I've got to talk to him! Oh, please, Colonel, what road did he take?"

"My dear, he is hours gone. There is no possibility that you could find him." He searched for some way to take the stricken look off her face. "I am assigned to Second Corps, and he is in Fifth Corps—but one never knows in war. I may run into him. I would be honored to carry a message for you."

She looked at the passing men, their uniforms grimy with the powdery dirt stirred up by tramping feet, hundreds and hundreds in columns seven abreast following the beloved Old Flag, rifles aslant, the sun that poured down on them turned into rainbow prisms of light by the tears in her eyes. They were marching down a long, dusty road that would be the last road for many. Vail was going, too; he was already far beyond her reach, and she had sent him away with a lie.

Dust from the moving columns had blown in her face, and the tears she could not stop traced dirty paths down her cheeks. She said, "Thank you, Colonel, but it was something I had to tell him myself."

Chapter 47

Carey came home to Marin in the simplest possible way. Sherman's army rolled back the Rebels and smashed through Georgia from Atlanta to the sea; three days before Christmas, Sherman presented Lincoln and the country with the city of Savannah and moved on into South Carolina. As cold rain was falling during the last days of February, a detachment of Union troops freed their miserable, starving comrades held in the Confederate prison at Florence.

Carey watched the blue-uniformed soldiers pour in through the gate, and tears streamed down his face. He was too weak to get up and run to them as men more recently captured were doing. He had had much time to think during the galling months of captivity and had come to the conclusion that his assumption of a false name had been a stupidity second only to his enlistment, for his family must have long ago decided he was dead. Pride was a luxury that had been stripped from him along with everything else he valued except his life. He told the first officer he saw that he was General Severance's son and begged the man to notify his father that he was alive. Before the day was out Stuart received a wire in Virginia from General Sherman himself, and that night Marin read the telegram from Stuart telling her that her son was coming home to her.

She was at the dock when they carried him off the steamer, kissing him, touching his face and hair, cradling him in her arms until they put him in the ambulance. He was brought directly to the house on E Street and she and Logan set energetically to work to cosset him, feed him, and bring him back to health and youth again.

Once he tried to apologize and explain why he had done what he had done, but she only smiled, her eyes brimming, and put her finger to his lips. "No explanations, darling. Don't look back ever again. We're going to get you well and strong, and then we shall take you home."

But as the days went by, Carey remained listless, and he gained little weight, although his appetite improved. He's so thin and pale, Marin thought, stricken to the heart. What images moved constantly in his mind? What horrors had he seen, what nightmares did he suffer? He told her that Mateo had been killed and then never mentioned him again. He asked about Vail and Dan and Charles, and she told him that Vail and Charles were somewhere with the Army of the Potomac and, reluctantly, that Dan was dead. But he merely nodded, seemingly unmoved.

Stuart, on a flying trip to Washington, stopped by to visit. He strode into the room full of hurry and energy and sat down at Carey's bedside. "Well, sir, aren't you the fine one! I suppose you know you just about drove your mother around the bend." He said it severely but with a twinkle.

"Yes, sir. I'm sorry." Carey answered, averting his eyes. It was strange. He had wanted so much to impress his father, and now the opportunity was here—Stuart was full of approbation and asking to be impressed—and he could not talk.

"Tell me about the Georgia campaign. Were you at Dalton and New Hope Church?"

"Yes, sir."

"What about Kennesaw Mountain? Sherman was wrong to try direct assault there. He should have outflanked the enemy."

"Yes, sir, I guess so."

"But he's proved his worth overall. He certainly outsmarted Johnston."

"Johnston is a fine general though, sir. He made us pay."

"He's well enough. What about Atlanta? Was it a stiff fight around there?"

"Pretty stiff. I got captured just a couple of days before we took it."

Stuart grew serious. "How did that happen? Were you overwhelmed?"

"I was stupid. I was in a henhouse picking up some eggs when this girl—she was about Belinda's age. Reminded me of Belinda some. She had a gun on me . . ."

"A girl captured you?"

Marin began, "Stuart, I really think . . ." but he waved her to silence.

"She didn't exactly capture me. That is, I took the gun away from her, but when we got outside—well, I hadn't been paying attention, and the other fellows had been chased off by some Reb cavalry. They just took my rifle—"

"They just took your rifle."

"Yes, sir."

"I see." Stuart drew on his gloves and rose. He looked down at Carey's drawn face. "I recommend you eat hearty, son, and you'll be back on your feet by the time I see you next. We'll have some fine times reminiscing."

Outside Carey's room he said again to no one in particular, " 'They just took my rifle.' Jesus, God." He shrugged into his greatcoat.

Marin followed him to the door. "Can't you stay for supper?"

"There's a war on, Marin," he informed her, as if she might not be aware of this salient fact, "and I want to be with my troops when the end comes."

"You think it will be soon?"

"The South is wearing down, they can't hold out much longer—though they die hard, I'll give the devils that. But everyone at headquarters believes it'll be over by summer, and then I'll go home and run for senator. How'd you like to be Mrs. Junior Senator from California? Eh? You'd enjoy that, wouldn't you, madam?" He grinned, pecked her cheek, and swept out to his waiting horse. She stood in the doorway, and he looked back, waved once, and cantered off.

Late that night she sat by Carey's bed, watching his sleeping face. The war over. It was a idea hard to take in, for war had begun to seem a normal way of life—the constant ache, the sense of loss, the lengthening casualty lists, and the fear that a particular name might one day appear. The war over, and then . . . ? Her grief over the lie to Vail had diminished a little as time passed, and it looked as if he might come home safe. It was a necessary lie, held to so stoutly for so long. Since the day of Carey's birth she had kept the vow she made and scarcely allowed herself even to think the truth for fear it would slip out. Papa was right—you should not lie to those who love you, and God knew she hadn't wanted to—but if Vail knew for certain he would want Carey to know; above all he would want that. Watching Carey with Stuart tonight, his shadowed eyes, his sharp-featured, haunted face, she wondered what it would do to him if he found out that his father was not his father and his mother not the good woman he believed her to be. His world would turn upside down and he would despise both her and Vail. She had been right to lie.

Stuart's prediction came true sooner than he had thought. Peace feelers were out and the two sides testing each other all through the month of March. Lee's depleted army was now a thin line behind the miles of entrenchments at Richmond; the powerful adversary that faced him grew stronger with each day. The capital was bound to fall, and he knew it; his men were almost out of rations, yet he could not bring himself to surrender. Instead he retreated, abandoning Richmond and Petersburg to the Union forces. Grant raced after his prey and trapped him near the little Virginia town of Appomattox Court House. There the guns ceased firing, the sabers were sheathed, and the regimental flags, the cavalry pennons, the bonny Stars and Bars went down and ragged, starving soldiers began to stack their weapons. Many wept. Others simply turned away and began the long walk home.

The great parade went on for two days, people laughed and cried as their men marched by, and cheers rang lustily in the warm May air. Public mourning had ended, flags no longer flew at half-mast, and although the tongue still tripped when people tried to say the new name, Johnson, when they spoke of the President, they could not feel anything but joy and triumph when Abraham Lincoln's great armies came swinging victoriously down Pennsylvania Avenue. Marin and Logan stood in the crowd and watched, flesh crawling with excitement. They waved little flags, sang "Glory, hallelujah" along with the rest, and wept tears of happiness and relief.

Marin was in a quiet glow of contentment, for Vail was in town, and with luck she would see him before the day was over. Her joy would have been complete if only Carey had come out on this second day of celebrating to watch his own army, Sherman's veterans, go marching by. But he had said he did not feel well enough and, oddly, did not seem to mind not being there to cheer his old comrades. At least it seemed odd to Marin.

"You'd think he'd want to see them, wouldn't you, Logan?" she said as they were walking home after the parade.

"He doesn't want to think about the war, I guess," Logan replied, and then said half to herself, "He doesn't feel the way we do. We can't expect him to."

At the house a letter waited for Logan, and she picked it up with a sharp stab of hope, for it was from Kitty. Maybe she had word of Ethan's whereabouts. So far there had been none.

Swiftly she scanned the opening lines, and then said, "This girl is beyond belief. Listen to this, Marin."
She read aloud:

Dearest Logan,
Well, it's over, and I say *good*. I never did think the pesky war was a smart idea, and I have been proved right, as I'm sure Ethan will agree if he is still in one piece. Now, Logan, I shall tell you in strictest confidence, when we heard that Old Abe had been "polished off," we went mad with excitement and have been having the *grandest* time celebrating our heads off—but very much in secret, of course. S.F. is draped in black, and there have been a thousand and one mournful speeches by public officials, but the Chivalry is in a spasm of delight. When the news came, we pulled down the shades in the middle of the day, locked the doors, and played "Dixie" *very softly*. And we sang and danced and toasted each other in champagne, and one of the gentlemen took a bottle and poured it over my head, which was a terrible waste, so I stuck out my tongue as it dripped off my nose, and a lot of it ran inside my dress and tickled all the way down! Maybe you will think we are dreadful, you being on the other side, but I say, Down with all Tyrants! Was that what Booth said? Maybe you should burn this after you read it. I don't want policemen knocking at my door! Papa says it's a very good thing we are out here in California, for the South is not going to be a nice place for a long time. I'm glad, too, for I expect everyone is very poor and boring down there. But it is over, thank the Lord, and you will all be coming home soon, even my darling Ethan. I can't wait to see him (if he is still alive, that is), or you, Logan. Come home soon.

Your affectionate
Kitty

"She's right. You'd better burn it. We don't want policemen knocking at our door, either."
Logan looked up, stunned by the truth of Marin's words. "And only a few months ago they suspected me of—I believe that girl has taken leave of her senses, or she never had any to begin with." She knelt before the hearth, struck a match, and watched the letter curl into bright orange and then turn black. She dusted her hands and looked sideways at Marin. "I feel so guilty, just as if I really were a conspirator."
"Don't even say that word," Marin whispered in agitation.

There had been many midnight knocks on Washington doors since the assassination of President Lincoln, and according to rumor, anyone who had so much as a passing acquaintance with John Wilkes Booth or with Mrs. Surrat and her boarders had been dragged off in chains, even women and old men.

Marin looked nervously at the little ball of ash on the hearth, got down on her knees, and poked it into crumbled dust. "There, no one can read it now. Tomorrow I am going to to buy tickets for the trip home."

"But Stuart won't leave yet."

"Stuart can stay and play politics all summer as far as I'm concerned, but we are going to get out of this town before the police remember you or Kitty writes any more idiotic letters. We got here without Stuart's help, if you recall, and we can get home without him. Jeremy can help with Carey."

Logan flushed and avoided Marin's eyes as she murmured, "Yes, of course."

Immediately Marin was on the alert. "Well, what is it?" And then, with suspicion mounting, "What do you know that I don't?"

"Not a thing. It's just that—now don't get mad, but I have a hunch that Jeremy might not be going back home with us."

Marin's mouth popped open, and the air went out of her in a rush. "What bee has he got in his bonnet now? You'd better tell me, Logan Severance."

Logan shrugged and said miserably, "I can't. I promised."

Marin shot her a withering look and stormed down the hall to the kitchen. Jeremy was sitting on the back steps putting a second coat of polish on his new knee-high boots.

She slammed the door loud enough to make him jump. "What is this nonsense about your not going home with us?"

"Miss Marin, you oughten to sneak up on me like that. It's wearin' on my heart."

"Bother your heart. We're going home as soon as I can arrange it, and make up your mind to it, you are going, too."

He began to buff his boot again. "No, ma'am, I reckon I ain'. I promised Ornelle I'd come back soon as the war got finished and marry her, and tha's what I'm gonna do."

"Marry Ornelle? Stars above, Jeremy, why?"

He looked up, his dark eyes soft. " 'Cause I love her, that's why."

She sat down beside him, marshaling her arguments. "That girl is nowhere near good enough for you. You're an educated man, you have great potential, and she—well, she's the bossiest creature it's ever been my misfortune to meet. I admit she's not bad-looking, but you could get lots of . . . What are you grinning about?"

He shook his head, the laughter coming from deep in his chest. "Nothin' atall. I know what Ornelle is better'n you do, if you'll excuse me. I'm gonna educate her myself, teach her to read and write and speak proper. She's smart, she'll learn."

"She's smart, all right, and you'd be a good teacher, but you can't deny her character leaves a lot to be desired. How can you love a woman like that?"

He sat down the boot and looked at her directly. "Ain' no explainin' about love, is there? It just hits us, boom, and there we is, lovin' 'cause we just can't help it, ain't that about the size of it?"

A blush stole into her cheeks and she looked away. "I didn't know you were a philosopher."

"I ain', but since meetin' Ornelle I've been thinkin' about love a lot."

She sighed and said grudgingly, "Washington isn't the best place for us to be just now and I'm very anxious to get home but if you can make the trip quickly, we'll wait. You go on down to Montrose, marry the girl, and bring her along. We can use another maid."

"Thank you kindly, Miss Marin, but Ornelle and me got other plans. We ain' gonna be a coachman and a maid anymore. I got money saved and investments, too. We're gonna get out of this country, try somewhere else, where things is better for colored folks."

"Leave the United States? Why, Jeremy, how could you? You're free, you've been free all along. Didn't Mr. Crown get that all settled for you? Didn't we all fight as hard as we could for you? We won, didn't we? And Ornelle is free, too. White folks fought a war for people like her. You're both of you free now, forever and ever."

"Well, ma'am, I figure war or no war it ain' gonna be real healthy around here for us. White folks *say* we're free and all, but they ain't gonna change what's in their heads, not for a long while, maybe never. Deep down most of 'em don't like us much. They don't want us around unless we're waitin' on 'em, and I don't care much fer livin' where I ain't wanted. Me'n Ornelle's gonna go to Hawaii or mebbe down to South America and start us up a business. We's gonna make lots of money and lots of babies, too." He chuckled. "Fine fat black babies, a whole raft of 'em that ain't never gonna know whut it's like not to be good enough. The O'Connell family's gonna be good enough, yes, suh."

He meant it. There was a tough fiber in him that her best blandishments could not touch. No use to argue or entreat or get mad. She had lost her temper once when a valued servant wanted to leave, and it had only brought hard feelings and estrangement, and Petra had left anyway. She looked at Jeremy with a piercing sense of loss, remembering the day she'd first heard him singing that old slave song and seen him rise up from his hiding place like a genie out of a bottle, each of them so scared of the other that they could scarcely breathe. "Miss Sophy will miss you. Everyone will miss you. Oh, Jeremy, *I'll* miss you horribly." The tears welled, and she threw her arms around him.

Surprised, pleased, he patted her shoulder gingerly and said, "There, now, missy . . ."

She kissed his cheek and wiped her eyes and promised him any help she could give and did not add that she still thought Ornelle was a baggage who would bring him nothing but trouble and was not at all in his class.

Chapter 48

For Marin the first Christmas after the war was one of determined zest and gaiety. All her men were safely home at last, and the new year was going to be the best her family had ever known. While peace had not brought perfect happiness or swept away all problems, worries would be set aside for a little while. At Christmastime you could sing and drink toasts and try to believe that life could now go on as if it had never been interrupted.

Christmas week contained a round of dances and parties in town for those who cared to attend—oddly, many of the veterans did not—and then it was New Year's Eve. The family gathered again to eat and sing and usher in the new year together, and to send up private, individual prayers that the days to come would be better than those they had recently lived through.

Charles Towle had survived privation and hardship suprisingly well, although he came home thinner, quieter, more withdrawn. But months of Sophy's loving care had restored much of the lost weight, and on New Year's Eve the preoccupied, troubled look in his eyes was less noticeable. He sat with his little son held close and frequently ran a hand over the boy's blond curls. Sophy stayed near him. Once she reached out to touch his eyes and nose and bony chin, to "see" him and assure herself once more that he was really there, and he smiled and kissed her fingers as they passed over his lips.

Watching them, Stuart remarked to the room in general, "Look at those two lovebirds. Charles, you set a bad example for the rest of us old married men."

Everyone laughed politely. Stuart was a jovial host tonight. He had been in an excellent mood all week, ever since returning from his most recent visit to Longridge. Since coming home from Washington, he spent far more time with his father than he had before the war, and Malcolm, as vigorous and ambitious as ever, welcomed his younger son's companionship. For a man of Malcolm's advancing years it was a comfort to realize how in tune he and Stuart were in every small matter, to be able to travel to Monterey or San Diego on business and know that Stuart would cheerfully and capably take over at Longridge. Recently Malcolm had gone all the way to Mexico City and had returned after two months to find the ranch humming, with every detail just as he would have it. Stuart had returned to San Francisco from this latest visit in the best of moods, kind to the servants, generous toward Marin, amiable with Carey.

His present good humor was a great help, for he spent time with Carey, enabling Marin to push to the back of her mind the worry about her son's odd behavior and devote all her energy to making this holiday season the best in memory. Stuart's forbearance was such that he never once taxed Carey with the circumstances of his capture or probed for details of battles or prison life, but was willing to sit with him in comfortable silence and think his own secret, contented thoughts. He had considered Marin's apprehensions about the boy and dismissed them long ago. She was all wrong thinking there was something the matter with Carey. His color was good, he had filled out remarkably and had suffered no wound. True, he'd had a rough case of dysentery and pneumonia in prison and hadn't gotten as much as he wanted to eat for quite a while there, but he was all over that now. Naturally Carey was quiet; real men didn't brag about their exploits at war, but as for his being nervous, that was all in Marin's head. What could possibly prey on the mind of a strong, healthy boy of seventeen?

What was hard for Stuart to understand was Carey's tolerance toward the one man who had put a dark blot on the family honor. Ethan had finally found his way home in October, the last of the men to come back, and they had all waited apprehensively for the authorities to pounce on him for his part in the *Mary Mulhane* affair. But no knock came at the door. Those captured on that disastrous night had received light sentences, and no one really knew how deeply Ethan had been involved in the plot. In any case the war was won, the Rebels were beaten to the ground, and in San Francisco at least the mood was to let bygones be bygones. High society was still dominated by those whose hearts had been with the South, and Kitty and her brave warrior-husband were welcome in the best parlors.

But to Kitty's disgust her warrior-husband wasn't interested. He would not attend parties and let the ladies fuss over him, he would not talk about his adventures or explain how he got the fascinating scar on his jaw, he called her friends a gaggle of geese, and instead of going to work at Gentry and Callendar he was talking about getting a plot of land far out in the country and raising horses.

"A horse farm!" she had screamed at him during one of their frequent quarrels. "You must be out of your mind. What would I do on a farm?"

Ethan had replied sardonically, "Clean out the stables. You ought to feel right at home with the horseshit."

An expensive china vase sailed past his head and shattered against the wall. He left with Kitty's insults scorching his ears and went over to his sister's house to sit in the kitchen watching Mrs. Victoria shell peas and conduct a desultory conversation with Carey. Neither ever mentioned the war or the moment on a sunny day near Atlanta when their paths had crossed. They talked of small, homely things; they played with Angus, who had grown ancient but still watched them alertly and tried to gambol like a puppy; they went down to the stable to discuss the attributes of Marin's new carriage horse. It was apparent to the least observant that war had changed Ethan, but no one knew if the change was deep or permanent. No longer did he come home roaring drunk or risk large sums at monte or poker, and if he visited bordellos, none of his friends knew of it. He lived most of the time in faded canvas pants and an old leather jacket, looking in Kitty's scathing opinion "like a trashy good-for-nothing." Ethan had answered, more to himself than her, "Which means I'm just about good enough for you, my sweet."

His looks had altered in other ways. No longer was he the rakish blond god that Kitty had lusted after and forced her father to buy.

His hair had turned from gold to silver, and the full, gray-streaked beard that covered his face when he arrived home had been shaved off to reveal a deeply furrowed face with loose skin hanging at the jawline that had once been so hard and firm. "And he's barely forty," Logan thought with an ache in her heart. She wanted to take him in her arms, stroke his head and cradle him like a child, but she had not the right. He often sought her out for conversation though and it was balm to see the shadows in his face lift as they talked. It was balm, too, the way his eyes followed her on New Year's Eve. She felt guilty delight that Kitty had not come to the family party, so much delight that the sadness always inherent in the death of a year did not weigh on her and she drank several cups of punch and giggled so much that Ethan smiled, too, and accused her of being tipsy.

For Marin the melancholy of the ending year was heavy indeed. The years were going down like ninepins with no hope that soon things would be better. Vail had been home since early fall, and never once had he alluded to what had happened between them in Virginia or even tried to see her alone. He, like the other men, seemed to be at a crossroads, undecided as to which road to take or unwilling to step out onto it. Of course he was tired and out of tune with peace, of course it wasn't easy to come back from war and killing and fit into civilian life again, but he could let her know that he still cared and was planning for the time when they could be together. Just how he was going to accomplish it she couldn't quite see, but it had to happen. She could not live in silent restraint forever. In the past it had been possible to nourish her lonely life with the occasional glance, the accidental touch of hands, the private talks, but not now, not after that night. Surely it had meant as much to him as it had to her. It had changed her forever. Now she wanted him not only with heart and mind but with her body, too, and she could not settle for less. He must feel the same, and never in his life had he been backward about taking what he wanted. Couldn't he go to Stuart and say—what could he say? How could divorce be made to seem advantageous to Stuart when it would destroy his political career with one stroke? Well, there had to be a way.

Across the room Alida, almost fourteen and giving promise of her mother's beauty, sat next to her father and leaned against his shoulder, her hand in his. Marin, watching, wished with all her heart that she, too, could kiss and caress him openly, could announce to the world that she loved him.

It was almost midnight. James asked Marin to go to the piano to play "Auld Lang Syne." The clock struck the hour, everyone sang lustily and then exchanged hugs and kisses amid laughter and furtive tears. In the confusion Vail pulled her up from the piano bench, and his arms went around her, dear and warm and familiar. His lips brushed hers in a brotherly kiss, and what she saw in his eyes made happiness leap up in her. James called out to her to play "Juanita," currently his favorite song, and she sat down again at the piano, thinking exultantly that 1866 was going to be the best year of her life.

It didn't start out well, however. Sitting at her old desk in the little office on Montgomery Street, she faced up to the job she had been putting off ever since coming home. After looking over the ledgers without comment, she read through the papers Michael put before her while he tried to decipher the expression on her face.

He shifted in his chair. "It hasn't been easy, Marin. The market's volatile as hell."

She looked at him, her eyes unreadable. How large he had grown. Compared with the lean, tough fighting men she had become accustomed to, he seemed soft and overfed. The slow, earnest, hardworking boy who had loved her so long ago had passed from view, and opposite her sat a thick-necked man with pale, manicured hands and a face that had settled into cautious, acquisitive lines. Michael was cutting his coat according to the cloth these days.

She read through the papers again, although she knew exactly what was in them. In her absence Michael had gradually been nudged into the role of manager of the day-to-day activities at the store and the warehouse while Tyler Winfield made the decisions that had always been hers. Winfield's Bank had advanced two loans, loans that clever management could have avoided, and Tyler was close to having a controlling interest. It would be years before she could dig her way out of this hole. Now Tyler was dangling another loan, an "expansion" loan, before Michael's eyes, and he wanted to take it.

She laid the papers down. "You should have shown me these before."

"You didn't want to see them, Marin. What with coming home and getting Carey settled, you said . . ."

"I know what I said. You should have told me what was in them."

"You think I did wrong about that last loan. But you weren't here, you don't know the circumstances."

"However, I do read figures remarkably well. If things had been managed properly, neither loan would have been needed. And now you want me to take another loan, this time for seventy-five thousand dollars, God in Heaven."

"That's the thanks I get," he spat out, and began to pace. It was hard to swallow being reprimanded by a woman, especially when he had a sneaking suspicion she was right. "I worked like a dog for you . . ."

"You worked for a very good salary and a piece of the company."

"A damned small piece."

Her eyes flashed. "You were pleased enough to get it when I made the offer." She leaned back and passed her hand over her eyes. "Oh, Michael, let's don't quarrel. I grant that you did the best you could . . . That is, you did very well in a difficult situation. Tyler is a slippery snake. I check my purse every time I say good morning to him. Now take off that scowl and let's be friends. We've got to work together if we're going to push him out."

"You think that's possible?"

"We're going to push him out and slam the door on him. I didn't work the last ten years building something for my children just to see that smooth operator snatch it away." Brave words, but Tyler wasn't easily pushed and at the moment he had the whip hand.

She leaned her chin on her hands and looked up at Michael. "Our debt totals only a little over twenty-seven thousand. Even if we couldn't scrape it up, why borrow nearly fifty thousand additional? Something else is on your mind."

He sat down in the swivel chair, his brocade-encased stomach protruding over his belt, and swung idly left to right and back again. Suddenly he leaned forward. "Boilers, Marin, that's what's on my mind. Three months ago Harvey Taggart, the owner of Taggart Boiler Works, shot himself. Did you know that?"

"I read it in the paper. He was about to go broke."

"Last week Mrs. Taggart came to me with a proposition. Her debts are paid off, but she hasn't a dime to her name. All she's got is the machinery at the works and her foreman, Denby Burwell, who knows boilers backward, forward, and sideways. He has an idea for a new type boiler, a water tube boiler that will produce higher steam pressures than any on the market today, and if it works every steamship company will want it. Mrs. Taggart's got no money to commence operations but if we were to back this new boiler she'd be willing to take a small piece of the profits in exchange for the use of her plant and equipment."

Marin's mind was racing. She knew Denby Burwell slightly. He had been a drinking companion of Usual McIntyre's before Usual gave up the drink for Mrs. Tierney. He had learned his craft with an English firm that built marine boilers for the British navy, and Usual said he knew more about boilers than any six other boilermakers in San Francisco. Boilers were a good deal more prosaic than rare art objects but what moneymakers they could be. Riverboats and, increasingly, oceangoing ships relied on steam for power. There were growing needs for industrial boilers, and when the railroad came through—as it soon would now that the war was over—boilers would be needed for locomotives. The prospects were limitless.

"If Mr. Burwell's boiler is so good," she inquired cautiously, "why did Mr. Taggart commit suicide? Couldn't he have held on a little longer? He knew more about the boiler business than we do."

Michael spread his hands. "Why does anybody kill himself over money? Why did Harry? I've never understood it. The new boiler wasn't ready and Taggart was under pressure from his creditors, but that's no reason for a man to blow his head off. Maybe something else was eating at him. We can't know. Whatever it was, we shouldn't hang back when a chance like this comes knocking at our door. What do you say, Marin?"

Once before she had gotten into deep trouble by accepting a loan from Tyler. Never again would she make a decision of such magnitude without first talking with Vail.

"I'll think about it, Michael, and let you know soon."

"As I told Mrs. Severance, a boiler is like a pot on a stove. You've got a tank with water in it and a fire under it to heat up the water, except that with a pot the steam from the boiling water evaporates into the air. In a boiler you trap the steam, and it exerts pressure trying to get out—the higher the temperature, the higher the pressure—and pressure means power. You just conduct the steam to where you want it to do its work, and there you are. Simple."

Vail tapped Denby's blueprints. "I understand the principle, but this looks very different from a tank."

"That's my improvement. To begin with, this is an upright

boiler, a marine boiler for steamships, but it could just as well be turned horizontal for locomotives. Instead of a tank it has copper tubes to hold the water, distilled water only. It will heat higher and quicker, and higher pressure means higher speeds and lower coal consumption. Now, tubes aren't just my idea. There's others in the business that have tried it, too, but this one's going to work."

"Why yours, if the others haven't?"

"The problem in marine boilers is weight. I've got one row of four-inch tubes here, but the rest are reduced to two inches. That cuts the weight and increases the pressure."

"How much time before you could be in production?"

"We could have a half dozen boilers built, tested, and ready to install in six to eight months."

"With what kind of investment?"

Denby shoved back the old bowler hat he wore indoors and out and rubbed his forehead. He was a slight man with the accent of an educated Englishman and a reputation for both an unlimited capacity for liquor and unswerving honesty. "I should have to say, as I told Mr. Morgan, fifty thousand dollars to get rolling, which is a very great deal, I am aware."

"Could Mrs. Severance and I have the use of your office to talk it over?"

"Oh, certainly. Shall I leave the blueprints here? Very good. Please take as long as you wish."

Denby shut the door, and they were alone in the chilly little room.

"Well," she said, "what do you think?"

"It's a high-stakes gamble. If you had extra money lying around, I'd say do it, but to borrow from Tyler, no."

She nodded, her own thinking confirmed. And how to bring up what she wanted to propose? He'd been so touchy since coming home. Hesitantly she began, "Would you consider . . . that is, Alida's money . . ."

". . . is Alida's money, not mine."

"It would be a good investment for her and I'm sure she would want to do it if you explained it in the right way."

"I'm sure she would, too, since she is only fourteen and believes that I am God. Her money stays safe in land and government bonds until she's old enough to manage it herself." He looked again at the blueprints spread out on the table and began to smile. "However, I might consider a roll of the dice."

Her eyes flew to his. He wasn't rich. How could he take the very risk he advised her against? But in his face was the old reckless sparkle she had not seen since before the war, and in spite of warning common sense, her spirits shot up.

She said, "What about a joint venture with Gentry and Callendar, each of us to put up half? The company could continue paying interest on the old loan just as we've been doing and borrow only twenty-five thousand."

"Don't take another dime from Tyler. Pay off your debt and get free of him."

"But that's exactly what I'll do, pay him off out of the profits." She leaned over the blueprints spread out on the table. "Vail, I have a feeling about this. It's going to be a huge success, and wouldn't it be grand to be doing something together . . ." She shouldn't say it, the man was the one who ought to say it, but she plunged ahead, "We'd have an excuse to spend time together, and I just don't see how we can otherwise . . ."

Her eyes avoided his, and a blush crept up her cheeks. He reached out, and she was in his arms, clinging to him and whispering, "I thought maybe you didn't love me anymore. Oh, Vail, I can't live like this, never touching you, hardly even seeing you, always hiding how I feel."

He tipped her face up and wiped away a tear that rolled down her cheek, and as he did, he bent and kissed her wet, red lips. One prudent thought crossed her consciousness—What if Denby comes in? But his kisses were so sweet, his mouth was caressing her closed eyes and cheeks and throat and then covering her own mouth again in a different, compelling way, and she no longer cared about Denby or anything in life but the feelings that were shaking her, the spinning darkness of mind, the need to give and give. This was what she had to have, his loving—gentle, tender, fierce. She felt him tense and try to put her from him, and she clung tighter and whispered, "Don't let me go. I'll divorce Stuart, I swear I will, only don't let me go!"

He pulled her arms away from his neck and crossed them in front of her. "He'll never agree to a divorce. He has to have you and the children every time he stands for office."

"I'll figure a way, I'll talk him into it somehow."

He pushed her a little distance from him and released her hands, his face grim. "Stuart won't divorce you, especially not if he thinks I want you. There is a way, if you'll do it, but I don't think you will."

"Oh, you're wrong. I'll do anything you want."

"Will you? Then live with me openly. There's nothing he can do about it but come after me, and I can deal with that."

She leaned against the table and stared at him. "What would people say?"

Slowly, thoughtfully he said, "It doesn't matter. I nearly died in the war, I got old in the war. Waiting to live is a bad idea, and I won't do it any longer. Marin, we can have each other if you have the courage for it."

To face an outraged world with every door closed to her, but to face it with him. To fall asleep in his arms and wake up with him beside her, to reach out in the lonely watches of the night and find him there, to look across the dinner table and see him smiling back at her. The years were hurtling by as swiftly as lightning in a dark sky . . .

She said, "Darling, let me talk to Stuart. If he refuses a divorce . . . well, then, I'll find the courage. Let's go see Mrs. Taggart and offer her a partnership."

That night she caught Stuart alone in the library. He was at the desk writing a letter, and he must have been asking someone for a favor because several previous attempts lay crumpled on the floor. He looked especially handsome tonight. The lamplight flattered his thin, straight nose and strong jaw and gave deceptive warmth to his eyes. Strange that once she had thought him the most beautiful man in the world and now for all his fineness of feature he was repugnant to her. The face she loved was aggressively harsh, with a big, hooked nose and gray eyes that glowed with love for her. And behind that beloved face was a mind of depth and complexity that Stuart could never attain.

With elaborate idleness she searched for a book to read. Her hand hovered over *The Scarlet Letter,* then passed rapidly on. Take a book, any book, but not that one. Blindly she picked out a volume of Emerson, making a slight noise as she pulled it from the shelf, and Stuart sighed and rattled his papers to show he did not want to be disturbed. Except for his visits to Longridge he was home all the time now and would continue to be unless the next election sent him to Washington. The constant contact had rubbed them both raw. But nothing must annoy him tonight. Somehow she had to get on his good side tonight.

She sat on the sofa and gazed at the open book, making no sound as she turned the unread pages, polishing careful phrases in her mind. He must never guess her real reason for suggesting divorce. He'd hang on to her forever, just out of meanness if he knew she wanted Vail in his place. She sat with tension building, her hands steady on the book, while he wrote on. Would he never finish? Was he going to scribble all night?

It was after eleven when he put down his pen, pleased with the result of his efforts. He took an envelope, addressed it with care, stuffed the letter in it, and sat back. "It must be a good book."

From far away his voice pierced her thoughts.

"What?"

"I said, it must be a good book," he repeated in the tone he used when addressing Delphine or reprimanding the children.

"Oh, yes! I recommend it. Uh—are you finished with your letter?"

"Finally, yes, and a good job, I think."

"I've been wanting to talk to you, Stuart, but you're always so busy . . ."

"Never too busy for you, my dear," he assured her, hoping she wasn't about to ask for more household money.

She looked at him from under silky, arched brows. Her black eyes were soft, her hair burnished in the lamplight.

"Stuart, I've been thinking seriously about you and me. The war has changed us, we've learned so much, grown up so much . . ."

By God, she was going to suggest a reconciliation. Well, he'd have to disappoint her; he wanted no part of it, for he no longer loved her. It was flattering though.

"Go on," he encouraged, wanting to hear her say it, and she took heart at the warmer note in his voice.

"We were only children when we married. At least I was a child. I didn't know the kind of person I would grow up to be. Neither did you."

It was true, and he'd often thought the same thing himself, but somehow he didn't like the sound of it on her lips. What the hell was brewing in her sneaky little mind?

She took a breath. The moment had come. "Stuart, we ought to get a divorce."

He stared, wondering if he'd heard right. She was looking at him hopefully and her words were very clear. A divorce. And he had thought she wanted him back, the bitch. He didn't want her, but by Heaven she ought to want him!

With control that he felt to be masterly he inquired, "Why now, after all these years?"

"Well, the children are grown, and . . . you're still young, Stuart. You should be free to find another woman—someone who'd make you a much better wife than I've been."

Yes, and I've found her. How I'd like to throw that in your beautiful, smug, withholding face.

"How considerate of you, Marin, always thinking of my benefit, always searching for ways to make me happier. I'm overcome by such thoughtfulness." He started out smoothly, but almost immediately his voice began to rise. How dare she try to cast him, *him*, off like an old shoe when it was he who ought to be kicking her out. All these years she had had his name, his reputation, his protective presence—though she hadn't been a wife to him since Belinda was born—and now she wanted to be rid of him. Why? His mind, never agile, leaped under the goad of wounded vanity to the correct conclusion. She wanted . . . yes, by God, she wanted the very thing she pretended to offer him. She wanted somebody else. The idea was so galling that at first he could not organize his thoughts. Then the certainty that had been hovering at the edge of his mind, too unspeakable to acknowledge struck with full force.

Slowly, he said, "You underhanded hussy, it's Vail, isn't it? It's Vail, before Heaven!"

"Stuart, how can you . . ."

His voice cut through hers. "He's the reason you threw me off, isn't it? How many years have you been sleeping with him behind my back?"

She was on her feet. "You accuse me . . ."

"You thought I didn't know. You thought I couldn't see you mooning after him like a common slut. And him, I know him. He'll take any woman he can lay hands on, even a cold shrew like you." He laughed. "What a challenge it must have been for him, trying to warm you up." That hit where it hurt, he thought with vicious pleasure. Not for one moment did he believe that she'd actually slept with Vail. He'd kill them both if she had. But she was too frigid, too hard-hearted and ungenerous. Even so, she'd been indulging in some florid, romantic daydreams about his charming brother. Why else was she gaping at him like that with all the color gone from her face? Suddenly his anger drained away; he felt nothing but disdain. In a voice oddly calm he said, "I'll never give you a divorce. I couldn't be elected dogcatcher if I did. You are my wife, and you'll stay my wife as long as you live. Don't ever mention the subject again."

After he left the room, she stood for a long time staring at the closed door. Did he actually believe . . . no, he had simply reached for the worst insult he could think of. If he really thought there was anything between her and Vail, he would have done more than shout. But his answer was no, as she had known in her heart it would be. So now, she must do as she had promised Vail—find her courage.

Chapter 49

To Stuart there was nothing squalid in an illicit love affair, if it was his own. He had discovered that deception and pretense were wonderfully exciting, and clandestine meetings a potent aphrodisiac. His sexual drive had never been powerful; always, in the past, he had preferred the aggrandizements of the public arena to those of the bedroom, yet now, with his affair with Glenna at its height, he was in a constant state of sexual readiness and often could scarcely wait until he was inside the bedroom of their little house to strip off his clothes and wrestle her onto the bed. This hidden, tiny house was, after Glenna, his chief joy, for it made possible the secret, sybaritic, voluptuous life he was living. Glenna had arranged it so cleverly, too. She was clever about everything and he admired her tremendously for it.

She had found the house far out on the road to San Jose, hidden behind a thick stand of trees; she had engaged a Chinese named Wong, who cooked well, kept the house immaculate, did the laundry, tended the garden, and, best of all, was slightly dense and spoke very little English. Stuart and Glenna were Mr. and Mrs. Smith to Wong, who took the large amount of gold Stuart ungrudgingly paid him at the end of each month, mumbled what Stuart presumed were words of gratitude in his heathen tongue, and grinned happily. It was the only emotion Wong ever displayed; no expression of shock, amusement, or even interest showed in his bland face no matter what thumps, grunts, or moans issued from the bedroom. He continued to cook serenely in the kitchen, knowing that when they were finally through, they would have ravenous appetites and want a large meal served to them in bed.

Most of the time the house was Wong's private domain, for Mr. and Mrs. Smith seldom visited more than twice a month because Glenna's excuses for shopping expeditions to the city were limited. When Stuart complained that he could barely endure the empty, meaningless stretch of time between, Glenna smiled. "Dearest, it would look odd if I were gone from home too often. And anyway," she added archly, "you might tire of me if I came over every week."

"Never! Never could I tire of you, my sweet, my precious, my delicious, juicy little pumpkin!" He flopped on her again, groaning with delight, and she submitted with a cry of pleasure that could be heard as far as the garden.

Eventually, sweating and breathless, Stuart rolled over and began to play with Glenna's long, brown hair. He wreathed it around one bare breast, leaned back to observe the effect, then took a fistful and began to braid it. Idly he said, "You will never believe the proposition Marin handed me last night."

Instantly on the alert at the mention of Marin's name, Glenna said merely, "Oh?"

"She wanted me to give her a divorce."

Glenna's brows lifted. She raised herself onto one elbow and gazed at him. "That is mad. What did you say?"

"I told her I'd see her in hell first. Well, that isn't exactly the way I put it, but she got the idea."

Glenna lay back on the pillow, her brows knit. "Why would she even mention such a thing? If she doesn't care for her own reputation, she knows it would ruin your career."

"She doesn't care a snap of her fingers for my career. She just doesn't like being married. And I know damn well she's got a yen for Vail."

"I always did suspect there was more than meets the eye between those two."

"Not much more than meets the eye—I'll bank on it, for I know that girl. Cold as an iceberg when you get down to business. And Vail is a lustful swine, interested in nothing but the carnal. They'd be an odd pair, all right. It makes me laugh to think of it. Not like us, my pet . . ."

He ran his hand over her plump bottom, and she sighed.

There was a light rap at the door. "Velly quick food now," came Wong's singsong.

"Damn," muttered Stuart. "What time is it?"

Glenna stretched out a bare arm and located his gold watch on the bedside table. "After five," she whispered, and giggled. "We have been here for three hours. Go let him in."

He hopped out of bed and strode naked to the door. He liked to walk around the house with no clothes on; it heightened the sense of freedom he felt in this secret hideaway and he had no more sense of being observed before Wong than he would have before a cat or dog. He unlocked the door.

Wong was kneeling in the hall, the dinner tray on the floor beside him, his eyes wide and desperate. Stuart looked up into the rock-hard, vengeful face of Malcolm Severance.

"Father . . ." He backed across the room until he was against the wall and could move no farther, huddled over, trying to cover his nakedness with his hands. His shirt lay on the chair beside him, and he snatched it and held it in front of the sinful part of him, a middle-aged man, a father himself, a congressman, a general of the army, cringing not so much as a man caught bedding another man's wife but as a naughty little boy found out in a childish misdeed. "Father, please . . . let me explain . . ."

He saw the gun barrel and heard far away a woman screaming. He saw a flash, and a shower of pain exploded inside him. "Oh, Father," he said, and slid slowly down the wall into darkness.

When Charles came out of Stuart's bedroom, it was after ten o'clock. His back ached, and his fingers, now that his work was over, felt stiff. Wet days and nights in cold, drafty tents, poor food, and constant surgery had left him with aches that would be with him as long as he lived. It had also left him with memories of too many men torn apart by gunshots. How he wished God would grant him the favor of never having to look on another bloody, sundered body.

Wong had been less dense and had known considerably more English than Stuart imagined. He had also known exactly where his employer lived and so had been able to locate a wagon at a nearby farm and drive Stuart home as soon as the carriage bearing Malcolm and his erring, fainting wife had disappeared down the road. But as efficient as Wong was, he did not have medical training, and Stuart had continued to bleed profusely on the jolting ride.

Charles walked to the upstairs sitting room where they all waited. Dear Marin. She looked so pale, as pale as Logan, who sat patting her hand absently. James and Vail were talking quietly by the window and did not see him enter, but Marin did. Her eyes, huge and stunned, fastened on his face.

She was thinking, This is what the Severances have come to. Stuart killed by his own father. Malcolm a murderer. Stuart and Glenna . . . oh, it isn't possible.

Charles came to her and knelt down. "He's lost so much blood, Marin, and the wound is in a very touchy area, but if we can fend off pneumonia, he should recover well. I must warn you, though, he will probably never ride a horse again."

Logan gave a great sigh and closed her eyes. "Who cares about horses? He's going to live! Oh, thank you, Charles."

"Thank Vail. If he hadn't got the bleeding stopped, Stuart would have been dead before I got here. Thank the war, too. Odd, isn't it, how good can come out of a great evil. But for what I learned about wounds in the war, I couldn't have coped with this tonight."

Vail had come away from the window and was listening quietly, his face impassive. "Did you get the bullet out?"

"Most of it. I may have missed a fragment or two, but that shouldn't cause him too much trouble. It penetrated the pelvis, lodged in the thigh, and did considerable damage to muscles and ligaments, but it could have been so much worse. The groin area is filled with blood vessels—that's why the bleeding was so copious, Marin, and the bullet grazed a very delicate area. Stuart's—ah—natural functions are affected, but I am nearly certain that with time he will be restored to full vigor."

James limped across the room, shaking his head. "What kind of a man is it who could try to kill his own son, no matter what the boy had done? I will never understand Malcolm Severance if I live to be a hundred."

"I'm not sure he did try. To kill him that is. Rather, I believe he had severe punishment in mind."

"Why," expostulated James, "the man fired point-blank at short range."

"Yes, and he's a good shot. Stuart would have been dead on the spot if he'd aimed at his head or his heart, but he didn't. He aimed at the groin, and while it could have been a mortal wound if mishandled, it was far from certain to be. I think Malcolm meant to fix Stuart so he could never commit the same crime again. Fortunately he failed."

Marin sat hugging her arms, her nerves stretched to the breaking point by the insanity of this night. Events were chaotic, out of joint, and the knowledge frightened her, as did any circumstance she could not control. If Tyler had not dangled his loan before Michael, if Michael had not pressed the boiler investment on her, if Vail had not agreed to go in on it and come to the house tonight to explain the deal to James, then Vail would not have been here in the precious few minutes when the blood was pouring out of Stuart and his life hung by a thread. It was the night Belinda was born all over again. But for a series of unconnected events Vail would not have come on that other night either and she and Belinda would have died.

She took the brandy someone handed her and swallowed a little of it, lightheaded with relief. Stuart was not going to die. There would not be another grave added to the many that had gone before, nor a trial for murder with the children's grandfather in the dock. She had not loved Stuart for many years and often wondered if she had ever truly loved him; at times she actively loathed him. More than anything in life she wanted to be free of him, and yet—she did not wish him dead. Then, after the first surge of blessed relief, memories began to rise up; Stuart, always so quick to pass moral judgments on others; Stuart, storming after Sophy and doing his best to kill Wes Morgan as he leaped stark naked out the window; Stuart, the good son, caught in bed with his father's wife.

She got up quickly and went to the window so that no one could see her face. The thought passed through her mind that Stuart had just generously provided her with perfect grounds for divorce, but in this moment she could not even rejoice. She could only picture her stately, unbending, self-righteous husband caught flat-footed and bare-bottomed with his flatulent dignity in shreds. She turned her face so that the others could not see and fought a rising desire to laugh.

The town shared Marin's amusement. When word first went out that Stuart had been shot and gravely wounded, there was general shock and consternation, for he was both a prominent politician and a war hero. But although no one who had been present in Stuart's house the night of the shooting talked, the details spread swiftly in the mysteriously efficient manner that succulent gossip always spread, and by noon of the next day everyone knew who had shot him and why, and where the wound was located. As soon as the news came that he was in much discomfort but recovering, the necessity to keep a straight face was removed, and the town burst into a guffaw that reverberated all the way to San Diego and even reached Stuart on his bed of pain. He writhed with the knowledge that people were laughing and there was absolutely nothing he could do about it. The incident was too serious to hide, and, worse luck, there was a witness. Wong must have talked his head off. Stuart ground his teeth when he thought of Wong and entertained himself by imagining the various tortures he would inflict on him.

The police lost interest in the case as soon as Stuart's recovery was certain. Malcolm could hardly be arrested for assault with intent to commit murder; as Charles had said, if you meant to kill a man, you shot him through the heart, "not smack in the balls." So William Purcell, the banker and Stuart's close friend, said, wiping tears of laughter from his eyes. If the district attorney really wanted to prosecute Malcolm, a charge of assault with a deadly weapon could be sustained, but to get a jury to convict, that was the difficulty. He was defending his home, wasn't he? A man had a right to do that. That was the considered opinion of the gentlemen.

Their wives, ladies all, indulged in speculation that was a good deal more carefully phrased but nonetheless enjoyable. Many of them had felt the sting of Glenna's tongue and had resented the airs she gave herself. She was such a self-righteous woman, ever quick to point out the shortcomings of others; it was a genuine pleasure to see her paid off in her own coin. The fact that she was Stuart's stepmother added a vaguely incestuous touch that made it all that much more delicious. What happened to Glenna after Malcolm got her home was also the subject of much conjecture. Would he lock her up, would he divorce her, was she pregnant? That last was the most interesting prospect. What relationship would such a child have to Malcolm? To Stuart's other children? One other question loomed large in the ladies' minds but was never hinted at by any of them—what must it be like to fling restraint overboard, meet a lover in a hidden rendezvous, risk all for love? It was a question they could not mention to each other or ask Glenna or even directly acknowledge to themselves, but in their secret hearts most of them imagined that it must be thrilling.

Stuart hoped fervently that by the time he was well the whole awful contretemps would be, if not forgotten or at least superseded by some more current tittle-tattle, but when he was finally able to limp out into the world he found that it was still considered the best scandal to hit San Francisco in ten years. Not that anything was ever said to him. Friends solicitously inquired after his health, brought him the softest chairs, and helped him in and out of the buggy he now rode in instead of sitting a horse, but he knew they were laughing behind his back and hated them for it. Ridicule struck him with particularly wounding force, for beneath his assured exterior his self-esteem was frail. He was a laughingstock, the butt of jokes the moment he left a room; he had let Glenna down when she needed him most and God only knew what her position was at Longridge. Worst of all, he had failed utterly as a son. The absurdity of the thought did not strike him; he had failed as a son the first time he took Glenna, so many years ago, but somehow it had seemed all right as long as Father did not know. Never until the day he died would he forget his father's face, stern as an avenging archangel, bringing him to judgment and then carrying out the sentence. There was no forgiveness in that face and never would be. He was stricken from Malcolm's book just as Vail had been. Worse than Vail.

And as for Marin, he couldn't figure her out at all. Not a word of reproach had passed her lips since the moment he came back to consciousness in his bedroom and found her tidying his bed. In the days that followed she bathed him, fed him, helped Charles change the dressings on his wound while he burned with mortification, never once referred even obliquely to the circumstances in which he got the wound, and in general behaved with saintly forbearance. She even fashioned a seat cushion for him and measured him several times to make sure the fit was right. As soon as he could, he ordered the buggy hitched and had himself driven downtown; better to face a snickering world than more of his wife's solicitous ministrations.

One late afternoon he sat alone on the porch swing, Marin's damned seat cushion (which he found surprisingly comfortable) pillowing his sore underside. The wound was healing well but was always tender, and sometimes, like today, it took a notion to throb unbearably. The ache in his mind was considerably more painful. Since Marin flatly refused to do it, he had prevailed on Logan to go out to Longridge to see how the land lay. She had gone reluctantly, the only one of Malcolm's children who was still allowed into the house, had spent an awkward hour there and returned with news that gave no comfort. Privately she had spoken to Malcolm of his son's profound remorse and his hope that he might someday be forgiven, and Malcolm had replied, "I have no son," and refused to listen further. However, he looked in rude good health, as vigorous and forceful as ever. Glenna, on the other hand, was a shadow, her round face thin and wan, her hands twitching nervously in her lap whenever she was not pouring coffee or serving cake. She had little to say beyond yes and no and how kind, and she kept an anxious eye on her husband to see how he took even those brief remarks.

"You don't think he's abusing her?"

"Physically?" said Logan, shocked. "Oh, Stuart, how could you think such a thing?"

"But he's making life hell for her all the same, just like he did for Mother. There are other ways to beat a woman than with your fists. It's not as if he really cares about her, it's his damned pride that's hurt." He slammed his fist on the arm of the swing. "I suppose he won't see me?"

"I fear not. One day, no doubt, it can all be ironed out, but not yet."

Thank God. His heart quailed at the prospect of looking again into his father's eyes and seeing the justifiable contempt there. What was it he had said just before he pulled the trigger? *And a man's foes shall be they of his own household.*

Logan was sitting on the step at his feet. She rose and kissed him. "Try not to worry, dear. He'll forgive eventually. He must, as he's a Christian. And while Glenna is in an unpleasant situation right now, it will pass. Time will heal even this." She went into the house thinking, Oh, what a shabby, untrue platitude that is. He won't forgive if he lives to be a thousand.

Stuart, brooding on the porch, muttered to himself, "'A man's foes shall be they of his own household.' I must look that up sometime."

He was still sitting staring at his feet when the front gate clicked and Marin came up the path. She had been to town on some kind of business—she never told *him* what she was up to—and was wearing a new dress of emerald green taffeta that gave her white skin a creamy glow; a little straw hat trimmed with lace, green ribbons, and tiny flowers perched on her red hair. She looked extremely pretty, and he groaned when he saw her. She was so damned sweet and polite and would undoubtedly ask how his bottom was feeling.

But she did not ask. Instead she came lightly up the steps and said without preamble, "Stuart, you must move to a hotel today. After the disgraceful way you've behaved, I cannot continue to live in the same house with you. Have the buggy hitched up; I'll go pack your bag."

He sat looking at her, his mouth open. Move to a hotel? Just like that—here's your hat? Who the hell did she think she was, ordering him out of his own house, which he had built with money he couldn't afford to spend because Vail had threatened to tell Father . . . But he didn't want to think about that. He got onto his feet, hobbled into the house, and struggled up the stairs, muttering an oath with every step. She was in his room, putting his shirts and undergarments in a case. She hadn't even waited to take off her bonnet.

He slammed the door. "What do you think you're doing? Put

those things back!" He grabbed the shirts and threw them into the drawer.

"Don't be childish, Stuart." She took the shirts up, folded them neatly, and placed them again in the case.

"Damn it, woman, you can't turn me out of my own house! I won't go."

She turned and met his furious eyes. "You have humiliated me—betrayed me before the whole world—and I cannot bear being subjected to your constant presence when it only reminds me . . ." She dug for a handkerchief and put it to her nose. "Either you leave or I must, and I don't think anyone would expect a mother and her children to be put out of their home when it is the husband who is the guilty party." She walked to the door. "Finish your own packing. I was only trying to help. Just remember, I expect you to be out of the house before suppertime."

He stood in the middle of the room, looking at his half-filled bag, dazed by the sudden swiftness of her attack. Before this afternoon she had shown not a sign of anger at his behavior, even though in all justice she had a right to. She had nursed him with kindness, anticipated his needs, and never uttered a word of recrimination. He might have known it was too good to last. Something had changed her since she had gone downtown, and he would give his right arm to know what it was.

He found out very soon. The next week as he sat in the hotel restaurant after breakfast, reading the morning paper, a stranger in an ill-fitting frock coat walked up to his table and doffed his tall, dusty hat. "Good day, sir. Be you Mr. Stuart Severance?"

Stuart nodded, wondering what the man was after. Before he could begin the painful process of struggling courteously to his feet, the stranger said, "No need to get up, sir. This is for you."

The man was gone, threading his way past the tables and into the crowded lobby before Stuart could speak. With an odd, premonitory chill he opened the paper and discovered that Maria Catherine Severance, the wife of his bosom and mother of his children, was suing him for divorce.

Gerald had made it very clear to Marin during her conference with him. "Get Stuart out of the house, and don't waste time doing it. Adultery is most certainly grounds for divorce, but it must not appear that you and Stuart have cohabited as man and wife after you knew of the adultery."

"But I wouldn't . . . Stuart couldn't . . . not right now. Charles said so. And everyone in the family knows we have separate bedrooms."

"All well and good," replied Gerald, ignoring her blushes, "and we can call Charles as an expert witness if necessary. Even so, this divorce is not in Stuart's interest. I don't want to leave any opening for him to impeach the grounds."

"How could he? The whole world knows what he did. He can't deny it."

"Perhaps not, but I believe in taking all precautions just the same."

Gerald was proven right when Stuart stormed into his office and threw the papers he had been served on the desk. "You can take this back and eat it, you smarmy little runt. She can't do this to me, by God!"

Gerald folded his hands and inquired, "Just how do you propose to stop her? Adultery is grounds for divorce in this state, as you, having once been a state legislator, must know."

Stuart leaned his fists on the desk, his outthrust chin in Gerald's face. "You're goddam right I was a legislator, and I know your only witness is a sneaky little chink, and chinks can't testify in court, not against a white man."

"How true, how true," Gerald agreed, and added silkily, "but you are forgetting that in addition to Wong there is another witness. Your father is quite competent to testify and, I suspect, will not be at all averse to doing so. In any case we will subpoena him."

"You wouldn't call Father."

"I must. Even if you were to agree to it, divorce cannot be granted either by default or by your own admission of wrongdoing. The court will require proof of the facts alleged as ground for divorce, and the only other person who could corroborate them would be your stepmother. I feel that chivalry demands we call only upon your father. Don't you agree?"

Stuart left Gerald's office a humbled man. Marin would have her divorce, and his political career would be finished. Any man, no matter how venal, could win high office if he presented the public appearance of a good family man; no man, however upright, could be elected if he was divorced. It was over, the dream of becoming governor or senator and perhaps one day climbing up to the most exalted office of all. It was over, and all because, standing on a riverbank on one long-ago day, a boy too young to know better had said to an adoring black-eyed, red-haired girl, "I love you . . . come to me, for the rest of your life you come to me." What a fool that boy had been, what a muddle-headed booby. Because of the decision that simpleminded ass had made eighteen years ago, a man was cut off from the woman he really loved and forever barred from the heights he could have reached. He drove back to the hotel, seated himself gingerly in the bar, and drank until he fell off his chair and had to be carried up to bed.

Chapter 50

Two days after a final judgment of divorce was entered in the case of *Severance* vs. *Severance*, Marin and Vail stood before a minister and were married with only family members and two outsiders, Gerald and Michael, as witnesses. They then departed immediately on a honeymoon trip to White Sulphur Springs, leaving behind a town rocked by the spectacle of a divorced woman's shocking-enough-in-itself marriage to her former husband's brother before, as Charlotte Winfield put it, "the ink was dry on the divorce decree."

Charlotte went on to point out that while Stuart Severance had sunk to the depths of depravity, a truly virtuous woman would have forgiven him instead of going through a public trial that brought all sorts of ugly deeds into the light and then, the moment she was free, happily flouncing off with another man. Charlotte's friends agreed. If wives sought divorces every time their husbands strayed, few marriages would remain intact, and where would the sanctity of home and hearth be then? Everyone knew that men were weak vessels and it was up to the woman to maintain the morals of society. Marin's stubborn insistence on divorce and her quick remarriage gave rise to a number of piquant possibilities, which were hashed over zestfully whenever two or more ladies got together for a good chat.

Charlotte was entirely right about Marin's pleasure in her new marriage, for in fact she had never been so happy in her life. The only shadow on her days was the fear that always accompanied great happiness, the fear that something would happen to destroy it. She worried that a horse might throw Vail, although she knew he was very nearly as expert a horseman as Ethan; she worried that somehow a duel might be provoked with some stranger who happened to be a better shot than Vail—the laws against dueling were still honored in the breach, not the observance. Most of all, she worried about Stuart. The trial, his father's testimony, the fresh spate of gossip afterward, the humiliatingly few votes he had garnered in last fall's election, had left him in an odd, embittered frame of mind. During the year it had taken for the divorce to become final, he got drunk in public, visited whorehouses openly, provoked quarrels with men who had no wish to fight him. And now she was married to Vail, the brother who had always bested him. In her worst nightmares she saw him stalking Vail, leveling a gun, and shooting him dead.

When she told Vail her fears before the wedding and reluctantly suggested delaying it for a while, he said simply, "Oh, my dear, while you're alive, live."

"Just leave everything to fate, is that it?"

He touched her face in a light caress. "Honey, I've seen too much death to live in terror of it. It comes when it will, and there's little we can do about it. So many times in war I asked myself, Why the other fellow and not me? I never did find a good answer." His arms went around her. "All I know is I am alive and you are alive, now, this moment, and that's all we've got. I want to marry you and live with you, and to hell with Stuart and the rest of the world."

The ardor in those words and the happiness in his eyes when the preacher said they were man and wife were treasures that she carried with her like a delicious secret to be taken out and enjoyed in quiet moments. He looked happier in the days at White Sulphur Springs than she had ever seen him and it delighted her that she was the cause.

The resort was an ideal place for a honeymoon. They walked under the oaks beside a crystal mountain stream that eddied into quiet pools on its rambling way down to the river; they stood on the little bridge over the stream, watching fish slip smoothly through the clear water; they took a picnic lunch and rode out into the countryside, content with only each other for company. And every evening there was a party in the ballroom, where they could dance through the night if they chose. For Marin each lazy day was suffused by a rich, golden haze, every night Vail's arms held her safe, and life was sweet as honey in the comb.

This coming together after their marriage was different from the time in Virginia. Then the opportunity had fallen on them, unexpected, a dangerous, illicit interlude snatched in the face of war and death with no hope that such a moment would ever come again. Now they had declared themselves before the world, and at last they had the right to be alone together behind a closed, locked door and do whatever they wished. It was not that they did nothing but make love in the sanctuary of their room, although in the first feverish days it seemed that there was nothing else in life worth doing; it was the luxurious freedom, the blessed privacy that was important. They could choose their moment, for they had all their lives before them. When they did make love, it was with quiet passion, for the violence of their need had hushed to a more tender and enduring rapture. Once, in a burst of daring she suggested that they go up to their room even though it was only early afternoon. With no concealing shadows to cover their nakedness she expected to feel as wanton as Kitty Winfield but discovered that daylight made no difference. Vail was her lover and her husband at night or at midday, whether they were eating or dancing or talking or in bed. It was so simple and so good.

Sometimes, instead of going downstairs to the dining room, they ate supper at the table by their window and listened to the sound of water flowing over stones and the mockers in the oaks tossing out complex trills to celebrate the coming night. Eventually the evening song would be complete, and the birds would dart upward across the sky, their wide, white-striped wings flashing in the fading light.

Sometimes it was pleasant to lie close in bed, watching through the open window as the stars came out and talking idly of the traveling they would do after the children were gone and the new venture with the Taggart Boiler Works was on its feet. Marin felt a glow every time she thought of Denby Burwell and his invention. A boiler was such an unglamorous, commonplace machine, but it generated power, the overriding necessity of modern life; financial success always came when you produced something that everybody had to have. And success would do more than secure the future for her and Vail and the people who depended on them; it would free her forever from Tyler Winfield. She could pay him off and kick him out, and what a pleasure that would be.

And she could do it only because of Vail. His money backed the project, his emotional support gave her the courage to gamble. Light from the half-moon fell across the bed, and she could see him dimly outlined, one arm under his head, the other holding her. For so many years she had slept alone; now the best part of the day came when she climbed into bed and nestled against him, feeling his length and size and warmth with the greatest satisfaction. She had survived the storms of life and had reached safe harbor; she had been lost for a long time and had come home.

She raised up so that she could look into his eyes and lightly brushed his lips with hers. "You belong to me absolutely. I'll never be lonely again. Isn't that wonderful?"

A strand of her hair fell forward. He ran his fingers through it and smoothed it over her bare shoulder. "Yes. Except that it isn't true."

"What do you mean? Of course it's true."

"Marin, no one belongs to anyone else. We are always alone. Anything else is mostly illusion."

She sat straighter, her eyes wide with hurt. "Don't you want to belong to me? I belong to you."

"No, honey, you don't. I can't have all of your mind and soul any more than you can have mine. We give as much as we can to each other, and maybe it's more than we've ever given before, but it isn't all, and you know it. There's always a part of us that we can't share with anyone even though we want to."

Her mind closed against the truth of it. There was a core of brutal honesty in him that drove her crazy sometimes. He could say such painful things without blinking, and the fact that they were true only made it worse. "It's not so," she argued. "You'll always be with me, and I'll be with you. And we've got the children and Papa and Logan . . ."

"But we don't, any of us, belong to each other. We have only ourselves. That's why we form attachments and build fires of affection, to keep out the cold. I love you because you fill my need. You love me for the same reason. With parents and children or brothers and sisters, common experiences and memories hold us together, and we may love greatly, but there are limits, because that is our nature." He stroked her cheek and said in a kind but uncompromising way, "I don't say this to hurt you but to make certain you see things straight. I'll be here for you when I can for as long as I can, but don't depend solely on me or on anyone but yourself."

Stubbornly she cried, "But it isn't all illusion . . ." and he drew her down and held her against his chest.

"No, it isn't, not all of it. He kissed her wet eyes and her earlobes and the tip of her nose. After a time her tears stopped, and once again they gave themselves up to each other, striving in the hush of the night to build higher fires to hold at bay a cold, uncaring world.

When they returned to San Francisco, Marin went her way, aware of the chatter about her and unruffled by it. She had known it would be like this—her actions were too unconventional not to provoke gossip—but the talk would die down as newer scandals came to occupy people's minds. Meanwhile life with Vail was too precious to allow the clacking tongues of envious women to spoil it. Not since childhood had she waked with such joy and looked forward to each new day with so much energy. It can't last, she thought, superstitiously apologizing to any jealous gods who might be watching. But it did last.

Belinda and Carey now lived in Vail's house, too, and Marin had what she had never dared to hope for—a life with her children and Vail together as a family. She could look around her dinner table and see Alida and Belinda, grown close as sisters during the bad days after Celia died, whispering together about the decoration of the big bedroom they shared; she could see Carey, too serious and earnest these days, relax a little as he talked to Vail. Watching them, she had the sense of home and safety that came when one was inside a snug house while a storm raged outside. Now, no matter what storms raged, she was safe inside this circle of people she loved best.

Not that life was trouble-free. Behind apparent dutiful acceptance Alida felt pangs of jealousy and Marin knew it. How like Celia she was—a tranquil exterior and an obstinate will. Of course it was hard for her to accept a kindly aunt's suddenly turning into a stepmother who took her father's time and attention, but surely she would come around when she saw that her place in Vail's heart was secure.

One other small cloud on Marin's days was Denby Burwell's struggle with his boiler design. It had taken much longer than he predicted to get the thing working properly, but now the machine was complete and ready for testing. High pressure with safety was the crux of success, for the steamer companies were mad for speed; at one time or another they all raced, although they swore they wouldn't, and there had been too many explosions in which passengers died. William Purcell had seen Denby's boiler, and Vail had had several long conferences with other members of the board of the Golden West Steamship Co. If they installed Burwell boilers in even one Golden West steamer and the boilers demonstrated their superiority, every other steamer company would have to have them, and the money would flow in!

On a deeper level there was one other worry that continued to plague her as the lovely spring days went by, an apprehension that nagged at the back of her mind in daylight and rose up into terrifying proportions in the blackness of the night. Finally, late in

May, the thing she most feared came about—the inevitable encounter with Stuart. He had not been seen around town in months, and she had begun to hope that he had gone away to start life over in some far place where his recent humiliations were not known. One evening she and Vail went to the Taggart Works near Broadway wharf to watch Denby run the second of his tests. They stayed for over an hour, and while he was still tinkering with the pipes, they went out onto the wharf, intending to walk to Gentry and Callendar's water-front office where Michael was working late. Fog had drifted over the harbor while they were inside.

They turned down a short side street. Ahead in the obscuring gloom a man came toward them, walking with an odd, halting gait. Marin's heart froze. He was here, he hadn't gone away. She had known it was too much to hope for. Why must they run into him now, on this dark, lonely street with no one else to witness an attack; why now, when everything was going so well and she was so happy? Thank God she was here, too; she might be able to draw his rage away from Vail and onto her. Thank God for the little gun that Vail, like most men, carried in his coat pocket. Instinctively her hand dropped from his arm, leaving her free to move.

Stuart recognized his brother long before he saw his face. The great height outlined in the dim light, the massive shoulders, the distinctive, free-swinging movement of his body. Once he, Stuart, had also walked effortlessly, before the constant ache of damaged muscles and ligaments caused him to shuffle like a damned crab. And her. Once, in the early days, she had clung possessively to his arm the way she'd been hanging onto Vail just a moment before. Well, that wouldn't last long. Probably she'd reject Vail soon, just the same way she'd rejected him. Probably she was planning to do it even while she was cuddling up to him.

Ahead, gray vapor swirled about the flickering light of a street lamp. Marin and Vail passed under it, and Stuart saw her face. She was scared! Not for herself—she'd always had courage—but for Vail. How sweet, how enchanting that she was scared. But Vail wasn't. He looked his usual bold, unworried self, as at ease as if he were out for a Sunday stroll and not walking down a dark passage toward a man he knew hated him, a man whose wife he'd stolen. Stuart, dismissing his own contribution to his downfall, thought bitterly, It's her fault. But for her, I'd never have turned to Glenna and Father wouldn't despise me. But for her, I wouldn't be scuttling along like this, and that puking girl at Madame Colette's wouldn't have laughed at me last night. Charles says there's no physical reason, but what does he know? It's all her fault. Vail doesn't have any such trouble. He can bed her anytime he wants to. What a pleasure it would be to pull out the Colt and blow that cocky look off his face, blow him to kingdom come. *That* would hurt her!

They came abreast. Stuart bowed stiffly and passed on. Marin swallowed and resisted the temptation to look over her shoulder. As they turned the corner, she glanced back down the dark street. Nothing was behind them but the obscuring fog. She laid her hand on Vail's arm again and said lightly but with a tremble she could not hide, "Thank goodness that's over. I guess he's not going to try and shoot you after all." Vail did not reply, and she looked up. His face was thoughtful and turned a little away from her. In surprise she said, "You didn't expect him to, did you?"

"I thought he might toss me a few insults or scuffle around some, but shoot me? No."

His calmness nettled her. She'd been so frightened for him. "I don't see how you could be so sure. Stuart's shot any number of men dead and never blinked an eye, men he wasn't half so mad at as he is at you."

"I know."

He said nothing more, and Marin hurried to match his long, absentminded stride, mulling over the singular relationship between Vail and Stuart Severance.

Even before they were married, Marin had itched to get at Vail's house and, at the very least, rearrange the furniture, but when they came home from their honeymoon, she hesitated until he assured her that the house was now hers to do with as she wished. It was a man's house, for Vail had built and furnished it; Celia had considered La Gracia her real home and had made few changes. After much thought Marin replaced the draperies, had her piano brought over and installed in a place of honor in the large parlor, and turned a small sitting room into a dining room where she and Vail could eat together when there were no guests. There she stopped, content for the time being. It was good strategy not to make too many changes as long as her relationship with Alida was on uncertain ground.

The armed truce between her and her new stepdaughter continued as summer came on, and then something happened to Alida that drove her father's marriage from her mind. Jim Porter, Carey's friend from prison days, arrived in San Francisco. Jim was thirty-two years old, a vast, sophisticated age; he was battered and insouciant, with a devil-may-care gleam in his eye; his strength and cleverness had saved Carey's life. Alida took one look and fell madly in love. After that wondrous event she was so busy keeping her newfound love secret, writing in her diary, and trying out new hairstyles before her mirror that she had no time to be jealous of Marin.

Jim's presence cheered Carey, too, and that encouraged everyone. He had never quite recovered from the withdrawn moodiness that accompanied him home from the war and had recently turned worse. One morning while Marin and Vail were in White Sulphur Springs he had found Angus lying unmoving in the straw of an empty stall in the stable. As James said, in an effort to comfort, the collie was about nineteen, a great age for a dog, and he had lived well and brought joy to them all for many years. Carey had nodded and agreed and wiped his wet face, wondering why he was crying for his dog when he had not cried for so many lost friends. He buried Angus near the summerhouse and sat out there often, staring down at the bay, but after Jim arrived in town, his dark moods came less often.

Though a man of quiet temperament, with a cynic's outlook on life, Jim was bowled over by the exciting tempo of life in the city. He prowled the waterfront watching ships arrive laden with exotic goods and depart for ports all over the world, and he loved to talk with Carey about the possibilities for adventure somewhere beyond the seas. Marin knew such talk was meaningless but it always unnerved her.

One night at dinner after Jim had poured out his ideas about the riches to be gained in Australia, she remarked, "What notions you have, Jim. Ask Ethan about Australia, and he'll soon set you straight. It's a dreadful place, dry and dusty, and every other man there is an ex-felon. It was a penal colony, you know. And the gold boom is over. I think you'll find San Francisco is the place of opportunity for an ambitious man. Would anyone like a second piece of pie?"

Later that night in their bedroom she said to Vail, "Jim is a nice enough man, but he's a bad influence. Did you notice Carey's eyes when he was running on about Australia?" She was seated at her dressing table, giving her hair the hundred strokes it had received almost every night of her life. In the mirror she saw Vail smile.

"I thought it was Jim's influence on Alida you were worried about. Luckily he has sense enough to keep her at a distance."

She smiled, too. "I remember when I was fifteen. Oh, my, do I remember. Poor baby, she'd die of humiliation if she even suspected we know. Now Belinda just flirts with all the boys and doesn't pine for anyone."

"I can't imagine Belinda pining. She's much too tough."

Marin bent forward to that her hair hung down over her face and continued to brush it vigorously. "About Carey, Vail, you give him a talking to, diplomatically, of course. He respects your opinion so much. Just make it clear that he's to go to Harvard and then step into the business and no more talk about Australia." She raised her head. "Vail?" But he was in his dressing room and hadn't heard a word she'd said. She tied her hair back and climbed into bed. Today the Burwell boilers had been installed in the *Princess*, Golden West's luxurious new side-wheeler, which the steamship company was counting on to beat out all the competition in the run from San Francisco to Sacramento. That was something to put under her pillow and dream about.

Chapter 51

The next day, Sunday, was James's birthday, and he celebrated it with his nearest relatives—all except his daughter-in-law, Kitty, who had a dreadful headache and begged to be excused. Whenever there was a gathering of her husband's family, excruciating headaches invariably attacked Kitty. These diplomatic indispositions were a source of considerable amusement to her in-laws, and as she had sent little Ty and Dottie in her stead James was satisfied and she was not missed.

He was satisfied with all of life today. With only two mighty efforts he blew out the seventy-six candles on the cake while his family cheered and applauded. At the table his eyes rested fondly on his two much-loved daughters and the fine men they had married, men who were among his closest friends. Not many elderly gentlemen could make such a claim about their sons-in-law. His own son was in attendance for a change instead of off on a tear with a wild hair up his ass, and he was seemingly in a calmer, more reflective frame of mind. Could it be that Ethan had grown up at last? All the grandchildren were present, too—the little ones, Jefferson, Ty, and Dottie, staring at the bonfire on the cake with shining, awe-struck eyes, and the two young beauties, Belinda and Alida, chatting with the children and enjoying their excitement. And Carey was smiling and singing "Happy Birth-day" more loudly than all the rest. It was a joy to see Carey laugh heartily again.

The candlewicks had gone black. Logan brandished the long saw-toothed knife and began cutting the cake. James watched her, feeling great affection for the gentle, intelligent woman who ran his household so efficiently. There was a sprinkling of gray in the fine brown hair, which she wore drawn back severely from her narrow face, a face marked by heartache and loss. She looked every year of her age, her status as an old maid was immutable, yet her laughter was still as buoyant as a girl's, and behind her spectacles her lovely gray-blue eyes could still shine with a soft light. Just now she was handing Ethan his plate of cake, and when he looked up and thanked her, her cheeks turned as beautiful a pink as Belinda's. Love couldn't be bidden. James sighed, and a little of the brightness went out of the day. Some, like Logan, made do with crumbs, but it was beyond him how they managed. He was never satisfied with less than he could grab, nor were any of the Gentrys.

After the party James thanked them all for their gifts and good wishes and volunteered to return Dottie and Ty to their mother on his way downtown for an evening of poker with his cronies. The carriage waited at the front gate, and he limped down the walk and climbed into it without assistance. His new outfit was natty and across his bright plaid waistcoat swung the new gold watch chain that was one of his birthday presents. His thick silver hair was parted in the new center style, and on it sat a black felt bowler with a rolled brim.

He is certainly the *dernier cri*, thought Marin, watching through the front window as his carriage rolled off down the street. He looked younger at seventy-six than he had in his fifties when he was struggling back to life after his stroke. With a rush of pride she thought, Knock us Gentrys down, and we come back stronger and feistier than ever!

Just as she let the drapery fall into place, she caught sight of Carey riding around from the side of the house on his big horse. How manly he looked, how strong his young face was, and how silly of her to want to run after him and warn him to button up against the night air and not stay out too late. She had no idea what he did when he went into town, but he never came home drunk or even smelling of liquor. There were other amusements though, gambling and so forth, things she didn't want to think about in connection with her boy. She wanted him to be normal, of course; she just didn't want to know any details.

The house was very quiet after the excitement of the party. Vail and Charles had gone down to the stable to admire Ethan's new horse, a fast, powerful animal, the first extravagance he had allowed himself since coming home. Marin ran her hand over the new velvet draperies Logan had made. It was a satisfying feeling to know that this house was now entirely her own—Stuart had been forced to sign over the deed as part of the property settlement—and her family could remain sheltered in it forever. Delphine and young Jeff had been put to bed and Belinda and Alida were upstairs exchanging girlish secrets. Marin's mind moved back through the years to the miseries and fears and foolish ideas about life and love that she had harbored in her teens. She thought, I wouldn't be their age again for all the tea in China.

Humming, she went back to the parlor to settle down with Sophy and Logan for a comfortable chat.

Belinda and Alida were upstairs, but at the moment they were not exchanging girlish secrets. They had gone up to the attic, a favorite playroom since childhood, and were dressing themselves in the old clothes stored there. The child that still lingered in them loved to play dress-up, especially in the outdated but low-cut and glamorous ball gowns, so much more tantalizing than the demure dimities and organdies they were restricted to.

Digging through the trunks, the girls had fallen joyfully upon two old gowns, one blue silk and the other deep emerald satin, which Marin had worn years ago with devastating effect. They had hooked each other up and pulled the bodices as far down as they dared, and were now singing a waltz and circling dreamily around the attic, hands held out, eyes half closed, in the arms of imaginary lovers.

Suddenly Belinda plopped down on a dusty trunk and gazed morosely at Alida, who was at the moment in a moonlit garden being kissed by Jim Porter. "This is stupid."

Alida opened her eyes but kept dancing. "Why? I'm having a wonderful time."

"You just think you are. Look at yourself, dummy. You're jumping around a dirty attic in Mama's old dress with nobody but a *girl* cousin for company. Jim Porter is miles away, probably in a bad house right now and not giving you a thought."

Alida came to an abrupt halt. "He gives me thoughts all the

time and he would never go to a bad house. He's much too pure and high-minded."

"Ha! Men are all alike." Belinda had heard matrons say that many times, and although she was not sure what they meant by it, the remark fitted her present sour mood perfectly.

Having been kept in the pristine state of ignorance considered essential for young ladies of good breeding, she and Alida knew next to nothing about men and even less about sex. They were guiltily aware that some activity that no one ever talked about went on between gentlemen and ladies after they were married. Although they had discussed it with every other young girl they knew and searched through every book they could lay hands on, they had found out very little, and most of what they thought they knew was wrong. Underlying their ignorance was fear. With the clear, hard, mistaken logic of the young they reckoned that whatever it was must be very terrible. Why would it be kept so secret unless it was too revolting even to speak of?

Alida stood in the middle of the floor, hands on hips, and scowled at her cousin. With the years she had grown less mild and credulous, and she no longer took Belinda's tempers and teasings lying down. "I think you're hateful. And you needn't say vile things about Jim, because I won't listen." With considerable satisfaction she added, "Your skirt is filthy."

Belinda jumped up and slapped at the pale blue silk now marred by dust and shreds of rope. The trunk she had been sitting on was far back in an alcove, bound by many lengths of heavy hemp tied with thick knots. She looked at Alida and saw the same thought in her eyes.

They broke several fingernails struggling with the knots, and then, because she knew Carey had left the house, Belinda slipped down to his room, located a bowie knife in the pocket of a pair of pants left lying on his bed, and quickly, quietly, ran back up the stairs.

"This ought to do it," she announced, and began sawing at the heavy rope.

"Let me try," Alida begged, but Belinda shrugged her off. "I'll have it here in a second if you'll just stay out of the way. There!" The last strands broke, the rope slithered to the floor, and she lifted the lid.

"Oh!" The cry came from both girls.

Before them, lying in perfect folds, was Rose's wedding dress. Reverently, as if the dress were a fragile body, they lifted it from the trunk. The rich satin slithered and shimmered, creamy white in the pale late afternoon light that fell through the attic window.

"It's Grandmama's wedding dress," breathed Belinda. "See the cunning little tucks around the waist and the gores in the skirt? Mama has described it to me a hundred times. She was married in it, too, the first time, that is, to my father, but she wore a crown of flowers on her hair because Grandmama's old veil was torn. Grandpa was very sick then, and Mama and Father wanted to get married right away, so it was just a simple wedding."

With one finger Alida caressed the cloth. "Look at the bodice. I'll bet anything the lace is Valenciennes." She was seeing herself in just such a dress, standing before a priest with Jim Porter gazing at her in adoration. She looked at Belinda. "Do we dare?"

"Me first," said Belinda. "It's my grandmother's."

The reasonableness of this was beyond dispute, so Alida helped Belinda out of Marin's blue silk ball gown and then lowered the lovely old satin over her head.

"Oh, my!" Belinda twisted to look at herself. "Oh, it fits exactly. Well, pretty nearly. Oh, where's the mirror? Now if I only had that veil. Even if it isn't perfect, we could get the idea."

Alida was already on her knees, digging down through layers of Rose's other gowns for the veil. "It's not here. Maybe they threw it away." She lifted out the last of the clothes. "Look at this."

She got to her feet with an envelope in her hand, and Belinda craned her neck to read the slanting script. "Miss Logan Severance. It's just an old letter of Logan's. Shall we read it?"

"That wouldn't be nice." Alida turned it over. "Anyway, it's sealed. Do you suppose she never read it? Or didn't like it and sealed it up again? Shall we just leave it here?"

"We ought to give it to her. Maybe she's forgotten all about it. Here, I'll take it."

Alida snatched it back out of reach. "I found it, I get to do it."

Together they ran down the narrow attic stairs to the second floor and then down the broad staircase leading to the front of the house.

As they reached the bottom, they heard Charles say, "Who are you marrying, honey?" Acutely embarrassed, they peered down the hallway and saw Charles and Vail smiling at the trailing wedding dress.

The back door slammed, and Ethan came in from the kitchen. "Bless me, who are these strange lovelies? I think I'll abandon my wife and run away with both of them."

"Oh, Ethan," giggled Belinda, feeling foolish, but at the same time terribly attractive. "This is Grandmama's wedding dress. See?"

"I see. And your mama will have a fit if she catches you in it. Better scoot upstairs before she sees you."

This was wisdom, and the girls recognized it. Alida gave the envelope to Vail. "Daddy, we found this letter of Logan's in the trunk. You give it to her."

"Let me see that," Ethan said, and took it out of Vail's hand. He looked at it for a long time, as though there were many more than three words to be read on it, turned it over much as Alida had upstairs, and stared at the seal. His tone, the sudden tension in his pose made the girls look down and avoid each other's eyes. Somehow the fun had just drained out of the afternoon. Ethan looked queer—his face so flushed, his lips so white, and all the laughter gone from his eyes. They wished that they were back upstairs and had never come down.

Ethan handed the envelope to Vail. "Do as your daughter says. Give it to Logan."

Alida and Belinda turned and scurried up the stairs, their voluminous skirts held up to their knees for swift movement. In the attic they stripped off the fancy clothes and did their best to return the contents of the trunk to the condition it had been in when they opened it. But they could not get the dresses refolded in exactly the same way, and dimly they realized that they never would, not if they worked for the rest of their lives.

Logan tore the flap partway, hesitated, and Ethan said, "Go on." She ripped it open, took out a paper closely written on both sides, and read it silently, color flooding her face and then fading, leaving white patches on her cheeks. At the end she lowered the letter to her lap and sat with head bowed.

Softly, cuttingly, Ethan said, "Couldn't you at least have opened it before you decided against me? Couldn't you dig up the courage to even do that?"

Her head came up. Her cheeks were fiery again, and her eyes were filled with tears. "I never saw this, Ethan. Not in my life."

"Don't lie to me. I gave it to Marin, I told her . . ." He looked at his sister, sitting so still in James's wing chair in exactly the position she had been in when Vail walked into the parlor with the letter in his hand. Her black eyes were enormous in her chalk white face, her mouth was open, as if she would speak but could not. Ethan's hand closed into a fist and went up. Then his fingers relaxed. In a mild, almost puzzled way he said, "You promised to give it to her."

Marin's mouth opened wider, to explain, but the words would not come.

Vail sat down on the hassock beside Logan. "May I see it?"

Without a word she gave him the letter. He read it through and handed it back. Absently she folded it and stuck it in her pocket, took off her spectacles and stuck them in, too. She got up, looking around in a blind way, unable to think what to do next. Ethan's hands came down on her shoulders and spun her around so that she had to look at him. "What would you have done, Logan? Would you have come to me?"

"I don't know," she said, dazed. "I . . ." The tears welled up and spilled over. "Oh, darling, I'd have come. I never dreamed you felt that way, I never dreamed you could, not about me. Yes, yes, I'd have come!" She was in his arms, sobbing against his chest, and after a little while he led her out of the room and left the others sitting there.

They stayed in the library across the hall for a long time. Not a sound of weeping or talking reached the four in the parlor. Marin still sat hunched in the chair, her face blank with shock, thoughts flying helter-skelter through her mind as though a bomb had exploded there. Vail . . . she must talk to Vail alone. Oh, why didn't Sophy and Charles go home? Vail must understand, she must make him understand why she had done it and agree that she had been right. He was so close to Logan, so protective of her. He would never forgive. But he must . . . how could she live if he didn't forgive her? Oh, God, what a thing to happen. She had almost forgotten the letter in the trunk. Why hadn't she burned it when she had the chance and then this ghastly moment would never have come. Oh, she had to get out of here, she had to go home and explain. But Vail only sat and smoked and showed no inclination to leave. Why didn't he say something—ask for an explanation or shout and upbraid her? Even denunciation would be better than silence.

Sophy spoke to Charles in a low tone, and he nodded and went upstairs. In a few moments he was back, carrying his sleepy son. Sophy came to Marin and pressed her cheek against her sister's. Marin seemed not to notice. She sat staring at the floor as if she found something of interest in the pattern of the rug. Ordinarily Sophy would have kissed Vail, too, but the tension she sensed as she came near him led her only to murmur good-night and follow Charles out.

Marin stirred. She sat up and turned her eyes toward Vail; what she saw in his face caused her to look down at the rug again.

The door opened, and Logan came in. Her hair was ruffled, and the tip of her nose had turned a delicate pink, but her eyes were dry and there was something altogether new in her face. In a matter-of-fact voice she said, "Ethan has been planning to start up a horse farm, and Uncle James has offered him Little Mountain—the house and the land that is left. He was going to wait until summer, but now . . . He believes he can do well in the horse business, and so do I. It's what he likes and what he knows. We'll move out there tomorrow."

The import of the words hit Marin so hard that for the moment shame was blotted out. "But he's got a wife and children."

"Indeed he does. Just think, it could have been me and my children." It was not accusation, only musing wonderment.

Marin jumped to her feet, struggling to think. A cyclone was blowing through the hushed room, blowing away everything. Then, of a sudden, her motives came back with full clarity, and she began to speak, laying out her arguments like a lawyer before a jury, striving to show Logan why she had done what she had done. Striving to show Vail, too.

"Logan, I know it looks strange now, but remember what Ethan did. He abandoned Papa to go running after gold, and even when he knew Papa and Mama were sick and there was nobody to run the ranch he wouldn't come home. Then he suddenly came back, just dropped in out of the sky after being gone for years without a word. He flirted with you for a while, just long enough to drive Dan away, and then ran off chasing Kitty because she had a rich father. He didn't even like her, he just wanted her money. Vail, you know it's true."

Vail said nothing. She couldn't read his face. She went on, "Then, two days before the wedding, he came to me with that letter. He'd decided he didn't want her, he wanted you. I told him to give it to you himself. I said, 'Ethan, this is no way to treat a woman,' but he wouldn't face up to it. So he gave it to me. I thought if you read it you'd believe him—but I didn't, not for a minute. I didn't trust him. He would have run off and left you, Logan, when he wanted something else, just as he left Kitty when he went off to the war. Eventually he abandons everybody. I thought if you never knew about the letter, you'd marry Dan and someday we'd read it together and laugh about what a narrow escape you had. I thought it was best . . ."

She looked into the worn face of her sister-in-law, a face she knew as well as her own. They had been girls together, had lived in the same household through the years, had quarreled and worked and laughed together, had wept over the graves of those they loved and suffered through a brutal war together. Marin's hands went out in appeal. "I only meant to spare you heartbreak. Logan . . . darling, do you understand?"

Logan's eyes were wide. She said slowly, "I understand. You played God with my life and Ethan's, took away my youth and my chance for happiness." A sharp trumpet of anger sounded in her voice. "I am going to live with him at Little Mountain—yes, unmarried, because there is no other way, and we'll find whatever life there is left for us."

"What if you have children? They would be . . ."

"They would be my own. But don't concern yourself. I'll never have a baby now. I'm too old. You took that from me, too."

"You—why, you're barely forty. It could happen."

"Not to me. That part of my life is over. But if children were to come, I would thank God for it even though people would say they were bastards. That's another charge against you." Logan stopped, her hand at her mouth, appalled by her own words. She shook her head. "But I'm wrong to blame you. I was a coward. I should have fought for him, he should have made me listen. No, I shouldn't blame you." She went to Vail and kissed him. "Come to see me," she whispered, and walked out.

Marin sat on the stool, looking after her. That was the woman who had once annoyed her for refusing to launch an assault on life; but she was also the woman who had chased across a continent after a married man in the middle of a war and even consorted with spies in an effort to locate him. Mild, unassuming Logan had fires unguessed within her. She was a Severance, as tough and bold and passionate as ever her brothers had been, with the courage to face public scorn and live as an outcast. She wanted, too, and was determined to have, regardless of cost. And she was coldly unforgiving, as the Severances always were. She had said, "I shouldn't blame you," but she did and always would. Sometime, after the first shock had passed, Marin would tremble again for what Ethan and, more importantly, Vail felt about her, but at this moment she could see only Logan and the lack of love or even mercy in her homely, kind face.

The ride home had been a silent one, and the house was quiet, too. Belinda and Alida, frightened by the tension between their parents, went upstairs without a backward look. Mrs. Moon had laid out a cold supper, as she always did on Sunday night, and Marin and Vail sat down at the dining table but ignored the food. The terrible look that had been on his face when he read the letter was gone, but that meant nothing. She knew him so well. The angrier he was, the calmer and more rational he became. Better to have it all out in the open right now.

She said, "Do you think he's good enough for her?"

"I think he's flawed, like me, like all of us. He isn't the man I'd choose for Logan, but, Marin, it isn't my choice. Or yours. If you had given her the letter and told her what you thought about it . . . but you didn't. You let Ethan go into a loveless marriage and Logan go on never knowing how much he cared. It was a bad mistake, but I can understand it. There's something else, though, that I wonder about. When did Winfield's Bank pay off the company's debt that year? After the wedding, wasn't it?"

Oh, God. He saw what Ethan had never seen. Better to speak the truth, all of it, exactly as it happened, even if it made her look bad. She couldn't fool him if she wanted to, and she didn't want to.

In a low voice she said, "The night of Harry's funeral I stayed late at the office, feeling so down, like we were finally licked. We'd had bad times before, but Harry had been there then. I never knew how much I depended on him until he was gone." With chilling force it came back to her—the loneliness of the night, the bleak hopelessness, and then, out of the blue, the astonishing offer from Tyler. "I had a visitor that night. Tyler Winfield. How he found out I'll never know, but he had our debts figured to the penny and knew exactly who we owed. He offered to pay off all the creditors if I'd make him a silent partner and give Ethan a job. I could see what was eating at him. His precious Kitty was bound and determined to marry Ethan, and he couldn't stop her. He finally came up with another forty thousand, and we made the deal."

Vail said something under his breath, and she hurried on, the words tumbling out. "I know how it looks—like I handed Ethan over to Tyler without a thought. But I didn't. I showed Ethan the books, I told him to go over them carefully. It was all there for him to see, but he wouldn't bother. All he wanted then was Kitty and plenty of spending money. So I thought, if that's the way he wants it, all right. Then he did one of his typical flip-flops just before the wedding." She gripped her hands tightly. This was the hard part.

"It looks terrible, I know. If he'd left Kitty at the altar, Tyler wouldn't have come through with the money. Did I think of that? Of course I did. But it wasn't the reason I hid the letter. Before God, Vail, it wasn't. I would have burned it if that were the reason. I've never lied to you. I never would."

"Never?"

Her eyes fell away. "Not about anything important."

"Strange. I would have thought my son was important, yet you looked me straight in the eye and swore in that same convincing way that he was not mine. What has always puzzled me is why you've stuck to your story so tenaciously all these years. Why lie when I was going back into the war? Why keep up the pretense after we were married? I will never understand it."

She stared at him, for a moment confused. Why was he suddenly talking about Carey?

"You're wrong. I told you the truth. I can't—I can't help it if it wasn't what you wanted to hear."

He crushed out his cigar in his plate and looked at her with cool eyes. "I've always known Carey was my son. In a way you told me yourself."

She opened her mouth to contradict, but no words came. After a moment she got out, "When did I ever say such a thing?"

"The night he was born. Women in labor talk a lot. That's why midwives always know the best gossip in town."

"Did Dr. Cutter . . ."

"Joe said nothing. But he had help that night."

A night she had not thought of in years, a night of grinding pain and surpassing fear. A night when she had walked into the path of a wild stallion and Dr. Cutter had worked to save her and her child from her own foolhardiness. A woman had been there through it all, wiping her face, gripping her hands, speaking in a low, comforting voice, and listening while she babbled.

"Petra. How did she dare."

"She had the odd notion that I ought to know. At any rate she told me what I was certain of anyway. He looks like me, Marin."

"He looks like his grandfather."

"No, it's me he looks like and is like, as much as any son ever was like a father. It's always been a mystery to me why the whole world didn't see it. Perhaps they did and kindly turned a blind eye to what they shouldn't notice."

She pressed shaking hands to her face. Her skin felt hot, as with fever, and her body trembled. Caught out at this, of all times, in the biggest lie of her life. She had been caught out all these years without knowing it, and there was nothing to be said, no twisting and turning that could get her out of it. From out of her childhood James's words came back, the young, strong, black-haired James who had sat her on his knee and said, "You must not tell stories, chicken, for people who do become known for it. Then when you are telling the truth and most need to be believed, no one will believe you." James, farsighted, wiser than she knew, had tried to teach, to warn, to protect her from herself, and she had not understood him. Trust, he had said, was the thing. "Deal the cards faceup with those you love. You'll pay dearly someday if you don't."

And now someday had arrived. She had told the absolute truth about the letter, and Vail did not believe her. He believed she had kept that letter secret not out of love for Logan but for Tyler Winfield's money. She could protest and plead and tell her story again and again, and she might never convince him. But she had to try.

She took a deep, long breath and softly said what was so hard to say. "All right, I did lie. Carey is your child." With the words spoken at last, relief and release came over her. "Of course he's yours. Why do you think I love him so? But I had to lie from the beginning. Papa was so sick, and I couldn't talk to my mother. I thought I loved Stuart, so I got him to marry me."

"Why didn't you come to me?"

"I didn't know you, not really. I thought—I believed you didn't remember that night, and I was so scared of anyone's finding out." Her voice broke. "I thought I'd been such a bad person."

It was the one thing she could have said that would reach past the coolness to sting his conscience. He had been so completely in the wrong, and she, in her innocence and stubborn pride, had been so brave. "Couldn't you have told me after you were my wife? What difference would it have made to anyone but me?"

"I should have, I know that now, but . . . I started pretending before he was born, I made a vow to God never to tell. If anyone had known, if Stuart had guessed . . . it scares me, just remembering. If Carey found out, what would it do to him? What would he think of me? I wanted to tell you, but I couldn't." He said nothing, and his silence pushed her on. "I've told you the truth about the letter. It wasn't for Tyler's money. I only meant to save Logan heartbreak. Please, darling, do you believe me?"

In a quiet, almost meditative way he answered, "I don't know."

• • •

Early the next morning Ethan loaded Logan's trunk, her rocking chair, and the quilts she had made herself onto a rented wagon and, with her beside him on the high seat, drove down to the ferry, crossed to the Contra Costa, and began a new life in the adobe house that James had built for Rose so long ago.

Before they were halfway across the bay, the entire town not only knew that Ethan had deserted his wife and run off with Logan Severance but was also conversant with most of the details. It was scandal of such delicious proportions as to pale Marin's divorce and remarriage to insignificance.

For Marin the affair was a nightmare she lived through every day and every long, lonely night. On the surface all was normal between her and Vail. They ate together, slept in the same bed, talked of household matters and Denby's progress on the boilers. But beneath the superficial talk was a silence that Marin could not bear and did not know how to break through. He never mentioned the sore subject of Carey. He never referred to the letter, never reproached her for the heartache she had caused his sister or mentioned the gossip sweeping the town about Logan's new, unsanctified situation. He also never touched her except for a perfunctory kiss when he left the house and never talked about anything that was really on his mind. If only he would say something, even something that cut to the bone. Would he go on like this, so polite and distant, forever?

Two weeks after Ethan and Logan's departure Vail crossed the bay to visit them. Marin knew he was going, for he mentioned it casually at the breakfast table. All day she busied herself at home, listening for the sound of his horses's hoofs in the road, for his key in the lock, for his footsteps in the hall, afraid yet uncertain what she feared. How would he feel when he actually saw Logan living out there with a man not her husband? It was one thing to know it was going on, another to have it thrust in his face. And what would Logan say about her? Would she accuse Marin again of ruining her life and urge Vail to leave her? Oh, that was the great fear—that he would leave, walk out on her just as Ethan had walked out on Kitty.

He arrived home long after dark. Alida had gone with Belinda to a party. Marin had given the servants leave to retire, and the house was very quiet. She served his supper herself in the little dining room where they often ate alone and then sat down and tried to eat her own food. It was tasteless and flat. She must speak to Mrs. Moon. Vail would not want to come home if the food was bad and the servants sloppy and his wife a wicked deceiver.

He said, "The house is in remarkably good shape, considering how long it's stood empty. Your father built well."

"Yes, Little Mountain was well built. I must go over soon and see how they've fixed it up." He said nothing. "Do they have enough furniture? Papa's attic is filled with perfectly good pieces they could have." Oh, dear, she shouldn't have mentioned the attic and the variety of objects stored there.

"They have enough for now. I believe they prefer to buy their own things as soon as they can afford it."

A clean slate with nothing to remind them of the past. She could understand that. "Would you like dessert? There's cherry pie."

"No, thank you."

He put down his napkin and rose. She remained in her chair while he went across the hall into the small parlor and shut the door. Then, gathering her courage, she got up, thinking to follow him. The full, short sounds of a violin being tuned stopped her. After coming home from the war, he at first would not take his violin out of its case, since their marriage, though, she had enticed him into playing duets with her in the big parlor. She would sit at the rosewood piano that had been his gift so many years ago and he would stand beside her, his eyes on his instrument, a scowl of concentration on his face, coaxing his unpracticed fingers into doing as he wished, swearing at a difficult passage, laughing in triumph when he produced the sound he wanted. Those evenings had been so happy, had brought them so close that afterward they could go to bed and love each other with even greater joy.

But since the letter—life was now divided into time before and after the letter—since the letter he had not touched the violin, and she had not dared suggest it. Now, tonight, he had turned to it again. The melody was a silver line, soaring, sweet. Abruptly it halted in midpassage.

She waited for what seemed a long time. He must have given it up. She crossed the hall and opened the door, driven by need, not knowing what she was going to say. It was the same parlor where once she had caught Petra Victoria lounging in a lace negligee while Vail played. She did not like this room.

The violin lay on the table. He was standing by the hearth, staring into a fire that was almost out.

"Vail?" She closed the door and moved hesitantly toward him. A bright orange coal fell through the grate and flared in the gray ashes, and the flickering light and shadow made his face seem very grim.

She came closer. "Vail, please talk to me." And then in a nervous tumble of words, "Oh, sweetheart, I can't bear to have things like this between us, so polite and empty. Call me anything you like, but please don't shut me out. I know . . ." She rubbed her hand across her cheek. She must not cry. "I know what I did was bad. I should have given that letter to Logan and let her decide. All—all I can do is say I'm sorry and I'll never do such a thing again. Sometimes I'm not quite as straightforward as I should be—I know it—but I am trying so hard to be better." Uncertainly she touched his sleeve, her voice dark with pleading. "Vail, I love you so. I've loved you and waited for you so long. Please, darling, can't you forgive me?"

Still he did not look at her, but he reached out and pulled her to him. The cloth of his coat was smooth against her cheek, the muscle beneath it hard. She could hear the beat of his heart, hear her own breath, ragged with anxiety. He lifted her chin and looked into her eyes so long, so searchingly that she knew every cranny of her mind, every hidden, secret thought must be plain for him to see. Then he bent and kissed her lightly, and she reached up and touched his face. With that brush of her fingers his arms went around her, her head tilted back, and her lips began to part under his as the old, sweet drowning sensation swept her. His body trembled against hers, his hands dug into her flesh; he seemed to have forgotten how little she was, and his arms hurt her, she could scarcely breathe. There was desperation in his hands and lips, as if he were trying frantically to hold on to something of great value, something that might slip away. She was shaking with exultation. He loved her in spite of what she had done. He still needed her, wanted her, could not do without her.

The grip of his hands eased. He drew back and smiled at her, the familiar, loving, tender smile. Tears of relief and happiness spilled down her face, and he held her in a quieting, comforting way and rested his cheek on her hair. Inside her the last knot of fear dissolved, for she was welcome once more in his arms. She could not see his eyes, thoughtful, faintly sad, gazing down into the last embers of the fire.

Chapter 52

The maiden voyage of the beautiful new steamer *Princess* was scheduled for Saturday afternoon, and Michael would be making the trip up to Sacramento City as the representative of Taggart Boiler Works. On Saturday morning a party was held aboard the glistening new paddle wheeler. Champagne and a buffet lunch were served to the city's leaders and those most closely connected with the building of the *Princess*, followed by a tour of the boat.

"It's a floating palace," William Purcell announced as he ushered the awed guests into the ornate, three-hundred-fifty-foot saloon. Sunlight shot through the stained-glass skylights and caused rainbows of color to dance on the white walls and the velvety Brussels carpet and the faces of people wandering about the immense cabin. In the dining room fine silver and English china made to order for the *Princess* rested on snowy linen. There was even a barbershop and a tobacconist's shop for the gentlemen. As the guests were led below, the boat's great bell bonged resonantly, and William Purcell remarked that it had been specially cast and weighed three thousand pounds.

Below decks were the engines, built for the high pressure to be produced by the eight Burwell boilers. *Eight* boilers, Mr. Purcell emphasized. There was no other eight-boiler steamer on the river. A murmur ran through the spectators as they craned to see. The machinery had been artfully draped so as to make it seem as nonutilitarian as possible, but those gentlemen with an eye for such things stated that it looked most impressive.

Marin agreed. The boilers were especially handsome, so pristine, so virginal, yet promising such strength and power. She was in an excellent mood this morning. Now that the bad feeling between her and Vail had been straightened out, the whole world looked newly polished, and adding to her sense of well-being was the set-to with Tyler Winfield last night, the first no-holds-barred shouting match she'd ever had with him. Always in the past he had remained suave and glib even when bitterly angry, hiding, always hiding his real thoughts behind a winning smile and a tongue as smooth as butter. But last night his mood had been vicious when he came to the office, for he had just left Kitty in a state of hysterics so extreme that she had required Dr. Anderson and sedation—Tyler would not allow Dr. Towle in the house because he was married to a Gentry.

Kitty had alternated between hysteria and cold, storming rage ever since Ethan ran off with that middle-aged spinster woman, and Tyler could not see where it would end. His days were spent watching his daughter suffer the snickers of her friends; he passed the sleepless nights inventing painful afflictions for the Gentry-Severance clan. Since it was the way his mind worked and where his power lay, he dreamed mostly of financial destruction that would leave them in squalid poverty, but often, especially in the weary hours toward morning, he contemplated various multilating physical tortures and seriously considered murder if it could be done without implicating him. It was not that he wanted Ethan to come back to Kitty; she was once more in the bosom of her family where she belonged, and must never go away again. But the present situation was intolerable. The whole town was on its ear at the spectacle of a man abandoning a wife who had everything to recommend her—youth, beauty, charm, and a rich, accommodating father—for a hag like Logan Severance, and setting up housekeeping with her across the bay in monstrous, brazen disregard of God and society. It was insult beyond insult and must be avenged.

In this state of quivering fury he had come to see Marin at her request last night, and she had informed him that all monies owed by Gentry and Callendar would be paid to him on Monday next and he would then have no further interest in the company. He had looked into her triumphant eyes and thought how pleasurable it would be to put his hands around her white throat and squeeze and squeeze . . . It was those thrice-damned boilers, that's what it was. They had proven successful, and payment from the Golden West Steamship Co. would be forthcoming as soon as the *Princess* sailed. It meant that this scheming unregenerate woman, who obviously felt no shame for the atrocities of her perverted brother, had beaten him at last. Tyler's investment in Gentry and Callendar had been in the beginning no more than a means of controlling Ethan and in that regard had been spectacularly unsuccessful, but his acquisitive nature was such that he had come to desire the company for its own sake. And now that this thing had happened to Kitty and he needed it as an instrument of vengeance, it was being torn away from him.

"It shall not be!" he had shrieked, almost jumping up and down in frustrated rage. "You unnatural woman, how dare you speak to me so when I have thrown away money in order to help you . . . when I have worked unselfishly for the good of all, never thinking of my own interests. Your piddling company will sink like a stone without me behind it!"

"Mr. Winfield," Marin replied with a brilliant smile, "don't you lose a wink of sleep over our problems. We will manage without you somehow," and she had handed him his hat.

He looked at it as if he'd never seen the thing before. In a low, harsh snarl he ground out, "I warn you, my reach is long. You will find yourself beset on every side in ways you never dreamed of. I will not rest until you and your ilk are destroyed."

For one bad moment unreasoning fear gripped her. Never underestimate the strength of your enemy, some wise general had said; he might have added, Never underestimate your enemy's hatred and desire to harm. Winfield's Bank was small, but who knew what connections he had with other businesses, who knew where his tentacles reached?

The little office where they stood glaring at each other had been recently swept out by the janitor, and dust particles still floated in the air. A mote tickled Tyler's thin nostril. His partrician nose wrinkled, his upper lip quivered, he threw back his head and sneezed. Marin's fear dissolved in an explosion of inner laughter. Nothing could make a man look more foolish than a sneeze. There he stood in his fury, no all-powerful nemesis but only a meager, narrow man with a meager, narrow mind, shaking his fist at fate and promising revenge. Well, hadn't she done the same herself when life had gone against her, and much good it had done. Life rattled on its uncaring, unfair way, despite her ragings. And so it would with Tyler.

He was wiping his nose with a large, white handkerchief and muttering, "Beg pardon, dear ma'am," out of incongruously polite habit.

In the same spirit she replied, "Not at all," while her mind leaped ahead. He had no power over her for he had no influence with the Golden West Steamship Co. If he could have prevented it, the contract for the boilers would never have been signed in the first place. Every cent Vail had in the world had been risked to back this venture, and the risk had paid off. Concealing both anger and laughter, she said, "I would prefer we part friends, Mr. Winfield, but if that is not to be, please deliver any future threats to my husband. He will know how to deal with them," and she had walked out and left him burning in the quiet, dusty room.

All in all, it had been a first-rate set-to, and she was still exhilarated by it as she followed William Purcell on his tour of the magnificent new steamer. Vail and Michael toasted each other with champagne and agreed that the *Princess* was a marvel, and then the three of them climbed to the promenade deck as high above them the silver whistle tooted experimentally. The whistle was custom-made and had seven notes so that a melody could be played and then a rich chord struck loud enough to tell the entire town that the *Princess* was coming. Marin inhaled the crisp, salty-sweet air. Outward, just beyond the Golden Gate, heavy fog lay piled in great gray billows, but within the shelter of the bay a blue sky prevailed and the water was as sparkling as a jeweler's bag of diamonds. Oh, it was a grand boat and a grand day!

Only one nagging hurt marred her happiness a little. This morning on their way to the wharf she and Vail had passed Ethan on the street. She had not seen him since the awful moment when he had looked at her and said in a puzzled way, "You promised to give it to her," and then had led Logan out of the room. She wanted to talk to him and beg forgiveness, hard as that would be. She wasn't good at humbling herself, but she would do it for the love she bore all those involved. At the sight of Ethan's silver-gray head she had readied a smile, but he had averted his eyes and walked past as if he didn't know her. The rejection was as sharp as a slap in the face. Discomfited, she glanced at Vail, but he was looking ahead toward the waterfront and seemed not to have noticed. As he often did, he had forgotten her shorter stride, and she had to hurry to keep up with him.

Gradually the flush of humiliation faded from her face. Ethan was still mad at her, but surely he would get over it. He was her brother and they had always understood each other—and, besides, he had made plenty of mistakes in his time. His faults were quite as numerous as hers. She wished she could talk it over with Vail. His reassurance would shore her up. But better not. In spite of the warmth of their reconciliation, this one matter was still tender and had to be handled gently. Later on, when the wound was completely healed, she would go over to Little Mountain. It would be good to see what Ethan was doing with the ranch. Horses were what he loved and what he knew, as Logan had said, and he would probably make a great success of the business.

In this optimistic frame of mind she hugged Michael, made him promise to come to see her the moment he was back from his trip, and descended the *Princess*'s gangplank with Vail. On the wharf they parted. Vail had something technical to talk over with Denby, he said, and she was to wait for him at the office.

She was at her desk toting up figures on a long bill of lading when she heard Vail's footsteps on the stairs. Strange how she knew instantly, with the first creak of the bottom step, that it was Vail. He moved so lightly and swiftly, so differently from other men. His voice was soft as he spoke to the clerks in the next room, and when he walked into her private office and shut the door she felt the delicious shock of pleasure that always came to her when she looked at him. It was as though raw energy passed from him to her, electric, breathtaking, exciting her as nothing else could.

She smiled in welcome. "I'll be through here in just a minute. Did you and Denby get your business finished?"

"Just about. There is one problem." He sat on the edge of the desk looking singularly untroubled. "Denby's a trifle worried about the amount of pressure the boilers will take. He wants the captain to keep it under a hundred and thirty today."

She swiveled around in her chair. "But the specifications say a hundred to a hundred and sixty-five pounds."

"The specifications give a theoretical maximum, but these boilers have only two rows of four-inch tubes. The rest are reduced to just under two inches to lower the weight. For safety's sake Denby wants the pressure kept low on the shakedown cruise."

"Pooh. Denby's nervous, that's all."

"Maybe. All the same we'll warn the captain to stay below a hundred and thirty pounds' working pressure. There are rumors all over town that the *Western Belle* is going to challenge for a race today."

"Racing's forbidden. All the owners have agreed to it."

"Uh-huh. Odds are five to one on the *Western Belle*."

Five to one. That meant that in spite of the glamour of the *Princess* the canniest gamblers in town were betting against the new design of the Burwell boilers. If those boilers failed to deliver on the maiden voyage, with all eyes on the *Princess* and money riding on her success or failure, no other steamship company would touch them.

"Vail, we mustn't say a word to the captain or anybody else. There isn't another boiler on the market that can go above a hundred and fifty pounds. We can offer at least fifteen pounds more, and I'll bet we could go up to two hundred with no risk. Our whole selling point is speed. If we don't have that, we have nothing the old line boilers don't have."

"Even so, we can't be a party to an explosion."

"Very noble of you, considering that every dollar you own is tied up in the Taggart Works. Do you want to be wiped out?"

"No, and I don't think I will be." He grinned. "That's how I can be so noble. Really, it's not as great a gamble as you think. All Captain Hadley has to do is let it be known that he refuses to race, in accordance with company policy. The boilers will prove themselves in time."

She got up, slamming her fist into her palm in agitation. "I won't agree to it. Speed and safety are the captain's responsibility—let him use his own judgment. You're wrong about what it would do to us if those boilers don't perform. If the *Princess* comes dragging into Sacramento City behind the *Western Belle,* nobody's going to listen to our explanations. The word will be out that our boilers are no good, and we'll go bankrupt."

An odd look came into his eyes. "You're not thinking clearly. Doesn't it occur to you that it would do a good deal worse for our business if the boilers did explode? Who would buy them then? And there is one other consideration. Have you ever seen what happens to people when a boiler blows? Do you know what they look like when they've been skinned alive by steam?"

His tone was one of casual inquiry, yet she felt a sudden need to explain. "Naturally I don't want anything like that to happen. I just don't believe there's any danger."

"Denby does."

She turned to the window and looked blindly into the street. Perhaps he was right and she was wrong, but she was so scared that this new venture would fail, so scared of what Tyler would do if he wasn't paid off. Yet what was all of that against the speculation in Vail's eyes when he looked at her?

From the direction of the wharves a horseman pounded into town, slapping his lathered horse with his sombrero and scattering chickens pecking in the street. Several endangered pedestrians shouted and shook their fists after him, but Marin paid the commotion outside no heed. Against all her instincts she said, "Whatever you say, Vail. If Denby thinks it's a risk, then of course we can't take it. You go tell the captain now. There's still time."

There was a loud thump of feet on the stairs and a very brief discussion in the outer office. The door burst open, and a short, wide-built Mexican with heavy thigh muscles swelling under his tight leather pants gasped, "Your pardon, Señor Severance. I look everywhere for you!"

"Why, Cosme, come in," Marin said in surprise. She had not seen James's old foreman in years. The last she had heard was that he was working at Longridge.

"Good afternoon, Miss Marin. *Gracias.*" He took a step into the room, his hat held politely against his chest, and smoothed down his dusty black hair. "Señor, I come from Longridge, where there is very bad trouble. Miss Glenna says for you to come quick."

"What trouble, Cosme? You know my father won't allow me on the place."

Cosme lowered his head. "Ah, señor, he will not say nothing. A bandit robbed the safe, and your father, he is lying there with his face shot off. He is dead, señor."

Marin drew an involuntary breath, unable to absorb the words. Malcolm dead? Impossible. She looked at Vail. He did not appear to believe it, either.

"Dead?" he said. "Father?" He turned away.

Without moving his feet, Cosme leaned to one side and peered at him. "I am very sorry to bring such news, señor, but Miss Glenna . . ."

"How is Miss Glenna?"

"Ah, she is very strong, that one, but a little upset and crying, as is proper. I am very sorry about your father, señor. He was a hard man, but I honor him as one who treated me with respect."

"Thank you, Cosme. Marin, you'll have to talk to Captain Hadley. Will you do that for me?"

"Of course, darling. I'll tell him." She went up on tiptoe to kiss his cheek. "Send a message if you need me."

She watched him go, thinking that Cosme must be mistaken. The lord of Longridge, that hard-hearted, pigheaded man. How inconceivable that he could be dead, like any other mortal. From the look that had been on Vail's face, she knew he found it inconceivable, too.

Chapter 53

The maids and the cook, frightened, subdued, were huddled in the kitchen, all except Teresa, who opened the door, curtsied, and scuttled away. Glenna came toward him, her hands held out in a beseeching gesture. Her eyes were protuberant with shock, her face was paper white.

She clutched his lapels. "Oh, Vail, how can it be? What am I to do?"

Gently he detached her hands. "Where is he?"

"In the—the office. I can't go back in there." She shuddered and squeezed her eyes shut.

"You don't have to. Sit down and wait for me here."

The ranch office was a room between Malcolm's library and the front parlor, a large room, for Malcolm had considered it the nerve center of the ranch and spent most of his time in it when he was not on horseback. Ledgers filled three long shelves, and against the wall behind the big walnut desk stood the safe. It was a fireproof Chatwood safe made of high-carbon steel two inches thick, with a lock of the latest design. It stood open, unlocked with the key Malcolm kept on his watch chain, and was empty of all but a few letters. He lay on the floor beside the desk, his arms flung out. Blood had trickled into his thick, white hair and was congealing there. Of his face only the broad chin was distinguishable; the rest was a bloody pulp.

When Vail came back into the parlor, Glenna asked with a quaver, "He is dead?"

"Yes." He picked up her wrist and held it. "Is the liquor still kept in the dining room cabinet?"

"Liquor? Oh, yes. I have the key about me somewhere . . ." She fumbled vaguely at her waist. "Here it is."

He unloosed the ring of household keys from her belt and went into the quiet dining room, its table already set for supper. In a moment he came back with a small glass. "Drink this. It will help."

She shook her head. "I do not drink spirits."

"Of course not. This is for medicinal purposes. It will have a calming effect on your nerves."

"It will? Then I suppose it's all right . . ." She took a swallow, gasped, and coughed violently into her handkerchief.

Vail sat beside her while she wiped her eyes and blew her nose. When she was done, he said, "Can you tell me how it happened?"

She pushed back the hair that hung loose on her forehead. "Your father was working in his office—he does that often in the afternoon. I was resting in the bedroom, the front bedroom upstairs. I heard a shot and came running down. I called to him, and when he didn't answer, I went into the office. He was . . . he was . . ." Her stomach heaved, and she pressed both hands against her mouth.

"A little more brandy," Vail held the glass to her lips.

She took a sip and grimaced. "Thank you. I'm better now."

"Did you see anyone, hear anything?"

"I was—I was paralyzed. I just stood there. Then I heard the sound of a horse being ridden away. I ran to the window and saw a rider disappearing into the trees down by the meadow. I called to Teresa, I told her to get the men and chase him, but everyone was gone. I forgot that today they were taking cattle to the wharf for shipment. You know, the best hotels in the city use our beef, and they slaughter it fresh over there."

"Yes, I thought I tasted Longridge pot roast the last time I ate at the Oriental Hotel."

"Did you really?" Glenna said uncertainly, confused by the gleam in his eyes. Surely he wasn't joking at a time like this, but with him you never could tell.

"Do you mind if I talk to Teresa?" He was already on his feet and walking out the door. She answered, "Why, no, of course not," to an empty room.

In a little while he was back. He sat down beside her, and she wished he would take her hand again and hold it in that comforting way, but he did not. He asked, "Was there much money in the safe?"

"I don't know exactly. Mr. Severance was not forthcoming about his business affairs, but we have had two recent sales of beef, so I should guess perhaps ten thousand dollars."

"In coin?"

"Mostly, I'm sure. Mr. Severance distrusted paper money."

"A heavy load for a man on the run. Have you notified the sheriff?"

She looked at him blankly. "No. Should I have?"

"You must. There's been a robbery and a murder."

"Murder," she breathed. "Yes, I see. We must call the sheriff."

"Glenna, would you tell me one thing more?"

"If I can."

"Why did you send for me instead of Stuart?"

Slowly she raised her eyes. "Because it seemed indecent—unfair—to Mr. Severance to have Stuart here after . . . after . . . Well, you do understand, don't you? Then, too, I believed you could handle the situation better."

Stuart arrived before the sheriff, leaving his hotel the moment he got Vail's summons. He stood in Malcolm's office, looking down at the remains of his father, with horror on his face.

"Let's get out of here," he said in a suffocated voice, and they walked out onto the porch together.

Stuart sat down heavily on the top step. Vail leaned against the porch railing and gazed down toward the meadow. It was after ten o'clock and a thin moon hanging low on the horizon gave light enough to outline the woods on the far side of the dark stretch of grass, the woods Malcolm's killer had fled through.

Stuart said, "When I was a child, I thought he was the strongest, grandest man in the world. More than anything I wanted to be like him." He clasped his hands between his knees and lowered his head. "Later on, when I found out I couldn't be, I just wanted him to approve of me. You know?"

Vail sat down beside him. "I know."

They sat for a time in silence. Stuart made a low, disgusted sound and shook his head. "Jesus, what I did to him. It must be the worst thing a son ever did to a father."

"I doubt that. We both have regrets, but there's one comfort. If you or I had died first, he would have had plenty to regret."

"I never gave Glenna a thought in the old days, never even saw how attractive she was. We were just sitting and drinking coffee together one evening, and one minute we were talking about Father and family matters, and the next minute we were in bed. I never meant it to happen. I wasn't even sure how it did happen. Can you believe that?"

"I can believe it."

"He never forgave me. I had this idea that someday after a long time had passed he would come around and we'd be friends again. Now it will never happen. I can't believe he's gone."

"I know what you mean. He ought to come storming through the door about now, full of righteous anger, and tell me what a rotten son I am. I had a vague hope about us getting together again, just like you—though I didn't know it until tonight—but it was a foolish hope. His mind was set, and he never would have changed."

Stuart fished a cigar from his inside pocket, struck a match on the step, and drew deeply until the cigar tip glowed. He tossed the match away and blew a lungful of smoke into the dark. "How are things with you and Marin?"

"Fine."

"Good, good. You think I ought to talk to Teresa, huh?"

"I think her story completes the picture. Hear what she has to say before the sheriff gets here and starts tromping over the place."

Teresa was in the kitchen with the other servants. The night was warm, but she huddled in a chair close to the stove, her face solemn and strained. Her dark eyes rolled when Vail asked her to repeat the events of the afternoon to Stuart, but she was trained to obedience and so tried her best to comply.

"I was by myself, sewing right here in the kitchen. Miss Glenna says the sheets mus' be finished by tomorrow, an' I still 'ave three to stitch." She cast a worried eye at the heap of linen on the kitchen table. "Don' see how I'm gonna get them finished tonight."

"Tell Señor Stuart what you heard."

Teresa's smooth brow wrinkled in concentration. "There was a boom, very loud. I think, 'The men are gone. Who is hunting?' Then I hear 'Malcolm, Malcolm!' but still I don' pay attention because I think they are at it again. She always yells like that when he hits her."

Stuart's head snapped up. "He hit her?"

"Oh, yes, señor. W'enever she did not please him, he scolded her with the words of God and said she is a bad woman, and sometimes w'en he is very angry he hit her."

"You saw this with your own eyes?"

"No, señor. But I hear them yelling an' him hitting an' each time he hit her she screams. One time he threw her against the wall, and she is crying and saying, 'Oh, Malcolm, Malcolm, you are too cruel!' I saw the bruises afterward w'en I was hooking up her dress, big purple bruises on her back an' her legs—he don' ever hit her face."

"When did you leave the kitchen?" Stuart asked in a low voice.

"She calls, 'Teresa, come quick, the *patrón* is hurt!' So I come running, an' she says, 'He took the money, he is escaping. Get help, get the men!' I say 'They are all gone, Miss Glenna,' an' she says, 'Oh, God, they are,' an' falls down in a swoon."

Stuart seemed past further inquiry, so Vail asked, "Did the man ride past the kitchen?"

"No, señor, he wen' the front way, down the hill to the woods. I could not hear him way back here, but Miss Glenna could."

Malcolm's house was silent. His body had been removed by the undertaker. The women servants were asleep in their beds after an all-night vigil. The vaqueros were clustered in the bunkhouse beyond the corral, talking quietly, their normal boisterousness tempered by the *patrón's* death and the questions of the sheriff. The sheriff himself, portly, red-faced, and running for reelection in the fall, had departed with his deputy shortly before dawn after giving Glenna his oath that he would soon locate and hang the culprit. Vail returned to town.

Stuart and Glenna sat at the kitchen table drinking freshly brewed coffee. The sheets Teresa had been unable to finish were folded neatly and stacked on a chair.

In the morning light Glenna looked haggard. Her eyes were red-rimmed from weeping, and fatigue caused her face to sag.

Stuart said, "Go to bed, Glenna, before you fall down. You must get some rest."

"I'm not tired, dearest, and how can I rest? I keep thinking, if only I had not taken a nap yesterday, if only I'd been downstairs, I might have frightened that man away."

"More likely you'd be dead, too. You must not blame yourself."

She poured a second cup for each of them. "I want Mr. Daniels to preach the funeral. Mr. Severance had a very high opinion of his sermons. The stone should match your mother's. That would be right, don't you think?"

"It's very generous of you. I'll order it today." He coughed to clear his throat. "However, I am embarrassed for funds at present, and they'll want a deposit."

Glenna set down her cup. "You shall have the cash before you leave. It will all come out of the estate. And, dearest, never again will you lack anything money can buy."

Stuart looked down at his large hands. "The money. It occurred to me, but I feel guilty as hell for even thinking of such things at a time like this. Half to you and half to me, he told me once, but I expect nothing. I assume he destroyed that will after . . ."

"I assume so, for I could not find it anywhere. However, there was an earlier will, written during the war, after you were promoted to general and your prospects were so promising. He left a small bequest to you and to each of the grandchildren, even Alida, but the bulk of the estate to me. I still have that will."

"You have? Good Lord, I would expect him to have destroyed that, too."

"One might think so, but in fact I have it."

Stuart leaned back in his chair, stunned by this information. Slowly he said, "You take my breath away."

"Indeed. So you see, dearest, you have no worries. Anything you need will be yours." Glenna's voice lifted and became brisk. "For the present you are to stay in the city, but after a decent interval—six months is long enough—we will be married. I plan to keep Cosme. He is an excellent man, don't you agree?"

"Excellent." Stuart's mind was whirling. He had come to terms with himself regarding the divorce from Marin when he finally recognized that it had been a blessing, well disguised. The titters of the town had been almost as hard to bear as the loss of political office, and for a while his jealousy of Vail had known no bounds, but as time passed, he found that bachelorhood was a splendid way to live. Every day he enjoyed it more. He went where, as, and when he pleased, with explanations to no one, and was even engaged in a small business venture that he hoped one day would put him in comfortable circumstances. He had come to believe that being married to a driving woman was the worst fate that could befall a man, far worse than penury or public humiliation. Marriage to anyone was the last thing in his mind. Glenna, despite a few flaws, was a fine woman, and he still admired her, but during the past months of freedom he had come to wonder if his feeling for her hadn't been admiration and sheer physical attraction rather than the profound, committed love a man should feel when contemplating marriage. He didn't want to make the same mistake he'd made with Marin.

"Dear Glenna," he said, and stopped. How to make his attitude clear without wounding her? "Dear Glenna, our love was beautiful, and it will remain one of the treasures of my life. My regard for you as a woman of honor and probity is of the highest. However, in all honesty I must tell you that I do not plan to marry again for a long time, if ever. I have tasted the dregs of bitterness and have struggled to my feet again, but I am still groping, still searching. I do not plan to marry."

"My foot," said Glenna quietly. She rose and leaned her hands on the table. Her face above him was a stranger's face. "We will marry in six months. You will run again for senator with my backing, and you will win." She slid into the chair next to him, put a hand over her eyes, and sighed deeply. When she took her hand away, the stranger was gone. Her eyes were tear-filled. "Oh, my dearest, this has been a dreadful time. I hardly know where I am. What am I to do with this enormous ranch, how can I manage Cosme and all those men out in the bunkhouse? Mr. Severance has provided generously for me, but how to handle the money, the investments, the land? He taught me nothing about business. How can I manage without a man to guide me?"

It was true, all true, and he hated to see her cry. Her hand was so small and white, her touch brought back so many memories. What a woman she was to have endured these past hideous hours with such steadiness. She was entitled to speak some sharp words. A lesser woman would have lost her composure long ago.

Yet even as he embraced her a question that had troubled him earlier crawled from a shadowy recess of his mind. Though he quickly buried it, he knew it would abide, monstrous, obsessing, vile, ready to rise up and torment him to the end of his days.

Chapter 54

High above Marin the *Princess*'s melodious silver whistle was singing and her bell clanging urgently. Black smoke rolled from towering smokestacks, and the boat shivered with restrained energy; steam for the powerful, high-pressure engines was building up in readiness for a swift departure. Passengers crowded the rail, waving hats and handkerchiefs to friends on the wharf. A wedding party swept up the gangplank; below, a friend called out a teasing remark, and the groom laughed, and kissed his bride, who put up her hands to cover her blushes and then crinkled her turned-up nose and giggled. A group of circus performers had boarded earlier and were clustered together at the bow, drawing stares from everyone.

There were soberly dressed men, too, traveling to Sacramento City on business, and many had their families with them. Children, excited almost beyond endurance by the marvelous boat, raced across the deck and climbed onto the rail for a view of the dock and the other boats. A little girl stood on the middle rung and hung precariously far out over the water. Her mother, a harassed-looking woman with a baby in her arms, dragged the child back and scolded her. There were other passengers, too. Thirty-five Chinese laborers had been brought on board early in the afternoon and were stowed discreetly out of sight in the hold, along with the circus animals.

Marin started up the gangplank, jostled by hurrying, late-arriving passengers, her blood stirring with the excitement around her. I wish I were going, she thought, and her mind turned back to another four o'clock sailing so many years ago. Bells had been pealing then, and whistles shrieking. Somewhere a calliope had tootled merrily, brass bands had played then as they were playing now, and she and Vail had sailed off up the Sacramento in search of Sophy and discovered so much more in the process. How young the two of them had been, and how many years had been wasted before they finally came together. If she had those years back, how differently she would live them. But it was no use to mourn the past. She must snatch the present and make it the best it could be.

She looked up. Far above her in the wheelhouse Captain William Hadley was looking down benevolently on his mass of passengers and his crew scurrying about their last-minute tasks. He saluted his wife and three children standing on the hurricane deck, and his eldest son and namesake almost burst with pride and looked around to see if everyone realized that he was the captain's son. Marin pushed forward toward the stairs. Even here on the lower deck she could see the gleaming gold braid on the captain's uniform. He seemed to look directly at her, and she waved, but his eyes moved on. In this throng she was indistinguishable from the passengers. She fought her way up the stairs, and as she gained the hurricane deck and started toward the steps leading to the wheelhouse, she was stopped by the second officer.

"Your pardon, ma'am. You can't go up there."

"Sir, my husband and I own the works that made the boilers for the *Princess*. I must speak to the captain."

"Oh? Where is your husband?" he asked, looking past her.

She smothered exasperation. So often she had to fight past the infuriating masculine belief that only a man could deal with business affairs. She said, "He was called away on a family matter, but I am his representative. Please, it's essential that I speak to the captain before you sail."

"I'm sorry, you should have come earlier. No one is allowed in the wheelhouse at sailing time, but I'm sure Captain Hadley will be pleased to have you at his table at dinner." He touched his hat, closed and locked the little gate that kept the unanointed away from the wheelhouse, and started up the steps.

"Wait!" Marin cried. The idiot with his grand uniform and shiny brass buttons thought she was just another silly society matron trading on her husband's position to gain the company of the captain. Oh, for the muscular strength of a man. She would burst through that gate, shove that arrogant sailor aside, and bull her way up to the captain as Vail would do, as any man would do. But as it was she had to use other means. "Please," she called after him, "you don't understand. It's about the boilers . . ." Everyone was looking at her. She couldn't stand down here and shout loud enough to be heard over the whistle and bell that the marvelous new *Princess*'s boilers had better be kept at low pressure or they might explode. That would empty the boat in a hurry.

"Marin, honey, what are you doing here?"

She spun around. "Oh, Michael, I never was so glad to see anybody. Will you make that fool open the gate and let me up there? I've got to see the captain before the boat sails."

Michael laughed. "So it's the captain you're after. And here I hoped you'd got tired of Vail and wanted to run away with me."

"Don't tease, Michael, I have a problem." She lowered her voice. "Denby wants the pressure held to no more than a hundred and thirty until we see how the boilers perform. He thinks there might be some danger of explosion."

"Don't say that word." He glanced around hastily, herded her away from the nearest bystanders and whispered furiously, "What's the matter with Denby? Those boilers have been tested a dozen times. What's he want to do, ruin us?"

"He's careful, that's all, and he's probably right. Vail wants the captain told that there can't be any racing on this trip."

"Oh, does he? Why didn't he come here and do it himself then?"

Her eyes dropped. "He got a message less than an hour ago from Glenna. They had a robbery out at Longridge and Malcolm was shot. He's dead, Michael. Vail went over to do—whatever has to be done."

His face went blank with disbelief. "Shocking," he said after a moment of thought. "Was Vail upset?"

"Yes, he was. Malcolm was his father, and I guess he can't help feeling something."

"Truth to tell, all I feel is relief. Glenna's had a hard time with the old bastard the last year or so. I shouldn't say it, but I'm glad she's free. Maybe I ought not to leave town, maybe I ought to go see her."

"You've got to go, you're the company's representative. The funeral won't be held for two or three days, and you'll be back by then. Vail will look out for Glenna."

"I know it, but I ought to be there, too. I'm her brother, all she's got left in the world."

How strange it was, Marin thought. After the vicissitudes of their lives and in spite of the different paths they had taken, Glenna and Michael were close in spirit, whereas she and Ethan . . . She pushed the thought away. "You can't let us down. Glenna will be fine, I promise."

The final bell rang, and on the upper deck the first mate blared through the bullhorn, "All ashore who're goin' ashore!"

Michael put his arm around her. "You're right. I have to go. And you'd better get off quick or you will be riding up river with me." He kissed her cheek. "I'll tell the captain no racing, though it hurts my soul. I had fifty bucks on the *Princess*."

Together they hurried downstairs, and Michael hoisted her onto the gangplank just before it was drawn up. She lifted her skirt and ran down; from the wharf she turned and looked upward. Michael was at the rail, waving his hat. She waved back and climbed onto a barrel for a better view.

A cheer went up as the enormous paddle wheel began to move. Water hissed as the wheel buckets dipped and scooped, water gushed down the wheel, leaving a frothy trail as the boat backed from the wharf. Nearby, other steamers were moving from their moorings, but most eyes were on the *Princess*. For all her size she backed and turned more quickly than the older, clumsier boats and she was away, steaming northward toward San Pablo Bay with flags fluttering proudly, black smoke billowing from her twin smokestacks and thinning into gray wisps in the fine breeze, the melody of her whistle drifting back over the water, the gilt letters that spelled out *Princess* glistening in the light of the lowering sun.

Like a swan sailing the smooth surface of a lake, its power disguised by its grace, the great white boat slipped past the islands of Suisun Bay and entered the delta region, where the Sacramento and San Joaquin rivers converged and countless marshy islands and bayous floated in the hazy evening light. The other steamers had not been sighted since San Pablo Bay except for the *Western Belle*, which dropped from view only when the *Princess* rounded a curve and reappeared moments later in ungainly but determined pursuit. The *Western Belle* was steaming under high pressure; thick smoke poured from her stacks, and fiery sparks blasted upward with each increase in power demanded by her captain.

To First Officer Morton the sight was a constant irritant, and twice he suggested that the *Princess* order up more steam. The cheeky challenge put forth by the captain of the other boat incensed him—and, besides, he had money down with a betting parlor. But Captain Hadley had not a touch of the bellicose about him. Unlike some captains, who prided themselves on their two-fisted toughness, he was a conservative, steady man with a profound awareness of his responsibilities to his passengers and his company—a difficult man to taunt. It was the reason he was the senior captain of the Golden West's fleet and the reason he had been entrusted with its newest and grandest steamer. He agreed completely with his company's no-racing policy. Below, the band was playing for dancing, and couples were strolling hand in hand on the deck. Dinner had been served, and the monogrammed silver and china had been washed and stowed in locked cabinets. He sent the first officer for his son, Billy.

The *Princess* kept a neat distance ahead of the *Western Belle*, adding a bit of speed whenever the gap narrowed, never allowing the other boat nearer than a mile, while Captain Hadley explained the instruments to his son and allowed him to briefly touch the wheel.

Billy, breathing hard, relinquished that marvelous wheel and looked downriver. "Father, they're awfully close on us."

"They won't catch us, son. Our fine lady is designed to move through the water with less resistance than that old tub. We can leave her standing still anytime we choose, but"—he winked, "we don't choose, do we?"

The *Western Belle*, snorting like a stertorous bull, was less than half a mile away, and passengers on the decks below were crowded at the rail, hurling imprecations at their pursuer and looking upward at the wheelhouse. Like Michael and the first officer, most of the men aboard had money down on the *Princess*.

Captain Hadley ordered more steam, the steady rhythm of the engines increased slightly, and the *Princess* moved ahead.

First Officer Morton laughed exultantly, but in the next ten minutes the gap closed again, and he shouted, "Sir, we're well under our safety margin. Let's give 'em a look at our stern!"

The captain smiled, but shook his head. "Let them come up if they're fool enough to try. Look at their stacks." Flame was belching from the *Western Belle*'s twin smokestacks, illumining her deck. She came up beside the *Princess*, chugging furiously, her boilers red-hot, and from the bridge her captain shouted, "All show and no go!" as his boat edged ahead.

Captain Hadley called down to the engine room for more steam, and Billy, his eyes shining, cried, "Oh, Father, are we going to race them?"

"No, son. Just pull out in front a tad. See that bend of the shoreline ahead? Past there the river narrows, and if they beat us to that point, we'll ride their wake for five miles before we can pass them. That would give our people a rough ride, and we don't want that, so we'll pull ahead here and let the *Western Belle* bounce and bump."

The thrum of the engines intensified, and the *Princess* slipped effortlessly ahead as the officers of the *Western Belle* watched in red-faced fury. The captain, a man known for his volatile temper, shook his fist and shouted down to his engine room, "More steam! More steam!"

Billy leaned out the window, laughing in delight, feeling like a king, so high was he and so free, with the night wind riffling his hair and the *Western Belle* slowly falling behind. "Father," he shouted, "that captain'll bust a blood vessel before he busts his boilers!" and as he spoke, a great boom smashed the quiet air, startling waterfowl resting in the marshes along the shore, hurling tons of water, mud, wood, metal, and bodies skyward with a blast of fire that lit the dark sky. From the bridge of the *Western Belle* the captain cried in horror, "Oh, blessed God!" and the second officer crossed himself.

The wheelhouse and the hurricane deck of the *Princess* were gone, blown skyward in a blast of fire and scalding steam. The entire center section of the boat was engulfed in flame, and people ran screaming, their clothes on fire, to jump into the cool depths of the river and be swept away by the strong current. Other passengers, who had been farther from the blast, clawed and battered their way toward what seemed the safer section, the bow. Mothers called frantically for children who had been blown into the water at the first blast. If a man stumbled, he lay there, trampled by the stampeding mob.

A second boiler exploded, and slowly, slowly, before the

stricken eyes of those on the *Western Belle*, the *Princess*'s towering smokestacks collapsed with a roar, trapping the Chinese laborers and the circus animals lodged in the hold. The smell of burning flesh was strong on the wind, and the cries of those who had been blown or had jumped into the water were heard more faintly and then not at all. From the sky a hideous rain fell— flaming chunks of wood that had once been fancy scrollwork, fragments of jagged metal, the entire side of one boiler complete with copper tubes, a cabin door with hand-painted porcelain knob still intact, scraps of furniture, baggage, pieces of glass. Bodies crashed into the water and disappeared or were tossed hundreds of yards onto the shore. A woman in a ruffled silk dress landed on the deck of the *Western Belle* near the feet of the captain. He ran to her and discovered that her head was gone. In the water a man riding a piece of wreckage dragged a child from the water and paddled shoreward. A circus pony, the only creature to escape from the hold, thrashed toward the opposite shore, climbed out, and fell to the ground, its flanks heaving.

The sky had gone crimson, and the glow could be seen for many miles up and down the river. In the bloody light the *Western Belle* pulled survivors from the water and set parties ashore to scour the banks for the living and the dead. Twenty minutes after the first explosion the *Princess*'s cracked hull gave way, and she sank with a final, gurgling rush. For another hour the *Western Belle* continued the search for survivors, aided by the *Triumphant*, which had been two miles behind on the trip upriver; then the boats turned, and headed back to the city, tolling their bells in grim announcement.

In her bed Marin lay sleeping lightly, half listening for Vail's footsteps in the hallway, although she knew he might not be back until morning. She thought—or dreamed—of Malcolm, vivid and powerful, threatening her in some unknown way. Abruptly she came to complete wakefulness and sat up, vague unease transformed into galloping fear. Those were boat bells tolling in the night, tolling as boat bells never did except in case of disaster.

A warehouse on the waterfront had been turned into a hospital, but swarms of frightened relatives pleading for news outside the door prevented her from driving up to it. She abandoned the buggy without caring that it and the horse might be stolen and plunged into the crowd. "Oh, please!" she begged of the people around her, "what boat, what boat?" and someone answered, "They say the *Princess*. My sister was on it . . . my sister . . ."

Across the street at Broadway wharf the *Western Belle* and the *Triumphant* rode at anchor, and stretcher bearers were carrying the last of the victims down the gangplanks. The covered forms did not move or cry out in agony—the casualties who could still be helped had been taken off first. People rushed forward, straining to see, and a sturdy few reached out to pull blankets back, hoping against hope that the bodies beneath were not the ones they sought. Most turned away, shaking their heads, but from one woman's throat tore a wail of grief, and she sagged to the ground. One of the stretcher bearers, a tall, dark-haired young man, looked down grimly, stepped over her, and moved on through an opening path as the throng shuffled back reluctantly. Marin called, "Carey! Over here!" but her voice was drowned by the tumult around her. She fought her way to the entry and stepped inside. What she saw caused her to clutch at the door to steady herself.

Lanterns hung high on walls and rafters cast a yellow, uneven glow that made the shadowy corners even darker, and a groaning arose, as sickening a sound as any she had heard during the war. The injured lay on pallets on the floor, and doctors, called from sleep, moved among them, examining with eyes and hands and administering laudanum and comforting words. Across the barn-like room Charles Towle bent over a man who lay on a bale of hay, and Marin went to him like a child to its father, hoping he would tell her this madness was not so bad as it seemed. But his face, when he looked at her, was austere, and he said only, "Are you here to work? Good. Hold this man's arm while I tie the splint."

After that she simply went where he went and followed his orders without thought beyond the moment. Life was only here, only now, in this dim light that did not hide the horror, in this great room that smelled of hay and coffee and hides and blood and burned flesh. Some of the injured lay in opium-induced stupors, some still moaned, others sobbed quietly or mumbled to themselves. The burn victims were the worst, and of them the most terrible were those who had been scalded by superheated steam as the boilers erupted. As clothing was removed, skin came with it; the lucky ones fainted with pain, others shrieked and cursed and begged the doctors to shoot them. Vail's words returned. "Have you ever seen what happens to people when a boiler blows? . . . Do you know what they look like when they've been skinned alive by steam?" Now she knew, now she knew.

There was no way to tell the hour. Time seemed to have stopped, and morning was no nearer than it had been when she first stepped inside this hellhole. The room was hazy with the smoke of many lanterns, and shadows shifted erratically on the walls, long, thin shadows that bent and rose as those on their feet moved slowly among the groaning mass of injured on the floor. Bend, lift, give water in tiny sips, spoon laudanum between quivering lips, close staring eyes, provide decent cover, softly order the body removed. The floor was less crowded now. So many had been taken out. The rumor was that two hundred were dead or missing and that many bodies would never be found, for they were lodged against some buried tree branch or sandbar in the river or washed out to sea. She rubbed eyes that stung with lantern smoke, not tears. There were not enough tears in her for this.

Across the room she saw Jim Porter helping remove the dead, and once she talked briefly with Carey. He had happened to be on the waterfront when the boats came in tolling their bells and had gone to help, as had other men in the vicinity. She thought to ask him why he was there at such a late hour, but a doctor called her and she went to him. Later, when she looked around, Carey was gone.

Dawn came, and no one knew it inside the windowless warehouse. The lanterns burned on. To avoid stepping on a sleeping woman, Marin squeezed between a stack of barrels and one of the posts that supported the roof, and her skirt snagged on the rough wood. She bent to free it and looked into the face of the man on the pallet near the post.

"Michael?" she whispered, and thought fearfully, He is dead.

His lashes fluttered and lifted. He smiled in recognition. "Hello, honey. Am I in the Pearly Gates?"

Relief flowed through her. He did not appear to be burned, and he could still joke. "You're far from heaven, my dear. Where are you hurt? Can I do anything for you?"

He ran his tongue over dry lips. "I sure would like some water."

"I'll be back." She hurried to the water bucket and brought him a dipperful. "Just a little. Don't gulp." She wet her handkerchief and mopped the soot away from his eyes and nose. "There, now you look like a raccoon."

"But a handsome raccoon."

"Oh, indeed." She passed her hand over the splint on his leg. "Are you hurt anywhere else?"

"Naw, I feel fine except when the damned leg starts to throb. My ears are still ringing, though. God, what a blast."

"What happened, Michael? Was there fog? Did the boat run into something?"

"It was clear as a bell, and we were sailing along pretty as you please."

That ended what little hope she'd had that the boilers had blown as a result of collision. Any boiler could explode if a carelessly handled boat ran into something. Still she had to ask, "Surely it wasn't the fault of the boilers?"

"Surely it was. They blew sky-high. Blew me ashore, and I landed pretty hard, but it probably saved me. I could hear the poor devils screaming who couldn't get off the boat."

She sat down on the floor beside him, cross-legged under her wide skirt. "But you weren't racing. Why would they explode for no reason?"

He grinned, his teeth a slash of white in his blackened face. "We were piddling along sedate as a lady in church with the *Western Belle* tagging us all the way. Then she got uppity and tried to beat us to the narrows. We picked up speed, quite a bit of speed—ah, Marin, you should have seen that *Princess*. She moved like a racehorse under the whip. Everyone was cheering as we pulled ahead. A man was doing a cakewalk up at the bow, and we were laughing and throwing pennies. The next thing I knew, I was lying in a marsh on top of a couple of ducks."

It was the way explosions always happened. There was never any warning.

She glanced around and said in a lowered voice, "I heard the wheelhouse went straight up and they couldn't find the captain. It sounds as if he was racing."

"Well, of course he was, honey, just a little. He had to get to the narrows first."

"Oh, but he didn't! Captain Hadley was such a responsible man. How could he do such a thing after you warned him?"

Michael closed his eyes as pain caused his jaw to clench.

She whispered, "Is it your leg? Shall I get you something for the pain?"

He let out his breath in a long exhalation. "I'm all right. Listen, Marin, I'll tell you the truth. I never said anything to the captain."

She stared at him. "Michael, you promised."

"I know, but—I thought Denby was wrong. God, I was on the boat, too. Do you think I'd have taken a risk like that if I believed those boilers wouldn't hold up?"

She shook her head helplessly and put her hand over her eyes. More to herself than to him she muttered, "I don't know what Vail will think. I *promised* him. Now things have come out just the way he was afraid they would. Oh, I don't know what I can say to him. "

"Tell him the truth. Tell him I said I'd take care of it and I didn't. But not a word to anyone else or we might be held liable. Let the captain take the blame. He's gone anyway, so it can't matter to him. Say, my leg hurts to beat the band."

His broad face was shiny with sweat. Soot ran in damp streaks down his cheeks and dripped dirty gray splotches on his shirt collar. Alarmed, she hurried to the table that the doctors had established as a dispensary and came back with a bottle and spoon. She counted out the drops and poured the drug into his mouth. "Go to sleep," she whispered, "and never mind what I said. You did it all in good faith."

She had thought he was almost asleep, but at the word *faith* he opened his eyes and clutched her arm fiercely. "You don't understand! I never meant to tell him. I just said I would to get rid of you. Oh, Marin, I've struggled so long, first with the damned farm and then the damned store, and I never made more than a living. Think of the money we'd have made if those boilers had worked. We couldn't crawl upriver and let that old scow beat us. We had to prove we were the best, you know we did." His fingers dug into her arm to emphasize each word, and then his hand dropped away. His eyes closed. When his breathing was deep and regular, she got to her feet and tried to compose herself before leaving the sanctuary of the shadowed corner. She and Michael were a pair. Never before had she realized how closely their thoughts ran. She started slowly down the aisle between the rows of maimed, suffering people thinking, Vail was right. Nothing is worth this. If only Michael had kept his word. If only . . .

It was almost ten o'clock in the morning when Charles told Marin she could leave. Only a few of the injured were left in the big, lantern-lit room. The dead had been removed, and most of the living taken to private homes. The unlucky had been deposited in the hospital.

As Marin walked to the door, two other nurses passed her, and she heard one say, "I'll stop by church on the way home and say a prayer for all the poor people." She thought, I should do that, too. Send up a prayer . . . but we send it up to silence. He sees the sparrow fall, He sees us fall, but never puts out His hand. We get on a boat that's going to blow up, all unknowing, we step into the street and are run down, a disease we can't understand comes out of nowhere, we get in the way of a maniac with a gun—there's never help, never warning, just a great silence. All those people are dead: Captain Hadley and his son and the man cakewalking in the bow and most of the passengers who laughed and cheered and tossed him pennies—men and women in the middle of onrushing lives, babies and little children at the beginning of theirs, and every one of them loved and needed by someone. Maybe this is Hell and we don't know it. What could be more exquisite torture for creatures like us? We imagine and remember and fear and want to live, we love other people so much and know we'll lose them someday. Such pain, such pain, far worse than any fiery Hell the preachers have thought up.

She walked out of the dark warehouse into the brilliant midmorning sun. Brazen sun to shine so shamelessly on this melancholy world. No use even to look for the buggy and the horse. They would have been stolen hours earlier. Instead of starting on the long walk home she crossed the street to the low wooden wall of the wharf. Diamonds of sunlight quivered on the surface of the bay. It soothed her, it had always soothed her, the sparkle and the soft slap-slap of the dancing water as it moved against the pilings and the rocking boats.

It was here that Vail found her, sitting on the wall, looking out at the bay. He kissed her lightly and sat down.

She laid her hand on his. "How are they at Longridge? Was it very bad?"

"It wasn't pleasant. He was shot at close range by someone who opened the safe with his key. The gold, his papers, everything was gone." He looked so tired that her heart ached for him. He had had a far more terrible night than she.

She said, "You were right about the boilers, utterly right. Have you heard how the explosion happened?"

"I couldn't find Denby—God knows where he is—but I stopped by Bill Purcell's office and got the official line. I also talked to some of the crew of the *Western Belle*. They said the *Princess* was under full steam when she passed them."

"I can't imagine Captain Hadley racing. He was such a steady man."

"Especially after you gave him my orders."

She looked at him directly. "I got down to the dock just before sailing time and they wouldn't let me go up to the wheelhouse, but I ran into Michael, and he promised to take care of it as soon as they got under way. When I heard those bells tolling last night, I knew—I just knew. They brought Michael in. His leg is broken. Oh, I hate to tell you this. Vail, he never told the captain. He thought Denby was being overcautious, and he wanted us to be first into Sacramento. He was hurting so, I couldn't scold him, but I told him it would be hard to explain to you. He said to tell you the truth, it was his fault, but not to mention it to anyone else because we might be held liable." Hardly breathing, sick at heart, she waited. Would he accept her word?

He said, "I'd like to talk to Michael."

They found him in his room at the boardinghouse recently opened by Mrs. Tierney, propped on his bed, his splinted leg resting on a pillow. Someone had cleaned him up, and his color was better than it had been when Marin last saw him, but his face was pinched with a mixture of discomfort and gloom.

"Oh, hello, Vail. Marin, clear off those chairs. Mrs. Tierney's very good to me, but she hasn't gotten around to straightening up the mess." He watched Marin move his clothes. "Say, Vail, I'm sure sorry about your father. Did you find out what happened?"

"He was killed by a shotgun blast, and the safe was cleaned out. Glenna says she heard someone riding away."

Michael shook his head. "Hard to believe. How is Glenna? Does she need me?" He grimaced at his leg. "Not much I can do for her just now."

"I think she'll manage. Let's hear about you."

For the first time Michael looked at Vail directly. "Marin told you, huh? Well, I did promise her. But, before God, I thought Denby was wrong. I suppose you're sore as hell. You can beat me up if you want to, as soon as I'm back on my feet."

"It was dumb, Michael. I thought you were smarter than that."

"It was a gamble, that's all. Haven't you ever lost a gamble? Sure you have." Michael's eyes roved over the small, shabby room. "I thought I was through with places like this. I was going to move to the Oriental Hotel. We're busted now, aren't we?"

Vail shrugged. "It's too early to say. Bill Purcell is talking about changes in the boiler design as soon as we find Denby, which means the bank is still backing us. They want to recover their investment. Remember two years ago when the *Eugenia* blew up? It was raised, repaired, the name was changed, and it's doing service on the river every day with a full passenger load. Everyone's forgotten about the blowup."

Michael pulled himself up in bed. "If you're right, that's the best medicine I've had all day. Now, how about I get Mrs. Tierney to bring up some coffee?"

The clock on the mantel marked the hour with a melodious chime just as it did on any ordinary night. Exhaustion had driven Marin to sleep during the afternoon but now she was wakeful and was busying her hands with needlework, an activity she disliked. Vail sat across from her in his big chair, silently reading newspaper accounts of the accident, and a momentary sense of peace and contentment came over her. With him she was home, her life had meaning; without him there would be only emptiness.

This morning with Michael there had been no mention of the maimed and the dead on that boat, but the truth was he would never forgive Michael or trust him again. Did he doubt her, too? Had he gone immediately to talk to Michael because he distrusted her version of events? Marriage always hung in such delicate balance—giving, taking, asserting power, backing down. It was like a human body, its state of health varying with time and circumstance. Looking at Vail's face in the lamplight, she had the odd feeling of seeing it clearly for the first time in many years. How he had changed from the rebellious, lusty, trouble-seeking youth who had infuriated his father and attracted all the girls so many years ago. He was now a tough-minded, uncompromising, disciplined man who would not allow himself to stray, from a decent path and would not allow her to stray, either. From now on, if she was to keep his love, she would have to work very hard at being honorable and show by every word and action of her life that she was honest and worthy of trust. And a stony, narrow path it would be. No quibbles or evasions or pretense, not even the comfort of an occasional social lie, for even a little lie could so easily slip over the line into a big one. No taking tiny tucks in the truth or bending it slightly even though there was no other way to make people do as they should. It would be like going into battle unarmed. How could she be upright and scrupulous all the time when she had to deal with people like Tyler? Tomorrow she would have to meet with that snake, somehow convince him to wait a little longer for his money, and do it honorably.

The clock struck the half hour. Nine-thirty. She went on poking the needle into the heavy cloth and pulling the thread through. A horse trotted into the drive and she looked up. Cool night air swept the parlor as the front door opened and Carey came into the room, bringing with him a vitality and quiet exuberance that made the future seem suddenly brighter and more hopeful. The light of my life, she thought as she kissed him. How young he was and full of energy, how firm his cheek under her lips. He smelled of fresh salt air, and the fog had curled his dark hair into the ringlets he hated.

He pulled the hassock to a position between them and sat down. His eyes were Vail's eyes in shape but black like Marin's, not cool, clear gray. He sprawled on the hassock, big hands held loosely between his knees. His long arms had developed a heavier muscle, but his shoulders were only half the thickness of Vail's and his chest remained flat and thin, more the chest of a boy than of a man. He still has filling out to do, thought Marin with motherly awareness, but, oh, what a man he is going to be. Just like his father. The thought leaped up, and she glanced at Vail, knowing he must be thinking the same thing. Thank God it was out in the open between them at last.

Carey grinned at them both. "I saw a good-looking pup on the wharf today. A sailor was trying to sell him. I almost brought him home, but then I decided not to."

"Why not, honey?" Marin asked, going back to her needle-work. "You ought to have another dog now that Angus is gone."

"It wasn't a collie, for one thing, and I'm spoiled. I can't replace Angus. Oh, maybe someday, but it's kind of like losing your wife. You might get another one eventually, but it would take a long time."

Marin laughed. "A fine thing, comparing a wife to a dog."

"Mother, as you once pointed out to a lady we all know, Angus was superior to a lot of women. Funny, isn't it, the way that sailor walked up and asked me to buy? It almost convinced me to take the pup because that's the way we got Angus. Vail, do you remember the day you brought him out to Little Mountain? Mother has told me a hundred times how you took him out of your saddlebag and gave him to me and then asked her if she minded."

"I remember," Vail said, and smiled.

Carey shook his head. "I can't recall a time when that dog wasn't with me." He studied his big, bony hands. "Well, I didn't come by to talk about Angus. I can't be at Grandfather's funeral, Mother. I wish you would explain to Father for me."

Marin sat up. "Why not? I know you haven't been close to him lately, but the whole family will be there. It will look strange without you."

"Oh, it isn't that I was mad at him or anything like that—and I'm sorry he's dead. I understood Grandfather pretty well. There was about as much use getting mad at him as fighting a hurricane. You just get out of the way till it passes. But, you see, I won't be here."

Cold spread over Marin like an icy wind, chilling her to the bone. "What are you talking about?" Her voice sounded hard because she was afraid.

Carey looked her squarely in the eye. His face had gone pink with discomfort, but his jaw was set. "Jim and I have been hired on the *Star of Ceylon* and she's leaving on the morning tide. That's why we were down at the dock last night when the *Western Belle* came in. We were making arrangements."

Marin swung on Vail. "Did you know about this?"

"No. Where are you bound, Carey?"

"China. That's where you went, so I want to go, too."

"Vail was a good deal older than you," Marin pointed out with a little laugh that told her son what a foolish child he was.

Carey's eyes, wide and serious, returned to her. "I know, but I've been through a war, and that makes a difference. In battle and in the prison, there were so many times when I thought I was a dead man, but I came through. Now I remember all the fellows back there in the swamps and the forests, and I know that each day since the war is a bonus day for me. I can't waste it, Mother. I want to see the pagodas and the exotic birds, and—well, I just want to find out about things. There's so much out there that I'll never see it all, but I want to try. I was going to take off and write to you later but I did that before and it wasn't right. I should have faced up to you. Please understand, Mother." *Release me, Mother. Give me your blessing, and let me go with a smile.*

Panic rioted in her, and her face felt stiff with the effort of hiding it. She did not see Vail's eyes watching her. Carey must not go away, not again. If she could somehow get him alone for just a few minutes, she could tell him anything. Plead, weep, tell him it would break her heart, tell him she needed him desperately in the business or even that she was sick—tell him whatever was needed to keep him home.

He looked so young, sitting there on the edge of his seat, waiting for the words that would set him free, and he was hers. From the moment of his birth she had known him and she knew him now to the marrow of his bones. For all his experience of war and the world, cynicism had not set its bitter stamp on him. He was still malleable. If she was clever and careful, she could do anything she wished with him, mold him and keep him at her side forever.

She looked into his earnest, honest dark eyes, shining with hopefulness and love and trust in her, and thought, Oh, my son, I love you, too.

Of all the difficult things she had done in her life, this was the hardest. Her lips moved into a smile. "I think it's wonderful, Carey. Go see everything out there. But be sure to come back and tell us about it."

He flushed with pleasure and relief and jumped to his feet. "I sure am glad you feel that way, Mother. I'll come back real soon, and I'll write all the time." He gave her cheek a smack and began to pace the way he had always done when he came to her with exciting news. "The *Star of Ceylon* is a great ship. She made San Francisco from New York in ninety days, only one day more than the *Flying Cloud* back in fifty-one. Our first port is Hawaii and then—China! Probably we'll see a lot of the islands while we're out in the Pacific, and we're going to Australia, too. Ethan told me all about the kangaroos and the kookaburras and the dingoes. After Australia maybe we'll go on to Europe and New York. Won't that be great!"

He promised once again to write constantly, and they went with him out onto the front porch. He kissed Marin. He shook hands with Vail, and then his arms went out and he hugged him hard. Once again he kissed Marin, and she leaned against him for a moment, her hands on his wide, strong back, and he patted her shoulder lovingly. Then he strode down the path to his horse waiting in the drive and vaulted into the saddle.

"So long," he called. "I'll write." And he cantered off.

She went down the steps, wanting to run after him, and stopped halfway down the path.

Evening fog lay on the city, curling its smoky tendrils down streets and alleys, blotting out the lights of town. Below the hill, hidden in the blanket of moist air, the waterfront bustled with activity. Even now cargoes were being loaded onto ships riding gently at anchor, lights on tall masts gleaming eerily in the mist. In a few short hours those ships would be moving silently on the tide, outward bound through the shrouded Golden Gate and across the Pacific to the other side of the world, carrying those on board far, far away from those who loved and needed them.

Good-bye, she said in her heart. Moisture from the wet air clung to her hair and caught the light streaming through the open door. Vail came to stand beside her and together they looked down the dark street to the point where Carey had disappeared.

She said, "I'll never see him again."

"Yes, you will. He'll be back in a year or two." Gently he pulled her closer so that she was resting against him. "I'm proud of you. It's hard to let him go but nothing else would have worked, not for long. He'd have left someday soon no matter what you said, probably with a lot of bitterness. This way he'll come back."

He was proud of her. It was the greatest praise. His arms were holding her and that was all she needed.

He brushed away the tears still shining on her cheeks and said, "It's cold, Marin. Come back into the house."

About the Author

DIANE AUSTELL is a native Californian and has always been interested in the dynamic history of the state. Her ancestors came to America before the Revolutionary War and her family's history is interwoven with the development of the country. Coming from people who express themselves through the written word, she was lucky enough to have their letters and diaries to draw upon in the writing of this book, and many of the events in it parallel their experiences. In 1849 her great-great-grandfather came to the California gold fields with his brother and found a rich gold deposit. Leaving his brother to guard it, he went to town to record the claim and returned to find his brother murdered and claim jumpers in control of the claim. He returned to Illinois in time to fight for the Union in the Civil War while other family members fought for the South.

Ms. Austell lives with her husband in Southern California on cliffs overlooking the Pacific. They have two children.

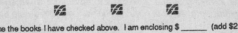

FANFARE

On Sale in February

New York Times Bestseller
TEXAS! SAGE

☐ (29500-4) $4.99/5.99 in Canada
by Sandra Brown

The third and final book in Sandra Brown's beloved TEXAS! trilogy. Sage Tyler always thought she wanted a predictable, safe man . . . until a lean, blue-eyed drifter took her breath, and then her heart away.

SONG OF THE WOLF
☐ (29014-2) $4.99?5.99 in Canada
by Rosanne Bittner

Young, proud, and beautiful, Medicine Wolf possesses extraordinary healing powers and a unique sensitivity that leads her on an unforgettable odyssey into a primeval world of wildness, mystery, and passion.

LATE NIGHT DANCING
☐ (29557-8) $5.99/6.99 in Canada
by Diana Silber

A compelling novel of three friends -- sophisticated Los Angeles women with busy, purposeful lives, who also live on the fast track of romance and sex, because, like lonely women everywhere, they hunger for a man to love.

SUMMER'S KNIGHT
☐ (29549-7) $4.50/5.50 in Canada
by Virginia Lynn

Heiress Summer St. Clair is stranded penniless on the streets of London. But her terrifying ordeal soon turns to adventure when she captures the glittering eyes of the daring Highland rogue, Jamie Cameron.

FANFARE

FANFARE

Sandra Brown

_____ 28951-9 TEXAS! LUCKY .... $4.50/5.50 in Canada
_____ 28990-X TEXAS! CHASE .... $4.99/5.99 in Canada

Amanda Quick

_____ 28932-2 SCANDAL .... $4.95/5.95 in Canada
_____ 28354-5 SEDUCTION .... $4.99/5.99 in Canada
_____ 28594-7 SURRENDER .... $4.50/5.50 in Canada

Nora Roberts

_____ 27283-7 BRAZEN VIRTUE .... $4.50/5.50 in Canada
_____ 29078-9 GENUINE LIES .... $4.99/5.99 in Canada
_____ 26461-3 HOT ICE .... $4.99/5.99 in Canada
_____ 28578-5 PUBLIC SECRETS .... $4.95/5.95 in Canada
_____ 26574-1 SACRED SINS .... $4.99/5.99 in Canada
_____ 27859-2 SWEET REVENGE ....$4.99/5.99 in Canada

Iris Johansen

_____ 28855-5 THE WIND DANCER .... $4.95/5.95 in Canada
_____ 29032-0 STORM WINDS .... $4.99/5.99 in Canada
_____ 29244-7 REAP THE WIND ....$4.99/5.99 in Canada

Ask for these titles at your bookstore or use this page to order.
Please send me the books I have checked above. I am enclosing $ _____ (please
add $2.50 to cover postage and handling). Send check or money order, no cash or
C. O. D.'s please.

Mr./ Ms. _____

Address _____

City/ State/ Zip _____

Send order to: Bantam Books, Dept. FN, 414 East Golf Road, Des Plaines, IL 60016
Please allow four to six weeks for delivery.
Prices and availablity subject to change without notice.   FN 16 - 12/91